CW00687175

# The Col_____
# Supernatural and Weird
# Fiction of
# J. Sheridan le Fanu
# Volume 8

# The Collected Supernatural and Weird Fiction of
# J. Sheridan le Fanu
# Volume 8

Including One Novel
'A Lost Name',
One Novelette
'The Last Heir of Castle Connor',
and Six Short Stoies
of the Ghostly and Gothic

J. Sheridan le Fanu

LEONAUR

*The Collected*
*Supernatural and Weird*
*Fiction of J. Sheridan le Fanu*
*Volume 8*
*Including One Novel*
*'A Lost Name',*
*One Novelette*
*'The Last Heir of Castle Connor',*
*and Six Short Stoies*
*of the Ghostly and Gothic*
by J. Sheridan le Fanu

FIRST EDITION

Leonaur is an imprint
of Oakpast Ltd

Copyright in this form © 2010 Oakpast Ltd

ISBN: 978-0-85706-159-1 (hardcover)
ISBN: 978-0-85706-160-7 (softcover)

**http://www.leonaur.com**

Publisher's Notes

In the interests of authenticity, the spellings, grammar and place names
used have been retained from the original editions.

The opinions of the authors represent a view of events in which he
was a participant related from his own perspective,
as such the text is relevant as an historical document.

The views expressed in this book are not necessarily
those of the publisher.

# Contents

# A Lost Name

## CHAPTER 1
### MARK SHADWELL OF RABY

Raby Hall stands near the old London road, in an inland county. You see but the great door and a portion of its front as you look up the broad straight avenue, with its double row of gigantic old beech-trees at either side. Its brick is red and mellow; black beams of oak, well jointed, and with carved inscriptions, bar the old walls across, and broad windows, with more small square panes than I dare number at a venture, return the sunlight when it nears the horizon like a thousand wintry fires.

The ground slopes downward from the front of the house, clumped with grand old trees, and rises in the rear, so forming those unequal and wooded uplands which overhang the old road with a distant and sombre outline for many miles.

The ancient park wall flanks a long stretch of the road, and, leaving it, slopes upward with a snake-like winding, and loses its gray line, at last, among the distant woods. In this wall, upon the high road, are set the four great piers of the grand entrance, surmounted by the demi-griffins, with wings elevated (carved, in a style of true heraldic audacity), which the Shadwells of Raby have long borne as their crest.

This place has its ancient family traditions—its nooks and solitudes of transcendent beauty—its romantic story—and its famous gaze-lady, or as antiquaries will have it, ghaist-lady, whom, had Holbein illuminated the pages of that once magnificent family history—now forlorn and expiring, he would have introduced again and again, with her mysterious star and melancholy beauty, in a new Dance of Death.

The old house and place, as you pass by, strike you as being handsome and interesting, but a little *triste* also. There is something more than an air of quietude about them. It does not amount to decay, but over it all broods the melancholy of neglect.

It was sunset when Mark Shadwell's steps echoed across the solitude of the paved stable-yard. The master of Raby had killed some weary hours and a few rabbits among the distant woods. His weather-beaten velveteen frock, his gaiters and wide-awake, would have been discarded by many a dandy gamekeeper, but the bearing of the slight tall figure, and the pride and refinement of his still handsome features, were worthy of the old name he bore.

"Hallo there! anyone! take these away to the cook," he called, as a boy emerged from the stable—"Here, you! and, have the letters come? That will do—don't know;" and Mark Shadwell, having thrown him his bag, with a sour look, and without a word more, strode from the yard, and so, thinking uncomfortably, with a knit brow and downcast look, to the hall door.

It was the sight of those winged demi-griffins, which are repeated in Caen stone, surmounting the low pedestals at the end of the balustrade at either side of the steps, that recalled him.

He raised his eyes, and came to a halt, and looked with a sour smile from one to the other. He scoffed at his heraldry now and then.

"Thank you, very fine fellows! A pair of vapouring rascals! Thank you both. It is very agreeable, I'm sure, to be received by two such distinguished personages at one's doorsteps every day, upon my life—*very*! What terrible fellows you are! I don't know, however, that between you you'd keep out a bailiff or a dun, by Jove! A good washing, too, would do you no harm. For such very fine gentlemen, don't you think you are rather dirty?"

All this time Mr. Shadwell of Raby, with his foot on the doorstep, was choosing a cigar—not with the countenance of a man about to enjoy a comfort, but with the sharp and peevish look of a sick man selecting his anodyne.

His was a style of face that accorded with the gloom of a proud and vindictive spirit. Dark as a gipsy's was its tint; finely traced eyebrows, dark brown sullen eyes, the whites of which showed a little fiercely against the tint of his complexion, added to this gloom and beauty. His mouth, small and finely-shaped, showed likewise, in contrast with his dark tint, a very white and even set of teeth. These points of beauty made his smile of irony or anger, I think, more painful by reason of a latent discord.

When he had lighted a cigar, he strolled slowly toward the farther angle of the house, and stopped under a projecting turret, a window on the second story of which stood open.

"Hallo! Sherlock, are you there? Carmel, I say! Carmel Sherlock!"

He stood expecting, with his cigar between his fingers, and in a moment there appeared at the open window a pallid face, not young, with long lank black hair and large dark eyes. This figure in the *chia'r oscuro*, who placed his thin hand on the window-stone, and looked down with the tired and dreamy air of a man called away from a task which still occupies his brain.

"Yes, sir, here," he answered.

"Come down for a few minutes, can you?" asked Mark Shadwell.

The pale face looked down, rather dreamily, and then away over the distant landscape, and Carmel Sherlock put his hand to his temple, thinking, and answered nothing.

"I say! d'ye hear? *Will* you come down?" repeated Shadwell.

"Down? yes, sir; oh yes! certainly."

And Carmel Sherlock stood erect, and, passing his fingers through his lank black hair, he turned slowly from the window. With a little shrug and one of his dreary smiles, Mark Shadwell thought: "That fellow's growing madder every day, hang him! *He'll* go next, I suppose, just because he's some little use—of *course!*"

Mark Shadwell walked back, smoking, with his eyes on the

gravel, and one hand in his pocket, slowly and rather circuitously, to the door-steps, and, seating himself on the balustrade, he smoked on with a bitter countenance, till Carmel Sherlock appeared.

"Well, did you look into that?" he asked, uncomfortably.

"What? which, sir?"

"The—the—that thing of Roke Wycherly's—the mortgage," he answered.

"Oh yes! I've settled that."

"I wish you had," sneered Mark, "it's something—a great deal, I dare say, by this time" and he paused anxiously, looking hard at his companion.

"Twenty-two thousand three hundred and twelve pounds," replied Carmel Sherlock, "besides silver, eleven—seven—yes, eighteen shillings."

"Ah—I see!" said Shadwell, growing pale, and throwing away his cigar, though it was only half smoked—"I see. Come along."

And he walked a little way under the beech-trees, the tops of which still caught the ruddy sunlight, toward the great entrance and the London road.

"But how, I say—how the devil *could* it have run up to anything like that in so short a time?"

"I wish it wasn't; but figures, you see, there's no avoiding them: they close in like fate," said Sherlock, with a shrug and a deep sigh. "They're odd things, figures, they'll never knock under—they're omnipotent—you can't squeeze 'em—they'll break your head or your heart—but they won't swerve." Carmel Sherlock rubbed his hands slowly together, and smiled oddly along the grass, as he said this, perhaps only in admiration of the little people, as he often called these self-same figures.

"It's nothing to laugh at, d—— you—what's there to laugh at? Suppose I'm ruined!" said Shadwell, savagely.

"Laugh! did I? I'm sorry, sir; I didn't mean—laugh, indeed! *I* don't laugh, never; I *never* laugh, sir; and I *am* sorry, I tell you, sir, I am."

"Well, you *ought*, I think, at all events. If I'm smashed, I don't see exactly what's to become of you—*I* don't, do you?"

"Ruin, I do see—ruin—*I* should be ruined, if you were smashed. I'd break my heart, sir, upon my honour;" so said Carmel Sherlock very earnestly, and stopping short in his promenade. "I should utterly break my heart, sir, unless— unless I could be of use ;" and, having thus spoken, he heaved a sigh, so deep it was nearly a groan.

Mr. Shadwell looked at him. "You're a very odd fellow," he said. "You wouldn't be half so odd if you ate and drank like other people, instead of living on tea and tobacco. How old are you, Carmel?"

Carmel Sherlock looked dismally on the ground, and, instead of answering, kicked a bit of rotten wood that lay in his way before him.

"How old are you?" repeated Shadwell.

"Too old to marry, if that's what you mean—too old, sir— too old to think of it." And he pulled off his felt hat, and beat it slowly on the side of his leg as he walked on; and looking up towards the sky, he shook back his long lank locks. "I'm very well here—I don't want much—I'm very well."

"Very well—of course you are. While I can fight the battle, you shan't want—you shan't indeed, Carmel."

Mr. Shadwell looked rather kindly as he laid his hand on Sherlock's thin arm; and that *distrait* companion said in a low tone, looking straight before him:—

"He's very kind—very kind—he's half ruined. He ought to sell."

"Selling is out of the question," said Shadwell, sharply.

"Selling?" echoed Sherlock. "I was just thinking you might; it was in my head, sir, when you spoke—exactly."

"I told you before, I can't sell; you don't understand land; it's only a life estate, except that seven hundred a year that Roke Wycherly has three times over, d—— me; and if it really is twenty-two thousand pounds, I can't pay it, nor get it, by heaven!"

"Sir Roke Wycherly, Baronet—I know—of Scarbroke. Twenty-two thousand three hundred and twelve pounds—and some shillings—not worth mentioning. I shall have all the balances finished tomorrow—all that's due; life's such a dream, sir."

"I wish it were: dreams, indeed! my neck's broke trying to pay interest and charges and everything—curse it! Better for a fellow to be dead, and out of it all!"

They had turned off the avenue into a wooded hollow. The sun had now set; there was still a red and golden glow in the sky, but the long shadows had spread into twilight, and the air was chilled.

## CHAPTER 2
### IT GROWS DARK

"Roke Wycherly, a nasty dog! the nastiest dog in England. I always thought him an odious fellow. He has let that money run up for a purpose, I know he has. He has never had a thing to trouble him—the beast! And look at me! why another fellow would put a pistol in his mouth, and blow his head off!" This was spoken with a bitter oath.

"That's it, there!" muttered Sherlock; "you mustn't. Oh no, no! It's a *mistake*; it's—it's like a bubble gone out; the same thin shell of water and the same little puff of air will never meet again. Body and soul—body and soul—better together! Oh yes! I've thought about that."

"Thank you," said sour Mark Shadwell.

"Dreamed!—ay, I dreamt about him two or three times lately; stiff in the corner, with a star of blood."

"Who?" said Shadwell.

"Eh?" answered Carmel.

"Your head's full of green tea and tobacco; of course you're always dreaming—it's the way fellows make themselves mad, by Jove!" said Shadwell, turning towards home.

"Mad! well—ha! that isn't likely to come, sir, to a quiet man like me, with plenty of work, and no great care—except one— except *one*," answered Carmel Sherlock, softly.

"Pooh! not mad; we're all mad, for that matter; I mean you

fast and watch like a monk, or nun, and you live on tea and smoke, and you've put yourself in training to see visions; you've gone in for that sort of thing."

"Here they are, sir; I'll go," whispered Sherlock, with a quick side glance, at the same time drawing away from Mr. Shadwell's side.

"Who?"

"The two ladies—here, sir, here—*there* so said Sherlock, pointing with his finger stealthily across his breast.

They were not goblins; very much the reverse. Two young girls; in this twilight you could see but their slender outlines. There was a sneer on Shadwell's features as he saw them. The sneer perhaps was for Sherlock. It did not brighten to a smile, however, as the young ladies, chatting musically, approached. His face grew gloomy and forbidding, on the contrary, and he looked as if he wished them fifty miles away.

These young ladies—Rachel Shadwell and Miss Agnes Marlyn—were talking as they drew near, and suddenly were silent on seeing Mr. Shadwell, and as they approached the point at which their path crossed his, they slackened their pace timidly, almost to a standstill, like people approaching a door within which they know is a dangerous dog.

"You shouldn't be out so late—damp and cold. Get on—get on—get home," snarled Mark Shadwell at his pretty daughter, and, with a make-belief of lifting his hat to Miss Marlyn, he waved them on towards the house.

Sherlock sighed profoundly, and he and his patron slowly followed in the steps of the young ladies, who viewed with so much awe the man of acres and of debts, of whose moods they know something.

Whenever the practical psychology of love becomes a subject of scientific inquiry—as barren metaphysics now are—and learned professors are told off to note, lecture, and, if they will, experiment on its unexplored wonders and universal power, it will come out that mystery is at the bottom of it all. Nature teaches all manner of beautiful duplicities to girls—sinuous and

13

subtle as the emblem of wisdom. It is strangely sweet, I think, to see a pretty girl, with downcast lashes and listening smile, communing enigmatically with her thoughts. With a slender wand she leads away the giant to her dungeon; man's imagination is her subject, and her wand is mystery. Wonderful girlish nature, in which the false and the true, the beautiful and the deadly, are always contending! The spell of thy power is mystery; we follow a voice in the air; a beautiful apparition that speaks not; the slaves of the unrevealed; and so we are thine till the hour comes of thy broken talisman and subjugation. The serpent, the serpent! The poison and the healing; the guile and yet the wisdom; the cruelty, sometimes, and the fascination! And when in the midst of this cold, proud, anguine empire comes "the charmer," though his pipe please not me, all is in an hour changed and disarmed by his ungainly music; there is a gliding to his feet, a gazing, a winding about his arms, and the creature is poisonless, docile, captive.

"I did not think your news would be so bad as that," said Shadwell, abruptly.

"I did not know, sir," said Sherlock.

"It *is* bad, I can tell you, and *very* bad. Now, the next thing he'll do, he'll begin with an attorney. I know what he's about; he knows I understand him, and by this time he's chuckling over it. Now just think—the whole thing—the scoundrel!"

Carmel raised his lean pale face toward the stars that were beginning to blink in the deepening blue.

"You're not an astrologer?" sneered Shadwell.

"Astrologer? no. Oh dear! certainly no—only what you call a fatalist," said Carmel, still looking up.

"A Mahomedan?" suggested Mark. And Carmel sighed very deeply, as he said, "I wish I were."

"The paradise, perhaps," scoffed Shadwell, angrily; for Sherlock's occasional inattention to his complaints, and even to his blasphemies, exasperated him. Some vices are indulgent to their like when repeated in others. But with egotism it is different. No one is so hard on the selfishness of another as a selfish man.

14

A quick shrinking glance Carmel shot on his companion. "Eh! eh!" he said, and then drew a long breath, and walked on in silence by his side, looking up at the stars as before. "He doesn't mean it—he didn't—he doesn't," he murmured. "Mahomedans are too nearly Christian for me—nearer than the Church of Rome, I think."

Shadwell laughed a short laugh under his breath; a bad and joyless laugh, it seemed.

"A fatalist—yes, yes—that I am—a fatalist, as you say," said Carmel, answering nobody.

"I'm with you, so far. We'll not quarrel on religion, I think."

"Yes; it's quite plain. I'll show you the principle any day, sir, you choose to come to my room—I haven't time to finish it now—with algebraic proof, the exact sciences. A creed should rest on numbers, you know, not on imagination; fancy is the decorative faculty, but number is demonstration—and demonstration is fact—the whole thing is necessity. According to the doctrine of Chance, there is *no* chance. The whole of the stars up there; it's all *coercion*, and yet it's all chance, don't you see? Chance is only limited rotation, you know; and the combinations of rotation itself are limited—and—and—don't you see ?—it ends in coercion."

Carmel had come to a standstill, and, with his white countenance smiling upward on the stars, and his hand on his patron's arm, was gabbling now with extreme volubility.

"Ay, ay, I dare say! capital algebra, capital science, I'm quite sure," answered Shadwell. "I don't trouble my head about that; my creed is, dust to dust—so there's an end o' it. Come along."

"I suppose there's *some* way out of it," resumed Mark Shadwell, on a sudden—he was thinking of his money troubles, not of his creed—after an interval, "Without a bullet this time—but what's a fellow's life worth? Look at that bat flitting there—zigzag—free as air—lots of flies—snug nest—everything—nothing to trouble him. Lords of the creation, indeed— such rot!"

Carmel's large eyes followed the wavering flight of the bat; and he murmured, "Oh! that I had wings—"

"Like a bat?" said Shadwell.

"Good poetry, sir, here and there, in the psalms," continued his companion. "Oh! that I had wings like a dove," he repeated with a strange sigh and a smile.

"Or a *demi-griffin*—hang them!" said the master of Raby, again snarling at the mystic brutes that seemed to mock him, with an elaborate burlesque, whenever ruin came as near as it stood at present. They were by this time at the hall-door, and, pushing it open, Shadwell paused and said:

"And, I say, you've done enough today. You must come down, you *must*, this evening, and read some Italian, or whatever it is; do you mind? They'll be very glad to see you."

"Shall I?" murmured Carmel, looking to the sky with a doubtful smile and one hand raised.

"Of *course* you shall; don't I tell you you must? You're tired; mind you come," he added with a nod, as he left him, and crossed the hall, thinking of something else; while Sherlock, with his peculiar pallid smile, stood at the foot of the stair, with the tips of his fingers to his lips, looking after him.

## CHAPTER 3
### THE BARONET SPEAKS

"Shall I?" repeated Carmel, with the same rapt smile and sigh, standing like a beautiful spirit at the gate of Paradise, with its light upon his face.

But as with sudden pain his features contracted and darkened. "Tut, tut, tut, Carmel! whither so fast? Not bad enough, eh? Ha! ha! why I'm all *burnt*—burnt. Scrivener, fiddler, fool! No, no; up to my crib, and draw forth my pitying angel, and scrape her into screams and sobs of consolation." And with this idea, evidently tickled, he laughed oddly to himself, running up the stairs three at a time.

The gallery was dark, and only the dim sky of a moonless night faintly defined the outline of his open window as he entered his room. He was groping for a match; but desisted.

"No," he thought; "this is better—beautiful neutral tint, on which my eyes will paint images! while, let me see, let me see—*can* I find it? ay, here thou art! while thou dost wail and quiver in the dark—my spirit!" And, at the same time, he swept his bow across the strings of the violin, and in low, wild, tremulous notes, standing with his shoulder against the window-case, and gazing out upon the blank, he made a dirge-like and wandering voluntary, which proceeded unbroken, though he sometimes sighed, and sometimes talked to himself, and sometimes laughed a little.

In the meantime, as Mark Shadwell approached the door to which he was walking dejectedly, his eye was suddenly caught by the post-bag on the oak table in the hall.

The letters! the hated letters. They never had a pleasant tale to tell. He emptied the bag on the table, and with a shock that suspended his breath, he saw at a glance a large square envelope, addressed in the hand of Sir Roke Wycherly.

Five years had passed since he saw that hand before—five years of mutability and death—through which they two had come alive, reserved for the events that were coming.

"R. Wycherly" at the left-hand corner of the envelope identified the writer. But Shadwell needed not the proof. Love has its instinct of recognition, but fear a still subtler one. Shadwell feared this baronet, who was his remote cousin, his creditor, and who had, moreover, a fancied claim to a portion of that estate, every acre of which was needed to keep him from ruin.

Mark Shadwell's features grew paler as this envelope looked him in the face. A crisis of some sort was coming. Roke Wycherly would not have taken up his pen to write to a man whom he despised—as he did every unsuccessful man—whom he had always rather disliked, and who, he knew, hated him—without some special business on hand. "He is going to demand his arrears of interest, and to open an attack upon my title, and perhaps to hint at a compromise. A compromise I what compromise could there be which would not ruin Shadwell?" All the time that he was thus trifling with his own suspense, he would have taken another man by the throat for retaining his secret. He looked at the large red seal, and back again at the front of the address. The letters were thick, and the lines ran up at one end with an ominous scowling squint.

"That letter means mischief," he thought, and thrust it unopened into the bottom of his pocket, pinched hard between his finger and thumb, and he stood irresolute: he was thinking of reading it elsewhere, but he could wait no longer; and, glancing over his shoulder and around, like a man on the verge of a crime, he broke the seal and read Roke Wycherly's letter. It ran thus:

Dear Mark,—Look on to the foot of this note, and then say, can you believe your eyes? Yet it is I indeed! I wish to see you, and am myself so much abroad, so little, therefore, likely to meet you in town, or elsewhere in England, *casually*, that I must ask you to permit me to make a *certainty* of it by looking in upon you at Raby. May I? I shall be running northward, in two or three days, to Scarbrook. My wish would be to pull up at your door as I pass. It is very impertinent, I know, to say so, particularly to ask admission at so short a notice, when fifty things may make it inconvenient or impracticable. See how I approach you! Pray stand on no ceremony with me. If you can't see me this time, I shall know you *really* can't. If you *can*, can you manage also a corner for my man? I have been a little of an invalid—though, understand, not a troublesome one— for now upwards of a year. Drop me a line to this place, and pray remember me particularly to my kinswoman. Amy, and my best respects to my other kinswoman, your daughter, whose acquaintance I hope to make. Again, pray requite me as little ceremony as I use, and believe me, dear Mark, yours ever,

Roke Wycherly.

——'s Hotel, London.

Shadwell's hungry eye devoured all this with a rapid glance. He read it again. "There is absolutely nothing in it, but that he wants to come here. Does he? It's not for *my* good, then, that's

18

clear; what can it be for? To see the place, to sneak, and pick up information about the property? It isn't that—no, it isn't that—what could he ask? what could he learn? No! it isn't."

Shadwell had read this letter with his broad felt hat overshadowing his still handsome face. It engaged him so thoroughly that he forgot the other letters lying on the table, and, crossing the hall in deep thought, or rather abstraction, he walked out into the darkness and solitude to ruminate undisturbed, for this enigma troubled him.

As he loitered with downcast looks under the broad front of the old house, he was startled from his reverie by the ugly wailings of Carmel's fiddle from the turret-window.

"That's you, Sherlock! Hollo! Stop your caterwauling, will you? Do you hear?"

"I do," said the gentle voice of Carmel, from above.

"Well, he's coming; I'm going to write for him. He'll be here in a day or two; I'll write to ask him—and—I don't know what it's for," he added, a little inconsistently.

"Sir Roke Wycherly—aha—I thought," said the oracle from above.

"Ay, Roke Wycherly, who else?" echoed Shadwell.

"Oh no! Oh dear, no! True—no one—ah! ha-ha!" said Carmel, with something between a shudder and a laugh. "Ho dear! can't you keep him off?"

"Keep him off! why the devil should I? I'm not afraid of him, I suppose," said Shad- well, fiercely.

"Oh no! oh no! of course; but I am; *I'm* afraid. I wish, sir, you could keep him off, you know."

"Why, it's I who am bringing him here! Keep him off? D—n him!" snarled Shadwell's voice, defiantly.

"Bringing him? Oh yes! Bringing him here—yes, sir. I'm *afraid*. It's a very dark night. It's the shadow. I wish I could keep him off—tut, tut!—is not there plague enough?"

And speaking these words, I suppose in a reverie, he drew his bow across the strings again, and produced a long-drawn discord.

19

"Will you stop that d——d noise?" cried Shadwell, sternly. "Light your candle, will you? I'm going up: and get out the paper about that cursed mortgage, do, and I'll just look at it, as far as you've got."

"Pardon—pardon—I wasn't thinking; light, to be sure, sir! I beg your pardon—light, to be sure, sir. It *is* dark—awfully dark! If I were a fanciful man, I'd say this violin made it darker, and the news darkest of all. Wings, wings, sir, and moral shadows!"

Shadwell, you may be sure, did not wait to hear these sage reflections out, and, as he ascended the doorsteps, the glimmer of a match from Carmel Sherlock's window showed that he was lighting his candle.

## CHAPTER 4

### MARK SHADWELL'S ANSWER

So Mark Shadwell mounted the stairs of Raby Hall in the dark, and at the end of the lonely gallery entered the turret room, where Carmel Sherlock awaited him standing, with a solitary candle lighted.

"By Jove!" murmured the master of Raby with his accustomed sneer, when he stepped in and looked round him. He always forgot when he had been a few weeks without visiting it how odd the little room was—a segment of the wall circular, the rest polyhedric and crooked. "What a perverse little closet!" one would have exclaimed. And stranger still were the furniture and decorations. Near the window stood a high, slender, lock-up desk, on four slim legs, and with shelves beneath laden with a litter of papers and ledgers. Carmel kept the accounts of the estate, and many cross accounts, and scores of interest, and other complicated debit and credit entries, and did his work standing before the tall desk. Over the tiny fireplace hung an ancient steel crossbow and four tobacco pipes of various fashions, long and short; an unframed small Madonna, antique and precious, in Carmel's eyes, picked up in an old lumber-room of an out-of-the-way London tavern, for such a trifle as he could afford, and which he almost adored, in which he saw resemblances, and recognised, he fancied, a master hand. There were shelves of books, too, not half a dozen modern ones among them, and those of that "philosophic" school which bears no amity to revelation. Coverless folios, yellow vellum-backed *quartos*, and some diminutive black letter and others, dark and warped by time, and looking like great burnt squares of gingerbread. Against the wall, too, hung his beloved fiddle, and a variety of other queer decorations, so that one could understand Shadwell's reflection, "It's like nothing but a corner of a madman's brain."

"Light that other candle, will you? and give me all the light you can, and let me have a sheet of paper, and—ay, there are pens and ink."

At the desk Shadwell wrote standing:

Dear Roke,—Your friendly note charms me. I shall expect you. Any day you like best will equally answer us. We can't make you as comfortable as we could wish; but roughing it in a poor man's country house you will make excuse. I write so briefly lest I should lose a post. We have some pretty good trout-fishing here. Our shooting decidedly bad—unless you care for killing rabbits. On the whole, I can't deny the place is rather slow; but you'll forgive it, and believe me,
Ever yours sincerely,<br>M. Shadwell.
P.S.—What you say of your health distresses me. But, boasting little else, the air of Raby at least is excellent, and really does wonders for some people.

"Oh! d——n the fiddle!" exclaimed Shadwell, interrupted by the renewed minstrelsy of Carmel, who, startled with bow suspended in his fingers, gazed with a pained alarm on his patron.

"Fiddle—fiddle! he said fiddle!" murmured Carmel, in sad and gentle accents, for it was a foible of his to fancy everything he possessed a *chef d'œuvre* or a miracle.

"So he did," repeated Shadwell, with a sharp nod.

"A—yes; but, this is—a—yes, do but look at it—this is a Stradivarius. I was lucky, sir—amazing— ha! yes. I paid only twenty-four shillings for it!"

Shadwell sealed his envelope, and offered no comment.

"And it is worth three hundred guineas, sir," continued he, almost whispering the estimate to his beloved violin.

"I wish you'd sell it," said Shadwell, drily, for he hated its music; "and if you can get half what you gave, I advise you. Come, let me see what you have done."

"Sell it? So I will—ay, sir, when its term of servitude is done. I shan't want it after a few weeks. There is a secret about those violins—Prometheus; the Statue of Memnon. If the history of Saul and David be as true as that of George the Third, there was a Stradivarius who made harps then—harps. Spirit is vibration, and vibration is music. I have thought upon that, sir. I can explain—"

"Thank you, I'd rather have the balance of the mortgage account," replied Shadwell.

"Oh!—ah!—to be sure, sir, I beg pardon—not quite made out, though. Roke Wycherly —Sir Roke. Coming! Tut! tut! tut! Ay—well, yes—such dreams! And potential letters, too. Would you like the window shut, sir?"

As he spoke he was selecting and getting together the notes required by Mark Shadwell.

"My father died of fever at Easterbroke; my poor mother at Rochester, and my dear sister at Wyden—all great losses— dreadful, sir, dreadful—one at Christmas, that's Yule—the next on Easter Monday, and the last on the Royal Oak day, we used to call it—the anniversary', you know, and the villain who robbed me was Robert Eyre Yardley. Where I was knocked down by the cab, and my rib broken, was Regent Street, and there are no end—no end of them. So I have reason to hate those letters E, Y, and R; and they are doubled in his name, and the rest—ay, here's the account deducted—Sandford's—and the rest are O, K, W, C, H, L—and they are *your* unlucky letters, sir. I'll show you."

"Much obliged—some other time," said Shadwell, drily, taking the papers. "Will you tell Jack Linton to run down to the town and post this letter?"

"Ha! this is it—ay, ay—my God! won't you think, sir?" said Carmel, throwing back his long black hair, and fixing his eyes with a stare of pain and fear on Shadwell.

"We'll post the letter, and think after," said he.

"R—Rachel, that's another—the worst, perhaps," whispered Carmel, clasping his hands as he left the room dejectedly.

"That fellow's cracked—he *is* mad," muttered Shadwell, looking after him. If he had been in better spirits he would have laughed; as it was he contented himself with a hope that Carmel's figures were right. And Carmel, much troubled, re-entered the room.

He passed his hand through his hair, and groaned as he came behind Mark Shadwell's chair softly, and laid his hand on the back of it, saying:

"I think, sir, if you knew all—such dreams! He came into my room at dead of night, like a great cock—ha, ha! you will laugh, you will—with a bloody comb—head, eyes, neck, all bloody, sir, taller than the door, and crowed. I knew it was he—such a crow, it pierced my brains, sir. I knew it was he, though I never saw him."

"He's not a bit like a cock, though—a cox-comb, perhaps. So do shut up your poultry, and help me to understand this."

While Mark Shadwell in Carmel's room was busy over these accounts, in the drawing-room sat quite alone a very pretty woman—though no longer young, still girlish—with the transparent and delicate tints of an invalid in her oval face, large eyes and long lashes, and such a pretty mouth! Though the face was very sad just now, you could not help feeling how brightly it might smile. Pensively she lay back in her low-armed chair; her thin pretty hands lay extended beside her, and her head a little on one side, with that peculiar dejection which strikes us so plaintively in pictures of medieval martyrs. Her hair, brown and wavy, was seen under that pretty little lace *coiffure*, with a dark-blue ribbon running through it, which reminded one of the old mob cap.

Pearly-tinted, slender, pensive, there was still in that fragile creature an air of youth quite wonderful in the mother of a girl now just eighteen.

This girlish, fragile, pretty matron was Mark Shadwell's wife— the still young mother of that pretty Rachel, who was their only child. Well might she be sad, thinking of the hope and love she had given in vain. It was one of those mysterious passions exacted by fate, never to be requited. Nineteen years ago, just two and thirty, in the prime of manly beauty, he seemed to her in all things a hero. His love was a beautiful but false adoration—so eloquent, so passionate, so graceful. Where was it now? Long burnt out, cold ashes, years ago—gone before their first child was born. What so terrible as this fatal fidelity of a neglected love? Wrongs will not murder it, nor desertion starve it. Wildly it prays to be changed to loathing—entreats that it may die, and curses itself for loving still.

As Amy Shadwell leaned back in her chair, her look was lowered to the ground beyond her tiny feet, and on her face that strange look of pain along with that light or smile, I know not which it is, that we have seen so often on the faces of the youthful dead.

Her thoughts were now wandering to Rachel and her governess.

"My darling, it is well for her—a gentle and loving person— affectionate and playful—Agnes Marlyn. She would be good to her if I were gone. She loves me, I hope. But this *triste* place! Will she stay—will she stay long?"

Just now the door silently opened, and Agnes Marlyn, like an evoked spirit, stood on the threshold with some flowers in her hand, doubtfully; and it seemed as if from within that old oak door-case, as from a stained window, a flood of wonderfully rich tints entered the room.

Pretty Mrs. Shadwell looked up and smiled.

"Come, dear—come, you dear kind Agnes; and flowers, too! You always think of me, you good creature."

Agnes heard this greeting with a beautiful dimpling smile, standing under the shadow of the doorway, and, as it seemed with a blush of gratification, and her long lashes were lowered over those dark, soft, clouded eyes, so impossible to describe. And closing the door, with the ends of her fingers, she approached the table with her flowers, gently.

## Chapter 5
### Agnes Marlyn

"Pretty flowers! All yes! and sweet!" mild Amy Shadwell, with a smile. "Charming! a thousand thanks, kind creature!" and she touched Agnes Marlyn's pretty hand caressingly as she placed them in the little glass that stood beside her.

Agnes answered only with the same smile, looking all the time down upon the flowers which she was adjusting.

"And where have you and Rachel been? Aren't you a little late?" asked pale Mrs. Shadwell. but with her gentle smile.

"Late? oh! very late, Mrs. Shadwell. I am so sorry. My watch, I think, went quite wrong. I was so afraid you would have been anxious and vexed, only you are so good. We were at Hazelden, so far away in the park, and the sun was nearly set when we came to that pretty ruin, Wynderfel—is not that the name? and so we came so fast—so fast—and were late, notwithstanding; and I am so sorry." Miss Agnes Marlyn spoke in a particularly sweet low voice, with a slight foreign accent, and a little slowly; altogether the singularity was very pretty. But although she had passed many years of her life at a French school, which she had left only a few months ago to come to Raby, she seldom spoke a French idiom, and then I think it sounded interesting.

"And where is my other truant? You're not tired, I hope?" asked Mrs. Shadwell.

"Rachel? Oh! Rachel's in her room, coming immediately. I don't think she was; she said she wasn't tired," said Agnes.

"And you?"

"I?—oh! never tired of the beautiful country—never tired walking. To wander always among the trees, to feel the blowing air and the grass and flowers—so charming under the foot—is my paradise, I think," said Miss Agnes Marlyn, in her low sweet tones, looking with a happy flush as if she could see her beloved woodlands, flowers and dingles, through and beyond the oak panels.

"But I'm so afraid you find it very dull, my poor Agnes—your pension, your companions, the pretty French town and gardens—"

"Ah, *Madame*, never was I so happy! The lonely country to me is sweetest. I never have cared for noise and gaiety. I have lost my father and my dear mamma early, when I was still a little girl, as you know. I never was anywhere so happy since then, because I never was with one so kind—never with any one I so much loved as you; but—pardon, *Madame*—I am, I have been, too audacious—I have for a moment forgotten myself."

"Forgotten your foolish shyness, I hope," replied Mrs. Shadwell, smiling on the affectionate and grateful girl. "Yes, Agnes, you must trust in me more than you have done. I think you like me; I know I like you. I should like to make you another dear child of mine."

The beautiful girl rose up with a flush of subdued rapture, her arms extended in a glad surprise; and with a smile of welcome the pretty and fragile mistress of Raby also rose, and, in the effusion of the moment, gently folded her young dependent in her arms.

Beautiful Agnes Marlyn! Lithe, tall, ineffably graceful! With a kind of sigh she gave herself to that embrace, and lay in it a second or so longer than she need, perhaps.

In fairy lore we read of wondrous transmutations and disguises. How evil spirits have come in the fairest and saddest forms; how fell and shrewd-eyed witches have waited in forest glades by night, in shapes of the loveliest nymphs. So, for a dream-like moment, one might see, under the wondrous beauty of the girl, in that spell of momentary joy, a face that was apathetic and wicked.

Amy Shadwell did not see it. As the girl drew gratefully back, with downcast look, there was nothing in that sensitive and splendid beauty but the light of a tremulous happiness.

"Oh! *madame*—Mrs. Shadwell—I cannot say—how can I?—half what gratitude I feel for all your goodness. I hope I may please you, and do my duty by your dear child, as I pray I may. My fate has been so solitary, even among many companions; no one to care for me—no one ever to love me. Contempt follows poverty like its shadow: amidst seeming equality, I was despised; amidst a crowd, I was alone."

Miss Agnes Marlyn here hastily brushed her handkerchief to her beautiful eyes, and Mrs. Shadwell again spoke words of consolation; and again the young lady's gratitude was eloquent.

"Do I not hear the piano? I think Rachel is playing. Shall I go, *Madame*? it is her hour for practising."

So, kindly, Agnes Marlyn was dismissed.

As she passed through the hall, Agnes paused at the table where the letters lay, about a dozen, littered together, as Mark Shadwell left them. She glanced over her shoulder, and listened for a moment; many doors opened on the hall—and, all being still, she ran her fingertips rapidly among them, and turned them over and about. There was one addressed to her, written in a constrained, it might be a disguised, hand. Quickly, with a handsome smile—a smile a little cruel—she hid it away in her breast. Again she glanced and listened, and then with a rapid eye examined the others. There was not another that interested her. And in a moment more she entered the room where Rachel was at the piano.

Ten minutes later Mark Shadwell passed the same table, and suddenly recollected the letters. There were two for his wife, one for Rachel, and—wasn't there?—there certainly *was* one addressed to Miss Agnes Marlyn, in a peculiar hand, and with the London postmark. Where was that letter? It had, somehow, a little interested Mark Shadwell; although that interest had been instantaneously suspended by the sight of Roke Wycherley's note.

Mark Shadwell now, in his turn, looked sharply round. Who

had been meddling? Well—time enough. Meanwhile he would see his wife, and let her have hers.

He had been a man of fashion in his day, and, though the vase was broken, "the scent of the roses" hung round it still. There were handsome features, though the light of youth was gone, and a distinguished air; and poor little Mrs. Shadwell still believed that his beauty and fascinations were unrivalled.

He had been a man of fashion, and something more—a rake, a gamester, a prodigal. There were much worse men, I dare say, but he was bad enough.

She smiled her timid welcome as he entered now. He did not choose to see it. Is any pleading sadder than an unanswered smile?

"Two letters," said he, drily. "If they're half as pleasant as mine, they'll help to make your evening agreeable."

"One is from old Mrs. Danvers, and the other from my cousin, Sophy Mordaunt," said Amy, as she glanced on the envelopes.

"Oh, indeed! then no doubt they'll turn out quite as amusing as I expected. I've had a very charming one, also—and from a particularly charming person."

And having sneered thus far, in his dreary way, he paused, and said: "Guess who—there, you may as well give it up—you never could—it is your old admirer, and my old creditor, Roke Wycherly. He tells me he has been suffering—no doubt miserably, with twenty thousand a year, and all Europe, and its pleasures, of which, poor devil, he avails himself in turn—suffering most cruelly—ha, ha!—and he's coming here; no doubt because we are so entertaining, and so fond of him—and the shooting so good—and he likes rabbits so excessively—and. Upon my life, if these aren't his reasons, I can't guess at any other—only I'm quite sure he means me no good, and I think he can do me a mischief, which he probably intends; and, therefore, we must make him as welcome and as comfortable as we can, and, no doubt, he'll pass a charming week. And pray tell the people to get his room ready; and his man is coming."

"How soon, dear, does he come?" she asked, with a rather

dismal look.

"I suppose in a week, or a fortnight—perhaps the day after tomorrow; I dare say he does not know himself—whenever he likes, in short—and that's *my* news."

And, with these words, he turned and left the room.

## CHAPTER 6
### SOME MUSIC

He walked into the room in which Rachel was playing, her governess sitting by her in the attitude of one reading the music over her shoulder, but with a look that passed through the page far away, and was dark and dreamy. Hearing the step, they both looked round.

"Pray, go on—I've come to listen. I don't interrupt, Miss Marlyn, I hope?"

"Oh, no, Mr. Shadwell, certainly not!" said Miss Agnes Marlyn, smiling and embarrassed, and in her low tones.

"I'm very glad. I like music and young people, and should be sorry to be turned out. Go on, Rachel."

So the music proceeded; and Mark Shadwell, throwing himself carelessly on a sofa, looked on Miss Marlyn with a secret interest. Though she seemed to be looking altogether on the music, and he could see but the up-curled edge of her long eyelash, she felt his gaze, and was secretly flattered, perhaps amused.

"That will do, Rachel, for a moment," said he, after a time. "The piano's very well, but, Miss Marlyn, don't you sing? I'm sure you do—I can't be mistaken,—the formation of the throat—you need not look down, I assure you it's very beautiful; but I can't be mistaken. Do sing a little—sola, duet, anything you like—pray do."

"Very happy, sir," said she with a modest awe. "But I had only a very few lessons when I left Darmonville, and I—I hardly dare sing before you."

Sing, however, on a little encouragement, she did, very prettily, a little French song; and Mr. Shadwell applauded with both hands, and thanked her, and said:

"Quite a charming voice! I *had* no idea—or, rather, I had an idea, and a very correct one, as it turns out; but I never heard you sing a note before. How strange! such a voice! and yet, to say nothing of us, you can deny yourself, and live in silence! Candles under bushels—I've no patience with that cruel sort of modesty—cruel nightingale! And, by Jove, what a blessing music is! I don't mean, of course, that noisy, formal, heartless business, that young ladies sit down to at the piano, but *music*—be it art or nature—the thing that stirs our feelings. I do assure you, King Saul was never so much under the shadow of his demon as I was when I came in here; and David's harp was nothing to that song. I do assure you, quite seriously, I am very much obliged."

Now there really was some savour of truth in this—Mark Shadwell did feel more cheerful; but I don't know that it was all the music, or very much, although he liked dropping in there and listening.

"You came to us in April, wasn't it. Miss Marlyn?" he asked. "You've been our guest six months; and my wife says you'll be sure to grow tired of us before long. She hopes not, you know, and so do I; but I am afraid it is a slow place—isn't it, rather?" and he laughed in his sardonic way once more.

"I told Mrs. Shadwell tonight, what is really true," said Miss Marlyn, gravely, "how much I like the quiet of this place, sir; I do *indeed*."

"Well, I'm sure I'm very glad; it's more than I do," he replied, peevishly.

"Oh, dear, Rachel, that is nine o'clock!" exclaimed Agnes Marlyn, as the clock in the hall struck the hour, and glancing at her watch for confirmation. "Yes, indeed! Rachel, dear, we must go. Your mamma will expect us in her room; and the books are in the schoolroom. Goodnight, Mr. Shadwell."

"Goodnight—goodnight," said he. "Oh, by-the-bye, I forgot—there's a letter—just one word—Rachel, you can run and get those books; don't be a minute." And Rachel, accustomed to obey, did as she was bid. "You know, you *do* think this place nearly intolerable. It must be insufferably dull."

30

"I have told you the truth, sir," said Miss Marlyn, with just the least indication of being offended.

"Ha, ha!" laughed Mr. Shadwell, in an under key.

"It is very well, sir, for the great or the wealthy to enjoy the world; but for such as I, what can it give? The same routine—the same solitude—and a thousand mortifications. If I did not like this place very dearly, I need not stay. I have told you the truth." And saying this, those clouded eyes of hers dropped to the carpet, and Mark Shadwell thought her colour was a little heightened.

He looked on her for a moment with a sombre sort of puzzle.

"And," he said, resuming, "there was a letter addressed to you—it came by this evening's post; I laid it down in the hall with the rest, and, by Jove, I can't find it."

He was looking still very steadily at her as he said this.

"Oh, thanks!—I *took* it," said she, raising her eyes and looking full on him.

"Ho! I had no idea," he said, fibbing, with an air of innocent surprise. "I'm so glad it's safe."

"Yes, it was from a very kind old friend. As I came into the hall, it and two others were on the ground, and I picked them up, and saw one addressed to me; I hope it was not wrong, but I took it. I am very sorry—I ought to have asked first; but, indeed, Mr. Shadwell, I intended to have told you the moment I saw you, and most stupidly, I forgot. I am very sorry; pray forgive me—won't you, sir?"

She was fibbing, too; but wasn't it pleasant to be asked, in such low and sweet tones, to forgive so very beautiful a creature?

"Oh! to be sure—no harm—none in the world. You were quite right, perfectly; I only wished to—to *tell* you; but it was your own, and I hope it may turn out pleasanter than mine do. When I was as young as you, I used to get some very pleasant letters indeed. You know quite well the sort of thing I mean—you all do; and I think you *are* a bit of a rogue—you all are." He spoke in very low tones, and looking full upon her, and smiling, showed his set of small, even teeth, that looked a little wicked, and seemed to like prolonging this little talk.

"I never tell a lie, Mr. Shadwell," said Miss Agnes Marlyn, with a proud humility, and downcast eyes.

"More than *I* can say; more than any other girl can say, that is not a literal saint. Are you? I hope not, I'm sure; they're so disagreeable and censorious; but you must not be vexed, you know. We are good friends, Miss Marlyn, aren't we?"

And he laid his fingers on her arm, which hung by her side, and they glided down her wrist to her hand, which he took.

"You'll shake hands?—there, now—we're friends, aren't we?"

There was something almost tender in this friendliness, and Miss Marlyn, raising her beautiful eyes with a look of timid wonder, which seemed preparing for one of recoil, withdrew her hand, and said:

"There was no quarrel, I hope, sir. I hope I have said nothing of disrespect; I should be very sorry of it."

"No—nonsense! Disrespect, indeed! what do you look so surprised at?" said he.

"I—I thought—you never spoke to me so much before at a time, Mr. Shadwell, and—I thought—we are all a little afraid, sir, of you; I thought you were proud, sir, and severe—and—pray do not be offended."

There was a kind of reproof in this. Shadwell thought; he looked gloomily in her face, without quite understanding her, and then he laughed.

"Proud and severe!" he repeated, reflectively, with an odd smile, like a man looking on his own miniature; "that's not so bad. Well, perhaps I am; yes, I *am*—where I'm crossed, that is; ay, by Jove! proud and severe as the fiend himself. Come along, Rachel—what have you been about?" he called, raising his voice as he heard her step coming. "Goodnight, child; goodnight, Miss Marlyn," and he threw himself back on the sofa, with a gloomy countenance, and without a glance after either.

# CHAPTER 7

## IN AMY SHADWELL'S ROOM

When Rachel ran into her mamma's room to bid her good-night, she found her busy with old Dorothy Wyndle, the house-keeper. A guest of any importance at Raby was seldom heard of, and such an arrival produced a sensation. Here was a consultation as to where to place Sir Roke, which interested Rachel, whose curiosity was all alive.

"Hey! ma'am, it's thirty-six years since he was here; my blue-eyed beauty I called him then. He was a very pretty boy, golden hair, dearie me! and them blue eyes, and his pretty pink cheeks; nice slim little figure, a tidy-made little fellow. His poor mamma came here that time; a nice creature she was, and I hear he grew up very tall at college. Him and Master Mark here, they used to ride out on their little rough ponies to see the hounds at cover, like yesterday, and sometimes they'd quarrel a bit; nothin' very bad, though. Shall I fill you out a cup o' tea, ma'am?"

"Thanks, Dolly," said pretty Mrs. Shadwell, smiling. Old Dorothy's prattle amused her, as she leaned back in her cushioned chair.

"They boxed one night, they did, poor little fellows, him and Master Mark, and I threatened I'd complain; but they made it up—ha, ha, ha! Oh! he was noways spiteful, was Master Roke; a nice little fellow!"

"How old was he then?" asked Miss Rachel.

"Well, dear, he wasn't much; about eleven, or twelve, or thirteen, I'd say, but it's a good bit agone; it's thirty odd years—thirty-six, or thirty-seven, I think. Thirty-seven and thirteen. He'll be past forty now! Aye, dear, dear!"

And she uttered these ejaculations in a prolonged note, which implied the wonder and regret of a discovery, and which a man might have conveyed by an equivalent whistle.

"Ay, ay! it will be—forty odd—you're good at figures, Miss Rachel. Hey, dear! that's too old for *you*, miss; ay, it would not do! I was thinkin', when I heard of him comin', and he so pretty, it was, maybe, after Miss Rachel he'd be lookin'; but she's very young, and forty—I don't know! What do *you* think, ma'am?"

"Why, Dolly, you foolish old thing! I believe he was in love with mamma!"

Her mamma laughing, shook her head, and old Dolly said generously:

"Well, Miss Rachel, you know, it's as *you* like, not as *he*, and you may like him well enough when you see him, who knows? and forty-six or fifty's nothing. Hoo! tut! nothing at all, if you knew."

And thus encouraged, Rachel threw back her pretty locks, and laughed heartily as she dropped into a chair.

"And *was* he courting you, ma'am?—was he *really*, now?" inquired old Dolly.

"I don't know, Dolly, I'm sure; they said he was," answered she, laughing again.

"I shouldn't wonder—no, I shouldn't; for I mind the first time I saw you, and I think you were the prettiest lass I ever set eyes on in all my days ever."

"Old Dolly is a partial witness, I'm afraid," said the sickly lady, smiling prettily on her, and from her to her daughter.

"No, she isn't, mamma; she's an honest old thing, and if she said anything else it would be a wicked story, for at this moment you're the very prettiest person I ever saw."

"My foolish little Rachel!" said her mamma, smiling very fondly on her.

"No! I'm your wise little woman; you know I am; you always say I am, except when I praise you." And with these words Rachel threw her arms about her mother's neck, and kissed her again and again.

"He's a bachelor, ain't he, ma'am?" inquired Dolly Wyndle, recollecting on a sudden that she was imperfectly informed.

"Yes; an old bachelor," said she.

"Not so old but he has lots o' time to marry in," said Dorothy, recurring, I suppose, to her original plan.

"It's quite true, Dolly; they marry at all ages: never too old," laughed her mistress.

"*Never*! *That's* what I say, ma'am, isn't it? and he's awful rich, ain't he?"

"There are much richer men; but he's very well."

"And will it all come to Master Mark if he dies without no children?" asked she.

"No, nothing; not a guinea."

"Well, that's bad, it is. I wish he *would* take a fancy to Miss Rachel here: who knows?"

"Come, Dolly, we must not talk nonsense. He's an old bachelor, an invalid, and has been very wild—I believe, wicked—in his youth, and I don't believe would be likely to make a wife happy; and it would not do to talk that kind of folly: you mustn't."

"Well, it is a pity, and she so handsome, shut up in this place—it's awful lonesome, you know; and I was looking at her, I was, t'other day, dancin' so pretty, and the governess; and, quoth I to myself, 'Well, an' if a Lunnon lord was to see that he couldn't but fancy her.'"

And up jumped Rachel, laughing. And the girl threw her arms round the neck of her laughing mamma, and bidding her a fond goodnight, ran away to her bedroom.

"A wild little creature, Dolly! Thank Heaven, she's so merry! What would this place be without her, I often think? Poor little thing! I sometimes pity her; and yet it is better, perhaps, she should never have known any but this melancholy place, seeing she must live in it," said Mrs. Shadwell.

"*Melancholy*! Well, now, I don't know. What's there so dull in it? It's a fine place, ma'am—beautiful trees; and Hazelden!—it's ten years, ye wouldn't believe, since I saw Hazelden, though 'tisn't a mile and half along the park—and Wynderfel! old walls they be, and them old graves there! I mind the last time I was there—ten years it is—ha! ha! ha! Dearie me! Wynderfel! I think it's the darkest wood anywhere on English ground, near Feltram, there, goin' down by the hollow, I'm sure on't. And them old walls with the ivy: that's the spot, nigh hand, where old John Gildford saw the Evil One, wi' horns on's head, sitting on the pixie's stone!

"Often I heard old John tell it when I was no longer than the leg o' the table there; and a steady man was John, and a godly; ye don't see men so gi'en to church and sermons now as John Gildford. Ye don't mind old John, do ye? No, no! He was gone— Oh! ay—long afore your time! Old master respected John Gildford very much, and gev him as good a coffin, a'most, as he got himself, when *his* turn came. Straight bed, ma'am, then, and narrow house, fits rich and poor—all's one; sleep sound, without no turn nor start, when work's done, till mornin', in sure and certain hopes ye know, ma'am, what they put on the gravestones; that's what we're to look to.

"Parson Temple preaches beautiful on that; he's a good man, is Parson Temple. I like to see him comin' to Raby, I do; and I wish, ma'am (lowering her voice), master liked him better. I wish master took more after his mother; she was a godly woman, she was, poor thing! I wish he would, and a thought less after the poor old master. God forgi'e me! not any wrong I mean; only neither on 'em cared for such like, nor minded church nor sermons—nothing, a'most; but good men—mind ye! I don't mean nothin' wrong—and I'm talkin' ower much," she wound up briskly, "and work to be done, like an old talkin' fool, as I be!!"

And so the question of quarters and commissariat was once more entered on with her accustomed vigour and clearness by energetic old Dolly.

## CHAPTER 8

### MISS MARLYN INQUIRES

At the beginning of the present chapter it was very late. The old clock at the stair-head of Raby had struck twelve some time ago. Agnes Marlyn had been sitting up in Rachel's room, gossiping with her about many things, as young ladies will sit up together sometimes in a chatty mood; still she was there, narrating French adventures and experiences, describing rural scenes and school vexations, happy hours and regrets, tyrants, and friends, oh! so dear, and all the story tinged with that sentiment, so sad and pure, which she knew how, with tones and looks, almost without the help of words, to shed, like a sunset light, over her little gossipings.

She had now got up to bid her companion goodnight, for the twentieth time, yet she still hesitated for a moment.

"So there is someone coming here—have you heard?" asked Agnes, as she stood by the little dressing-table in Rachel's room.

"Yes, Sir Roke Wycherly," answered the girl.

"Sir Roke Wycherly!" repeated Miss Marlyn, slowly; "what a very odd name!"

"Yes, an odd name," answered Rachel, who was brushing her rich fair hair before the glass, "and, I fancy, an odd person, too."

"Ha, ha! there are so many odd persons in England," said Agnes Marlyn. "Sir Roke Wycherley:—an old friend of your papa's, I dare say?"

"An old friend! yes, a cousin. They were at Eton together, mamma says, and he's an invalid."

"A cousin?"

"Yes; some kind of cousin. I suppose, having been schoolfellows, he and papa are very fond of one another."

"I am sorry he's coming," said Miss Marlyn.

"Why? What are you afraid of?" said Rachel, gaily. "I think it a blessing—I really do: quite a mercy anyone coming; although, I dare say I shall be horribly afraid of him; but I'm very glad, for all that."

"I am sorry," repeated Agnes Marlyn.

"And why?" reiterated Rachel.

"Why? I don't know: that is, I *do* know."

"Well?" said Rachel, looking over her shoulder, and expecting an explanation.

Agnes laughed suddenly, paused, and then said, in her usual tone:

"I *am* sorry, and I'll tell you why. I like quiet; I love this so quiet place; I love you; I love your mamma; there is no one coming can make it happier."

"And do you like papa?" asked Miss Rachel, a little abruptly.

Agnes Marlyn looked at her rather oddly, and laughed again. The girl was looking at herself straight and frankly in the glass as she arranged her soft golden hair.

"Your papa! I am sure he is a good man, but I cannot say I like him, for I do not know him: and, to say truth, I think I am a little afraid of him—and so are you, are you not?"

"I *am* afraid of him. I always was; and yet he never was cruel—no, of course, not cruel!—I mean, he never was harsh; he was never unkind to me," said Rachel.

"Nor ever kind," said Agnes Marlyn, and laughed once more.

"He's so clever!" said Rachel.

"How do you know? He never speaks to you," said Miss Marlyn.

"Mamma says—that's how I know—he was quite different when he was young: very gay."

"Gay, was he?"

"Gay spirits, I mean—a witty man—and very much admired; but, you know, those creditors—who are always distracting him about money—they have made him so gloomy: things they call mortgages. Horrid cruelty, *I* call it, to torment a fellow creature the way mamma says they worry papa!" said Miss Rachel, with spirit.

"Nine men out of ten have debts, dear," said Miss Marlyn. "He ought to be happy: he loves you and your mamma very much."

Miss Rachel looked round from the glass upon her handsome companion. She saw nothing in her countenance but a listless melancholy.

"Yes, of course, he loves mamma very much, and that, I dare say, makes him suffer more, because he knows she must suffer with him."

"That is very generous," said Agnes Marlyn.

Again Rachel looked at her, but no sign of irony appearing,

she turned again to her glass, and a little silence ensued.

"But, my dear Rachel," resumed Agnes Marlyn, "though he is so generous—"

"I did not say he's generous, though I dare say he is," said Rachel; "of course he is—too generous, or he would not be so much worried with debts as he is."

"Well, I mean so good, and all that; yet, I think he is a very stern man; and you must not be angry, but I am always afraid of him, and would rather not see him coming—would rather not meet him, and I never feel quite at ease while he is in the room."

Another pause followed.

"And you are afraid, also," added Miss Marlyn.

"I said so—yes—but afraid is hardly the right word; it is more a strangeness. When I was a little thing, I was always told to be silent when he was in the room; as long as I can remember, he was always melancholy and—"

"Cross," suggested Miss Marlyn.

"Cross. No," replied Rachel, whose pride was touched by this girl's daring to criticise her papa so boldly; "he has a great deal to vex him, and—and—let us talk of something else."

"Well, Rachel, we are very happy here: I love this old place, so grand and forlorn, for I, too, am a melancholy person like your papa, more perhaps, and I love this solitary Raby better, I dare say, than he does; I love you, Rachel, as I said, and I love your mamma; I wonder does she love—no, not love—*like* me!"

There was inquiry in Miss Marlyn's plaintive tone, but it was like the inquiry of a soliloquy, in low and dreamy notes, with her fine eyes lowered to the table, and her pretty hand to her chin.

There came a little silence here. There were moments when Rachel felt oddly towards this young governess, a disposition to challenge and snub her suddenly. Why should there be loving and liking so soon? what, in seven months' time, had she done for them, or they for her, that could found a serious sentiment of that kind? Was it a suspicion of a sham, with the impatience that accompanies it? She could not tell; only, having finished the arrangement of her hair, she leaned back in her chair, with her chin a little raised and her eyes nearly closed, and answered nothing.

Miss Marlyn sighed softly, and looked full and sadly on her pupil, and said, as if she had divined what was in her mind:

"I am, perhaps, a fool to talk of loving and liking."

"I don't expect you to like me much, or love me at all, on so short an acquaintance," said Rachel.

"Yes, that is true; you are all so good to me, I forget how short it is: it is gratitude that makes attachment in a day. I owe it all to you; you can owe none to me—so it is."

Agnes Marlyn said this with a sad sort of sincerity, that touched the girl, who opened her blue eyes, and placed her hand kindly on that of her governess.

"What can put such things in your head ?—you are not to talk so," said Rachel, repentant.

"And I shall leave you soon—yes—yes, dear, not voluntarily, but it must be; you cannot long need a governess, in effect—it is almost time I should go."

"But I must have some friend with me here always, mamma says, and she would prefer you to any other—she says so, and so should I, Pucelle," answered Rachel; "therefore you are not to fancy that, because I have no sentiment, I don't like people, for I like you—I do, indeed; I like you *very* much ."

"No sentiment! I fancied the same of myself once," said Miss Marlyn, "but it needed only time and affliction to prove to me that I had—time will make a like discovery to you, dear Rachel."

"I hope not, Pucelle ;" she called Agnes by that name, from a fancied resemblance to a pretty old print in her bedroom. "Mamma says that all romantic people are unhappy."

"That is true," said Miss Marlyn, with a sigh; "I am romantic; you are too young, dear Rachel, to understand the force of that word—I am unhappy—I care not for money—I care not for the world."

"I like you the better for that, Pucelle," said Rachel; "I hate to see people always making up sums, and counting their gains and losses; and, besides, the Bible says it's wicked to love money, and I don't know, really, why they do, or what they can want of all the money they are always wishing for."

And Rachel thought over these propositions; being very young and innocent of tradesmen's bills, and, I dare say, it was one of her axioms that one's house, and one's meals, and all that sort of common-place, came by nature.

"Yes, I have been a fool; I have lived too much from my heart, too little from my head. It is very necessary to be a little selfish. I will try; but, *hélas*! I know I shall not be able—so impetuous!—so volatile! so foolish!" and, with these words. Miss Marlyn stamped her foot lightly on the ground, and pressed her shut hand to her brow.

"Agnes, I think I'm like you, I'm sure I am," said Rachel. "I know, at all events, I like you for that kind of feeling, and I hope you may never succeed in changing your character. Don't try; you'll only injure it."

"Ah! thank heaven, then, there is one person on earth who does understand me. Yes, Rachel, you do. Goodnight, dearest; it is very late." And with a kiss, she hurried from the room.

## Chapter 9
### Mark Shadwell Engages a Secretary

Beautiful Agnes Marlyn, with her candle in her hand, as she trod lightly along the passage towards her chamber, looking with one stealthy glance over her shoulder toward the door of her young companion, which she had just softly closed, might have furnished a painter with an image for some spirit of a bygone and guilty beauty, haunting those old galleries, and visiting the curtains of midnight sleepers to shape their dreams; for there was in her large dark eyes, and in the curve of her eyebrows, an evil care—something wild and dismal—as she glided alone along the gallery in slippered feet.

Raby Hall is very old, as you know; the buttery and the spicery still bear their traditional names there. It was re-edified in Elizabeth's time, and has been little altered since. It could hardly be said to be, now-a-days, inhabited at all. Mark Shadwell and his few retainers occupied their nook of warmth and life in this great and forlorn structure; but the light of habitation was lost in the waste of general darkness, like the gleam of a homestead on a moor. Miss Marlyn's weaknesses were not, however, of the superstitious kind. She might be walking amidst those desert places where evil spirits inhabit, but she did not care about such things. The fears of that beautiful girl, such as they were, were all of the earth, earthy; therefore it was only with that kind of start which may occur at anytime and anywhere that, on turning the corner of the gallery leading to her room, Miss Agnes Marlyn suddenly met Mr. Shadwell.

There were not two steps between them as they met. He, like her, had his bedroom candle in his hand, and in his other he carried a dispatch-box, charged with those weary papers—the multitudinous children of his early follies, the inexorable tyrants of his matured years. John Bunyan's Christian did not walk under a heavier load than that little dispatchbox. It bent Shadwell with his face to the earth—it half broke his heart.

He stood before Miss Marlyn—now for a moment scarcely feeling it—with a surprised and haggard countenance, candle in hand, and stared at this timid beauty for some seconds before he spoke.

"By Jove, Miss Marlyn! I did not expect to see you again tonight. I'm afraid I startled you. It's very odd."

Of course it was very odd. It was one o'clock, and Miss Marlyn and her pupil were usually in bed at about ten. But he could not be very angry, for he laughed ever so little, and Miss Agnes Marlyn said, in a contrite way that was very pretty:

"I am so sorry, sir; I have been sitting up with Rachel much too late. We really quite forgot the time, and I am very sorry, Mr. Shadwell, and I hope you are not displeased."

"Displeased—*I?*" said Mark Shadwell; "quite the contrary. There, you need not look puzzled, I'm quite serious—I'm glad I met you. What are you afraid of?"

"I'm not afraid, Mr. Shadwell."

"No, you're not such a fool." He laid his "dispatch-box on the window-sill beside him. "I said it was odd my meeting you, because it happened I was at that moment thinking of you, and very selfishly, too. May I go on?"

"I'm so tired, sir; perhaps in the morning," Miss Marlyn began, with a very low curtsey.

He looked on her with a bold sort of admiration, as he might on a pretty picture.

"I like that," he said; "one of the old French curtsies, that our grandmothers used to make; a beautiful curtsey, by all the graces of Versailles. It ought to be made in brilliants, powder, and brocade; one of the curtsies that have lingered in quaint old corners of France, where the vulgar sweep of the Revolution never rushed."

"Goodnight, Mr. Shadwell," she said, dropping her eyes very gravely, and "addressing herself" to pass him.

"Pray not, for a moment. You need not reprove me; how do you know I deserve reproof?" said he, a little sharply.

"Reprove, sir? I merely wish to pass," said Miss Agnes Marlyn, holding her head high, and looking straight before her, beautifully sulky.

"So you shall; can't you wait a moment? You seem to fancy I'm a fool. I'm no such thing. I'm perfectly sober, perfectly serious; and what I have to say, I fancy, you'll think not of the slightest consequence, though you may think it a bore. I want to know—you'll really do me an essential kindness if you will—*will* you consent to be my secretary?"

"I don't know, Mr. Shadwell, what you mean," said the young lady, gravely.

"Literally what I say," he replied, a little drily. "You need not be in such haste. Really, in this house there's no sort of oddity in my venturing to say a few words on so dry a subject when we happen to meet just for a moment. I say in this house, because it's such a solitude that there is really no difference between one hour and another, no matter where one may be; and, therefore,

I may as well say what I wish, here and now, as in precisely the same sort of solitude tomorrow morning."

Miss Marlyn looked haughtily over her shoulder—one would have fancied for succour, but no one appeared.

"I have never practised the duties of secretary, sir," she said.

"But you can write a good hand, and you can write a clever letter, and—I never pay compliments—I'm quite past that happy time of life. You'll find I'm a mere man of business—though a very indifferent one—and I assure you, Miss Marlyn, I make my request, odd as you may fancy it, with the most respectful seriousness, and I shall be very really obliged if you will be so kind as to grant it. Pray, a moment. I've considered it. I'll tell you in a word how I am circumstanced. My daughter, as you see, though she's clever, I believe, knows nothing.

"My poor wife—her state of health, you know—can't be of the slightest assistance, and I'm literally overwhelmed with letters. Carmel Sherlock—the queer fellow you've seen here—he's a capital accountant, and knows how every tenant on the estate stands, and the park-book, and all that, but he could no more write a letter than he could make a watch; he has no brains, and there's an end; and upon my honour, if you won't give me a lift. Miss Marlyn, I don't know what's to become of me. I'm not jesting, very far from it, and I'll release you now, only begging of you not to refuse without at least considering; and if you've no objection, I should be so very much obliged if you could copy two or three letters for me—not very long; and,—but I see you'd rather put off saying till tomorrow; so I shan't venture to delay you longer. Goodnight, Miss Marlyn."

"Goodnight, sir."

He picked up his dispatch-box, and she glided away, light in hand, swiftly down the gallery, like the bleeding nun, whose figure must have been very pretty, and her action also, to have been mistaken by a lover for *his* Agnes.

Mark Shadwell looking after her, held his candle, as it were, to light her down the corridor, forgetting that it was unnecessary.

As she passed out of sight his handsome face gleamed into one of his satiric smiles, and his even row of teeth glittered strangely after her in the candle light.

He shrugged.

"How exactly they are, one and all, made after the same pattern! What pains they take to hook us first, and then they let us play ourselves! She mistakes me, though. A stoic—quite above that, d——n her!" This indefensible execration was pronounced, not angrily, but with a little laugh, and a shake of the head.

And late as it was, Mr. Mark Shadwell whistled low a few bars of an old-fashioned air as he walked to his bedroom, where he set down his box with an angry crash on the table, and weary, bitter, and sullen, got into bed with a yawn and a groan; there awaiting the uncertain visit of slumber, as the sick man at the pool of Bethesda might the descent of the Angel.

## CHAPTER 10
### MISS MARLYN LOCKS HER DOOR, AND UNLOCKS HER DESK.

That girl, Agnes Marlyn! It was like a dream his meeting and talking with her. Why had he stopped her there? He almost laughed as he lay thinking of his folly. He had done it without a thought. She looked so lovely he could not pass her by without a word. "I'm not quite sure that I understand that girl. She was not intended for a governess. If her mother had not died—if her father hadn't,—unlucky for her, poor little devil! She's sweetly pretty If Jack Marlyn had lived—a clever fellow, and a staff appointment—that Indian war would have made him. I don't quite understand her. Her mother—her mother was a demirep, wasn't she? Mrs. Marlyn, someone told me—who was it? Someone did. And a French boarding-school. Ha, ha, ha! I wonder what sort of school it is!"

He thought in this vein, perhaps truly, that he did not understand her quite. He fancied she had thrown herself very much in his way. "And what did the gipsy mean by her dignity and stuff tonight? She must have known he had no notion of carrying her off like a Sabine *belle*. I do believe their whole life is such a system of counterfeit and affectation, they don't know themselves when they are in earnest and when they are acting."

And so this brief glimpse of flowers and sunshine closed, and the thick folds and dun fog of his cares broke over and rolled in, and he lay among the shadows of his gigantic mortgages, planning far-off battles and new combinations.

Half-undressed by this time, Agnes Marlyn, having bolted her door, unlocked her little desk—an odd little desk—of some dark wood inlaid all round with small rings and leaves and flowers of brass—a pretty little desk, perhaps made after some old traditional pattern in vogue two hundred years ago, and still known to humdrum craftsmen about dreamy old provincial towns in France. I wonder whether it was a lover's gift—the offering, perhaps, of an adoring worker in brass and rosewood—his *chef d'œuvre*, love-sick, and utterly Quixotic, and he was blest in thinking that so much of his labour was really bestowed on her, that, in very truth, her pretty fingers every day opened and closed that desk that he had worked at, and dreamed, and sighed over so long.

Miss Agnes Marlyn took the letter she had that evening received. It was open; she was not now about to read it for the first time. Standing by the table, with her bedroom candle raised in her left hand, she read it over again with a sort of smile, subtle, contemptuous, amused, yet anxious.

Twice she read it, and the same strange quiet smile again stole over her features. Then she thought profoundly, then for the third time read the letter through, and turned round the back of the envelope, and looked at that, and so at last locked it up again, and when she was nearly undressed, she fell into deep rumination, sitting on the side of her bed for nearly ten minutes, and did not recollect herself until the chill recalled her.

So with a little shudder up she stood, shook her beautiful dark tresses round her shoulders, and gathered them into a few great folds, and prayerless, got into her bed, extinguished her candle, and laid upon the pillow her small head, full of the vapours and chimeras of that letter.

Poor Mrs. Shadwell, that confirmed invalid, appeared not at breakfast. The party consisted of Miss Marlyn, Rachel, Mark Shadwell, and Carmel Sherlock. It was not always a cheerful meal.

Sometimes the master of Raby chose to talk, and then the room became animated a little. But the party stood in awe of him; he would sit in a lowering silence, dark as a thunder-cloud, and people asked for "butter," or "more sugar," in whispers. But this morning he spoke, placing beside him the last letter of the batch which had reached him by that morning's post.

"No letter for you, Miss Marlyn, this morning," said he, suddenly raising his eyes.

"Mine are very few," said Agnes, without raising hers.

"Much to be pitied, you are; you like, of course, to get lots of them. I remember when I liked them. By Jove, I do!" and being bitterly amused, he laughed; "Rachel there, never gets any. No friends, Rachel? So much the better, girl. I had lots of friends, I know, and some of them helped to pigeon me, and others are never done plaguing me, and I can't recollect one that ever did me a kindness!"

"There is, there is, sir, a humble friend," said Carmel Sherlock, looking full at him, rather sorrowfully, with his large eyes; "one friend that would gladly serve you, if he could—if he *could.*"

"Oh! pooh! Carmel, my good fellow, I know that, of course; I was thinking of the fellows who write letters and tease one. I reckon on you, of course," replied Mark Shadwell, impatiently; "but you see. Miss Marlyn, that letters and friends are not quite the blessings you young people take them for. Life is made up of illusions, devilish disagreeable ones—the breaking up, I mean, and discovery, when you come to see things as they are. 'Tis not the golden age, by any means, I can tell you that; nor Arcadia even, nor a pageant, nor even a holiday."

Agnes Marlyn did not breathe a sigh and look plaintive, as an indifferent *tragédienne* might at these words, but she raised her beautiful mysterious gaze gravely to his eyes, and looked like one who had heard a melancholy truth which was to her no revelation.

"Sometimes, of course, a friend does turn up; once, perhaps, in a life," said Mark Shadwell, returning Miss Marlyn's gaze steadily; and she lowered her eyes in a proud and pensive reverie.

"There's Sherlock, I think I may reckon on Sherlock; you need not say, I *know* it. But, by Jove! I don't know many more; I'm not certain I know *one*—ha, ha, ha!"

Mark Shadwell spoke of Carmel Sherlock as if he had bought him body and soul by some enormous service. This way of talking and thinking was generated by poor Sherlock's immense and simple gratitude for very small benefits. He had picked up that dreamy creature in distress, and brought him here to Raby, where for light wages he received from him very useful services, and a loyalty and gratitude that had the extravagance almost of insanity. It rather pleased Mark Shadwell to figure on these easy terms in the character of a benefactor. He could not for double the sum have procured from any other man half the work, yet I believe he honestly fancied that he was, on the whole, the saviour of Carmel Sherlock—that in a freak of disinterested good-nature he had rescued him from the miseries of a world for which he was unfit. Mark Shadwell, therefore, received his allegiance graciously, and applauded his gratitude.

He was beside in especial good humour with Carmel Sherlock this morning. He had relieved him immensely respecting his arrear to Sir Roke, which turned out to be an enormous mistake by reason of the rent-charge payable out of Queen's Hockley by the baronet, which Mark Shadwell, a lazy man of business, with ideas all at sixes and sevens about his affairs, had quite misapplied in his reckoning:

"Well, I thought it could hardly be; I told you I was surprised. It went out of my head, because, you see, I never got a farthing by it, and I fancied Lewis's agent got it."

"It ought to have been brought into the account—yes," said Carmel, "I never heard of it till today. The attorney's letter—the Demon of Socrates—you know, sir, a sudden thought—a thought, an impulse."

"Wherever there's an attorney, there's a demon, of course. There was no danger, for Dolby and Keane have it all up in those d—d tin boxes of theirs; but I'm glad it's off my mind; hang it, it's a mountain gone. And see, Carmel, will you ride down and try and make out what those fellows at the mill want, for I'm hanged if I can make anything of it; and take Will Byers along with you: he's sharper than you or I: and make a note of what they say."

Carmel, always pale, paler now than usual, stood by the door, which he held open for the young ladies as they left the breakfast room.

"Yes, certainly—yes, sir," he answered, with a little start.

"And the sooner the better," said Shadwell briskly. Whereupon Carmel, with a sigh, turned, and shaking back his lank black hair, walked slowly to the hall.

"Miss Marlyn—I beg your pardon—one word—just a moment, please," said Mark Shadwell, following her with this summons from the door; "will you come, just for a moment, to the study?"

The young lady turned.

"Your papa wants to speak to me, Rachel dear. I shall follow in a moment."

Shadwell, with a swift step, reached his study, and by this time was leaning with his elbow on the chimney-piece. He felt a little oddly; a return, though very faint, of those boyish flutterings which he vividly remembered now, though he would as easily have suspected a relapse into kites and marbles. This sort of embarrassment somehow wounded his pride. He heard the rustling of her dress at the door, and a little tapping.

"Come in, please," said Mark Shadwell, with a look and tone a little more haughty than he was accustomed to address to her.

And the young lady entered, carrying her head a little high, and with eyes lowered to the floor, and a flush on her cheeks, and he fancied a faster heaving than usual under the folds of her dress that came up to her throat.

She stood very gravely near the door, expecting, with downcast eyes, and looking quite bewitching, he thought.

## CHAPTER 11
### THE MASTER AND THE SECRETARY.

So *bewitching*, indeed, he thought her, that he paused for some seconds, gazing on the beautiful picture.

She still looked down, standing at the study-door. Whatever the cause, there certainly was a bright flush at her cheek, a short, slight, quick breathing he had observed, and her attitude somehow indicated suspense, and had, he fancied, an indescribable alarm and prettiness.

"Miss Marlyn," he began, "you made me a kind of promise last night, didn't you?—when I by good fortune met you for a moment and told you my distresses—that you would be so really good as to give me a little help, don't you remember? so I want to know—I'm afraid it's very unreasonable—whether you could now and then copy a paper or write a letter for me? You have no idea what a real kindness you'd confer upon a very tired and overworked poor devil."

Miss Marlyn had grown a little pale, and drew a long breath— or sighed. I know not whether the deep and sudden respiration was due to a sentiment or only to a sense of relief

With a faint tumult at his heart, that yet half-vexed him, the morose-recluse of Raby witnessed these evidences of a confusion, so flattering to the vanities of a man no longer young.

"Perhaps I am too unreasonable," said Mark Shadwell, in a lower tone; "and, perhaps, you forget all about it?"

"No, indeed, I do not forget," answered Miss Marlyn, in tones as low, and raising for a moment her eyes to his; "I ought to have said at once I should be most happy; it will be a great pleasure to me to undertake, always, any service where my duty is owed."

"That's very good of you, very kind. Miss Marlyn. I'm quite serious. I am really very much obliged. I've a paper here; I must send a copy of it to Dolby and Keane, and I'm afraid it is an awful bore, but really I don't know how to find time, sometimes— you've no idea."

"I'm only afraid I shan't do it well, sir—I'll try—I'll do my best, and you won't be vexed, please, if I fail."

The young lady spoke so deprecatingly that Mark Shadwell felt obliged to encourage her.

"I promise you, whatever you do, I shan't be angry, in fact, child, I *couldn't*, I call you child because you are really a second daughter here, and I am bound to take care of you, you know, and to make you as happy as I can; so, don't fancy I'll blow you up if you make a mistake; and I've a theory that mistakes are made by ugly people, and nearly all the mischief in the world is due to them; and, you know very well, you don't belong to that order of beings. I dare say many a poor fellow will have reason to wish you did before all's over."

The lady still looked down. You could not have told from her face whether these speeches pleased or vexed her, only she looked embarrassed, and that look was very becoming.

"I think you're impatient to go," said he.

"Miss Shadwell is waiting, sir," she answered.

"Call her Rachel, why don't you? and pray don't say *sir* quite so often. I wish you to feel at home here, quite at home—I really do, and shall fee I myself very much complimented if you will consent to drop that odious term. You know your dear father was a very dear friend of mine (Mark improved this bygone intimacy for the occasion). One of my very dearest friends, and it really is quite ridiculous your calling me sir as you do. This is the paper, not very long, you see—thanks; and you know you are my secretary now; and you shan't call me *sir* any more—and now goodbye—and I'm really very much obliged."

And he took her hand before she saw it, and pressed it for a moment to indicate how much obliged he was.

And now she was gone, the door closed, and he was alone in the room, where it seemed to his dazzled eyes the tinted glow and outline of that beautiful girl still remained where she had been standing. How was it that she seemed so much more beautiful than ever? How was it that this soured and sullen man of the world, a *blasé* rake—a stoic— a sceptic, quite philosophically regenerate, as he boasted—past the age of illusion and impulse—felt on a sudden so strangely? Are we ever past the age of impulse and romance? Is not the insensibility of age in this respect but the resignation of despair? Once persuade a man, no matter whether he be fifty or sixty years old, that he is regarded for any reason, say his wit or his fame, by a young and beautiful woman with the sort of interest he has long despaired of inspiring, and what boy so romantically wild as that old fellow?

Here was Mark Shadwell, some nine-and-forty years a wonderfully preserved man, not without remains of his early beauty; a man, indeed, early hardened in the ways of pleasure; and yet a new and fresher interest had visited him; a sentiment long-forgotten, curious, absorbing now and then.

He leaned on the chimney-piece, looking towards the door, not thinking, hardly dreaming, the state was too still—as gods are painted reposing on rose-tinted and soft golden clouds, in self-satisfying contemplation. So, leaning on the cold and polished stone which he felt not, Mark Shadwell, in entire mental inaction, in the luxury of one vague idea, reposed in serene beatitude and elation.

But this state is transitory as the glow of sunset, and the chill and twilight of Mark Shadwell's customary depression stole over him.

The discovery of the real state of his account with Sir Roke Wycherly was an immense relief. His spirits had expanded for a time, but quickly the vague sense of danger with which Sir Roke's meditated visit had before been associated returned.

He had known Roke Wycherly well and long, better than he knew himself—always selfish, a cold, hard heart. What on earth did he care if the inhabitants of Raby were one and all dead and buried? Nothing. Why, then, did he propose this visit to Raby, forlorn and dull? This troubled him. There was some little question, he could not recollect what, he had never understood it, about his title. There had been a correspondence about it in his father's time, reserved, laconic, and defiant. It had subsided, and nothing came of it. But he remembered well how transformed his father was pending that unpleasant controversy, that he grew gloomy, fidgety, and silent; that he shut himself up a great deal in the library, and addicted himself to solitary walks, that his temper was short and dangerous, and that no one liked to go near him unnecessarily.

The whole thing had made an impression on his childish imagination as a picture of great suffering—a shadow of that outer darkness—an inkling of the worm and the fire—with which the bilious old Rector of Wynderfel, in his loud and hollow tones, used to threaten so awfully on Sundays.

The alarm had passed away; his father had emerged from the horror of great darkness; and he heard no more of the debate of title-deeds, fines, and recoveries. But he had once since then looked into the correspondence in the chambers of Messrs. Dolby and Keane. It left an unpleasant impression. There was that kind of dipping and drawing together which is seen between cloud and sea when a water-spout threatens. It did not actually form, but cloud and sea were there; and here again was a menace: what else could it mean?

"He'll come, and he'll go; he doesn't know what to do with himself—used up; so he runs down here, as fellows descend into a lead mine, or go to Norway, for want of something new—just for the chance of a new idea. Too much ease, too much money, too much pleasure—life grows tiresome—ha! ha! It's but a choice between life and death. Death, of the two, I should say, is the most tiresome. And they say he has been tapping at your chest."

Vaguely, but substantially, as this soliloquy runs, flowed the current of Mark Shadwell's reasonings, as he strove to shake off the unaccountable uneasiness that returned as often as he thought of Roke Wycherly's visit.

There was an old quarrel. Sir Roke, when they were both young, had outwitted his kinsman in an affair of the heart. It had nearly taken a tragic turn, but friends interposed, and an unnatural duel was prevented. So years had passed away. Mark Shadwell, proud and vindictive as he was, had, in his way, forgiven this and many other trespasses; and they had "buried the hatchet," which might yet be disinterred.

## Chapter 12

### The Walls of Wynderfel

Far away beyond Hazelden—beyond haunted Feltram—beyond the ruined manor-house of Wynderfel—next evening, Mark Shadwell had wandered through the rabbit-peopled woodlands with his gun. The sun was setting, the birds whistling their vespers from a thousand boughs, as that gentleman, with the fatigue of dejection, sat down upon the rude stone seat—a relic of other times and their hospitable care for the wayfarer—which still stands in the now solitary region of the old park, under the roofless gables of Wynderfel.

He was looking up at its grey walls, his eyes wandering listlessly from window to window, and from one tall, smokeless chimney to another, over which the jackdaws were wheeling. Dismally he looked upon the relics of the old manorial residence of generations of Shadwells, before the Raby estate had united itself with Wynderfel by marriage. He was thinking, as he looked, that the Shadwells of those days must have been very great people.

It was the finest house of its time in the county. What lots of chimneys there were! and he thought how hospitable the place must have looked when they were all smoking; and how those empty windows were once pleasant with pretty faces—the Shadwells were a handsome race;—and the stables, and kennels, and offices, among whose silent buttresses the alder and hawthorn were growing now, were astir with horses, dogs, and hawks; and from his readings in Walter Scott's romances, he peopled the deserted courtyard with jesters, knights, falconers, and a masquerade of old-world splendour.

"And all this was ours! And what is left us now? What would they think of Mark Shadwell, of Raby, I wonder, in this costume, without a guinea—a seedy recluse—who never knows one year whether he's to have a house over his head the next?"

Mark Shadwell raised his eyes again, lighted a cigar, and grew serene and contemplative as he smoked it—less bitter about himself—more wrapt up in the tranquil glories of the past.

The memory of pain is short-lived. Retrospect is sunny; the best days always in the past. The illusion runs beyond our own short lives, into other centuries, among buried generations; and we look on their relics as those of a golden age, when times were plentiful, and men all kind, and women beautiful, and heads and hearts never ached.

"Merry England it was then!" said Mark Shadwell, lowering his cigar: he had read an extract from an essay on the subject somewhere. "So it was! No gambling; none of those cursed places where you're robbed; no debts; plenty of fun; plenty of everything; and old families where they should be! Now it's all mortgages, and tradesmen, and upstarts, and money, and smash!"

He was obliged to stop, for, as his eloquence was kindling, his cigar was dying out, and he was fain to replace it between his lips and puff a little anxiously until it was aglow again.

There is a state of pleasant and active observation of passing things; a state also of dreaming, a state of thinking, and another state for which in due time metaphysicians will find a name quite distinct, in which there is a mental silence—thought and fancy nowhere—in which the eyes will rest unmoving on a tree, or distant hill; the mind a blank, in utter, yet strangely pleasurable, apathy.

In this state, smoking, with his eyes on the shield and Shadwell arms over the arch of the wide door, Mark Shadwell heard a voice close by him at the stile; a voice he did not like—quiet, low, and a little stern—a voice which was unlike his angry nature, for it was cold, and which always fired his pride, for it was, in its very tranquillity, commanding.

"Mr. Shadwell, I think? How d'ye do, Mr. Shadwell?" said the voice.

Shadwell had turned towards the speaker before the sentence ended, and saw the Reverend Richard Stour Temple, Vicar of Rydleston; a man of middle height and thin, with a pale face, closely shorn, and dark, steady grey eyes. The level light of the setting sun shone across his features with an odd abruptness of light and shadow; the smile of greeting on his thin lips was slight and cold: his dress, though natty, had seen work, and was fashioned rather after the High Church manner.

"Oh! Temple; how d'ye do? Charming evening for a ramble, isn't it?" said Shadwell, without rising. He did not like the vicar.

"Sweet evening, yes," said the vicar, extending his hand. Shadwell gave him two fingers to shake.

Mr. Temple had generally a word to say when he met Mark Shadwell, and so he seemed to have now, for he paused, and leaning rather than sitting on the bank, close by the old stone seat, he looked down upon the squire as his master at Eton used, when he meditated a lecture.

"Very sweet evening," he resumed: "a little tired though;" and the vicar with his walking-stick knocked his dusty gaiter slightly. "I find my walks tell upon me more than they used; it's a good way to Pennelston: I've been to visit a tenant of yours, Abel Ford; poor man, he's dying; you have not heard, perhaps? You ought to look more, I think, after your tenants, Mr. Shadwell; it's not right."

He spoke this very quietly, with a little nod, and with reproving eyes fixed on the representative of the Shadwells of Raby, and of this old Wynderfel, whose long shadows were stretching over the turf beyond them.

"You've told me that pretty often," said Shadwell.

"No doubt; and you think me impertinent?" said the vicar, gravely.

"I do," said Shadwell, the indulgence of whose morose temper had grown upon him in his solitude.

"And yet, Mr. Shadwell, it is but my duty. The man is dying; I've been praying with him—the office of the church ;" and he touched the coat pocket in which lay the book. "I don't think he's properly attended to; he's poor, and has no wife, and his daughter has not turned out well, you know."

"No, I *don't* know; and if he is not attended to, I can't help it: I can't attend him, can I?"

"If you told your steward to speak to his cousin, who lives near him, he would look a little after him; he had no one last night to give him a drink," said the vicar.

"You churchmen are always for saddling men with duties. You don't ask what are their privileges—estates, indeed—tenants! You know perfectly well I'm a mere receiver over all this for others; you treat me so; you know devilish well, sir, you would not talk to me as you do if the estates were unencumbered, and I where I ought to be."

Thus spoke Mark Shadwell, with an angry eye upon the vicar, and then laughed scornfully to himself, turning his head slowly away.

"I've many faults, I dare say, but I don't think cowardice is one," replied Mr. Temple. "I thought it right to mention the circumstance; you can do as seems good to you."

"I can *not* do as seems good to me. How can a fellow do anything without money? Such rot and nonsense!" These latter words were muttered contemptuously to the grass at his feet, but the vicar heard them, and Mark Shadwell did not care whether he did or not.

"When that old building was raised, Mr. Shadwell, our social relations were better understood," said the vicar, turning up his face toward the gables and gurgoils of Wynderfel, with a cold smile.

"I dare say," said Shadwell. "Gentlemen, for instance, did not give their advice in those days till it was asked for."

"Except churchmen," said the vicar, "whose thankless duty it is, uninvited, to instruct, to exhort, and to warn. Those who most need advice are the last to ask it. Were we to wait till erring mortals invited us to reprove them, our calling were vain indeed."

"Well, Temple, I dare say you do fancy you are doing your duty—I'm *sure* you do; and I assure you, though you talk sometimes about things you don't quite understand, and give me all sorts of impracticable advice, I respect you all the time, so you'll forgive my gruff talk, I can't help it; but, upon my soul, if you expect a poor devil like me to look after all those tenants, and find nurses for them when they're sick, and fun for them when they're well, you're going rather too fast for me: I tell you once for all, I can't; I can do *nothing* for them; I never have a guinea to bless myself with; half of them are better off than I am; I wish you'd tell them to look after *me*, by Jove!"

"You know, Mr. Shadwell, as well as I," replied the vicar, gently and coldly, "that you might do a great deal more than you do: in the case I mentioned, for instance, but having mentioned it, I can do no more."

"Well, I don't care if I do what you say; I'll send down there tomorrow. If you'd just ask people quietly, and not mind lecturing, you'd often carry your point better, d'ye see? You're not vexed at my saying so?"

The vicar smiled and bowed with a serenity in which one might have suspected a little contempt.

"Thanks, at all events, for your compliance with my present request," he said. "There was one other, I have often urged it, you perhaps remember?"

"Upon my life, I can't say; there have been a good many," answered Shadwell, darkening again.

"It is not much; that is, not much trouble; it was only this, that you would read just six verses of the New Testament every day."

Shadwell looked at him and laughed, as one might at a foolish saying of a child.

"I beg your pardon—you'll forgive me, but it sounds so odd; I know you mean it well, but it does, because I don't believe it; I think your New Testament is all a myth; Christianity is simply a philosophy which has survived other and better ones, just because it has condescended to ally itself with the principle of superstition, which is part of human nature."

The vicar, for the first time, looked sadly; he shook his head, and for some seconds silently watched the now fading splendour that duskily flooded the wake of the sun that had gone down. There was in the sight something funereal that accorded with his thoughts.

"It's nothing new, you know; I've told you the same thing pretty often, and that's the foundation of our relations. I live in your parish, but I'm not your parishioner, though we are very good friends, don't you see? You're a Christian; I'm a philosopher," said Mark Shadwell, who was conceited of his smattering of Greek philosophies. "I don't say I'm a Platonist, an epicurean, or a stoic; *nullius addictus*, I don't deal all in one shop; every man who thinks frames a system for himself. I'm an eclectic philosopher, if you please, and I'm very well satisfied with my credo!"

"I have argued it with you pretty often, Mr. Shadwell. I had hoped that time and reflection might have opened your eyes; there's an hour coming for. each when we shall need more than the speculations of men."

"We all need more than we're ever likely to get," replied Mr. Shadwell; "but what enabled Socrates to meet death as he did, is enough for me."

"I'm not arguing it, mind. It is not a question to be settled in a five minutes' talk over a cigar, but I should be very happy if you would discuss it fully with me, or even if you would read a few books which I'll be glad to lend you."

"Thanks, no. The death of Socrates and the morals of Hume; I don't think your calendar and martyrology can show much better. I'm content."

Mark Shadwell, if not exactly content, was self-complacent; he lighted another cigar, and puffed a little smoke into the air, fancying that he had floored his opponent, who rose as if to go upon his way.

"And as for me," resumed Shadwell, lowering his cigar, "I can't say, of course, what sort of death I may die, but my life, I venture to say, is as moral as any parson's in England. I don't drink, I don't play; I live like anchorite, every way; I don't even curse or swear, to signify, and I could give that up, if I liked. I hardly run up to town twice in the year, and then, upon my honour, it's only for business; you say I've no experience of Christianity, I say *you've* none of philosophy. I haven't a passion left in me, by Jove! Of course, a fellow can't help getting riled a bit, sometimes, but every other way I'm as cold as a marble block. Take one of these, on your walk, won't you?" And Shadwell tendered his cigar-case.

"Thanks, no; I never smoke," said the vicar.

"If you were, as I am, looking at that old house, and remembering what *we* were there, once on a time, you'd know what it was to feel as I do," said Shadwell, pointing at the old walls with his cigar.

"No greater waste of time than regretting, except, perhaps, wishing," said the vicar; "I must get on. Your young people—Miss Shadwell, I mean, and her governess—are drinking tea with my sister. So I'll say good evening."

Shadwell stood up and waved his hand to the vicar's valediction, and the vicar smiled his cold smile and nodded, and his swift and wiry walk soon carried him under the white-thorns and scattered ash-trees through which the path descends. Mark Shadwell remained with his foot on the stone seat, smoking and looking after that disappearing figure.

"Good man—awfully conceited—curiously disagreeable; I wonder how he made love to Amy, long ago, when he was at her feet. I dare say he frightened that poor old fellow, Ford, to-day, half out of his wits, with his Beelzebub, and his hell, and his visitation of the sick. How these poor little prigs do delight in frightening people!"

It was a delightful, balmy twilight, and Mark Shadwell was in no mood to return to Raby for a little time, so he smoked on, and the bats came out from their ivied nooks in the walls of Wynderfel, and the stars began to glimmer in the deepening sky.

## CHAPTER 13
### BONNIE AND RABY

As the Reverend Stour Temple said, the young ladies of Raby

were that evening drinking tea at the vicar's house.

In the pretty country about Wynderfel, there are few prettier things than the vicar's house, which is old and lonely, standing among dark elm-trees, on a gentle eminence, built of time-worn white stone, with a flight of broad white steps leading up to the fluted doorway. In front, spreads a little carpet of short grass, pleasantly relieved by clusters of roses and sweetbriars, and several small beds of brilliant flowers. A tall double hedgerow marks the line of the narrow road in front, from which you can see, peeping among the old trees and underwood, the arched gateway of the farmyard, and the smaller arch of a little belfry, and the pigeons are often seen fluttering and wheeling in the air, above the dovecot, and the great dog, Drake, lying before the steps, on summer days, blinking and dozing, and snapping lazily at the flies.

Stour Temple, the vicar, is the master of this dwelling of rural quiet—that is to say, he pays the bills, but exercises little other lordship, leaving the government pretty nearly altogether in the hands of his dear maiden sister, Barbara, who takes into counsel her brother, the vicar's junior, I think, by about a year, beloved of both, though seen with different eyes.

This brother is Roger S. Temple, and as unlike as may be to the slim dark vicar. I am going, young ladies, to describe a fellow, by no means handsome, who, nevertheless, from some celestial qualities, has always seemed to me almost beautiful. He violates all the canons of your heroic statuary, as you shall see, if you read on a little. But, on the whole, knowing that in age, ways, and form, he is likely to fall under your displeasure, I would advise your looking another way, and passing by what concerns him. Happy am I to be able to write of him in the present tense still, and yet to know that these lines will never meet his honest eye, or wound his innocent soul, for he reads no books but those half-dozen samples of the old sentimental novel, which his sister. Miss Barbara, keeps in her bookcase, and these so much at his leisure, that by the time he reads "*finis*" in the last, he is ready with a fresh interest for the title-page of the first.

He is fat, and round, and high-shouldered—clumsy, I must allow—no longer an athlete, and when, for instance, he ran after his hat, on the stormy day in October last, suffered more, and was longer in recovering, than he ever divulged. His face is the kindliest, though homeliest, in the world. It is a fat and expansive countenance, somewhat brown; there is not an angle in it, anywhere. He has no moustache or beard. His lips and chin are shorn and bluish, with a fat kind dimple here and there. He is somewhat bald too; a baldness not glaring and complete, a little softened and downy, and those remnants of what was once crisp black hair at the sides and back are grizzled, and now very much dashed with white. Round little light-blue eyes, as innocent as they were in the cradle, are his, with next to no eyebrows over them.

At a cricket-match, thirty years ago, some of his upper teeth were smashed, and time has, somewhat prematurely, removed the rest, which, to his kindly smile, gives an infantine character, though some people, when he smiles, fancy rather that he looks like a fond old nurse, charmed with the prattle and gambols of the children toddling about her chair.

Everyone likes Roger Temple. He never said an ill word, because he never harboured an ungentle thought of mortal. He is no more conscious than his sister Barbara, who actually thinks him still young, as well as beautiful, that the dew of his youth has quite evaporated, and that it is now drawing toward evening with him. He is soft-hearted and romantic, and, but for his shyness and certain panics that come over him, would have been, no doubt, married long ago.

As it was nearly sunset, and tea early, Miss Barbara was by this time standing at the drawing-room window, which commands a view of the hollow, now glittering its last in the golden evening sun, through which lies the path from Wynderfel.

"I don't see a sign of them, do you, Bonnie?" This was an ancient, pet name of my friend Roger. "Oh! he's gone," she said, looking round, "perhaps to meet them—but no, poor darling, he's so shy."

So she looked out again for a time, and then compared her watch with the old French clock over the chimney-piece. It was hardly time yet; but fatiguing as it is, few people can, especially in the rural solitudes, where an arrival is an event, and from a window with a distant view of the hoped-for approach, refrain from watching.

Miss Barbara, whose fingers were tired holding her golden glasses to her eyes, with a little sigh, put them down and turned from the pretty view, and sat down at the piano.

It is an instrument which has seen better days, like the good lady who loves it. It has an old-world air, and its ivory notes have got a mellow golden tint, and are hollowed with a wonderfully long course of Mozart and Handel, and variations interminable, garrulous, circumlocutory, and mazy enough to have unsettled its wits. The little oval landscape over the notes, has lost its youthful complexion, and acquired an antique melancholy tint; the varnish has cracked into all manner of tiny wrinkles, and if you strike a loud chord, and listen, you hear the whole instrument audibly wheeze after the effort.

But to her it is a peerless piano, beloved with the sad yearnings of irrevocable youth; on any other the old music would lose its life and charm; forms gather round it as she plays, and when she ceases, remembered tones murmur in her ear. Maiden sister Barbara had many offers, and might have been well married; but there was one that was not to be. The same music stool, the same little oval landscape, the same music, the same instrument and its reedy chords and faded harmonies, as her thin hand calls them forth in the summer evenings, sound sad and sweet in her ear, as choirs of far-off angels.

When she had played for a while, up got Miss Barbara again, and walked down the hall-door steps and to the little grass-mound, about a stone's throw to the left, on which she took her stand. The big dog, Drake, got up and shook his ears, and followed her lazily to the point of observation, whence, sitting with cocked ears and sniffing nostrils, he made his official survey also: and flanked on the other side by the splendid old lime-tree that over-shadowed them, Miss Barbara, with her golden glasses to her eyes, looked out earnestly for her guests.

"Oh! you're there!" exclaimed Roger's kindly voice, approaching, and turning, she saw him with his smile drawing near at a little trot, which subsided to a walk. "I've been talking to Dolly in the poultry-yard," he resumed, as he arrived, a little out of breath, upon the eminence, where Miss Barbara received him with her most attentive look, for he had plainly something to tell, and Drake fidgeted in his place and looked on him kindly, and licked his lips with just the least little tip of his tongue, and brushed the grass back and forward with his tail as he sat, indicating his willingness to give up his place and kiss hands, and make himself generally agreeable, if it were thought desirable. Roger's countenance darkened with the sad and earnest expression which it always wore when business was approached, and he laid his hand gently on his sister's wrist—"I've just been looking at the two turkeys, Raby dear, and I really think it looks very like pip."

"Really?" echoed Miss Barbara.

"I do, indeed, upon my word!"

"Poor things!" exclaimed she; and they looked gravely into one another's eyes.

Roger shook his head, closed his eyes, and with a little sigh, said:

"It's a nasty thing, *pip*."

"Awful!" said Miss Barbara.

"I can find nothing wrong in their food; I really. Raby, can't account for it, and I've told Dolly what she ought to do, and she's very careful, you know, and as the food is all right, I hope the others mayn't take it."

"I trust not; and sufficient to the day, Bonnie dear," she replied, brightening up, for she remembered her guests, and she glanced over his wardrobe with approval.

"How handsome you look this evening, Bonnie!" exclaimed his sister, looking at him with a proud smile of affection.

"You must not say that. Raby dear; no, you mustn't, you make me too conceited; no, Raby, you mustn't," replied he, shaking his head and smiling violently.

"I *want* you to look well tonight, and you know why?" she said with a smile and a nod.

"You're always quizzing, Raby: there's nothing, I assure you," laughed Roger rather sheepishly; "now, really, upon my honour."

"You want but this, and you're perfect;" and she placed a rosebud in his buttonhole.

"Thank you. Raby dear," he said, with a smile, patting her cheek very gently, "you're always so pleasant ;" and he kissed her cheek fondly. "But, really, and upon my honour—well, you won't believe me, you never will. Raby, you're such a rogue."

"By the bye, where's Charlie?" inquired Miss Barbara, suddenly recollecting.

"Gone to fish, I think; he took my rod and flies; but he knows you expect friends, and he's sure to be home in time."

"Yes, I'm sure he will, he *wouldn't* disappoint us; and I want him and Rachel to see one another; it's more than three years since they met last," said Barbara, who was addicted to that romantic school of match-making which makes no account of prudence, and had this evening two affairs on her hands—one, the little project she had just suggested; the other, a romance which she had imagined, in which Agnes Marlyn, all unconsciously, and honest Roger Temple, willingly enough, figured as partners.

*Sure never a hall such a galliard did grace!*

It was these romantic situations which quickened her hospitable instincts this evening, and her gentle soul yearned to see them all happy together.

"Here they are, at last!" exclaimed she, joyfully. "Run down, Bonnie, and meet them; fly, darling, and I will go in and ring for tea, and have everything ready by the time you arrive."

With a throbbing heart honest Roger Temple, at that odd little jog-trot which constituted his mode of "flying," set forth, and not caring to be unbecomingly blown at his arrival, he subsided, as usual, into a walk, and so smiling gloriously, he approached the two young ladies who were drawing near.

## CHAPTER 14
### CHARLIE MORDANT

Their cheerful welcome over:

"My dear," said Miss Barbara to Rachel, "I'm so glad I've got you here; it was so good of you and Miss Marlyn to come! I told you in my note I had an old friend to meet you; it isn't Bonnie, of course you understood that. It's—*shall* I tell you? Who do you suppose? It's Charlie Mordant; yes, indeed, came on leave yesterday morning. He'd have gone up to pay his respects at Raby, but I wasn't quite sure that your papa would wish it. His uncle—I think there was some unpleasantness—was not a favourite of Mr. Shadwell's; and then Sir Roke Wycherly being his guardian, or patron, or whatever it is, I fancied would not be a recommendation, as I know there had been a coldness there too, and I thought it better we should wait a little and feel our way."

"I really don't know, I think, I'm sure papa would have been very happy, and I know mamma would. We had such a charming walk here, everything looking so beautiful, and we stopped for ever so long, did not we, Agnes," at the stile? We admire this pretty place; it looks so wonderfully, just in these tints, and in the sunset light! If we had brought our pencils and colours we should certainly have stopped there, and made sketches."

"And spoiled our tea, wicked creatures! But it is pretty, certainly, quite *beautiful* from some points of view," acquiesced Miss Barbara. "I'm very glad Miss Marlyn saw it to such advantage. Bonnie darling, show Miss Marlyn the photographs."

My fat friend skipped to get the book, and placed it before the object of his admiration, and forthwith the ladies began to discuss the "photos" with animation.

"Bonnie dear, you must find my microscopic photo, you know the one I mean," said Miss Barbara, eagerly. "Yes, thanks; now, here it is, Miss Marlyn; look at it. I'll give you the magnifier presently. Now, examine it closely; is it a human being, or is it a building, or is it the Ten Commandments, or is it a cow?"

If Miss Marlyn had seen how conscious my fat friend, Roger, looked, she would have had an inkling of the truth, but she was politely scrutinising the atom.

"Oh, no!" cried Miss Barbara, "don't turn the back; you shall read that afterwards: do you make out anything?"

"It is so wonderfully minute," said Miss Marlyn, with a pretty frown of puzzle.

"Well, do you give it up?" cried Miss Barbara, with a delighted little signal to Bonnie.

"It looks a little like—is it?—a lighthouse, with the lower part dark, in deep shade, and the upper lighted; is it a lighthouse?"

"Well, what shall I say? It answers some of the purposes of a lighthouse; *I've* found it so, at least; it guides people in uncertainty, and it's a very fine object, *I* think, and it is luminous, and looks bright, always; a lofty, symmetrical structure."

"It can't be a statue, then?" conjectured Agnes.

"Or a water-spout?" suggested Rachel, who was now peeping over Miss Marlyn's shoulder.

"No! it isn't a water-spout; it's nothing so uncertain, nor a statue, though it might make a very fine one, I think," answered Miss Barbara.

"It would make a statue! then it is a block of white marble, *I* guess, with the lower part in shade," said Rachel.

Roger moved a little, uneasily.

"Well, that's your guess; and what do *you* say. Miss Marlyn, you must fix on something—anything, just for a guess," said Miss Barbara.

"Give her the glass. Baby darling," murmured Roger, who was in a painful state of bashful excitement, and wished the ordeal over.

"I'll tell you what I think it is," said Miss Marlyn, in this sudden light, forgetting her data, "it's Kemble as Hamlet; the picture in the National Gallery, with the skull. I fell in love with it!"

Here Roger changed colour a little, and cleared his voice, as if about to say something.

"Not a word, Bonnie, for your life," entreated his sister.

"Well that's *your* guess, an auspicious guess," said Miss Barbara, who had been rubbing the little lens in her handkerchief, and now placed it in Agnes Marlyn's taper fingers.

The young lady took it, applied it, and beheld honest Roger, looking more than commonly fat, in evening costume, with a white waistcoat, and smiling with all his might full in her face. An incredulous little shock for a moment expressed itself in Miss Marlyn's countenance, and then came an irrepressible fit of laughter.

"It's a horrid thing," said poor Bonnie, smiling plaintively. "I know you think it frightful."

"Tell me, dear Miss Marlyn, what amuses you so much?" inquired Miss Temple, a little anxiously.

"Thinking of our absurd guesses—a lighthouse, a waterspout, a skull in Hamlet's hand—how dreary and awful! and now it turns out to be something so cheerful and happy," replied Miss Marlyn; and then added in a sad tone, leaning back in her chair, so that Bonnie only could catch the murmured accents— "so very cheerful and happy, that sad people wonder how it *can* be so! Don't you think, Mr. Temple, that people who are always tolerably happy, are a sort of blessed monsters, who have reason to be thankful to heaven, above all others?"

"Yes, indeed!" said honest Roger, affecting a little sigh.

"Then you suffer—you—who seemed to me so light-hearted. You, also, have your secret griefs, like others?"

I am afraid that Miss Marlyn was quizzing him. And Roger, who was one of the serenest and cheeriest of mortals, was led into a silent prevarication, for the good fellow, for a moment, tried to look miserable, and sighed again. But what was he to do? Misery seemed to interest Miss Marlyn, and could he forfeit his chance?

"And what are these initials?" asked Miss Marlyn, changing the subject suddenly, and looking on the back of the photograph—"R. S. T.; they are yours, are they?"

"Yes, *Roger*—Roger Temple is my name!" said he, with an indescribable softness.

"*Roger?*" she repeated; "I thought it was *Bonaparte!* I've certainly heard your sister call you Bonaparte, haven't I?" said Miss Marlyn, cruelly, I am afraid.

"Oh! I think it must have been Bonnie," said honest Roger, with an ingenuous blush; "an old pet—I mean *nick*—name that she is fond of. *I* call her Baby, still; I do, indeed!"

"Then you were children together!" said the young lady, much interested.

"Yes, indeed; playmates in the nursery," said Roger, with a sigh, and a smile of innocent sentiment, and his head a little on one side, as people sometimes incline their heads in such fond retrospects.

"Our maid, long ago, used to call Bonaparte, *Bony,* and I suppose it was that, but I really was quite sure I had heard your sister call you Bonaparte!"

"What about me?" inquired Miss Temple.

"Only a mistake of mine. I've been asking the meaning of these initials, and now I know the 'B' and the 'T,' of course; but what does the 'S' mean?" asked Miss Marlyn, innocently.

"*Segrave*" said Miss Baby, shortly, and looked very grave.

Roger dropped his eyes, and coughed, and flushed a little, uneasily; and a momentary silence overtook the party.

I only know that, in the baptismal registry, "R. S." is expounded to mean "Roger Sidebotham." The calling these names to a helpless infant was, in this case, no wanton cruelty. The old original Roger Sidebotham was a bachelor, a City personage, and East India director, who obtruded himself as poor Bonnie's godfather, and accompanied the proffer of his spiritual parentage with some mysterious intimations of an intoxicating character.

But he married; and compensated his godson with a cadetship in the Company's service.

The dream of a million was gone, but the brand of "Sidebotham"' clave to him like the leprosy of Naaman the Syrian. It galled him. He hated it. It was one of the very few bitter drops in that pleasant syllabub which filled his cup of life. It certainly is not a pretty name. But he had brooded over it, and grown morbid, and had come to abhor and dread it as a spirit does the cabalistic word that has power to degrade and torture.

It was some relief to him when his sister Barbara, in her indignation, insisted that he should never sign himself "Sidebotham" more, but take instead the name of his admirable uncle, Segrave, who had left him a rent-charge of twenty pounds a year.

Still "Sidebotham" weighed upon him like an evil secret, which, sooner or later, time would bring to light: and thus it was he winced and coloured under Miss Marlyn's harmless but cruel question.

"Segrave is the second name," repeated Miss Barbara, who could not endure to leave her little speech, even for a moment, in the attitude of an untruth: "that is, *at present*; formerly, I mean originally, it was different."

"Oh!" said Miss Marlyn, turning again with a gentle interest to Roger Temple. "And what, then, does the initial 'S' really mean?"

Miss Marlyn's question, I have sometimes thought, was pressed with a cruel knowledge of facts.

"Don't ask, Miss Marlyn—pray don't!" said honest Roger, very much flurried; and, dropping his voice to the tenderest murmur, he continued: "I must, if you desire it: I can refuse you nothing: but you won't; I can't describe how it would pain me, I hate the name so much; and I know the effect that names have in prejudicing people. I've felt it myself; I know it; I *have* felt it myself; and I know, if you were to hate it as much as I do, you would always associate me with it: it is such a shabby, odious name. Side——"

He was as near as possible letting it slip out, and looked at her now with his round, innocent eyes in such woeful terror that, in spite of her efforts, she did laugh a tremulous little laugh.

"I don't understand you, Mr. Temple. What *can* you mean by that, and looking at me with such an expression? You have really excited my curiosity, and I *must* know what you mean—really."

"Ah! no, Miss Marlyn—*pray*, don't!"

Just at that moment, to his indescribable relief, an interruption occurred, by the entrance of a tall, handsome young man, of a frank and animated countenance.

Miss Barbara had announced his step in the hall, with a sudden smile, and—

"Here comes Charlie!" and, as he entered, "At last! Charlie, at last!"

"I'm awfully late, I'm afraid; but it really isn't my fault. The boy you sent with me, Roger, brought me such a round! We had never been there before. I really thought we never should have got home again. I don't know which blundered most. Nobody could have told which of us was the guide."

The end of his sentence he spoke a little slowly, for his eyes had wandered to Miss Marlyn, and from her to Rachel; and looking still at her, with eyes that lighted up suddenly, he asked, in a low tone:

"Is not that Rachel Shadwell?"

The young man was instantly at her side as she stood by the piano, that wonderful relic of Miss Barbara's youth, where she had been turning over a volume of quaint Arcadian songs, full of Daphne and Chloe, and flight and pursuit, and pipes and echo, such as were sung a generation before Barbara Temple, though, in her old-fashioned childhood, she had learned to trill them.

"I'm so delighted: I had not an ideal" said he, a swarthy glow on his handsome face answering the brilliant blush of the girl, who was smiling very merrily, and, holding her pretty hand, he continued looking in her beautiful blue eyes:

"You do look so—well, Rachel, and you've grown so tall;—I'm so glad you're here!"

"I *thought* it would be a surprise—ha, ha!" said Miss Barbara, gleefully, "and to *someone*"—with a very arch glance at Charlie—"a rather pleasant one! Has she not grown very much?—she's just the nicest height in the world—taller than *I*, I'm quite certain."

"Oh, no!" disclaimed Rachel, who, whatever she might think,

was obliged to disavow that presumption.

"You have," said the young man, in very low tones. "I could hardly believe it; and I think just that height is so beautiful!"

"I should be more obliged," she said, laughing, "if Miss Temple had not just paid me that pretty compliment." Indeed, could anything have been prettier than the round and slender figure of the girl, as she leaned on the old piano, that had played in its day so much music for the young?

"How pretty they look together!" whispered Miss Barbara in the ear of her brother Roger. "But *I* know two who would make a still prettier couple—in *my* mind," she added, with a fond little laugh and a tiny tap on his sunburnt cheek. And honest Roger, smiling with bashful delight, kissed his sister's cheek stealthily, whispering in her ear, "Now, don't; you mustn't quiz me, Baby."

It was in my mind a delightful craze that kept these people young. I have seen conscientious people slyly trying to *un*-deceive others into mortification, and to rob them logically of their blessed blunders, forgetting what a mysterious world it is, and how much of our enjoyments depend upon illusion. Let, then, that tenderest love that is a little blind linger still within the sacred walls of home; and cherish the absurd but beautiful mistakes that exercise the kindly admirations, and celestial affections, and unconscious gratitudes that make its spell remembered in distance, and after the flight of years, like an early gleam of Paradise.

Good, active housewife, kindly Barbara, of the wheezy piano and loving dreams, what a good mission is thine! What would thy brothers be without thee—resenting everything for *them*, nothing for thyself? Though Stour Temple laughs, I think it pleases him that the person who places his slippers at the study fire, and pours out his tea, believes implicitly that he ought to be Archbishop of Canterbury—believes always what an unjust outer world it is, and shakes her head, and musters her powers of patience, when she remembers that her high-spirited, gifted, handsome brother Roger has returned from India without a fortune, or a title, or even a colonelcy.

He was a failure; but was he ever allowed to feel or even to perceive it? Stour Temple, also, with faculties, and reading, and energy, was here a castaway, upon a desolate strand, and growing old; but was not the sunshine of the same admiration making the air about him cheerful and warm? Oh! beautiful hallucinations of women's affections, utterly wild and unjust, sweet as angels' consolations, balm of our wounded self-complacency, still seeing a beauty and youth under the hollow mask of years, and still predicting good times to come, after the game is quite lost and over, and harbouring a delightful confidence in the talents that are—nowhere. How many a wounded wayfarer by the bleak paths of life would break his heart and die were it not for thy misplaced admiration, *thine* inextinguishable enthusiasm and cheerful mercy, pouring in ever the oil of an unconscious flattery, and the blessed wine of hope!

## CHAPTER 15
### GOODNIGHT

"I was going to say I should not have known you, Rachel," said Charlie Mordant; "but I can't say that, for I think I should know you anywhere and almost at any distance—ever so far away. But it is nearly two years since I saw you, and you have grown so tall, and yet you are little Rachel Shadwell still—the same, yet not the same, but always the same to me, and I know I'm talking nonsense; but I know what I mean, though I see you are laughing at me." He smiled, and was speaking very low.

"*Was* I laughing?" said the pretty girl, who was leaning lightly on the ancient grand piano. "I always laugh when a sentence gets entangled—particularly a fine one. So perhaps I did laugh, though I really wasn't conscious."

"You never said—well, no matter," he began, and she saw him glance quickly round, and, being satisfied that their little talk was not overheard, he resumed, "and you never said you were glad to see me. Very ill-natured of you, I think, considering what old friends we are, and that I've been half-way over the world since I saw you; isn't it?"

"Why, yes, of course I'm glad to see you."

"it's very odd what a pleasure you take—I don't mean you, in particular, but all of you—in bewildering and mocking us men. I never know when you're in earnest. You're so awfully insincere, and take such a delight in it. What can be the pleasure of it? It *is* so odd!"

"If one's known to be insincere, one's incapable of deceiving any longer, and nobody has any right to complain, don't you see?" urged Rachel, ingeniously.

"Well, I'm not good at arguing, but I know this: I wish you'd honestly say you're glad to see me, for I'm awfully glad to see you."

"Yes, honestly, I am glad to see you."

"Well, that would be very pleasant if you did not laugh while you say it; but no matter. I'm very glad to see *you*. I've been nearly two days here, and I assure you it has seemed like two months, for Miss Temple would not allow me to go to Raby to see you and Mrs. Shadwell. I don't pretend to say why, but you know if she wasn't a little fanciful and peremptory sometimes, she would be too perfect. She's the dearest old woman in the whole world, and I forgive her all she has made me suffer; but she would not allow me to pay my respects, either, and here I've been pining, and now comes this little compensation, and I'm so happy! And I could not have believed you could have grown so much; you are quite a tall girl, Rachel, and so—so very—but you were always pretty—lovely, I think, and as saucy as ever."

Rachel laughed again at this plain-spoken compliment.

"I've grown so awfully brown—like a gipsy, almost. I suppose you didn't know me when I came in?" said he.

"Oh yes; I should have known you perfectly, but great arrivals are always proclaimed beforehand, and Miss Temple took care to tell us all who was coming, when we heard you knocking the hats and sticks about in the hall."

"You'll soon be a young lady of the world, Rachel; you'll be coming out and all that. I suppose you'll go to the hunt ball this year, won't you?" he asked.

"I don't suppose I shall; I don't know, really. Papa does not like our neighbours, I think; he lives so entirely to himself, quite shut up, but *you* know—"

"Yes, I know. What lots of people he does hate, to be sure! That is, I mean, you know, I don't think he likes any of the county people. I remember very well how he used to avoid them two years ago, before I went away, and I know some of them did not like him; and so, I suppose, he's as solitary as ever. How awfully slow you must find it at Raby!"

"My aunt Pleydel wrote to mamma offering to take me out next year, if she would let me go to her."

"Oh yes; she's in the centre of all that, isn't she?"

"Yes, I believe so; but I don't think I should like it. I don't think I could endure that kind of life."

"A country miss, is that it? But you'll find you'll get into it wonderfully; you all do when you have the opportunity. I hear you are going to have a visitor at Raby."

"Oh yes! Sir Roke Wycherly."

"He's my guardian, you know."

"No, I didn't know."

"I dare say he forgets it himself; though, no, he can hardly do that, for he signs the cheques twice a year for my annuity. I sha'n't be of age, you know, till I'm five and twenty, and then I succeed to— nothing!" and Charles Mordant laughed as cheerfully as "if nothing" meant ten thousand a year. "When my second horse broke his leg in India, I assure you I really don't know what I should have done, if it hadn't been for that capital fellow over there," and he nodded very kindly towards Roger, who was talking some very soft nonsense to Miss Marlyn. "I met two or three fellows that knew him in India—by Jove, how they did speak of him! I never heard a fellow so praised; they all *loved* him. There was a poor fellow with a young wife who got into a scrape—put his name on bills or something for a fellow, and was let in for five hundred pounds, and would have had to sell out if Roger there had not pulled him through—he's an awfully nice

75

fellow, though he's such a guy. I wish Sir Roke was half as nice, but they say he's an awful old scamp."

"Sir Roke Wycherly!"

"Oh yes; there are all sorts of stories about him. They say he killed an opera dancer in one of his tempers at Paris."

"Oh, come! you don't believe that?"

"Well, no, I don't, perhaps. But anyhow, it shows what a devil a fellow must be when things of that kind are seriously whispered about him. Do look at Roger—he's awfully gone about that girl—very pretty she is—Miss Marlyn—isn't that her name?"

"Yes; Agnes Marlyn. I think her perfectly lovely, and she is such a sweet girl—charming!" said Rachel.

"So Roger seems to think. What a muff he is! The best fellow in the world; but he *is* a muff, and I think I should not like him half so well, by Jove, if he *wasn't* a muff," said Charlie, who was watching with an amused interest the progress of his wooing, in which he smirked and blushed like a schoolboy.

"She looks attentive, doesn't she? and she makes play with her eyes. Very fine eyes she has got, by Jove! He's making an impression; I swear to you he is."

"I'm glad you think so," she laughed. "He couldn't do better, and if Agnes is to marry, I should be so glad she was settled so near us."

"Look at him—do look at him! He's so bashful and enamoured! it is quite delightful!" said Mordant. "What fun that girl's having! she's greening poor Roger so awfully—I mean, making such a fool of him."

"Oh, do you think so?" dissented Rachel.

"Think! To be sure she is."

"You don't know her; that's the reason you say so."

Charlie laughed.

So that evening his romance was prospering with honest Roger. The *purpureum lumen* of his youth glowed round about him in a Tyrian halo. The seven ages of man to him were a myth. He had stopped short at the third, where youth indites verses and sighs like a furnace. No man was ever more unconscious of his years. Like the good monk in the old legend, who followed the song of the celestial bird, from bush to brake, from hillock to running stream, over bosky uplands and through rocky glens— led on by its warblings from hour to hour, till the day was spent and sunset came, and, returning to the convent door, found that fifty years had flown, and his life was over—so our friend, beguiled by the music of a wonderfully happy and loving soul, went unsuspecting and sweetly cheated on and on, and the flight of his years seemed to him but as an hour. And old age, when it overtakes him, will lead him by a flowery path to the grave, still incredulous.

And, now the hour of leave-taking had come, gay and kindly voices, and kisses often exchanged in the hall with Miss Barbara, and a lawful consignment of the young wayfarers to the time-honoured escort of honest Roger Temple, and of his subaltern, Charlie Mordant, succeeded one another, and away went that pleasant party on their moonlighted way to Raby.

## Chapter 16
### A Meeting at Wynderfel

Three stories high in the roofless walls of Wynderfel is the stone-shafted window from which hangs, like a beckoning arm, a long tendril of ivy. Over that window-stone a poor Lady Mildred ever so many years ago, threw herself, or was thrown— dreadful, whichever way. It is still pointed out, and called the Lady's Window. You can see the quiet stars through the stone-framing in which, once, like a ghost, she stood for a while, and vanished with a shriek. It is something of a Cumnor Hall story.

Mark Shadwell, the philosopher, was entering into the spirit of his bivouac on the limestone block, under the walls of Wynderfel. He swallowed the thimbleful of brandy that was left in the flask, and lighted a third cigar; and admired the thin film of silver that the moon was throwing over the singular landscape.

The philosopher was looking up at the Lady's Window, thinking idly of poor Lady Mildred. "A devilish fine girl, I dare say!" And conjecturing what her style might have been—dark or blonde, with blue eyes or brown—and thinking what he would have done had he been the cavalier who used to bribe the porter, and enter the courtyard by night; and he lowered his eyes to the empty arch in which that ill-starred lover had stood so long ago, and he saw the figure of a horseman standing in it motionless and black against the moonlight.

Up rose Mark Shadwell, grasping the barrel of his gun hard in his hand, and called "Hallo!" rather fiercely.

"Ha!" cried the horseman; and there ensued a little silence.

"I say, who are you?" challenged the stoic.

"Ho !—Ah !—dear! Mr. Shadwell? So it is!" exclaimed the voice of Carmel Sherlock.

"And what the devil brings *you* here?" answered his patron.

"Returning from the mills, sir. All right—everything," answered Carmel, in his odd, gentle way.

"Why, this isn't your way—unless you mean to ride over the stile—is it?" replied Shadwell, tartly.

"Near—only near—not quite, sir; but I longed to see Wynderfel. I could not refrain. I hope it is no harm. I longed to see Wynderfel once more," replied Carmel Sherlock.

"Well, I suppose you've seen all you're likely to see, by this time—and there's no good in sitting there stock still, like a caricature of the sentry at the Horse-guards," said Mark, who resented being startled.

"Under the archway—yes, sir. But this, sir, *this*—these are places of power—where a spell is left—or a spirit is held in prison—the stone hand with the key in it, over the gate of the Alhambra—this arch, sir—you know the inscription on the stone of this doorway—that was carved by a spirit in torment—a patient hand—the perseverance of passionate misery, looking backward on eternal remorse, and forward on eternal despair. It has the thought that came with Mildred here, and returns with the gaze-lady, and is mixed with my fate, sir, and yours—and has blighted your house—and I feel the presence of the spirit while I read it, and loiter under this arch."

If Mark had not been smoking, he would probably have

stopped Carmel very early in this meditation.

On a broad stone by this doorway, cut deep and rudely, like an inscription on an ancient prison wall, anyone may read these odd quotations:—

*Longe fac ab eâ tuam.*
*Ne des alienis honorem tuum, et annos tuos crudeli.*
*Dedes ejus descendunt in mortem, & ad inferos gressus illius penetrant.*

The meaning of which Latin words we find thus expressed in our bibles:—

*Remove thy way far from her.*
*Lest thou give thine honour unto others, and thy years unto the cruel.*
*Her feet go down to death; her steps take hold on hell.*

"Should you like to ride home? You'll find the horse quite fresh, sir. Will you take him?" said Carmel.

"No, thanks; you'd better get home yourself. You're always turning up in out-of-the-way places. By Jove! in the days of Wynderfel they'd have taken you for a warlock, and burnt you some fine morning. You never do anything like anyone else. What the devil's the good of being so queer?"

"Queer! am I, sir? Well, I dare say; but I only wanted to look at the old house. I've been dreaming such odd dreams about the Lady's Window, and all sorts of faces, so confused. I wished to look at the place again to try and understand them, and what it all may mean."

"Well, if I were you, I'd come down in the daylight, or get my bed down here, and sleep, if you like it better. Capital place for dreaming dreams and seeing visions; but just for tonight, I'd get home and have some supper."

Carmel Sherlock had dismounted as Shadwell spoke these jeering words, and led his horse across the intervening space.

"I know Sir Roke Wycherly's face, sir. I saw him once when I was at Sidney, at Cambridge. I wish I did not dream at all, or could remember my dreams clearly. *His* face is always there, and there was something last night I saw about the Lady's Window up there," he pointed with his finger at it; "something, but I can't recollect it—I can't. Only he was there, and you, sir—you *were*, my God! climbing with a body like a black monkey's, and your own face."

"Ah! thank you," said Mark Shadwell, with a nod.

"I hate them. It was quite clear the whole thing as I dreamed it; but it all went to pieces as I awoke. I'd give an eye or a hand, sir, almost, I could gather it up again, for I know it's true, whatever it was, and I under- stood it—true and dreadful, sir. My face and forehead and hair were wet, and I cold as death when I wakened. It's worth knowing, if I could but recover it!"

His fingers were laid on Mark Shadwell's arm as he whispered this, and his pale countenance and large eyes gazed into his face with a near and frightened scrutiny, as if imploring a hint or a conjecture.

"What the devil are you afraid of?" asked Shadwell, with a laugh that sounded oddly in his own ears. "Dreams, indeed! Pretty stuff! By Jove, I often wonder you don't set up for a fortune teller, or a prophet, or a new Evangelist. Pity to put your candle under a bushel when you might make such a good thing of it."

"I thought, perhaps, I might recover it if I looked at this place; but no, no, I can't find the clue; these voices in the air, sir, if you don't write down what they say while it's in your ear, you lose it. You may as well follow the wind or try to paint the clouds of last year, or seek for a smile of Cleopatra; it's all gone. But oh, sir, I wish he wasn't coming!"

"Yes, *Wycherly*, it's very alarming, isn't it?" acquiesced Shadwell, with one of his ironies, as he watched the smoke which he had just blown from his lips dispersing.

"Sir Roke Wycherly, baronet," resumed Sherlock. "Yes, it's bad—it *is* bad; there's something bad about it, sir, his coming here. I fear him—I misdoubt him, I do—I fear him," murmured Carmel Sherlock, looking up at Lady Mildred's window, and

80

through it at a lonely planet shining clear in the sky; "I can't win it back, any way; it won't come: it's enough to make a man mad."

"Quite enough. I don't wonder you're so much afraid of Wycherley; he is such a formidable fellow, with his asthma, and his dyspepsia, and his drops, and his caudle—enough to frighten a giant, by Jove!" observed Mr. Shadwell, getting up. "You may as well get home, and I'll talk to you by and by."

"The horse?" said Carmel, again offering the bridle to his patron.

"No, I'll walk, I tell you— I'd rather," he said; and Carmel Sherlock, throwing first a dreamy look around him, and then looking down in thought upon the ground, led the horse away through the archway, and Shadwell soon heard the clink of his hoofs as he trotted briskly along the little by-road below the old walls of Wynderfel toward Raby Hall.

"That fellow will be stark mad some of these days; by Jove! he is mad! He'll be up in a madhouse so sure as I stand here. I wonder how long the poor devil will last before he breaks out!" muttered Shadwell, in that vein of soliloquy which was customary with him whenever he had just closed an interview with his eccentric assistant; and having settled this point with himself, as he did at least once every day, he watched the flight of a bat for a while, and had even a thought of shooting it, only he did not wish the trouble of loading. Then he reflected what a cross-grained world it was, and how he had been twice interrupted in that most unlikely spot, which three persons seldom passed in a week, and then he began to think of Roke Wycherly.

"It's an odd thing, devilish odd—that fellow's always maundering about here, and dreaming and fancying some mischief is brewing; and I can't get the same thing, by Jove! out of *my* head either. And hang me if I can think of any mischief he can do me. What can he do to injure me? If he were thinking of a lawsuit, it could do him no earthly good coming down here. Inquiries—evidence—stuff! He's no such ass as to think he could do it. That's the work of some fellow bred to attorney business. Devil a thing can he do to hurt me by coming down here; and yet, ever since I opened his note, it seems to me that I've been as mad, by Jove! as Carmel Sherlock, almost. I feel there's some d——d mischief gathering, and I can neither shape nor prevent it."

With his gun over his shoulder, Mark Shadwell mounted the stile, intending to pursue the lonely walk to Raby. But at the summit of it he paused, looking over his shoulder, for he heard voices approaching from the other side of the smooth sward in front of Wynderfel.

Female voices sounded pleasantly in the dewy night air, and there were men's voices also. He guessed whose they were.

"Rachel, is that you?" he called. There was no answer. The talkers were absorbed in each other and themselves, and the merry voices and laughter still approached.

"Miss Agnes is there also," he commented, in an undertone. "Pretty Miss Marlyn! what are you saying, I wonder? That's young Mordant, of course; yes, seeing them home. I wonder they didn't drive. Well, I'm not sorry; it will help to prevent me from thinking as I go."

So down he came from the stile, calling "Rachel" again as he went; and soon, with an answer, the party of four came round the distant corner of the old building, and Mark Shadwell greeted them and joined in the walk homeward.

## Chapter 17
### A Moonlit Walk—Another Step

There was a momentary chill and shadow as Mark Shadwell joined the party. The garrulous merriment subsided, and a short silence came, during which nothing was heard but the tread of their feet on the pathway.

Mark Shadwell inquired for Miss Temple—asked Charlie Mordant when he had come, and how long he was to stay— asked honest Roger how the cob he had bought at Raby did his work.

And with these questions and answers, the conversation flagged again, and the party walked on in silence.

"Five abreast is a little too much for this path, isn't it?" said Shadwell. "You shall lead. Go on, Temple; you and Mordant take care of my daughter, and I'll take charge of Miss Marlyn."

And, in compliance with this order, his daughter and honest Roger, with a longing, lingering look and a great sigh, and young Mordant, walked on, while he and Miss Marlyn fell a little behind.

Mark Shadwell strode on beside Miss Marlyn. He did not speak; a topic somehow did not turn up at once. He saw from the comers of his eyes her elegant figure moving beside him, with a little space between; he saw her features, too, clearly enough in the moonlight, and that she was looking straight before her, rather downward as she walked, and very gravely.

"Rather a damper, I'm afraid, my appearance just now? You were talking very merrily, I think, as you came round the corner of the old house there," said Mark Shadwell, after a little silence.

"Yes—that is, I believe we were," said Miss Marlyn.

"And what was all the fun about?" he inquired.

"I really forget, sir" she hesitated.

"Now, you're not to be *sir*ing me, do you mind," he urged, in a low key. "I told you before, that your poor father and I were very, very dear friends. If you want to vex me, of course I can't help it; but unless you do, you really mustn't treat me so very formally. I sometimes think, Miss Marlyn, that you are a very haughty young lady."

Haughty!—really?" replied she. Yes, haughty," he repeated. We never know ourselves, I believe; but that does surprise me, Mr. Shadwell," she said, looking downward on the path before her; and Shadwell fancied he could, with his side glance, detect a trace of an enigmatic smile.

"They smile to themselves, when they think we're not looking; what are they dreaming of, I wonder, when they do it? It's very becoming," he thought.

"I tell you what, now—you know you're my secretary, and we are on confidential terms, and you must listen to me—and

I do say, you are as haughty a little queen as ever swayed the sceptre of empire."

"You don't think so, sir?" said Miss Agnes Marlyn, very gravely.

"There! *sir* again! Well, no matter; I say I do. I'm quite serious. I'm a reader of faces and of character, and understand the psychology of gesture and motion also, and I say that pride is your strength, and—weakness."

Miss Marlyn threw upon him in the moonlight another earnest look of inquiry, which was he thought, wonderfully handsome. He looked at her a little more directly and smiled; whereupon her brief gaze was averted again, her dark clouded eyes were lowered to the path before them, and he could see her long eyelashes; and he looked a little while in silence, and then he said:

"The reason—one reason—why I say you are so haughty, is this: that you keep me so at arm's length. All very well, of course, if I were a young jackanape; but I'm not—I'm an old fellow."

There was no remark.

"Old enough, at all events, to have that daughter," and he nodded toward Rachel. "And, besides, even if I had never known or cared for your poor father—who, I've told you very often, was my most intimate and dear friend—I am, and I feel it, and I wish to Heaven *you* could understand it too—I am, in virtue of your position under my roof, your guardian. I'm not jesting; I'm perfectly serious. I consider you as my ward; and you'll see, should you ever need it, there's no trouble I should shrink from, no exertion I'm not ready to make in your behalf. I know it's easy to say all this, and not very likely, you'll think, perhaps, that my services will ever be needed; but, by Jove! I mean what I say, and I wish they were, that I might prove it."

"You are too good, Mr. Shadwell," said she: and the low and very sweet notes in which these words were spoken, he fancied, touched him.

"Yes, you'll see it; I regard you as a second daughter—I do, I assure you."

Miss Marlyn made no answer.

"And, in some respects, you could fill a place in my confidence, which a daughter cannot," he said, in a very earnest, but a lower key.

Miss Marlyn looked at him for the first time quite direct, with a wondering and almost startled glance.

"I do not understand, sir," she said.

"No, of course—how should you?" said he. "But there are lots of things I can't talk to Rachel about, even if she had sense to make it worth the trouble, on account of her mother. Why, you look as if I was going to talk treason and blasphemy, whereas I was really only going to speak very sober good sense."

And saying this, Mr. Shadwell laughed a little, and paused for a reply: but Miss Agnes offered no remark, and looked down as before.

"What I mean is this—you see I'm talking quite frankly to you; as frankly, in fact, as I expect you always speak to me—I say, what I mean is just this: there are subjects on which I can't talk to Rachel, just because they involve a discussion of her mother's prejudices and unreasonableness—and she has more than one woman's share of both, *I* can tell you—you'll understand better the sort of thing I mean by and by. You see, I mean to be outspoken, and hide nothing from my secretary; other fellows would mince the matter, and take a roundabout way of conveying their meaning; but with you, I go straight to the point. She's delicate, she's peevish, she's exacting."

"She's very kind to me, sir," said Miss Marlyn, sadly.

"Of course she's kind—of course she is; I'd like to see any one in my house treat you otherwise than kindly. But I mean, and you'll find it, she's no more good in the house than a picture, and she's a sort of worry beside; and she can't, she never could, enter into my feelings. I was an ambitious fellow—I had plans for life—I wasn't duller than other fellows who have got to the top of the wheel since—but she was all against it; such a drag, a dead weight, I never could move—all for a quiet life, and, by Jove! she has got it—ha, ha! If it hadn't been for her, I'd have been member for Halford twelve years ago; but she was in the way—a woman can knock those things on the head, you know. Now Miss Agnes Marlyn, if you marry a fellow with any 'go' in him, and any brains, while you live, don't tether him down by the leg to a post at the back of a rabbit warren, as you see me here."

This was a theme on which Mark Shadwell was more eloquent than exact. Perhaps his poor wife, in her ill-requited idolatry, had pleaded against his early maunderings about public life. But she had not had much of her own way in other matters; and I suspect that Mark's earnestness, or, at least, his opportunities, had not been quite so inviting or so strenuous as he chose to believe.

"I don't think, however, Miss Marlyn, that you are the kind of person who would want sympathy with a daring ambition."

For one moment Miss Marlyn glanced upon him a kindling look— something wild, fiery, admiring. It was like the last face seen in a dream as a man awakens, gone quite in a moment; for the young lady's look was again downcast, almost sad; but that wild, glad, momentary look haunted him—it was inspiring.

"She's wonderful!" he thought. "By Jove! a glance like the pythoness! She's a fine creature! There's no woman worth a fig that has not a vein of the tigress in her."

He walked beside her, quite silent again for a little way, and thought how handsome she looked. That look of strange admiration seemed burning in the darkening sky, on the grass, on the dark background of distant foliage—wherever he gazed.

"I say no one can get on alone—it is not meant; one's own applause won't carry you through—one must have sympathy. I might have been differently placed in the world now, if I had secured it," said Mark Shadwell, aloud; "and I can't tell you how much obliged I am for—well—for your consenting so good-humouredly to be bored with my confidences. You understand now what I mean? I wish I could requite your kindness any way. You can hardly estimate the extent of it, because you have never known what it is to be in a solitude like this, without a human being to talk to upon the very subjects that most interest you—and I'm a fellow that can't talk to reeds and purling streams—and you have no idea how a secret preys on one, like that animal, by Jove! the Spartan fellow hid under his robe, and that devoured his flesh while he concealed it."

Mark Shadwell talked as if he was immensely grateful. He felt, on the contrary, that he was conferring an immeasurable obligation. He was thinking how flattered the young lady must be by this graceful condescension of his confidence. He wished to please her. The philosopher may have suspected some little sentiment mingling in his goodwill; and if there was, why should he not amuse himself a little? Heaven knew he meant no harm! he knew himself too, he hoped. Had he not outlived his follies? Of course it is pleasant to look at a beautiful girl, as you look at a flower or a picture. His statuesque admiration was very free from danger; he was not like the poor little woman who fell in love with the Apollo Belvidere.

They were now approaching the timber that groups high and dark about Raby Hall.

"And so," said he, "it is a bargain. In all your plans, and in all your troubles, whenever they come—and may Heaven avert them for many a day!—I'm to be your adviser and helper, to the extent of my poor power, do you see? and you, in return, are to listen to all my wretched secrets, and give me your advice—instinct is better than experience, it is always true—and we are to be true friends—real friends; and I shall keep no secrets from my secretary, and she's to make me her father-confessor: so that's agreed!"

And with these words, drawing nearer to her side, he took her hand and pressed it.

"It is agreed, isn't it?" he repeated in a lower key and more earnestly.

She laughed a little, and said "Yes;" and he thought she blushed as she laughed. Yes, she did blush: he was sure she blushed a little; and she did not draw away her hand, as Becky Sharp or Miss Jenny Bell might have done. "There were none of their false pruderies—no leaven of the shark in Miss Marlyn. She was genuine;" he thought.

That little blush was like the sparkle and flush of champagne in his veins and in his brain, as he went to his study that night.

## CHAPTER 18
### A LETTER CONCERNING MISS MARLYN

Mark Shadwell knew that Sir Roke Wycherly had a sly taste for satire, and he had no fancy to figure more amusingly than he could help in the pleasant stories he was sure to tell of his visit to Raby. With therefore as much activity as a proud man might, and with some grumbling and some sneering, he pushed on preparations for the reception of this kinsman, whom, as we know, he neither loved in his heart nor spared in his talk.

The evening after his moonlit walk, a letter reached him from Sir Roke. It terminated suspense as to the reality of his intentions, by fixing a day for his arrival.

He had begun to think that something had happened to change Sir Roke's plans. He had been better pleased than his pride would allow him to confess to any one, that there was a chance of escaping this visit altogether; and had the letter been one to tell him that on a certain day an execution would be in his house, it could hardly have left, for some minutes after its perusal, a more disagreeable impression.

"That mad fellow, Carmel, has made me as nervous as a sick old woman, with his croaking. This comes of living in a solitude, with no one but rabbits and women and madmen to talk to. What the devil *can* it signify whether Roke Wycherly comes, or no? He's not a ghost, or an evil spirit, or even a conjurer; a commonplace fellow, with nothing in him but money and selfishness. Well, he says he'll come—and so he will, and he'll go—and there's an end."

And thus framing his mental protest against the auguries of Carmel Sherlock, he rose from his chair, and thrust Sir Roke's letter into his pocket, with contempt in his countenance, and an odd misgiving at his heart.

There was among the letters on this occasion a French one, addressed, in a little round hand, and with very florid capitals, to "Madame Shadwell," which Mark took the liberty, without hesitation, of opening.

It was from the principal of the French school, and concerned Miss Marlyn.

"My secretary, by Jove! Let us see."

And thus saying, with an altered countenance, he read this official communication.

He now recollected that his wife's application to the mistress of the boarding-school, for information respecting the young lady's qualifications, had been only provisionally answered by a sort of deputy, who had spoken in the highest terms of her. Mark scanned this supplemental letter with a keen curiosity.

The principal of the establishment had been absent for some time, it seemed, in consequence of ill-health, at Vichy. She apologised for the long delay, and proceeded to answer Madame Shadwell's inquiries one by one.

It struck him that this letter was much colder, and more guarded, than that which had come from Madame de la Perriere's representative. With respect to intelligence and accomplishments, indeed, it spoke of her much in the same strain; but with regard to those moral qualities about which inquiry had been made, there was a kind of reserve that rather piqued than alarmed his curiosity. Madame de la Perriere had nothing to censure in the morals of Mademoiselle Agnes Marlyn, and, though she was still a very young person, she trusted that in her new situation she would be steady, and approve herself worthy of confidence.

As to whether Mademoiselle Agnes Marlyn was likely to grow weary of her present position in consequence of its solitude, she did not feel herself competent to pronounce. But for a person so young as *mademoiselle*, she thought a secluded place much more desirable than one of a different stamp, and would certainly advise no visiting or other relaxation of the rules of her residence in Madame Shadwell's house. And she thought that *madame* would find that the accustomed quietude of her daily life would conduce to the young lady's efficiency in her situation.

He read these passages several times over. He could detect, nothing positive in them. Their tone, however, persuaded him that Miss Agnes had required a stiff rein while under Madame de la Perriere's authority.

"But then she says she has nothing to censure. The pretty rogue has been just wild enough to cause uneasiness, and there she was pulled up. I'll go into the schoolroom and talk to her a bit."

So resolved Mr. Shadwell, and, entering that room, found Miss Marlyn alone at her desk.

The young lady rose as he entered, and laid down her pen.

"Dear me! what a reverential courtesy!" said he, laughing. "What has become of Rachel?"

"Mrs. Shadwell sent for her. Shall I call her?" said the young lady, with another little reverence, and moving towards the door.

"On no account," he replied. "I don't require to look at that great girl to be reminded how old I am, and I am not so often favoured with a *tête-à-tête*, that I should wish to cut it short in a moment. Sir Roke Wycherly's coming. We are quite sure of him at last. He'll be here on Monday. That's my first bit of news; and the next is, I fear you were rather a wild little woman at school, for I've got a letter in my pocket that tells all sorts of fibs. It comes from Madame de la Perriere. I'll only tell you it's by no means so good as the note we had, eight weeks ago, from Mademoiselle de Chatelet. I'm telling you the truth, upon my honour; and I'll leave you till tomorrow to guess what's in it."

As he spoke *mademoiselle* blushed, and for a few seconds her colour grew more and more intense, and then suddenly it waned. She became so pale that Mr. Shadwell half repented his jocular experiment. He could not tell whether she was nervous only, or angry, or very much frightened.

"Come, you pretty little scapegrace, you must tell me honestly the entire history of your school adventures. Mind; I am your confessor—tell the whole truth, and upon my honour I'll give you absolution."

She dropped her eyes, and looked much more like herself.

"I may have enemies, sir—it is possible; but my conduct has been always irreproachable. If there be malice, I defy its worst. Madame de la Perriere can testify of my conduct if she will. It is terrible to have to assert of one's self those things which are taken for granted of all ladies. I am a child of calamity—an orphan—in some measure, always at the mercy of my employers; but powerless and unhappy as I am, I have yet some rights, and one of them is that of hearing distinctly whatsoever may have been urged by another to my prejudice. Only tell me what it is, and I pledge my life I refute it. Have I not, sir, a right to hear my accusation?"

"Why, see where you're running to, you little madcap! Who on earth talked of accusation? I assure you there is nothing of the kind," said Shadwell.

"You did, sir," replied the young lady, in a clear and rather bitter tone. "if you did not use the word accusation, you conveyed it. You said that falsehoods had been written of me."

"Did I? I do believe I did; but you might have guessed by my manner that I was not serious."

"I did not guess, sir," said the young lady.

"By Jove! She's awfully offended," thought Mark Shadwell, who had expected quite different relations to arise on this little conference. Miss Agnes Marlyn held the higher ground, and he was actually apologising.

"Well, I'll tell you exactly the truth, and you'll see how mere a nothing it really is, and you mustn't be vexed with me, though it was very stupid jesting as I did. I had a letter from Madame de la Perriere, as I said, and I fancied it a little cold—that's all. I do assure you there is not a single story or complaint in the entire rigmarole; but there is what I said—it's cold, and for that reason I shan't mention it to a human being but yourself, and I'm sure you'll not be vexed with me for telling *you*?"

There was a little silence here.

"I knew you wouldn't—I knew it." He touched the back of her slender hand as he spoke; it was almost a caress.

"There, now, she's reasonable child. She's not going to be one of my troubles."

He raised her hand and pressed it for a moment. "We are good friends again, aren't we?" he said in a low tone.

"You are very good to me, Mr. Shadwell," she said, after a little pause; "but I've just been thinking that I had better resign my situation here, and go elsewhere. May I say so to Mrs. Shadwell?"

"Why, what on earth can you mean? Go away? By Jove! wouldn't that measure be rather sharp and short ?" said Mr. Shadwell, rather aghast.

"I am sure you did not mean to insult me, Mr. Shadwell, but it seems to me that your confidence in me has been shaken by that letter of Madame de la Perriere," said Miss Marlyn. "I know well what pain it will cost me to leave Raby; but suffering is not new to me."

The young lady spoke with a decision that alarmed Mark Shadwell.

"You'd hardly use me so ill as that," remonstrated he. "If I conveyed anything like what you say, I'm very sorry, and do believe me, I never intended it. You must try me a little longer. It was very thoughtless of me to mention the letter. I remember when I used to care about what people said; I don't now. I've felt nervous myself when I thought stories were told of me—I mean lies, of course."

"Everyone has enemies—very few have friends," said the young lady. "I lost my mother very young; when I lost my father, I was fourteen years old." Miss Agnes Marlyn was speaking as it were in a melancholy dream, and you would not have supposed that she was conscious of another person's presence. "Madame de la Perriere found herself in charge of an unfriended orphan. I have laboured to requite her kindness. I have much more than repaid her. It is not her fault—she cannot help it—that she can

92

attach herself to none but people of rank or fortune. I have neither; of course she speaks coldly of me."

"But I told you, that letter is our little secret, yours and
mine—not a soul else shall ever hear of it; and I give you my
honour I never for a moment attached the slightest importance
to it. And I beg your pardon for having named it to you."

Miss Marlyn looked at him for a moment with eyes very
grateful and humble, and said:

"You are too good to me, Mr, Shadwell."

"Don't say that *now*; make trial of me first, and then pronounce whether I wish to serve you," he answered in a low tone,
and accompanied his words with that fierce and handsome smile
which showed his small white teeth. Then he left the room,
and Miss Marlyn looked for a moment sternly on the oak door
through which he had passed, listening, and quickly shut and
locked up the desk at which she had been writing.

Then standing with her finger to her lip, she listened for a
while, and, having thought a little, she hurriedly reopened her
desk and tore up the letter she had only an hour ago elaborately
written, and with a match set fire to the fragments on the hob,
and saw the last spark out.

Notwithstanding the confidence she always professed in her
Raby friends, this young lady's ways, I think, were cautious and
secret.

## CHAPTER 19
### FIDDLE AND THUNDER

A thunderstorm that evening came down over the distant
forest of Hazelden, and the glen of Feltram, over the old man-
or and woodlands of Wynderfel, and down the wild slopes and
brakes of the neglected park of Raby. It was to the music of the
distant thunder that Miss Marlyn, standing at the window of the
schoolroom, read a very short note which had come with the
other letters in the Raby postbag from the village.

Whatever indecision she may have experienced about her
other correspondence, there was none about this. She glanced at

the little clock over the mantlepiece; she had only time to trace a few hurried lines in reply, which accomplished. Miss Agnes, with a light and swift tread, and carrying her little desk which never left her bedroom but in her own company, put on her humble little dark grey cloak and black hat, and glided along the gallery without meeting anyone, and down the great staircase. She was just entering the vestibule when a side door opened, and she was encountered by the last person in the world whom she would have liked to meet.

"Going out!" exclaimed Mr. Shadwell, with a look of such honest astonishment as made her feel how necessary an explanation was. "Going out! Have you quite lost your little head? What do you think of *that?*" The question followed a brilliant flash of lightning. "And do you hear that?" he added, as the nearer thunder rolled over their heads.

"Is it very foolish?" she said, with a deprecatory little laugh. "I delight so in thunder and lightning; is anything so magnificent?"

"That's all very fine, but Farmer Dobbs down there had two cows killed by lightning last year; besides, don't you see the rain?"

He had opened the hall door a little, and some heavy drops had already fallen upon the steps.

"The rain! Oh yes, indeed!" she said.

"Rather a damper, I should say," suggested he.

She laughed again.

"Then I suppose I'm not to go out—absolutely?"

"Certainly not," he replied, lifting his finger; "I'm very angry at your having thought of such a folly"—he was speaking in a low tone, and with a smile—"but, naughty as you are, I can't bear to kill you quite. I won't allow you to kill yourself; I really can't make up my mind to lose my secretary so soon. You must only look from a window, high and dry," he insisted.

"With the fate of Farmer Dobbs's cow before my eyes," she laughed. "Oh, how grand!"

She paused, as indeed he did, while this new peal ran over

their heads, and rattled and rebounded among the distant hills. "How awful and glorious!" she murmured, when it was over. "Can we wonder at its being taken for the voice of God?"

"And the moon for a green cheese, and the Pope for an oracle, and an electric crack for a verse in the Bible. I never wonder at anything. None of your heroics with me, little rogue ;" and, with a laugh he drew back into his room, and closed the door.

On the stair Miss Marlyn paused, with a changed countenance. She was terribly in earnest about the short letter which was to travel by that night's post. It *must* go. She would have walked twenty miles through the thunderstorm to post it. She could have walked down now, and passed on her way through the other door to the town; but, coming or going, she was sure to be observed. She must lay her account, with Mr. Shadwell's hearing of it. What would he think? She could have easily confessed her folly, and pleaded her girlish Quixotism, had it not been for the unlucky *rencontre* at the hall door. He was shrewd and suspicious, she intuitively felt, where feminine motive was concerned. Henceforward, were she now to go, he would watch her with an eye of scrutiny and doubt. That would never do.

She looked at her little silver watch—a present from a prodigal English bagman, an adorer. It was still reliable, having hardly entered on its second year. Time pressed. She dared not ask a servant. The antipathy of that race to the governess order was against it, and she had made no confidences among them yet. The old panelled oak clock, with hour-glasses and scythes, and bald Father Time, with his forelock, and the hours carved in bold relief, was ticking stolidly above her at the stair-head. Four minutes faster than her new silver watch was this grim old monitor. It was distracting.

Suddenly she remembered Carmel Sherlock.

During the months she had been living here, she had hardly spoken fifty words to that queer shy person; and yet she trusted him thoroughly, though, metaphysically, she treated him as an enigma not worth studying.

In another minute she was at his chamber door and knocked.

95

There was a quavering and wailing of the precious Stradivarius going on within, an odd accompaniment to the thunder without, which prevented her first and second summons from being heard. At the third, the fiddle suddenly was mute, and Carmel Sherlock, with the instrument under his arm, stood pale and amazed in the half-open doorway, and gazed in the face of the handsome girl from under his lank black locks.

Without ceremony. Miss Agnes Marlyn entered, and shut the door.

"Can you get away down to the town, and nobody see you?" demanded the young lady, hurriedly.

"Ay, to the town? Pray sit down, Miss Marlyn; this is a great honour," replied Carmel Sherlock.

"Thanks, no; I'll stand, please. I've come to ask a great favour; and, if done at all, it must be done quickly. It's just what I said, that you'll go down to the town for me this minute; can you, Mr. Sherlock?"

"Surely—yes—who's ill?—who?" said he, anxiously.

"No one; it's to oblige *me*—a *great* obligation, Mr. Sherlock; you must promise to mention it to no one."

"Ay? how? What am I to promise?"

"Secrecy," she answered, "only that. It's the merest trifle— next to nothing— only to go down to the village. I would do it myself—I was going—but there's a difficulty."

"Afraid of that?" said Sherlock, pointing up with an odd smile, as the blue glare of the lightning, followed by the reverberations of the thunder, startled her again.

"*Not* afraid of that; I was going, but was prevented by an accident. I feel, Mr. Sherlock, that I can trust you. Will you accept my confidence, and do me that great service at a very trifling cost—the walk to the village? I'm sorry it's raining."

"I'll go, yes—oh dear, yes! "

"And promise, upon your honour, never to say *what* you did, nor that you went at my request; do you promise?" As she spoke. Miss Marlyn laid her hand upon his arm, and looked with a dark entreaty into his eyes. The little chamber was obscured by the storm, and the successive flashes, as they talked, illuminated the stern features of the girl, and, in their livid light, bereft them of their colour.

"I do—oh yes—certainly—upon my honour. I thank you, Miss Marlyn, for your confidence; I do, and it is wise—truth lies at the bottom of a well. I'm very deep."

"You are to put this in the post—that's all;" and with these words she placed the letter in his hand.

Setting it down upon the table, "My God!" he exclaimed, staring at it with a horror that made her begin to fear he might know more than she had suspected.

"What's the matter, sir?" said Miss Marlyn, a little fiercely, and turning very white,

"It's very odd—we were playing a farewell;" he spoke this to his fiddle, looking it grimly in the face. "It came very freely—of itself, almost. It wasn't for nothing; it's all a system of echoes and reflections; no power ever lost, every force made to exhaust its utmost value. You call it omens, I call it economy. And the letter—good God, ma'am!"

Saying this, he poked the Stradivarius towards it, as if he expected to learn something of its spirit through that semi-intelligent medium.

"There's the letter—you've promised to post it—you may, of course, play me false—*will you?* There's not one minute to lose, if you mean to keep your word."

"Look there, at that clock," said he, nodding towards the dial of his Dutch clock; "it's right to the twentieth part of a second. I may stay here six minutes longer, and yet be in time to post it—but I'll never post it, unless you first answer me a question."

"Then, sir, you've deceived me, and I shall take my letter away," said she, loftily, extending her hand towards it. If she expected to change his purpose by this appeal, she was mistaken. As a lurking spider pounces on a fly, his lean hand seized the letter.

"Your letter's become *mine*," he said, with a cunning laugh, which gave place to an expression of savage menace, as he added:

"By Heaven! it's mine, except on that condition."

Miss Agnes Marlyn was now pretty well in a corner.

"I'm not going to put a pistol to my head for you, miss," he said, wagging that head grimly, as he searched her with a suspicious glance.

"What do you mean, sir?" said the lady, frightened into something like fury. "How *little* I knew you!" and as she spoke she stamped on the floor.

"What do I mean?" he repeated. "I mean that Rachel—Miss Rachel Shadwell—wrote that letter; and, by Heaven! it's mine."

"Miss Rachel Shadwell did *not* write a *line* of it. She does not know of its existence. I *swear* it!"

"Who wrote it?" demanded he.

"*I*—upon my sacred honour, *I!*—there. I've placed myself in your hands; you can't, in generosity— in common manhood, you can't betray me."

"I won't betray you! I believe what you say—every face is glorified by truth—I saw truth in yours as you spoke—I was half mad; no wonder."

Carmel Sherlock walked once or twice, with a kind of shudder, up and down his little chamber, and threw open his window and stood at it for two or three seconds.

"If I thought," he said, returning suddenly to the table and eyeing her with a new access of suspicion, "that she was writing to that man to accept him for her husband—that is, without her father's knowledge and consent—I'd take my own course."

"Young ladies, sir, don't do such things—it's simply impossible. You said, sir, you believed my word of honour. It was I who wrote the letter; it concerns no member of this family but myself, and no other knows of its existence."

Carmel drew a deep breath of relief; he looked up and then down, and stroked the back of his friendly Stradivarius, and "Oh dear!" said he gently, with a smile. "Miss Agnes Marlyn, you've wrung my heart. Only in a dream—only in a dream."

She looked uneasily at the clock.

"Two minutes still," said he, reading the dial. "I won't fail you. I'll prove it—only not yet, for I intend to put myself in *your* power. I'll be to you transparent; you shall have my pure but dreadful secret. I'm sure you are good—beauty is the surface of goodness, and nature never lies."

Tenderly and reverently he replaced his beloved fiddle in its berth, and whispered some words to it, she fancied, as he did so.

"And now," said he, as he took his coat and hat, "not for this trifling service, and the secrecy I promise, but for all I will yet do for you, and for the sake of humanity, you will share with me that lock of hair—I heard you tell her, on Thursday last, you wear it in your locket."

"Rachel's? yes; *here*. Take it all; I can get more."

He took it to the window for a moment.

"Yes, it is—oh! it is—in my hand!" He gazed on it as it lay in the hollow of his palm, with an incredulous rapture. "Lie there—lie there—and oh! Miss Marlyn, you'll speak to me of her sometimes? you'll tell me about her when we meet? Now I must go."

He was gone as he spoke; and Miss Marlyn found herself alone in this odd little room, and bethought her how awkward it would be if anyone—say, worst of all, Mr. Shadwell—were to surprise her there. So, listening at the door, and hearing no step near, she made her escape to her own room by a different route, and there, for the first time, her agitations over, with the volatility that belongs to all clever people, broke into laughter, peal after peal, over the ingenuous confessions of Carmel Sherlock, and the conquest of her unconscious pupil, who shared with his fiddle the mysterious devotions of Mr. Sherlock.

## CHAPTER 20
### SIR ROKE AT RABY

On the night I am now going to speak about, there was a pleasant fire in the old-fashioned drawing-room of Raby Hall, for a change had come, within the last day or two, in the weather, and the evenings were cold.

The long suspense about the baronet's visit was ended. Sir Roke Wycherly had arrived with his servants at twenty minutes past nine, and was now making his toilet. His host stood before the fire alone in the drawing-room, awaiting his appearance.

Mark Shadwell's temper had not been pleasant all that day. He looked round on the faded upholstery of the room with a sulky acerbity. He was angry with the furniture, angrier with his guest. Few things could more have galled his pride than to administer the hospitality of Raby to his cousin, Roke Wycherly.

The door opened—Sir Roke entered. It was more than seven years since they last met. He saw a change in his host, who saw probably a greater one in him.

Sir Roke Wycherly entered smiling. He was tall; he was lean; he had an easy wig on—a wonderful deception—which, however, deceived few people; his eyes had that peculiar haggard character which I have seen in those of some profligate men, showing a great deal of white. He was a little rouged, and cautiously whitened, I think; and was there not something odd—a little line of black, was it—under his eyelashes? altogether, in that long, and when you saw it near, shrivelled face, an odious pink and white effeminacy prevailed. His dress was quite unexceptionable, with an air of quiet fashion. Paradoxically, the man of pleasure looked older, and the man of cares and discontent younger, than his years.

"Very glad to see you, Roke," cried Shadwell, advancing with his best smile. "Very welcome; a great many years, Roke, since you've been here."

"A thousand thanks—don't remind me—a thousand thanks, dear Mark. I've heard of you very often in my wanderings, though we don't write letters; and you, I dare say, have heard of me."

"I never hear of anyone; I never see a human face. I take in one newspaper, and that's all my society, except the interesting inhabitants of this house; so I confess I have *not* heard; but I *see*, Roke, which is much better, and I'll not allow you to take the airs of an invalid."

Sir Roke laughed, and bowed a little, and shrugged, and shook his head.

"I've had a shake or two, though, but never mind; and do tell me, how is Amy?"

"Wretchedly, always—miserably, poor thing! other *poor* fellows' wives can give them a lift in country quarters like these—play tunes, or talk, or make tea, or play a rubber of backgammon, now and then—how charming, you'll say—but those are gaieties for other houses; poor Amy is not equal to any such exertions."

"But, really? Do you mean—" began Sir Roke, in a sympathetic key.

"I do, indeed; she's a perfect martyr to ill-health; can't come down this evening to see you."

"How very sad! and your daughter?"

"Oh, Rachel's as robust as you please; she'll give us our tea just now, I hope; she ought to be here."

"I've seen her, and she's sweetly pretty," said Sir Roke.

"Oh! met on the stairs," suggested Mark.

"No; in town, at a very old friend's, old Lady Mary Temple's," he replied archly.

Shadwell looked at him, thinking either he or Sir Roke must be mad.

Sir Roke laughed quietly.

"A *carte de visite*—a photo—my dear Mark; the prettiest thing I ever saw in my life almost; you know what a whimsical fool I am when I take a fancy. I followed a cameo I saw at the Paris exhibition to Florence—where they told me the fellow was who bought it—I did, upon my honour, and from that to Rome, and back again to Paris, where I got it at last; and, by Jove! if that photograph had been taken from the cameo, or both from your daughter, my cousin Rachel, they could not have been more like; and I should be ashamed to tell you—the confession's so ungracious—how much that *carte de visite*, and my restless curiosity, have had to do with my visit to Raby."

They both laughed. There was a little vein of earnest in Roke

101

Wycherly's jesting; there was also, as Shadwell knew, a whimsicality in his fancies, and a pertinacity in their pursuit, of which he could himself have cited instances as eccentric as that of the cameo.

"I've reason to be obliged to her, however, though you mayn't, for having led you to this stupid old place, where there's next to no shooting but rabbits, and almost no fishing at all, and, in fact, nothing but air and landscape to offer."

"So much the better; I never was much of a shot, and I always hated fishing; and if you had no end of both, I'm in no condition to try either at present. What I really do enjoy and require, is the perfect quiet you seem to dislike, a saunter in your park ( he was going to say a ride, but he hesitated, not knowing the state of Mark's stables), and the delightful bracing air of these uplands. It's devilish odd, Mark, but it's true, if you get a knock anywhere," and he touched his waistcoat with his fingers, "and begin to grow a bit hippish, you get a sort of liking for the old places, and for the old faces too, Mark; *I* find it so."

And he smiled and shook his host's hands,, promptly.

I don't think he was quite lying when he said all this. There were bits of truth jumbled up in it; and Mark Shadwell, who knew him well, began to think a little better of him, and to remember vaguely how characters are sometimes mellowed by time: and not a romance, but a worldly castle-in-the-air associated with this Roke Wycherly, very agreeably began to build itself up in crimson and gold, as the clouds do in sunset.

"Do you remember that thing from Horace *Qui fit, Mæcenas*, it begins—that I had to repeat at the end of the Christmas half, for old Beaks? I can't get further now, but it means that every man quarrels with his own place in life, and envies his neighbours," said Sir Roke.

"Suppose we exchange, then?" said Mark, with a pleasantry that had something of a sneer in it.

"More easily said than done, my dear Mark; we flies don't get free of our cobwebs so easily. There's some truth, *I* can tell you, at the bottom of the cant about money and its cares; there *is* trouble about it. By Jove, Mark, I often think I have too much of it!"

Mark thought he could help him off with a part of his burthen.

"Ha, ha! you're laughing Mark—I know you are; but it's true for all that. When my poor dear father put me on my allowance, and I made it do, I think I enjoyed things as I never did since, because I paid for them, and felt the price too, I can tell you. Now that I have everything *gratis*, as it were, the world has lost its flavour. I've often thought how much more enjoying a fellow would be with a smaller income; I don't say I'd have nerve to reduce mine by a guinea, but I *do* think it, Mark, just as fellows who drink too much, envy those who haven't the habit, though they can't give up a glass of their daily quantum, don't you see?"

And having concluded his little oration, Sir Roke yawned gently behind his hand, and closed his eyes languidly for a moment.

"And, I tell you what," he resumed quietly, "anyone who has been knocking about as much as I have, grows tired of it, d'ye see, and likes quiet."

"Well, that's a liking I can gratify, for devil a soul one sees here from one year's end to another," said Mark, with splenetic jocularity. "Oh! this is my daughter," he said, as she entered the room with Miss Marlyn. "Rachel, this is your cousin, Roke Wycherly."

The baronet approached, smiling, with something foreign, a little ceremonious, in his manner, and took her hand deferentially, and told her he had been wishing, a long time, to make her acquaintance, and asked her a number of trifling questions, and listened to her answers—it seemed to her with a degree of respect and pleasure that was to the young girl still new and very flattering.

The manner was indeed silken, the voice very low and sweet; she felt that she was treated like a person of importance, and worth pleasing. But there was nothing very engaging, she was conscious, in the sickly and somewhat long countenance that was inclined with an unchanging smile over her.

The matter of pigments and enamel and wig and teeth apart, she could not quite discover where lay the peculiarity in that countenance, which generated a feeling of distrust, and something of the nature of antipathy; she felt only the general effect, which was contracted and deceitful. In those blue eyes was the peculiar light of exhaustion, and about them a multiplicity of small complex lines of cunning and cruelty—a sickly cheek, a wasted look, and a smile that was artificial and unpleasant, and always there.

It was thus with a mixture of feelings that Rachel regarded him. There was also a sense of pity. The tall thin figure was narrow chested, and stooped a little, and Sir Roke coughed once or twice a slight cough, which Mark Shadwell, too, had observed.

"She is my cameo," murmured he to Mark, when he again took his stand beside him on the hearthrug. "She's perfectly charming!"

"Do you think so?" said her father, flattered in spite of himself.

"Oh! you *must* see it, yourself," he insisted; "she's perfectly lovely!" and his eyes rested on her again, as she sat talking to Miss Marlyn, at the tea-table. "And the young lady beside her?"

"Oh! that's Miss Marlyn; you remember poor Marlyn of the Guards?"

"*Henry* Marlyn?" suggested Sir Roke, looking still at her. "Yes, poor fellow!—his daughter."

"Dear me!" exclaimed Sir Roke, with more wonder than was quite called for. "He's—he's—sold out, didn't he?"

"Sold out, yes, and dead some years—poor Marlyn! My wife took an interest in her, and got her here. She knew his wife, you know—she died some time before him—and that poor girl was working for her bread in a French school, when Amy heard of her, and brought her here. She's a kind of—I can't call her governess—instructress and companion to Rachel."

"She's pretty, but at disadvantage where she sits; very few girls would bear that contrast," said Roke.

"You're fatigued, Miss Marlyn—you've been taking one of those horrid long walks," said Shadwell, approaching the table; "you ought not to allow her, Rachel; you see she's quite pale."

"No, indeed, sir," said Miss Marlyn, suddenly blushing, so that her cheeks and neck and temples were dyed in the same brilliant tint, which was again succeeded by an unusual pallor; and Mark Shadwell was pleased to see how an unexpected word from him could agitate her. He did not want his cousin, Roke, however, to observe it, and, turning to rejoin him, he found that he had accompanied him to the table.

"Will you introduce me?" he murmured in Shadwell's ear.

"Sir Roke Wycherly," said Shadwell, presenting him.

"I had the pleasure of knowing some of your family, Miss Marlyn, a great many years ago, before your time. I had no hope of meeting a daughter of my old friend in this part of the world. And so you're a great pedestrian, are you? A very dangerous ac-complishment," he continued, transferring his address to Rachel, "in young ladies; you are such enthusiasts in whatever you take up; you always overdo it—you do—a little tea, please."

"They do, indeed," he continued, addressing Mark, as he stirred his tea beside him at the fireplace. "You must stop it, pray do; they kill themselves that way—I assure you they do. How very well your daughter looks just in that light; do look—quite lovely, doesn't she? You must positively stop it."

And so for a time they chatted, till the young ladies departed, and Sir Roke, being undisguisedly sleepy, took his departure also to take possession of the stately old bed in which he was about to pass his first night, since boyish days, at Raby Hall.

## Chapter 21

### Sir Roke Wycherly in His Bedroom

Sir Roke Wycherly's man, the grave and gentleman-like Mr. Clewson, had spent nearly two hours in his master's bedroom, accompanied by Dick Willock and Mrs. Wyndle, in reversing and recasting the whole of that provident housekeeper's dispositions for the comfort of his gov'nor, as he called the baronet.

He moved about and inspected and countermanded and adjusted with a quiet but sublime sense of responsibility, which impressed the imaginations of the simple people of Raby. There was no question whether the thing was right or wrong *per se*, or easy to accomplish, or next to impossible. It was simply to be done, quite inevitable, and to be set about with silent and resolute resignation.

The dressing-table was too near the window. The bed must be got four feet farther from the fire. Mr. Clewson had to place beside it, among other things, the lamp invented particularly, as he informed Mrs. Wyndle, for his master, by "Mussier Lumbell," of Paris, which there was but one other in all the world the same, and the empress had that, and by experiment he showed them how when it was. thrown ever so little out of the perpendicular it extinguished itself with unerring precision, and there were little tinted glass globes, rose-coloured when the baronet was in the dumps, and green when he wished to read. He had been offered, himself, forty guineas by Mr. Budisman, of London, to take a model of it, but he couldn't allow it for no money; for we were put under obligation of honour in writing to Mussier Lumbell. So he showed the lamp and all its tricks with a grave pride and condescension, and the rustics admired with awe and curiosity.

There was a little thermometer which he hung at the farther side of the bed, away from the fireplace, and which it was his duty to maintain at a given point, at dressing hours and bedtime. He got Dick Willock to "obleege" him with a hammer and some tacks, and he actually went down upon his knees to tack some neat little strips of *gutta-percha* to the door next the carpet, to protect the baronet from those draughts and eddies which he feared like the fanning of the wings of Azrael. Though so great a gentleman, Mr. Clewson was not a bit proud. "He put his hands to things quite ready!"

There was a most elaborate and splendid dressing-case, which he had only time to disclose generally. They were dazzled. The spirit of magnificent dandyism had been stronger upon the baronet when he purchased it some twelve years ago. In some respects he had sobered, and illusions of that kind had subsided since then. The lust of the eye and the pride of life had since been dimmed and cooled a little, in the first solitudes of the valley of the shadow of death. And the other box, very neat, but by no means gorgeous, polished oak, bound with brass clasps, a chest, with a thick brass ring at each end for handles. Yes, evidence of the panic and chimeras of the *dominus ægrotus*.

The medicine chest which the wonderful Doctor Vandevelde of the Brunens of Nassau, physician, magician, impostor, who yet unquestionably wrought sanitary miracles, induced so many of his rich patients, to his advantage, at all events, to purchase. The medicines were mysteries from his own laboratory—extracted, compounded, procurable in no other *sanctum* or den in all the world. They saw there more tinctures and drops than *Lord Ogleby* ever dreamed of.

It was only a gaze of a few seconds. There were German words on the inside of the cover, and the bottles were queerly shaped, with eccentric stoppers, and might have held the famous Bottle imp, or even Asmodeus. "Dear me!" exclaimed Mrs. Wyndle, who had herself a housekeeper's taste for quackery, and admired this exquisite chest accordingly.

The baronet's dressing-gown and slippers were displayed before the fire, and were a little shabby—very shabby, in fact, for so great a gentleman. Very grand when new, no doubt. But they had got rubbed and old; and lessened with a sense of disappointment and relief the immense distance which Mrs. Wyndle had felt widening between her and the great man, and brought him down, in one point at least, to the level of mortals.

It was past eleven o'clock as Mark Shadwell wished good-night to his cousin, Sir Roke, at the threshold of his door. The baronet smiled and waved his hand, and shutting his door, his face was all at once leaner and more haggard, and he yawned dismally; and his dreary eyes looked restless and fierce as he turned them from place to place in the chamber, and asked Clewson if the water was there and everything right, and screamed at him, with a curse, to know "where the d—l he had hid away those drops, and why on earth they were not on the table" and told him, with an oath, he was not "worth his bread and butter."

Sir Roke had nerves and a liver, and had been twice or thrice, in a gouty panic, to Vichy. His charlatan at the Brunens had given him a habit of swallowing these drops and other physics. But although in this, as in his fastidious appreciation of feminine beauty, he resembled *Lord Ogleby*, he bore no other resemblance to that high-bred type of invalided English chivalry.

He "cussed and swore hawfle, he did," Mr. Clewson said, and he well knew that fact before he entered his service. But such missiles break no bones. All things were taken into account in Mr. Clewson's salary, which would have made many a hard-working vicar, to say nothing of curates, open his eyes.

So now Mr. Clewson, with a countenance as meek and reverential as if a bishop had just blessed him, pointed out with a bow the identical drops which Sir Roke had overlooked, close to his own hand.

"And, please. Sir Roke, your dressing-room is ready," said the man, with the same reverential inclination indicating the door.

"*No*," snarled Sir Roke; "*no*, just get me to bed, will you? I'm tired to death by my d—d journey in that rumble-tumble machine."

Sir Roke began to inspect his features in the glass which the man set before him.

"As tired as a ghost, by Heaven! I look as if I had pulled it all the way myself. By Jove! this d—d place will kill me."

There was a pause and he muttered:

"How young he looks! I might be his father, almost—*to-night*—always grumbling—the most good-for-nothing fellow on earth. Never thanked God for a mouthful—no more than *I*; and, by Jove! he looks a dozen years' younger than he is; good-looking—a devilish deal better looking than I fancied he could be; and, I dare say, thinks himself an Adonis. We'll see. I'm awfully cut up. Those cursed roads. I must have something. You've got that *curaçoa*, Clewson? Well—here—*here*! *will* you?" and he tapped angrily on the table beside him. "Yes, I do look awfully seedy. I don't think I ever looked so seedy in my life. D—n you, do *you*? Just the sort of thing to happen to me. Will you give it, or not?"

He leaned back in his chair and sipped the cordial a little,— and ended by swallowing what remained at a gulp. His squire stood by his elbow with the high-shouldered foreign bottle; Sir Roke held the glass towards him and had some more.

"Take it *away*—*will* you?" said he, still leaning back. "Yes, I feel a little more naturally now ;" and he stooped forward and again inspected himself in the mirror. "And look—see—yes, one would say now, there's a little blood left in me."

And he held up his head and almost simperedy he thought his pink cheeks so becoming; and this, and the glow consequent on his "nip," as Clewson called it, made him feel wonderfully comfortable for a few minutes.

"*You* look a little tired also, Clewson; they gave you your supper, I hope?"

He was so busy about the rooms, he had not had time yet.

"That's very bad management, Clewson; you did not get your dinner, either—those little commissions for me. You ought to be more alive, Clewson—old traveller, you know. Just get me to bed—we'll not be very long—will you? and then just wait in the room there, till you see I'm asleep; and then, for goodness sake, do be off and get something. The merciful man, you know, takes care of his servant, the Scripture says," said he, looking up at the cornice in a peevish reverie.

Sir Roke did not know very much about the Scriptures, no more did his man, and so the quotation passed muster. And as the impulse of the *curaçoa* subsided. Sir Roke's benevolence abated, and before he got into bed, I'm sorry to say, he was snarling and swearing and never alluded to Clewson's supper again.

Old Wyndle was a good-natured woman, but I think no stimulus short of curiosity would have kept her up and awake in her room to give Mr. Clewson his supper, which was keeping hot before the fire.

She could see that Mr. Clewson, great a gentleman as he was, was something of a slave, and stood in awe of that bleak, savage, selfish temper; that he was afraid of Sir Roke, who yet seemed "such a nice gentleman," "and spoke to her in the gallery so friendly;" and as the clock chimed half-past twelve, and at last struck one, and she grew uncomfortably sleepy, she wondered how great folk could be so hard on their servants; "and that poor gentleman, Mr. Clewson, looking just like he was going to faint with hunger—nothing else—and he not daring to swallow a scrap o' cold meat, afraid he should smell it. Smell it, indeed! How *could* he smell a san'wich? Lud 'a mercy, sich noses! And he, poor gentleman! down on his knees, to make everything ready, and himself not able to stand! There's usage for servants. And I remember the poor old master—how he'd look a'ter his horse, when he'd come in himself, many a time I mind it. That was for a horse—and here's now for a man. Who'd a' thought, wi' his pretty blue eyes, he'd ever 'a bin so hard, an' a good-natured little fellow he was?"

When Mr. Clewson did come to the housekeeper's room, with his tap at the door, "Billie Winkie, the dustman," had been with her, as she was wont to say to the children long ago, when blinking, and yawning, and nodding set in, and he thought the old woman looked, at least, ten years older, and he, *she* thought, "fairly worn off his feet." But supper is the great restorative—sleep, we know, is "great nature's second course"—the first being what we have mentioned; and Mr. Clewson, for whom and his gossip she had waited for so long, was now quite a new man, and, though grave and sedate, was yet energetic and wide-awake for the ten minutes that followed, over his tea, which, late as it was, he preferred to any other beverage.

There was nothing cynical—no sort of animus in Mr. Clewson's little sketch of his master—neither was there flattery. If it was not a prepossessing picture, it was not Mr. Clewson's fault.

"Well, he's none o' that left—no—he ain't soft nor good-natured, mam, ain't Sir Roke; but the situation's good, mam, very good; if it wasn't, no one would keep it. He allows a good deal o' liberty in off times—so you gets through your work punctially he doesn't care if the old boy had you. He pays liberal, and he passes on a deal o' things—'ansom things—to the person as fills my situation. It is a huncommon good situation, but it requires a very superior person to fill it; he would not keep no one helse, and no sich person would keep the place if the hemoluments was less than what they are. *Wild*? Well, I don't know what you mean, quite; he's very reg'lar, mam, and he has his pleasures, I do suppose, like other gentlemen—*more*, I dessay. His 'ealth? It was bad two years ago, but I don't think there's very much amiss now, if he would give over them drops and physics. He can go through a deal of amusement and pleasuring when he likes, he can. That's private to himself, of course."

"Between him and his Maker, poor man!" interpolated Mrs. Wyndle.

"Quite so, mam; and I don't know nothink o' the matter," said Clewson, with a quiet decision, which seemed to shut that subject up.

"You've heard him, now and again, I dessay, talk o' the old place and people?" suggested Mrs. Wyndle.

"Which o' the old places do you mean in particular, mam?" inquired Mr. Clewson, who recollected several haunts, both in Paris and London, which had disappeared from time to time.

"I mean *here*—Raby—Wynderfel—and the old family, and old friends—simple folk, like myself—he used to like old Dolly Wyndle, pretty, little, soft fellow he was; running to my door every hand's turn, for a bit o' cord, or a handful o' saltpetre—you wouldn't suppose how they used to bum it—or an apple. I want this, Wyndle; and, Wyndle, give me that; and so 'twould be; wi' his pretty blue eyes—and I often wondered if he talked of old Wyndle ever?" and she paused.

"Well, as for places, mam, he never likes no place for. long; and I don't think he cares for no one—not that cup o' tea," replied Clewson, not satirically, but gravely, as stating a metaphysical fact.

And with this and some more gossip, Mr. Clewson took his leave. And as he might easily miss his way, old Dolly Wyndle conducted him to his door by the back stairs and gallery; and he paused and listened at the door, and opened it as softly as a thief might; and whispered his *adieux*, and on tiptoe entered his room, and shut the door slowly and soundlessly, as if his life depended on Sir Roke's sleep, although the dressing-room interposed between his bed and his master's.

## CHAPTER 22
### CARMEL'S WALK TO WYNDERFEL

Sir Roke came down to breakfast in high spirits.

There was always a place for Carmel Sherlock, who seldom contributed, except when a chance question invoked him, to the conversation. Unnoticed he came and departed, like that domestic apparition in the red coat, who harmlessly haunted the meals of the German forester's family in the story.

Sir Roke looked at him; perhaps he expected an introduction, the party was so very small. But Carmel Sherlock was apparently seen by none of the people there, except when Miss Marlyn, with ever so faint a smile and a nod, from time to time handed him, or received, his teacup.

Shadwell had again to apologise for his wife's absence. Miss Marlyn was as silent, nearly, as Carmel, except when, in an undertone, she spoke a word or two to Rachel. But Sir Roke chatted very gaily, and had no end of stories and anecdotes to tell, which were quite new, at all events, to Rachel, who—her shyness vanishing—listened and laughed, and questioned, and thought Sir Roke's conversation wonderfully charming.

Mark Shadwell, sometimes inactive during this discourse, was yet pleased. A very odd idea had got into his head. He knew how unstable Roke Wycherly was, but also how violent and imperious his fancies were. He was drawing towards that age at which men are ruled by sense rather than imagination—when they prefer the essential to the conventional—and, with an instinctive acquiescence in the conditions of contracting life, determine to live with the least degree of respect that is decent for fame and custom, and with the most rigorous attention to self. This is the age at which a man, defining with terrible precision what he wants, dispenses with all the frivolous, and even the respectable incompatibilities—not because his object is dearer, but his sacrifice is less. The value of this one residual idea is dominant, because all the rest have been tried and found wanting. It is the age at which *roués* project the domestic serenities, and marry milkmaids, and fancy that thatched simplicity and ancient faith, and plump innocence, with rosy cheeks and a white skin, are worth finally trying.

He has had all that this fashionable, pharisaical, rascally world can give him. His iron safes are full of the counters which are its circulating medium. He has discovered, however, that they are not convertible at the great Bank of Happiness, and he is resolved this time to try his own way. Though all the Rules, aghast, throw up their hands and eyes, and the enraged Prejudices protest till they choke, he *will* have one chance for the *summum bonum* he has always missed. He will set about it, with a cynical enthusiasm, in earnest, before the appointed hour comes, and he must yawn and simper his last, and leave the lights and fiddles forever, and go down and let the undertakers get on his last mufflers in the cloak-room, and the pale waiter at the door cry, "Lord Newgate's hearse stops the way!"

For so great a philosopher, Mark Shadwell was, I am afraid, unduly vain, and even conceited. He thought himself more of a genius than he was. Had he measured his powers more accurately, he might have perceived that his obscurity was not quite so purely an unlucky phenomenon. Had he known how many men, all round him, with twice his intellect, and ten times his knowledge, were working, without a single brilliant chance or a hope of distinction, for daily bread, with a manly resignation, he might have been a more contented and a less useless man; but his own mental superiority was an axiom of his system. Success was his birthright, and that he had it not was due to the perversity of a monstrous destiny.

Sir Roke Wycherly was no genius either: in some respects, a shallower man than Shadwell; in others—rather, perhaps, from temperament than intellect—decidedly the stronger. His host, however, no doubt, well knew how to measure his early companion's strength and weakness, and his character was bare before him.

He knew that Sir Roke's fancies were absorbing and violent; but he also knew that he was cautious and secret. These qualities were, at times, opposed, and here was a situation in which their action seemed directly so; yet he could not quite conceal the interest and admiration that were growing upon him.

Fortune owed Mark Shadwell a great compensation. Were the tables about, at last, to turn, and was this visit, the prospect of which had filled him with perturbation, to open a way to a strange but simple reparation?

"What's become of Carmel Sherlock?" asked Mark Shadwell of anyone who might choose to answer.

"I did not see him go; but he *was* here," answered Agnes Marlyn.

"Oh! I know; though it might have been yesterday for anything he said; but he can't have been here ten minutes: he must have gone more than half an hour."

"He sat over there?" inquired Sir Roke, indicating his empty chair. "I was going to ask who he was. Fine eyes, hasn't he?—rather remarkable head?"

"He's a genius of a particular kind, if you like them," said Shadwell.

"No, Mark, I hate 'em all. I suppose they're good for geniusing, but they're fit for nothing else. Does he paint pictures, or what?"

"Upon my life, I don't know. He does a little at everything—he geniuses, as you say; but what I keep him here for is to keep my accounts, and, though he's a genius, he does it very well."

"He's going to put me in a poem, or a picture, or something," said the baronet. "I never was so scrutinised in my life—*quietly*, I mean—for I don't think he knew that I perceived it. But he has got a great pair of lamps for eyes. They don't do for peeping; it's always a stare or a glare, by Jove!"

"So, child," said Mark Shadwell, half an hour later, stopping his daughter, who was running downstairs in her walking things, and smiling on her, with a kind of approbation, "our guest amuses you! I don't wonder; very agreeable, isn't he? He always was very good company; and, I can tell you, he thinks you—Well, I won't tell you *all* he thinks of you; but he has been quite opening my eyes on the subject of your perfections and 'Where are you going? I told him you'd show him the old bridge of Raby. Can you tell me where Sir Roke is?" he added, addressing Clewson, whom he saw crossing towards the back stairs.

"Sir Roke is writing his letters in his room, sir.

"Oh! well, after luncheon, then," said he, tapping her cheek with his finger-tip, and smiling. "You *are* looking *extremely* well."

So away she went for her walk with Miss Marlyn, who awaited her on the steps; and, as she went, she was pleased and wondering, for her father had never taken so much notice of her in her life before.

Carmel Sherlock was not among his accounts when his patron sought him that morning. He had gone away fasting, having swallowed only a little tea. A solitary walk over wild and sylvan slopes, and through many a forest hollow, of ivied rock and ash and thorn, with his broad-leafed wide-awake hat on, and his rugged walking-stick swinging in his hand—you'd have thought he was walking with an object. But that straight line of march and rapid stride had none. It carried him to the deeper solitudes of Hazelden. Beginning like a mountain gulley in the woodlands, it wound and deepened under crag and shadow until it became stem, precipitous, and dark as that glen in which the ill-starred marksman of the Hartz cast his enchanted bullets.

Utterly solitary and solemn—the haunt of the wild cat, the owl, and the fox—it simulates, even at noonday, the silence and gloom of night. With a little plashing of unseen water far below, with rocks, sometimes broken, sometimes rising, sheer as the walls of Rhenish castles, their fronts stained with lichens or clasped and hooded with ivy, and their long chinks and crannies green with moss and hanging pellatory;—their steps and chasms are gripped with the roots of straggling trees, and their beetling summits over-topped with mighty boughs and brooding foliage.

Here, at last, he paused, in another world, as it were, and awoke from the dream of life, such as it had been.

There was the hustle of faded leaves high above him, and the indistinct plash and moan of waters far below. Seated on a step of rock, in a high nook of this great cathedral, he began his wild self-examination and confession and adoration.

"All the earth doth acknowledge Thee, the Father everlasting! *How*ever, *what*ever, *where*ever, I must, and *do*! Abandoned to general laws, or marvellously seen by Thee, and all my hairs numbered! The spirit sounding—motion life! Were I to drop from this height, 'twere only into the lap of Nature, to beat my brains out down by the brook there—*there*—in a moment, if I chose"—he was looking down—"I should be alive again, deluded in the next; and here, and now, I still may see her, and hear her—there—and forever my anguish wouldfollow me. Rachel! Rachel!"

He called her up and down the ravine, as if he thought a spirit would answer, with his hands clasped. Some large bird flew from below into deeper shadow down the glen. "Away—away!—fly—fly away, whatever you are! Everything flies from me! Rachel! Rachel! She's gone—she's *gone*! Rachel, you'll never hear me! I come in and out, and to and fro, like a shadow —no one turns, no one cares—and I, who have watched her from her childhood like a spirit, am to her—*nothing*, and never could be—never, never could be!—and now the thing I knew and feared so far off has come up suddenly, and I have seen Death face to face! No one ever dreamed it, nor ever will, except Miss Agnes. And so it is here—suddenly, but foreseen. The coming calamity repeats itself in thoughts and signs, dreams and other ways. My soul went out to meet it. I met it, and saw it on its journey far off a thousand times. She is glad, and my benefactor is happy—and *I?*—I can't complain. I can blame *no* one—not even *myself!* It *was* to be, like death, and no one could help it!"

And thus on and on, with a monotony that was yet various, like the solemn sounds of the solitude that surrounded him, Carmel Sherlock talked down through the sheer darkness to the rocks and trees, as the Knight of the Sorrowful Countenance had once done, long before him, in another forest.

## Chapter 23
### The Baronet Writes to Dear Adderley

Sir Roke was in his room, writing to Pepys Adderley, Esq., a young fellow of forty and upwards, who had tried a little of many things and places, and broken down everywhere. An Eton man—always in a good set—full of the idle energy of adventure and pleasure. He had seen the last guinea of his little patrimony fifteen years ago. He spent two years in the Levant. He visited Australia, and wrote home flourishing accounts of his growing fortunes to his old mother, from whom he requested a sum of money a few months later. He has been seen at California. He has written three sketch books of travel; the longest is in two "sparse" volumes, as his publisher terms them, and he still owes something to his printer.

I don't know that Adderley's pedigree would bear sifting; but he has always been among men of rank and fortune. He likes good *entrées* and good wines, and other people give them to him, though he's not pretty, not witty, and not good-natured; but being a used-up man of fashion, with gay spirits, whose pride would stand a good deal of rough handling, with seasoned modesty and obliging morals, who thoroughly knew the town, and the world, he suited Sir Roke precisely, and had been, under the rose, his comptroller, master of the horse, and what you please, ever since his little visit to the baronet had commenced at his pretty house at Richmond, more than three years ago.

To this gentleman, whom he had despatched to Scarbrook to await his arrival and administer for him in the interim, he was now writing thus:

My dear Adderley,—No one is more ready to admit than
I the immense value of your time; and therefore I merely
hint that, if you *could* waste a very few minutes in improving your valuable letters, they might be applied with advantage in *forming* the words of your sentences, which at
present axe only *indicated*, and in thus saving me an infinity
of fruitless trouble. I would also suggest that if, instead of
thinking *after*, you would take the trouble to think *before*
you write, it would obviate the necessity of those frequent
erasures and interlineations which further complicate the
problem of speculating upon your meaning. I write at
present to beg you won't go to races or any other d—d
thing, just for a week.

By that time I shall be at Scarbrook; and pray don't leave,
as I may write by any post, and arrive the train after. Write
to this place up to Saturday. I shall go to town on Sunday,
and remain there till Tuesday, or perhaps Wednesday; you
may expect me on either day. It is just possible a friend
may precede me. Suppose we call her Mrs. —— (any
name you please, only tell me what), and you receive her
as your married—any relation you please—a mere *lark* as
you say—but the rustics must not be offended. Have you
any objection? We sha'n't remain many days at Scarbrook,
and you shall never see that dull spot of earth again. She
must be received with respect, observe, being, I assure you,
a lady. Her maid will accompany her. Let me have a line,
*legible*, by return of post. Let my people make everything,
in a small way, as comfortable as possible. I don't understand the object of what you call 'roughing it.'

Ever, dear Adderley,

Yours sincerely, R. W.

Sir Roke came down and talked with Amy Shadwell, whom
he found at last in the drawing-room. The pretty Amy of long
ago, with the large hazel eyes—those eyes would always be pret-

ty—and the slender figure, and white delicate hands, and her pretty even teeth, and the early pleasant smile; but how very delicate she looks! there can be no mistake here—poor little smiling thing! She'll not be a trouble very long to Mark!

Mark, her first and only love, whom she still loves, and thinks the handsomest and the cleverest man on earth, whose looks she watches by stealth, for whom she hazards little hesitating smiles on the chance, just the chance, of wiling him back, even for a moment, to the illusions of bygone days, and luring him into one answering smile. Poor little smiling thing, with always the same load at her heart!

I wonder whether any woman, except a very coarse one, ever met a man who had admired and pursued her once, and not beheld her since, for an interval say of ten years, without a secret shrinking and a pang: she would rather remain unseen, leaving the early image in its place un-shivered.

Sir Roke Wycherly advanced and took her hand with a smile that admitted no shock and no decay. He sat beside her at the sofa with an air so tender and respectful as testified that the romantic gallantry of chivalric days was not over.

They talked a great deal of all sorts of things, and of old times, of course, and he said some pretty things, at which she laughed, but was pleased, and repeated them after to old Wyndle and pretty Rachel, and laughed more. She knew it was flattery, but spoken by the man who once felt it, there was still the ring of a romantic sincerity in it.

She talked to him of course a great deal about her demi-god Mark, and he listened, I am bound to say, respectfully; and he thought within himself what an odd arrangement of nature it was that women do go on liking particular fellows. It answers some end, he supposed; but it did seem to him a mystery, worshipping fellows like Mark there, who has not cared a pin about her for ten years or more.

"What a pretty creature she was, sweetly pretty!" Sir Roke thought; "very gentle, and rather agreeable. She seemed to me positively clever when she was young. What fire and point a brilliant eye lends to a *bon-mot!* How their good looks tint and lighten up their conversation! Mark will be looking out for a wife—he'll try for money this time—I'll back him to get a woman with money. Wonderful fellow he is; his hair—what a mystery the hair is"—Sir Roke had a great deal of trouble with his whiskers; we know that the upper tresses grew, hair by hair, in the studio of the great M. Picardin of Paris, and had ceased to cost the baronet any anxiety—"a wonderfully preserved fellow, as good-looking almost as ever he was, and the estates and a very good name, the Shadwells; it's time he should make a push somehow—great advantage to my pretty little friend Rachel, pretty little girl, the Miranda of this solitude—I wonder where they are." He was by this time in his room, and rang his bell for Clewson. "Find out where the young ladies are, will you? and if they have gone out for a walk, in what direction, and get the people to show you, so that you can point it out to me, *will* you?"

In the interim Sir Roke made an inspection before the mirror, and some little repairs and embellishment, and then walked out, as unexceptionably got up as he would have done in Mayfair.

"I've no fancy for killing birds," he used to say, "or deer, or fish, or myself, by Jove! a little delicacy in boyhood saves one from all that, and I never could contract, thank Heaven, a taste for the drudgery and butchery of what they call their sports, fiddling with worms and taking fish in one's hands, or killing a great deer as big as a cow, or breaking my neck in pursuit of a stinking fox! I'm not ashamed to say I'm a bit of a cockney, and don't care to kill my own meat, and like to be clean; and I look on the country as a very decided bore, a place where we get our flour and beef from, and go when we're sick; but I'm altogether of Captain Morris's way of thinking about the grove of chimneys and the sweet shady side of Pall Mall."

## CHAPTER 24

## UNDER LADY MILDRED'S WINDOW

Miss Marlyn's dress is very nun-like, made high up, with broad plates, quite simply. She makes them herself, I think—the material nothing remarkable; she affects greys—silver greys, I think we call them—which look as if they were shot with silk, but are not: grey, nun-like, I say, but with just a little bit of colour below her full white throat, generally a small knot of crimson velvet. I can't be quite sure; just a few inches of soft and intense colour, harmonising, the French know how, with the shy elegant grey. It is the most humble, quiet, piquant thing in all the wardrobe of cruel love, Everything is in keeping.

The little bonnet she used to wear—nothing—*straw*; but there is a *tournure* in it, as in everything she wears; and the croquet gloves she pulls on so carelessly: is the prettiness theirs, or is it all in the slender hands they cover? Her dress might have been shorter without violence to the fashion—*mutabile semper*—of that particular season, but it would have lost its conventual quietude, and when some cruel chance for a moment shows her boot, you see the slenderest boot, the prettiest foot in all the world.

When this young lady took her walk today with Rachel, it seemed to her pupil that she was not in her usual spirits, or, truth to say, temper. She was silent, or stopped her companion's overtures to conversation with short and dry answers, so much so, that Rachel asked her whether she had vexed her. Whereat Miss Agnes looked full at her on a sudden with her deep grey eyes, and laughed.

"*No!* what makes you think that?" she answered.

"Your silence and your manner," replied Rachel.

"Well, I *have* been silent, I believe, and I really don't know why; but my manner?" said Miss Marlyn.

They were by this time under the grey walls of the ruined Manor House of Wynderfel.

"Yes, Pucelle, your manner," repeated Rachel.

"Well, Rachel, I did not intend—I did not even perceive it—

*there*, won't you?"

And she drew her towards her and kissed her, and then held her from her and looked for a moment in her face with an expression which Rachel did not understand.

"Vexed with *you*; good God! what a notion!" she exclaimed, with a sharp disdain; "what in the whole earth *could* I be vexed with you about? Come, do pray let us talk of something else." There was a little silence here, and with a slightly changed manner she added—"You know, dear Rachel, I love you."

"Shall I tell you about Lady Mildred?" asked Rachel.

"Do," answered Miss Agnes; and Rachel related the story.

"It's a very pretty, sad story—love and jealousy—poor thing!" said Rachel, by way of epilogue to her tragedy.

"Lady Mildred, what a goose!" said Miss Marlyn.

"Ah! you don't think so, Pucelle," answered Rachel.

"From that window?" inquired Agnes, and she stood up and looked through her little glass at it. She did not smile, she looked without sympathy or interest, as she might at the "drop" of a prison at which a convict had been executed.

"A high window," she said at last. "If she did go about it. Lady Mildred was quite right to do it effectually, don't you think? An odd fancy to live in a garret, though! I did it once, because I could not help it. Old La Chouette we used to call old De la Perriere. De la Perriere, indeed! Her real name was Roque, and her father was porter in a dirty old house near Notre Dame. She put me into one; but I'll never sleep in a garret again."

There was something both cynical and dismal in Agnes Marlyn now, that was quite new to Rachel, and which somehow made her feel uncomfortable, and even nervous.

"It was not a garret, however, in *our* sense," he said. "It was, on the contrary, a very fine chamber; look to what a height the roof rose above it, and look inside with your glass, and you'll see a wonderfully carved mantelpiece. There is a great stone with the Shadwell arms, and I don't know how many quarterings over it. It was quite a splendid room."

"And if she was so comfortable, why did she kill herself?"

asked Miss Marlyn.

"She was wild with grief, and love, and jealousy, poor thing!" answered Rachel. "She was cruelly ill-used, and has haunted us, you know, ever since."

"I don't pity her a bit," said Miss Marlyn.'

"You don't!" exclaimed Rachel.

"Neither will you, when you know better," replied Agnes. "How can you interest yourself about a fool?"

"Why a fool?" asked Rachel.

"Because she was jealous, and a greater one for killing herself. If she *would* kill someone, she should have killed him. But he was not worth it."

"I think, Pucelle, you want to shock me," said Rachel, after a little pause; "why do you talk like that?"

In fact, it was something wicked in Pucelle's face rather than in her words, which were, like those of young people, often loosely spoken, that vaguely startled Rachel Shadwell; but people don't always take the trouble to analyse their impressions.

"Oh! everyone talks what they don't half mean sometimes. I think all that business up there was miserable folly," said Agnes Marlyn. "She was an *imbecile*, that's all. It would have been murder, of course, to kill him, and murder's wicked; but it was worse to kill herself. It's a world of tyranny."

"What do you mean, Pucelle?" asked her companion.

"I was tyrannised over ever since I was a wee thing like that," and she laid her left arm across her breast, and locked it in her right, like a baby, with a laugh.

What a wonderfully pretty strange nurse she would have made!

"*You* like babies, dear little sweet things, you know," she continued, and laughed again,—not pleasantly, Rachel thought. "As long as I can remember papa used to box my ears for anything or nothing, every day almost, and lock me up in a dark room; and after my mother died, often half-starved me, when I knew he had money enough in his pocket for his pleasures."

"Agnes, dear, I thought you loved him!" said Rachel, with

wide and sorrowful eyes.

"So I did, I believe, in spite of it; I don't know why—he did not deserve it. Perhaps because he was lively, and amused me sometimes, when he took the trouble; and he was a man, and we like to be ill-used by men. It seems to suit—nature designed it, I suppose—slave and tyrant. But the idea of being *jealous* of a man!"

And she smiled along the daisies at her feet, in a listless contempt.

"Madame du Barry was a very wise woman," she continued; "she did not know what that sort of jealousy meant; she never teased the king."

"Was she a good woman?" inquired Rachel.

"*Yes*," answered Miss Agnes, with decision. "I read her life in my garret, once; she wrote it herself. She had no Tartufferie about her, and was good-natured—that's what I mean by good."

"But was she really good?" asked Rachel. "Yes—well enough—good and wise in her way, I suppose; how should I know?" replied Miss Marlyn carelessly.

"And who was she?" inquired her pupil.

"She was one of Louis the Fifteenth's wives, when he died."

"One of his wives!" repeated Rachel, as not having heard her rightly.

"Yes; kings have as many as they choose," Agnes laughed. "Upon my honour they have. King David had, and every other king that was worth a rush, ever since; as many as ever they choose. Why do you stare, child? I'd tell you no end of things—all true—only you'd tell them again, and get poor Pucelle into trouble."

She had two or three pebbles in the palm of her hand, which she was throwing with tiny jerks into the air, and rolling them about, and looking intently on them all the time she spoke, so that Rachel saw nothing of her eyes but their long lashes.

"I should not like to hear anything I might not tell mamma," said little Rachel, spiritedly.

Her simplicity may amuse town-bred young ladies, but they

will excuse her, remembering that she had not their advantages, and that her young mother had been her near and sisterly companion.

"No, of course not—what a little fool! Your mamma, of course; I tell everything to your mamma myself," said Agnes, quietly, still rolling the little pebbles in her hand. "All I say is, that no woman ought ever to make a fool of herself about any man; and no woman but an idiot, absolutely, could think of hurting herself for jealousy."

"They say that jealousy is a sign of love," argued Rachel, in support of the sentiment of this legend of Wynderfel, which had seized on her imagination. "Wives always love their husbands best." She thought she saw the light of a smile cross Agnes's downcast face at these words. "And if they did not love them best, why should they marry them?" she added, arguing resentfully with that smile.

Agnes Marlyn looked full at her for a moment, with laughter in her deep dark-grey eyes that she did not understand; and with the end of the daisy she had plucked from the bank close by, between her fingers, she knocked the pretty tip of Rachel's nose, as one of Titania's fairies might have done, with the tiniest little tap in the world, and almost whispered:

"Mademoiselle Simplicity!"

They sat down for a time, in silence, on that old stone bench which I have already mentioned. It was the drowsy time of day, when the afternoon san is warm, and the air hardly stirs. Rachel had a book with her, and turned over its leaves, and laid it down.

"Let us come to the ruin—the chapel, I mean, close by," said Miss Marlyn, getting up listlessly. "We'll sit under the window, in the shade of the ivy; it's pleasanter than here,"

## CHAPTER 25
### SOME ONE LOOKS IN AT THE WINDOW

The ruined chapel of Wynderfel stands on the slope behind the Manor House, embowered among grand old trees. A broken stone fence, here and there half obliterated, surrounds it; and a few stooping thorn and elders have straggled within it; an ancient yew-tree—which has witnessed, no doubt, the old funereal splendours of the Shadwells, whose burial- place this chapel was ever so long ago—still maintains its sombre supremacy in the centre of the long disused churchyard.

Agnes Marlyn's conversation had somehow frightened Rachel. Up to this she had seemed always playful, girlish, like herself; a sort of malign revelation had taken place. She had mistaken her; her sympathies were not with the child. The young girl felt she was making a mock of her; knew that she was the stronger; that she was mistress of a knowledge that was not good, and whose nature she had not apprehended. She was not as high as she thought, but more dangerous. She could not define all this; it was such an overpowering impression as comes in a dream, and there was a sense of sorrow and degradation mingling with her fear.

In an evil world the evil is the more potent spirit, and overawes the good. We have not faith enough in Time, the vindicator; how few, even in Eternity, that will adjust all equities! The *present* is the inheritance of evil. We instinctively know this, and the knowledge clothes its fascinations and cruelty in terror and power.

The first imperfect manifestations with which Evil hints its presence, touch the eternal antipathies of human nature with a frightful thrill. The ideas of danger and pain foreshadow its approach. Neither is there any such thing as a long hypocrisy; sooner or later the features of Evil appear with unmitigated distinctness. It is self-revealing, like Good, but manifests itself sooner, because its power is of *time*, and the other of eternity.

Agnes could not help it—did not care. As in the dead body the blood will gravitate hither or thither, as the body lies, and in due time show itself on the discoloured skin, so it is with evil. Its law is, when the time and place arrive, to come to the surface. There was a pain at her heart, which she would not acknowledge, and the nature of which her proud spirit scorned.

The mood was upon her, and the self-revelation the expression of her pain.

Rachel hoped that her companion would not renew her dismaying talk. They entered the old churchyard, and threaded their way among half-buried tombstones, upon a soft undulating sward, untufted and untangled with those rank weeds and dark high grass, that so painfully indicate the recent graveyard.

Rachel would have gladly seized some subject of conversation far removed from that which had just ended. The objects that now surrounded them might easily have suggested one. But somehow it would not come at call; and before she could find it, Agnes Marlyn began.

"Girls take fancies, of course," she said; "*I* could take a fancy to a man, but fall in *love* with him—no more than with a wolf or a shark!"

She sat down on the great stone of the eastern window, where, in old days, the altar had been; and just before her pretty feet, nearly buried in the unequal grass, stretched the tomb of Sir Hugh Shadwell, who *hic jacets*, with the customary patience and virtue. He was the hero of the Lady Mildred drama: "*Eques auratus, vir præclarus*," reposing in hope, and greatly mourned. The eidolon, carved in *bas-relief*, in white marble, once gilded and painted, now lies in the parish church of Raby, removed, two years ago, for better preservation, to that site, from Wynderfel chapel, which, however, still enjoys the distinction of Sir Hugh's personal presence, and the custody of his bones and epitaph.

"There's no man ever lived, or ever will, could make me, for jealousy, prick my finger-tip with a needle, much less die for him. Men come into the world to support women—women to please men with their beauty, and be supported; men to ill-use them, and they to deceive men. Whatever they marry for, they are sure to plague one another before the game is over. The Sabine women we read about in the Roman history yesterday— much love and romance there was there! And they made as good wives as any. Don't you see, *ma belle etoile*? The woman finds the pot, and the man the pullet; neither can get on without the other—and there's the secret of romance. The woman runs after an establishment, and the man after a pretty face. It's quite true; ask your papa."

Rachel looked with haughty surprise at Miss Marlyn.

"Or any other man," she continued, "they'll all tell you the same. Every girl should hold herself ready to marry the first good *partie* that offers—you, for instance, should marry Sir Roke Wycherly, if he asks you."

"*I*—Sir Roke Wycherly!" almost gasped amazed Rachel.

"Come, come, you can't pretend, dear, not to see that he has fallen in love at first sight, poor old gentleman!" laughed Agnes, a little drily.

"I really think, Agnes, you are mad yourself, or trying to make me so; either *that,* or you have been mystifying me all the morning," said Rachel, vexed and bewildered. "I should be very glad to be assured of that."

"A drowsy day—a little sultry," said Miss Agnes, standing up, and with clasped hands extending her arms with a listless stretch. "Mystifying? perhaps mystifying myself too. Whenever you talk sense, quite in earnest, you are very likely to talk some nonsense along with it, at least *I* do; but, on the whole, you'll find I'm right. You'll find what I say true, and why not? What objection to Sir Roke? Marry him, if he asks you; I don't say he will, though. But he has waited a long time, poor gentleman! and he deserves a young wife. Yes, marry him, he deserves it; I like to see a rich, old, selfish bachelor suitably married to a young, spirited, clever wife, who is also beautiful; a very interesting game ensues."

Again she stretched her arms as before, and added: "All I pray is this, that if he does ask you, you'll do me the justice to say that I urged you, as strongly as I could, to marry him."

"I suppose this is all a joke," said Rachel; "but it is not a kind or even a good one, Agnes, and I beg you'll talk of something else."

"I'm tired talking, suppose we read?" said Agnes.

"Yes, certainly; I should like it so much," answered Rachel, eagerly. But here arose a delay, for she had forgotten her book on the stone seat beyond the Manor House. "I'll run and get it!"

"Yes. I'm lazy-tired—I'll stay here." said Miss Marlyn, a little ungraciously.

So away went Rachel, through the arched doorway under the belfry, and across the little enclosure. The sound of her retreating steps died away, leaving Agnes Marlyn in silence and in deep meditation.

A voice, oddly connected with her thoughts, hard and snarling, quite close, on a sudden startled her. Sir Roke Wycherly was at the window, looking through upon her, with a very angry countenance.

"Charming retreat—did not expect to see *me*—nor desire, possibly. Where's your companion, pray?"

"Gone down to the ruined house," she answered, with a sudden change of colour.

"Coming back?"

"Oh, yes."

"How soon."

"In a moment, I think," she answered.

"In a *moment!*" he repeated. "Yes, I thought I saw her run down there, and I've only a word to say. I'm not a boy—I'm not a fool—I'm, on the contrary, a pretty sharp old fellow, and no subject on earth for child's play; I shall remain here till Tuesday—not a day longer—for I must be in town on Wednesday morning, d'ye see? I merely mention this, because I'll decide within that time; there's nothing unreasonable. 'No,' is very easily pronounced, and I merely object to being trifled with. Before your face I have evinced a very natural admiration for your pupil; of course, it is observed.

"What a *fool* you are! Pray excuse me. I say Tuesday, for of course *I* must make up *my* mind, whatever other people do, and I won't endure any caprices, nor run myself into the smallest trouble, I assure you. I allow myself to that day, not an hour longer, to decide in. What's that? Is she coming? Well, that's enough for the present. If you want to tell me anything, I'll find an opportunity—not altogether I—*you* must assist; but, of course, I shall be much obliged and flattered by a conference, and, I may as well say, frankly, I don't quite understand you, Miss Marlyn."

"Nor I you, Sir Roke Wycherley," answered the young lady, coldly.

"Yes, you *do*; I beg pardon, but you *certainly* do—you can't possibly *mis*understand me—you can't be such a *fool*—excuse me. You do understand me, and you understand *perfectly* every incident of my conduct."

He paused.

"Is she coming?—eh?—I'll go down and meet her;" and, for the first time, he smiled, though his smile was neither a warm nor a bright one, and he kissed the tips of his fingers, and waved them towards her, and disappeared.

Miss Marlyn looked after him, very stern and pale, with di-lated and brilliant eyes. Then she drew a long breath, so that the folds at the neck of her grey dress rose and fell, and she looked down on the tomb of Sir Hugh Shadwell, at the foot of which she was standing; you would have fancied that she was reading the epitaph, and that her smile was tinged with the dark cyni-cism which such be-pufferies of defunct bad men will raise.

And she murmured, "He's very angry;" and with the point of her parasol was poking away the moss from the projecting edges of one of the black-letter words, on which she smiled. She had something of Mark Shadwell's philosophy about the Sir Peter Teazles of this mad world.

"He's very angry!"

She smiled more, and looked closer at the moss, and worked more diligently. What a pretty "Old Mortality" Sir Hugh, the *nir praeclarus*, had found!

"Candescent," she murmured. But these attentions were not for him, or even for this tomb. She was using him merely, in a state of preoccupation, as young ladies will living men, I am told, on occasion, as softly as if love-passages were being whis-pered between her and the recumbent Sir Hugh; but she was only quoting her little *quarto* dictionary, playfully. "'Candescent—growing white—applied to metals at a white heat.' Ha! he does look very angry!"

She thought she heard voices, and listened.

"Yes, here they come!"

And with her pretty cruel feet she stepped lightly up the limbs and across the face of the helpless Sir Hugh, and sat down in her old place on the window-stone, and whisked her parasol to her side, where it lay between two fingers of her slim glove, and laid her other hand upon the carved stone of the window, looking out pensively upon the sad and solemn picture, and quite arranged for the coming surprise.

## CHAPTER 26
### A PARTY OF THREE

They were not quite so near as Miss Marlyn thought. Sir Roke hated brambles and stiles, and cursed stepping-stones, and always suspected grass of damp, even in the fiercest glare of July. He picked his way, therefore, and spared himself all the trouble he could. "What the devil pleasure can there be in sitting in that beastly churchyard? So *like* women! With a garden and flowers and everything at home, they come down here to sit in a dirty paddock, wetting their feet, and breaking their legs over tombstones!"

He had nearly reached the ruined house of Wynderfel before he espied Rachel returning with her book. He lifted his hat and smiled with all his fascination. "My long walk at last is rewarded," said he, gallantly. "I surprised Miss—Miss—your friend, in the picturesque little chapel you have chosen for your shrine— pray, allow me." He would have taken her book, but with a new sense of things, the fruit of Miss Marlyn's exhortation, a shyness mingled with dislike, she declined his aid, and, a little disconcerted and annoyed, pursued her way accompanied by the polite baronet, who chatted agreeably and murmured his little flatteries by her side. She was relieved, however, of the apprehension that he would attach himself to them during the remainder of their ramble; he had no notion of doing so.

There was a change in Rachel's manner, which, though decidedly the reverse of flattering, yet both pleased and amused him. Oddly enough it struck him as in the highest degree auspicious.

He stood in the little archway under the belfry chatting agreeably, holding his slender umbrella crook upward, and corresponding in his niche with the antique monumental bishop at the other side, in bas-relief, crosier in hand, and Lilliputian angel on his shoulder: possibly Sir Roke had his spiritual prompter at his ear also, if people's eyes could see such things.

"When I was here—only ten or twelve years old," said Roke, agreeably, looking about him, "I remember, with Mark, getting into the darkest glen I ever saw in my life—even in Switzerland—with a deep pool of water in it. I do assure you, the sides were so perpendicular, and the place so dark, it was like being at the bottom of an abyss; and there was a tombstone on the grass there—I remember it as if it were only yesterday—a female figure extended—do you remember?—cut in black marble, I think—with her hand so—"and he held up his open palm by his shoulder; "and there was a star on her left hand—that I can swear to."

"Oh! to be sure, that's the glen of Feltram; I've peeped into it often," said Rachel, forgetting her reserve. "You know it too, Agnes. Yes, indeed! it's an awful place, and the tomb of Lady Mildred—all alone, poor thing!—now, nearly four hundred years!"

"I remember Mark and I grew awfully frightened there, that day—the tombstone and the solitude and darkness," said Sir Roke. "So we did," repeated the baronet, amused. "I recollect our shouting to frighten the kites, or hawks, or whatever they were, up in the trees; certainly it was a wonderfully dismal spot— and the echo, high among the precipices every time we shouted, sounded not like a repetition of our own voices—we were boys, you know—but like a female voice imitating an echo; and, by Jove! we got it into our heads it was the dead Lady Mildred, who had got up among those awful trees. Mark saw that I was frightened, and I saw that Mark was frightened, and so we made a race of it, and ran for our lives."

"And does she haunt the place?" asked Miss Marlyn, dreamily, feeling, or affecting an interest in the story.

"Oh! dear, yes!" interposed Rachel, eagerly. "She's called the Gaze-Lady—I told you, I think, Agnes—and she bears an unrelenting hatred to our family."

"Exactly," acquiesced the baronet. "I recollect when we got home, there was an old woman—a superannuated housekeeper or something—I quite forget her name, but I remember her appearance perfectly—an old, lean, yellow woman, with a shake in her head—that used to sit in a great armchair by the fire, in the housekeeper's room—and she lifted up her hands—I remember so well— in horror at our audacity in venturing into that haunted recess, and threatened us with being kidnapped by the evil spirit, and told us such a long story about the ghost, and its malignity, that we were frightened half out of our wits. The Lady Mildred—the gaze-lady, you know—is the evil genius of the Shadwells, and returns in the flesh, at long intervals, to compass their ruin. I give you my honour, Mark's mother, your poor grandmamma, believed every word of it as religiously as she did her Church-catechism. She has told it to me fifty times. Did you never hear the story?"

This was to Rachel, who answered—"The gaze-lady? Oh, dear! I've been hearing of her all my life. Old Wyndle has stories about her—and Mr. Sherlock, of course, believes in her— and the other evening Mr. Temple—the vicar—was talking to mamma, and he says the legend would make a fine subject for a poem. She has visited our family, he says, twice—old Wyndle says, a great deal oftener."

"I know it all at my fingers' ends, better than Temple," said Sir Roke, "because I heard it at the age when little fellows are easily frightened, and remember better than we do afterwards. Have you told your friend? Really, Miss Marlyn, it's worth your listening to. This Lady Mildred, owing the Shadwells an eternal debt of hatred, is the spiritual minister of their destruction."

"Oh! and how does she contrive it?" gently said Agnes, still looking as in an odd dream along the scattered daisies, beyond the marble armour of dead Sir Hugh; and Roke Wycherly, with a gallant smirk, replied—

"Well, they say she comes like a beautiful woman, and very plausibly—more as if a chance brought her, than by design—and so she grows into an influence which she uses, with a fiendish wisdom, to entangle and beguile, and draw them into those dangerous currents of life which are strewn with dead men and shipwreck. Now, to leave metaphor, the first visit of this lost soul in the flesh, was made in the shape of a young Italian widow, of noble birth and fortune, and marvellous loveliness; and this creature took possession, as it were, of the wife of the then Shadwell of Wynderfel, and a pretty dance she led them all— such feuds, and litigations, and forfeitures!—ain't I right. Miss Rachel?— that was more than two hundred years ago, and she shook off nearly half of the estate, and established enmities, and in fact, worked like the father of evil, till her hour came, and she departed, *she* said for Italy, but our wiser forefathers knew it was to a still more ardent climate."

"But really, there did come an Italian lady?" enquired Agnes Marlyn.

"Miss Marlyn won't allow the supernatural; but I think, Rachel, we can vouch for the fact of the Italian lady's visit?"

"Oh! mamma says she heard there was once a portrait of her," said Rachel, enthusiastically.

"Heard!" laughed the baronet, "why I *saw* it—that old woman with the palsy, and a face as yellow as a gourd—used to shew it to us—what was her name ?—Dinah Ponder—wasn't it?—in one of the bedrooms—but it had grown so black by time, she could only see here and there a very brilliant complexion, and an intense carmine in the lips."

"I wonder where it is!" exclaimed Rachel. "It was in the year 1640, a hundred and ten years after the death of Lady Mildred—and then you know in 1750 she came again, that was exactly a hundred and ten years later, and that time my ancestor found her—a young English novice during her probation in a con- vent near Vienna—and he took her away, married her, and brought her home; and she bewitched him—as that goblin always does—and involved him in all sorts of ruin, and that was the last visit of the gaze-lady; but the old prophecy says, you know, that she was to return for the last time in a hundred and ten years more. Wyndle knows it, and all the old people, Mr. Temple says, between Wynderfel and Applebury."

"Yes, I've heard it often when I was a boy, can you repeat it?" said Sir Roke.

And Rachel repeated these rude verses:—

*Though Shadwells be churlish of old,*
*And the maid lie stark and cold,*
*In five score years and ten*
*Ye'll open, and I'll come ben.*
*In a hundred years and ten*
*I'll find the door again.*
*In ninety and a score*
*Again I'll come at the door;*
*And then we'll measure the ground*
*And the Shadwells no more be found.*

"So you see it is at intervals of a hundred and ten years she returns; and the next time will be her last visit," said Rachel with that eagerness to believe the marvellous which belongs to the young.

"Seventeen hundred and fifty—eighteen hundred and sixty—so she's due now!" said the Baronet with a smile.

"You're going to sleep, Agnes," said Rachel reproachfully.

"Torpid and drowsy," said Miss Marlyn shrugging with a smile and a little shudder. "I was falling into a trance, I think."

Sir Roke has talked enough now to shew that he was quite on his usual footing, he had nothing particular to say, nothing whatever to Miss Marlyn, no reserves or embarrassments, quite frank and chatty.

The baronet did not remain more than five minutes longer, and walked home to luncheon in decidedly better temper than he had set out.

## CHAPTER 27
### WHAT DOES SIR ROKE MEAN?

Mark Shadwell, like other solitary and discontented men, was given to building castles in the air. He had reared and tenanted many in his day; and once in occupation, he held to his tenancy, against all hints and even processes, with admirable tenacity, until the castle fell. He was not exacting in the matter of proof; very light material sufficed for their construction. Now, as we know, he had a theory in hand: like one of the old cage-work houses, it stood in outline first, and Mark found brick and mortar as often as Sir Roke Wycherly talked, to build in the interstices.

Mark liked making a cumulative case of this kind. As he and his guest stood on the hall-doorsteps today, for instance, admiring the long files of lofty timber that darkened the avenue, the baronet's talk went off on other matters, and at last he made quite a little homily upon the dissipations of the gay world and their effects on the habits, characters, and worth of young ladies; and then he harangued on the graces of simplicity in such terms as satisfied him that he could only be thinking of Rachel.

After dinner, over their glass of wine, again, Sir Roke made a picture of domestic, not rural life, which he contrasted in his own way with the sort of life he had hitherto led. Perhaps he really felt what he said, for of late his qualms and panics about his health had very much spoiled for him the flavour of his old life. It was merely like a spoken reverie, but was enough to contribute to the masonry of Mark's *château*.

"You must not grumble, Mark," said Sir Roke again, "if you knew but all, you are better than I, with broken health, and no pursuit, and no tie, and placed on a d—d regimen, and forbidden nearly every enjoyment on earth! How would you like that?"

Sir Roke was grumbling, in his way, now, and exaggerating, as grumblers will.

"My money never did anything for me, to speak of. I never sat for any place; politically, I'm no more than you. I *could*, of course, if I had liked it, but I never cared."

"You might have put me in for Dowcastle, instead of that

fellow Dingley. I might have done you some credit, and I would not have played you the trick *he* did, at all events," said Mark, in whose heart that wrong had long been festering.

"Now, that's very true, Mark, so I *might*; but you know you did not hint it till it was too late: however, that sort of thing can be made all straight by and by; our parliaments don't last forever."

Here was another sign of an auspicious change, for Mark knew very well how sharp and short had been Sir Roke's answer to the meditation he had employed in this matter of the borough of Dowcastle, and how he had pointedly said that "he wished Mark Shadwell were informed, once for all, that he did not think him in any respect suited to the House of Commons."

That evening as they stood near the fire in the drawing-room. Sir Roke sipping the chocolate which the accomplished Clewson prepared, for he was a little afraid of tea, and coffee was interdicted, said Mark, very low, on a sudden—he had been looking in a long reverie at Miss Agnes Marlyn, who was at the piano—

"She *is* beautiful!"

Mark's solitude had given him careless habits. As Sir Roke glanced at him with his shrewd, hard, mean eye, Shadwell would have given something to recall his words.

"Your daughter? Upon *that* question I shall certainly be found among the ayes."

"I think Miss Marlyn beautiful, at least very pretty, don't you?" said Mark drily, and trying to rally. He was aware that Sir Roke knew perfectly whom he meant, and it was less suspicious to be frank.

"Miss Marlyn?" repeated Sir Roke, "oh! I know; yes, very well, very pretty indeed, very, but her style is by no means so uncommon. My cousin Rachel's beauty is more exquisite and more heavenly, I maintain."

Sir Roke was a little near-sighted, and through his tiny Parisian glasses he covertly inspected the young lady at the piano for a moment, and then putting them down, he said to Mark:

"So you admire Miss Marlyn; and I'm not surprised, she *is* very pretty."

There was nothing in this speech at all remarkable, nor anything tangible in the manner of its utterance; but Mark was stung by it. He knew what was passing in Sir Roke's mind, and he fancied that he was aware of that fact and amused at it.

Mark Shadwell did not quite understand the pain he felt, nor even in what particular nerves it was seated. He had no more pretensions to morality than other men who had lived, like him, an early life of dissipation. It was not worth his while to wear a mask before Roke, who knew him as well as he knew Roke; but a sentiment was combined with his mere admiration of Miss Agnes Marlyn; she was growing dear to him. If he had looked this secret in the face, I do not say that he would have had nerve to act as he ought; but he must have seen incidents in the situation enough to appal him.

His pride was wounded on a sudden. He had unveiled to the lynx-eyed cynicism of Roke the secret which was almost a secret to his own soul. He was angry with him, angry also with himself—yes, very angry with himself—for was he not a philosopher? had he not long ago renounced the illusions of his youth? was he not a friar of the order of David Hume, as well as a theologian of the school of Voltaire?

Of the two men who stood side by side on the hearthrug, I am quite sure that Sir Roke was the worst. Both of the earth earthy, unennobled by the only influence that can improve our sorry moral plight—Mark's nature, with its great faults, perversities, and early stains, was yet the better.

He had never been the cruel epicurean that Roke was. Generous and even tender impulses had visited him sometimes, and occasionally disturbed his selfishness, and something of passion had mingled in his early profligacy. Even now he was living partly in a delusion, and he loved, in his sharp debates with the Reverend Stour Temple, to challenge that severe censor to pick a hole in his morality. He liked sarcastically to pit himself against the vicar's best parishioners. He would have liked to make Roke speak out what he knew was in his mind, for the sake of answering him according to his temper. But Roke would do no such thing. He would enjoy his suspicion discreetly with an insulting reserve.

Miss Marlyn was playing still. Sir Roke approached Rachel, who, I suppose, did not receive him encouragingly, for in a few minutes he glided to the piano, and stood by the side of the performer. He beat time with a little wave of his hand, and smiled and whispered something; a compliment on her music, Mark assumed.

What he really said was this: "So you've been doing me a. kind office, with your pretty companion? she won't speak to me—she won't *look* at me. What sort of person must she think me? You must allow me to view this in my own way, and to regard it as of the best imaginable augury. Pray remember how very soon I shall be ordering my wings and be off to town. Was I very ill-tempered, today? I hope not."

Here came a great roulade, and the bass grew very loud; so that he contented himself with smiling, and marking the time with a little oscillation of his hand.

Mark Shadwell, standing by the chimney-piece with his coffee-cup in his hand, looked at his invalid wife, to whose side by this time Sir Roke had transferred himself

"That sneering beast thinks every fellow like himself. I *never* lived a life like his. I despise a man who does."

His glance wandered to Miss Agnes Marlyn, and then dropped to the ground; he leaned on the mantelpiece, and his reverie was of the afternoon, some time ago, when in that irregular apartment, hall, vestibule, all in one, of the Star and Garter, in the quaint High Street of Raby, waiting to see old Brent about his cob, the 'bus from the distant railway station set down a passenger at the open door, who entered in her cloak.

He knew nothing of her—he had forgotten all about Miss Marlyn's intended arrival. He saw a plain dress, but a wonderfully beautiful girl; and he made way for her as for a princess. There is an impulse, not of admiration simply, but of *respect* in our first sight of a beautiful woman; because we intuitively reverence power of every kind, and beauty in a woman is power. The momentary scene was fixed in his mind for ever. In the shadow of that homely hall, so queerly misshapen, doors and galleries opening on it, the clumsy stairs mounting through an arch on one side, the bow-window of the bar projecting at the other, had appeared this young figure, and face, and all was glorified by her beauty.

"I have been like a *father* to her—a guardian—the shabby fellow!"

Mark Shadwell mentally presented himself with the most unexceptionable certificate; and with that in his pocket, glanced a contemptuous defiance at his kinsman, who smiled and chatted on, quite unconscious of the lightning that forked and flickered so near him.

## CHAPTER 28
### CARMEL SHERLOCK KNOCKS AT AMY'S DOOR

Mrs. Shadwell went early that evening to her dressing-room. Dolly Wyndle, their usual conference ended, had gone about her business. With solitude came dejection. The sick lady, supporting her head upon her thin hand, began to think of what would be when she was gone. "Agnes Marlyn will not desert my poor Rachel; wise above her years, and kind, I don't think Mark will disturb that. But then she is so young a creature; every way, difficulties. Perhaps Mark will go up to town and live there, as he always wished, leaving them here. He will marry very soon:" a pain thrilled her, though she smiled a forlorn little smile. "I wonder whether he will ever think of his poor little Amy! No one will ever love him so well again;" and her eyes filled slowly with tears.

Poor little wandering soul—troubled about many things! Then came the thought of death. Oh! was her failing health, or the coming of that ghastly change, a frightful dream? A horror of great darkness, and the fears of death had fallen upon her, and there came the shuddering and wailing of panic. To this, an awful calm succeeded, and she lifted up her clasped hands, and her eyes and her trembling heart to God in dumb supplication.

Many sensible people had long set down pretty little sick Mrs. Shadwell as a fool—yet she had accomplishments—could draw—was a musician—was, as the phrase is, "well-informed,"— could tell a good book from a dull one—and talked when her spirits served, pleasantly and intelligently about most things. But though not a mental, I am afraid she was a *moral* fool. She had not courage to fight any one—to wound any one—to suspect any one—to hold her own, in short, in this world of cunning and ferocity; and when she lay down at night, she was troubled to think that anyone, on earth, was "out with her," and busy with little plans for reconciliation.

And had she not given herself up to an idiotic idolatry of a husband who could no longer see any good in her priceless love, or, pleasantness in her un- conscious adulation. Eyes had he and saw not, ears and heard not, and yet her worship never flagged, and she sat by a dead love in that wildest and saddest insanity which will not believe in death, but watches, and hopes, and waits for its awaking .

After a while, in the silence that followed, came a sudden knock at her door.

"Who's there?" she asked, startled, for she heard no step approach the door.

"I, ma'am, I—Carmel Sherlock—shall I come in?"

"Come in."

And Carmel entered, looking very pale—looking, indeed, like a man, faint from pain.

"Thank you, ma'am, you're very good. I've something on my mind—something to say;" he closed the door, jealously looking at her all the while, with a troubled face, and his large eyes dilated with fear. "Don't be frightened, but I must go, ma'am; I must leave Raby. The place where I've been so happy—dreaming— *dreaming,*" he groaned.

"What is it? What do you mean, Mr. Sherlock?" asked she, surprised.

"I'm come to say, I must go, ma'am—I *must*," and he groaned again. "I must go, and I don't like to tell Mr. Shadwell—my benefactor—because it would cause a—a struggle; he would try to keep me; and if he were to succeed—oh! if!—I won't look at it; I must go *tonight*."

"Pray, Mr. Sherlock, be quite frank, and do let me know your reasons."

"Oh! ma'am—my dear, good lady, you mustn't ask—I can't. It isn't—it isn't to be told."

"But Mr. Shadwell will be so pained—you will be an irreparable loss. I really don't know what he's to do, if you leave him. Surely you'll consider him—I know you will."

"I will—I do—I always do—Oh! ma'am, I'm not ungrateful. I should have been cast away upon the wastes of life, but for him. I owe him all—my life—my life—but this would never do; it scares me; it won't be battled with or denied—just—just a whisper that has caught my ear."

"One word of all this I can't understand," said she; "I hardly think you intend I should."

"Better not," he said, and clasped his hands hard together. "So many years, and to *frighten* you at last! No, no! it could not be."

"If anything has happened to make you less happy than you were, I think you ought to tell me. It's very odd, and hardly kind to think of going away without assigning a reason; there's nothing that could possibly frighten me in any you are likely to give." She paused; but though she said this, she did feel nervous as well as curious; there was so much anguish in Carmel's dark stare.

"It *would* frighten you," he whispered; and looking round the cornice of the room, he laid his hand on his head, as if to control some pressure there. She remembered the sarcastic bulletins with which Mark Shadwell often favoured her, to the effect that Carmel was growing decidedly madder and madder every day.

"Now, I've made up my mind, Mr. Sherlock," said she, with something of her old spirit, and shocked to think of his leaving at such an hour; "you'll stay tonight, whatever the cause; you won't go—at my earnest request, and as a kindness to me-you'll remain!"

"She does not know," Carmel groaned, "she doesn't, what she's doing! Why will she ask it—*dis iratis*? Oh! madam, you mustn't—oh! spare me that one command!"

"I will ask you—I do—you must not go tonight—I *insist* upon it—don't think of it: in the morning you will see things differently. I entreat you to grant me this one kindness."

There was a pause of a few seconds.

"I *will*, madam," said he, shaking his head, nevertheless, as if he had said "no."

"The day after tomorrow—you must stay till then; there are many things, you know, to arrange—you mustn't go till then. Promise this—you *shall* promise—I know you will!"

And, with these words, poor Mrs. Shadwell, who in her energy had risen from her sofa, took his hand kindly, and repeated her entreaty.

"I will, madam, I obey you in this; I promise—take it—my hand—*cruentum!* There Good God, madam, my hand!" He withdrew it, and looked into her eyes with a very odd stare, and muttered: "Well were it for that man that he had never been born! My hand—it looks all wrong to me! I wish, ma'am, you had ordered me rather to get it smashed in a mill-crank!"

"Till the day after tomorrow, you have promised to remain," she said, passing by this odd parenthesis. "I am satisfied now, and thank you, Mr. Sherlock, thank you very much—and goodnight."

"Goodnight, ma'am. I am constrained—"He paused, with his hand on the door-handle, and looked at her as if on the point of speaking; after a few doubtful seconds, however, to her relief, he changed his mind, and, with a great sigh, he said merely "Goodnight, ma'am," and left the room, closing the door gently, leaving her a great deal more excited and agitated than she had fancied herself during the flighty interview he had just given her. Odd he always was; but now his language, like the incipient mutterings of actual insanity, was wild and ominous. She was grieved and shocked, and felt on the point of bursting into tears.

143

"Poor, kind, gentle Carmel!—what can it be?" she wondered, as she stood very pale, where he had left her.

Very glad she was to hear a step approaching. This time it was her husband who entered.

"Oh, Mark, I'm so glad you have come. Poor Carmel Sherlock has been here, and seemed so excited and strange."

"I told you. Amy, he's odd—you don't see so much of him as I do—a little bit mad; you would not believe me," and Mark laughed. But his merriment in her ear was not reassuring. It sounded like laughter heard in a dismal dream.

"Oh, Mark, dear, you could not laugh if you knew how very strange he looked, and ill. I'm so afraid there's something very seriously wrong."

"Now, come," said Mark, a little inconsistently, "you must not be absurd. You fancy Carmel's mad—he's no more mad than you or I. He has very odd ways, I grant, and theories—it's merely solitude and reading, and this vile wilderness; but with that dreamy way of his, he's as wide-awake and sharp as any lawyer in Westminster—you may take my word for it. I know him better than any man living—at accounts and business with him every day—as sound and clear a head as any in England—no more mad than the Lord Chancellor."

Mark was, in fact, arguing with himself, and blowing and brushing away the little suspicions that were, as his frightened wife spoke, gathering over his own mind.

"I promised to play a little piquet with Roke in his room tonight," he resumed; "he asked me. You remember what I said yesterday about him—you do, of course. Now, all I say is this—you'll leave it entirely to me; and, mind, there's to be none of that talking him over, you know, that women are so fond of; by Jove! I only wonder any girls ever married—they sit like a secret committee on every fellow that pays them the least attention, and pick him to pieces, and laugh at him, till I wonder how any of them can have the face to marry him, and I'm certain that's the sole reason why half the disappointments take place that do. Now, mind, you mustn't allow it, nor any tattle of old Wyndle's, and Miss Marlyn must not be laughing with her over Roke's wrinkles, and nonsense, if he has any. All I say is this—just leave the matter in my hands. Ill speak to Rachel myself, if she's disposed to be foolish—she sha'n't be allowed to sacrifice herself. There aren't six girls coming out in London, next season, who'd refuse Roke Wycherly. Pretty stuff! Of course she's to be quite free—but—that's all."

Mark was talking more this night to Mrs. Shadwell than he had done for five weeks before. His head was full of this grand scheme, and it must be admitted, not without some colour of evidence.

"I'm glad you think, Mark, dear, that our darling Rachel should be left to herself if it should."

"Of course, that's precisely what I say—leave her to her own decision. I'm certain, if Roke isn't pulled to pieces and talked over, as I've said, she'll decide like a girl of sense. She's not an idiot, I suppose."

And so on and on Mark talked, every now and then, by way of parenthesis, admitting that he spoke on hypothesis. At last there came a pause, during which the thoughts of both, by one of those odd coincidences that we sometimes recognise, returned silently and suddenly again to Carmel Sherlock. The lady was first to speak.

"Carmel Sherlock seems to have made up his mind to go."

"To leave us, do you mean?" asked Mark, looking up sharply. He could not spare Carmel.

"He wanted to go tonight, but promised to remain till the day after tomorrow. He would not tell me his reason. Don't you think, Mark, you should see him tonight?"

Now Mark had already made up his mind to do so. He said, therefore: "I don't see much good in it; but if you wish it, I will. We've had a long talk. Amy," he added, with the air of a man who had done a gracious thing, and knows it.

"Oh, Mark, darling! it's very happy—it's like old times;" and as she spoke and smiled, her large eyes filled with tears.

He patted her cheek, and kissed her, not ardently, but kindly, and smiled on her encouragingly, and, said he: "You often mistake me, Amy. You think me cold and ungracious, when, Heaven knows, I'm only plagued to death with my worries and disappointments."

"It's kind of you, *darling*, to say so. I knew it—I was sure of it," she said, putting her pretty hands on his shoulders, and looking up in his face, and smiling and crying at the same time; and, smoothing her hair with a caress, he looked down in return with a relenting commiseration that was strange to him. "I don't know why I'm crying. I'm such a fool; I'm so happy, Mark. Don't mind my crying—I can't help it. I never was so happy, I think."

Few acts, as we know, are done on a single motive, and the origin even of our emotions is not always absolutely explicable to ourselves. Something of compunction, a sudden recoil to self-upbraiding tonight in the drawing-room, as I mentioned, prompted a recognition like this; but I do not know that the impulse would have had strength at this hour to bring him to her room, had it not been for the necessity he was under of finding someone to listen to his confidences and speculations respecting the intentions of his kinsman.

He went away, pleased with his own great attributes and with that instinct of self-approbation which stood him instead of a conscience, altogether gratified and glowing.

## Chapter 29
### A Hand on Roke Wycherly's Door

Mark, candle in hand, walked down the sombre passage charmed with himself. He thought it a pity that the Reverend Stour Temple, that well' meaning, bigoted vicar, could not witness his triumph of philosophy. He had made a condescension to that poor wife who, with all her infirmities, was so infinitely his superior. He had patted her cheek, smoothed her hair, kissed her, and was in a manner reconciled. Yes, reconciled; for was she not always and unaccountably, as it were, in disgrace?

Gross are we, and measure our virtues and our gratitude, not by the motive of the service, but by its magnitude. Always reversing where it suits us the moral of the widow's mite—not even by the magnitude of the service, where that will not do, but by the wild gratitude of despair.

Our theatric virtues strut their hour, and the applause of the gallery roars above them. But God sees with an awful eye, and it is the whisper of self-suspicion that reverberates before His throne in thunder. He knows the dynamics of all morals, and measures the momentum of good-will, not by visible results, but by the unseen obstructions it has overcome.

Mark Shadwell had observed a shyness in Rachel's manner towards the baronet which led him to think that Sir Roke must have talked in a strain of gallantry. All the better—proof upon proof. He was also in high good humour with himself, and confident in his philosophic self-control. Prospects were brightening. His debts could not plague him as they had done any longer; and was not the House of Commons opening to receive the coming man?

All a-glow with this moral tipsiness, who should he encounter at the turn of the gallery but his daughter and Miss Agnes Marlyn?

He paused for a moment, said a few words, and bid them goodnight. How was it that this Agnes grew more and more beautiful every day? The girl is gentler, shyer, different somehow. He had seen her eyes follow him in the drawing room when, at least, he *thought* she fancied he did not observe her. He had seen her blush, he could almost swear, twice on meeting him unexpectedly. There was something submissive, sad, strange in her manner of late. How she liked working for him, and tried to please him! and how beautifully gratified she looked when he thanked and praised her! Poor little thing! Just a fancy. Well for himself—for *all*—he was so coolheaded a fellow! Well that he had burned his fingers, and seared them so early that he could afford to play with fire!

"My secretary certainly is beautiful! How interesting—how sad! Who could withhold his compassion?"

And he sighed. Who sighed? A benevolent philosopher simply; in that sigh, exhaled only ardent pity. He walked on with the image of that beautiful secretary before him. He knocked at Carmel Sherlock's door, and opened it. That eccentric gentleman rose suddenly to his feet as he did so. He spoke not—only gazed with a pale frown across the table, as if on the entrance of a thief in the night. A book was open before him. Oddly enough, it was the Bible.

"Didn't expect me, Sherlock? Passing this way, so I just looked in."

"Thankful, sir, always when you do."

"Reading?"

"Yes, sir, reading—the Bible, sir."

"Hey? that's something new, isn't it?

"Oh dear me! No, sir. As good philosophy as you'll find anywhere, and more ancient. I like it. I always look into it. Why should the Bible be the only book we can take nothing out of? There is something in every book—every ancient book—written when it was troublesome to write, and no one read but the critical."

In the midst of his scepticism, Mark Shadell had a lurking awe of this mysterious book. In the tremendous perspective which it opens, there was no pleasant place for him, and he shut it down with something between a curse and a scoff.

"Ho! That will be very agreeable news to the vicar," said Mark sarcastically.

"There's the Christian trinity, you know, and the Platonic, There's a fundamental triplet somewhere, sir, or the triplet would not rule as it does. If there is a noon, you see, there must be a forenoon and an afternoon. In limited life, which is the first progress, the acme will have its antecedent and its consequent. The order is, desire, fruition, satiety, or, in other words, incipiency, power, decay—that is, you know, childhood, manhood, age. I see, sir, you are listening."

"Yes, certainly," said Mark, who had been thinking of something else.

"And you follow me—quite?"

148

"The devil I do!"

"Don't you, sir?"

"Pray lead on, my good fellow. I'm stuck in the mud; but never mind, I'm doing my best."

"But the *un*limited life triplicates also," said Carmel, unconscious of Mark's banter. "Self-evolution is exhausted in three. There is no mutation after the worm, the grub, and the fly. The act of death, you know, is the labour of the man in the flesh, and the bringing forth of the intermediate man, who in turn evolves the man immutable. It is the law of fermentation—saccharine, vinous, acetous. Two processes of life, leading up to finality. This present state in the flesh is the first subterranean germination of life, compared with the next, feeble, inapprehensive, and ugly."

"And yet I've seen some rather pretty specimens," said Mark. He was speaking in the glow of that beautiful phantom of Agnes Marlyn, which still stood before him, though laughing at Carmel.

"This self-evolution, in triplet, is a moral law, desert, judgment, execution; the moral life is self-evolving. It projects a second state from its first, and a third, which is final, from the second," said Carmel Sherlock, looking vaguely downward, and tracing slow lines with his finger-tip along his pallid forehead.

"People grow from indifference to like one another; eh? and so on?" said Mark—he was thinking of Agnes Marlyn still—"and fall sometimes into indifference again. That's a great discovery—is it in the Bible?" Mark was quizzing him gravely.

"Just this now," continued Sherlock, lifting his tattered Bible and reading—"*When lust hath conceived, it bringeth forth sin; and sin, when it is finished, bringeth forth Death.*"

"In the Bible that, is it?" asked Mark, smiling.

"Yes, sir, here, in the Epistle of James. The Triplicate self evolution, lust—sin—death!" answered Carmel; and read the awful passage again, aloud. "I'll show you how that must be—"

"Well, I believe we'll not mind tonight. I told you before, my creed is dust to dust," said Mark.

"Don't you believe in a resurrection?" asked Carmel.

"Of the body?" inquired Mark, preparing to go.

"Yes—I do—of the body," said Carmel.

"*Nous verrons*," said Mark; "and for the present, I must remain in darkness; I mean, I can hear no more tonight."

It was clear that Carmel did not mean to open his plan of going away, and Mark was now satisfied that Sherlock's idea of leaving him was one of the many vapours that rose in his solitude, and, crossing his mind, dissolved and came no more.

"What a fellow that is!" he thought, sneeringly, as he retraced the gallery alone. Mark was not quite in the contemptuous mood he fancied. That text had an odd mystic sound in it that was uncomfortable. There had risen something dark, now, a little in the way of that glowing phantom of Agnes Marlyn. In the midst of Carmel's babble, a pale, pure face had looked in at the door and startled him. In the midst of his gentle maunderings, a stern diapason had broken in, and rang still in his ears.

So Mark shook his ears, and hummed a tune lightly, and went and paid his visit to Roke Wycherly in his dressing-room; they chatted pleasantly, and then they played piquet.

Mark won—what some people would think a considerable sum—it was only some twenty pounds. It was nothing in the scale of old exploits. But guineas were welcome as drops of water in the desert to needy Mark, and is it not always pleasant to win?

"You'll come tomorrow night again, won't you?" said Sir Roke as he smiled feebly in Mark's face from his easy chair.

It is not always the loss, but the mortification of defeat that tries temper. Roke did not care for this game, nor for any other, for its own sake. He rather wished that Mark should be pleased with his visit, and was glad that he had won. And Mark's feelings towards him got into a state of equilibrium. He fancied as he left him that he could even come almost to like Roke. On such small things do likings and antipathies depend; and is not this just considering how seldom the great things turn up, if ever, and how minute are the bits which make up the mosaic of a whole life?

Very late that night, Sir Roke, whose sleep was light, awoke. He fancied he heard a step on the gallery floor. He listened, with an ugly frown, on his pillow. And then— he could not be quite sure—he heard a hand laid softly on the panel of his door, and brushed gently along it. Sir Roke lifted his head. The hand seized the door-handle and began to turn it gently.

"Who the devil's there?" cried Sir Roke on his elbow, and stretching his lean neck over the side of the bed.

There was no answer. He thought he heard breathing. He was sure he heard a soft retreating step. He was one of those persons who can't endure any trifling with the sanctity of sleep; it made him furious. Spluttering some ejaculations which I don't repeat, he had already got the bell-rope in his fingers, to ring up Clewson and take his revenge upon that harmless slumberer, when, on a sudden, his mood quite changed, the bell-rope dropped back upon the wall.

"By Jove, it's possible— quite—what a fool!" And he jumped out of bed in his long nightshirt and silk nightcap—a figure something like that of the Knight of La Mancha, when he fought his nocturnal combat with the cats, if you can imagine that Christian gentleman with a very wicked smirk on—and wrapping his silk dressing-gown about him, and forgetting night air and all else, he opened his door softly, still smirking in the dark, and looking and whispering up and down the gallery, "I'm here, does anyone want me?" and so at last to bed again, rather cold and cross.

## Chapter 30
### Mr. Clewson Confers With Carmel Sherlock.

Mr. Clewson had formed a slight acquaintance, in the housekeeper's room, with our friend Carmel Sherlock, and had often, to Mrs. Dolly Wyndle, expressed his high estimation of Mr. Sherlock's erudition and wisdom, for he had quoted languages which that gentleman had never heard before, and ventilated theories, the futile endeavour to comprehend which had a rather fatuising effect upon his practical intellect.

He met Sherlock next morning on the back stair, by the great window on the landing-place, and respectfully wished him good-morning.

"Ho! sir, I hope you slept well," said Carmel, looking woefully in his face. "For my part, sir, I've had a bad night—no sleep—only a *thought*—the same—*one* thought—a load, as you lie, always increasing, like the *peine fort et dur,* till it breaks your heart. Sir, it's like the drop of water—tick, tick, tick —on your brain—that the Inquisition invented; and you must go mad or submit, sir, eh?"

"Quite so, sir," assented Mr. Clewson, who apprehended but vaguely. "My gentleman, he always takes hopium, in little lozenges like; I can give you two or three—or try counting up a thousand or so."

"I don't want sleep, sir. It's only that, don't you see, if the idea would change; but all one thought, never pausing, like one fiddle-string in your brain, and a bow as long as forever, drawn on, and on, and on—it's too much—you're sure to submit; it has you at last."

"Just so, sir, a want of variety; every one tires of sameness like. I do uncommon," said Mr. Clewson.

"When does he go?" said Carmel.

"Sir Roke?"

"Ay, yes—Sir Roke—he should go today," said Carmel.

"I don't think Sir Roke has no notion of going so soon," answered Mr. Clewson.

"He's here for no good, sir," said Sherlock.

"You really *think?*"—inquired Mr. Clewson, and with a shrewd look, and something like the dawn of a smile.

"Can't you get him away? In God's name get him away!" urged Carmel, laying his hand upon his arm, and grasping it with a little shake.

Mr. Clewson smiled a little, and said he:

"It's not me takes him, but rayther him that takes me, sir."

Carmel sighed, and said:

"Look, sir; every man has a side to the light, and a side to the dark; his shadow goes with him. I wish he had stayed away. Can't you do *anything?*" said Carmel in great trouble, as it seemed.

Mr. Clewson shook his head, amused at the idea.

"My sleep, sir, while I had it, was all like a church window, with dreams glowing all over with allegories. I told my beloved master something of it; but I'm worn out, sir, I'm tired."

"And what may be running in your mind,, sir?" inquired Mr. Clewson, being curious.

Carmel looked at him suddenly, with a contracted and suspicious gaze, and dropped his eyes.

"About what?" said Carmel, drily, looking up again.

"I mean about Sir Roke, sir," said Clewson.

"I know nothing about Sir Roke Wycherly; and so you're going to stay? Well, you know, you ought to go and see something of the scenery—Wynderfel and Hazelden—and other places worth seeing. Will he go away tomorrow?"

"Sir Roke?"

Carmel nodded.

"Well, I know no more than you, Mr. Sherlock; I never know, sir, except a haccident, where or when we're agoing, until he gives me the order to get things ready and pack up."

"Something came into the house with him."

"You *may* say that, Mr. Sherlock; all them portmanteaus and boxes—awful particlar—no one living, sir, has a hidea what it is, I tell you."

"Troublesome, sir," acquiesced Sherlock.

"Rayther, I should say, a few," answered Mr. Clewson, shaking his head with a pathetic comicality.

"And don't you know what he came here for, Mr. Clewson?" asked Carmel, with a bitter smile.

"No, I don't, sir," answered Mr. Clewson.

Carmel looked at him.

"*No*, really, sir. It may be many things. I don't know. I give you my honour," he averred, and shook his head.

"Well, *I* know," said Carmel, smiling darkly out of the window. "He's come here for a wife."

"Oh, oh! I see. I'm not a bit surprised. I *thought* so," answered Clewson, who *was* very much surprised, and uneasy too; for he could not say how such an event as marriage might shake him in his place, and his place suited him; and, in fact, was on the whole a good deal better than any he was likely to get again. Therefore he was shocked, though he did not believe it.

"And who—who may he be a-looking after?" inquired Mr. Clewson.

"Miss Rachel Shadwell," answered Carmel, hastily, as if he were mentioning a dead friend, and still looking straight out of the window.

"I partly guessed it; there's several things has led me to that opinion. Is she likely to turn out a hinterfering person, do you think?"

"Miss Rachel is perfection," said Carmel.

"I didn't mean nothing contrary," said Clewson.

"Think of such a man as that coming to marry her!" said Sherlock.

"Well, it *is* a lift for her," observed Mr. Clewson. "A very desirable halliance. He's took a vilent fancy, I dessay; he's that sort."

Carmel repeated, rather to himself than to his companion:

*L'amour arrive en chantant,*
*Et s'en retourne en pleurant.*

"You may have read that—why not? French. Yes, he knows French; it's in the *Morte d'Arthur*, and it's very true." And so Mr. Clewson went up and Mr. Sherlock down, and the little conference at the large window on the lobby came to an end.

The Reverend Stour Temple paid a visit early next day at Raby. The two young ladies, Sir Roke, and Mark Shadwell, were at luncheon very sociably; and at this irregular meal, the vicar joined them in the dining-room.

Mark did not like the vicar, but he welcomed him courteously.

"You remember Roke Wycherly? Roke, *you* recollect Temple, at Oxford?"

Sir Roke gave him two fingers, and one of his bleak smiles, as he looked up at him from his chair.

"Charmed to see you. Temple; it's so many years. Pray don't count them. And you're at Ridleston, here, Mark tells me. You were good at most things; you pulled a very good oar, and I remember you were a capital wicket-keeper. No cricket now-a-days, I dare say?"

Stour Temple smiled with a sad and supercilious complacency over these recollections of his prowess.

"Never played since I took orders. I suppose I could not stop a ball now. I've an objection to clergymen playing."

"I don't see why they shouldn't," said Sir Roke; "they want exercise as much as laymen, I fancy, and it would prevent their growing so fat as some of them do."

"My duties afford me exercise enough," he replied, with a smile; "by the time I get home, I shall have walked fourteen or fifteen miles."

"I wish they were all as active as you. Temple, I've a fellow down at Scarbrook; he rides at a walk on a horrid cob, and he's as fat as I don't know what; never visits his people, nor doe s a bit of good, from one year's end to another. I wish the brute would get his apoplexy, and make a vacancy for a useful man like you."

The Reverend Stour Temple looked not flattered, but very grave, and even stern, and Mark thought, with some pleasure, that he was on the point of rebuking the baronet, whose temper might have exploded under that liberty. But it did not come, *then*, at least.

The Reverend Stour Temple had not been five minutes in the room, indeed, when Mark perceived that there was something upon his mind. He was silent and thoughtful, and being an abstemious man, luncheon was to him a ceremony quickly over.

"How pretty the old Tower of Raby and the village look from the summit of the wood!" said the vicar, awaking from a reverie, and speaking apropos of nothing. "There's a market there today. I crossed the uplands, and you can't think how pretty it looks, lying among the trees and enclosures beneath you. It would almost repay the walk, if you would venture so long a ramble," he smiled, as he spoke to Rachel. "There are very fine clouds, too, today, for a background; such towering piles of vapour! I should have suspected thunder, but that it would be too soon. It's hardly ten days since we had that thunderstorm."

"More than a fortnight," said Mark Shadwell.

"Ha?" said the vicar. "Time cheats us, Sir Roke, in the country."

"Suppose we make that our walk?" said Rachel, addressing Miss Marlyn.

"Mr. Temple says it looks so well. I should like very much," she said, with a timid glance towards the clergyman.

He made, however, no sort of answer to this little overture, and said to Mark:

"I crossed from Pennelston; that poor man I spoke to you about died this morning."

"Oh, did he?—poor fellow!" said Mark, with a slight flush, and looking at the landscape through the window. He thought Stour Temple's cold eyes were upon him, and I rather think he had forgotten all about the farmer of Pennelstone and his wants. "Very sorry, poor fellow! You mustn't go, Temple, I'll be back in a moment, only to write a note in the study."

This Mark Shadwell said with the intention of seeing the vicar no more that day; for he was always uncomfortable in his presence, and so had made a step or two towards the door, when the vicar said:

"Will you excuse my asking just two or three minutes with you, in the study? only a word or two."

"Certainly," said Shadwell, as cheerfully as he could, "whenever you please."

He crossed the hall, vexed and in a petty suspense that irritated him, shut his study door rather sharply behind him, walked across it, pulled out an old quarto, and read with a sour countenance, on its back, the harmless inscription, "*Histoire des Voyages, tom. 8.*," and having read this inscription several times over, he threw it on the table a little roughly. "That fellow's a sort of irritant," he said. "I never met him yet that he hadn't something to pester about. I wonder what it is *now?*"

Intuitively Mark Shadwell felt that it was something more than usually annoying.

## CHAPTER 31
### A WARNING WORD

The vicar, meanwhile, loitered away a few minutes beside Sir Roke in the dining-room window, to allow Shadwell time to write his imaginary note.

"I had heard. Sir Roke, that you were here."

"Oh!" said Sir Roke, with one of his smiles and faint bows.

And I should have been over here to pay my respects before now, had my time been my own."

Sir Roke smiled and bowed a little, and laid his hand upon the vicar's arm:

"My dear Temple, I should not have stood on ceremony with you," said he. "I meant to run over to the Vicarage—which, I am told, is quite a little Paradise—and see you before I left the country,"

"Very good of you," answered the vicar. "I've been anxious to see you from the moment I heard you were here. I've been wishing very much to speak to you." He looked on Sir Roke for a moment as if he were on the point of opening his case, whatever it might be; but the young ladies were chatting in the room, and, after a moment's reflection, he continued: "I came today hardly hoping for an opportunity, and I thought it, on the whole, a better plan to write what was in my mind, and—I've put it in this letter."

Sir Roke nodded affably as he took it.

"And, I'm afraid, it's tedious; but will you kindly read it through?" said the vicar.

"Certainly—rely upon me—every syllable—and give it my

best attention too," answered Sir Roke, graciously.

"That's all I ask, Sir Roke," replied Stour Temple.

"How grand that fellow looks! That letter's to ask me for the presentation to Scarbrook; and you'd fancy he was going to ask my leave to build a church or an hospital. Sanctimonious rogues!" So thought Sir Roke, and said aloud, "I'll not open it *now*, dear Temple; I'll wait for a quiet opportunity; isn't it better?"

"Certainly!" acquiesced he; "and it's time I were going."

So the Reverend Stour Temple took his leave, and went direct to the well-known door of Shadwell's study, and found that gentleman awaiting him impatiently.

"Well, Temple, what is it? I've been playing the devil somewhere, or you wouldn't have something particular to tell me. Pray go on; I'm prepared for something uncomfortable," and he laughed a little viciously.

"Sorry my mission is not generally pleasanter," said the vicar; "but you mistake me now. I'm not going to blame anyone. I've sought this opportunity only to say a word of warning."

"Well, thank you—I'm all ear," he replied, as gaily as he could.

"I have had a letter from a friend—a resident at Darmonville—and I think I'm bound to tell you that it concerns Miss Agnes Marlyn , now domesticated in your family, and that it conveys a rather—in my mind—a *very* unfavourable impression of that young lady."

"That's very odd!" said Mark, sharply, and looking rather aghast.

"Not so odd in a *French* boarding-school as it might in an English one," said the Reverend Stour Temple. "Recollect, I say only unfavourable. What I have to report does not amount to criminality. God forbid I should seem to intend more than I have warrant for; but her conduct there was characterised by great deceit and unpardonable indiscretion."

Mark Shadwell looked full in the vicar's eyes, rather pale, and he seemed altogether more shocked than a man of the world might have been expected to be, on learning that a young governess had been, in matters of mere decorum, a degree less discreet than seemed fit to the Reverend Stour Temple.

"It seems odd we should hear it in this roundabout way; and it strikes me as a little too vague and intangible to consist quite with the laws of fair-play—to say nothing of charity," said he, with a rather dubious sneer, after a little pause.

"It reaches you in a circuitous way, because Miss Marlyn was recommended in the absence of the principal of the school, Madame de la Perriere, who, rightly or wrongly, was afterwards reluctant to disturb Miss Marlyn's position here, hoping that she would conduct herself with more discretion in your house."

"And nothing could be more unexceptionable," interposed Mark Shadwell.

"And so far from being vague, the statement is very precise indeed. The young lady is ascertained to have let herself out of the school at night, on no less than five several occasions, by means of a key improperly obtained. On three of these occasions she met the friend or agent of a gentleman, whom Madame de la Perriere says she believes, or hopes, to have been seeking her privately in marriage; and on the two last occasions she met the gentleman himself, in the house, however, of Madame Du Bois, a shoemaker. This woman used to meet her at the wicket of the school-garden, conduct her to and from her house—so they say—and remain in the room during the entire interview; and, with the exception of this piece of—what shall I term it?—this Madame Du Bois was always accounted a person of unexceptionable good conduct.

"These are the facts, so far as they are known; and, to that extent, they seem to me positively reprehensible as well as *suspicious*; and it seemed to me right that you should be made aware of the particulars of the impropriety of which the young person now placed in an intimacy with Miss Shadwell is capable."

"Well—ha!—yes—I still can hardly believe it. If Miss Marlyn is not a fit person to be here, what business had those people sending her? Of course, if we begin angling for stories and gossip, we'll get enough of them. I think I did all that was right when I applied to the head of the school; and there has been a very good account of her, and she has been everything we could wish since she's been here; and I do wish people would not wait until all the expense has been gone to of bringing her over to this delicious place, and then begin collecting—I mean sending over—the tattle of an idle French town, and expect me—who haven't a guinea, by Jove!—to throw away money by handfuls, for no better reason."

"The occurrences I have mentioned are perfectly ascertained," said the vicar, whose cold self-possession was never ruffled by Mark Shadwell's hard words. "If the statement consisted of mere gossip, as you suppose, I should not have troubled you with it—I should not have repeated it anywhere, and I should not have given it a moment's consideration myself; but all I have related is *true*; and were I the head of a household in which Miss Marlyn filled the delicate and important place which she occupies here, I should at once withdraw my confidence, and no consideration would induce me to retain her services."

"Yes, that's all very fine!" said Mark Shadwell; "nothing easier than managing imaginary families, and lecturing other people on their duties, and practising all the virtues of the Decalogue by proxy."

Mark Shadwell was always irritated by the officious morality of the vicar, and by his unaffected serenity under his attacks. It was an assumption of superiority, and galled his pride.

"Of course, I'm a mere child," he went on, "I know, and quite below the serious notice of a divine of the Church of England; but I may be supposed to know something about my own affairs. Miss Marlyn is, so far as I can see, quite a lady. We have found her perfectly satisfactory, and she has been a companion to my poor wife in her solitude, and very kind, and I really don't know how *she* could get on without her."

The Reverend Stour Temple remained provokingly silent and attentive, and, as usual, Mark's choler rose.

"And I don't see, with you, that, making common allowance

for exaggeration, there's any case for turning this young lady adrift on the world; I think, on the contrary, it would be monstrous. Of course, I'll consider it; I'll talk it over with my wife. You have not spoken to her, have you?" he asked, sharply.

"Certainly not," answered the vicar.

"No—*I'm* the proper person to do that, I fancy."

"Of course," said the clergyman.

"And, in fact, I shall leave the whole thing very much in her hands."

"I've done now, I hope, at least, my duty; and, I may add, a very painful one. I did not seek the information I have communicated; but, having received it, I could not in conscience reserve it from you."

"No—well, it's off your mind now, and *we* can best advise about it, don't you think—my wife and I?"

The vicar answered nothing, he only bowed; and said he:

"I sha'n't interrupt you further, I must go; how long, by-the-bye, does Sir Roke remain here?"

"Two or three days."

"Farewell."

Mark Shadwell walked with him to the steps, and standing above his *demi-griffins,* nodded and waved his hand, with a very sombre smile, to the retreating vicar.

Mark was indeed very much disturbed. Ha had not the slightest notion of telling this story, elaborately, to his wife. "Women do run away with things so." Neither had he a thought of dismissing Miss Marlyn. But a responsibility was cast upon him which he hated; also a doubt troubled him to a degree which he could not have anticipated. How had the vicar learned this? He might know a great deal more; that is, detail—particulars, which, although they did not affect the moral of the story, yet interested him intensely.

"I say, Temple," he called after the vicar, following him; "one word."

The clergyman turned about and paused.

"I forgot, you'll be returning this way, sha'n't you?—just

about our dinner-hour—you must come and dine with us—you really *must*."

"You're very good, but I fear—"

"Pray do—it will be really a kindness. I make it a point; you *won't* refuse."

"You are very kind," repeated Stour Temple, looking down for a moment on the grass by his feet, and thinking.

"Yes, you *will* come?"

"Very well—*yes*—many thanks," said the vicar; and with a second farewell he took his departure, and Mark Shadwell stood for a while looking after his receding figure, not knowing, quite distinctly, why it was that so trifling a story had so utterly confounded him.

## CHAPTER 32
### THE VICAR TAKES HIS HAT

Sir Roke Wycherly took a little desultory walk with the young ladies, and was very chatty and agreeable; directing, however, his conversation principally, as perhaps was natural, to Rachel, who was beginning to get over the little shock of her companion's absurd conversation of yesterday.

It was not until Sir Roke had ended, for that bout, his compliments and gaieties, and put off his smiles and his walking coat, in his dressing-room, and collapsed on a sudden into that bitter, peevish, and formidable man of snarls, scowls, and wrinkles, with whom Mr. Clewson had to do, that he saw and remembered the letter which the Reverend Stour Temple had placed in his hand. He enjoyed a certain sort of psychology, and broke the seal with an anticipation of amusement.

Nothing akin to amusement awaited him, however. The supercilious radiance with which he had opened it vanished before he had read half-a-dozen lines, and gradually his face darkened and corrugated like that of an angry monkey.

Mr. Clewson, making arrangements at the dressing-table, heard distinctly the hissings and splutterings of the high pressure.

Sir Roke folded the letter but half read, and with a hand that trembled with anger, thrust it into his dressing-gown pocket.

The fact is, there was a shadow of disappointment, if not of dismay, in the rage that agitated Sir Roke's countenance.

"Upon my soul, Mr. Stour Temple, you've got on a bit since I had last the pleasure of meeting you! You are one of those saints whose religion is made up of fire and brimstone, and impertinence—you think you may insult any one in any way that pleases your vulgar arrogance, provided you do it in the name of the thirty-nine articles."

If at this moment Sir Roke had encountered the vicar, he would have given him a piece of his mind, together with some expletives better omitted. But the baronet, except when his virulent temper overcame him, was a particularly cool man: without natural affection, without impracticable resentments, with all his malignities under the supreme guidance and control of convenience.

By dinnertime he had cooled down perfectly. Disliking the vicar intensely, he was not in the slightest danger of meeting him with any evidences of irritation.

The Reverend Stour Temple was there, and sat beside Amy Shadwell, with whom he talked, and very little with the other guests: unusually grave, and, at times, abstracted; and was not Mark Shadwell more silent, too, than usual? Had it not been for Sir Roke, indeed, the tide of conversation would have ebbed utterly, and all lain flat, black, and dismal.

"I think you walk too much. Are not you overdoing it a little. Temple?" said his host, observing his look of fatigue. "Take some sherry—that light wine is nothing when one's tired."

"Thanks," said he, "I *am* a little knocked up. Two years since I shouldn't have found that walk too much; I'm afraid I must acknowledge the band of Time, and shorten my walks."

"Charming walks—a temptation always to do too much. But the air here is quite an elixir; *I* feel it so," said Sir Roke, who ignored decay, and abhorred mortality, and was always disposed to be testy when those ideas were pressed into prominence.

"That death is a stranger here," said the vicar, "and the Bible so far justified, is I think in nothing more clear than in the difficulty we experience in presenting the event,, as a fact, to our understandings; the great truth is written in awful characters in every churchyard; proclaimed in every hour's retrospect by the broken and disappearing ranks of early friends; printed day by day, among all the vulgarities of life in every newspaper; every black-craped hat or bonnet we see is a signal that the dread event has happened recently and near us; all nature speaks by signs and allegories, and all our social relations, with a tremendous distinctness, of *death*; and yet how hard it is, for five consecutive minutes, to accept it as a certain incident of our position! so that we have reason to thank God for those other intimations of its approach, which are furnished in the evidences of decaying vigour and subsiding life."

"Isn't it—surrounded as we are with blessings—an odd subject to select for thankfulness?" said Sir Roke, with a little shrug and a bitter smirk. "For my part, I thank Heaven for quite other things."

"For other things, and for that, also, since die we must; well that we should have every help to keep it in mind, for judgement follows death, and here sit we three; and very trite it is, but true, that this time twelve months one of us may lie in the grave!"

As I have said. Sir Roke hated death worse, I am afraid, than worse things, and he thought the vicar detestably ill-bred in pressing the topic as he did. The baronet, therefore, could brook this no longer, and he took up his parable, and said:

"Quite on the cards, though *I'm* a great deal better than I was this time last year; and growing better, too, every week, thank God. I'm sorry *you* can't give so good an account of yourself. But whatever happens we must bear it, you know, and there's no good, that I can see, in plaguing one another about possible occurrences, which are certainly not meant to turn us from the business, and blessings, and—and duties of life, till they do come. Life's our business, and *meant* to be our business, here, in my opinion. It's no news, you'll pardon me for saying so, to tell us we're to *die*. Death's no *discovery*: I'm to die, and *you're* to die. *You're* to die as well as Mark there. I hope you think about it, if it does you good. Your death's your own affair, whenever it comes, and mine's mine; and I don't want to plague you and Mark about it, and I *won't*." And Sir Roke took the claret, filled his glass, and looked across the table a little defiantly at the vicar, who sat under fire like a veteran.

"When I want medical advice, I send for a doctor," said Sir Roke, softening a little, and descending, as he did so, to a hackneyed parallel—"and when I want religion I'll send for a clergyman, and for none would I more readily than for *you*. But I think for myself, you understand, upon these subjects. The genius of our Church is liberty, you know; that's my view."

Thus Sir Roke wrested the conversation forcibly into another channel. Mark dropped in, and the vicar dropped out, and so for a while rather uncomfortably and with a sort of effort, of which they all soon tired, the discourse dragged on over their wine. Each had matters connected with the other to think over, and the conversation was often on the verge of subsiding into silence.

As Sir Roke and the vicar walked into the drawing-room side by side, the baronet said in a low and friendly tone:

"I read your note, my dear Temple, and you must pardon me for saying, I've seldom been so much puzzled, and so much amused; you've fallen into a most diverting mistake. I could not think, at first, what you meant; somebody has been mystifying you."

The vicar looked in his face with a very grave surprise, but made no answer, only bowed.

"I'll take an opportunity tomorrow; I'll go over to see you, and I'll make it as clear to you as daylight; there never *was*, you could not have *conceived*, anything more preposterous. I wished to say so much now; I don't choose my friends to think worse of me than I deserve—even for an hour."

Sir Roke laid his hand in a friendly way on the arm of the

vicar, who, however, looked down still without returning his friendly glance, and with the expression of a man who is distressed, and wishes an irksome subject at rest.

"You won't say you believe me, but I know you do, and I'll make you confess it tomorrow, when I see you. In the meantime, although, upon my honour, you have been quite in the clouds upon this subject, I assure you, I respect and I like you, Temple, for having written as you did—I do indeed."

The Reverend Stour Temple bowed very gravely again. Sir Roke might as well have spared his flatteries. There was no response.

## CHAPTER 33
### A KNOCK AT SIR ROKE'S DOOR.

Mark Shadwell talked a good deal with the vicar in the drawing-room. The ladies made music and sang at the piano. Sir Roke was smiling and agreeable, and flitted from Rachel to her mamma, and from her mamma to Rachel again. Mark Shadwell shaking himself now and then free of his perplexities, almost wondered why he was so disturbed, wondered with a feeling at once of ridicule and fear, half hated himself as he looked at Agnes Marlyn, who acquiesced with a cold unconscious pride in the neglect to which she seemed abandoned that night, half hated her, yet in his compassion, he was tempted to go over and tell her how sweet her music was, and rescue her from the prolonged insult of that neglect, but somehow his heart failed him. Mrs. Shadwell on a sudden perceived it, praised her music; and asked her the usual questions about it and its composer, and so forth; and shortly after, Miss Marlyn, with a few whispered words to Mrs. Shadwell, and a smile, glided from the room, happily unconscious, it seemed, of having been overlooked and forgotten.

Ten minutes later the vicar took his leave, and the little party broke up. Mark Shadwell walked with him to the gate. They strode along silently for a good way.

"Sir Roke seems to enjoy his visit very much," said the vicar at last; but like a man rather asking a question than stating a fact. "Your quiet rational life must be a change to him."

"And you wonder how he can endure its dullness?" said Mark, with a laugh; "so do I, but anything may be endured for a day or two, and Roke does not mean to stay longer."

"Oh! has he said so?"

"Yes—why?" asked Mark, struck by something in his companion's tone. "I think he said he meant to go on the day after tomorrow."

"Have you any idea where he goes then?" asked the clergyman.

"To Scarbrook, I think; you seem to take an interest in him, Temple; do you think of sending him a tract on death and judgement, or some little reminder of the sort? I'm sure he'll read it."

"I sha'n't trouble him with tracts, because I know he would *not* read them, and *would* think me a fool, and so any little chance that our conversation of tonight, or of any other time, might have, would be lost."

Mark smiled to himself, thinking that Stour Temple had actually thought over the tract, and been busy about Sir Roke's spiritual concerns.

"I'm afraid you may as well leave that erring and straying sheep to walk his own way, a perverse disciple like me, only I don't think Roke has any philosophy, except the hand-to-mouth one of extracting from life, day by day, all the pleasure he can, a rule which, except indeed in coming to Raby, I don't think I ever knew him offend against. I've some reason, however, to think that he begins to find that way of life a little tiresome, and he's talking of a quieter one, but I don't know: have you often known a man of that kind settle down and many?"

"Yes, I've known two or three; not that they all make good husbands," answered the vicar.

"I dare say not; so have I, some," said Mark.

"They don't always make good husbands," he might have said, "but they do make good settlements sometimes ;" and that

I am afraid is what he was principally thinking of.

"When will you be coming this way again, Temple?" asked Mark, who wished to ask him more closely about the story of Miss Marlyn's schooldays, and yet somehow could not this night.

Temple smiled.

"I wish you would look in a little oftener," said Mark, who interpreted that smile aright, and felt the rebuke more than his pride would quite acknowledge.

"Thank you very much, but my walks are very uncertain; their direction is often controlled by that most capricious, humanly speaking, of all influences, sickness."

"I'd ride over tomorrow or next day, If I thought I should find you, but you're so uncertain, and I really want"—he lowered his voice unconsciously—"to hear anything more you may happen to know about that story you mentioned today."

"I don't think I have anything to add," said the vicar.

"Well, I ain't going to ask you tonight, but you'll look in when you can, won't you?"

The vicar promised, and they shook hands and parted.

"The most officious fellow in England! Well-intentioned, no doubt; but he's always making me uncomfortable, and I suppose other people also. I wish Roke would present him to Scarbrook. I wish he could keep his scandals to himself. I don't think he'd come all that way to tell me anything pleasant—delight some fellows take in tormenting their neighbours!"

Thinking of many things, he sauntered back towards the house, and was surprised to find himself so soon again on the steps.

The little game of piquet in his dressing-room amused Sir Roke, and soothed his nerves for bed.

"Well, what do you think of Temple?" inquired Mark, as he shuffled the cards.

A hard shrewd glance Roke shot at him, but Mark's countenance had nothing alarming in it, and his eyes were upon the cards.

"Oh! Temple's very well, if he wasn't always talking shop, you know. He's very well, but too much shop," replied Sir Roke, cutting the cards. "He used to be clever—sang very nicely, didn't he? And he wrote verses, I think, and was an accomplished fellow before he grew so dismal. Everything good in its place; let him preach in his pulpit, I've no objection, but I do object to—I lead, don't I?—I object to sermons, and d—d disagreeable sermons after dinner."

And with this remark Sir Roke entered on his game; they played as usual; the baronet lost, and, when he had played enough, he thanked Mark, paid his losses, and yawned gently behind his hand.

"Very good of you, Mark, to get my nerves in tone, and enable me to sleep, by this little game. You'll come to-morrow night? I'm afraid it must be my last—what the devil's *that?*"

Someone had pushed open Sir Roke's door a little bit, and closed it again softly.

It was near one o'clock by this time.

"Someone at the door," said Mark, getting up and opening it.

"No one there," said Mark; and he listened. "No, it was a mistake."

"No mistake," said Sir Roke, testily.

"I mean that someone mistook the door, and got away again on finding out his mistake," replied Mark Shadwell; "who on earth could it have been, though?" He bethought him, and again he looked out and listened. "Whoever it was, all's quiet now!" and he closed the door on the gallery, bid Roke "goodnight," and went out the other way.

Sir Roke Wycherly was not in a pleasant mood that night, as Mr. Clewson was made aware. It was a phase of exasperation that tried that gentleman's politeness severely, a sort of dumb madness as to all utterances but revilings and curses—in which he indicated his orders by signs, and resented a misapprehension in such terms as would make a good curate's hair stand on end, and suggested the prudence of some such fumigation as that potent one we read of in the *Book of Tobit.*

These tempers excited Mr. Clewson's curiosity, for they were seldom wholly capricious, when they reached that pitch of intensity; but depended for the most part on some exterior cause.

He wrote a letter at last. A curious observer of the human countenance would have noted an unpleasant flickering; the ironical lights and dismal shadows of an angry and malicious face, as he penned it, and read it over. It ended, however, by his putting it into the fire. It did not satisfy him, and looking woefully tired, he at length got himself into his bed, toned and tranquillised by his tinctures or drops; and looking like the corpse of a man arrested by death in the moment of revenge, he lay worn out and bleak on his pillow.

This letter may have been to the Reverend Stour Temple, or to quite another person. I don't know. It will never be known till all secrets, great and little, are proclaimed.

It was three o'clock and the house quite still, when on a sudden Sir Roke was wakened, he fancied, by a noise. His nerves were jarred upon, and his heart thumping at his ribs as he wakened, as will happen with irritable men under the imperfect action of laudanum. He had just collected his wits, and remembered where he was, when he heard the handle of his door tried again from the outside.

Up jumped Sir Roke with the nimbleness of anger, resolved to clear this matter up; stealthily he got into his dressing-gown, lighted his bedroom candle, and drew near the door, and exactly as he again heard the handle of it cautiously turned from without, he turned the key in it, and candlestick in hand, with his head a little stooped, and features peaked and corrugated with anger, he confronted Carmel Sherlock, who stood before him, very pale and haggard, in his ordinary careless costume.

Like a somnambulist wakened, he recoiled in a kind of horror a pace or two, and then stood with his great dark eyes gleaming back the light of Sir Roke's candle upon the baronet.

# CHAPTER 34

## MORITURUS

Neither spoke for a while. At length, raising his candle a little, so as to disclose those odd confronting portraits more sharply, Sir Roke said, with a pallid grimace which sarcastically travestied a smile:

"I've been obliged to you, sir, I think, more than once for this kind of attention?"

"Very likely, very *certainly*," said Sherlock, just above his breath. "It must be that you lock your door."

"Pray, sir, do you want anything in my room?" repeated Sir Roke, in the same constrained tone, and with the same angry smirk.

"No, sir, no. I've no business, certainly. It's a happy thing, sir, you wakened me," said Sherlock, looking full at him as before, and with a sort of shudder he went back another step.

"Then you've been walking in your *sleep*, sir, I suppose?" said Sir Roke, intent on mentioning the case to his host, with whom he felt very angry for having such a person in his house.

"Walking in my sleep, sir? Oh, no! that's double life; no, never, sir. Lock your door. I hope you will—do, sir—double lock and bolt."

"Your advice, sir, is immensely obliging," said the baronet, with the same sneer, but somehow fascinated by the sublime impudence and unintelligibility of his visitor, and unable to break away at the moment.

"No, don't fail; every man changes his theories from time to time, and looking among the ancients, I think the Sadducees were wrong, and there is some place like hell—"

"And I should say a likely way to settle one's mind upon that question would be going about to people's bedrooms at this hour of night, and getting yourself mistaken for a robber. Pray, sir, don't come here anymore. Goodnight." And so saying, with a burst of anger at himself for having played the fool for so long, he shirt the door in Carmel's face, and locked it; and he cursed his audacious disturber with intensity, and rang up Clewson; and blew him up, not reasonably, for allowing every d—d fellow that had nothing better to do to hammer upon his door for half the night, and ruin his health; and he demanded of Mr. Clewson what the devil he was good for, and whether he fancied he would go on keeping him for nothing, and so forth.

So in his wrath he marched and counter-marched Mr. Clewson, put him on fatigue duty, made him get on his clothes, and mount guard in the gallery outside his door. He made him share the bitterness of his own involuntary vigil, and strained his patience very nearly to the cracking point, and did not permit him to revisit his bed until sleep began to approach his own, and he wished him out of his way.

Sir Roke was one of those gentlemen who utterly pooh-pooh the idea of hell. He cultivated vague ideas of his Creator's beneficence, which had been unconsciously his epicurean comfort in many an incipient qualm about futurity.

"Hell, indeed! vastly good of him to call me out of my quiet sleep to tell me his ideas on that agreeable chimera; d—n the mad brute!"

Many fat good-humoured fellows smile at hell, if they do not sneer. And many bad men class it with Styx and Tartarus—a bugbear and a fable. Eating, drinking, dozing, comfortable friend! Willing to take a luxurious view of your Creator, and to make the day of judgement a good-natured sham. God is good, you say; it cannot fare so ill with us. He is the God of love and of mercy, and of every good and pleasant thing. Alas! most certainly He is also the God of every evil thing—the God of pain, of madness, and of death. Look around on the gloom of this transitory world. If here and there is a broken light of heaven, are there no glimmerings and shadows of hell? Are there not the hospitals, the madhouses, the prisons, the graveyards?

Is there no such word as incorrigible? Are there not criminals whom no punishment and no fear can cause to cease from troubling, whom nothing but final loss of liberty, or of life, the completest loss of liberty, can render harmless? Persons who have educated themselves into a systematic and irrevocable enmity to their race, to fair play, to God—persons to whom we award imprisonment for life, and leave them, at the end of it, morally where we found them—not to be trusted with liberty? There we leave them, and there we should find them, if life lasted twice or twenty times as long, or through eternity.

We see this in our own economy, and can we not understand the possible necessity of "spirits in prison" forever, by the committal of God? If a perverted man be here so immutable, and will, with his limited powers and opportunities, inflict so much upon his fellows, how would it be with the opportunities of an everlasting life, and the magnified faculties of a being raised in power?

But Sir Roke Wycherly felt himself better and stronger every day. Though still an invalid, therefore, there was no reason he should think of another world yet, or trouble himself with any unearthly speculations. Very much of the earth, earthy indeed were his thoughts just now. A young lady, he thought, was fooling him. With a preposterous ambition playing fast and loose with him, he had grown more eager and incensed than perhaps he ever had been before in a similar pursuit. And worthy of admiration is it in such enterprises with what a devilish perseverance and energy obstacles will inspire the most supine and despicable of men.

Over the evil and the good, the hale and the sick, the jocund and the sad, the morning rose, and the slanting beams of sunrise blushed and glittered across the valley. The songs of happy birds greeted the dawn; rural labourers awoke, and the pleasant sounds of life were heard all round. A new page was opened in the *Book of Life*, on which all sorts and conditions of men were to write their indelible inscriptions—their falsehood or truth—their virtue or wickedness, to be folded back in its turn, and see the light no more until the seal shall be broken in the glare of doomsday!

"What sort of person is that Mr. Sherlock, who sometimes comes in to breakfast?" inquired Sir Roke, after that meal, of Rachel Shadwell, with whom he was now chatting by the window. "An odd being he seems to be."

"Oh! so odd, so simple and clever, and so really kind, and gentle, and affectionate," she answered, forgetting her reserve, in a kind of enthusiasm; "poor old Carmel; he taught me—let me think—ever so much. He taught me writing, and arithmetic, and French, and Italian, and some German, and some music too; I'm very fond of good old Carmel Sherlock."

Sir Roke listened politely, and then with a shrug and a smile answered:

"An Admirable Crichton! but he keeps very late hours, and visits people's apartments very oddly."

Rachel stared, and Sir Roke laughed gently.

"Yes, I assure you, he made me a call last night, and knocked me up, between three and four, to advise me to keep my door locked, and to instruct me in some of his admirable theology. I don't know that I shall adopt his theology, but his advice about locking my door I certainly shall."

"Yes, he is very odd," she answered, joining slightly in Sir Roke's laugh. "But he's very grateful."

"Odder still!" remarked the baronet.

"Papa has been very kind to him, and he is so devoted; I really think he would die for him."

"Oh! He *must* be very much obliged, indeed, and very romantic also, because dying for a friend is a sort of politeness one can't repeat. Life is a bird in the hand, which, if you let it fly, never returns. How charming the sun is today; how brilliant your flowers look!"

He pushed open the glass door which opened on the gravel walk, and paused. It was, however, so very genial a day that he was prepared to venture without his hat. He looked up, and waved his hand a little in the air, to be quite assured of its temperature.

"It is—yes—a charming day."

And he invited her to redeem her promise, and tell him the names of half-a-dozen flowers which he particularly affected, and forth went Rachel, "herself the fairest flower;" and her father, looking through the window, observed with a reserved satisfaction the little scene, and fancied a tenderness in Roke's manner, as he took the flowers from Rachel's fingers, and a sentiment in his smirk that pleased him infinitely.

Why was Mark Shadwell's head so full of the little comedy for whose opening scene he had rung the bell, and which he watched with an interest which perhaps no one but its cynical hero quite detected? He had never cared for Rachel; he had grown indolent and unsociable in his rural solitude, and he had no very active desire to return to the glare and excitement of his early life. But this great marriage would be a mortification to many on whom it would delight the proud and wounded recluse to retaliate the contempt with which he fancied they had treated him.

Rachel, besides, cost him money, which his discontent exaggerated; and she was, somehow, in his way. As for Miss Marlyn, she, he was sure, would not like to leave Raby—no, she should not go. Amy would require a companion, and Miss Marlyn would remain their guest. Poor Amy! their marriage had been a great mistake—such were his conceited ruminations. A woman of mind and ambition would have been a wife to comprehend, and to promote the fortunes of such a man.

Sometimes Mark Shadwell's monstrous ambitions were relighted for an hour. He was, in his dreams, an M.P., high in office, the most brilliant reputation in England. His evening receptions crowded by personages and celebrities of all sorts, and certain personages peremptorily *excluded*—yes, that was a pleasant thought—sweetest drop in his mantling cup of nectar. These gorgeous dreams, however, it is but justice to say, were only occasional.

There were others worse, perhaps, but less fantastic, in which the scene was laid after the death of poor Amy—an event oftener in his mind than that pretty, fading, adoring little wife could have believed possible. That occurrence would be to him a liberation, and with it he connected a romance.

Miss Agnes Marlyn! Who so fit to be the wife of a man so

gifted and aspiring as he? Clever, beautiful, energetic, how she would help to push his fortunes—how popular she would make him! What a little diplomatist she would be. How graceful, how elegant, how beautiful! Who could do the honours of his house when fortune should begin to shine, when he should sit for that borough which Roke had promised, so charmingly as she?

But these visions of active ambition, as I have said, depended on certain moods, and states of spirits, which were not always, nor indeed very often, his. And in his normal condition she was simply his future wife. Agnes Marlyn! without a guinea! Oh, Prudence! What a thought for a man not far from half a century old. Time was when proud, handsome, highly descended Mark Shadwell would not have admitted such a dream. But solitude makes us less worldly, and more self-indulgent.

## CHAPTER 35
### LETTERS ON THE HEARTHSTONE

Mark Shadwell was away that day among his woods and rabbits. During luncheon they heard the distant pop of his gun. His other shooting, thanks to the poachers, for Mark had long ceased to pay keepers, would not repay a trial. But his rabbits increased and multiplied; they swarmed in the burrowed woodlands, whose shades and solitudes accorded well with the indolent and dreamy habit of his discontented mind.

When he got among the knotted roots, the steeps and shadows of these sylvan uplands, he generally loitered away the whole day there. But on this occasion Mark had miscalculated his ammunition, and was out of powder early enough to make it worth his while to go back and replenish his old-fashioned powder-flask.

Things were brightening for Mark, and his head was full of pleasant chimeras. Had it been otherwise he would probably have loitered among the woods, powderless and morose, for the remainder of the day, with no occupation but his cigar.

Upstairs, in one of a suite of unfurnished rooms, Mark Shadwell kept his guns, fishing-rods, shot, and powder, and thither he went. Three rooms open *en suite*, and, contrary to his custom, and without any particular reason, he entered the first.

Standing near the window, with a shock, he saw Agnes Marlyn and Sir Roke Wycherly. The baronet was speaking in a low tone as he entered, and instantly was silent. If Mark had shot him with a pistol, he could not have eyed him for a moment with a stranger stare and gape. In another second the young lady had vanished through the distant door. Mark stood stock-still in the doorway, gaitered, in his rusty velveteen coat and wide-awake hat, with his old-fashioned shot-belt across his breast, looking very pallid and foolish.

Miss Marlyn was gone, indeed, in a moment. But her face, with its strange look of *guilt*, was it? was caught and fixed in his brain.

If they had been allowed even one moment's preparation, I dare say the beautiful Miss Agnes Marlyn and the withered Sir Roke would have met Mark with countenances so serene, and an air so plausible, that he would have been puzzled, and prepared to accept, or at least entertain, any explanation they might have chosen to offer. But Mark Shadwell, whom they had reason to believe to be more than a mile away at that moment, was standing, even before they saw him, in the doorway, and gazing at them with a countenance in which they both saw consternation and menace.

Sir Roke—a man of the world inured to such small reverses, disciplined in dissimulation, and blessed with presence of mind— was quite himself before Mark had half recovered his shock.

"I thought I heard your voice, and I wasn't wrong—just this moment, coming out of my room—and I fancied it came from here," said Sir Roke, gaily, with his withered, impenetrable smile: " and as I entered at one door. Miss—Miss—what's her name? came in at the other. Ha, ha, ha! I'm always in luck; I fancied she mistook *me* for *you*, and came in for instructions—your secretary, isn't she? A very good idea; very agreeable; I quite envy you. She made so many apologies, and looked ready to sink into the earth—ha, ha, ha! I think she said she writes your letters."

"Yes, my letters—that is, sometimes. You both thought, of course, that I was still away, shooting in the woods," said Mark, fixing his eyes, with a strange look, upon Roke, and speaking in a measured way.

"I really had not been making conjectures on the subject—I can't say, of course, how the young lady had been employed; for my part, I fancied, as I crossed the gallery, that I heard your voice *here*, and, the door being open, I walked in. I hope I have not done very wrong. I was making my excuses to the young lady when you came in; I must have heard your voice as you came up the stairs."

"No, that couldn't be; I did not speak—some mistake," said Shadwell. "I've come in to get some powder. Should you like to take a gun for once, and try the rabbits?"

"No, thanks; I was just going out for a walk. Have you any notion where I should find my cousin Rachel?"

"Not the slightest," said Mark, shortly.

"Well, I must only try. Pretty landscape that;" and Sir Roke, as he spoke, waved his hand towards the window, and smiled from the distance through it in such a way as ought to have made the flowers turn their innocent bells and cups towards him, and the birds sing more sweetly. .

Thus smiling—with a little nod—Sir Roke was gone, leaving Mark Shadwell standing there, with his empty powder-flask rather tightly held in his hand.

Mark's look was cast down on the floor, and there was a very angry tumult of suspicion, and other dark passions, at his heart. He entered the other room, where his powder and shot and fishing-tackle lay locked up in a press. It was simply the impetus of his first intention that carried him on, for powder and rabbits were now quite out of his mind.

On the middle of the floor of this room he stood with downcast eyes, and darkened face, I cannot say thinking, but rather stunned, and with the elements of fury indistinctly rolling in his breast.

He walked to the dim windows, stained with the old patterings of rain, and looked out, without an object. A pleasant female laugh sounded from beneath, and he saw Miss Agnes Marlyn talking with Rachel, on the grass. She seemed gay and at her ease, and the sight—suffering as he was—stung his pride with a momentary agony.

As he entered the room just now, and surprised her and Sir Roke in conference, a truth, though undefined, quite incompatible with accident or honesty, shocked him in their faces, transitory as one gleam of lightning, but fastened, with a dazzling chemistry, forever in his brain. All Sir Roke's rubbishy explanations—lies, lies, *lies*! How near he had been to tell him, at one moment, that he *lied*! He was glad now that he had not. To betray his rage would have been a humiliation. Was it possible, after all, that there was some truth in Roke's explanation? No, it *could* not be. That one look that met him was detection.

With a sudden resolution he turned and walked swiftly across the room, along the silent gallery, and direct to Miss Agnes Marlyn's room.

That room was simple, neat, nothing out of its place. Not a letter was lying about. He espied that little desk, inlaid with circles and *fleur-de-lis* of brass, quaint and rather pretty. He tried it, and found it locked. He tried his own keys, but they would not do. Mark Shadwell! Was it possible? in his governess's room, a shabby spy and detective!

There was only this extenuation: he would have done precisely the same had her eyes been upon him. No; he was no spy, but the grand inquisitor, in his power and fury. He was not to be baffled by that artful little lock; his anger found a rough and ready way, and he carried the reserved and pretty little desk to the hearth, and with force, measured by his fury rather than its strength, dashed it upon the stone.

Delicate and obstinate little lock, decorative brass clasps, neat dovetailing and glue, all burst into wreck in a moment, and away flew, with a tiny clatter, broken bits of sealing-wax, a pencil-case, a seal, and two or three keys, over the floor; the letters lay among the wreck, and them he gathered up into a little pack, and laid them, methodically enough, on the small table near the window. There were not twenty in all. There was his wife's gentle letter, which did not seem to hire, but to invite, Miss Agnes Marlyn— the beginning of all this!

The rest were in French; a few of two years since—adoring, fierce, sublime—from the constructor of the desk whose wreck lay on the hearthstone, violated. There were three in English, and they were from Sir Roke—the envelopes addressed in another, or a disguised, hand. The sneak! Mark gasped, and ground his teeth, unable to find a term of execration bitter enough for the man and the occasion. I don't know that Sir Roke would have thought *his* procedure deserving of a much better one.

He read them carefully. Their meaning reached his angry brain but slowly, so many images excited and interrupted him. One of these letters, he thought, said, without seeming to say, that Sir Roke could not marry. Good Heavens! The sublime audacity of that little gipsy adventuress.

Had it not been for Mark Shadwell's own dreams about the baronet, would he have regarded Miss Marlyn's castle in the air with a contempt so exasperated and virulent? He actually laughed, with a kind of rage, over the idea.

He could not quite make out their relations by means of these three letters, two of which were very short. Sir Roke called her "provoking," "cruel," "unintelligible." He talked of "encouragement" and "unreasonableness." He said he had hoped that he had made "his difficulties and his hopes better understood." He said, in another place, that he "honoured her motives"—hypocritical villain!—and that he knew, "so soon as she arranged that interview which she had promised," he could "entirely satisfy, not only her honourable scruples, but her *conscience*." That he meant "altogether honourably, and she *knew* it."

On the whole, thus much was clear: whatever the origin of their intimacy might be, that Sir Roke had come to Raby with no other object than to see Agnes Marlyn; that, as appeared from the tenor and date of one of his letters, she had evidently consulted him as to whether she should come to Raby. He fancied, from some faint allusion, too, that she had been describing him—Mark Shadwell—amusingly! What he would have given for a copy of the entire correspondence! It was enough, however. She should leave Raby peremptorily; and he would tell Roke, in plain terms, what he thought of him.

Thus resolved this proud, reserved, conceited man. His heart was wrung with a terrible mortification.

## CHAPTER 36
### ALONE, YET NOT ALONE

When Mark Shadwell first picked up Sir Roke's letters, he was trembling with eagerness for a collision with the shabby author of them. He could hardly wait patiently to read them through. But his pride helped him now. He had been spelling over these letters for more than ten minutes, and by the time he had mastered their contents, he was cool enough to act more in accordance with his haughty character.

The letters were now in his hand. But he had changed his mind. It would be time enough to talk to Roke by and by. It would not do to make a fracas about a little governess. It would be *agony* to betray that other disappointment. To no one—even to his wife, hardly to himself—could he endure to define that fraudulent insult. If, indeed, Roke had meant it—for there might have been something of chance; but no, it was a premeditated deception, and intended to mask his real object—what name could adequately describe such a man?

Mark had the letters in his hand; but he knew all they contained, and there was no need to satisfy any one, but himself upon the matter. He looked down on the coy, little, murdered desk, dislocated, gaping on the hearthstone, bleeding a stream of ink from its broken bottle; and his impulse was to tear the vile letters across, and fling them upon it. But that would have been but accumulating evidence of his irritation; and, instead, he placed them on the other letters that stood like a pack of cards, ready to be shuffled or cut, on the table.

Down stairs went Mark again. A quarter of an hour had done

a great deal fox him. Powder, shooting, gun, he forgot. From habit, he took his stick in the hall, and sallied forth, with quick strides, to stun the sense of pain with exercise. The sun was gone down from his sky, and the future a chasm.

Away to the sylvan solitudes he had lately left, he strode. Along their slopes and sides, under the congenial darkness of the branches, he walked, and sat down at last, at the entrance of a glade, upon the trunk of a prostrate tree. The summits of the wood were touched by the level beams of the declining sun, which here and there broke ruddily through the hoary stems of the forest.

"To think of that d—d old satyr—old in health, in strength, and in brain—whatever he may be in years—coming down here upon such an errand! He always hated me, I think; and I'm sure I always hated him—with *reason*. He never had a kind thought in all his days, or a sympathy, or a human feeling; his heart—a cold lump of stone—*always* the same. A boy—*what* a d—d boy he was! I'm glad I gave him that licking at Scarbrook. I gave him one good licking—ha, ha!—thank God! I wish old Weals had not come between us; I think I'd have killed him then. It *was* a good one. Everyone was glad. I hope to God he remembers every blow. The devil, they say, haunts Wynderfel. Does he? If there be one, I shouldn't wonder. I wish he'd pay Raby a visit, and take away what belongs to him."

He glanced through the distant opening in the wood, down which was visible a glimpse of the grey walls of Wynderfel, a grass-tufted chimney, and a mullioned window, through which the sky of sunset dimly glowed.

The rustle of withered leaves in the fitful air, and the evening song of the birds, accompanied incongruously the long and bitter denunciation with which Mark Shadwell amused or scared the wandering spirits of the wood.

"And that girl—the idea!—can she possibly fancy that Roke Wycherly could seriously think of marrying her? Roke Wycherly marry her! Is the minx mad? Roke Wycherly, the hardest screw in England, sacrifice himself to the ambition of a little adventuress!"

This unjust man, Mark Shadwell, cruel to some, almost loving to others at times, on the great voyage, every knot of which is irrevocable, without helm or compass, in which a mistake is worse than running on the shore of the Cyclops, had no misgivings about his missing chart and empty binnacle, but drove on in the dark, before wind and sea, with the confidence of madness.

I have thought of Mark Shadwell as of one altogether worthless, because his name calls up always a rueful image of an adoring little wife—faded, neglected, despised. Perhaps, in some measure, I have wronged him, and condemned him too sweepingly. There remained a residuum of compassion; at moments the remembrance of his early feelings returned, and sometimes a qualm of compunction visited him. His daughter Rachel, I believe, he loved, although he usually spoke to her but little; and a stranger would have fancied, from his looks and taciturnity, that she was in perpetual disgrace.

His sullen demeanour was however, but the expression of his pain—of a profound and angry ulcer. Had he been in reality the character which he affected—a philosopher—and cheerfully made up his mind to seize the opportunities of happiness that lay neglected about his path, he might easily have been, not only a merrier, but a better man.

Sometimes, considering the sort of education he received, and how inflexibly species are formed by circumstances, I almost wonder that he was not a worse man than we find him. The more I marvel at his delusions, the more I admire his moderation. Considering how preposterous was his estimate of his powers, I am amazed at the modesty of his demeanour. Considering how much ruin he fancied his marriage had involved him in, I wonder, selfish as he was, at his toleration of his wife. Much that was odious there was in him, but vestiges and rudiments also of good.

If it had not been for his angry pride, always on the watch, and ingenious in imagining insult, he might have lived on terms with his neighbours. As it was, he had surrounded himself ,' with quarrels and antipathies, and lived in a haughty isolation in which he yearly grew more morbid and embittered.

The sun by this time had gone down behind the crest of the distant wood, and Mark Shadwell, who had meditated a long and solitary ramble, and had not meant to see Roke Wycherly, or, if he could, any other human face again that night, sat rapt in his gloomy visions; in Swift's phrase, "*rolling resentments and framing revenges.*"

The crows had glided from the burning west, across the yellow and sea-green sky of evening, home to their leafy roostings in the forest of Wynderfel, from whence their cawings sounded now faintly like the roar of a distant sea.

Mark Shadwell sat looking on the sod between his feet staring in a wicked dream. You would have said he was looking into an unseen grave, upon the face of the man whom he hated. When he looked up, upon the saddened sky of evening, his thoughts for a while were toned with a corresponding melancholy, and then on a sudden came a ghastly despair.

"Why did that d—d girl's image take possession of me? Yes, she has—she has; while I was cheating myself with dreams of superiority and indifference, I was becoming the slave of a creature whom I understand and despise, *and hate*, and yet whom I love. My God! it is true; I could shoot her dead at my feet this moment, and then myself. To think of that d—d, sneaking, sickly, smirking villain! A plan—a scheme—in league, both, to use and cheat me. Away she goes! How she'll stare when I bid her be-gone! I'll do it coldly too—give her no reason."

Up he got, and paced down the slope of the wood in the direction of Wynderfel, and found himself at last, in the twilight, by the ruined chapel of the old manor-house, among the half-obliterated graves and tombstones.

How beautiful the silvery glimmer of the moon shows in the grey twilight sky! How thin and airy looked the tall walls and gables of old Wynderfel in that deceptive light! Through the old graveyard Mark Shadwell sauntered, dim as an evil spirit, and entered the silent courtyard of the ruined manor, and looked about him in a dream.

Of the different forms of temptation, those ascribed distinctively to the world, the flesh, and the devil—the latter, which deal with the malignities of human nature, are awfully exaggerated by solitude. In many ways, it is not good that man should be alone. Human society is perhaps the ordained prophylactic against the horrors and cajoleries of that unseen society that broods and pines in desert places. Undisturbed in solitude, the corrosive action of these murderous passions bites deep. The evil spirits who lust for possession, there way-lay and overpower their prey; any companionship is better than that. Better that the mind should be ruffled and rippled by the breezes, and even lashed by the storms of life, than lie dead and smooth to reflect the starless sky.

As the twilight deepened, the angry thoughts in Mark's mind grew more vivid; so that at last he was almost scared at their intensity.

"Ten years ago I should have done it, had he so insulted me, but no one fights now; let that thought away, then—let it away. I like it too well—*do* I? He's not worth it; let it go, or let it *come*, if it will."

And with this invitation a figure appeared through the opposite archway, so opportunely as to make him start. It paused, and Carmel Sherlock spoke:

"Mr. Shadwell! Here, sir? and I thinking of you."

"I ought to have known you," answered Shadwell, gruffly; "you're always in out-of-the-way places. I've been here but once before this year, and you met me from under that very doorway."

"When I come to Wynderfel, I always pass under that same archway, sir; I feel that I should violate fate if I entered Wynderfel by any other way but that. Some day or other I shall see something there, or hear something, or meet it *there*—good or ill—essential to my destiny."

"But, I say, what the devil brings you here?" interrupted Shadwell, savagely; "if you want *me*, I'm in no mood for nonsense, and can't talk now."

"Nor I—tomorrow," moaned Carmel.

"Well, *do* speak, and have done."

"I'm glad, sir, for I wanted to say a word."

"Out with it, then, I say, and have done with it—or, keep it to yourself, if another time will do," said Shadwell, turning away impatiently.

"*Where the carcass is, there will the eagles be gathered together,*" said Carmel, following by his side.

"Yes, I know that's in the Bible," sneered Mark; "but I don't exactly see the application."

"There's an idea that lies dead in the brain, sir, and round and over it bloody thoughts keep wheeling," said Carmel Sherlock.

"What the devil's that to you?" said Mark Shadwell, stopping short, with a furious turn.

"I did not say—I hope, *nothing,* sir, nothing; but eagles—vultures, rather. What a bird a vulture is! Prometheus chained, I think, and the vultures come; I can fancy him shake his head at them in his agony, and spit at them, and strive to fright them off with yells, but they keep circling lower and nearer—he's partly dead and partly in hell—did you never feel the death of hope and the hell of jealousy?"

Mark looked at him for a moment in the imperfect light. "Neither the one nor the other, thank you; had not you better get home, and eat your dinner?"

"I was going to say farewell," said Carmel. Farewell," said Shadwell. I shall leave Raby," said Carmel.

"Well, now, pray do, just go and eat your dinner, and you'll be ever so much better; and we can talk about your going tomorrow morning. *No,*" repeated Shadwell, silencing Carmel Sherlock's incipient speech, imperiously; "you sha'n't say another word on that subject till tomorrow morning; I say *no*, I *won't* hear it."

And so saying, Mark Shadwell turned from him suddenly, resolved to shake him off, and strode away through the ruins.

# CHAPTER 37
## MISS MARLYN IN AN ODD MOOD.

"What does that d—d fellow mean by his talk about jealousy, and all that stuff?" thought Shadwell, in a rage. "What can he be poking about? he's not a spy, nor a traitor, nor a *witch* neither; I venture to say he has not a notion what he means himself." Still a suspicion was in his mind that Carmel had divined something of the truth, and he was angry with him, angry with himself, and his wounded pride lay writhing under a sense of exposure.

Mark Shadwell had no care in his present temper, for the decencies of hospitality, and had his solitary mood continued upon him, Sir Roke might have looked in vain at dinner for his host.

On a sudden, however, the image of Agnes Marlyn was before his imagination, and an impulse determined him irresistibly homeward. He would see her—in what mood, his passions and thoughts were too confused to resolve. So, skirting the now darkened forest, he walked sullenly towards the house of Raby.

About the same hour. Miss Marlyn and Rachel were walking under the rows of grand old timber that flank the avenue, towards the house. Agnes has been laughing and talking in unusual spirits. It was not gaiety, however; it was excitement.

"I wish, Agnes, dear, you were always so merry."

"I wish I were," answered Agnes, with a sudden change. "Though just now my laughter sounds in my ears like an idiot's. Why should I laugh? life is simply terrible for me. What would have befallen the bird who found no rest for the sole of her foot, if there had remained no ark for her to return to? It is different for you—you have a home—but *I* Come, we won't think."

"And you have a home, dear Agnes, while I have one; you know very well that we all like you, and I love you, although I don't know quite whether you like me."

"That's all romance, my dear little girl, and very pretty; but it's not true—don't start—I'm sure you think it's true, but it isn't. Sentiment and liking are all very fine, but they are subject to mutation, and are transitory. It's very nasty, I know, but quite true; there is nothing solid but property—ha, ha! and *I* have little more than my thimble; and life is a rough, and a wide, and a cold sea to cross, and I'm no witch, and I can't sail in a sieve—and—what do you advise me to do? Isn't it a pity there are no Protestant nunneries, where girls who must become old maids, and perhaps tenants of the workhouse, as things are, might dedicate themselves to comfort and seclusion, and escape the mortification of public celibacy and penury?"

"I never know, Agnes, when you are jesting; but I am serious—I mean, indeed I do, every word I have said."

"So do I, Rachel, dear, every word. I feel this evening—what shall I say?—enterprising. I think I should like to masquerade in male attire, as other girls have done, and enlist—or go to sea. You read the other day an Irish story, about a man sitting on a stone that was sinking in the middle of a bog, and who gratefully accepted the offer of an eagle to fly him out of his dilemma. Now, my dear, this Raby is all very well. It's pretty, and pastoral, and romantic, and what not? I like staying here, but how is it to end? You will be marrying and running away; I shall be growing old, and finally, I shall be left alone to sink in the bog. Yes, this Raby is the stone, and I feel it already sinking under me, and I should be obliged, I think, to any fowl or monster, a Pegasus or a goose, willing and strong enough to fly me out of it."

"You certainly speak plainly, dear Agnes, though I think you might speak a little more kindly," said Rachel, who was hurt.

"Come, come, *ma chère*, we must take care of ourselves. There's nothing unkind in being honest. There's not a creature on earth who cares for me, and therefore I must the more particularly care for myself."

Miss Agnes laughed, Rachel thought, a little more bitterly than she need, as she said this.

"I told you that *I* like you, Agnes."

"But you *don't*, dear."

Rachel stared.

"No," laughed Agnes, "you *can't*; how can you like a person you don't know, and me you can't know. There are things about me I don't know myself, and what I do know, you don't. Come,

188

be honest, Miss Rachel, don't we mystify one another all we can? do I know you quite? and how can you know me?"

"Well, you know best," said Rachel; "I suppose we are all hypocrites."

"More or less," said Agnes, quietly; "you talk of liking me! No one likes another, unless they love them through all their follies, tempers, and crimes. None of these have I shown. But how can we tell that your liking would stand that strain? Suppose I were to leave Raby tonight, and you never hear more of me,, would you still like me? Mr. Sherlock, you know, you mentioned is going, no one knows why or whither; I don't mean to elope with him, but I don't think that sort of flitting a bad idea."

"I hope he is not going; I don't believe he is; I am so fond of poor old Carmel Sherlock," said Rachel.

"Not so old," interposed Agnes, disagreeably.

"You are determined to laugh at everything tonight," said Rachel, "but the place would not be like itself if he were gone, and I can't think he will go, he's so kind and affectionate."

"Not like me, who am odious enough to think sometimes of myself," said Miss Marlyn, in her odd bitter mood. "Well, if he goes, we have still a resource in that charming vicar," Miss Marlyn added, with an irony that was not playful.

Mr. Temple, you mean?" The Reverend Sour, or Stour Temple; yes, what an agreeable man—what a gentleman—how pretty!" and she laughed.

"Mamma likes him very much."

"He admired your mamma very much, I believe, once on a time."

"I dare say—everyone did who saw her when she was young, and I think her quite beautiful still—but I don't see what that has to do with what I'm saying. Mamma thinks him a very good and useful clergyman, and so do I, and so does papa, although they sometimes disagree about things."

"And oh! that funny old bald foozle, that fancies himself a lover," said Miss Marlyn, with a sudden recollection and a laugh.

"Who?" asked Rachel.

"*Bonnie*—who but our charming friend, Bonnie? She should have called him Bauldie, if it must be Scotch, after the young man in the *Gentle Shepherd*, that stupid book; I'm so glad we have done it."

"Oh, Pucelle! you must not laugh at Roger Temple," pleaded Rachel.

"I *must* laugh at Roger Temple! at everything! I should die in this place else, and why should not he be laughed at like the rest? Preposterous old fool!"

Somehow there was a desecration here in Rachel's mind. She was shocked, and a little disgusted; but, after all, Roger Temple was a difficult case to fight, for she could not conceal it from herself that he *was* preposterous.

"Take care," said she, "he is in love with you."

"Well?" said Miss Marlyn, with an odd smile, that showed the glittering edge of her even teeth.

"You may marry him yet."

"And suppose I do, does that make any difference? I shall love, honour, and laugh at him—*selon les règles*—still."

By this time they were crossing the hall, now nearly dark, and entered the room where they were accustomed to read together, and here the faint glow still reflected from the western clouds afforded them an imperfect and melancholy light, through the still open window.

"There is this comfort in having no one to care for you, that you have no one to control you. There is not a person on earth who has a right to command or even to question me, and so, child, I'm perfectly free and—perfectly miserable. It *will* cost me a pang, many a pang, to leave Raby, as leave it I soon shall, but fate, and pride, and despair, ordain it. I hate myself for going— I'm different from you, Rachel; you can't understand me, if you could *you* would hate me also. No, don't kiss me, it is folly, you shall never kiss me more. I suppose you think me mad; for the last four hours I have been walking and talking in a dream, and yet I am not mad, and it is all a reality, only I have taken a resolution that has nearly broken my heart—don't ask me, I'm talking because I must talk, but it is not confidence, and I'm no worse, not an atom, and no better than *you*, than all others, who act according to their circumstances, and opportunities, and necessities, and I'll never talk of it to you more. A beautiful sunset it must have been! how it glows! There were sunsets like it two thousand years ago, and will be again two thousand years hence; and my story is an old one, and will turn up with a different heroine—generation after generation there is nothing new, and things are no better and no worse than they were, and than they will be always,"

Agnes spoke wildly, though quietly; and Rachel was startled by her manner, which was resolute, and defiant, and excited. Curious as Rachel was, and even alarmed, she instinctively felt that, at least just then, it would have been vain to ask for an explanation. So, at the window, as Agnes gazed upon the dying flush that still glowed in the west, Rachel looked in her face. The lurid light fell across her great mysterious eyes like a glowing bar. Rachel long saw that beautiful face—touched with an upward light—looking sinister and blinded, and she said:

"Don't look that way, Pucelle, it's so odd."

"How, *ma chère?*"

"So changed, I mean."

"Perhaps I am changed."

"Turn away from that light."

"I'm looking at "Wynderfel, and thinking of Wynderfel," said the beautiful girl apathetically.

"But that light is so unbecoming," persisted Rachel.

"Unbecoming—oh?" murmured the young lady with a smile, and a satire faintly returning to her face, and she did turn and looked with a tiny nod—arch and dismal, also—on Rachel, who took her hand, and in silence for a time, side by side, they looked out on the fading landscape. In Agnes Marlyn's face there was melancholy without softening. The far-off gaze, and those delicate features looked sad and stern—no sympathy—no yearning.

"Come, Pucelle,—I won't have you look so sad and cruel,"

said Rachel with a little laugh. "You shall look like yourself."

And with fingers interlaced, as they had been standing, she raised Agnes Marlyn's hand and leaned her head lightly on it—the attitude was fond and even caressing.

There was a short silence, the light was fading, Rachel raised her head, and in a minute more she said:

"An odd little scar you have got, Pucelle, in the middle of your hand."

She was looking at a little white scar on the palm of Agnes Marlyn's hand. Agnes still looking out, held her slender hand, palm upward, wide open for Rachel's scrutiny.

"But it really is," she continued, with growing curiosity, and with a little laugh she added, "why it has just five little rays, the star of Bethlehem, you know, and your left hand, that's the mark of the gaze-lady."

Without changing her attitude, Agnes also laughed a little.

"I did not think of that," she said. "I got that when I was a very little thing—I don't remember—someone told me, getting over a fence, and I leaned on a sharp stake—yes, so it has—one, two, three, four, five," and she smiled for a moment. "That star of Bethlehem burns sometimes, I can tell you—it pained me today for instance—all the time we were talking in that little chapel."

She sighed, and with a little shiver, drew her hand away suddenly, and her cloak about her. Then Rachel, without an attempt to stay her, saw Agnes Marlyn leave the room.

"She is angry, I think; what can have happened? I have said nothing to vex her. She'll tell me all by and by. She can't seriously mean all that she says. Yes; she'll tell me the cause, I dare say, and she will be like herself again."

Rachel fancied she thought all this, but she did not, for the dark laugh of Agnes chilled her with a strange presage of evil.

## CHAPTER 38
### Venus Δύσερως, Farewell.

The window was open; the rich odours of the flowers exhaled on the evening air, and the rose-tinted western lights, melting into the deep sky of the coming night, inspired that luxurious melancholy which is, for the young, the poetic foreshadowing of the sorrows of life. Rachel, leaning against the side of the window, looked out upon those fading piles of cloud that crowned the solemn landscape, and experienced the influence of the hour and the scene. From under the boughs of the ancient clump of trees that stands nearest to the house, emerged a figure, and slowly approached the window at which she sat. "Only I, Miss Rachel; only I, your old tutor," said the well-known voice of Carmel Sherlock.

"Oh! Mr. Sherlock?" she said, kindly.

"It is a long time, Miss Rachel, since we read French and German, and Italian."

"Yes, very long; but you have been so busy."

"A long interruption, Miss Rachel."

"Too long—a great deal," she said.

"All goes on and on, Miss Rachel; and that time sickened and died, and a new time is come; and that, too, will die, and be succeeded by another, and another; the first perishes, there is no unknitting the fruit, and expanding it into the flower again; there is no folding the flower, and shutting it up in the seed again. Nature makes no step back—never looks over the shoulder—never."

"Well, sha'n't we resume our Italian soon? we must begin again—soon—very soon," said she.

"No; not soon—*never*," he said, very sadly.

"Never! Why?" asked Rachel.

"You see. Miss Rachel, they all believe, one way or another, in that *palin-genesis*; for my part, I can't believe but that, somehow, I shall see the light again, and see my love again. Petrarch met, I think, his Laura when he died. How beautiful those lime-trees look, where I read *Tasso*, long ago, to you, when you were a little thing. I love these solitudes, and when I die, I'll come— yes, I'll come again—not to be seen—only to wander here, by the old lime-trees where I read *Tasso*, long ago. Or at Wynderfel, where sympathy grows among the brambles and ivy-tendrils, and the wind among the high gables has a pitying sound, where I may chance to meet that poor lady who died for her love; and I would tell her—my God!—all my misery. The sordid idol!"

She listened to this rhapsody, as she had to others from the lips of the same maundering prophet, not understanding, only in kindness. His lonely habits had taught him quite to dispense with dialogue, and his spoken meditation flowed on:

"That was her girlish thought—to die. Yes, once worshipped, always a divinity—*always*. Break the poor heart—*that* was the shrine. Shatter the brain, where the image always stands in light; it is so only that love can break the idol, and extinguish the tapers of a vain worship. I hear that scream—sometimes—so far away—at night! Yes, indeed, by Heaven! like one wild note of distant music—the past and future in it. I've stood a whole night, at the window listening. It hardly lasts while you could count a slow *ten*—swelling on and on, louder and louder, till it stops in silence. That one note is a concert from Paradise and Tartarus; it fills a whole night, to a man who will think; the hours fly after it, pursuing like waves to drown it. Nature hastens to hide it away; the morning comes before I am aware."

Carmel looked with a despairing eye over the wide landscape toward the disappearing glow of sunset, as you might fancy a shipwrecked man upon a lonely raft gazing towards that fading light in the space of ocean.

"What a pity! Love does not meet love in this world; follows a phantom and unreal voices, and, finding itself alone, dies. A hard case it is. Love crosses love, like ships at sea, each on a different errand, over the waste of life; the narrow horizon coming up and disappearing. Miss Rachel, it is terrible! the affections all so minute and intense, and nature and time so vast and vague— all love so individual; it may be never, in the revolution of time and the changes of worlds, never to meet again. You need not tell me; I tell myself. I *know* it; it is unreal. I have created it; but it is irrevocable—an irreparable mistake. I have found it out, but am none the better. Satan has come, and I have tasted of knowledge; and so—*forth* from Paradise forever. The wide world; the dark night! Little Miss Rachel, with the golden hair, how long it seems since I taught you to write! I don't blame you; I never did. It is nature that is cruel—kind, but also *cruel*. The bird will fly—nature is vigorous—the bird will fly! All pain, and pleasure, and illusion, come to an end. Instinct, the inspiration of our birth, alone inflexible. God whispered to each creature when he made it, and God is immutable."

Carmel looked down, and up, and stamped upon the ground.

"The hoary Satan!—the old dragon!—with poisonous tongue and golden scales, lying under this moon awhile, basking and panting in a gluttonous dream. The reptile!—the murderer! There is a spear of light for him. His sun shall be darkened, and his moon turned into blood. When he moves, the skin of the earth quivers under him. The elements that gave him birth abhor him. But my hand I hold palm upward. My robe is white. The fossil reptiles are extinct. Leave the monstrous generations to the vindicator. Death. Out of the castle I go, and close the gate after me; into the night, the forest, the waste—never to look back—only hoping for some spot where a worn out man may die! The journey—the descent; and oh! at last, the fountain of forgetfulness, and the cold sleep of death. I hope, Miss Rachel, I have not been ungrateful—that is, quite unprofitable."

"Unprofitable! no one was ever kinder or more useful," she answered.

"That is all," he said, sadly.

"And if you were to leave us, I really don't know how papa could manage without you; and as for me, almost everything I know I have learned from you, my kind teacher."

"Ah! yes, the Italian—the French; these will go on, and she will remember, and sometimes say, I learned these from that poor Carmel Sherlock, who went away, and was heard of no more."

"No; I will say I learned them from that kind Mr. Sherlock who would not go away, because he knew it would make us all sorry; who stayed with us, and is with us still, and will never leave Raby."

Sherlock with both hands leaned on the window-stone, as a drowning man might hold by a rock, and she thought he looked steadfastly in her face. She could not see his features distinctly in the deep shadow, but it seemed to her that he was weeping.

Her heart bled with compassion for the kind creature who had been so gentle with her through all the inattention and way-wardness of her childish years, and she wondered how one who never gave a moment's pain to others should inflict so much, and, as it seemed to her, so causelessly, upon himself.

"I'm going, Miss Rachel; I've come to say farewell. I'll leave Raby perhaps tonight, perhaps in the morning; but I'll see you no more."

"Really!" exclaimed she, in a kind of consternation.

"Really, Miss—if there should be such a word as real where all is visionary. So, Miss Rachel, goodbye."

"No, I'll *not* say goodbye," said she; "and you sha'n't go—good, kind Carmel. I don't think I should know Raby without you; so, goodbye, it shall not be."

"Well, Miss, what will you say?"

"I'll say goodnight, as usual."

"Very well, Miss," and he held out his hand timidly. She gave him hers. "It will do; yes, better. Goodnight, Miss Rachel; for *night* it will be."

He hurriedly kissed her hand, and repeated faintly, "Good-night!" and he walked quickly away along that front of the old house, and was lost to her sight, before she had quite recovered from the surprise of the strange familiarity, if anything so sad and timid could be so called, of his parting salutation.

"Poor Carmel! is he really going? And so grieved; he seems quite heart-broken. Has he heard any very bad news from his people at home? Surely he ought to tell us; papa might be of use, and advise him; and he ought to know that we all feel for him, and with him, in all his troubles."

So she murmured to herself, as, leaning from the window, she looked after the disappearing figure of Carmel Sherlock.

He walked round the two sides of the house, and by the small projecting tower, I may call it, in which his quaint apartment lay.

"What an oddity—poor old Carmel!" said she, with a little shrug and a smile, as he disappeared.

"Spirit of light and beauty!" said he, with a moan. "Henceforward for me, the long, dark winter of the north! The hour of flowers and of light I shall see no more."

Up and around he looked; he was taking leave of everything that night.

The front of the house, with the hall-door, and the winged demi-griffins keeping guard, with fierce crooked beaks, and talons, and expanded wings, were all in deep shadow by this time. He stood upon the steps—the door partly opened.

"What is the meaning of these things?" pondered Carmel Sherlock, whose mind like all others too strongly infused with fancy, was easily and powerfully diverted by any object that invited for the moment his imagination.

"These griffins, which heraldry has found—not created; the eagle, the lion—a combination whose origin goes back into mystery: an Assyrian image, proceeding, perhaps, from visions. What is its meaning—what is its force? What latent power and action on the world of spirits? See *here!* this great family of Shadwell—the Shadwells of Wynderfel; all through the County History growing greater and greater till they came here, and passed in and out between these carved dreams. Not a breath—not a sound—enters the door but through them; and how have they dwindled ever since! wane and waste!—peak and pine! Ha! what's that?"

"Well! what is it?" said Shadwell, surlily, who had nearly reached the doorsteps unperceived, on his return. "Perhaps it's I; will you allow me to get by?"

"I *saw* it, sir!"

"What did you see?" demanded Mark.

"I swear I saw it pass and enter the house!"

"Suppose we follow it," said Mark. "I think it did right at this hour."

"Only a shadow—a degree darker than the rest; your evil genius or mine; an influence, about no good—

*—Things that love night.*
*Love not such nights as these.*

"Do, pray, allow me to go in, or go yourself," said Mark Shadwell, looking much angrier than his words implied.

Carmel Sherlock drew back.

"One meets you everywhere, except where you are wanted. Don't you think you might sometimes look into the books upstairs; the accounts will be in a precious mess, if you do nothing but study the picturesque and see ghosts!" and so speaking, with an angry look at Carmel Sherlock—a look charged with violent and unspoken wrath—he entered the house.

"See, how angry he is; he can't help it. He does not see the cause; he only feels it—my benefactor!"

Carmel Sherlock hesitated at the threshold, and, with a shudder, entered, and went up alone to his room.

## Chapter 39
### Agnes in Her Bedroom

Miss Marlyn took a candle and went upstairs to her room. In the hall she passed the open door of the drawing-room, and from within, a gaunt figure beckoned her, silently with a smile; affecting not to see Sir Roke, she passed on, but he overtook her at the foot of the staircase.

"You did not see me?" said he, with the same smile, and in a very low tone.

She stopped short, and looked full on him with rather fierce eyes, and flushed cheeks, and said: "Yes, sir, I did."

"You did? Then you *cut* me! Cruel, isn't it?"

As he spoke, the baronet glanced back into the hall and up the stairs vigilantly.

"You said, sir—you promised, upon your *honour,* that you would speak to me no more during your stay at Raby. I don't much care—but if you will speak—speak aloud."

"I should not have spoken at all, had you deigned to smile as you passed," he said gallantly, and glanced again quickly, but no one approached; "why did you not come in for a moment to the drawing-room—I don't frighten you, I hope."

"You can have nothing to say, sir, you *know* you can't; do leave me at peace while you stay here; let me collect my thoughts, if I can."

"Well, you are a *very* odd—"

"Very odd, perhaps," she said, turning away to pass on.

"Yes, a most capricious and charming little witch," said he.

"Very common-place, perhaps. When I've made up my mind, though I suffer, I debate no more. If that is odd, it should not be so," she continued, taking no note of his parenthesis.

At this moment a distant step was heard, and Agnes went her way, and Sir Roke glided quietly again into the drawing-room, where, standing on the hearthrug, he looked up at his own distorted shadow, dancing over the ceiling, and the reflected flicker of the fire, on the distant cornices, with an unpleasant smile.

At times, indeed, this evidence of satisfaction was heightened to a quiet laugh; he had not been in such spirits since his arrival at Raby. He was disposed to be charmed with everything. It was a little excursion into savage life, and he liked the notion of roughing it, as in this case, without any essential sacrifice of comfort. He smiled, he laughed, it was no habitual homage to the genialities; but in his solitude, the expansion of a genuine comfort and elation. He even spoke peaceably that evening to Mr. Clewson.

He looked at his watch—still a quarter of an hour to wait. He rather enjoyed his dinner at Raby—country fare, and no French cookery, very odd, but a new sensation, and he was hungry, as invalids are oftener than they will always allow.

He thought he heard Mark Shadwell's step crossing the passage outside the door; he placed himself so as to see. It was Mark, returning from his walk. The guest was but dimly visible as he stood within, in the uncertain light of the fire. Mark saw him.

"Ha!" exclaimed Mark Shadwell, stopping short.

It was involuntary. He had not expected to see Roke Wycherly, who seldom descended from his dressing-room so early.

This faint "ha!" had in it something of the gasp with which a man might discover an escaped cobra unexpectedly on his hearthstone.

I think each would have been equally well pleased to have escaped this recognition. But Mark's ejaculation had been too loud, and the recognition was inevitable.

"Charming evening—delicious sunsets you have in this part of the world," said Sir Roke; "you have just the right quantity of vapour; your colouring is perfectly splendid. I don't know whether it is always so at Raby, or only that I am very much in luck. I wonder our artists don't study sunsets more than they do."

Mark had come into the drawing-room. The last faint flush had nearly died out in the west, and the flicker from the fire chiefly lighted up the room. It showed how pale his face was, and glittered on his fierce eyes, as he looked in a kind of abstraction on his guest.

"Sunset—yes," he said; "I suppose so. I never understood art, or whatever it is. I dare say we have."

"It was particularly beautiful this evening," said Sir Roke.

"Oh, yes, I do recollect. I believe it *was*. You're alone here? I hope I'm not very late."

He looked at his watch, and compared it with the clock over the chimney-piece.

"I believe it is *I* who am unusually early," said Sir Roke. "We had rather a good game last night; but you pigeoned me, Mark. Suppose you look in on me tonight, and give me my revenge?"

"No, thanks, no," said Mark, drily, and even sternly.

Mark's attempt to talk and look as usual had broken down. In that sort of accomplishment the more artificial man beat him easily. But had Sir Roke known the adventure of the little French writing-desk, and what awful eyes had peeped into his foolish little letters, the acting would not have been so easy.

"No, and why not? haven't I an equity—a sort of right to my

chance?" laughed Sir Roke, persuasively. The fact is, he reckoned upon the opportunity of the little game and conversation to remove the uncomfortable impression which he knew the surprise of that day had left upon the mind of Mark Shadwell.

"I'll *not* play tonight, thanks," he said, abruptly, and looked for a moment in Sir Roke's face, as if he meditated saying something unusual; but he checked himself, and added, only more in his accustomed way: "I've but a few minutes to dress—sorry to run away and leave you alone; but we shall all be here in two or three minutes."

And glancing again on the dial of the clock, as he might on the face of a man he hated, he disappeared.

Sir Roke leaned with his elbow upon the mantelpiece, and smiled into the old-fashioned looking-glass over it, and laughed a little.

"That fellow is perfectly wild, and ashamed to say what's the matter with him. He's great fun—delicious, isn't it? Trying to smile, pale with rage, he'd like to fire a bullet through my head; he's so jealous, and he dare not hint at the cause of his fury. Capital comedy! Inconvenient, perhaps; so we'll quiet him tonight—quiet him tonight—we must part peaceably."

Miss Agnes Marlyn meanwhile had gone up the stairs, and reached her own sequestered room. She shut the door, and candle in hand, surveyed her beautiful features in her modest looking-glass; a little flushed her cheeks were, unnaturally bright her eyes. She had never seen that expression in her face before— excited, defiant, a little wicked and handsome, with a peculiar beauty. The strange look of disdain and shame and triumph met her from the homely glass, and a feeling of admiration thrilled her, and she smiled with a baleful divination.

"Yes, you are beautiful," she whispered, looking sidelong on herself. "There's no one *so* beautiful, and beauty is power. Agnes! Agnes! *is it wise*? Yes, *she stoops to conquer*," she repeated with the same bitter smile, reciting the title of the play that lay open in the ragged little volume upon her dressing-table: "her little foot will yet rest upon the neck of the man who thinks he has subdued her. Yes, Agnes, what others have done without more cleverness, and with half your beauty, *you* shall do. There is a brilliant future."

A momentary trance and a sigh, and then she glanced at that homely little silver watch that recalled her present poverty, and it suddenly reminded her that it was now near the dinner hour, and then she made a rapid toilet; and crossing the floor with her candle in her hand, the light fell suddenly on the ruin of her little desk.

There were men and women, I dare say, on whose murdered bodies she could have looked with more composure than upon the fragments of that outraged desk.

Who had done that?

When Robinson Crusoe saw the footprint on the sand, and felt that his solitary dominion was invaded, and that perhaps the secrets on which his life depended were discovered, he was not, for the moment, chilled with so grim a horror.

"*Who* has done it?"

She stood erect, looking down on it motionless and pale, with a scowl of fear.

Could she have laid it on the mantelpiece, and the cat—that ubiquitous marauder—have knocked it down upon the hearth-stone?

The hypothesis was a momentary relief—momentary only—for she remembered well having returned as she was leaving the room that day, and unlocked it to read a sentence in one of her secret letters, the exact phraseology of which she had forgotten. She distinctly remembered the very spot on the table where she had left it locked.

"Good God! who has been here?"

She kneeled down and rummaged among the debris of the rosewood, broken glass, pens, little seals, keys, and the rest, for a second or two.

"Not a letter left. The villain!"

And up she started like a spectre, still staring on the ruin, and accidentally placed her hand upon the letters on the table.

"Oh! ho—ha; here they are," she gasped; and I think if her training had been at all different she would have said "Thank God!" She felt as if she were on the point of fainting.

"I see it all now, that stupid maid. Yes, Mary dropped it, and here she has placed the letters together."

As she murmured this comfort, smiling with pale lips, she raised the little packet of letters.

Alas! here was consternation anew. Miss Marlyn was one of those persons born with the genius of neatness, and no letter of hers ever returned to its berth in her desk unsheathed in its proper envelope. But here they were—all disarranged—a few in their envelopes. The greater part just doubled up as they had been laid down by the careless hand of the person who did not think it worthwhile, it seemed, to conceal the evidence of the outrage.

The three letters of Sir Roke Wycherly lay at the top of the little pile, all out of their envelopes, and one had plainly been crumpled together in a strong hand as if in anger.

Agnes Marlyn fenced with the conclusion no longer. The thing she had feared—the moment she saw the wreck upon the floor—was no longer disputable.

More accomplished sinners than she would perhaps have been little dismayed after a few minutes, and bethought them of a mode of darning their broken cobwebs. But Miss Agnes Marlyn had some attributes which rather marred her art. There was a fiery vein of passion in her nature; also there was an odd pride, which reared and shied at trifles, of which others would have made nothing. To deceive with her was easy. It was from the vulgarity and detail of clumsy mendacity that she recoiled. She would not construct a card castle of lies that might fall flat at any moment, and leave her stolen *bijouterie* exposed. Her lies were chiefly of reserve. She had not quite the evil humility for a system of positive falsehood; her arrogance recoiled from the risk of failure, and who was worth the degradation.

"Who is injured? *I* He thinks it fine and tragic, this outrage of a brigand. Oh, *quel gentilhomme!* I will not go down this evening."

She sorted her letters—after all they were not very many—she tied them up, and placed the little parcel under her pillow——

"I will keep guard over them here."

The dinner-bell rang; she heard it, and flushed suddenly with a flashing glance towards the door.

"The idea! To think that *I*, after *this*, should sit down at the same table!"

She did not collect or disturb the fragments of her little desk; she looked down upon them with a bitter smile.

"Let them be as he left them, to reproach a *robber*!" she said.

Then she sat down at the dressing-table.

Storm is not a term to describe the state of her mind. The analogy was rather in the lurid glow, the rolling smoke, and the sudden glare of a crater.

"Whatever vacillation there may have been, whatever chance, he has ended all."

Then came a knock at her door: it was a servant, to tell Miss Marlyn that the little party were at dinner.

Miss Marlyn had a headache, and could not leave her room.

A few minutes later Rachel came into the room. I don't know in what channel Miss Marlyn's thoughts had been running at that moment; but she rose very pale, and turned her large eyes on her companion, with a feeling like a shudder.

"Oh, *you*?" she murmured.

"Yes, Agnes, dear; you do look very poorly—you should lie down—can I do anything for you, you poor little thing?'

"Nothing, dear; *no*."

"I'll stay a little with you, at all events.'

"No, dear; don't stay!"

"But you do look so poorly—I *can't* leave you."

"You must leave me; yes, dear, you must," said Agnes Marlyn, in a cold, almost a repulsive tone.

"Is it really pain, dear Agnes; or have you heard anything that grieves you?"

"I've heard nothing—no news—pain is the shortest word."

"But are you vexed with me?" pleaded Rachel.

"Not the least, dear child—no—*pain* expresses it very well," said Agnes Marlyn.

"If you really mean pain, poor little Pucelle "

"Don't call me that—nor any other pet name," said Agnes, abruptly.

"Something has vexed you, dear Agnes, and I am sure you will tell me what it is; but if you are suffering—if it is pain—you must lie down."

"No—no—no, child; you're very good, but you bore me. I won't lie down; I shall remain here—and I shall remain alone. They'll wonder what detains you—pray go. By and bye, you'll hear me talked over, I dare say; you look at me as if I had two heads,"—Agnes laughed coldly—"but you will; and I don't care many pins what's said of me! It's well they can't hurt me, or dash me to pieces like *that!*" and she pointed, with a fierce and bitter smile, at her desk.

"Why, it's broken—your little desk—who did it?"

"Cowards!" said Agnes, with a quiet scorn.

"I can't make it out; what has occurred? who dared to break it? do tell me. You *must* tell me what has happened," exclaimed Rachel, shocked and excited.

"Pray go down, there's a dear girl, for I'm not going to tell you anything about it; no, not a word. I may, though, for I'm sure it will be a pleasant story. I shall choose my own time, however; and now I've said all I mean to say for the present—whatever my pain may be, solitude is the best cure for it. Goodbye!"

"You won't allow me to remain, then?"

"No!" said Agnes, decisively.

Rachel looked wounded.

"Very well, Agnes; will you allow me to send you some dinner here?"

"What a question! how it shocks the sentiment of the situation!" answered the young lady, mockingly. "No, Rachel, seriously, I have been startled, and made angry, made almost faint, and that kind of thing does not leave one much appetite—and pray do believe me, dear, once for all, I choose to be alone. I know you mean kindly, but I must insist on it, and so goodbye, or goodnight, or whatever you please to make it."

"Well, then, as you will have it so, I will go; but you'll allow me at least to send you candles, for you are very nearly in the dark?"

Agnes made no answer.

"And I'll run up and see you just now and again," she said.

Still the same ungracious silence.

"Goodbye, dear Pucelle; I hope I shall find you a great deal better."

And as Pucelle made no sign, after another little pause, Rachel Shadwell ran down the stairs again.

## CHAPTER 40
### BICKERING

The dinner party at Raby that night was not quite so small as you may have supposed; Miss Marlyn's place was unexpectedly filled by the vicar.

The Reverend Stour Temple had to call on his errands at out-of-the-way times, as his parish business and long circuits brought him to the doors where they were to be done, unseasonably. He did not enjoy his occasional dinners at Raby. The loving little party at home, with its quaint admirations and perfect harmony, contrasted sweetly with the gloom and comfortless severity of Raby. He had no hope, either, of being of any use to Mark. They never approached the one subject on which the vicar wished to talk with him without uncomfortable results. Mark was conceited and irritable, and, where his superiority was touched, insolent.

The vicar was too unbending—shall I say proud?—for his meek and patient calling; and, provided he spoke the thing that was true, he did not perhaps care sufficiently how or when. This great embassage is addressed to creatures weak, volatile, and violent; and needs a diplomacy the wisest, the most sensitive, the most patient. Perhaps, though the vicar was not conscious of it, the fault was not altogether Mark's, that, when they met, they parted no better friends, and with no progress made.

"Ho! Temple! I'm glad you're here; I'm *very* glad!"

"Many thanks! I've just been making inquiries and leaving a note—here it is—from my sister, with a message to Mrs. Shadwell."

"My wife sha'n't have the message from anyone but you; you shall deliver it yourself, and stay and help me to entertain Roke Wycherly."

"You are too good; but they expect me at home."

"The old excuse, but it sha'n't do now," said Mark, quickly.

"And another; I have not walked today, but ridden, so my poor pony stands, with his bridle fastened at the doorsteps; he has carried me twenty miles today, and awaits me, I dare say, impatiently enough."

"We'll make him comfortable here; we've room enough, I promise you, and though you mightn't suppose it, there is some corn and hay, and I undertake a comfortable supper."

"I'm afraid——" said the vicar, smiling, and shaking his head.

"Don't refuse me this time," said Mark, with an odd entreaty in his manner, which the clergyman observed, and the more that Mark was not very hard to put off with an excuse on ordinary occasions. It struck him that Mark had some special reason for pressing him. There was a little hesitation, and Stour Temple's dark eyes looked for a moment with a grave inquiry in his face.

"Yes, I see you will, you're going to stay; you *won't* refuse," said Mark Shadwell, and prevailed.

So the after-dinner *tête-à-tête* with Sir Roke Wycherly was avoided, and no wonder Mark Shadwell disliked it.

There was something excited, Stour Temple thought, in his host's manner, which suggested a suspicion of a quarrel; but Sir Roke's ease and gaiety rebuked the idea, and the vicar, still fancying that there was something wrong, did not know exactly what to think.

He was not a man, however, to be a bit put out by the suspicion of a quarrel, and he chatted quite as usual during dinner, and was glad to perceive that whoever else the persons in disgrace might be, Mrs. Shadwell and Rachel were just as usual.

Miss Marlyn, the only absent person, had a headache. Had Mark Shadwell taken some decided step respecting her, and was she about to leave Raby? Yes, Mark must have had a scene with her, and her headache was a result of it. He looked at Rachel's innocent and pretty face, and he was glad. He had an ill opinion of that beautiful Miss Agnes, and she knew it.

When the ladies departed, these three gentlemen began to talk. They were not well assorted. The vicar was not a flexible man, and Mark Shadwell was in one of his moods. So the conversation ran not smoothly on, but jolted and dragged, and made sudden starts and stops.

The baronet seemed in high spirits. He was amused, he was affable, he was gay. The vicar might have observed that Mark talked little to him, and that his eye was surly, though he did his office, as Sir Roke's host, rather ceremoniously—a coldness, an elevation which amused Sir Roke, I dare say, and the suspicion that it did so made Mark angrier. But the vicar was not a man of observation, and took no trouble to theorise on what he saw. His account to his sister was:

"Sir Roke was very chatty, and seemed better than when I last saw him; he leaves tomorrow. Mr. Shadwell was a little out of spirits."

"And Sir Roke goes away tomorrow?" said his sister.

"Yes, and I'm very glad he does."

"Glad, dear! And why glad?" asked his good sister, a little curious.

"I don't think that Raby is the kind of place that suits Sir Roke, I don't think he cares for their society."

"Dear me! and Mr. Shadwell so agreeable a man when he chooses."

"Very agreeable—as I am—in this out-of-the-way corner of the world; but not so agreeable, I am afraid, to a man who sees and hears clever men in the capitals of the world."

"But why are you glad he is going? That, I'm sure, is not your reason—I mean, your only one."

"You are right, dear, and I'll tell you my other this day twelve-month, if I remember it; sooner, perhaps, but not tonight."

At present, however, he is one of the party of three, and the conversation which devolves chiefly upon him and Sir Roke has just taken this turn:

"He was one of those fellows," said the baronet, "who are, by some people, emphatically styled gentlemen."

"Don't you think that's rather a vague term, now-a-days at least? It had a meaning, no doubt. Would you undertake to define it *now*?" interposed Mark Shadwell, suddenly. The vicar fancied a suspicion of a sneer in the question, and was rather confirmed by the lines of Mark's countenance as he asked it.

"It's too complex an idea for me," laughed Sir Roke, with a shake of his head. "Temple must give us his idea—do, pray."

"Don't you think old Chaucer has given us a fair outline of a gentleman? you remember:

*"A knight there was, and that a worthy man,*
*That from the tymé that he ferst began*
*To ryden out, he lovede chyvalrye*
*Trouthe and honour, freedom and curtesie,*
*At mortal battles had he ben fiftene,*
*And foughten for our feith at Tramassene.*
*And though that he was worthy, he was wys*
*And of his port as meke as is a mayde.*
*He never yit no vilonye ne sayde*
*In all his lyf, unto no maner wight,*
*He was a verray perfight gentil knight."*

The vicar concluded his little recitation, and Mark Shadwell repeated:

"*Truth and honour.* Yes, there's the foundation; what do you think of Temple's definition?"

"Not mine—Geoffrey Chaucer's," said the vicar.

"Yes, truth and honour; yes, to be sure, the basis—truth and honour," repeated Sir Roke, with a pleased acquiescence which provoked Mark Shadwell, who intended a sarcasm. "A very good picture of a gentleman, indeed."

"Considering it's so old," said Mark. "Don't you think we have improved upon it, however?"

He meant this for Roke, but the vicar answered in good faith:

"I don't think we have. Christianity and chivalry were the standards; we have Christianity still as the great social rule, but chivalry is but the shadow of a tradition—the two elements entered into the character of a gentleman, and the decay of one has not improved the combination. Don Quixote is very near my idea of a gentleman."

Mark Shadwell laughed low and sarcastically, looking at his wine-glass. I don't know what was in his mind, but Sir Roke fancied that he intended a ludicrous allusion to certain points of resemblance between him and the tall lank knight of La Mancha. It did not sting him. He thought he understood the motive, and Mark's malice amused him therefore. So said he to the vicar:

"Yes, as well as I recollect him, Don Quixote *is* a gentleman—that is, a gentleman gone mad."

"But the more mad he is, the more severely are his high qualities tested. If they stand that strain, they would stand almost any," said the vicar. "A man whose diseased imagination surrounds him with trials and temptations imaginary though they be-and comes through the ordeal pure, is a thorough gentleman; a mean man would break down under the trial. You see so many men, not actually mad, but hypochondriac, moping in out-of-the-way nooks, who fancy themselves ill-used, and their neighbours in league against them."

"Really, that's very amusing; and I suppose grow quite unlike your ideal?" There was a malicious twinkle in Sir Roke's eye as he said this that made the vicar pause, and perceive that he described a character not unlike his host's.

"Yes," he continued, a little put out, "the character requires so much—such elevation—temper no less than honour—that walking in the light which needs no concealment or deceit."

It was now Mark's turn to approve, and the vicar beginning to feel indistinctly that he was, in vulgar phrase, somehow "putting his foot in it," wound up by quoting Buckingham's fine lines on the death of Lord Fairfax:

*Both sexes' virtues were in him combined.*
*He had the fierceness of the manliest mind,*
*And yet the meekness, too, of womankind:*
*His soul was filled with truth and honesty,*
*And with another thing quite out of date.*
*Called modesty.*

And so the vicar's lecture ended; and Sir Roke observing that the clergyman suspected some uncomfortableness between him and his host, assumed at once a more frank and genial tone, and so ten or fifteen minutes more passed without any renewed symptom of disturbed relations between Mark Shadwell and the baronet.

## CHAPTER 41
### AN EXORCISM

In the drawing-room the Reverend Stour Temple found himself standing with his teacup in his hand beside Mark Shadwell.

Mark was looking down on the faded pattern of the carpet, lost as it seemed in a gloomy rumination; so that when the vicar, for want of something better to say, remarked: "Miss Marlyn has not made her appearance, I see," Mark Shadwell looked up with a vague smile from his sombre reverie, evidently not knowing what the vicar had said, and he therefore repeated his trifling remark:

"Oh no! a headache, I think, or some young lady's excuse."

"I know—yes," said the vicar.

"Oh, to be sure; she sent us word at dinner," said Mark; "I've been thinking about *that*," he added, after a pause, in a lower tone.

"About, do you mean, the "The——" Reverend Stour Temple hesitated, and Mark continued the sentence: "The letter you told me of, I—I'm thinking it over—I don't say that anything ought to be done in a moment—but I am."

The vicar inclined his head attentively as Mark spoke.

"I have," said he, after a sufficient pause to ascertain that Shadwell was not going to add anything, "a great objection to volunteering advice." The vicar had notwithstanding, I think, rather a weakness in favour of advising, and that, too, in a somewhat commanding tone. "It's only in cases where my duty distinctly imposes that task upon me that I ever venture it, and when I did so in this particular case, it was simply because I saw how grave it was, and how very much more serious it might become."

"Yes, I quite understand your view of it. I've been thinking over it; we'll see, and—and as usual I have other things to trouble me. Did you see Carmel Sherlock this evening?"

"No, I have not seen him—not for some time. He's quite well, I hope?"

"Oh yes. That is, as well as usual—always odd. you know. Either I am growing a greater fool than I used to be, or he's madder, for he makes me sometimes, in a lonely place like this, with nothing ever to cheer, and a great deal perpetually to press upon one's spirits—he makes me sometimes quite nervous—upon my honour!" And Mark laughed a little uncomfortably. "Not that I think him a witch, you know; but he has a knack of saying exactly the most unpleasant thing that it is possible to say—just the thing to jump with your own hypochondriac fancies, and to help this depressing place to make you nervous and miserable. Did you ever feel as if the devil had got about you?" and he shrugged and laughed again.

"The devil, unhappily, is about us all," said the vicar.

"Yes, yes, to be sure; that's the doctrine," acquiesced Shadwell. "By-the-bye, Temple, do you want timber for that barn-roof? I've found some I can cut, to thin the wood. I've a right to that, you know, though those agreeable fellows, my creditors, say I've no right to cut one of my own trees."

"Thanks, you're very good. I'll ask my people when I get home; but I rather think they've got the timber. Very much obliged to you, all the same."

"It's there for you, if you do want it, remember," said Mark. "Do you recollect some—let me see—five or six years ago, when you used to read some verses of the Bible and say a prayer, when you were here in the evening, before you went away?"

"I make it a habit everywhere, except where I am distinctly forbidden by the master of the house," said the clergyman.

"Yes, of course, you know, where there is no sympathy; but it came into my head to ask you tonight—I can't tell why; I should like it, though I can't go quite with you myself; *won't* you, tonight?"

"As I told you already, I need but permission," said the vicar.

"Can you. Temple, throw any light upon it?" interrupted Sir Roke's voice from the other side of the room. "Was there ever really such a lady as Pope Joan?"

So the vicar was called off to that odd chapter in history, and delivered his little essay upon it for the amusement of Mrs. Shadwell.

What was it that made the room more than usually gaunt and gloomy that night? Was there less light than usual? It looked so much too large for the people assembled there, and so dismal.

Miss Marlyn's absence, and the uncertainties and surmises which her slight excuse suggested to several of the party, who knew something more than others of real relations, were depressing, and everyone knows how contagious dejection, or even embarrassment, is.

"I've asked Temple to revive an old custom," said Mark Shadwell, a little later. "He used to read a few verses of the Bible before he left us, and, thinking it over, I'm sure it can do none of us any harm, and you always wished it. Amy."

She smiled. She looked so happy and grateful, that Mark Shadwell, had his nature, or even the moment, been different, would have been touched. It was a point on which she had often timidly pleaded, and been always brusquely overruled by her husband, who cursed the vicar's twaddle summarily, and told his wife she must go to church for that sort of thing, as he was resolved to have no more of it in *his* house. So now this sudden change seemed to her a concession, and she was full of wonder and gratitude at his goodness.

Mark Shadwell, I dare say, did not exactly himself know why he wished it. The violence of his agitations, and some thoughts that had crossed his mind that day, had shocked him. He was impelled, perhaps, to try what a sudden return to old associations might do for him. Perhaps, without his suspecting it, there was less of the metaphysical and more of the superstitious in it, and that he had a dim idea of his house requiring this sort of religious exorcism and fumigation.

Very small was the vicar's congregation—morally, however, in nowise more or less motley, I dare say, than any other assembled ostensibly to listen to the good words that fall from reading-desk and pulpit. In a different mood, Mark would have enjoyed what would have struck him as the ludicrous in the situation. Sir Roke submitted with an excellent grace. Like a polite man about to be bored by a well-meaning friend, he composed himself to the attitude of attention, and threw the reins, I suppose, on the neck of his fancy, and thought of what he pleased.

Mark, I think, really listened with a closer attention than his pride would have admitted.

The Reverend Stour Temple, with his Bible before him, delivered a brief lecture upon charity.

First, came Paul's beautiful and also terrible definition of charity, so hopelessly, as it seems, above human attainment, yet the ideal to which every man must, with all his strength, soul, and mind, aspire, or leave his heart open to the intrusion of those awful sojourners whose residence there is—death.

"*Out of the heart proceed evil thoughts—murders;*" and "*whosoever hateth his brother is a murderer.*" The *hater*, then, comes distinctly, in God's judgement, under the condemnation of the *murderer*; and what is the fate of the murderer?—"*All murderers shall have their portion in the lake which burneth with fire and brimstone.*" Seeing, then, the awful capaciousness of this term "murderer," it behoves each of us to search, with a fearful eye, and the clear lamp of an honest conscience, every neglected nook of his heart, lest one such frightful guest should lurk there. How mad one day's negligence in this respect! How thin the partition between us and the tremendous phenomena of eternity! *"Set thine house in order, for thou must die!"* The messenger comes *"as a thief in the night."* We all expect warning. But the language of God promises none— *"Thou fool! this day thy soul is required of thee." "Son of man, I will take away from thee the desire of thine eyes—at a stroke."*

And so on, till having concluded his little discourse, he took his leave, and Mark Shadwell accompanied him to the hall door. If Mark had been in his usual mood, his sense of the ludicrous would have found food enough that night, for when they reached the steps, from the half-open window of Carmel Sherlock's lonely chamber came the long-drawn quaverings of his Stradivarius.

"What sounds are those?" said the vicar, pausing, with his hand on his pony's mane.

"Nothing; only that queer fellow, Sherlock, making his horrible music," answered Mark, with a kind of dislike that had none of his usual briskness in it.

"Very weird, odd sounds! Has he a genius for music?" inquired Stour Temple.

"I don't know—I don't care, I mean; I suppose he has, but I hate the melancholy-caterwauling he keeps up there; that is, when I'm in specially low spirits, as I don't mind saying I am just now. I wish, Temple, you weren't going away—I wish you could stay here tonight."

Temple laughed, and shook his head.

"I'm serious—I assure you I am, and I rather liked your little sermon tonight; how do you know you mightn't do me some good, if you would stay?" added Mark Shadwell, with a dreary half-jocular entreaty.

"A thousand thanks for your hospitality, but it's quite out of the question; my poor sister, the most nervous being on earth when my hours are concerned, is sitting up for me, and I have tried her courage as much as I dare, in staying so long as I have; and I have got an early call to make in the morning, exactly in the opposite direction. So I must say goodnight, you see, and very many thanks for an evening which, for many reasons, I shall long remember with pleasure."

"Goodnight, Temple, since so it must be; we did not quarrel once tonight, for a wonder, did we? and I am, I assure you, very sorry to lose you."

And they shook hands much more cordially than they had for a long time, and Shadwell stood by his winged demi-griffin, looking after the receding shadow, that was losing itself in the deeper darkness of the trees that over-arch the avenue, and listening to the faint clink of the horse-shoe on the broad way. He waited till he heard the iron gate open and close, and the sound of the horse's hoofs growing more and more distant, till he could distinguish them no longer.

About the same time Carmel Sherlock's dismal minstrelsy quavered into silence, and looking up, Mark Shadwell saw him standing at the open window, leaning out, with his precious fiddle under his arm. He was looking towards the moon, which was beginning to rise, and towards it his other arm was extended and his fingers moved with an odd beckoning motion. Mark fancied that his face wore a fixed smile all this time.

In his then mood he beheld this greeting of his crazy steward with a strange sense of disgust. The last thing he would have chosen would have been a talk with Carmel Sherlock just then. He drew back, therefore, into the hall, and swung the massive door to with a heavy crash. The picture of Carmel, as he saw him last, stretching, in fancied solitude, from his turret window, and just touched by the dawning moonlight, gathering, as it seemed, its rays with his finger tips, and smiling with a sinister idiotism, remained with a strange tenacity ever after on his brain.

He walked back towards the drawing-room, and paused. There burned in that great wainscoted hall but a solitary candle, at which people lighted their bedroom candles which stood

216

there. He intended to go to his room, without again seeing Sir Roke. It was a small pleasure to him to inflict this rudeness of omission.

The smiling image of Carmel Sherlock was still before his retina as he pondered for a moment with his hand on the candlestick. "Every question," thought he, "is a dilemma for a poor man—a relief, in one sense, that Sherlock should go; but how on earth am I to get on without him?" Even to himself he did not like to admit that Sherlock was so good a bargain, and that great benevolence of which Carmel's simple gratitude made him a little proud, so commercially prudent, and, in fact, so selfish.

"Very good lecture Temple gave us tonight," said Sir Roke's voice near him.

"Yes, I believe so," said Mark, looking toward him.

"Quite intelligible, at all events," said Sir Roke, lighting his candle; "but they are very odd people—our clergymen, aren't they? They talk always as if they had the direction of death and damnation, by special appointment, in their own hands, and seem to forget that they are subject to both like other mortals, and that their warnings and threats apply to themselves with at least as much force as to their auditors. By the bye, won't you come in just now, and have our little game of piquet in my room?"

"I'm afraid I can't manage it tonight," said Mark, coldly.

"You've been carrying all before you, you know; you owe me a chance; though, you are so deep—I mean scientific—that I'm afraid a shallow poor devil like me has no chance with you."

Mark fancied an under-meaning and an irony in this speech. There may not have been any, Sir Roke's smile was never very genuine. Mark's glance fixed for a moment obliquely and sternly on those insincere eyes of the baronet's, and he said: "Well, as you seem to make a point of it, perhaps I shall."

"That's right—that's friendly; I don't think, really, I could sleep, now, without my little game first, I've so got into the way of it," said Sir Roke, passing on, and up the stairs with a little nod, and a smirk over his shoulder.

# CHAPTER 42
## VIOLINA

Mark Shadwell knocked at the door of his invalid wife's room; she was in her dressing gown, sitting up in her bed, as she held her accustomed consultation with old Wyndle, when he came in.

"Don't send her away—don't interrupt," said he, "I'm in no hurry; in fact, I have next to nothing to say."

Shadwell took up a little book with 1641 on the title-page— George Herbert's poems, which he knew not, and opening it at haphazard, he read:

> *As I one evening sat before my cell.*
> *Me thought a starre did shoot into my lap,*
> *I rose and shook my clothes, as knowing well,*
> *That from small fires, comes oft no small mishap.*
> *When suddenly I heard one say,*
> *Do, as thou usest, disobey,*
> *Expel good motions from thy breast,*
> *Which have the face of fire, but end in rest.*

He had no sneer now for this, as he might a day or two before. He had been fooled by another, and might possibly, in this graver matter, have been fooling himself. His vanity was prostrate for a time, and his confidence in himself had received a shock. How many "good motions" had he "expelled from his breast!" Well, here, at last was a good motion he was about to act on. He would not "disobey," as he was wont. But *was* the "motion" celestial, though its effect might be so? Did it not, on the contrary, proceed from jealous fury, revenge, and wounded pride? I believe, notwithstanding, that Shadwell thought he was about to act from cold, stern principle here, and rather respected himself therefore.

He turned over and read:

> *Come away.*
> *Make no delay.*
> *Summon all the dust to rise,*

*Till it stirre and rub the eyes;*
*While this member jogs the other,*
*Each one whispering,*
*"Live ye, brother?"*

"Ay, ay, the resurrection; grant us that, and doomsday, and a great deal follows," muttered Shadwell, with a dejected scoff.

"Goodnight, Wyndle," said Mrs. Shadwell.

Mark looked a sullen farewell, and nodded in reply to old Wyndle's courtesy. He got up and shut the door, and said he, not sitting down, but leaning, with his elbow on the chimney-piece:

"I came intending to say—or rather to ask you—whether you think—that Miss Marlyn."

He stopped—he had not shaped his sentence well—and was near saying more than he had quite made up his mind to say.

"Miss Marlyn! Is there anything unpleasant, Mark dear?" exclaimed she, in great consternation.

"Well, it is only this—I have been seriously turning it over in my mind whether we should have her here any longer; and, in fact, I have pretty nearly made up my mind to part with her."

Mrs. Shadwell gazed at him in a sort of alarm.

"Yes," he continued, "all these things cost money, and I really don't see what good she is doing here; I'm sure she's teaching Rachel nothing. I doubt whether so young a person has often learned enough to *have* anything to communicate, and certainly she can't have the authority of an elder woman."

Mark was already faltering in his purpose. An hour ago, he had made up his mind to dismiss the young lady peremptorily. He meant to tell his wife that he had reason to believe that Agnes Marlyn ought not to be harboured in their house, and to support this by relating Stour Temple's story. He knew that this step would irrevocably commit him to dismiss her, and now was not quite equal to the task of plucking out the offending right eye, and casting it from him. At a distance, even a little one, he thought the effort would cost him nothing. But now that he had come up to it, he quailed.

"Well, Mark, darling, I hope you have very much underrated what Agnes Marlyn has actually done for her. She certainly has improved her playing wonderfully, and she speaks French quite fluently now. Have you tried her lately?"

Mark felt the inconsistency of his answer.

"No, not very lately; but generally, I mean, I am not satisfied. I think they spend their time dawdling about the place, and I dare say Miss Marlyn does just whatever best pleases Rachel, and you know there is no money to throw away, and I thought I'd tell you what I was thinking about—what I *am* thinking about—though I shan't discuss it tonight." He spoke this as brusquely as if she had combated his authority. "I'll tell you more—tomorrow, perhaps. Goodnight Amy," he said, abruptly and calmly enough.

When he had reached the door, Mark Shadwell suddenly relented, and returned to his wife's bedside.

"You haven't been looking well tonight. Do you feel better. Amy?"

"A little tired; but it won't be anything, thank you, dear Mark."

"Better now, aren't you?"

"Oh! much, since I lay down. And now tell me, Mark, darling, how *you* are. I'm so anxious. You have been looking miserably all this evening."

"*I?* I did not know—not worse than usual, I suppose? But I shouldn't wonder."

"Yes, indeed, and very careworn, my poor Mark. I have been very unhappy about you."

Mark looked at her first with a dark sort of doubt, and then laughed faintly.

"I'm not going to die, or drown myself Amy. After all, I take pretty good care of myself; nothing can happen me that will not reach us all pretty equally. I'm worried, of course—always that; but not ill—at least, that I know of."

"I was so afraid there had been some ill news—something very bad threatening; but there's nothing."

"No, nothing particular—nothing. Sometimes one's spirits go down. Everyone feels that. You can't control your spirits— they are sometimes worse than at others. Everyone knows that sort of thing. I sometimes wish. Amy—that is, I'd give something I could believe all that." He tapped with his finger the Bible that lay on the little table by her bed. "But believing, unluckily, isn't a matter of choice any more than loving. No—I assure you there's nothing bad—nothing, in fact, whatever, but just a sort of fore- boding that makes me fancy I should like to have something to go upon—I mean *belief,* idolatry—anything. But," he said, with another little laugh, which she fancied was intended to cover a more serious meaning, of which, perhaps, he was half ashamed, "I dare say *you* pray for me, Amy, and that is better. Goodnight, dear." And he kissed her, and departed.

With a solitary candle burning in his odd darksome room, the window opened wide, and a broad slanting moonbeam making a great diamond-shaped diagram of light on the floor, the still landscape lying broad and misty under the moon, vis- ible through the open casement, and the chill night air floating softly in and out, and waving the candle-flame faintly, our friend Carmel Sherlock was passing the hour in a feverish listlessness.

That night his fiddle—I beg pardon, his Stradivarius—would not play exactly what he wished, but seemed to take the control of the music, and by an irresistible influence to draw his bow and infuse odd vibrations into his elbow, which resulted in such wild, shapeless, and lamentable melodies as half startled the crazy fiddler himself.

"Hal ha! That was good!" he would say, with a start; holding his Stradivarius up suddenly, and looking it in the face, so to speak, with a suspicious smile . "*I* could not do *that.* It wasn't I. No. Ha! ha! You think I don't know when it is you and when it is *I.* Bravo, Cremona! Bravo, Stradivarius!" and with a scowling smile he shook the bow, which he held upright over his shoul- der, at the fiddle. "You or I *master?* You're growing too much for me—a man who floats on passion—without a will; a nota- ble victory, forsooth! 'I'd smash you sometimes, only you sha'n't think you can frighten me. I think you are panting a bit, are you? Well,, hang there a little while, and recover from your epilepsy, poor little lost thing! Who knows—who knows?"

I don't know whether Carmel Sherlock ate opium. His face had that night the peculiar pallid sheen which De Quincy describes as the special symptom of the ecstasy so attained to. A homelier poison for the nerves was on his table—potent green tea—cold, Chinese fashion; no milk, no sugar, the cup of madness!

A tiny cup of old cock-china, and a cracked and venerable little teapot of the same date: these old-world things he picked up where he could, and treasured and loved to live among them; they kept his fancy stirring, and tinted and shaped his dreams. Tiny as was the teacup, if you had sipped its measure, once filled with the awful elixir which was his habitual solace, it would have covered your darkness with gliding pictures, bereft you of sleep for a night or two, and introduced you to strange quakings. When I look at that old teapot replenished with its fatal infusion, standing on his table, I think I see, not a teapot, but Carmel Sherlock's magic-lantern.

"I think I've found out your secret," said he, with a laugh, and an odd cunning in his glance. "Dark, is it? There is illumination here. *Books.*"

Standing before his bookshelves, he was gently tapping the backs of the tomes with the end of his fiddle-stick. "What"— looking all the time askance at his *Stradivarius* suspended from a nail like one of Bluebeard's beauties—"What says Virgil?

*Nam, quæ prima solo ruptis radicibus arbour*
*Vellitur, huic atro liquuntur sanguine guttæ,*
*Et terram tabo maculant—*
*—gemitus lacrymabilis imo*
*Auditur tumulo, et vox reddita fertur ad aures.*

"Not Violino—Violina, are you?—*feminine,* wilful, hysterical. Ha! *Traitresse*—beloved, mysterious Violina—have I touched the secret of your birth? Wince and tremble—tremble and wince.

Yes, it is in the old, old legend, as untraceable in the days of Augustus as now. Ah! Violina, my companion, beautiful fiend! You are *detected*. Listen, tremble. No one hears, only you and I. Again in Dryden's verses:

*I pulled a plant; with horror I relate,*
*A prodigy so strange and full of fate.*

"Hearken! How foolish you look and guilty! Ha, ha, ha! You would have lived with me, and had my ear, and passed for nothing but an undesigning frame of wood, would you? Clever Violina! Listen! Ha, ha, ha! Ay, my mistress, to lead me on and on to Bedlam. Hearken:

*The rooted fibres rose; and from the wound,*
*Black bloody drops distilled upon the ground,*
*Scarce dare I tell the sequel: from the womb*
*Of wounded earth, and caverns of the tomb,*
*A ——*

"A—a *what*? Oh, Violina, listen! For I know you. Come—come, don't you? By heaven! you do look paler. Well, well, listen:

*A groan, as of a troubled ghost, renew'd,*
*My fright, and then these dreadful words ensued!*

"Now if you could speak, you'd say, 'Thank God! though he came *near* to finding it, he has not got the key of my mystery in his fingers yet !' Be not too sure of that, sweet wayward Violina I Come—come—rest, poor thing—rest awhile. But you would say, '*Nay, let me hear all now?*' I know your face so well; did I not see you smile once? Ay! I was a novice then—I dropped you, in horror, on my bed—and was afraid of you for five weeks after. Heigho! it has been an odd life. But come—come—why this *shame*! Foolish Violina, don't you see I am no more your dupe—the thing's impossible. I know you, shy Violina; say you see the eye of a corpse move, its face change into a fixed smile for two minutes time, with a meaning—a meaning suited to *your* thoughts; it is a corpse no more, but a devil. Ha, ha, ha!

found out, eh? In the wood of the tree—in the wood of the tree. How deep the root goes—and I so tired.

*Non era ancor di la Nesso arrivato.*

"Hark! listen! I say—it's coming.

*Quando noi ci mettemmo per un bosco,*
*Che da nessun sentiero era segnato;*
*Non frondi verdi, ma di color fosco;*
*Non rami schietti, ma nodosi e'nvolti*
*Non pomi v'eran, ma stecchi con tosco—*

"There it is—the forest—an infernal metamorphosis. The same thing only worse; not the tap roots only, but stems, boughs, foliage, all in hell. Dante's forest of suicides—trees that bleed, and moan, and speak; damned spirits—and *forever* is such a long time. Poor Violina! no such wood for a fiddle. Ha! rest now—rest. The ancient bidding—turn your face to the wall."

With tender solicitude he turned the fiddle softly with its face to the wall, whispering, with a frown of dark compassion: "Rest—rest—rest."

Then again to the open window he went, and looked out, long and in silence; kneeling with his elbows on the window-stool, and his chin resting on his hands. Oh! what a draught of moonlight, sweet, night air, sad and mysterious landscape, deserted of all living. Awful, lonely, beloved; darkness so soft, and lights so dim. In that imperfect light all vulgarities and unsightly things vanish, and the beloved scene presents the image of the dead—who are beautiful and purified by distance, and the dim medium of memory.

## CHAPTER 43
### MYSTAGOGUS

Half an hour passed, I dare say, in that sort of dream, and the moonlight seemed to grow insupportably pure, and the night air—like the water to the swimmer—met his breast with the thrill of a delicious shudder. So a solitary happiness stole over him, the most melancholy and serene—like that of a man who is about to make the last great venture, and die; and has already taken leave of all his miseries and complications.

"Henceforward you are my Ægeria—a phantom only; I shall see you in my solitude and darkness—a picture of light; I shall hear your voice, like notes of distant music, but no more conflict; the tumult of hope for ever over, and this wild heart is quiet; the first death has passed, and all now is remembrance—

*There are brains though they moulder that dream in the tomb.*

With this quotation Carmel Sherlock got to his feet again, took his pipe, and charged it with the biting tobacco he liked, and lighting it, and lighting his second candle also, read and smoked by the light of his candles. Read what? It happened to be the Bible—the Old Testament, for its poetry, philosophy, and profound knowledge of human nature—to him it was no revelation—all *man's* work—but even so, it was tranquillising and elevating. The fruit of the tree of life, we know, is for believers, but its *leaves are for the healing of the nations.*

He dipped into the Psalms; he turned over to Isaiah; and then passed away into the Cyclopean sublimities of Job.

He read, and smoked, and pondered; and came at last to a passage which lighted up his frowning face with a smile:

*This is the portion of a wicked man with God, and the heritage of oppressors, which they shall receive of the Almighty." "Though he heap up silver as the dust, and prepare raiment as the clay; He may prepare it, but the just shall put it on, and the innocent shall divide the silver." "The rich man shall lie down, but he shall not be gathered: he openeth his eyes, and he is not. Terrors take hold on him as waters, a tempest stealeth him away in the night.*

These grandly sinister words applied themselves; as he read them, each sentence seemed to rise up and point a weird finger at the man he feared and hated—wicked and wealthy. Again and again, over and over, he read them, till they seemed to gain slowly a power over him, and, with a gasp, he started from a dream that frightened him, and hurriedly he turned over the pages, and looked slowly about him; round upon the strange furniture and decorations of his crooked and dimly-lighted room, through the open casement once more upon the wide dreamy landscape, and then upon the dial of his Dutch clock, whose diligent ticking, exaggerated by the silence, was the only sound audible. He raised the candle to it and looked. It was near one o'clock. His eye glanced on the Stradivarius—Violina, with her face to the wall. He did not care, just then, to remember that she was there, and averted his glance quickly—was ever solitude so utter?

These ancient writings, which used to soothe him, like his narcotic weed, were failing him tonight. He turned back and read, after many others, this passage:

*Then a spirit passed before my face; the hair of my flesh stood up: it stood still, but I could not discern the form thereof: an image was before mine eyes, there was silence, and I heard a voice saying——*

As Carmel Sherlock read these words he raised his eyes, and they happened to rest upon the door, which now stood wide open, and a figure was there observing him.

It was Miss Agnes Marlyn, pale, with her candle in her hand, and gazing on him with large steady eyes. Carmel Sherlock rose to his feet, returning her gaze. I don't think he was quite sure that he did not see a spirit. He raised the candle, and stared at her in a way that, at another time, would have made her laugh. But now she did not smile. She looked pale, like himself, and only said "Hush!" and raised her finger warningly.

"Miss Marlyn!" he whispered.

"Yes; may I come in? or will you come to the door for a moment? I dare not speak aloud."

"Come in, yes. She's Miss Marlyn—these lights are flaring-you are not afraid."

He glanced at his fiddle, lying very quiet with its face to the wall. "Young ladies are afraid of ghosts sometimes—*I* used to be, but long habit, and," he looked along the floor, "never seeing them, don't encourage it—it's a fancy that might steal you out of your senses."

"I have come to you, Mr. Sherlock, to ask a kindness—a great favour—you did me one once."

"Yes—I know—in that thunderstorm, when I brought that letter for you to the post, and so, between us, we've brought not a man, but a vampire into the house."

"You were true to me *then*, Mr. Sherlock—in God's name, be true to me *now*! It's only a trifle, and there is not a soul in the house I can trust but you; I have not a friend."

"You are talking to a dead man; I'm no one's friend."

"I know you are kind, I know you are true; you can be a friend where one is needed; what I ask is, I assure you, but a trifle; promise me this, at least, that if you refuse me—which I hardly think possible—you won't tell anyone what my request was?"

Carmel Sherlock looked at her with a shrewd and shrinking glance, and walked across the room, looking down on the floor; and having stood for a minute at the open window, he returned, and said:

"If it has no relation whatever to Miss Rachel Shadwell—I—may."

"None; it's only a note, and I swear to you, it has no reference—not the slightest—to Miss Shadwell."

"Yes—yes—she says true; I remember—a note—go on."

"Just this—I'm making a great confidence, but I know you won't betray me; and even if I were not sure, I cannot choose, I must place myself in your hands."

"Fear nothing; there was a heart there," and he knocked his clenched hand at his breast, "now there's a stone. I don't know why I asked that question—no—go on—*nil admirari*."

"I want this note delivered tonight."

Was she ashamed, or afraid? I don't know which, as thus speaking, in a lowered voice, she hastily placed a little note in Carmel Sherlock's open hand. He turned frowningly to the candle, and, having read its address, turned ashy pale.

"Who put this in your head?" he said, with a ferocious and

horror-stricken stare. "Did you dream it—or *how?*"

"I don't know what you mean!" she answered very honestly.

"You are beautiful—yes; see how her colour comes and goes, with the beauty of a young Venus—warm, crimson blood—and beautiful shame. Listen to me: what put it in your head? I say there's foul play here. Everything pushing me on!"

It seemed to her that he trembled and looked faint. Her patience was on the verge of breaking down altogether, but she controlled her anger, for the case was urgent, and Carmel her last hope, although, as she said, the service was slight.

"Beautiful?—yes; the *genii* came in different shapes—a serpent, a boy, an old man, a girl. Is any man on earth so perplexed as I?"

"I implore of you," she whispered earnestly, "to give this tonight, without fail, into his own hand; and I trust all to your honour, no one on earth but you and he must know."

"Don't mind your dreams," he said, in a whisper. "Dreams are not sent from God, nor caused by him, but must be demoniacal, since nature is demoniacal, not divine. Come, come, don't *you* enter into the conspiracy."

"You can't suppose I understand one word of what you say," she said at last, a little fiercely; "I ask you, once for all, to deliver that note tonight. You must know *I* can't, and I have told you I shall be ruined if you don't."

"If you had said travel fifty miles before morning, I should have tried; but to Sir Roke Wycherly's door—until the sun has risen—I will *not* go. Why will you trouble me? I was serene."

"You won't give it tonight? Oh! won't you, Mr. Sherlock?"

"I won't give it tonight! What temptation is this, and whence do you come? I say *no!*"

"It ought to have reached him before nine o'clock tonight, I had promised it, and my silence he is to read as *no*, and he' is odd and violent. He may never forgive it. Oh! Mr. Sherlock, think; I can't, I won't do it myself, and if it is not done, what is to become of me? An enemy has read my letters—*there!* I've told you—and has learned that which he may use to ruin me, and there is no one to help me but that one bad man, Sir Roke Wycherly; don't you see how madly I trust you? and you won't help me, in a matter to me impossible, but for you as easy as to walk to that window. Oh, Mr. Carmel! Mr. Sherlock, *think!*"

"Yes, easy—*facilis decensus*—evil has come to many, in many shapes—you are warped by some dream—you have had a dream tonight—I don't believe in any exorcism—no, no, no!—they are too strong for us."

"Oh, Mr. Sherlock! do, for God's sake, do give him the note tonight!" She stamped, and wrung her hands in her anguish.

"How she persists! How cruel they all are! Take this with you then—the thing's *impossible!* Short is the way, but a gulf between us! False sibyl! you say, step boldly. What of the abyss? Have not the spirits charge over thee, in their hands to bear thee up, lest thou dash thy foot against a stone, and return blood-stained? Listen to your words, and say, are not they the song of a devil? No, no, you shall *not* prevail, beautiful Miss Agnes Marlyn! And you have lifted up the curtain, and showed me that other image. Oh, Rachel! Rachel! Rachel! See what a wreck she would make; this Ariel of the storm, flaming amazement, she knows not, or cares not, to what purpose."

Without another word, her beautiful eyes flashing, she extended her hand.

"Patience!" he said, "only a moment, I'll give it to you, if you like, but listen first; this is reason, this is business. He's asleep now! he's asleep! I—I *know* it! Look there, it's past one o'clock! he's asleep by this time, and I promise this, the edge of the sun shall not have appeared above that upland there in the morning one minute before I place it in his hand—don't be so crazy, young lady! if you're mad, I'm not." And with these stern words he darted a lowering glance at Miss Marlyn.

"Well, perhaps, *yes*; *do* so, we shall see." With these words she turned, and was leaving the room with a light and quick tread, but she stopped, and said: "Mr. Sherlock, I was going without thanking you; I *do* thank you, pray forgive me; but I am agitated and miserable, farewell!—and oh! do not fail me!" She clasped her hands, and looked on him for a moment with such eyes as are raised in shipwreck, and then was gone quickly.

Sherlock followed to the door, and listened with a raised hand and wide-open eyes.

"Not a sound! not a step! not a breath!" Then he paused again for awhile, listening.

"Foiled? ha, ha, ha! Well that the thought came as it did—ah, spirit, you hear me now?—God! what have I seen? What is a mortal creature among them? If a good angel—*come*, oh quiet, quiet! If an evil one, lead away into the desert. Oh, that I had wings like a dove! then would I flee away and be at rest. Can any man escape his destiny?"

So he closed the door.

"Ah, Menander! you say truth:

*Unicuique homini statim nascent*
*Adest Dæmon vitæ mystagogus.*

He looked round his strange room, stealthily, as if expecting to see the mystagogus of his life revealed; and then, sighing, he leaned his head upon his hand.

## CHAPTER 44
### SIR ROKE'S LAST NIGHT AT RABY

Mark Shadwell was in his study. It was all over between him and his secretary. It was all over, too, with his dream of a great alliance for his daughter. If he had been left to the dismal tenor of his life, if his vanities had not been excited, his ambition awakened, the hell of this reaction would have been spared him. Here he was deluded—insulted; alone with the worm and the fire—his despair and his fury.

Around him, on thin old oaken shelves, stood, tier above tier, the dusty tomes, some of which had furnished the now roof-less library of Wynderfel—before the Shadwells had migrated, in an evil hour, to Raby—all old enough, and some no doubt curious; but Mark troubled them but little. The nimble spiders spread their nettings across the shelves, and the tiny book-worm was busy with their pages, and heavy drifts of dust lay thick over their buried wit and wisdom. Mark was not a reading man at any time, but just now reading, or even thinking, was quite out of the question. There was only the dull pain of an inexpiable insult and the feverish yearning for revenge.

It was a kind of pleasure to Mark Shadwell, collecting every sheet of Miss Marlyn's writing, copied law papers, copies of letters, and tearing them resolutely into the smallest fragments and throwing them into the grate; and when not a fragment remained unsacrificed, he continued pacing the floor. Whatever his mind was revolving, he was as much startled when a knock came to the door as Carmel Sherlock was that night when Miss Marlyn appeared at his.

It proved to be his wife, wrapped in a dressing-gown.

"Ah! you?—why, what can have brought *you* here?" said Mark, recovering from his surprise.

"I couldn't sleep, Mark, till I came and told you that you are to do whatever you think best as to parting with Agnes. I shall be very sorry—but I know how harassed you are—and I think, Mark, you do her injustice."

Mark was inattentive as she spoke—preoccupied with his own agitating thoughts—but her last phrase rang upon the very nerve that tortured him—like a sentence heard by a man half asleep, without its context, and applied to his dominant idea without thought of improbabilities. Her husband darted a glance of suspicion upon her face. But that face was frank, earnest, and noble.

He was disarmed. He was silent for a time, a transient but vivid pity touched him for a moment. He took her hand and kissed it.

"I'm glad you came, darling, very glad. We can talk of all that another time—but I *am* very glad you came—though you mustn't stay longer, the room is cold—you must get to your bed, you must indeed. God bless you, darling."

He accompanied her to the door, at which he remained standing for awhile. At the foot of the great staircase she smiled and kissed her hand. He bid her goodnight again, with a strange gloomy smile, and waited till that faded apparition and the light of her candle had quite disappeared.

"I am—*very* glad," he repeated, stepping back into the room. "It would not have done had I gone to Roke's room. I might have said more than I intended; his sneering coolness would have led me on, and now I'll secure myself."

He locked his door on the inside, and placed the key in his *escritoire*, which he locked also.

"And now, Master Roke," said he, "I must think twice before I visit you; whatever accident brought her down to see me, she has saved me that annoyance—saved me from, perhaps—from something *very* bad."

Mark began to feel the nervous reaction which follows upon the subsidence of the malignant emotions. He had been talking to himself in the solitude of this room, and in the silence his own words seemed still to haunt his ears, like a dialogue of other voices urging him on.

He sat down by the smouldering fire, and leaning back in his chair, he closed his eyes. But there was that about him which scared away sleep. Now and then he muttered with a kind of abhorrence, "No, *no*, let him go—*let* him go."

And sometimes he would open his eyes, and look for a moment at the door, and then at the *escritoire*, with the keys of which his fingers in his pocket were playing, and then back again at the door, and so once more at the *escritoire*; and then, with a sudden shrug, like a shiver, he would start up, and walk about the room, and read the names on the backs of the old books, and so wander about for awhile, and then sit down again, looking ruefully into the embers; and then he would look at his watch—half past twelve, only!—and wonder how slowly the time lagged. And then, after a time, the same sort of thing would occur over again, and Mark Shadwell once more was wandering restlessly about his room; and he looked at his watch. It was now a little past one.

✦✦✦✦✦✦✦

Sir Roke Wycherly was in gay spirits that night. He amused

himself, thinking of his cousin Mark.

"The beast!" he thought. "He's quite wild about this little romance of ours. He has been bullying that pretty little rogue; there has been a row. I suppose he has put her in a devil of a passion—he'll not find it easy to frighten her, though—and her little *billet* has not come; it will, though. Mark won't come, quite past his hour, now, and I shouldn't wonder if my little note reached me, somehow, after all's quiet." And he smiled slyly and pleasantly towards the door. "I may as well wait a little—yes, and we'll get that fellow, Clewson, out of the way. Poor wretch! he does look awfully tired. I forgot him last night, and we are to be off tomorrow, and there's a great deal to do."

He was accounting to himself, good-naturedly, for getting Clewson out of his way. The well-trained Clewson did look a little surprised at this considerate dismissal. Glad he was to receive it, however. He made two or three trifling arrangements very quietly, and withdrew, and got to his bed, where he quickly fell asleep.

"Yes, poor devil! we'll do without him tonight; and—hey? was that a step? No—no—fancy."

He listened, notwithstanding, for a minute; and he got up very quietly, opening his door softly, and smiling up and down the gallery, with the candle high above his head; but all seemed quiet, and, so far as the light reached, was deserted.

"Not yet—not yet—I wager my life, it will be, though; only a word—a little bit of paper no bigger than a card."

By this time he had again closed the door, and was standing in his dressing-gown, by the card table, where lay the pack with which he and Mark were to have fought their battle—not their great one.

"If he had only come—I wish he would—a fellow in that plight is always amusing, and a little bit of quiet comedy would not have been amiss tonight—and that charming little woman. She would not have popped in her note at the wrong moment— far too clever to put her pretty little foot in it—and, egad! no great harm if she did. We shall be all far enough tomorrow, and the curtain goes down on a strong situation and a spirited tableau."

Then Sir Roke listened again, and again there was nothing. And he bethought him of a letter to that Pepys, Adderly, to whom he had written before, to expect him at Scarbrook. He wrote:

My dear Adderly,

I have next to nothing to add to my last letter, except that you may take as absolute, all that I then described as *probable*, respecting the little romance which has amused and piqued me for some time. I am going to town, as I said, tomorrow, and I sha'n't leave for Scarbrook till Wednesday; but your charming married niece, Mrs. Hyde, will reach Scarbrook, with her maid, on Thursday morning. You need not tell the people there that I'm coming down. I shall appear, simply by accident—you don't expect me—no one expects me. I think I have said quite enough. Make your niece, of course, as happy and comfortable as possible— but very quietly, please. I sha'n't stay there myself a week, and I shall be off before it becomes known; and now the whole plot is before you, and do pray be on the alert, and attend to these few plain directions.

Ever, dear Adderly, yours sincerely,

R. W.

Roke Wycherly shut up his letter and sealed it. "And now, I think all's ready," said he, lifting his hands with a little wave, like a man who has completed a piece of work and means to enjoy himself and rest. And then he listened again, but there was nothing—and he yawned.

"It will come before half an hour," said he. "What an affectation! The little gipsy fancies her hesitations impose upon me. Well, we must amuse them—why not a note, if she likes it?— only I'm growing uncomfortably sleepy. Hang their caprices, they *are* so selfish, one and all."

Sir Roke took up his *French Review*, but it made him yawn

more; and then, with his handkerchief, he touched his temples with *eau-de-cologne*, and then he looked at his watch that he had placed on his table, and muttered an execration upon the tortoise-pace of time—irrevocable time!

Too slow for you, its flight, Sir Roke! Is it?

And then growing peevish, he got up and opened his door again, and listened, and gaped dismally up and down the empty gallery.

You remember the passage in Faustus:

> *Mephistopheles.      I am not free; a little obstacle,*
> *I did not see, confines me—*
> *Thedruid foot upon the threshold traced.*
> *Faustus.      The Pentagram?"*

Sir Roke closed his door gently, but with a cross and dismal face. Again he looks at his watch. A quarter-past-one! And he sits down, and takes up his *French Review* again, and reads and nods, and reads a little more and nods again, and drops asleep in his easy-chair, with his back towards the door, and all became quite still and silent.

Pity, Sir Roke, no pentagram was traced upon your threshold.

Sir Roke's bedroom opens upon the great gallery, and in the same chamber, in the further wall, another door gives access to a dressing-room, beyond which, again, lies Mr. Clewson's bedroom, which opens upon a lobby at the head of the back-stairs.

Mr. Clewson was fast asleep. But the habit of attending his master's call at all hours throughout the night made his sleep light.

He was startled from it now by a sound from his master's room. It was a crash as if of something thrown with violence upon the floor, and broken to pieces. He sat up in his bed listening, and heard a furious gabbling, in which he fancied he distinguished the words "God" and "wretch." The whole thing hardly lasted a minute, and suddenly subsided.

Mr. Clewson, not knowing what to make of it, glided out of

his bed, and into the dressing- room. There was always a candle burning at night in the dressing-room, for if Sir Roke happened to want additional light, he was not a man to wait while his servant was groping for matches. Clewson took this candle in his hand, but there was light visible through the keyhole, and Sir Roke did not call him. He listened at the door, but he heard his master, shuffling about the room, he thought, in his slippers, and making his customary arrangements before getting into his bed.

So Mr. Clewson concluded that Sir Roke had accidentally knocked down one of the old china vases which the care and good taste of ancient Mrs. Windle had placed upon the mantle-piece. And he knew that Sir Roke, when an accident happened, could snarl and curse in soliloquy, with great spirit.

So Clewson went back to his bed, a little out of humour, and made a few cynical remarks upon the "governor's" delight in disturbing people. But being weary, his temper did not keep him long awake, and he was soon again in a sound sleep.

Things had promised fairly that night for Mr. Clewson's. slumber, but his repose was destined to be broken.

After some time passed in dreamless sleep, without a summons, without a start, Mr. Clewson on a sudden opened his eyes. There was a large window in his room, without shutters, and through it the moon shone brightly.

In this light Mr. Clewson saw a man, with a wide-awake hat on, standing a little way off, and the character of the face and figure were such that for some seconds he did not know whether he was waking or in a dream.

## CHAPTER 45
### SLEEP, AND HIS BROTHER DEATH.

He beheld Carmel Sherlock standing, not far from his bed, in the moonlight, ghastly, his eyes fixed upon him with a cold glitter. His hands were clasped together, and there was a steel curb-chain about one of them, to which two or three large keys were attached.

The newly-awakened man sat up in his bed staring at him, and neither spoke. But Carmel drew near, and in the broad moonlight he could plainly see that one side of his face was covered with blood, and that his features wore an expression of horror and menace. Mr. Clewson's fear increased, as Carmel Sherlock came silently nearer and nearer to him, so that, with an effort, he found his tongue, and said, but in an undertone, for even then the training of Sir Roke's servant prevailed,—

"I say, Mr. Sherlock, what is it? I say, sir—please—what do you *want*?"

There was no answer, but, he fancied, a faint groan; and he now saw that in Carmel's clasped fingers there was something more than the chain I have mentioned. He saw that his hands, too, were covered with blood.

"Why, sir—Mr. Sherlock, I say—my God! sir, you're all over blood!" said Clewson, freezing with horror.

Carmel Sherlock, like a sleep-walker awakened, recoiled at the sound of his voice, and as he did so, he dropped something from his hand, which rolled to some little distance on the floor, and his gaze was still fixed on Clewson.

"Blood—blood—I dare say! Do you know me?" he whispered.

"Know you—to be sure; but you're hurt, Mr. Sherlock, sir. You've got a knock over the head, or something," said Clewson.

"Yes, sir—I'm very ill."

"I'll help you, sir, to wash your head, Mr. Sherlock; and I've some plaster, sir; and your hand—it's cut, isn't it?" said Mr. Clewson, putting his foot out of the bed.

"Eh? who told you my hand's cut—*cut*? *That* it is, to the bone—to the bone!"

"I'll give you a lift, Mr. Sherlock, sir, and get it all right, if you please."

"Hush! Was that a *call*, sir, from Sir Roke's room—Sir Roke Wycherly, Baronet?" said Carmel Sherlock.

"No, sir—nothink, Mr. Sherlock—no!" said the man, listening nevertheless.

"A *jibe*, sir; an angel; shall we go and help him?" whispered Sherlock, wildly.

"But he *did* not call, sir! The smallest trifle wakens him—he was getting to bed, Mr. Sherlock, more than an hour ago. I'm sure I wouldn't wake him for somethink—he's quiet now."

"*Lethali somno exporrectus*," said Sherlock, and sighed. "Shall we come?"

"Where?" asked Clewson.

"To Sir Roke."

"I *tell* you, let him alone—can't you? He's *asleep*," whispered Clewson, testily.

"Ay, ay; *Homerus* **Θάνατον** *et* **Ὕπνόν** *Germanos finxit*. In there, sir, *frater, fratrem amplectitur*—brother embraces brother. My hand!"

"Let me do it up for you, sir; pray do?" said Clewson, again essaying to rise.

"No, sir, I'll manage it—blood, to be sure—let Justice drink it; it is the milk she lives on, if a man catches the blade instead of the handle! an image of life—the way of death—a topsy-turvy world."

All this time he was groping on the floor; and looking for what he had dropped. He found it, and stood up.

Mr. Clewson could not see it distinctly, for he thrust the hand that held it quickly under the breast of his coat, but he did see a momentary metallic gleam. It was either a very small bright-barrelled pistol, or as he inclined to conclude, a knife.

"Ay, sir, the altar of Justice; between this and there a path of blood—the *via lactea*—and there you'll find her sacrifice—like herself—blind, and cold!"

Mr. Clewson seeing Carmel Sherlock, about whose growing eccentricities the servants had been talking, now again approaching his bedside, with the same dreadful expression of feature, and the unexplained blood-marks, and a knife, as he thought, in his hand, could stand his uncomfortable sensations no longer.

"Jest you get away with you, please; don't mind a-coming to

me, sir. What brings you here at this hour? It can't be far from daylight."

"Ay, ay," said Carmel Sherlock, and a strange craft and suspicion suddenly appeared in his face, and his eyes seemed to read Mr. Clewson's thoughts with a dangerous scrutiny. "Ay, very unseasonable; but when a man cuts his hand, you wouldn't have him go on bleeding—blood is life, you know—when a friend could stanch it; so I came up the back-stair, and then hesitated to waken you."

"Well, I'll do it up for you, if you like," began Clewson.

"No, I remember I have got it—better plaster—in my own room—the best—and it's hardly bleeding now. Thanks, sir; thanks, good Samaritan."

"And what did you want of Sir Roke, sir?"

"Well, Mrs. Wyndle says, *you* told her he has a medicine-chest, with everything in it, and I thought you might bring me to his room quietly; but I remembered he keeps his door bolted, and we couldn't get in without disturbing him; and I don't care about it, sir, for it has turned out next to nothing; so I'll go to my bed—goodnight, sir,—I'm tired and sleepy."

Carmel, for a second or two after this little speech was closed, continued to fix a shrinking gaze on Clewson, and suddenly repeated his "goodnight!" and turned to depart.

"Goodnight, sir," said Clewson more civilly.

And the moment Carmel Sherlock had left the room and closed the door, cautious Mr. Clewson skipped noiselessly to it, from his bed, and bolted it, lest Mr. Sherlock should change his mind and return. That Mr. Sherlock was more than half-crazed was the opinion of the servants' hall. The plight he was in to-night was by no means reassuring, and Mr. Clewson was very well pleased, for the first time in his life, at the precaution of that old-fashioned falling bolt, which secured Sir Roke's door on the inside.

When he was about to step once more into his bed, his attention was arrested by a sound in the stable-yard, of which his window commanded a full view. To the window therefore he

239

returned, and thence he saw Carmel Sherlock cross the paved yard toward the stables.

It was a brilliant frosty moonlight; the walls, the ivy, the pavement, showed all in intense whiteness, and the figure of Carmel Sherlock, as he walked swiftly across the pavement, was sharply defined, and its shadow lay clear and black on the stones. A great stone trough stands in front of the huge old pump, and against its side lay a thick- pronged pitchfork, a broom, and a shovel, and the sight of these homely implements seemed to arrest his attention, for he stopped suddenly, and took up the pitchfork and turned it over in his hands, and then placed it leaning against the pump; and he took from the breast-pocket of his coat a knife— there was no mistake about it now—and turned haft and blade quickly about in his hands. Then suddenly he looked up at the house, at the same time thrusting the knife into his pocket again, searching window after window with his glance. Mr. Clewson stepped back quickly, forgetting that there was no light in his room.

His eyes having run quickly along the windows, Mr. Sherlock took the pitchfork again in his hands, and went direct to a little iron grating, which let off the drain near the stable-door, and having first tried to pass the knife through its bars in vain, he then, with the prong of the pitchfork, forced two of them a little apart, and so dropped the knife in, and then carefully readjusted the grating. Then he looked up again at the windows, and proceeded to wash his hands and face hurriedly, at the stone tank before the pump.

Mr. Clewson watched him, with much curiosity, through these processes; hoping that he had been about no mischief, well knowing what an oddity he was, and willing to suppose the best, yet with a most uncomfortable misgiving.

"When Carmel Sherlock had completed his ablutions he walked to the stable-door, unlocked it, and disappeared for a little, returning in a few minutes leading the horse he usually rode saddled and bridled. Mr. Clewson then remembered that he had heard that Mr. Sherlock, when he had to visit a distant part of the estate, sometimes set out as early as three o'clock in the morning. He watched him till he unlocked the outer door and led the horse out of the yard. Mr. Clewson looked at his watch, in the light which the moon afforded, and found that it was half-past three; and then he return to his bed a good deal quieted.

"He's a very quiet man, is Mr. Sherlock. I never heard of his quarrelling with no one. A nice man, and knows a deal o' book-learning, he does. It's just one of them early rides; and he's cut his finger, and he took his revenge o' the knife—he is sich a queer un. Well, he's broke up my night's rest a bit, he has—the fool!"

And with this remark, rather cold, Mr. Clewson laid himself surlily down in his bed for the third time that night, and was soon fast asleep.

## CHAPTER 46
### APPLEBURY CHURCH.

At the pleasant old town of Applebury there was a cattle-fair next morning. By daybreak the whole town was in a bustle; and the High Street, which expands near the old Town Hall into a great, irregular, paved square, was already thronged with men, women, and children, and stalls and booths of all sorts. Applebury is thirteen miles away from Raby, and only eleven from the Vicarage

Two cows and a troop of sheep, belonging to my friend the Reverend Stour Temple, were there; and his brother, honest Roger, had, by earnest entreaty, supported by the eloquence of Miss Barbara, who had long thought he wanted a holiday, persuaded him to ride to Applebury next morning.

Down the narrow road overhung by noble ash-trees, which enters the antique town from the north, while the pleasant morning sun was glittering on the old gilt vane and clock of the church-tower, rode, on their trotting nags, a little cavalcade of three,—thin Stour Temple, fat Roger, and Charlie Mordant. Honest Roger, smiling cosily, and jogging breathlessly in his saddle, young Mordant in high spirits, and the vicar's thin brown features smiling also pleasantly, and all the better of that ride in the exhilarating air of early morning.

A little way down they had to slacken their pace, finding themselves involved among droves of cattle, farmers on horseback, and pedestrians, all tending into the town; and Bonnie came to a walk with a very red face and a great sigh of relief.

"I told you, Stour,—now didn't I?—you'd like it," said honest Roger, when they sat at breakfast in the Bull Inn parlour, with the broad fat backs of two farmers, busy over a bargain, against the window-stone, and a view of the steep roof and gilded clock of the Town Hall, the noble old tree that grows there, and the ever-moving panorama beneath it, touched with the pleasant morning sun. "I see you are enjoying it, my poor fellow;" and smiling inquiringly into his face, he pressed his brother's knee gently with his fat hand.

"So I do, Bonnie," said Stour, with a very sweet smile, and pressing his own hand over Bonnie's kindly paw. "Very much; five years since I was in Applebury before. I never saw the old place look so pleasant; and I'm very much obliged to you and Barbara for making me come."

I think the kind blue eyes and fat smile of Bonnie, and the affectionate patting of his honest hand, had a great deal to do with the charm of the scene. "There's some good in you and Barbara, after all, though you are a pair of despots."

So said the vicar, still smiling; and in his heart there welled up the strong and tender love that would have said: "Bonnie and Barbara—brother and sister—my treasures! What are long walks, and now and then a trouble, and an obscure threadbare life, if only in the bright warm sunshine of your love, my darlings! For whom I bless God every hour."

"We are very comfortable, aren't we?" said Roger, with a delighted little chuckle. "We are enjoying ourselves immensely; we are so cosy—ain't we?"

"Awfully!" acquiesced Mordant. "What a queer little town it is! Lucky to have such a fine day. *There's* an odd name, isn't it? On that red board with the gold frame over there. Don't you see?—on that square brick house."

"Yes—yes—there," said Roger, looking across, and as he did so blushing an ingenuous crimson. The name was Amos Martyr. Charles Mordant had made his little remark in all simplicity; and honest Roger, who was a little near-sighted, I believe, fancied, though with amazement, that he read a more interesting name.

"Where is she? By Jove! you have seen some one," said Charlie, gaily, and running to the window. "I must see her."

"I didn't; upon my honour! No, she is *not* there."

"Who?" demanded Mordant.

"Come, who is she, Roger?" urged Stour Temple, who enjoyed his good brother's flights into the land of romance.

"That fellow has been at his tricks," said Roger, with a smile of bashful reproach at Charlie.

"*I* have?" exclaimed Charlie.

"Ho—ho—yes; do ask him what he has been doing over *there*," said Roger, smiling and shaking his head.

"I never was over there in my life! Upon my honour, sir, I never was," exclaimed Charles Mordant, earnestly, observing the direction of honest Roger's short arm, and not knowing what accusation might be intended by his fat friend, smiling sheepishly.

"Not you—you rogue! I say, Stour, ask him whether he knows how to use a paintbrush. By Jove! though, there's Dick Larcom and his son, with the cows," exclaimed Roger, interrupting his own rude and mysterious allusions. "Let us come out for goodness sake, and hear what offers he has got."

So forth they sallied; and in the hall Roger said in Charlie Mordant's ear:

"Isn't it delightful we got poor Stour to come with us, glorious fellow! And killing himself with work—a perfect slave; but you must run over, like a dear fellow, and make them take that thing down; it oughtn't to have been there at all—do, *do* now; and here's Dick. Stour! here's Dick Larcom with the cows."

So forth they sallied, among stalls and booths, and piles of gingerbread, and baskets of apples, in pursuit of Dick Larcom who was making his way to the green with the vicar's cattle. But the vicar, being less interested than as a wise farmer he ought to have been, and having an easy confidence that among his more skilled friends the cattle would be managed well enough, wandered away into devious lanes, and finally paid a visit to the old church, whose beautiful porch is so justly admired; and seeing that the door was open, the sexton being there employed in his vocation, the vicar stepped into the hallowed shade, taking off his hat.

This church of Applebury is, I think, about the darkest in England, the eastern window being of stained glass, and under the shadow of two enormous elm-trees. Coming out of the bright sun, this gloom strikes the visitor, so that one would fancy there was scarcely light in the building to read by. He stood for a little, just within the threshold of the door, looking up and around, as such visitors will; and, glancing at his left hand, some five or six yards away from the entrance, he saw a man, in a loose wrapper, with a hat in his hand, standing, and, as he felt, staring at him. The vicar could not see his features distinctly, only his white eyeballs, as in silence he watched him without motion.

One of the frequenters of this fair of Applebury the vicar took him to be, who had sauntered there, like himself, to see what the inside of the old church was like.

The man made a short, shuffling step or two backward, as if irresolute, and the vicar, fancying a recognition, instinctively made a step or two in advance, and saw Carmel Sherlock, just with that amount of surprise which in imperfect light induces a momentary uncertainty.

"You've come here for *me*, sir?" demanded Sherlock, in tones that were low and stern.

"Far from it," answered the vicar, with a slight smile. "I was a little surprised, on the contrary, to see you here; and indeed, in this light it is not easy to know anyone."

"I've been here longer—*in tenebris*—and everything is clear. I saw you distinctly; there is some of your cattle at the fair, sir—and so we have found one another. You had no news, last night, from Raby?"

"No, none at all," answered the vicar, looking at him attentively.

"Well, I've a message. There's no one following you, no one outside—no one watching us?"

And Carmel Sherlock, who had been drawing near, peeped from the door, and through the quiet porch.

"No, I'm quite alone here—my brother and young Mr. Mordant are at the fair; but what is the message?"

"Only this, sir; they want you at Raby; there is great anxiety there, sir—an unexpected calamity, and it is your duty to be there. You may be of use—it is a house of affliction, today."

"What has happened?—who is ill, or—who is it?" asked Stour Temple.

"I have nothing, sir, to tell more than—Ha! yes, I hear the horse."

"Where are you going now, Mr. Sherlock?" inquired the vicar,

"*Home*, sir," said he, with a start.

"Do pray let me know how I can be of use, and what has happened," pleaded Stour Temple, who was alarmed.

"They'll tell you when you get there—if they like. There's no more for me to say than I *have* said. Receive me as a messenger, sir, who tells what is needful, and no more. This morning, sir, Raby is a house of trouble, and you will be expected there. Leave this town, and be where you are wanted; that is my message. You will do as pleases you best. Ha! here it is."

And Carmel Sherlock stepped quickly through the porch, in front of which stood a horse saddled, a boy holding its bridle.

"I beg pardon, Mr. Sherlock," said the vicar, following and laying his hand upon his arm; "pray relieve me, if you can—pray tell me—if anyone at Raby is dead?"

"I've told you all I have to tell," said Carmel Sherlock, with a dark stare, and stamping with wild impatience on the flags. "Just *that*—they want you." And in another moment he was in the saddle, and. riding at a swift pace down the solitary lane that runs in front of the old church, was immediately out of sight. Stour Temple fancied he had never seen anyone, in full possession of his physical strength and activity, look so ill as Carmel Sherlock. There was also that in his countenance he had never seen before. Altogether, he did not well know what to make of him.

"Suppose the poor fellow's mad," thought the vicar. "I should have my ride to Raby for nothing; but no, it has not come to that—always eccentric, but quite sane—where he chooses to talk rationally. No, it is not a vision. Something has happened."

Now so it was, the vicar could no longer feel happy sauntering about the little town of Applebury, and back to the Bull Inn went he, and he called for the reckoning, and called for his nag, and he left a little note for Roger, who he knew was well furnished with money, accounting for his departure; and he mounted his beast, and trotted away by the old road that leads to Raby.

## CHAPTER 47
### THE DARK CHAMBER OF WHITE DEATH

It was little past ten o'clock when the vicar, amid the sweet and solemn landscape that surrounds Raby, approached the lordly gateway of that mansion, with the defiant *de-griffins*, with wings expanded, keeping guard upon its lofty piers. With an anxiety that increased as he approached, Stour Temple scrutinized the hall-door and the windows in search of some sign that might help his suspense to a conclusion. There was no one in the gate-house, an occurrence not rare in those disorderly precincts. He dismounted under the aerial shadow of the huge trees that embower the gateway, and led his horse in upon the stately and melancholy avenue.

Silent and lifeless the great old mansion stood before him, and door or window gave no sign. Who could it be? What had happened? The image that constantly presented itself to his imagination was horrible and piteous enough. Had that gloomy, morbid, miserable man, Mark Shadwell, made away with himself in one of his paroxysms of malign despair? and if so, what a spectacle of agony awaited him!

That poor weak lady, adoring that unhappy and ungrateful man, could she survive so frightful a shock? As he approached the other pair of *demi-griffins*, with upturned wings and monstrous eyes and beaks, awaiting him by the steps, and looked at the closed hall-door, his heart sank within him, and he felt almost faint as he anticipated the scene that was coming.

He threw the bridle of his pony over the comer of the balustrade that flanks the steps at either side, and rang the bell. He had to repeat his summons more than once before the door was opened.

"How is Mrs. Shadwell?" inquired the vicar.

She was pretty well.

"And Miss Shadwell?"

The same answer. But the servant was looking at him with a stern countenance, which indicated something untold and dreadful.

"And your master—*he's* well, I hope?" said the vicar, trying to read the man's answer in his face, as he put the question.

He was well, also. Stour Temple began to think that Carmel Sherlock's warning was but a symptom of his crazy state.

"Has Mr. Sherlock returned?" inquired the vicar.

"No, sir," said the man with a shake of his head, and a very odd look in the vicar's eyes.

"Can I see your master?" asked Stour Temple, who was willing to clear the matter up without more delay.

"I'll inquire, sir," said the man.

"Say it is *I*—perhaps he'll see me."

"Yes, sir."

And the man walked across the spacious hall to the library door. It was locked; and he returned, and said:

"He has locked the door, sir, please ;" and he looked as if he would add, "I dare not disturb him."

"Well—thanks—don't mind; I'll try myself if he can see me."

The vicar knocked several times, and on a sudden the door

247

half opened, and Mark Shadwell presented himself standing on the threshold.

"Ho! Temple? So you've come. I'm sorry—sent for—eh?"

"Well, yes; I got a kind of message, but very vague. I only heard you were in trouble," said Stour Temple, struck by something suspicious and stony in the countenance of Mark Shadwell, and looking into it with a dark and anxious inquiry.

"Trouble?—*I!*—well I can't say I am; come in." The vicar entered, and Mark shut the door. "Hardly trouble—but in a very painful situation. You did not hear about that—that—unfortunate fellow"—and saying this he averted his eyes—"Roke Wycherly?"

"No, nothing; he's—what is it?"

"He's—he's *dead*; and what makes it worse, he has been killed." Mark spoke nearly in a whisper, and looked very grim and pale.

"Good God!" exclaimed the vicar, while his face paled with horror, "do you mean he has been *murdered*?"

"Yes—there can't be a doubt. No one could have inflicted those wounds on himself; and he was not a man to hurt himself." Is he quite dead?"

Yes; it must have happened as early as sunrise. At eight o'clock he was cold. It's shocking, isn't it?—quite well last night, you know; and *now!* I could scarcely go in myself. I never could bear the sight of a dead person since I saw my poor father—it's a hateful sight; but I told them to leave everything as it was exactly, and nothing has been disturbed. There must be an inquest, of course. I'll have the whole thing searched out, and all as light as day."

"Certainly," acquiesced Temple; "and, depend upon it, you'll succeed—these things always discover themselves. I'm very sorry to find you in so painful and horrible a situation. If I can be of any use I shall be only too happy."

"If it is not too painful, I should be so much obliged. Temple, if you would just go and look at what has happened, and examine the room, and make a note of anything that strikes you. I should much prefer that all evidence of that kind should come from someone not an inmate of the house, and someone both intelligent and unexceptionable; people are talking, I dare say, already. When did you hear?"

"Well, it was at Applebury, this morning; there's a fair there."

"Oh, yes—quite natural; they were talking about it, I dare say," said Mark, in a low tone.

"No; I met Carmel Sherlock, who gave me your message," said the vicar.

"Carmel Sherlock! At Applebury? Good heaven! Then he's perfectly *mad*!"

Looking at Mark Shadwell as he spoke, the vicar could see hardly anything but his flaming eyes, and a face pale as death.

"I hope to God you arrested him?" Arrested him? No—why?"

"Why? Because he it was who indubitably murdered Roke Wycherly last night. Did you leave him still at the fair?"

It was now the vicar's turn to look horror-struck.

"Is it credible? Mr. Sherlock—so gentle and harmless," said the vicar, after a pause of several seconds.

"The man has been growing mad this long time—madder than any of us thought. Clewson's evidence—Clewson, Roke's servant, you know—is quite conclusive on that point. Was he arrested?"

"No. I tell you, no one, I'm certain, knew anything of it. It can't have been much past seven when I saw him. There did seem something very strange in his looks and manner; and he urged me to come here, as if he had a message from you; but he would not say what had happened. Would it not be well to give a hint to Cripps, the policeman in Raby, to look after the wretched man—I trust a lunatic—who had committed this dreadful crime?"

"So I was just thinking," said Mark, with a haggard start. "You saw him at about seven o'clock at Applebury fair?"

"Yes; he rode away from the church porch, where he seemed to have appointed a boy to meet him with his horse, in a westerly direction, along the quiet little road that passes there."

"How was he mounted?" asked Mark, ringing the bell.

"A strong bay horse."

"Ha! He rode the old black hunter from this—the horse you've often seen him on. He must have picked up the other at the fair, or hired it, perhaps. How was he dressed?"

"Very much as usual, I think; a loose outside coat, and one of those broad-leafed felt hats, with a low round crown, and— yes—a pair of those leather things, like jack-boots; and he was looking .very ill, indeed."

Mark shook his head, and smiled drearily.

"Ha! well he may," said he. "Tell Clewson to come here for a moment," he continued, addressing the servant who presented himself at the door, "and tell them to put the horse to the tax-cart instantly; and do you come back here in five minutes. I'm so much obliged to you. Temple, for this call. I'll just make a note of what you tell me, and send it, and Clewson's information, which I took this morning, to Cripps; and I'll tell my fellow to drive him over to Applebury, and put the people there on the alert, and I think we *must* catch him—don't you?"

"I'm quite certain of it; no fugitive, as a rule, can escape—the telegraph nets them round. There are two or three police at Applebury, and the railway not far; give them the description, and they will take care to transmit it."

"I do hope they may catch him—there are so many enemies—the people are talking about it? Not yet, I suppose—but they'd stick at nothing, some of them; they'd say I favoured that wretched fellow's escape. I'm so delighted you came. I tell you the truth, I felt miserably till you came. I think they must find him, and then it will all be cleared up; at the same time, mad the poor wretch is. Roke heard him at his door—he told us all about it—one night before, trying to get in, very cautiously— it's a very odd business—and he opened the door suddenly, and there was Sherlock face to face with him; and he seemed put out and half frightened, and talked some nonsense. You may rely on it he intended that night getting in, and murdering the poor fellow, as he did at last. But, be it how it may, could anything be more unlucky for me, surrounded as I am with slanderers; the d—d hornets will be all up, in a cloud, about my ears. But let them say their say; provided it is within the limits of law, they can't hurt me—eh? I'll be vigorous and energetic as the hardest of them. I pity the wretched madman, of course; but I could not—I couldn't connive at his escape—eh?"

"Of course not, my dear Shadwell; no one could be weak enough to fancy any such thing. You take the plain view. There are very few cases, indeed, in which duty is anything but simple."

"This is the key; the room is locked. I have not been there since early this morning, for a few minutes, with Clewson. He will show you the way, and point out everything to you. I sha'n't visit it again until the coroner comes. So many enemies, God knows what they might say."

"Well, I hope you mistake them," said the clergyman.

"I'd rather not trust them; I'll leave nothing in their power. Here's Clewson," said Mark, as the man entered, very grave, very quiet, with air and looks beseeming the dismal occasion: and I am sure he would much have preferred that the accident had not happened, for his place was a good one. "You'll move nothing; do you mind: everything is to be left precisely as you find it," said Mark, addressing Clewson, who with this charge accompanied the vicar, and led him by many rooms and passages to the back-stairs, which, having mounted, they unlocked the door of the room which had been Clewson's.

Now Mr. Clewson pointed out the spot where Carmel had stood, and he showed bloody footprints leading to it, through the dressing-room, more distinctly marked the nearer it approached to the scene of the catastrophe, the room from which it started.

The vicar hesitated for a moment at the door of the room where Sir Roke had slept; a sensation of fear and repugnance chilled him as he was about to step into the scene of crime. He opened the door. One window-shutter and curtain was partly open. It was a sudden change from the clear light of the dressing-room to the shadow of this chamber, which contained the object he almost feared to see. A cross light from a far window, leaving the greater part of the room in darkness, just touched an odd-looking figure that reclined in the cushioned chair, some way off, by the table.

"There?" whispered the vicar, interrogatively, indicating the indistinct figure with his hand.

"Yes, sir, please; in his dressing gown and slippers, with the cap on as he always wore when he put off his wig, which he had 'ung it on the small block, by the looking-glass. Sir Roke's caps, sir, was made to cover his ears, that he shouldn't take cold, he 'aving 'ad a bad habcess in his left ear, last year, sir, in Florence, where we was for three months "

"Is that door open?" whispered Temple, nodding towards the door that opens on the great gallery.

"We found it locked, sir, on the hinside; Sir Roke, being shy-like, or something, he usu'lly locked his door before he put his wig hoff."

"I'll go over and see," said the vicar, with a sigh that was nearly a groan: "we'll not open the shutter; we must move nothing. Hush!—yes!"

He was now standing about two steps away from the sitting, or rather reclining figure. There was Sir Roke, leaning back in the great cushioned chair. He had on a thick flowered silk dressing-gown, and a quilted white nightcap, that covered his ears, and was tied under his chin, giving a grotesque air to his costume. His chin was sunk upon his breast. Upon his thin lips was a faint piteous smirk; his eyes were fixed in a dim stare, as if upon something inimitably remote and awful. There was in this dead face a strange discord of fear and mockery. The narrow line of light from the partially opened shutter touched its features, and its odd white *coiffure*. The vicar had no notion that Sir Roke could have looked so old and worn; such a tracery of fine lines and wrinkles—lines of dissimulation and selfishness it seemed to him, as well as of exhaustion. In the thin high nose and almost transparent nostrils; in the thin lips and haggard face, was recognisable no one trait of manliness. You might have mistaken the face for that of a wicked old woman who had died whilst listening to an amusing scandal.

The right arm of the corpse was extended on the table, and the slender hand was cramped and drawn together as if in the effort to clutch something. The fingers of the other were closed on the arm of the chair.

The evidences of violence were only too apparent. Blood had flowed from the comer of the mouth, and stained the lip and chin with a black streak. There was a dreadful wound in the throat, nearly under the jaw, about an inch away from the ear—a stab with a broad-bladed knife or dagger. There was plainly another fearful wound on the breast, for the shirt, which the opening in the dressing-gown displayed, was cut, and immediately below this the white was stained with a broad red gush. There must have been other wounds, the vicar thought, for the carpet was saturated with a wide pool of blood.

With the frown of a horrible compassion, the vicar gazed in silence upon the image before him for some time.

"My God!" he exclaimed at last, with a great sigh, "who could have dreamed this of Sherlock?—so refined and gentle, and yet such a cruel villain! *Mad*, I hope, he may prove. What depths below depths in the heart of man. *Lord, in Thee only is safety. Thou Rock of Ages!*"

With clasped hands, the vicar, looking up, spoke thus, and then turned away, and treading lightly, and speaking low, from point to point they went together in the room.

Every now and again Stour Temple made a little note as he had promised Mark Shadwell. These little pencilled memoranda were after all but few, and were nearly as follows:

Sir Roke Wycherly's bedroom, examined by me, Stour Temple, Clk., in presence of Mr. T. Clewson, on ——, the ——, presented the following indications, &c.:
The carpet, to the extent of about a yard in one direction and a little more in the other, is saturated with a pool of blood, partly in front, partly at the side of the chair in with

the body reclines, and towards the right side of the body. This blood seems to have discharged itself from the body, partly through the trouser of the right leg, which is stained by it, and the slipper of the right foot shows marks of having been full of blood, which flowed over.

The fragments of a large decanter of cut-glass, lie on the floor, at the same side, and partly under the table.

The three shutters and curtains of the three windows are closed, with the exception of that which is farthest from the bed, a small portion of which is open.

The door of the room which opens upon the great gallery, is locked, and the handle of the key and the brass of the door bear marks of what appears to me to be blood.

There are footprints, indicated by blood, leading from the chair to the door already mentioned, and also to that of the dressing-room next Sir Roke's bedroom, across the floor of it, and upon the floor of Mr. T. Clewson's bedroom, the latter very faintly traceable.

On the carpet is a sharp-pointed knife, with a broad, wavy blade; it is very much marked with blood. The cloth of this table is dragged to one side. On the table is one letter, addressed, 'Pepys Adderly, Esq.'

There are pens, an ink-bottle, and a blotting-book on the floor.

There is a small table with a cloth on it, and a pack of cards, standing near the wall with no indication of having been disturbed.

There are four silver candlesticks on a small marble table at the left side of the body, the candles in which seem to have burned out in their sockets.

Stour Temple, Clerk,

And then the date.

Having completed his survey of these rooms, Stour Temple hesitated for a moment, and then returned and looked once more at the dead man, reclining in the chair. There were the fixed attitude, the odd smile, the awful clouded gaze. It is these returning visits after an interval of absence, the strange literality of the impression reproduced, the mobile lines, and transient gleams of living emotion, fixed where the moment found them, the immutable smile, the unchanged compression of the lip, the stem brow and changeless eye, that strike one with a sense of that awful anomaly in a world of life—the inexorable and irrevocable character of the change.

"As a thief—in the night! The thing which I greatly feared is come upon me," repeated the vicar, almost unconsciously, as he looked woefully upon this spectacle, "Let us go, Mr. Clewson, if you please."

Accordingly the Vicar and the servant *emeritus*, took their departure, carefully locking the doors, and these chambers and their tenant were abandoned to silence and solitude.

## CHAPTER 48
### THE EVE OF THE INQUEST.

"Well, you've seen it?" said Shadwell, gloomily, when the vicar had entered the study again.

"Yes," said Temple, very pale. "I'm almost sorry I *have* seen it. I shan't easily recover the impression. I wish I could forget it."

"I'm afraid I've been very unreasonable and thoughtless. I dare say I should have made my request to some other friend, although, except your brother Roger, I can hardly reckon another," said Mark, sourly.

"Pray, don't mistake me. I would willingly do a great deal more, and for people in whom I took a much less interest, in so deplorable an emergency. I only meant to say, how very awfully that scene has impressed me. But I do assure you I'm only anxious to be of any use in my power." And so saying, he extended his hand to Mark, who took it, and held it for a moment, looking gloomily at him.

"I wrote to the coroner at eight o'clock this morning," said he, "to entreat that he would summon his jury without any loss of time, and I have just had a letter from him to say they will be here at eleven o'clock tomorrow. Would it be asking too much if

I were to beg that you and your brother in this, as you say, emergency, would come here at that hour? Think as you may. I have enemies, and bitter enemies, some of whom will be no doubt upon this jury. I don't say avowed enemies—it may be even unconscious ones—but on this account the more unscrupulous. Of course such fellows as Mervyn and Desborough would be only too glad to reflect upon me."

"Reflect upon *you!*—I don't see how that can be, though," said the vicar.

"Why, they may say—that I ought to have dismissed that wretched Sherlock long ago—perhaps I ought. I don't pretend to say; the event at least seems to say so, but you know my motive in keeping him. You know how I trusted him with my own interests, and how impossible it was that any of us—crazy in some of his fancies as we might suppose him—could have believed that there was the smallest danger in harbouring him. He was, as you say, so gentle and patient, and with so much refinement and cultivation."

"Certainly; I never was so much shocked and astonished—the last man in the world I should have suspected," said Stour Temple.

"I can't go quite that length, however," said Shadwell. "He had his malignities, and I have heard some things since that induce me to think that he had conceived one of his intense antipathies against the man upstairs. He spoke in an odd menacing way about him to some of the servants, and I should not like the jury to tack a censure upon me, or any other insult to their verdict."

"And you wish me and Roger to attend? You may, with God's permission, reckon absolutely upon that."

"Thanks; one does not like to be totally without a friend to stand by one, you know, in the midst of such neighbours as I have about me.

"I've made some notes," said the vicar, holding his open pocket-book in his fingers.

"May I look?" asked Mark, extending his hand.

"Certainly," said the clergyman.

And Mark, taking it to the window, read these memoranda very carefully.

"You mention footprints marked with blood?" said Shadwell. "Clewson said something of them also. You mention here that they are traceable to the bedroom door which opens on the great gallery. Did you look out to see whether the marks were continued on the floor of the gallery?"

"No," said Stour Temple, "for there were marks of blood upon the key, and I thought you were so clear that nothing should ever be disturbed."

"Quite right! Thank you; exactly what I would have wished; but suppose we go now—it did not strike me before. We can take Clewson with us, and examine the floor,"

They did go and made their scrutiny, but not the slightest trace appeared.

Shadwell and the vicar paused upon the lobby. "God sends nothing in vain," said the vicar, laying his hand on Mark's arm; "even crime and death. His warnings are whispered to some, and spoken in thunders to others. This tragedy, does it not, my dear sir, speak trumpet-tongued to you? That wretched Mr. Sherlock had no religion, neither had that unhappy man who has perished by his hand. Is there not a double lesson in this? How near, even in its unlikeliest forms, death may be, and how vain are the securities afforded by unaided human nature against the access of even the most monstrous crimes! I have often talked on the subject of revealed religion to you; but what are the man's pleadings compared with the eloquence of these tremendous events? Lay the lesson, then, I implore of you, to your heart."

"I'm sure you mean well. Temple, I always thought so. But each man reads his own lessons for himself. I must read mine, as best I may. I don't suppose one man is better than another in the eye of God. It is all temperament and circumstance. I'll talk it over with you whenever you like, except *now*. I'm half distracted, that's the truth."

"I can well suppose it, Mr. Shadwell. Men of the world don't avow it, but there is too much real paganism—here in the light of the Gospel—to escape the most careless eye. Oh! Mr. Shadwell, think of this sudden death and sudden crime, and trust no more to the ever shifting illusions of scepticism, and to the fancied virtues of human nature."

Mark Shadwell was holding the banister with a hard grasp, and looking, with a contracted face, darkly on the ground, like a man in sudden pain, whilst the vicar spoke; and when he ceased he continued motionless, and seemed to listen for more of this homily for some seconds; and then, with a sigh, he said:

"Would you like to see my poor wife? She has been very low and nervous about this miserable affair, and I am certain would be the better of a few minutes' talk with you."

"If you think she would really wish it, I shall be most happy," assented the clergyman.

"I know it," said Shadwell, and led him along the gallery to the door of Mrs. Shadwell's sitting-room, where he found that lady, frightened, nervous, almost hysterical. Mark Shadwell had intended going in, but he stopped suddenly at the threshold, merely saying—

"Amy, I've asked Mr. Temple to pay you a few minutes' visit. He is here."

And angrily, you would have fancied, he walked swiftly away, down the gallery, and then to the left, and so down the stairs, and into his library once more; where, pale and exhausted, he threw himself into a chair, and with a deep groan he said:

"Black a thing as death is, I wish I were dead instead of him—I wish to God I were."

Stour Temple took his departure; Mark heard him cross the hall. He did not care to see him again; and he heard the tramp of his horse, as he rode away, and did not wish to recall him.

Mark had received one of those shocks which, for a while, convert men into the ideal of an anchorite. To fast, to watch, with one idea always perched or fluttering, like an imprisoned bird, in his brain; and one choking emotion rising from his heart—was his present doom. Pale, *distrait*, nervous, furious at time? when disturbed by message or question, or even a tap at his door, he occupied his library in utter solitude. Sunset came with its solemn glare; the cold moon rose, and sheeted the landscape in White. Mark lighted his candles and closed his shutters, and drew his curtains for himself. He hated the faces of his servants; they seemed to be reading him with prying eyes, and coming again and again on pretexts to his door for the purpose.

After one or two such calls, met with unaccountable bursts of fury, he secured the door. He stirred the fire. He sat before it, looking sullenly among its embers, and then peeping slowly back, over his shoulder, he would get up, and stand with his back to the fire, looking drearily from corner to corner, and then he would pour out a glass of sherry and drink it in haste.

Slowly wore the night away. He was horribly nervous. All kinds of fancies beset and startled him. He thought he heard the handle of his door turned, and stood watching it, with a freezing gaze, for minutes. He opened the shutters and drew the curtains of the window next him; but there was a tall plant just before it, that in the white moonlight took the shape of a man, standing there nodding and swaying himself slowly backward and forward; and look where he would, he still saw obliquely this teasing object, and could not rest till he had closed shutters and curtains again.

Later in the night came the distant howling of a dog—dismalest of sounds—and on a sudden he fancied he heard a sharp whisper at the window say *Wycherly*. It was the twitter, perhaps, of some passing night-bird, or a spray of the rose-tree brushing lightly on the glass. But he would have sworn that he had heard that ominous name so syllabled.

Chilled and fixed, he listened for its repetition, but it came not. He fancied then that it might have been uttered by Carmel Sherlock, whom he had begun to fear with a dreadful antipathy. He dared not open the shutter. He fancied he should see that strange face, with its eyes and lips to the window pane.

It was hard to move his mind from the hated subject under which it lay in a monotonous pain. An image was always before him. The only thought allied to life and action was that of the inquest that the day would bring; and there, too, among the sinister faces of unfriendly neighbours, was the same odious image.

To his sherry, for courage, Mark Shadwell often had recourse through that hateful night. At last, worn out, he fell into a slumber in his chair, from which he waked with a cry, he knew not why uttered. It was still in his ears, and the walls seemed ringing with it, as he looked about him. The candles were expiring in the sockets. He started up and drew the curtains, and was glad to see the grey light of morning through the chinks of the shutters.

*Oh! glad was the knight when he heard the cock crow,*
*His enemies trembled and left him!*

So now that first detested night was over, and the old house of Raby was dimly lighted by the dawning day that was to witness the inquest upon the body of the murdered baronet.

## CHAPTER 49
### THE CORONER

As the day wore on, strange faces began to appear. Men rode up to the door, and dismounted, sending their horses round to the stables. Broughams, dog-carts, all sorts of vehicles, drove to the open hall-door, and set down their masters. The coroner had come, and Doctor Lincott from Gilleston. The Reverend Stour Temple was there, and our honest friend Roger, his fat face charged with a supernatural solemnity.

Some stood on the steps talking of fairs and prices in a decent undertone, as people sometimes mention irrelative subjects at funerals. The hall-door stood wide open as that of an inn, and in the hall were various little groups, earnest and grave in their talk. Others were in the two drawing-rooms. Mark Shadwell was among them, pale and grave. Very formal, too, with those guests, whose dispositions towards himself he suspected.

And now the hour having arrived, the coroner opened his court in the hall of Raby, and the jury were sworn. He then told them what they each knew already—the nature of the inquiry, and the general character of the tragedy they were to investigate.

Then at his own request Mr. Shadwell was sworn, and informed the jury of the circumstance under which Sir Roke Wycherly had made his brief sojourn at Raby; he described the particulars of his parting with him on the fatal night; also, generally, the state in which he found his room in the morning on visiting it with Clewson, who gave the alarm. He mentioned, also, that the Reverend Stour Temple had visited it later in the day, and made, at his request, a note of everything that struck him as at all bearing on the subject of their inquiry, and he, Mark Shadwell, had done this, and also retained possession of the key of the room; the door of which he had kept locked, lest there should be any uncertainty as to whether the indications so supplied had been ever so little disturbed, either by accident or design.

He then described Carmel Sherlock: he was eccentric, hypochondriac, in some points a little crazed almost; but he was habitually gentle. He should not have dreamed of suspecting him of violence had it not been for the distinct evidence of Clewson, supported by that of the vicar, whose strange interview with him at Applebury he mentioned. It was, however, certain that Carmel Sherlock had conceived an intense but unaccountable antipathy to Sir Roke Wycherly, and that he had made no secret of that feeling, as only too many witnesses were ready to prove.

The coroner and jury then went upstairs to view the body and inspect the room. Shadwell accompanied them, as did Clewson, at his suggestion.

The master of Raby, pale but collected, pointed out to them what was most striking in the disarrangements of the room.

Clewson was sworn here, and described Sir Roke's habits.

"You say," said one of the jurors, "that Sir Roke Wycherly always locked the door opening upon the great gallery before going to his bed; but he had not gone to bed, he was still seated at the table when he was stabbed. What leads you to the conclusion that the door in question had been locked before the murder took place?"

"He usually locked his door before he removed his wig; he had a great objection anyone should see him without it. And the wig being took off, it's in that 'ere box, sir, and his nightcap on, I'm certain sure his door *was* locked."

"How do you account for the blood on the handle of the key?" persisted this gentleman; "does not it look as if the murderer locked the door after he had committed the crime, and with his hand bloody?"

"Well, it might be; but I think Sir Roke had locked it. No, he wouldn't by no chance, leave it open for no one to come in and see him settling of his wig. No, no, never; it could not be, sir."

"The murderer, then, must have been thinking of going out by that door, and stained the key with blood, and you think Mr. Sherlock must have entered this room, as he went out of it, by the other door, and across the dressing- room, and so through your room. Now recollect yourself. Did you hear any sound? Were you, that you can remember, even partially wakened by any noise in your room?"

"No, sir, not *in* my room."

"Are we to understand, however, that you were awakened by a noise before Mr. Sherlock's visit to your room?" interposed Mr. Mervyn, a tall, gaunt gentleman, with a high grey head, and the dress of another generation—blue coat and brass buttons, and a shirt frill, and gaiters buttoned up to his knee.

"Yes, sir."

"What was it?"

Clewson described what has been mentioned already,

"You went to sleep after this?"

"Yes, sir."

"And for how long did you sleep before you awoke again and saw Mr. Sherlock?"

"Well, it might have been an hour, and it might not have been so long."

"Could it have been so short a time as a quarter of an

hour?"

"It might, sir."

Shadwell here whispered in the vicar's ear, who nodded, and whispered something in the ear of his neighbour, Mr. Digges, who was upon the jury, and Digges asked the witness:

"Might it have been less?"

"Well it might, sir."

"Were you sleepy?"

"Very much so, sir."

"And dropped off again as fast as you were waked?"

"Just so, sir.

"A bit of a snooze, and then called up, as you might sitting in a chair?"

"Well it was, sir, very much like that."

As soon as they had thoroughly examined the room, the jury, led by the coroner, and accompanied by Mark Shadwell and the lookers-on, returned to the hall.

There was a good deal of evidence to show the ill-feeling which Sherlock seemed to cherish against the deceased.

Then came an odd part of the evidence.

Clewson had found upon the carpet, on entering the room in the morning, a dagger, or creese, with a sinuous blade, both the blade and handle of which were stained with blood, and a mark which resembled the pressure of a closed hand was also indicated indistinctly by a blurred brown stain.

Now this creese was the property of Carmel Sherlock, and what was still more to the point, it was proved to have been in his hand at about two o'clock on the night of the murder. The evidence upon this point arose thus:

Attached to Raby is a great old orchard, in the centre of which is a sort of small square tower of brick with a loft in it, which is known by the name of "The Watch." Some of the apples had been lately stolen, and some timber cut at night not far from the house; and to check these depredations two men had been stationed in "The Watch," who took it by turns to visit the woods that lie near it.

One of these—Will Hedgelong by name—was, according to this arrangement, sauntering near the house of Raby on the night in question between one and two o'clock. He saw a light in Carmel Sherlock's window, which, appearing through a piece of red curtain that hung at one side, looked like a fire in the room. Apprehending danger to the house, the man ran to the point from which the light came, and saw Carmel Sherlock leaning on the windowsill and looking out.

On seeing him Carmel Sherlock appeared to be startled, but after they had exchanged a few words, talked just as usual. He asked the man to wait for a moment, as he had something to give him. He saw Sherlock move about the room, and he came again to the window, and told him to go to the hall-door, where Sherlock met him. He came out upon the steps, having unlocked and unbarred the door. He had a wide-awake hat and a loose coat on, and a pair of leather leggings—the dress he usually wore when he rode any distance.

Carmel looked pale and flurried. Hedgelong thought there was something "queer about him, more than usual. It certainly was not drink." He gave him a note, with a request that he would give it to the servant to lay, in the morning, on the breakfast-table. This letter was produced, and read. It was addressed, "For the most honoured of the family of Shadwell, of Raby," and contained only these words:

"To that one, if any, who will be good enough to regret him, Carmel Sherlock, departing from Raby, worn out and disabused, with a heart full of gratitude and anguish, bids farewell."

As Carmel Sherlock placed this note in his hand, saying, "I have to ride to Wodely, early, and sha'n't be here, so don't fail," Hedgelong saw something shining in his left hand, which was the knife found on the bed in Sir Roke's room.

"What light had you to see it by?" asked Mr. Mervyn.

"It was full moon, and a clear sky, sir—very bright the knife was in his hand, careless-like. I saw it quite plain; the blade goes back and forward like a grig in the water, with a twist to and fro, and the handle's black, with two silver rings. I knew it, when I saw it in his hand."

"Had you seen it before?"

"Yes, sir. Mr. Sherlock showed it to me about three weeks ago; it was hung over his fireplace."

"Is that the knife?"

"It is, sir."

"Had he the knife still in his hand when he left you on the night on which Sir Roke Wycherly lost his life ?"

"No, sir. He saw me a-looking at it. I think he forgot it was in his hand, and he dropped it into his pocket, in haste. When he gave me the letter he stepped back, and shut the hall-door, soft like. I can't read. I did not know how odd the address on the letter was. It was about eight o'clock, it was; I gave it to the butler before it was known in the house Sir Roke was murdered. He looked on it, and shook his head, as much as to say there was summat queer in it, as I took it."

Now the oddity of the evidence respecting the instrument by which Sir Roke was deprived of life was this: the knife which Clewson had seen him secrete in the stable-yard was also produced, and proved to be a dagger which Sir Roke had purchased in Spain. Sir Roke did not carry it about his person. It happened to lie on his dressing-table. Clewson could point out the spot. He could swear that it was Sir Roke's dagger. It was as much stained with blood as the other. The drain was dry, and it had got no wet to wash the blood off.

"You heard voices, and a noise of something broken in Sir Roke Wycherly's room some time, you can't exactly say how long before you saw Sherlock in your room?"

"I heard something broke, and I heard Sir Roke's voice, and I heard him walking about the room when I went into the dressing-room."

"How do you know it was he who was walking there?" asked Mr. Mervyn.

"Well, I thought it must be he—"

"You can only say you heard steps—is that it?" said old Mr. Mervyn, with half-closed eyes, and inclining his ear.

"Well—yes—that's all."

"Was it your master's step?—did you recognise his step?" asked the coroner.

"I took it, it must be his step; but I couldn't swear."

"Did you mention that circumstance to Mr. Shadwell in the morning?" asked Mr. Mervyn, in the same attitude of shrewd attention.

"Yes, sir."

Mark Shadwell confirmed this statement with a nod of assent, but he was looking pale and angry.

"Then you heard a crash of something thrown down—you heard a voice or voices, and recognised Sir Roke's, speaking in excitement, and afterwards heard steps, you can't say *whose* steps, passing to and fro in the room, in silence?"

"Yes, sir, that's about it," said Clewson. Mark Shadwell, who sat close behind the vicar, leaning on the back of his chair, was now standing upright, and he said:

"You'll allow me, Mr. Coroner, to say a word. It seems to me that an imputation is indirectly thrown upon me, as if I had in my evidence suppressed what the witness Clewson told me in the morning. I need not tell you, sir, and others here, who know me better"—he glanced at the Reverend Stour Temple—"than ever Mr. Mervyn is likely to do, that I am incapable of suppressing anything in my evidence. I can't conceive a motive. If my attention had been called to that particular incident, I should, of course, have remembered all about it.

"What the man told me was simply that he heard a crash, followed, as he believed, by Roke Wycherly's voice, exerted in anger; be said it was his habit to talk by himself, and that a trifle like the breaking of that glass was enough to put him out of temper—he had a violent temper—that he went to the door and heard him—he did not then speak as if there was any doubt about it—walking about the room, that he returned to bed, and was wakened by the appearance of Carmel Sherlock, under the circumstances which he described, in his room; and that he could not tell how short might have been his interval of sleep when he was thus awakened. No sort of suspicion crossed my mind in consequence of this statement, and as to those knives, or whatever you call them, I've no clear conception what Mr. Mervyn imagines or surmises. I suppose he will let us know, and whatever it is, I venture to predict, it will turn out to be another mare's nest."

Mark Shadwell bent a sarcastic and agitated scowl upon the shrewd old gentleman, who said, with a cynical coolness:

"Pray, Mr. Coroner, allow me one remark, as a juror. I shall do my duty, and sift everything. I rather think it's important to know whether more persons than one were engaged in this atrocious murder."

"*Oh*, I *see*," said Shadwell.

"I'm sorry, sir, I can't hear you, Mr. Shadwell," said the coroner.

"You see," continued Mr. Mervyn, addressing the coroner, "here are two deadly weapons, each stained with blood, each used in this murder. If people see nothing odd in this *I* can't give them eyes, or brains."

"Now, I really must request—all this is quite irregular," said the coroner, beseechingly.

"*Odd!*" repeated Mark, grimly, and neither regarding the coroner's appeal nor Stour Temple's distressed look, which might have acted on him like a pluck by the coat. "The whole thing's odd, and I can't see why one particular singularity is seized upon for the purpose of suggesting that there is an undetected murderer still hid among this family, except for the odd satisfaction of inflicting pain upon me, by casting a scandal on my household."

"Now, Mr. Shadwell, I beg you'll observe this kind of interruption I cannot tolerate," said the coroner, growing peremptory; "we have been interrupted, gentlemen, by an altercation, and I must say I have heard no imputation to warrant any feeling—"

"It is indifferent to me what motives may be imputed in some quarters. I shall do my duty all the same, to the best of my power," said old Mervyn, drily.

"The better you do it, the better we are pleased," retorted Shadwell. These two gentlemen, who loved not one another, were growing more bitter as the dialogue proceeded, constantly springing up in gleams of anger like an imperfectly-extinguished fire, and causing the presiding functionary more trouble than the venerable chief of the nursery suffers, when children forget Dr. Watts's exhortations about "little hands" and "one another's eyes." But this subsided for a time, and the sterner business of the day proceeded.

While the examination of Clewson was continued, in course of which the letter to Pepys Adderly, which it was thought might possibly throw a light on the motive of the murderer, was read, the surgeon was upstairs, and made a careful inspection of the body.

The result of this was that he discovered three deep wounds, one about an inch from the extremity of the ear, nearly under the left jaw, entering the throat, and passing almost through the neck; another, a little at the left side of the breast, which had pierced the heart; and a third, with the same effect, about an inch below it. It turned out oddly that it was impossible to determine by which of the weapons the wounds were inflicted, for the length of each blade was the same, and although the creese looked the narrower of the two its wavy shape made up for this, and produced a gash as nearly as possible of exactly the same width. It was impossible then to determine which of these instruments had been employed, or whether only one or both, in accomplishing the murder.

In addition to these deep and fatal wounds, the palm and fingers of the right hand were deeply cut. There was also a severe contusion on the forehead and a cut there, but inflicted either by a blunt instrument, or by the fist of his assailant.

The jury returned to Sir Roke's room to view the body and the room again, and, after another minute scrutiny, they arrived substantially at this conclusion—that Sir Roke, having written his letter, and then read for a time, fell asleep in his chair; that, while he slept, Carmel Sherlock had entered the room to execute his guilty purpose; that, as he approached the chair, stealthily, the baronet awoke; that a brief struggle ensued, during which the decanter had been thrown to the ground, and the exclamations, imperfectly heard by Clewson, had been uttered, and Sir Roke almost instantaneously struck back in his chair by a blow on the forehead, had lain there stunned, while he was despatched by the three dagger-wounds which have been described, having clutched the blade of the knife in his hand during the struggle, and thus received those deep wounds in its palm and fingers which the surgeon had mentioned.

In this struggle, one or other of two things may have happened: either Sir Roke may have had his own dagger, for some reason, within reach—for he had already talked to several persons of a visit which had surprised him from Carmel Sherlock, who had attempted to enter his room on a former occasion at a very late hour at night, and whom, by suddenly opening the door, he had discovered and disconcerted; he might on this night have placed the weapon beside him, from a nervous fancy that Sherlock might repeat the visit which he had then attempted, and may have seized and lost it in the struggle—Sherlock wresting it from his hand, and in doing so dropping his own knife, and committing the murder with Sir Roke's, which he had secured.

Or the murder may have been perpetrated with his own creese; whichever weapon fell upon the ground, at the side of Sir Roke's chair, would have been as effectually stained with blood as if it had been actually used in stabbing him. This seemed the only way of accounting for Sir Roke's dagger having been removed by Sherlock. He must have picked up Sir Roke's, in his confusion, instead of his own.

Again by which door had the murderer entered the room of the deceased? Clewson swore distinctly that he heard the bolt which secured the door that opened on the dressing-room fall into its place while he was arranging the candle and some other things in the dressing-room. If this were so, access from the dressing-room was impossible. The murderer must have entered from the gallery, and after committing the murder, locked the door upon the inside, as the blood marks on the handle of the key attested. One thing was certain, that he had not made his egress through the same door. He must have raised the falling bolt, and let himself out through the dressing room. Clewson, who was accustomed to be called up at all hours of the night by his master, slept very lightly; no one, he was confident, could pass through his room without awaking him. Carmel Sherlock could not, he thought, have been many seconds in his room at the time when he first saw him.

And now the jurors trooped down the stairs again, silently ruminating; and having retired and considered their finding for some ten minutes, they returned with a verdict of wilful murder against Carmel Sherlock, for whose apprehension the coroner accordingly forthwith issued his warrant.

## CHAPTER 50
### ROGER TEMPLE SEES HIS LADY-LOVE.

When at length the house was cleared of these intruders, and left to the consciousness of late occurrences, and the gloom of death, Mark Shadwell, standing with Stour Temple and honest Roger in the hall, had hardly seen the last vehicle drive away, and disappear through the perspective of towering trees, when, lifting his head, he said to the vicar:

"Did you hear and see that long-headed villain?" Mark looked fiercely on Stour Temple.

"Whom do you mean?" asked he, surprised at this abrupt appeal.

"Old Mervyn, of course—stingy as he is, I believe he'd give a hundred pounds to improve this occasion to aggravate the misfortune and blacken the gloom under which my house lies—*think* of the wretch! The whole day long, but one idea in his head—to try and make people fancy that there were two murderers in this house! Whom could he mean to indicate? It could not be that fellow Clewson. There is no imaginable motive there, and he's a stranger—a mere sojourner—*that* would not disgrace me—whom could he be thinking of?"

"I'm quite clear,", answered the vicar, "that he did not think of any one in particular. I don't think even he fancies any such thing seriously, himself. He threw it out simply as a possible hypothesis on which to account for some puzzling circumstance s, which must have struck you also. If I, or Roger here, had mooted the same inquiry, you would not have suspected an unfair motive. It is, pardon me, my dear Mr. Shadwell, your own prejudice that reflects itself in mistaken imputations of his motives."

"Ha, Temple, you *won't* see!—that fellow goes to your church, and listens to your sermons, and gives you a half-crown now and then out of his overgrown wealth to divide among your poor—so, of course, he's a saint! May God unmask, and punish him!"

"Pray, my dear sir, do consider; only this moment, as I may say, descended from so awful a scene, and the presence of that mute and terrible witness of the vanity of earth and the victory of death," said the vicar, in the low tones of earnest expostulation; "I do assure you you wrong Mr. Mervyn. He may be no friend of yours; you make no secret of your feelings towards him: but I'm very certain he bears you no enmity."

"I'll make him speak out; he shall tell his meaning. I'm much obliged for his forbearance, but this is a limited household, and to set such an imputation afloat among them! Surely you see the malignity and cowardice of it as clearly as I do? But—no matter—the *cat will mew, the dog will have his day*; it may be my turn yet. I saw his nephew a short time since—Charles Mordant—is he still with you?"

"Yes; on leave. We are all so fond of him. I don't know whether he is going to visit his uncle this year! I fancy he has more liberty with us, and enjoys it more," answered the vicar.

"I dare say; I don't know much about him. Have you seen my wife today? I'm certain she'd like to talk to you a little. There's no good in my going; I'm as much put out by this odious business as she is, and I really don't know what to say to her. But you could—I have not seen her today, simply because I knew I should find her in distress, and should not know how to comfort her."

"Certainly, if you think she would wish it."

"Of course she would. I don't mean talking nothing but Bible; tell her the news, and anything to get up her spirits a little; I'll go upstairs to her room with you. I hope those fellows," he continued in a low tone, as they went upstairs side by side, "will come at once and take away poor Roke. You can't imagine what it is, having all that here, with so many nervous women in the house; and to be in charge of such a thing—I hate it. And then, I'm every way quite upset; and how I'm to get on without Carmel Sherlock God only knows. Here we are—I'm coming to see you, Amy, and I've brought a visitor with me; are you at home to us?"

"It is so good of you to come again today," she said to the vicar; "you must stay—*pray* don't go for a few minutes?"

He answered her little appeal and her beseeching look kindly, and Mark said:

"Having seen you, Amy, and asked you how you do, I take my leave; there are fifty things to be looked after, one more distressing than another—but it must be got through."

And dismally he turned and left the room.

"That dreadful inquest is quite over?" she said, in a very low tone, and looking at him as if she would have asked another question.

"Yes; and I think very satisfactorily—that is, so far as perfect distinctness is concerned. That poor, wretched man, you know," and the vicar shook his head, "mad man, I must call him—they found that the act was his—as we all knew before—and so, except for him, it ends; and he, from all we can learn, appears to be unquestionably insane."

"That any one capable of this should have been living in this house, talking to us, passing us on the stairs, and smiling in our faces, seems so frightful; and that the crime should have happened in this quiet household—so near to one's doors, and by a hand we all so trusted—is like a dream—or a frightful story!"

"I am haunted by that kind of incredulity myself," said the vicar, with a little shrug. "I can fancy how men who are beginning to grow insane, and are frightened by their illusions, feel. It really is by an effort that I can fix the truth in my mind as a reality, and believe in it."

"And how did Mr. Shadwell go through that dreadful ordeal?"

"Oh, just as we did—very well."

"He is more sensitive than you would imagine; anything that touches the honour of his house is agony to him. It was very-kind of you to come; he is not on happy terms, you know, with some of our neighbours, and he might have imagined affronts intended, where none were thought of; and a word from you would set it all right; and—*was* there anything unpleasant—did anything occur?"

"No—nothing—there was just a word or two between him and old Mr, Mervyn."

"Oh! Mr. Mervyn? What did *he* say?" asked she, nervously.

"Merely a few words, such as I might have said, or any other friend, but the spirit of which Mr. Shadwell mistook quite; and, in fact, take it what way one might, there was absolutely nothing in it to cause the slightest pain.

"Tell me—*do* tell me—if there was anything? I am sure you'll tell me."

"Nothing—really—just an impatient word from Mr. Shadwell, and a word of defence, or excuse, from Mr. Mervyn; but only that; and everything went on quite smoothly; no hitch—nothing: and now—except, of course, the impression that remains upon one's nerves—your trouble, on this account, is quite over."

"God grant it!" said she, with a great sigh and a look of great anxiety.

"And now I must tell you how they are at home; and what is going on in our little world round the vicarage."

And so the good man endeavoured to lead away her thoughts from the occurrences that had so awfully occupied them.

The hall door was still open, and our friend, Roger Temple, stood in the hall alone, looking from that elevation down the avenue, with its broad grass borders and solemn perspective of gigantic trees.

His jerry was on his head, his dark grey "zephyr," as he called his outer garment, loosely encompassed his portly form, and with the ivory crook of his stick pressed upon his fat chin, he looked with an innocent melancholy upon the prospect before him.

He had not, it must be allowed, much variety to amuse him; but, like more busy and bustling, men, he had something to think of. That which from outward seeming we often assume to be the dominant idea, is not always present in our thoughts, any more than in our dreams. I do not think that honest Roger was absorbed wholly by the tragedy of Raby. There was another drama in which his interest was nearer and more active.

As his fancy painted its scenes, and listened to its dialogue, with an interest that took no account of the time that was flying while he stood there, and amid his dreams kept him continually on the alert for sign or sound that might indicate the coming of that enchantress whose approach thrilled him, even at a distance, with an indescribable emotion, he looked about him, now and then, with a fat and simple sadness, and stood suspended, the handle of his cane removed from his expansive chin as he listened, and then sighed, and resumed his tender contemplation of nature.

On a sudden a door, in its deep oak frame, one of many that surround the panelled hall, opened. With an oblique glance, almost over his shoulder, this portly swain beheld it, turned, and with a sensation of delight and confusion, ready to sink rapturously into the earth, he saw his spirit.

In the shadow she stood. Did she ever before look so lovely, melancholy, beautiful? What clear and wonderful tints! Her rich, wavy hair, and deep, large eyes; and those lips, for which honest Roger could find no comparison but in the glow of the scarlet geranium petals in Barbara's garden, a discovery which, in a

274

moment of romantic confidence, he had trusted, with a bashful sigh, to the ear of his sister—that admiring and sympathetic
maiden—who assented thoughtfully and with energy, and then
plucked a sprig of that flower, as they stood together in the sunset air, on the steps, and placed it in his button-hole; whence the
enamoured fellow disengaged it, and looked on it with a sigh
and a smile, and kissed it with a gentle laugh and a blush, and
replaced it, saying:

"Ah, Baby! if she thought of me as you do—but I think it is
all a foolish dream."

And now, in the deep, oak frame, behind a film of shadow,
he saw his dream, and did not very well know for a moment or
two what he said.

With eyes lowered, she stood before him, and said in a low
tone, such as people murmur in a church porch as they go out:

"Oh, Mr. Temple, I'm so glad it is you! have they all gone
away?"

"All except Stour—my brother, you know—he's upstairs,
and I've been waiting here for him."

"Oh! And is it quite over, Mr. Temple?"

"Yes, it is over. Miss Marlyn; I fear you have found it a very
trying time—very agitating; you can't think how much I have
pitied you all this time."

"Very kind, Mr. Temple. It has, indeed, been a very awful
time. Would you mind—I've been so unspeakably anxious—
telling me just what happened?"

"At the inquest?"

"Yes, if you will; perhaps you'd come into this room for a
moment, and I can listen."

She stepped in—a melancholy, rather dark room—the schoolroom, with a shelf, and some lesson books, and two dingy globes,
and a very old piano, to indicate its old character; one tall window, never sufficient to make it cheerful, was darkened by three
or four elms, standing very near, in a clump, which threw their
gloom upon it.

"The door is open, so you can hear when your brother is

leaving," said the young lady, standing by the old grand piano, leaning on it with her slender hand. "You will kindly tell me what passed?"

"Only too happy—everything—as well as I can recollect it," said he, and he looked at her, and sighed, and then, in a very tender voice, he told the story of the inquest. He told it carefully. It happened that it had interested him intensely, and he remembered everything, and knew the people. Before he had got very far she asked him—

"Mr. Shadwell was present, wasn't he?"

"Oh, dear, yes. You see, you are so innocent of the ways of—of the world. I may say," he murmured, tenderly, "you don't know about these things; but he was a witness."

And so he went on with his detailed narrative, now and then sighing, and looking at that enigmatical young lady who was listening, as they say, with all her ears, while her slow glance darkly travelled over the floor.

When Roger came to the little altercation that had interrupted the quietude of the proceedings, she looked at him with a very odd expression. He saw it for a moment. It almost startled honest Roger, as, unexpectedly turning his eyes upon her, he met the glance. For so incontestable an angel, was it not the strangest look he could have imagined?

*A snake's small eye blinks dull and shy,*
*And the lady's eyes shrunk in her head,*
*Each shrunk up to a serpent's eye,*
*And with somewhat of malice and more of dread*
*She looked askance.*

Honest Roger had no turn for analysing phenomena or sensations; he simply saw that which dismayed him—felt there was something wrong, and stopped short, a little bewildered.

With electric speed Miss Marlyn saw in his honest face the shock which her look had given him; and that look had disappeared, and Miss Marlyn was looking down, softly and sadly, as before.

"Why do you stop?" she said, looking up sadly.

"I forgot, I think, what I was saying, for a moment; and I was afraid, perhaps, that the account of all this horrid business might have frightened you. Did it?"

"Frighten me! Yes, it does—that is, rather—it horrifies me, I should say, although it certainly shouldn't. If there were anything new to hear, indeed; but, you know, we had heard it all—all about poor, miserable Mr. Sherlock, who is mad, isn't he? and everything about that frightful occurrence; and—and who is Mr. Mervyn?"

"He is an old gentleman, with a very good estate. My brother likes him, and thinks him a useful man. I don't know much of him.

But you must have seen him at church two or three times, since you came here, though he usually goes to Maxton—a tall man, with a very white head."

"And—I don't quite understand what he meant—do you?"

"Mr. Shadwell thought he meant that two people might have been engaged in the murder."

"Oh? That is a very unpleasant idea; it makes one feel so unsafe. What do *you* think? what does the vicar say?"

"Oh, he does not think it—no one does; Mr. Mervyn doesn't, I'm sure; he seemed to have quite given up that idea before the inquiry ended. I should be sorry you were alarmed."

"But I'm not by any means; and I should be very much pained if you concealed the real state of the case through fear of frightening me. I hope you don't think me a coward, Mr. Temple, or a fool; I should be vexed at your thinking so meanly of me."

"But I don't—I couldn't; I wish you knew how I really think of you—*half* what I—I——"

"Then—oh, Mr. Temple, don't deceive me! Do tell me, I entreat, what is really thought about it."

"Nothing more, I assure you, than that Carmel Sherlock was the assassin—in fact, there is no second opinion about it; and I am so delighted that I happened to be the person to relieve your mind of any apprehension that any dangerous person might be still in your neighbourhood."

"That is so kind of you."

"I wish—I only wish—I wish ever so much—" said Roger, growing very hot, and tender, and hurried, and making a faint attempt to approach his short fat hand to her taper fingers.

"Yes, you have been always very kind—and very kind taking the trouble of telling me all this; and do, pray, tell me all the rest, you tell it so interestingly."

Thus encouraged, he went on with his narrative. He saw no more that shrinking gaze that, for a moment, had scared him—only the beauty that he was so tenderly enamoured of.

She listened, looking down, with a sharp and close attention, now and then fiddling nervously with a little black cross she wore; and at the end she said:

"I'm so much obliged. One grows nervous and excited so near to so horrible a scene; sure of nothing, fancying everything. I was always accounted brave at school, and I'm sure I'm no coward—that is, in the foolish sense; but still, everyone has imagination—even you men feel its power sometimes, and can pity us whose nature it is to look up in danger, and in trouble, to your strength, and counsel, and compassion. I have two friends here, Mr. Temple," she continued, a little incoherently, "two only—my pupil and companion, Rachel, and my dear Mrs. Shadwell—they are so good—otherwise I have none; and Madame de la Perriere—cruel to me when I was a little thing, a child, at her school, is my persecutrix still. I have discovered lately a cruelty of hers; and I cannot, as my dear Mrs. Shadwell advises, quite despise it. No, no! it is not for me that happy talent of contempt; falsehood and insult I can defy, for I am brave, but my heart is bleeding all the time. I think I shall leave Raby very soon. Perhaps, on earth, is some place where a poor and very unhappy girl may toil and live in safety. There are some kind faces I shall miss, and long remember—perhaps always."

"But—but—you're *not* going—you can't be *thinking* of going; what should they *do*—what should *everyone* do?" said Roger tumultuously.

He had taken her hand, in a tremulous agitation; and, at the same time, the vicar's step and voice were heard on the stairs talking to someone as he approached.

Miss Marlyn withdrew her hand suddenly.

"I've been speaking very foolishly—I have forgotten myself; pray, Mr. Temple, forgive me. Go, pray go—farewell, Mr. Temple; and a thousand very grateful thanks."

She placed her fingers to the open door, and drew it a little more open, so that honest Roger, who was lingering still in a happy confusion, could not fail to understand that he was dismissed.

"Farewell, dear Miss Marlyn, but only for a day or two," said he, with a great sigh, and a look of prodigious tenderness.

"Do—do go, pray," whispered the young lady, a little earnestly; and hearing his brother very near, with one longing, lingering look over his fat shoulder, he passed the threshold, and was established in the centre of the hall, and looking quite innocently, by the time the vicar stepped into its dark panelled area.

## Chapter 51
### A Distinguished Visitor Leaves Raby

Next day Mr. Pepys Adderly arrived. The Master of Raby received him in his study, and saw a man of some five and forty years, with an air of fashion, and a kind of languor and puffiness that suggested the idea of self-indulgence, and what is called good living.

He was, of course, properly concerned about poor dear Wycherly, because, in fact, he did not quite see, now that his patron was going to that formal and protracted supper, after the manner of Polonius, where the chief guest is not active but passive, how he—Pepys Adderly—was any longer to fare sumptuously every day; and, in fact, unless the baronet had done something for him in his will—a not very likely thoughtfulness, even if there was a will, which Adderly could not make out, and Sir Roke's men of business in London had not heard of—he might, before a year had passed, be very much puzzled to make out a dinner of any kind.

The vicar had come over to Raby, at Shadwell's request, to be present while inquisition was made for a will, in Sir Roke's room.

Mark Shadwell had placed seals upon the deceased baronet's desk, dressing-case, despatch-box, and every other possible depository of such a document which his room contained.

Mr. Pepys Adderly gave all the assistance in his power in this search; but it was totally unrewarded. There were not even letters. It was Sir Roke's habit, except when there was some very special necessity for preserving them, to destroy his letters on answering them.

Those which turned up were upon business accounts, memoranda of investments, an invoice of some pictures, bronze, and statuary—not a letter among them all but such as related strictly to business. Mark was relieved of an oppressive suspense when the search concluded without discovering one scrap of paper bearing the well-known handwriting of his secretary.

"And now," said Mark, who was looking very ill, so soon as they were again in his library, "what steps do you propose taking about the funeral? Where is he to be taken to?"

"Drayton, who is to succeed him, you know, would be the natural person, but he's yachting—in the Mediterranean—Lord knows where, and there's no one to direct. We don't know whether there's a will, and there's no one with authority."

"Well, you know, something must be done, and you and his solicitors can act—*I* won't," said Mark, harshly.

"There may be directions—where he's to be buried, and all that; it had better be quite private, I suppose?" said Pepys Adderly, patting the leg of his trousers with his walking-cane, and looking inquiringly at Mark, who merely nodded. "And where he's laid for the present, poor fellow! isn't of much importance, I should think. They'll be removing him, I conjecture, to some place, don't you think?"

"I can't tell at all any more than you," said Shadwell.

"No, quite uncertain; and I'm told there's an old family burial-ground where some of his people, long ago, were buried—a place near this called Wynderfel, isn't it? and it struck me it might lie there, as it were, provisionally—until—eh?"

"*No*," said Mark, peremptorily.

"Oh!—I merely mentioned it; but you think it wouldn't do?"

"No. You don't know, but it has been shut up as a burial-place for ever so long, and it isn't to be thought of. The remains must be conveyed from this, and they can lie, as you say, provisionally, wherever you, or those people who have been acting for him, think best."

"There are cemeteries—yes—the undertakers will know?" suggested Mr. Adderly.

"I dare say. You can have no difficulty; I decline taking any part in those arrangements, however. You'll be good enough to arrange with Clewson, his servant, and about the things he has got in his room."

"Yes—yes—certainly; and there will be people here tomorrow—about the arrangements—undertaker-people, you know. I suppose they can get in when they arrive?"

"Certainly," said Mark. "I only wish I could offer you a bed here; but we are all in such confusion in consequence of this miserable occurrence, and you will be much more comfortable down at Raby."

Pepys Adderly, I dare say, mentally acquiesced in this conclusion. At the best, however, it was a dismal bore, and I think he would have had no hesitation in cutting his dead patron in this extremity if it had not been for some hopes of founding relations with young Drayton upon the melancholy duties he was now performing.

Mr. Adderly had no difficulty in presenting a very becoming melancholy upon this funereal occasion to the people of Raby; for, as we know, "nothing dies, but something mourns," and here in this out-of-the-way part of the world, Pepys Adderly's soft raiment and sumptuous fare had been suddenly abolished by a madman. The claret, hock, and Madeira of his serene perspective had been smashed. The haunch he loved had been pitched into Tartarus by Carmel Sherlock—that most selfish of murderers. Mr. Adderly devoutly hoped he would be caught, and grudged him so quick and easy an exit as that through the drop. But his practical ruminations were chiefly concerned with the rising star. He knew little of Drayton—less he now felt than, considering his past opportunities, was at all justifiable.

His passion for yachting he could make nothing of. Adderly could not abide that recreation. To him it was simply being in a floating hospital, and he knew nothing about luffing and larboard, and all their horrid lingo. He had nothing for it, then, but to be sharp about these funeral expenses; to take on himself to discharge all the servants who would go at his bidding; to see that the cellar-books were all right, and to get up exact inventories of everything, and constitute himself the conscientious guardian and incorruptible agent of the unconscious heir, and by mastering detail, and cultivating for him a Spartan frugality during his absence, to lay the best foundation he could for a continuance, under the new *régime*, of his privileges and his office.

The next day came, and something was smuggled into the house, and people treading softly and speaking low were busy in Sir Roke's room.

When next Mr. Clewson saw his old master his dress was changed to white, and a border of white was round his face, and he was extended in a deep coffin lined with white quilted satin—robed, and fringed, and cased in the emblematic purity of white.

Mr. Clewson looked down on the familiar face of the baronet—more sharp, more sunken, more of the earth, earthy it had grown—a little streak of the sightless eye showed white in the shadow. Mr. Clewson saw the lines about the nostril and mouth that used to express themselves so dangerously when he snarled and cursed at him pretty regularly every night and morning. He had often made the phlegmatic Clewson intensely angry, and driven him to the verge of his self-command; but, on the whole, Mr. Clewson had been very sufficiently afraid of him.

Now Mr. Clewson was looking upon that mechanism, the spring of which was taken away, with a stolid but decent curiosity. He had now decidedly the advantage of that great gentleman whom he had feared, and a good deal hated, and in some sort admired. Mr. Clewson could see, and hear, and stand, and, after his fashion, think. A latent sense of the value of life communicated, as he looked on this odd image, a serene self-satisfaction and a tranquil glow.

As he looked on the mask that lay in the shadow of the coffin, a good many indistinct thoughts and feelings were also moving to and fro within the not very refined or active mind of Mr. Clewson, whose parents had been religious people; and left there some shadowy ideas of hell, which occasionally came into view like things traced in sympathetic ink, which show themselves only in certain temperatures.

"That's a really *beautiful* suit, it is!" said the soft diapason of Mr. Clothey, the eminent undertaker, as he gently brushed away some dust from the edge of the coffin with his handkerchief. "You never saw nothink of the kind more tasteful nor luxurious nowhere? That satt'n, sir, has stood us in fifteen four the yard, and heider down stuffin' and pillow. The style is the same which the hobsequeies of the late Marquis of ———. You've 'eard of that, no doubt, sir. We had that, you've 'eard—very beautiful thing it was. If he was the Dook of Wellington he couldn't 'av been got up more tasteful—the whole world 'eard of that, sir; we were in the papers, and spoke very high of indeed, and there wasn't no other 'ouse in England could 'av turned him out with the same finish and hellegance.

"This 'ere is one of the sweetest bits of cedar you hever seed, and this un's lead." He scratched it a little with the nail with which he indicated the successive rinds, as it were, in which the kernel of Sir Roke was enclosed. "Then the meeogny—the shell being hoak—we've turned out nothink prettier, and the family has reason to be gratified, which I say, is our *principle*; we never put in nothink but the very best of everything, and spares nothink to give satisfaction."

"It's 'ansom, sir, very," acquiesced Clewson, solemnly.

"'*Ansom!* why, there's not a dook but might be proud to lie in that, sir."

And so forth did they converse.

Two of Mr. Clothey's gentlemen remained at the inn at Raby, awaiting the orders of Mr. Pepys Adderly next morning. One of these gentlemen drank tea that evening obligingly with the servants at Raby, the other being entertained by old Mrs. Wyndle with the same beverage in the housekeeper's room, and with a great collection of anecdotes of the late Sir Roke Wycherly's boyhood, and two of the servants came over from the vicarage, and several neighbours also, who were brought up quietly by the back-stairs, and had a peep at the handsome upholstery provided by the tasteful house of Clothey and Clamp, and also at the forlorn baronet simpering fixedly through the thick satin and eider-down in which he reposed.

The next morning Sir Roke was gone. He set out in the grey of the dawn for the railway station, more than ten miles away. He was to make the journey up to London attended by Clewson, who was in charge of the luggage, and under the special care of the two gentlemen from Messrs. Clothey and Clamp, at whose establishment he was to pass the night on trestles, and thence in the morning to proceed to his destination in the dry and quiet vault where his grandfather and some contemporary kinsmen had been awaiting him for fifty years.

Sir Roke being gone, and Mr. Clewson gone, the obliteration proceeds. Beds and bedding are removed, bedsteads are taken down and transported to other places. The curtains unhung, the carpets dragged off the floor. That one with the great black stain upon it goes I know not where, but the stain has gone through, and dyes the floor itself in a wide black blotch with a map-like outline, which will not wash out. Three different days has the charwoman been at work upon it with hot water, and sand, and soap; but when the floor dries the stain comes forth to witness, and won't be put away or got rid of. And now these rooms are locked up. Mrs. Wyndle has the keys, and I suppose in course of time they will be haunted.

No news of Carmel Sherlock. A reward for his apprehension had been offered. The newspapers reprinted the description of his person; the police were vigilant, the telegraph transmitted scraps of information, and sent people on vain quests. Twice already had wrong persons been arrested on suspicion, examined, remanded, and discharged.

The winter was already heralding its march with gusts and storms, that roared through the tossing boughs of the forest, and began to strip the yellow leaves from their holdings, and scatter them impatiently over the sward. More wild and sombre grew the scene. Sometimes came a still and sunny day—a saddened remembrance of summer—throwing a melancholy lustre over the thinning and discoloured foliage.

The chilled air, and red sunsets, and shortened days betokening the decline of autumn, seemed to deepen the gloom of Mark Shadwell. More than three weeks had passed since the inquest, and still nothing was heard of Carmel Sherlock.

Mark had taken no step to secure a successor. He was making no exertion to supply by his own diligence the loss of his strange, but, on the whole, efficient steward. He was much more silent than ever, and looking ill.

When his newspapers came, he used to take them into the recess of one of the windows, and there con them over, every column, every paragraph; and after he had made his search, he would call to his daughter, if she happened to be in the room, and say:

"Look through it carefully, child, and try if you can find a line—anywhere—about Carmel Sherlock;" and when there was nothing, I think he seemed better pleased and more at his ease for the rest of the day.

In one of those red sunsets, wild and stormy, that have a character at once sad and threatening, Shadwell stood at the window, looking along the undulating plain studded with noble timber, and shut in on the left by the wooded uplands, towards Wynderfel, hidden by an intervening undulation, but showing in the red west the tufted tops of the old trees that stand among its ruins. He had been making his fruitless search as usual, in the newspaper which had just reached him—among reports, and *facetiæ*, and notices, and the other lumber that impeded him—for the missing and concealed Carmel Sherlock, and having failed, handed it to his daughter with the words:

"Run your eye carefully over this, and see if you can find anything about Sherlock."

He had almost forgotten that she was in the room, when Rachel said: "Oh! here's something!"

Shadwell turned sharply. "What is it? *Read* it."

And she read:

Plymouth Police.—A man answering the description of the villain Carmel Sherlock was arrested at Plymouth yesterday, on board the *William Ford*, bound for New York. As the vessel was only waiting for the tide to weigh anchor, the arrest was made necessarily with great promptitude. On being brought before Mr. Truefit, the magistrate, his worship asked him——

"Look on, *do*, and find—*was* it Sherlock? Here—*here*, child, give me the paper."

He spoke so harshly, and looked so pale and angry, that the girl was startled, and, as he snatched it from her hand, her eyes filled with tears.

"*Where?*" he said, with an impatient stamp. She pointed to the place.

He, as we say, devoured the news, and in a few seconds more, with a kind of sneer, exclaimed, pitching the paper aside: "Such rot!"

"It wasn't he?" she inquired.

"No; another blunder. I hope the fellow will bring his action, if he lost his passage: those fellows should be taught their business. This is the third time, by ——, they have pulled up a wrong person."

Though he spoke bitterly and with vehemence, there seemed

a sort of satisfaction too in his air. Was there a lingering regard for Carmel Sherlock, which excited a concealed sympathy with his stratagems, and exulted in his escape?

Mark Shadwell continued in silence to look toward the distant prospect, to which the red clouds of an autumn sunset formed a background. His thoughts were no doubt running in the same channel, for he repeated the name of Carmel Sherlock once or twice to himself, and then he said in a low tone:

"Wynderfel—that was his favourite haunt;" and he looked vacantly at his daughter.

"I should not be surprised if he were to come here," said Rachel. Perhaps she would not have spoken had he not looked at her so steadfastly, that she grew nervous, and felt constrained to say something.

"Who?" he asked suddenly.

"I meant Carmel Sherlock," she answered, half-frightened at her own audacity in speaking on a subject which seemed so much to disturb her father, of whom she stood so much in awe.

"You talk like a fool," said he, and looked again from the window.

She was in hopes that the dialogue had ended with that sharp speech, but she was deceived; suddenly he asked her:

"What makes you fancy that—who said it?" and he looked at her with eyes angry and earnest.

"The last time I saw him—the evening before—"

"I know—before he left; go on!"

"He took a kind of leave of me, as I sat in the window, and he talked as if he had a wonderful love for this place."

"Wonderful, indeed!" sneered Shadwell, dismally.

"And he spoke of a return, as if he would revisit it after death."

"Ho? That he may safely do."

"But it left an idea in my mind—I have been thinking ever since—that he would feel something like that home sickness that the Swiss are said to feel, and would be sure to return."

"I see; you are a very romantic young lady. Men, however, with constables and the hue-and-cry in pursuit of them, don't run into the lion's mouth in search of the picturesque. Sherlock is mad, I dare say; but he has the shrewdness of a madman. Come back *here,* indeed!" he muttered, still with a sneer and an impatient shrug.

And Mark Shadwell turned from the window, and walked moodily to the fireplace, where he leaned with his arm on the chimney-piece; and once or twice again he looked at her in dark meditation, and she fancied he was about to question her further, but he turned instead and left the room gloomily.

## Chapter 52
### A Strange Meeting

That night, with a message from her mother, Rachel timidly entered the library, and found Mark Shadwell at an open cabinet. He turned suddenly towards her, and she saw that he had a pistol in his hand. He looked angry and embarrassed, but said only, with an odd smile on his pale face:

"You see, I've been thinking of what you said, and am looking up my pistols; prudent, eh?"

There was, I suppose, something between fear and perplexity in her countenance, for he added:

"You need not be afraid; they're not loaded. Don't you know what I mean? Suppose Sherlock *should* come back here, as you said—quite mad, and want to murder *me?* Don't be afraid, I tell you; I don't believe anything of the sort. But people are sometimes made nervous by dreams; and your dream about Sherlock—for such it is—has made me a little bit fidgety—contrary to reason, contrary to belief; but this miserable month has unstrung me, and I'm growing like an old woman or a child."

And so saying, he fell into a dreary little laugh, and locking the pistol up again, resumed that sterner gravity that had grown habitual with him, and heard her message and answered it.

Mark Shadwell, alone in his library, was not reading, nor writing. He was darkly dreaming away his hours in vague schemes of change and self-banishment. A Canadian farm—a flock in Australia—a clearing in the back settlements. To sell Raby and the Wynderfel estates to some rich clothier, and thus scuttle the vessel that had been so long labouring and foundering in hopeless stress of weather, and let the rolling ocean of oblivion roar over the old name of the Shadwells of Wynderfel. Such was the staple of those vague thoughts which were always rising and revolving over the cauldron of his divination.

How was even his present painful position to be maintained? The huge, creaking, decayed machine—worked with a perpetual strain and increasing difficulty—had just sufficed to keep the deck of the used-up vessel above water; and who was to work it now that its engineer, Carmel Sherlock, whose screws and hammer and oil were needed every hour to prevent its coming to pieces, was gone?

Yes, there was one clever person—and diligent, too, when diligence was needed—who might do much, but of course not all to stay the threatened ruin: his secretary. But she was not to be thought of. Under sentence; with just a reprieve until more urgent distractions were allayed; and then, she, like Carmel Sherlock, should depart into darkness. Still he put it off, and off. And though his wounded vanity was sometimes stung almost to the pitch of hatred, and his arm lifted to strike, the blow was deferred and the sacrifice lived on.

This night, at the comer of the great gallery, unexpectedly, Mark Shadwell met Miss Marlyn. They had each their candles in their hands, and met face to face, with only two or three steps between.

Their eyes encountered for less than a moment, and Miss Marlyn's were lowered to the ground. Mark's gaze was fixed uncertainly upon her. His thoughts had been elsewhere. In such surprises a quarrel slips sometimes out of mind, like a loose page from a book; and it required an effort to recover the parenthesis. Mark did, in time to save him from the familiar sentence that was on his lips. He remembered all on a sudden the awful distance that was between them. Silently he drew a little aside to let her pass, and as silently, with eyes still lowered, but looking not abashed, but sad and proud—yes, very proud—she glided by and disappeared. Mark Shadwell felt oddly—a little chill, a regret, a pang; but, with a scornful smile and a frown, he turned and pursued his way.

He had not seen her; no, not since that dreadful night, which made the old house ghastly. No, not once. He had lived so entirely to himself, and his walks had been so remote.

He had forgotten how very beautiful she was, or rather how that beauty always impressed him. He shut his door sullenly, and as he set his candle down upon the table, he thought:

"So much beauty is *funeste* and ominous. It never was granted to the heroine of a common or a happy story. To me to look at her is pain. Ever again to suffer that d—d delusion to steal into my heart is impossible. That is the kind of person whom it is impossible not to love, or not to hate. Indifference is not imaginable. Well for me she chose to make me hate her. Yes, I shall settle that matter. She shall go. Let her play out the tragedy or burlesque which fate allots her in another theatre. Raby has seen the first act. My God! If she had never entered these doors he would not have come."

Mark Shadwell left the house next day alone at about noon. There are agitations of mind for which instinct seems to prescribe bodily labour and extreme fatigue. Mark walked rapidly. He chose the upland forest for his march. Its brakes, its steeps, and rocks enforced exertion, and its vast seclusion secured him against interruption.

The sun was near the horizon when, by a circuitous and lonely route, Mark found himself at last before the ruined walls and roofless gables of Wynderfel.

The level light glittered on grass and nettles, and on the ivy upon the walls with a tremulous splendour, flooding the sharp grey angles and nodding trees, now stript of half their foliage, with a sad and mellow glory that deepened by contrast the cold grey shadows stretching far over the slopes.

Not two months had passed since he had sat on the same

stone bench, looking on the same lonely picture of bygone greatness and earthly mutability, under the same sunset glow and shadow, and he was no longer the same Mark Shadwell. He looked years older, and turned towards these ruins a thinner, paler, sterner face.

Rapid walking is not conducive to thought. In fact, it is next to impossible while walking quickly to think in train at all. One reason, no doubt, why nature points to that expedient for relief in high mental excitement.

Now Mark's walk was over for a while; he was sitting on the old stone bench, looking upon the low-arched doorways, the mullioned windows, and those tall chimneys of Wynderfel, up which the ivy tendrils were creeping.

Quietude had hardly succeeded to his long and rapid walk when the image of that strangely beautiful girl, as she stood for a moment before him, like a lovely statue of shame and pride, suddenly, in the lonely gallery of Raby, rose before his memory, and furnished the theme of a long, passionate, and bitter meditation.

She haunted him, and yet he hated her—hated her for having used and deceived him. Was ever man so fooled and mortified? And yet there was that beautiful image, the fascination of which at times overpowered his vindictive rage. Wounded pride and passion mingling resulted in that malignant idolatry which we know as jealousy. Hardly conscious of the passions that entered into his. agitation, he was, literally, wildly jealous. Jealous of whom? Of that blood-stained, cold, smirking shadow whom he hated to think of Yes, a profitable conspiracy! Let them keep their tryst.

If Carmel Sherlock were here, he would say, "Let *her* go to him, or let *him* come for her." A sort of chill stole over him with this mockery, and at the same moment, like an apparition summoned by his evil thoughts, Carmel Sherlock stepped through the arched doorway of the ruin, and stood before him.

Travel-soiled and wild was the figure. Famine-stricken he looked. He extended his emaciated fingers, and directed his woe-begone eyes towards Mark Shadwell.

As a spirit rises, Mark Shadwell was standing upright, he knew not how, and freezing with a horror he had never known before.

"My good God!" repeated Mark, slowly, twice or thrice, in a tone scarcely above a whisper, gazing with wide eyes, and fixed as if he were cut out of stone.

Carmel Sherlock was equally motionless, and stood still with a countenance indescribably piteous; his lean hand extended towards him, palm upward, like a mendicant's. With a sudden gasp, Mark Shadwell stamped upon the ground, and cried:

"Murderer! miscreant!"

And at the same moment, with a step back, he lifted his hand from his pocket and discharged a pistol full at Carmel Sherlock. The explosion rang sharply among the echoing walls, and startled into a general flutter the sparrows in the ivy.

Carmel Sherlock staggered a step or two, as his arm dropped by his side.

Before the film of smoke projected from the pistol had ceased rolling in the air, almost simultaneously with the report, a cheery voice close by shouted, and steps were heard approaching on the narrow old road, which, just where it winds by the angle of the building, shows its pavement above the grass. It was plain from the tone that whoever cheered had no notion of the deadly intention with which the shot had been discharged.

Mark's hand was already in his pocket, on another pistol. But he did not raise it. The challenge that had just reached his ear arrested him. If he had seen the spectre of Roke Wycherly, he could not have turned on him a more horror-stricken scowl than he did on Carmel.

Sherlock's face winced with pain; with his left hand he caught the angle of the doorway, and a cold moisture shone over his forehead.

"Do, through the head, and let me die," said Carmel Sherlock, faintly. "I came, sir, for that, to be taken, to die—anything to end it."

"Hallo!" panted Roger Temple, now within a step or two of Mark Shadwell, and amazed, as well he might;

"By Jove!" exclaimed Charles Mordant, his companion, equally astonished.

"Glad you came up," said Shadwell, with a very pale face, and an attempt to laughs "Rather a surprise, isn't it? Here he is— *Sherlock*. I don't believe a word he says."

With this false and agitated smile he glanced from them to Sherlock, and from Sherlock to them again, and the smile quickly subsided, and darkened into a careworn scowl.

"What do you wish, Mr. Shadwell? Shall we take him?" said Charles Mordant, who had advanced within a step of Carmel Sherlock.

"The d—d fool!" said Shadwell, between his teeth.

"Yes, take me, shoot me; the grave is best. I travelled, sir, Mr. Temple, seven and thirty miles on foot since last night for this, and I came to Wynderfel to see it once more. I'll go with you, Mr. Mordant, Mr. Temple, wherever my master says."

"You shall come up to the house, then, and from thence to Applebury, and as you seek justice, you'll find it there," said Mark, savagely.

"Have we a right to take him without a warrant?" whispered honest Roger at Mark Shadwell's ear.

Shadwell made no answer. He merely said, "In a moment," looking still at Carmel Sherlock.

But Charles Mordant, who had not heard Roger's question, seized the wounded man by the collar.

Carmel started.

"Take your hand from my throat. Remove your hand, sir," said he sternly, but with a trembling lip.

"Don't mind," said Shadwell, addressing Mordant.

"No, time enough when I get to the gaol for *that*. I give myself up. No one takes me. I've come for the purpose; but you shan't drag or throttle me—let me die; but no profanation."

"Well, then, come to the house, your hurt must be attended to. I'm sorry, *very* sorry, but I could not help it. I thought you had something in your hand when you raised it. I wish I had known your real purpose," said Mark Shadwell, anxious, no doubt, that all should understand how he came to wound Carmel Sherlock. "Do you think you can walk so far?"

"In the arm," said Carmel. "I don't feel it now—it is not much—nothing, in fact." He looked pale, and spoke faintly, however.

"I'll fetch some water from the brook, shall I?" said Charles Mordant, and ran off, returning quickly with his flask filled.

"No," said Carmel Sherlock, "the bone is not broken—nothing. I wish it were through my brain, sir."

Some twenty minutes after this, the party consisting of Mark Shadwell, Roger Temple, Charles Mordant, and Carmel Sherlock, supporting his bleeding arm, entered the hall-door of Raby.

## CHAPTER 53
### Mark Shadwell's Offer

There were few words spoken till this odd party reached the house. Carmel Sherlock walked among them like a man going to execution. When he came to the door he looked up and about him, and entered the large hall with a great sigh.

Old Robson, the butler and *factotum* of the family,—who knew something about horses, a little of tailoring, and loved flowers and singing-birds, and, also, having seen service as an officer's servant at Quatrebras and Waterloo, pretended to surgery,—was, with this accomplishment, now put in requisition. He happened to be in the hall as they entered. His short white hair seemed to bristle up over his purple face, and his little eyes almost to start from their sockets, as he stared on Carmel Sherlock.

"Hey?—*Dear* me!" he ejaculated. "Mr. *Sherlock*?"

"Ay, Mr. Robson, the moth returns to the candle. You did not think to see me, sir?" said he, very pale and excited. "Shake hands! That was blood well spilt, sir—a devil cast out—Sir Roke Wycherly, body and soul!"

Robson, the fat old butler, with a shrewd face, drew back

without touching the hand he tendered, and Roger Temple answered emphatically, with mild reproof:

"There, Mr. Sherlock, pray don't. You mustn't talk that way, and you may injure yourself besides."

"He has been wounded," said Mark, sharply. "Don't mind his talking, but look to his arm; do you hear, Robson? and dress it if you think you can. You're faint, Sherlock—you must take something. Give him a glass of wine first, and then see about his arm," said Mark. He touched Temple on the arm, and said in his ear: "You'll kindly stay with him, won't you, for a few minutes? I must make out his committal—but I shan't detain you long."

And with these words he entered the library, leaving Carmel Sherlock seated in the hall with three people about him, and soon in the surgical hands of old Robson.

When Mark Shadwell got into his library and shut the door, he felt suddenly faint and overcome. He bolted it and opened a window, standing before it for a time. He took from a drawer a printed form of committal to the jailer of Applebury jail. But his hand was tremulous. He did not want criticism, and this odd scrawl did not look like his signature. He tore it up, and threw it into the grate, and looked sadly on the extended hand in which was this treacherous tremor. He must wait a little, and let it subside.

Shadwell went out again to the hall. It was empty; but he heard voices from the room at the other side. There he found Carmel Sherlock, with his coat and waistcoat off. He was leaning with his shoulder to the wall, and looking down with a dark apathy upon the floor at his feet—the only man present, you would have said, quite unconcerned in the discussion of his wound. That wound, as it turned out, was trifling. The ball had passed between his left arm and his breast, leaving a severe abrasion, but little more. Two inches to the right would have directed it through his heart, and ended some of his speculations in certainty.

"I'm very glad—I'm very much relieved," said Mark. "I'm certain, now, he could not have meant me any harm. If I had only had time, Sherlock, to think, I should have *known* it. Had you not better sit down?"

Carmel Sherlock looked up at Shadwell, and his large eyes rested on his face with a melancholy stare. At this look of reproach, Mark Shadwell's eyes contracted and were lowered for a moment to the ground.

"Ah, sir, even for a moment that such a thought should have crossed my benefactor's mind, dishonours me," said Carmel Sherlock.

"It was not a thought, Sherlock, it was a craze."

"A craze!" echoed Sherlock. "It is hard to pick your steps among unrealities and substances—*umbrâ pro corpore.* This house of Raby, sir, is full of false lights and false shadows; there is no true life possible in it."

"It was an impulse—not even a craze," said Mark Shadwell, with a strange eagerness. "If I had hurt you seriously, I should never have forgiven myself."

Sherlock sighed deeply.

"It is nothing, sir—I said so."

"No, thank God!" said Mark.

"I should have liked, sir, to fall by a friendly hand—by an accident. Where are my things?" he added, turning hastily, and getting on his coat and waistcoat. "I'm ready to go—I'm ready to go, sir. It is not the place, but the *way,* I hate. Those who like death don't like dying."

"Poor fellow!" whispered Roger Temple, shaking his head with a significant glance at Mark Shadwell.

"Yes," said Mark, with a nod, and beckoned Roger Temple into the hall. "You heard him talk—isn't it strange?" said Mark, looking darkly into Roger's honest eyes.

Roger lifted his hands, and shrugged his fat shoulders, saying:

"Poor fellow! isn't it horrid? It accounts for everything, I think, almost—doesn't it?"

Mark nodded, and said:

"I've known that a long time. He has no idea of deceiving;

but, at the same time, you can't believe a single word he says—half the things he relates are the merest fancies; and, no doubt, one of these delusions has been the cause of this crime—apparently so motiveless, and certainly so unlike him."

"If he's mad—" began Roger.

"Can we doubt it?" suggested Mark. "And I do trust, in the mercy of heaven, that he is quite mad. They can't think of hanging him," said Roger.

"We English like hanging people—sane men, if we can get them—madmen, if we can't. It's clear, however, they mustn't hang that wretched maniac."

"It was a horrible freak. What do you suppose was in his mind?"

"A lunacy—an idea of a duty, or a mission—heaven knows what."

"Poor, wretched fellow! Certainly he does look miserably," said Roger, pathetically; "and, by-the-bye, how are we to get him to Applebury?"

"Well, I've been thinking, and I fancy the best plan is to swear in some of my men as special constables, and let them go there in Wason's 'bus from the town here."

"You know you must not hesitate if you have not got messengers enough. I can go at a devil of a pace when I like it," said my fat friend Roger; "and I'll run down, if you wish it, to Raby about the 'bus, and—and I hope this occurrence today has not alarmed your young ladies," he added, lowering his voice tenderly.

"I'm sure I can't tell," said Mark, drily; "but I'm very much obliged for your offer. I don't know how I should have managed if you had not turned up. I think I'll talk a bit to that strange fellow—quietly by ourselves—he and I, and try and make out what fancy was in his brain when he did it."

"But you can't mean to be alone with him, he's not handcuffed or secured in any way; and, upon my honour, I think he looks quite mad!"

"I'm not afraid. I'll take care of myself—I'll try—he'll talk to me by ourselves; I'll try—yes, I think I'll try." Mark thus talking, they returned to the room where Sherlock and his two custodians were.

Shadwell despatched the servant for three men who were within call; and signing to Roger Temple and young Mordant, they, with some misgivings, left the room together, keeping, however, within easy hearing of any alarm.

"Carmel," said he, as soon as he had shut the door of this rather dark wainscoted room, "a pretty mess you have made of it! What devil possessed you to run yourself into this frightful fix?"

"I'm guilty," said Sherlock, with his hands clasped together, looking down with a scowl of agony.

"Of course you are guilty," said Mark.

"That is," continued Sherlock, "if guilt there be in seeking the life of a monster predestinated by infallible powers to a bloody death."

"Well, I shan't debate the question, call it how we may; that has passed which exposes you to death. It is all very fine speculating on death—like Pythagoras or Plato; but I'd like to know what we can make of it, but just the most dreadful thing we can imagine. If there is a futurity, it means judgement; and if there is not, it means annihilation. Now, why should you voluntarily run yourself into that iron trap?" said Shadwell, very pale.

"I think, sir, differently of death. Life is ghastlier. Nature points to a less dreadful life in death."

"Nature tells you plainly enough the value of life, by giving us the instinct to cling to and defend it, even in privation and torture Every man has, of course, some theory about that event. I have mine—you have yours; but we need not test it by martyrdom. If we could open the door, and look, and drawback, of course it would be all very simple. But that's an iron door, Carmel, with a spring lock, of which we have not the key. Once in we are trapped for ever. We have only a few minutes now to talk; as I said, I won't discuss it. Now I meant you to understand *me*."

"I do, sir—I *do*—all goodness," broke out Sherlock.

"Well—well, but that's not the point. I don't seek your life. What occurred today—if there's any good in swearing—I *swear* it was accident. I was more shocked than you when it happened. I don't know even *how* it happened; but so far from wishing you any ill, I'll prove to you that my first wish is to serve you."

"Oh, sir! did I ever question it?" pleaded Sherlock."

"I don't know—I hope not—only listen. I wish to save you. The door here is bolted; raise that window, and a dozen steps will bring you to the edge of the oak-wood you know so well. Hide yourself there in that impenetrable thicket till twelve o'clock tonight. I shall direct pursuit upon a false scent, and visit you at that hour at the old well with provisions, and I'll bring you money enough to carry you to America, or where you please. You must wait there for a little time, and I'll bring you supplies every night until pursuit begins to slacken; then you cross to France. I'll give you the means of disguising yourself; and you are not the shrewd fellow you have proved yourself up to today, if you don't make your way to a place of security. There, raise the window, and go."

Though Mark Shadwell spoke, or rather whispered all this, in slow, measured articulation, the signs of suppressed agitation were visible in his face, and his eyes were fixed on Sherlock more with the eagerness of a man begging his own life than the coolness of one merely offering an escape to another.

Carmel looked on Mark Shadwell earnestly, and raising his finger, he said:

"Eight days after I left this I was alone on the side of Penmon Maur, and a shadow of a cloud, shaped like a hand, pursued me upwards. I saw it on the low ground first, and my heart died, for it was shaped like the hand I dreamed of. It was gliding up the side of the mountain spread out, and I knew if it seized me it was a sign. All that man could do, to escape, I did; but it caught me near a wall of rock facing southward, and a darkness like night overcast me, and the thunder began—you remember. It was *then* that fate overtook me."

"For God's sake!" whispered Mark, "talk for once like a man of sense; tell your dreams tomorrow. Go now, and do as I've said, and leave me to tell my own story."

Mark Shadwell, whose face was darkened by agitation, pushed him by the shoulder, as he spoke, toward the window.

"*Then*, sir," continued Sherlock, "I would have died of cold, or famine, or fatigue, rather than forfeit my liberty. After *that* happened, I sickened of life, and began to long to give myself up—and so the longing grew and grew—until I could bear it no longer—and I came—and here I am, a willing prisoner-and resolved to be either on or off with death."

"I say, Carmel Sherlock, you had better do as I have told you," said Mark Shadwell, sternly, "I run a risk for your sake; you'll have no second chance."

"I have things to tell you about the death of Sir Roke Wycherly that will amaze you—but not now. If you come to me after I go to prison, I will tell you all."

"Don't be a d—d fool," said Shadwell, in a fierce undertone; "try the chance I give you."

"Forgive me, sir—I can't—I should come back tomorrow—I should go to the prison and give myself up—I can bear it no longer."

"Then you are a worse fool than I took you for," said Mark, with a ghastly laugh; and he looked for a moment as if he would have struck him, but he controlled himself; and he walked to the window which offered the means of escape, in vain—and he looked out for a time—and then turned and said:

"You won't let me be of use to you. I'm sorry, but it can't be helped, I suppose."

He paused, as if to allow Sherlock to reconsider his resolve, but there was no sign of change or hesitation; so he proceeded:

"You spoke of circumstances connected with Sir Roke's death that would surprise me. Well, you choose to go to prison, and to prison you go. But I'll see you there, and whatever these are; I ask but this—keep them for my ears."

"I shall seem to you in one sense a victim. I've had a partner, sir. I love this house, but I ought to hate it; sleep is haunted in it—whispers round the corners—ha! I know it."

"Well, if there is anything worth telling, tell *me*."

"Yes, sir."

"*Me*, mind."

"I know, sir."

There was in Mark's mind considerable curiosity respecting this, but also a stronger loathing; and so, whatever the revelation might be, he was glad to put it off to a more convenient season.

Mark went to the door as if to unbolt it, and with his hand to the brass, he paused. He looked at Carmel Sherlock for a moment, and returned a few steps quickly.

"Sherlock," said he, in a low tone, seizing his arm very hard, "you see how I have trusted you; how in my zeal to save you I have placed myself in your hands."

"Trusty hands—Gloving hands," murmured Carmel.

"Need I tell you that, of our conversation in this room, you must promise that not one syllable is repeated."

"No, sir, I'm deep and dark."

"And don't mistake me, Sherlock. In the presence of others I may seem harsh and unfeeling, but remember, under all disguises, I'm your *friend*. No, not a word;—only don't mistake me."

Again he approached the door, but turned in a kind of agony, and extending his hand with an imploring look toward the window, "Change your mind!" said he.

Carmel Sherlock shook his head, with a sigh that resembled a sob, but answered nothing.

"All's over then!"

And with these words Mark Shadwell stepped to the door and opened it.

Robson had already got three of the workmen into the hall to be sworn as special constables. The preparations were soon completed, and in their custody Sherlock departed for the prison.

"Vain trying to get him to talk coherently," said Mark, as he stood upon the steps, and the distant gate closed upon Sherlock and the men in whose safe keeping he was. "It is impossible now to separate his dreams from his facts. Hanging such a creature would be a mere murder, and it is impossible to rely upon any statement he makes—no matter in what good faith."

## CHAPTER 54
### JEST AND EARNEST

As they stood upon the steps, about to depart, Roger, who in the excitement of their strange visit had no practicable opportunity of inquiring for the ladies, repaired the omission. And Charles Mordant mischievously supplemented his politeness by inquiring particularly for Miss Marlyn, which threw honest Roger into a cruel confusion.

"Oh! Miss Marlyn?" answered Mark, quickly, with a glance in the young man's eyes. "I suppose she's very well. I hav'n't seen her for some days. I've had too much to think of. It's very unfeeling, I suppose, but I'm afraid I half forgot her existence; why do you ask?" he inquired, rather oddly.

"Miss Temple's sure to ask us. She admires Miss Marlyn immensely, doesn't she, Roger?—and I assure you Temple would get into an awful scrape if he could not give an account of her. You have no idea, and the consequence is that Roger is generally sure to inquire."

"What a goose you are!" retorted Roger, with a bashful little laugh and a shake of his head, and a jocular menace with his walking stick.

"Well," said Shadwell, drily, "you may tell Miss Temple that whenever anything goes wrong, my people are sure to tell me; and I fancy if they had anything unpleasant to report—a cold or a headache—I'd have been certain to hear it; and" he continued, rather more sharply, "I don't know that she's going to stay with us very long. I suspect she's rather too young to know much about her business."

Roger tried to smile still, but the smile was by no means cheerful, and he was looking down on the steps, and running the point of his cane carefully along the joining on the stones.

Mark glanced at him with an eye of scarcely concealed contempt.

"And I believe there's nothing more to tell about Miss Marlyn. And the fact is, I'm thinking more about that wretched man who's gone to prison; a useful fellow he was, and so gentle, and I can't conceive how he possibly could—though it may be intelligible enough—" he corrected himself, leaving his sentence unfinished. And he walked a little with them on their way back, and took his leave, and smoked at his leisure returning. By the time he reached the hall-door his cigar was out, and he cast the stump away with somewhat more violence than was strictly necessary.

"What a disgusting old fool that fellow is; past fifty, and Agnes Marlyn! Upon my soul!"

I don't believe he was thinking of himself. I'm afraid he was kicking and tumbling in the gutter poor Roger Temple's little romance.

"Clever young lady! I shouldn't wonder if she had been making a fool—but that's tinting a rainbow, and throwing a perfume on a violet—making a fool of Roger Temple. What a fool that fellow *is!*"

The effect of this little meditation was to send Mark Shadwell directly to his wife's sitting-room upstairs, where he found her.

"I've come to say a word about Miss Marlyn. It's absurd our continuing to keep her here. She's doing no good. There's nothing to stare at. I don't mean she's doing any mischief. I simply mean, at a time when I can't afford a guinea, it won't do to go on adding all that young lady costs to our expenses. If she were worth the money, I might try to get on a little, but she's not, and you know she's not. It's simply, she's kept here to talk, and laugh, and amuse. There, now you're preparing to cry, but there's nothing to cry *about*. If it does amuse you, hang it, do you think it can be any pleasure to me to stop it? It's only one more vexation. But I have not money to spend on anything of the kind. I told you so before, and I tell you so now; and you must see her Amy, and tell her so at once."

There was a pause here, and nothing was heard but the little tattoo that Mark was drumming with his finger-tips on the table.

"If you want her in the neighbourhood, why don't you place her somewhere—I mean, find her a husband," he said. "There's that clever fellow, Roger Temple. It's a pity he has no ideas, and no teeth, and no hair; but I venture to say that won't prevent any girl's marrying him, if she thinks he has a little money, and she can't find anyone with more, to oblige her. I think someone said—didn't they?—she and old Roger liked one another."

He said this with a sour carelessness. He hated Agnes, he was sure, and yet he was curious.

But Amy could only tell him that Roger was enamoured, without having excited any corresponding romance.

Well," said he, returning to his point, that's not my business. If she thinks she can do better, of course she won't have *him*. Only she must understand that, go where she may, she can't stay here. It ain't caprice, Amy—I may as well tell you—I must get someone in Carmel Sherlock's place. It's quite impossible for me to get through more work than I do; and I must have *one*, at least, where there's ample work for *six*, to look after the never-ending business of this miserable property; unless, indeed, we are prepared to see the whole thing go to pieces before a year."

What could Amy do but acquiesce?

"Of course, you'll do it your own way. I don't mean a scene, or a rudeness; I only want her to understand that she must leave Raby. I believe they get a month's notice, or something; but do it today. I shall ask you this evening what is settled."

So saying he turned to leave the room, and recollected, just at the door, to ask her how she was, and awaited her little story, without, I am afraid, hearing much of it; and then, with a rather absent—"I hope I shall find you better. Amy, by-and-by," he went on his way alone.

He heard, as he crossed the hall, faintly through the doors, the chords of the piano, and the notes of a sweet, well-known voice.

He stopped and listened with feelings bewildered, for a minute, and then, with a sigh and a sneer, passed on. Within were Rachel and Miss Marlyn, who had just stood up from the piano.

"Thanks, darling," said Rachel; "that is the saddest and prettiest little song in the world!"

"And the most appropriate," said Agnes, placing her hands on her companion's shoulders, and gazing with her large melancholy eyes into Rachel's face—"for it is a farewell."

"You are not to say that, Pucelle; think of me. What should I do; quite alone, in this great house and place—you cannot be so cruel."

"I am not cruel; and yet I am going to speak to your mamma about it today. I can't help it, Rachel. There are many reasons, and one is enough. I feel that I am *de trop* here."

"What?"

"Yes; I don't say in *your* way; but it seems to me that your papa has judged me unfavourably. He thinks that you and dear Mrs. Shadwell are too good to me; and he is jealous. He thinks me overrated; and so, I'm sure, I am. No; you need not protest. How can you or I know whether I am capable of teaching anything? and it seems to me that he has conceived a prejudice, not to be got over, against me, and so I am condemned in secret. I ask but for *light*. Who is my accuser; what the charge? I will not stay even to *fancy* that I am suspected. This is enough to determine me; but there are other reasons also. Heaven will not desert me!"

Her eyes were raised as she spoke. There we anguish and indignation in her appealing gaze to Rachel; she looked the embodiment of defenceless innocence; a more practised eye might have fancied something of the cold art of the melodramatic actress in the beautiful young lady.

"That, however, is one reason; as I have said, there are many. I am sorry I sang that song. It has put me out of spirits. The soldiers march away to the wars to gay tunes. I am away to the great war, and I'll go with pleasant music in my ears."

Down she sat laughing, and played and sung an odd defiant

little German song, with a wild, merry refrain, which Rachel did not understand, but the careless gaiety of which sounded heartless; the light of the old, cruel smile which she remembered, once or twice, when Agnes drifted away from her reckoning and knowledge into dark moods and associations which pained and half-frightened her, was there.

With a ringing chord or two, a wild *roulade,* and a silvery laugh, the music ended, and she stood up, still laughing.

The laugh passed into a weary "heigho!" and a rather dismal restless gaze from the window.

"It was very unfeeling, that little song, wasn't it?" said Agnes, looking at her with a sidelong glance, as she leaned with her slender fingers to her cheek.

This common-place little speech puzzled Rachel rather. The smile had vanished, like wintry sunshine chased away; but the sadness that had preceded it had not returned. There was no softness there. The eyes that were turned upon her were dark and cold, and just a suspicion of scorn in the features.

"Why do you look at me as if you did not like me?" said Rachel. "I told you once or twice, when you did it before. If you don't like me, I'd rather you told me so."

Miss Marlyn's eyes neither lightened nor softened at this appeal, neither did her dark, cold eyes swerve.

"I was thinking," said she, "of our expedition on which old *La Chouette*, I mean, Madame de la Perriere, despatched me—not for love, you may be sure—with poor little dried-up Mademoiselle Descatel, in charge of four of the girls who were coughing and wheezing in consumption—such a noise they made all night! The doctor said they must change the air; and La Chouette had nothing for it but to submit. So she packed us off to a place called Dromonville, and I think it was the oddest climate in the world. It was always either dense fog or brilliant sunshine; the sun was very little, the fog a great deal. We were only there six weeks, and two of them died there; it was ridiculous—poor things! We were very sorry, of course; but one could not help laughing—and that climate of Dromonville, with its dense fog and glare of sun, now and then resembles me. I'm in a frank mood, now—too frank, whenever my glare of sunshine comes. One great, fiery gleam in fifty days, and then all again in a thick white mist. No eye in nature could pierce it. My natural reserve, forty-nine days of fog—ha, ha, ha!" she laughed suddenly. "Isn't it funny?"

"I don't think it a bit funny. I think it was very sad about those poor girls," said Rachel.

"Very sad, to be sure! *and* very funny, if you had seen old La Chouette's face, and seen what a fright she was in when she found out that she had killed the two girls."

"I think it's shocking," said Rachel.

"So you should—I knew you would. It *was* shocking. And now with me, for the hour, the fog is rent a little, and that white, fierce sun of Dromonville shines through and hurts the eyes; you see, it is my candid mood."

"I don't think so," said Rachel. "I should call it your mood of—shall I say, affectation? I'm sure you are not like yourself when it is upon you. I like your real self; I don't like this."

Agnes was still looking on her with the same dark and not loving eyes; half, as it seemed, in abstraction, and drumming with her finger-tips on the window-frame.

"*There!*" she said, with a sudden smile; "I find myself still playing that heartless little air; pretty, I think it; but, as I said, very unfeeling of me."

"If you think so," said Rachel, who was growing a little cross, "had you not better stop it? I don't know the meaning of the words, so I can't say."

"Ho! the words? They are merely a comical, little vulgar lamentation over the difficulty of finding a lover, and bringing him to speak his mind; and now that I think, it *was* very unfeeling, considering that you have lost two very interesting lovers so lately,—Sir Roke Wycherly, who has been killed, and Carmel Sherlock, who has just gone to be hanged."

This brutal jest did not seem quite meant as a jest by Miss Marlyn. She did not laugh; she seemed, and looked, both pale

307

and angry.

Rachel retorted this sneer with a surprised and indignant stare. Miss Marlyn laughed; and Rachel, with heightened colour and haughty air, was walking out of the room when Agnes intercepted her, and stood facing her, with her pretty shoulders to the door. But, decided as was this procedure, her look and mien were quite changed.

"You won't go without forgiving me. It is just one of my odious tempers; the result simply of misery. I have offended you, Rachel, by my odious folly; I am going from Raby, and I cannot bear the idea of having wounded you. Oh, Rachel! may you never know half my sorrow!"

Thus began a little dialogue quite in a different tone, which ended in a reconciliation, and a little feminine effusion, in which these young ladies embraced; and then, after a very affectionate talk together. Miss Agnes remembered that they must run upstairs to see "dear Mrs. Shadwell."

They found that lady in trouble; she had this disclosure to make, which would quite satisfy Miss Marlyn, and save her the pain of announcing her own intention of leaving; provided that young lady knew her own mind. I don't think she did. However, if she fancied her mind was to go away, she changed colour notwithstanding a little, when she heard it; and she smiled, forgetting that a smile was hardly in keeping with her melancholy tone when treating the same subject downstairs.

"Do not, pray, dear Mrs. Shadwell; do not on my account suffer the slightest embarrassment or regret. I had told my dear Rachel that it must be, that I had quite resolved, and was about to leave Raby and my dear friends, because my going would be the best thing for all—was, in &c., as it seemed to me, a duty."

"How a duty? I don't see," said Mrs. Shadwell, looking direct at Agnes.

"Yes, she has been talking of going, but I hoped she would change her mind; and today she told me again she would go," said Rachel.

"Yes," said Agnes, gently, and still looking down, she laid her hand fondly on Rachel's arm; "and that *nothing* could alter me."

"But how a duty?" persisted Mrs. Shadwell.

Agnes raised her large, dark eyes sadly, and said: "Does not this command come direct from Mr. Shadwell?"

"Yes—certainly; but new expenses compel us to deny ourselves, for a time, every pleasure we can possibly dispense with," said she.

"Do not fancy, dear Mrs. Shadwell, that I am pleading against a resolution which I do entirely approve. I merely begged to know whether it had first moved from Mr. Shadwell."

At the same time she lowered her eyes again, and glanced along the floor, as if to hide a smile.

"Still you don't say *how* your going should ever have appeared to you in the light of a duty," said Mrs. Shadwell.

Agnes Marlyn continued to look down, and, as Mrs. Shadwell fancied, to smile as before. The lady looked at Rachel a pale, hurried glance, charged with a fear which she did not comprehend, and which was as quickly averted.

"I suppose," said Miss Marlyn, raising her eyes, "Mr. Shadwell would prefer seeming to send me away. You, madam, are *all* goodness, and Rachel I love; yet I had resolved, as I said, to go. He is offended with me, madam."

"Offended, child! no," said Mrs. Shadwell. "Why is he angry?"

"Perhaps, madam, I am too *good*. I mean, if I were more artful and less frank, I should please better. Mr, Temple, the vicar, said in his sermon last Sunday, that the world belongs for the present to the devil, and *his* children prosper best in it. May I now go to my room, madam? I shall have just one letter to write"

"Certainly, Miss Marlyn; but I hope you quite understand there is no idea of hurrying"

It was odd, but true, that in so short a time there had grown between Miss Marlyn and Mrs. Shadwell a distance and a formality.

"You have been always too good to me, madam," she said, pausing at the door for a moment, before she withdrew.

Mrs. Shadwell remained silent, nothing was heard but the little scribbling she made on the table with the tip of her crochet-needle on which she was looking sadly, as if she were tracing with it the epitaph of her lost child. Rachel was looking at her and thinking, with an instinctive feeling of alarm and uncertainty, of the ambiguous looks and language of her beautiful friend Agnes; and she was thinking, too, whether she any longer wished her to remain at Raby. As children see in dreams pale faces that impress them, they can't explain how, with a sense of malice and deceit, that startle them from a happy sleep in horror, so she saw stealing over that lovely face an unearthly light that chilled her.

## Chapter 55
### Miss Marlyn's Ruminations

Miss Agnes was not more consistent than, I suppose, other young ladies are. I think she smiled expressly for Mrs. Shadwell's behoof, and she soon began to fancy that she might as well have spared her the pain of that enigmatic gleam of satire.

Was it pride, or irritation, or malice? for, notwithstanding previous appearances, I don't think she liked Mrs. Shadwell a bit. At all events, she thought its effect had been a little more than was quite desirable. It was of course pleasant to sting that heart with the slender arrow of a new sudden pain. The woman was in her way—she owed her a debt of malevolence for the hypocrisies and flatteries to which she had humbled herself. She amused her satire in her scanty correspondence with her one confidential friend and school-fellow, clever Mademoiselle Du Chatelet, a wonderfully pretty brunette, with such exquisitely even little rows of teeth, and such a charming animation, at present established in London, not as yet in so solid or splendid a position as her many perfections would fairly claim. She presides, in fact, at the counter of Dignum's cigar saloons, and presents each gentleman who enters that resort of betting men, billiard-players, chess-players, &c., Hebrew and Christian, with a cigar and an ivory counter in exchange for his shilling.

I wish you could have seen those wicked sketches of Raby people and pursuits which amused the young lady who fills that dignified position at the cigar saloons.

These descriptions, were even they quite sincere? Did brilliant Miss Agnes go herself all lengths with her own satire? Were all her caricatures sure of her own comic sympathy? and did her "dearest Aurelie" know anything whatever of her real plans and feelings?

I rather think *nothing*. She had little sympathy with those people among whom her lot was cast. Fools they were in her eyes, each according to their folly, and some of them she disliked, not because they were odious, but because they were inconvenient.

Miss Marlyn, as she left Mrs. Shadwell's room and ascended the stairs, wore that serene Madonna-like air and expression which were so touching. But so soon as she got into the security of her own room it was plain enough that this young lady was very angry.

She had not an idea that her departure could be accepted as a settled thing, with so much coolness. It needed, she fancied, but a hint of such a step to plunge this family into consternation, and Mark Shadwell, with all his airs of formality and neglect, into secret dismay. Was vanity ever more mortified?

Miss Marlyn bolted her door, and sat down to commune for a little with her own heart, calling her head also into counsel. It was against Mrs. Shadwell and Rachel that her anger was chiefly kindled. In Mark's hostility there was something to flatter her. Did it not spring from passion—passion not dead, only disguised and perverted? For had he not, with the inconsistency of an undecided character, in the midst of vehement protest and ostensible change, in Bunyan's phrase, "lingered after" his evil yearnings and the ways of death, and kept her secret well.

She could contemplate Mark's condition with complacency. But it was otherwise in the case of the women. Of her own sex she was profoundly suspicious. Cowardice is our weakness, thought she, and our strength is treachery, these Shadwells are two fools; but with the usual duplicity, with all her caresses, that woman has been jealous for nearly two months, and the sneak dared not betray it to her husband or move me from Raby; and now he has talked, of course, of sending me away, and she submits—angelic submission!—and without consulting him tells me I'm to go, and so, she fancies, pins him to that resolve, "and Miss Rachel, of course, she knew perfectly what her mamma was thinking of. I'm not angry, dear, only amused," murmured Miss Marlyn, with a pale smile, in which was something both of malice and victory, as she gently rose and got her paper and envelopes.

But when she sat down, with her pen in her fingers, she found that she was not in the vein of letter-writing, and she drew a crowd of profiles instead all over the sheet of paper, all the time in a deep reverie, finishing the noses and other features with a touch so careful and delicate that one might have fancied she was etching for her bread and fame.

Looking carefully at one of these, which she held up before her eyes, she murmured, with a bitter smile, not seeing it, I think:

"Bauldie! what an idea! Roger Temple, I may come back to you, Bauldie, if everything goes wrong, in ten years' time. You'll be nothing the worse of the wait. You'll not have a tooth or a hair less, but you would not do to begin with; no, Bauldie, I must try my fortune before I spoil it. One brilliant chance already spoiled by a *coup* of ill fortune! Lady Wycherly, I should have been." She set her teeth resolutely, and tapped her little knuckles fiercely on the dressing-table. "He could not have helped it—nothing could have prevented. Well, we must only try again. He's quite gone—quite, quite, quite. I hate thinking of him. I'm always fancying that old face,"—she peeped over her shoulder,—"I have many years, and the game has many turns."

Here she hummed a little air, and a moment after she laughed. "Poor little Monsieur La Roque! with your *nez retrousse* and dolorous old face, what a lover you were, with your *chassée* and your *pas de sylphide*, and your little fiddle, my first lover, at fifty-nine years! You had your brilliant hopes all dashed in a moment by an impertinence of fortune. To be in the very act of winning two hundred thousand *francs*—the ball stopped—the croupier, with rouge on the tip of his tongue, and La Roque a made man, when down falls the house! and La Roque, croupier, roulette-table, company, candles, all, all—buried under fourteen feet of bricks, boards, plaster, tiles, and rubbish! Poor little La Roque! how you used to relate the tragedy and your own extrication, after eight-and-twenty hours passed between a hearthstone and a dead Jew, and yours and his discovery, reposing together like the 'Babes in the Wood,' only strewn over with a pack of cards, instead of leaves! Well, down fell *my* house also, at the moment of fortune, and—killed it, buried that stake; but I shall play again. I don't give it up, like you! What a wicked, insane, ridiculous creature I am! Is there another such on earth?"

And the young lady, who thus described herself, made a courtesy before the glass, and laughed gaily in her own beautiful face.

This young lady came down in a little while, saint-like and sad. But Mrs. Shadwell was changed, cold, formal, quite a different Mrs. Shadwell, on whose pained and averted face the sad, appealing glances of Agnes Marlyn were wasted.

I think the young lady had misgivings as to the good sense of her little experiment of that day.

"Your mamma is angry?" said Miss Agnes to Rachel.

"I never saw her angry; I have seen her offended, though," said Rachel.

"Well, offended; I did not mean that she is in a passion."

Rachel made no reply. They were now in the hall, going out for their walk.

"Rachel!" said Miss Agnes, in the tone of a person good-humouredly calling up a child from a nap.

"Well?"

"Come; why need we quarrel at present?"

"I don't understand you, Agnes; I don't want to quarrel; and I don't care to talk." And Rachel was silent again.

"Unsociable little woman! Because I have shown a momentary wickedness, for which I am sorry, you would put me in Coventry—your mamma would forgive me, but you can t," said Agnes.

"I don't think you had any business talking to mamma as you did, and looking at her, and smiling at her; I never felt so angry in my life," said Rachel, with spirit.

"You are not so angry with me as I am with myself; but I am unhappy, and misery is one of the many roads to wickedness, and so I have been odious; and then comes remorse—I am sorry. When you said I looked, and smiled, and talked, as I ought not, I might have said, as other girls would, 'what can you mean?' and looked innocently surprised, and all that; but I disdain that, and instead, I say, I am *sorry*."

Rachel looked at her, but there was inquiry and distrust in her eyes. Confidence dies, like love, from slight causes, and is sometimes as hard to give back.

"I see you don't like me; you will never like me again."

Rachel was silent.

"No—never—but you may forgive, and hear with me while I stay; and when you have experienced half the sorrow I have, you may understand how grief makes us bitter, and bitterness makes us impatient of all good restraints. You cannot like me, I see you cannot even forgive me, perhaps; but at least you may pity and indulge me for the few days that I shall still remain at Raby, and when I am gone, and your task ended, perhaps you will remember me less unkindly."

"Which way shall we walk, Agnes?" said Rachel, on whom this appeal of Agnes Marlyn's did not act quite as usual.

"You shall choose, Rachel; and you shall forgive me by-and-by," said Agnes. "*Do* choose?"

"I don't care, really;" and Rachel looked half-disposed to turn back, and put off her walk to tomorrow.

"Well, suppose we go towards Wynderfel?" said Agnes.

"I shan't go to Wynderfel again for a long time; I have a horror of that place. Wretched Carmel Sherlock was taken there, and wounded, and we met Sir Roke Wycherly there also. I hate it; I think it a ghastly place," said Rachel.

"And it is too far away," said Agnes, looking towards the dim summits of the distant trees that surround those old walls. The sun would have set by the time we had reached it; but suppose we just ramble a little among those trees close by; they are so noble, and the sun shines up among the grass between them so softly."

Rachel and Agnes walked on together.

"What a pity it is you don't know something of the world, my poor little Rachel," said Miss Agnes, looking toward the setting sun. "I don't mean the great world, or the bad world, but simply men and women—what our vicar calls human nature, and preaches about, although he doesn't know anything about it either; it is bad living in a solitude like this—living among affectations—it is not simplicity, it is not even ignorance, for every recluse knows all the time what she herself is."

"I am not conscious of being anything I don't seem," said Rachel.

"No, perhaps not; I dare say you know yourself very moderately; but you can take short, hard views of the few persons you meet; you can thank them as little as you please for what they do; the flatteries of a few dozen old servants who know they would not be tolerated in other houses; and the idolatry of your mamma—don't be vexed—make you fancy yourself a paragon. Living in a desert, in the midst of prejudiced admiration, *always* has that effect, it would upon me, it has upon you—and you think it is only natural and right that all the world should admire, and love, and pet you; but, my dear, the meaning of the *world* is simply equality—the human republic; don't you see *egalité, liberté, fraternité*! and with what measure you mete, it will be measured to you again."

"I think I saw papa this moment," said Rachel, drily.

"Oh!" murmured Miss Agnes.

"Yes, walking down there, among the chestnut trees, where we are going; hadn't we better turn? he might not like to be disturbed."

"Oh, yes—turn—to be sure!" said Miss Marlyn, a little peevishly. "Are we not curious people here, with all our simplicity, afraid of meeting one another; so many little rules and crotchets, formalities and distances, unconscious contempts, and absurd egotisms. Pray cry, *à bas* the whole thing! and *vive* the other true forms of common sense which I have named!"

She turned, and they walked in another direction.

"Yes, of *course*, if Mr. Shadwell was there."

Was Miss Marlyn beginning to sneer again? Rachel glanced at her quickly.

"Well! I look at you again; do I look very wicked, or very mad? I don't feel it. Here is. the translation of my little speech," said Miss Marlyn. "Your papa is my enemy, I am sorry to say, and being so, I should rather never see him more, that is all. Is it unnatural?"

"It is possible not to like another, and yet not be their enemy," said Rachel, gravely.

Miss Agnes looked at her for a moment, and then, on a sudden, her sense of the ridiculous seemed irresistibly moved, for she laughed, long and merrily, not a sarcastic laugh, quite the contrary, a perfectly good-humoured, and even good-natured one, and the more grave Miss Rachel looked, the more heartily she laughed.

Rachel struggled to maintain her gravity for a time, but the contagion eventually overpowered her, and she was constrained to join in her companion's laughter; and they laughed in rivalry till they almost cried.

"At last," said Agnes, recovering, but still breathless, laying her hand lightly upon Rachel's arm: "I've been lecturing you and you have been freezing me—so much satire, and so much dignity—and all thrown away, for we *can't* quarrel; no, Rachel, we can't, it is not in us. When we try it, laughter comes in, and the whole thing breaks down, and leaves us just as we were before, and—here we are.

And with these words her arms were about Rachel's neck,

and she kissed her; and Rachel returned the caress, saying:

"I do believe, Pucelle, you are right, and it is no use trying to quarrel-but you have been very disagreeable."

"And odious; and you have been just as bad. And now, see, the sun is within half an inch of Feltram hill, and you know, as the vicar says, we must not let him go down on our wrath."

So she kissed her, and was kissed again, and very amicably the two girls returned from their walk.

## CHAPTER 56
### SUSPENDED CHANGE

After this little escapade Miss Agnes Marlyn seemed very penitent. Loving and pleasant with Rachel, and very contrite in presence of Mrs. Shadwell, she was not content with this distant and imperfect expression of her regret in presence of her offended "benefactress," as she used to call her, but made long lamentations in her walks with Rachel, reproached herself, and was so *désolé*, and so engaged her companion to undertake her cause that Mrs. Shadwell forgave, and tried to forget the little scene which had seemed to suggest a suspicion if that kind of impertinence which no woman can tolerate.

She had indeed lost the place she once had in Mrs. Shadwell's affection. But she seemed content with the portion of regard that remained to her, and grateful for it.

"I'm going away so soon, going so *very* soon, we must not have a clouded hour till that which is clouded by parting."

There seemed to have grown upon her, with her penitential and loving mood, an increased dislike of Mr. Shadwell, a systematic avoidance of him, which might result chiefly from wounded pride, but which might also have a more malignant antipathy for its basis. The distant apparition of this gloomy man, the wide-awake hat, the short weather-beaten velveteen coat and the gun, approaching among the trees startled her, as the sight of the distant ranger might the wary deer, or turned her course as it might the flight of a bird. Often, as she or Rachel walked together, Agnes would, on a sudden, change the direction of their route, and perhaps, a minute later, Rachel would see the cause of this deviation in the distant figure of her father. In the house, too, the sound of his step would suffice to hush her music or her voice, and to arrest her step or withdraw it from the threshold of her door.

This avoidance, too, was not unobserved by the object of it, and, I think, it made him secretly angry. He was suffering now, and things that would once have amused, or at most piqued him, now filled him with fury.

A day or two had restored Agnes Marlyn very nearly to her former footing with Rachel. After all, there was nothing tangible to lay to her charge, and how could she keep up a quarrel upon a mere caprice of temper? In fact they were as good friends as ever; Agnes, when she pleased, could make herself very amusing and winning to her young companion, and now she did choose. So Rachel often insinuated a good word for Agnes in her occasional conversations with her mother. But Mrs. Shadwell made no answer on these occasions. She neither seemed pleased, nor the least disposed to discuss Miss Marlyn with her daughter, who wondered that her mamma, usually the most placable of mortals, could so resent a mere impertinence, already repented of with so much contrition.

By one of those instinctive processes which are accomplished in a moment of time. Miss Marlyn had undergone a transformation in the eyes of Mrs. Shadwell. Not all the logic of the subtlest sophist, not all the oratory of angels, could restore her to her former shape.

Agnes talked plaintively to Rachel of her approaching departure.

"I have written this morning," she used to say, "to my only friend in London, Mademoiselle Du Chatelet, whom I knew two years ago at Madame de la Perriere's school—too good, much too good, for that place. She gave up her situation there, being shy and grave, and is now housekeeper in an institution in London." The reader will remember that the "Institution" was the famous "Dignum's Cigar Saloons," and that her "housekeeping" consisted in presenting cigars and counters, with the prettiest taper fingers and dimpling smiles, with the prettiest little lace *coiffure*, and a perfectly Parisian get-up, across a table at the foot of the great stairs there, to the gentlemen who, from ten o'clock p.m., began to pass up that splendidly illuminated ascent. "I have entreated her to look out for me some little convenient nook, where I may very quietly hide my foolish head, until some situation, quiet, and perhaps more humble than my present one, turns up."

I don't believe, however, that her friend. Mademoiselle Du Chatelet, was conscious of any such intimation or request contained in any one of the letters with which her old friend, from time to time, enlightened and amused her.

Agnes Marlyn had herself, in a low musical minor, alluded hastily once or twice, in Mrs. Shadwell's presence, to her approaching departure. But Mrs. Shad well evinced no intention whatever of interrupting her preparations, or of discussing the subject with her.

Miss Marlyn's heart swelled, but not with any tender regrets, under this insensibility.

As in the solitude of her room she undressed that night, she smiled:

"The stupid little woman! with her airs and *hauteurs*. How I laugh at her! Is there, *madame*, never more than one way of reaching a point? It may not be so easy a matter to put me out of Raby. There are none of you here so holy that you frighten me. This kind goeth not forth so easily."

"Why does not that woman go about her business?" demanded Mark of his wife, rather savagely, next day.

"She says she's going immediately," answered she. "I have said nothing to delay her departure—I can't hasten it, you know, Mark, for even if I were to try to do so, I could not. She has a right to remain here nearly a fortnight longer."

"The devil she has!"

"I wrote down the date on which I gave her notice, as you wished"

319

"I hate that charming young woman," said Mark.

"Hate her?"

"Well, that's too strong—but I don't like her."

"I did not know that, Mark, you only said you thought her useless."

"I dare say. If she were useful, of course,—but then, she is not, so without fear of removing a valuable person, I may say that I dislike her."

"But why dislike her, Mark?" asked his wife, who had grown curious in some things, of late.

"Because I think she laughs at us; I don't care a farthing, of course. Do you like her?"

"I think she is a little odd—but I think Rachel likes her very much."

"You don't," said he.

"Why should I not?"

"Oh! come, you know you don't; and why do you look at me as if I had two heads, when I say I feel as you do?"

"I—I really did not intend, Mark "

"Ho! but you did it," said Mark, with a short laugh of scorn, who did not choose to be looked at either in that way or in curiosity. "You looked as if you intended to see through me, and read my soul."

Amy's usually pale face actually flushed a little.

"I had no such idea, I assure you, Mark."

"Yes, you had, I don't know what for, though, and I can't say I much care."

He walked over to the window, and stood there for a while looking out, and suddenly turned about, saying:

"I think you have all got a way of peering at me—I don't know what you want, it is the most offensive thing on earth. If there's anything you want to know, you've got the use of your tongues, I suppose. Why the devil can't you put your questions? I wish I could assure you. Amy," he added, with a change of tone, perceiving how frightened his poor little wife looked, "that there is nothing, neither ill luck nor good, concealed from

320

you. I hide nothing, absolutely, and you can't imagine, when one is harassed by never-ending real vexations, as I am, about which, heaven knows! I have never made a secret; how it pesters one to be watched and wondered at as if I were a witch, or the man in the 'Iron Mask!' I hate Agnes Marlyn, if you want to know, simply because I think she laughs at us."

"Laughs at us, Mark?"

"Yes, at our poverty and shabbiness, and all our miserable ways; this great gaunt wilderness of a house, with a handful of poor people living in a corner of it; and this desolate place, a dozen miles round, the picturesque and solemn principality of starvation. I quite understand her; you don't. Do you fancy I believe one word of her talk about rural repose, and sylvan seclusion, and all that stuff? A French girl! For *that* she is, in all her thoughts, and ways, and tastes. The idea is too absurd! It was quite evident to me from the first, that she alighted here, like a foreign bird, to fly elsewhere. Settle down at Raby, indeed! But it doesn't matter. In fact, I'm poorer than ever, and she can't remain here."

"I've been thinking, Mark, it is very bad for you living so entirely shut up as you do," said his poor little wife, prescribing, as good wives do.

"I'm going down to Raby today; there's a market there; rather a dissipation, isn't it? and I want to see three of my Feltram tenants—mine, I call them; I don't know why, I'm sure; very little of their rent comes to my share. I'm utterly sick of the whole thing. I must have rest; and so soon as I can get a clever fellow to help me, I'll ascertain exactly how I stand, make the best terms I can, and renounce Raby, Wynderfel, and all the rest, forever; and whoever gets them I hope they may burn their fingers, and break their hearts, like me."

The handsome figure and face of the Squire of Raby, when he showed in public, never failed in his own county to excite a curious, and for the most part a respectful wonder; and many eyes and whispered comments followed that haughty and solitary man, as he walked slowly through the main street of Raby.

Silently people made way for him, and many country farmers who owned no territorial relations with him, knowing vaguely what great people the Shadwells had been, the oldest blood in that region, touched their hats as he passed, and eyed him with interest.

Having talked with his farmers, he was now strolling homeward from the village, when he was overtaken by Doctor Stalton, trotting leisurely on his tour of professional visits. The doctor checked his pace to a walk on recognising Mark Shadwell. He was one of the few residents in that wide region whom the Squire could talk to.

"Well, doctor! we don't often meet on the roads here; I don't trouble them much," said Mark, with a gloomy smile.

"I'm very glad to see you about, however; it's a great pity we don't see more of you: I hope you'll excuse me! It is, indeed, Mr. Shadwell."

"They don't seem to like me particularly, when they do," said Shadwell, with an unpleasant laugh.

"Well, now, you know, Mr. Shadwell, you must be reasonable," answered the physician, with a smile, and a reproachful shake of the head.

"Reasonable! I should like to know when I was anything else," he replied, with a sour look at his outspoken companion.

"Well, it isn't reasonable, I think, for you to expect them, don't 'you see, to be neighbourly with you, while you hold aloof from them. You won't forget old scores and let old wounds heal. You avoid them, and refuse to take your place among them as a country gentleman, and—you mustn't be vexed with me—you shirk even your duty as a magistrate, and take a pleasure in letting them feel that you don't avoid them from indolence or shyness, but distinct from personal hostility; and then you wonder why they don't like you, and that, I say, is not reasonable."

"But I don't wonder. I don't expect them to like me; and, which is just as much to the purpose, it was they, not I, who chose those relations, and insulted me with a thousand petty, vulgar insults, just because they knew Raby owed money; left out of everything, never once in my right place. Why, there isn't a family in this county but ours, and just two or three others—you could count them, by heaven! on the fingers of one hand —that is not perfectly new. It is the most upstart county in England; I'm talking of the fellows who hold up their heads, now-a-days, as county families. Take old Mervyn, for instance, what is he? Everyone knows what the Mervyns were; Welsh gardeners at Raby; and a very good thing they must have made of our gardens, by Jove! I have the old lease of The Oaks, in George the Second's time, and he is called Thomas Merven—v-*e*-n, not v-y-n: that was a refinement," he sneered, "Thomas Merven, Gardener to Sir Soame Shadwell, of Raby, Knight; and old Mervyn pays me to this hour thirty pounds a year under that very lease: didn't you know that?"

And Shadwell laughed viciously .

"And there are the Jessons, and the Drakes—*that's* even more recent: city tradesmen—nothing the worse for that, of course, if they did not affect to lead the county. And you think I'm to bear affronts from people like that, and trot about the country from one court-house to another, to admire their liveries, and try to propitiate them. Upon my soul; sir, I'll do no such thing! I think they were ten times as deserving of respect when they were in their proper places, looking after grapes and asparagus beds, or standing behind their counters weighing figs— d—— them!"

"Well, of course, an old family has an advantage," begun the doctor.

"Very little; it's just something—not much: I'm not going upon that. All I say is, that people who get up among us, like mushrooms, ought not to affect airs of superiority, or to be surprised, if they insist on their money, at our remembering their origin. When did you visit Applebury jail last—no fever there?"

"No; very healthy just now. My last call was the day before yesterday."

"And did you see Sherlock?"

"No; he's not ailing."

"I shouldn't wonder if it burst out, all at once, in downright, furious madness. See what a time it has been smouldering, and no one suspected danger in it, till a life was lost. Have you formed any opinion respecting Sherlock's case—professional opinion, of course, I mean?"

"Well, I can't say I have; one has lots of things to consider. I need not tell you, that a fellow may be very eccentric indeed, and yet be perfectly free from madness."

"Is it one of the subjects you are well up upon—I mean, have you studied it particularly?"

"I can't say I have; I know it generally though, of course. If it turned out that there was madness in Sherlock's family, I should have very little doubt; but it is possible that his motive may have had nothing illusory about it; . and I doubt if there's a case strong enough to relieve him of the consequences of his act."

"Would there be anything odd, do you think, in my going over to the prison to see him?" asked Shadwell, walking beside the doctor's horse, and looking down on the road, in his rumination.

"Odd? I don't see how there could, if their rules allow it," said the doctor.

"No, of course—if their rules allow it—as you say."

"But," said the doctor, with a shrewd smile, "I don't say, mind, that were *I* concerned, I should like to see him."

"I don't understand," said Shadwell.

"I mean, you know, upon the subject of the Raby tragedy, as the newspapers call it," said the doctor, with a maladroit jocularity, under which the Squire of Raby secretly winced.

"I didn't know that the papers called it so," said Shadwell, a little drily.

"Because," said the doctor, not minding, "he might—such a queer fellow, you know!—let out something that might make a very hanging witness of you, don't you see? and I'd rather give him his chance, than have a hand in the fluke that hanged him. Eh?"

"Oh! as to that, I should not allow him to open his lips on the subject. Of course it was just that, having lived so long and served so faithfully, people might think it unfeeling, especially knowing that the crime was committed probably under the direct influence of disease, that I should never have looked in upon him during his imprisonment. I don't see that it can do him the least good, and I should much rather escape the pain of seeing him; but I may as well tell you plainly, that I should not like to be thought insensible or cruel in the case of this poor devil. It is simply a question—not of feeling, but opinion, what will people think?"

"Well, there are things for and against, you know," said the doctor, drawing his bridle and coming to a halt, for they had reached the gate of Raby. "People talk over everything, you know;" and as the doctor sat turned in his saddle, with his hand on his knee, he whistled low a thoughtful bar of a tune which ended in silence, and lowering his eyes from the yellow leaves of the trees at the roadside, he said:—

"There are situations in which it is not easy to say what's right and what's wrong, or how people will take anything

And so he took his leave, and trotted briskly away. Mark nodded and smiled his *adieux*, and then walked slowly up to the house, ruminating moodily.

## CHAPTER 57
### PURSUER AND FUGITIVE

As he approached his house the low evenings sun shone up from the western horizon, and flooded the air with splendour. From glittering ivy, from thickets, from the discoloured foliage of lofty boughs, the birds sang out their vesper lays and glorified the coming hour of rest and the Great Creator who cares for all His creatures. All nature far and wide glowed and saddened in this melancholy smile. The crows, high in air, glided in wide procession, with busy cawings, faint and airy, towards the distant woods of Wynderfel. The peculiar pleasant chill of autumn evenings sharpened the air, and the faint white mists came up over distant plain and hill.

A man with a sense of the beautiful is thrilled by such scenes and hours, but in certain states of mind it is with the pain of a discord. Shadwell stopped, and saw and heard the spectacle and sounds around him. The rapture of silent worship and profound enjoyment, which other men experience in such contemplation, in him was displaced by a dreadful impatience, a fatigue amounting almost to despair, and he groaned.

The old question was floating and tumbling in his mind to and fro, like a dead body rolled hither and thither in the sea. What was the purpose of all this? What was the meaning of this parade of joy, so insincere—of glory in the midst of pain and death? To what purpose, for himself or others, had *he* been brought into the world? or how could the Creator scandalize his benevolence by the production of such a complication of misery as Mark Shadwell and his surroundings?

Mark was one of those men who do not stick at a contradiction. Whatever good came to him, he thanked himself for; whatever evil befell him, he laid at the door of heaven.

As he leaned with folded arms wearily against a tree, an object met the eye of that volatile man which suddenly changed the tenor of his thoughts. He saw Miss Marlyn alone, for a slight cold kept Rachel at home that day, approaching by the path which led close by the very tree at which he stood, towards the house.

A sudden wish to meet her stirred within him.

The old dangerous interest was, for a moment, rekindled and mingling strangely with his resentment. In such situations and alone men are determined by impulse. There is no time for debate. Had she come up to the spot where he stood, he would at that moment have accosted and joined her, most likely, in her homeward walk.

But this one flagrant inconsistency—and blessed are those sages whose lives are not full of inconsistencies—was prevented by Miss Marlyn's suddenly diverging from the path, at right angles, and passing quickly out of sight.

"Ha! she saw me," thought Mark, "and she fancies I don't know that she saw me; or, perhaps, she wishes me to see that she avoids me. A heartless young devil she is. She's right to avoid me, though: she's wise. The guilty don't care to confront the judge. She does honestly wish to avoid me, and she sha'n't. She is walking now by the stile-path, and will reach the hall-door, she fancies, uninterrupted; but she is wrong. I will meet her at the two trees."

For the first time, for many days, with a petty object that really interested him for the moment, Mark Shadwell, with a faint smile of scorn, marched swiftly at the near side of the sylvan screen, bent upon intercepting the enemy.

When he came within sight of the two slender birch-trees that stoop together as if they had something to whisper, he slackened his pace to that dilatory and gloomy saunter in which he was wont to prosecute those objectless rambles which served to consume the time which he hated.

He was now again upon her line of march, and very soon she emerged, and the same graceful though muffled figure was again approaching him.

Once more, however, and earlier than before, he was detected. Nothing could be more natural than Miss Marlyn's divergence, more easy, more unconscious, and yet he knew perfectly that this *détour*, like the last, was made with the express purpose of avoiding him.

Is there such a thing as spontaneous drunkenness? This little occurrence suddenly sobered Mark. What had he been doing? He felt ashamed of himself; and the suspicion that Agnes Marlyn saw his pursuit, and deliberately mortified him with the humiliation of avoidance, made him angry, with that sort of anger, which, being mixed with self-disgust, is one of the most galling passions to which we are subject.

There are some men—not perhaps more conceited than others, but more proud and sensitive—whom it is not safe to pique, who grow haughty, repellent, and contemptuous under the arts which excite and allure other men. Mark Shadwell's self-love was wounded. He fancied that she would think him her captive, and secretly glory in his baffled pursuit. He was angry, too, with himself: for had he not found out that his indifference was not so absolute as he had begun to believe?

Later that evening he accidentally met and passed Miss Marlyn at the foot of the great staircase. He had presence of mind to regulate his looks and demeanour to that precise tone which would indicate a genuine and hopeless indifference. A very slight recognition, with just the shadow of a bow, a faint cold smile, and that slight air of abstraction which indicates thoughts remote.

Miss Marlyn was grave, reverential, penitent, he thought; and with downcast eyes she slipped by: the transit was quite mute. Mark thought he had decidedly the best of it. Could by-play be better than his, and *was* Miss Marlyn's really indifferent?—or, considering how clever an actress she must be to have practised so successfully so dangerous and protracted a deception, was it even *intended* to express indifference? Some wild thoughts were beginning :again to haunt him. But was he not a philosopher? Did he not believe in enlightened reason, and the omnipotence of will? What had he to fear?

As that night Mark Shadwell sat alone in his library, smoking slowly cigar after cigar, with one foot upon his fender, and his elbow on his knee, he took this spectre to task, and analysed himself, finding, if some clay, which he passed over lightly, also much good iron, and store of refined gold in the image which he worshipped; and he reasoned also with the phantom which troubled him, and finally resolved to invite it no more, but to banish it with an irrevocable exorcism and never more be under the spell of its cruel eye.

And then suddenly came the image of Carmel Sherlock on his lonely pallet in his cell, with his bandaged arm, and crazy thoughts, talking with himself, forlorn, moaning the praises of his "benefactor," and pining under a curse.

Then suddenly peeped a face, yellow, sharp with its hateful smirk, and immortal fixedness; and at that look he was again where he had been, sitting alone in outer darkness with his thoughts.

Mark Shadwell thought he heard a light step cross the hall toward his door. He held his breath and listened, looking over his shoulder, half expecting to see someone enter. But nothing of the kind happened.

He looked at his watch: it had grown late. The hour of rest had arrived for all but himself, and there was no eccentric, desultory spirit now in his house, such as poor Carmel Sherlock had been.

Mark was not now so nervous a man as he had been when last I described him in this same room on the eve of the inquest. He listened until he had satisfied himself that no step was in motion in the hall, and then he resumed his cigar and his ruminations. Mark preferred sitting up: he would have preferred going out, and passing the hours in a solitary march about the place to going to his bed, where his thoughts and imaginings were always the most troubled. In the night-time, in the attitude of seeking sleep, if sleep will not come, the afflicted man lies at the mercy of his thoughts, which hover over him, as vultures over the dead, and perch, and probe, and ransack where they will.

To smoke, and sip from time to time brandy and water, and resolve that he had done with Raby, that he had known too much of solitude, and drunk deep and long enough of its horrors, and must change all; go to some colony, and rough it there—but mix with men, it might be as moody and short-tempered as himself—still human beings, who would talk to him, exercise his thoughts, and—all the better—his temper, and prevent his growing morbid and atrabilious, as any man shut up in Raby must do.

And so he would turn over a new leaf, or begin a new book in his history, and bury the volume of his Raby existence, its isolation, visions, and horrors, certain fathoms in the earth.

If he could once shake himself free of this accursed old sprawling property, with its inextricable complications and awful debt in which he was immeshed, and under which he groaned and stumbled hopelessly, and set his foot on Canadian or Australian earth with a purse in his hand, and that hand free, there would be a career before him at last. Centuries ago *his* ancestor had left his Norman land and dwelling, and come here to Wynderfel.

Centuries before that, again, his ancestor had left his old north-ern home and found a new one in France. There were periods of decay and renovation. The serpent must change his skin, a great collapse, a great resuscitation, and then a long new brilliant life for the Shadwells of another hemisphere. So, full of his resolution, with perhaps a real flash of the old sea-king spirit-enfeebled by circumstance and by habit—he stood up with his back to the fire, chucked the end of his cigar into the grate, and frowned defiance in the front of imaginary obstacles.

In this silence, with the distinctness that belongs to small sounds at night, he heard the same light step cross the oak floor of the hall quickly, and stop at his door.

He did not move; he listened and watched the door frowning. Not the slightest sound or motion followed. Who on earth could it be? Conjecture failed him. Who could be up and about now? It was not the tread of Old Mother Wyndle; nor of his invalid wife. It was a quick, light, young step. The sharp faint click of the shoe was still in his ear. Agnes Marlyn was out of the question. Rachel not possible either. D——n it, whoever it was, why could not they open the door? He could not get it out of his head that his stealthy visitor was Carmel Sherlock. He had a strange idea of Sherlock's ingenuity and resource. He had managed his escape and concealment without accomplice or assistant, with a success, the completeness of which savoured of natural magic.

Pursuit was defeated; the police baffled. He never would have been taken, Mark was certain, had he not chosen to give himself up, and then he had himself selected the place and agents of his capture. "That fellow could make his way out of the jail, and into this house if he liked, and no one suspect him. He'd venture it for a fancy. He'd come back for his fiddle." In Mark's mind this crazy creature, whom he generally despised, yet in a vague way considered a wizard, excited his admiration and his fear, and the associations connected with him were horrible.

A sharp, light knock sounded on the study door. Mark felt oddly, chilled with the sense of a coming crisis. His instinct whispered truly. A crisis was at hand. Its angel stood at the other side of the door.

"Come in," said Mark, gazing with the frown of suspense at the door.

And in obedience to his invitation, the handle was turned, and the door gently opened.

## CHAPTER 58
### A SHRIFT

"Good God! is it you?" said Mark, in a wild whisper, quite forgetting his indifference and disdain, after an interval of utter silence.

He was amazed, as well he might, to see Miss Agnes Marlyn before him. Never did painted martyr, on oriel window, with arms crossed over girlish bosom, and head inclined, in the melancholy glory of her beauty and her fate, look lovelier or sadder than this vision.

There was no palm nor glory, indeed. This beauty was in truth more voluptuous than saintly. But Rafael could not have painted a sadder face.

It is said that the thoughts of the bravest man, suddenly wounded by gunshot, are seldom very clear. Perhaps that sort of shock and hurry most nearly resembled Mark Shadwell's.

"I couldn't think who it was," said Mark, after another pause.

"No, sir, of course, I have been quite out of your thoughts, you have had so much to think of, and you may have supposed that I had already left Raby," said Miss Marlyn, in tones of low sweet melancholy, which well accorded with the sadness of her looks; and as she spoke her eyes rested on the floor, and her delicate fingers still touched the handle of the door, as if she were uncertain whether her timid intrusion, hardly beyond the threshold, would be permitted, and ready, as it seemed, at a look, to vanish and come no more.

"Left Raby? No, I didn't fancy *that*. You don't go till the 30th, unless you prefer it. My wife tells me, however, that you wish to go on the 19th," said Mark Shadwell.

"Very good of Mrs. Shadwell; so good! yes, I told her so."

"Oh, yes!" said Mark, recovering his ordinary tone rapidly. "I know pretty well what is going on in my house; and this I must say, Miss Marlyn," he resumed, after a few seconds, "that you are about the last person, I should have fancied, who could have desired an interview with me."

As he said this, Mark suddenly remembered his little game of hide-and-seek that evening, and he bethought him, with a qualm of shame, what secret ridicule the dignity of his air was possibly provoking at this moment, and he subsided suddenly.

One momentary glance, however, from the corner of his eye told him that there was no gleam, not the faintest, of any such feeling in her sad features.

"Putting other things aside, Miss Marlyn, doesn't it strike you as a very odd time at which to seek an interview with me?" he said, a little sarcastically.

"In some respects very odd, as you say, Mr. Shadwell," she replied. "In others, in that one of probable freedom from interruption, the best possible time. The world—and stupid people who have but one rule and measure for all our acts, who take no account of character and never discriminate motive—would, of course, censure me, and charge me with an audacity which my nature utterly abhors. I see that smile, sir, but I don't fear it; before I leave this room, Mr. Shadwell, I will show you that if I come here at an odd hour, to secure an uninterrupted interview, I do so from the purest sense of duty. I owe it, I will not say to you only, but to your family. There is something which I must divulge, and I accept the risk, and, if you will, the sacrifice."

Mark Shadwell stared hard at Miss Marlyn, but her eyes were lowered as before.

"I can't form the faintest conjecture as to what you mean. Miss Marlyn. I don't pretend to read riddles; but I venture to say that were any accident to bring a third person to the room, don't you see how unaccountable it would appear?"

"I'm not afraid, if you are not, sir. With me it weighs as nothing in comparison."

Did she sneer? There was nothing but gentleness and sadness in her tone. He glanced again at her. No, it was not mockery—it was almost pathetic. It was a scene of audacious humility.

"Well, Miss Marlyn, do, pray, say what you mean!"

"Ah! Mr. Shadwell, have you not sent me a cruel message?" said she.

"I *have* sent you a message—that is, I have requested my wife to say that you must go," said he, grimly enough.

"Yes, a cruel message! And I ask why?"

"Why! Miss Marlyn. Do you seriously ask me why?" he answered, with fierce contempt.

"Ah! Mr. Shadwell, you are one of those who judge and punish your friends unheard," she murmured.

"Now you must excuse me, Miss Marlyn, but this is really too cool," said Shadwell, with a bitter scoff.

"Well, I will put two cases. Suppose I have been as foolish and wrong as you choose to think,—are people who do wrong never forgiven?"

"Go on," said Shadwell, smiling angrily.

"And suppose the alternative—oh! you must suppose it!—that, placing your own perverted construction upon letters which you took from my desk and read, you have understood neither the feelings, nor the purposes, nor the situation of the person whom you stigmatize. Nothing—nothing—nothing!"

"Upon my honour. Miss Marlyn, all things considered, I am tempted to think you have come here to indulge an odd vein of pleasantry," said Mark Shadwell, growing more severe.

"Pleasantry, sir? You *know*, while you say it, that I speak in agony!" murmured Agnes Marlyn. "Were your worst conjecture true, and I the wretch you suppose, still, in this murder, have I not sustained the loss of all a wicked woman's ambition? Pleasantry, indeed! you don't think it: you can't think it: you don't believe in that any more than you do in the rest. The whole thing is a monstrous affectation!"

"Pray, what have I charged you with?" said Shadwell, turning sharply on her.

There was a silence. He laughed and went on:

"Come, come, Miss Marlyn! you are not the first clever young lady I have met. I know something of the world, though I do live at Raby. No, no—it won't do."

And he laughed again.

She frowned a little suddenly, and said: "I can prove my innocence; I can prove more."

Shadwell shrugged, and, with a sneer, repeated the hacknied distich:

"*He that's convinced against his will,*
*Is of the same opinion still.*"

"Then it's vain pleading with you?" she said, imploringly.

"Quite," answered he, drily.

"You don't, and you won't believe one word I say?" she repeated, in agonized tones.

"Just so; I don't and I won't believe one word you say," he repeated, with insulting slowness, "and pray let that suffice."

He turned to the chimney-piece, to choose a cigar among those he had laid there: a signal to Miss Marlyn that he would be left to himself.

She raised her head and her eyes, and for a moment there gleamed on him a baleful light; her hand was raised from the door-handle; she was on the point of speaking, but refrained. The pale lips were silent; the gleam and the frown died away. Her eyes were lowered again, and her fingers once more hesitatingly touched the brass handle of the door.

"I'm going to light this cigar, Miss Marlyn, but not till you have quite done and gone away. I don't mean to hurry you, if you have got anything more to say."

He paused, with the cigar in his fingers.

"I must make, then, before I go," she said, in a tone of melancholy, and with a deep sigh, "one confidence—one last confidence; and, even here it must be *whispered*. Judge me by it."

As she spoke the colour receded from her face, and her tones became so strange, that Shadwell returned her gaze with something of excitement, while, quitting her place by the door, with quick, light steps, she crossed suddenly to the hearth, and stood nearly before him, looking in his face.

Shadwell returned her gaze with an involuntary frown, but lowered his eyes.

She drew nearer—a little nearer still, laid her hand upon his shoulder, and whispered for a few moments in his ear.

With a sound like a short laugh, he raised his face suddenly. But there was no smile there. It was distorted, and like a face of grey stone looking at her from the shadow. For a few seconds his hand was stretched towards her, and without a word, Mark Shadwell staggered backward, and would have fallen upon the floor, but that, luckily for him, the chair in which he had been sitting received him.

When he saw again, Miss Marlyn was still there. She was standing near, and looked pale and frightened. He got up with a shudder, and stood looking at her, unable for a time to get together the antecedents of this odd situation.

He did soon recover them, and sat down in silence, like a broken-hearted man.

The colour had now returned to her cheeks with a more brilliant glow, and she stood before him, with down-cast eyes, like a beautiful penitent who has just made a shrift of shame.

Mark Shadwell drew a long breath, and groaned.

"Why should it trouble you so? I have made my confession, and now you understand me: you will suspect your secretary no more. Poor Agnes Marlyn has told her sorrowful secret to none but one living creature. Now you know me—my courage, my constancy. Deal how you may—severely or compassionately—with me, you now at least know me, and will think of me, more lowly perhaps, but more highly too. I am reckless, but also true."

And, with one sad, fiery look of reproach, she left him.

As the door closed, Mark followed, and stood irresolutely, with the handle in his fingers. Perhaps he was on the point of recalling her. He hesitated for a moment, and then slowly turned away.

His ideas of the situation—his ideas of Miss Marlyn's character—had undergone a change.

## CHAPTER 59
### MISS BARBARA VISITS RABY.

Next day no one could have told from the air or looks of these two persons that anything unusual had occurred. Neither was there any outward sign of renewed confidence or amity between them.

The only event which happened was the arrival of Miss Barbara Temple, driven over in a curious little ancient gig, by Charles Mordant, from the Vicarage, to pay a visit to Mrs. Shadwell, and to persuade her to pass a few days with them, by way of interrupting a monotony which recent events had rendered unusually gloomy.

The indolence, or that which seems so, that accompanies ill-health, and habitual depression of spirits, however, prevented her accepting the invitation. The world—her little world—did not perceive it, but the apathy was that of a chronic despair—the sense of an insurmountable unfitness.

"I'm so sorry I can't persuade you; a few days' change of scene and air would do wonders for you. I don't know, my dear, how you have lived through the last terrible month," said Miss Barbara. "We have been, I assure you, all wonder, and pity, and I may say, admiration."

"Oh, my dear Barbara!" answered Mrs. Shadwell, "I wish I could take credit for the courage you impute to me. I'm afraid I have been, on the contrary, a great coward."

"Quite the reverse—a heroine. Amy; but you must not over-do it. As I often say to dear Stour, exertion must be recruited by repose, and the nerves must not be kept always on the stretch. It is not in nature to bear it, and—I hope you won't think it rude—for this, you know, is a magnificent place and park—quite a regal thing—and the house is so grand; but, just for that reason—now you won't be offended—it is, I always thought, a little gloomy; and, just now, after all that has so recently happened, you must find it quite awful staying here; at least, my dear, it is quite out of the question, your spirits getting up. Well, now, won't you think of it? *Do* come."

But no; it was vain pressing the point.

"Well, now, I don't know what I am to do or say; I shall appear so selfish, I'm afraid. But, I was so sure of you, that when I met Miss Marlyn in the hall—what a charming young person she is!—I ventured to invite her, intending that you, Rachel, and she should come all together, and stay a day, or a week, or a month, as you found it pleasant; and she seemed so pleased, and said so prettily, if you would permit her; and then—what shall I say about Rachel? I haven't seen her yet; but I should feel such a brute, asking them both to come away, just when you can least spare them."

"My dear Barbara, I should be so delighted; just for a day or two. Young people require a little change, and, of course, this place is very dull for poor little Rachel; and, as you say, particularly now. I should not miss her for that time, and I know it would do her so much good."

"Well, a thousand thanks! I know I am detestably selfish, but I can't help it, and I am so much obliged. Can you let them come tomorrow? I should have asked leave to take them away with me today, but our dear Bonnie—Roger, you know—who is the life and soul of our little party, does not return till tomorrow, and you have no idea how *he* would feel it," she added, archly.

"Well, dear, arrange it exactly as you like; only you'll allow them to return in a day or two, for, I confess, I shall miss Rachel, though I am delighted that she should go to you. It will make her so happy, poor little thing, and do her so much good."

And, this point settled, the two ladies entered into a very interesting conversation about Sir Roke Wycherly and the miserable Carmel Sherlock, with their heads very near together, as they sat by the fire in Mrs. Shadwell's room upstairs.

In the meantime Charles Mordant was very happy, for in the

hall he had met Rachel. I cannot say what they talked about, but I am sure it was as interesting as the conversation between the two elder ladies upstairs, for they talked rather low,—and a great deal pleasanter, for they laughed now and then.

The cob stood under the gig, in view, before the steps, without evincing impatience, which was fortunate, as there was no one to stop him if he had chosen to run away, and I doubt whether Mr. Mordant would have perceived the occurrence, if he had done so. Rachel, who had just returned from a solitary little ramble, had on her coat and such a very becoming little hat! She was to have come in to practise an overture with Agnes Marlyn, who by this time was waiting for her; but neither of the young people in the hall appeared to remember their business, until, on a sudden. Miss Marlyn entered the hall from a side-door.

As she exchanged greetings with Mordant, Miss Marlyn looked oddly and steadily at him for a moment.

"I saw Miss Temple as she went upstairs," she said, "and she was so kind as to ask me to the Vicarage. She intends having us all together—your mamma, and you, and me too. It is so very kind," said Miss Marlyn.

"Oh, yes," said Rachel. "I am certain it would do her ever so much good. I do hope she'll come."

"Oh, she must," said Charles. "She could not think of disappointing all her friends at the Vicarage so miserably."

Just at this period Miss Barbara came down the stairs, and spoke to Rachel, and told her what was settled, and that they were to come next day: and this little leave-taking over, she and Mordant got into their queer little vehicle, and drove away.

Miss Barbara Temple's head was still full of the awful details which she had just been discussing with Mrs. Shadwell, and, as often happens in this sort of preoccupation, there was a certain gloom and constraint in her manner, as she nodded again to Miss Marlyn, which impressed the young lady very unpleasantly.

Full of the anticipated visit the young ladies lay down that night to sleep. Very differently framed, however, were these anticipations. Miss Agnes Marlyn expected neither amusement nor pleasure, but she did expect in the little drama which she had nearly resolved on producing, to make my friend Roger Temple fill a *rôle* which might turn out to be a rather important one.

That evening, after dusk, Miss Marlyn knocked at the study door, and being told to enter, found Mark Shadwell there, as usual, moping in solitude.

Mark darted a glance, in which was a good deal of suspicion and alarm, at the young lady.

"I have called, sir," she said, very timidly, "to know whether I can be of any use in copying and writing letters, that is if, during the remainder of my stay at Raby, you will permit me still the duties of my old office of secretary?"

"It is very good of you. Miss Marlyn," said he, breaking into a doubtful smile. "I'll think of it; that is, if you really wish it."

"You don't doubt my sincerity, Mr. Shadwell?"

"You are an enthusiast," he almost whispered, but with a pained and averted look. "I say I'll think of it, but at present there is nothing."

He extended his hand; she advanced with a beautiful but strange confusion, and timidly placed her fingers in it. He held them for some moments, looking at her half-averted features, as if he was on the point of speaking. But he did not. He opened his hand, and hers was liberated, and she instantly left the room.

About the same time at the Vicarage, leaning back in his chair, with the slight pallor and listlessness in his face that betokens fatigue, the Rev. Stour Temple, his feet on the fender, was sipping that second glass of sherry which was the measure of his after-dinner wine.

Miss Barbara had come in to chat with him, as she always did when he came in late and tired to his dinner.

"I paid poor Amy a little visit today," she said.

"And found her pretty well, I hope?" he asked.

"Not very well; and she could talk of almost nothing but that dreadful business, you know. You must take another glass of sherry, Stour, darling; you look so tired—you sha'n't refuse."

"Hadn't I better take this first?" he said with a smile. "Impetuous darling—my ministering spirit," he said, patting the back of her thin hand with a very caressing gentleness.

"You don't take care of yourself, Stour, and you know if you overwork yourself, and won't take nourishment, you must simply be worn out."

"Well, darling, we'll see when I have done this; and tell me, has anything more been heard of the wretched man who is in prison— Carmel Sherlock?"

"Nothing; and you remember our little plan, two months ago, before all these horrors were dreamed of?"

"What was it?" asked Stour.

"To ask Mrs. Shadwell, and Rachel, and Miss Marlyn here for a week," said she.

"Oh!" said the vicar; "and have you?"

"Yes," she said, and paused, a little surprised at his manner, and at the grave look which he was directing, over his knees, into the fire.

"And have they refused?"

"Amy can't come, but Rachel and Agnes Marlyn are coming tomorrow."

She saw as she said this, in the vicar's dark face, the slight contraction which marks a sudden annoyance. Still looking into the grate, the vicar swallowed the wine that remained in his glass, and held it out towards his sister, who, glad to be relieved of debate upon this point by his momentary abstraction, replenished it instantly, and that with so honest a bumper that her brother, still ruminating deeply, was obliged to sip a little cautiously before setting it down.

"You are sure," they said they were coming, Barbara?"

"Oh, yes; quite certain! Amy said they should; but what is the difficulty, dear?"

"It is very unpleasant; but I could not possibly have Miss Marlyn here," said he.

"Why, my dear Stour, you surprise me!" said Miss Babie, with eyes wide open, and ears also, for she was not deficient in curiosity.

"No, indeed, Barbara, she must not come," he said, very gently, but in that firm tone which experience had taught her there was no gainsaying.

"Not come here. Miss Marlyn, my dear Stour? Why, she has been here fifty times."

"I know all that, dear Babie."

He got up uneasily, and stood with his back to the fire, looking towards the window-curtains. and thinking uncomfortably.

"No, darling, it would not do," he repeated, nodding twice or thrice.

"Do you seriously mean, my dear Stour, that we can't have Miss Agnes Marlyn at the Vicarage?"

"Quite seriously."

"And what on earth, Stour, can be the reason?" said Babie, also standing up, and expanding her hands in remonstrance.

"You must not mention it to anyone. I don't want to prejudice her—you promise, Babie?"

"Yes, certainly," she answered, with the air of one about to hear a secret. But nothing followed.

"What is it I'm not to tell?" she inquired at last, a little impatiently.

"You are not to tell anyone, except those who must know, that I said we could not have her here. I have written to make inquiry, and I may hear more favourably than I at present hope; but in the meantime we must not run a risk of injuring a person whom I only suspect."

"I thought you were going to tell me all about it, Stour?" she complained.

"If I can I will, dear, by-and-bye; but don't ask me at present."

"I really think you ought to tell me—I do. What on earth am I to say to her, or to Mrs. Shadwell?"

"It is very awkward, I know, dear Babie; but it is not my fault, and I don't see that my telling you more, just now, would mend the matter."

341

"And what am I to *say*? I don't want to know, except for that. I should not like to seem rude, you know, and it certainly would seem worse, quite brutal, my giving no reason."

"Yes, indeed, darling, the whole thing is very awkward. I ought to have told , you before, not to mind asking Miss Marlyn here, but I forgot. I think I will tell you all about it tomorrow or next day. You may not think it so serious; but I mentioned it to Mark Shadwell, with very strong advice as to how he should act, and our asking her here, and making her an inmate, would be at best an inconsistency, and a very glaring one he would think it."

Miss Barbara looked up at the drapery of the window-curtain, and then down on the carpet near her foot, a little anxiously. She thought that Stour had penetrated Roger's little romance, and did not approve. So she raised her kind grey eyes, and looking in his face earnestly, said,—

"You must tell me one thing."

"What is it, Babie?"

"You must tell me, dear Stour, has your reason anything to do with Bonnie?"

"With Bonnie? No, certainly," said the vicar, in unaffected surprise, followed by an involuntary little laugh. "No, darling, upon my honour! Roger has neither act nor part in the mystery."

Barbara was relieved.

"I wish I knew all about it"—here was a little pause—"I might very possibly be of use in clearing it up if I did"— here was another;—"but, as you tell me, I shall by-and-bye"—she concluded, having failed to elicit anything more from the vicar, "I only want your help for the present, dear Stour, to tell me, what *am* I to say?"

"The simple truth, darling; as, I think, you always do. I don't think you need write to Miss Marlyn, if you don't wish to do so; but just say—put it all upon me—that *I* see an insurmountable difficulty in the way of Miss Marlyn's coming here at present. Mrs, Shadwell may either say so in so many words, or she may keep Miss Marlyn at home on her own authority, without explanation. Of course, you tell Mrs. Shadwell that I, the most impracticable and secret of curmudgeons, refuse you a single gleam of light into the mystery."

In consequence of this little conversation, there went a note that evening, in Barbara Temple's hand, to Baby, which startled Amy Shadwell. There had been afloat in her mind just enough of that unpleasant misgiving which does not amount to suspicion, to give to this enigmatical note a force and augury which made poor Amy's heart sink, and kept it in a dismal flutter all night.

It was not much to have to say to Miss Marlyn that, on second thoughts, she would ask her to stay at Raby. There were fifty natural reasons to account for such a change of plan.

She had a vague terror, however, of its leading to a scene, and she felt that she had neither ability nor spirits for an encounter with that clever young lady, whom she did not quite understand—whom she had liked so much at first, and began now to fear, like one of those persons in a dream who undergo in its progress a gradual transformation, and end by holding us in the spell of a nightmare.

## CHAPTER 60
### MISS MARLYN TALKS WITH HER BLACK CAT

Mrs. Shadwell would gladly have got out of this unpleasant task; but one way or other it must be got through; and it was better to despatch it, than to let it continue to hang over her till next morning.

So she did see Miss Marlyn—who stood, though invited to sit, and listened submissively, in silence, during the few minutes occupied by the little conference. A brighter glow for a moment flushed her cheeks, on hearing that, for some reason which Mrs. Shadwell could not explain, which she approached and went away from, without touching. Miss Agnes Marlyn was not to accompany Rachel to the Vicarage next day.

At this point Agnes looked with keen, steady glance for a

moment at the lady, who instinctively averted her eyes. Miss Marlyn, however, evinced absolutely no emotion, except in those very trifling evidences.

"Is there anything more?" asked Miss Marlyn, in her lowest tone, and with the faintest light of a sad smile.

"No—nothing," said Mrs. Shadwell, who was embarrassed in the presence of the young lady who stood before her, smiling, patient, and so gracefully submissive, that her heart smote her, and she almost wished that Agnes Marlyn had been angry and violent.

It was a relief, however, that this little unpleasantness was over, and without giving pain, or exciting an angry thought.

But was this so?

Miss Marlyn ran downstairs lightly to the drawing-room, where she had left Rachel in the middle of a duet.

"Well, Pucelle, what was it?" she asked.

"Nothing, dear, only that I'm not to go with you tomorrow to the Vicarage," said Miss Marlyn, quietly sitting down beside her, and striking a chord.

"And why aren't you coming?"

"I don't know, and I don't care—I forget where we stopped; here, I think."

"Wait, Pucelle—don't mind that tiresome duet—and tell me, are you really not coming?"

"Oh, my dear, don't you know I'm not coming?" said Miss Marlyn, with a smile a little sarcastic and incredulous.

"No—I had not an idea that anything could happen to prevent it; and you mustn't suppose anything so treacherous as my hiding it, if I had known."

"Did I fancy any such thing?—Why should I, dear? What an odd, fanciful, huffy little creature it is! But, really, it is not worth talking about. I should not care to sojourn in that wearisome little place, and be so be-Bonnied as I was when we last drank tea there; nothing but its comicality makes it endurable, and the fun of the best joke wears out, you know, by repetition; and, in fact, nothing but the hope of being of some little use as a daisy-picker, could have prevented its being absolutely insufferable. I can't admire even the scenery there. I think it the only uninteresting spot in the country. To be sure, there is an object that does make the landscape interesting—I mean Mr. Charles Mordant, doesn't he?" and she laughed, and played half-a-dozen bars, and added: "What a beautiful blush, my dear. I wish he were here to see it."

"Pucelle, you talk like a fool!"

"And I such a rogue?"

"No—but I mean to say, that I can't conceive any girl caring the least for any man who has not first shown that he likes her better than anyone else."

"And doesn't he show it? Come, I never ask anyone to confess anything in this hypocritical world, but you know he does; and you know you like him— and now let us play this other overture."

And she began to play so brilliantly, and loud, all the time saying: "No—no—I won't hear; I'll listen to nothing but music;" that Rachel, half provoked, though she could not help laughing, did sit down and play the treble.

"You're not vexed, Pucelle; but I am—very much disappointed—and I sha'n't half enjoy my visit without you. *Are* you vexed, Pucelle?"

"I'm never vexed, dear—I'm not even curious—for I know perfectly how this little change of plan came about," said Agnes Marlyn, leaning back in her chair, and looking listlessly upward.

"No, dear, it is too long a story; I'll tell it tonight to my little black cat, who sits on the end of my pillow, and hears my complaint whenever I have one to make, and sometimes gives me a tiny bit of advice."

This black cat of Miss Marlyn's—allusion to which, in moods of sinister playfulness, was not unfrequent— it is right to observe, had no material existence, and was altogether an imaginary confidant.

"I hate that black cat, Pucelle; I wish you'd make it jump out of the window; I can't think it likes us, and I'm afraid of it."

345

Miss Marlyn laughed gently, with a sidelong glance along the carpet, and the glittering edges of her even teeth appeared with a pretty suggestion of malice, that made her for a moment appear like a stranger to Rachel.

"Part with my dear little black cat, with the yellow eyes, and sage counsel, and patient ears! Ah! no. It is such a little wise-acre, and so sharp, and has heard all my secrets, and is so very old a friend, and only the size of my hand, and never comes except when people use me ill; and then it comes crouching and clawing along my pillow to my ear, rubbing its little whiskers to the sheet, and tumbling so playfully, growling like a dear little tiger, or hissing like a tiny pet snake. You can't imagine such a darling; when I was at school, where old La Chouette used to knock me about as she pleased, even before that, when I was beaten and half-starved at home, from that time it was my solitary confidant—my own dear, little, black rogue—who listened to my poor little whimperings, and—taught me tricks."

Except in this little enigmatical speech, Miss Agnes Marlyn evinced no sense of wrong: and when the hour of rest arrived, she kissed Rachel at her door, and went to her room. She had not to pass Sir Roke's door, but she could see it as she went round the corner of the gallery swiftly, and glanced hastily at it over her shoulder as she quickened her pace. She was not afraid of ghosts, as most young people are. I suppose on occasion, however, she was capable of that kind of fear; but whatever may have been the tricks or menaces of her imagination when she saw that door after dark, I am sure she hated the sight of it.

Hurriedly she shut and locked her door. Her heart was full of bitterness; but she did not burst into tears, as young ladies under a sense of wrong usually do in the seclusion of their rooms. Perhaps the tenderness of early parental love, and the habit of being pitied, are needed to induce that relief, and Agnes Marlyn had no home affections to look back to, and had never enjoyed the luxury of being pitied. And so her training had steeled her against the necessities of sympathy, and the habit even of pitying herself.

Miss Marlyn sat for a moment before her glass, thinking and looking all the time at her reflected features. She liked looking at herself in the glass; and she knew she was beautiful; and she could do that and think also. Her beauty was her power, and the vivid consciousness of this inspired her thoughts, and quickened her sense of insult.

She had sat longer than she thought, and was a little chilly when she stood up to undress. Having gathered up her magnificent hair, her graceful limbs were quickly laid in her bed. She did not put out her candle; she liked thinking in this kind of light, with her small hand under her cheek. Her heart was full. An intense, cold anger was struggling in it, and yearned for some expression in act. She was turning over all sorts of things in her mind—talking, as her phrase was, with her little black cat. They had a long confidence, and it was late when she put out her candle.

Miss Marlyn was a clever person, and made theories, and often saw further into millstones than other people. She fancied a change of manner towards her when Miss Barbara had come down that day from her talk with Mrs. Shadwell. Who had brought about that change? and now she was in consequence forbidden to go to the Vicarage. Insult upon insult! Cowardly outrage! Very well. She was not a person to be stricken down with a blow of a fan, and walked over. She would talk for a time with her little black cat, and see what was to be done.

Next morning Miss Marlyn came down serene and beautiful, in good spirits even, for she had quite made up her mind, and saw her way a little in advance, distinctly. Up to last night, whatever she might say or write, she had been in a great indecision. A grain of passion had determined the equilibrium, and Miss Marlyn's future, for some chapters to come, was now distinctly written in those tablets of her little brain that retained inscriptions like adamant.

At the appointed hour away went Rachel, Agnes Marlyn standing on the steps, and smiling her farewell. When the sound of the wheels grew faint in the distance, she was still smiling, though looking down musingly, at her little foot, which, on the smooth Caen stone, was beating time, as it were, to the gentle measure of her pleasant thoughts. Then, awakening from them, she looked up at the clear autumnal sky, and abroad over the fair landscape. It was the sun of Austerlitz, the augury of conquest, and she ran in and amused herself with jubilant music, and some spirited marches, on the old piano.

Miss Marlyn read her novel, and took her walk, and sang songs to the jingle of the old instrument, which was abandoned to the wear and tear of practising; and, at the usual hour she repaired to Mrs. Shadwell's room, and was particularly gentle. and submissive, and, somehow, engaging. She offered to read to Mrs. Shadwell, who was beginning to relent; won, insensibly, by her melancholy, little attentions. Mrs. Shadwell, however, had a long interview pending with old Wyndle, but, fearing that a mere refusal would appear ungracious, she asked Miss Marlyn to come to her for half an hour, by-and-bye, and read a little then, if she still felt disposed. Miss Marlyn pathetically thanked her, and entreated that Mrs. Shadwell would think of some way of making her useful, during the very brief stay that remained to her at Raby.

The evening closed over that gloomy household, and darkness succeeded; and Mrs. Shadwell, looking to the little clock over her chimney-piece, saw that it was half-past seven, and remembered Miss Marlyn's promise.

Just then, the door opened roughly, and her husband entered. He looked pale and angry, and came over, silently, to the little table, which was placed beside her, and sat down at it. Then, suddenly, he said:

"What has become of Rachel?"

"She went today—I thought you knew—to the Temples, to pay a little visit," she replied.

"Well, she has returned by this time, I suppose?"

"No; she was not to return till tomorrow, or, perhaps, next day."

"Upon my soul, that's being rather cool!"

Mrs. Shadwell looked rather frightened at his angry face.

"I hope I haven't done wrong, Mark," she began.

"You have sent Miss Marlyn with her, of course?"

"No; Miss Marlyn is here,"

"Oh! and wasn't she asked?"

"Yes, dear Mark, at first, but that was changed afterwards."

"Changed, was it? So she has gone off without her governess," he said.

"But her governess couldn't be of the least use to her there, and you know you said you thought Miss Marlyn was unnecessary; and she's going away," pleaded she.

He stared at her very angrily, the more so, that he was a little puzzled by her very obvious rejoinder.

"Upon my honour! you're growing quite a debater, that's a vastly clever answer, only it don't quite demonstrate the wisdom of sending Rachel off alone, among such a set of muffs, to meet that fellow. Mordant; and I don't see what business you had to send my daughter away on such a visit without acquainting me with it."

"But, Mark, dear, don't you remember that you told me that I might always send Rachel there without troubling you about it?"

"I say, having asked Miss Marlyn, as the proper person, to accompany her, it was insufferingly impertinent withdrawing that invitation; it strikes me, if she is good enough company for you and Rachel, that Mr. Roger Temple, and Charles Mordant, and old Miss Barbara might venture to sit in the same room with her. Have you heard anything against her? I should be glad to know the pretext on which we are to be treated with that kind of insult. And recollect the effect such a snub, from such a quarter, must have upon the position of that young lady, in whom you professed to take an interest, and whom, I think, we are bound to protect, not only from common wants and dangers, while she stays here, but from damned impertinence and slander."

He thundered the last words, actually pale with anger.

"But, Mark, dear," she faltered, "there has not been a word

said."

"Yes, that's the odious cowardice of the thing, don't you see; there's always a risk of being exposed and punished if one does say lies of people; and don't you perceive that the work is just as effectually done, and far more safely, by letting the world know that the vicar and his family won't let a given young lady into their house, and decline to sit in the same room with her? Do you think it fair to Miss Marlyn that we should allow that? I don't, I can tell you, and I'll write to give them my opinion of it, and Rachel shall come home tonight." And with these ominous words he rose, lowering, and stalked from the room, shutting the door, with more emphasis than beseemed the chamber of an invalid.

There are two doors to Mrs. Shadwell's morning-room: one through which Mark had come and gone, opening on the great gallery; the other from a small ante-room, which communicates with a back gallery.

As Mrs. Shadwell sat there stunned and frightened, this latter door opened, and Miss Marlyn, with a book in her hand, entered. Mrs. Shadwell was in tears. Miss Marlyn's smile vanished—she stood still.

"Pray, come here. Miss Marlyn, and sit down," sobbed Mrs. Shadwell, vehemently, forgetting the coldness and reserve of the last week, in her agitation. "Now, I ask you. Miss Marlyn, have I slandered you—have I? Have I ever slandered you, or permitted any one to slander you?"

"Oh, dear Mrs. Shadwell! I could not imagine such a thing!" exclaimed that beautiful young lady, much shocked, apparently. "Slander me—slander any one! Utterly impossible!"

"Mr. Shadwell has been here, so amazed about that little visit to the Temples, and your not having gone with Rachel."

"Oh, dear Mrs. Shadwell! How very provoking. You have no idea how much I prefer being here, and you know I should have only been in the way there, and I should not have liked it at all; and I know they have not much room, for Mr. Mordant is staying there."

"And Mr. Shadwell is so vexed, and he is going to write, and to send for Rachel tonight; and so, I suppose, we shall lose the only friends that are left to us."

"But if you were to ask Mr. Shadwell not to write, surely he would not."

"Mr. Shadwell is very kind, so kind, you have no idea; but he is very firm, and when he thinks a thing right to be done, nothing ever moves him, he always does it, and I am very sorry. "

And Mrs. Shadwell broke down again, and when she looked up Miss Marlyn was gone.

In less than ten minutes more Agnes Marlyn returned, flushed, radiant, and so beautiful! She had prevailed with Mr. Shadwell, the letter would not be written, nor Rachel sent far, nor the arrangement with the Temples disturbed.

It was running so rapidly up the stairs that made the rise and fall of her dress show her quickened breathing, and that called that brilliant colour to her cheeks, which seemed to give a fiery softness to her eyes. Her words and tones were very humble; those eyes were cast down. There was the modest gratification of having done her benefactress a little service: a very timid pleasure and an indescribable pleasing sadness in her tones and attitude. And along with all this—imperceptible by all but that marvellous organ, the eye of a wife—was there not the baleful light of an insufferable triumph?

Ten-million-fold rather at that moment would poor Amy have accepted all the vexation that threatened than been so rescued. She recognised the extraordinary beauty of that girl. She felt, with a deep-seated agony, how facile had been her influence where she, even in better days, had failed to persuade. Like other foolish wives she worshipped the beauty and fascinations of a husband whom other people saw as he was, and she thought him irresistible.

*In black mourn I,*
*All fears scorn I.*
*Love hath forlorn me.*
*Living in thrall.*

*Heart is bleeding.*
*All help needing,*
*Oh, cruel speeding!*
*Fraughted with gall.*

With a heart wounded and resentful, she yet contrived to smile and thank her. She praised her reading, the meaning of which never reached her wandering thoughts, and heard the cadences of that sweet voice that stirred her heart with the anguish of jealousy.

When Agnes Marlyn had bade her goodnight, and departed, she looked in the glass with a pang, her retina still glowing with the radiant beauty that had just left the room. There met her the plaintive, faded little face, whose glory was over, and the large eyes, still beautiful, and to which, as she looked, the tears sprang. "Amy! Amy!" she murmured, slowly and sadly, with a mournful little shake of her head. All at once the change of years came up before her—the sense of the flight of her power—and the wild uncertainty of future times.

## CHAPTER 61
### CARMEL SHERLOCK IN HIS NEW ABODE.

That evening, so unhappy at Raby, was passing very pleasantly for Rachel at the Vicarage,

Barbara Temple had made, as she supposed, two people very happy. But, alas!—there were two others. Poor Roger was now, six o'clock p.m., expected momentarily, and disappointment awaited him.

Miss Barbara grew silent and nervous as the hour approached, and when Roger's fly drew up at the door, she actually grew pale, as she ran out to the hall to meet him.

"Oh! Bonnie, darling, I'm so glad, and you're looking so beautiful—such a colour!"

"Now, Babie, you rogue, you're at your old tricks—trying to make me conceited," panted Bonnie, with a laugh of fond gratification.

"But I do say, Bonnie, your colour is just what it was when

you were nine years old— quite beautiful!" repeated Babie, in a rapture, and still out of breath from the hug she had bestowed on him.

"I'm glad I'm looking so young—or—so- well, I mean," said Roger, in an undertone, smiling delighted. "It's just the little breeze—the air; and—and, hadn't I better run up and get off these things?" he added; and she knew, by the wandering of his honest little blue eyes towards the drawing-room door, whom he was thinking of, and with a pang she suddenly recollected.

"Oh! Bonnie, dear! I forgot—how shall I tell you?" she exclaimed, suddenly looking in his face quite woebegone.

"Good gracious! She isn't ill—is she?" he exclaimed.

"Oh! no—not ill; but she's not here," said Babie, looking in his face as if she expected him to burst into tears.

"Oh!—and they haven't come, after all?" murmured Bonnie, in a dismal tone of disappointment.

"Only Rachel, dear; Mrs. Shadwell couldn't come, and Miss Marlyn remained with her at Raby," said Babie with a little indirectness.

She saw that Bonnie was in despair, though his faded smile still lingered.

"Well, Babie; another time," he said, with a dismal hopefulness.

"Oh! yes—let us hope—let us hope!" exclaimed kind Barbara, evasively.

Honest Roger made a tedious toilet, and sat long over his fire. When he entered the pleasant, old-fashioned, little drawing-room, his brother Stour had come in, and Doctor Sprigge, who was of their little dinner-party; and he and the vicar were chatting with Miss Barbara quite cosily by the fire.

With that affinity which acts so irresistibly, Roger's eye instantly found Rachel, associated as she was with the absent Agnes Marlyn, and he drew near and greeted pretty Miss Shadwell, and turned away, with a melancholy yearning, to shake hands with the doctor and the vicar; and then to take Barbara's hand and pat it, and look sadly

"Ay, that's the place to catch it," said the doctor, overhearing him. "That moor's worth fifty pounds a year to me, in bronchitis and cases of that kind. Anything of an east wind comes down through the break in the mountains,—like a funnel—and sweeps Higmor. I never felt anything like it. You're all right here?"

And the doctor touched Roger's ample chest with a privileged poke with the top of his finger.

"All right there?" repeated Roger, whose attention had been wandering. "Ah! ha!—you rogue!" he murmured, with a sad smile and a shake of the head which the doctor did not understand.

"Roger," said Miss Barbara, getting up hastily, "I forgot to show you—come to the window—you must do something to the poor Persian lilac; the best branch was broken last night in the storm. See, Bonnie—isn't it a pity?"

Bonnie gazed.

"Yes, indeed; so it is," he answered, and a sigh followed.

"Why do you look so sad, Bonnie, darling?" she whispered.

"Sad? No; I was only thinking what a lucky fellow Charlie Mordant is!"

"Yes, Bonnie, dear, but other people will be lucky too—and happy; all that's wanted is just a little patience."

"Do you think—do you think she'll come tomorrow?" whispered Roger, holding Barbara's hand.

"I can't say, dear. I'm afraid not."

"She wasn't ill—you're sure?"

"Oh, no! quite well; and she seemed delighted at the idea of coming—I assure you she did. She looked so—so beautiful, and pleased."

"Did she—did she, really? Babie, you're a darling; you always see everything."

"And, I'm sure, she was much more disappointed than you are. I'm certain she's looking out from the window over Wynderfel Wood, in this direction, at this moment. I can picture her to myself—looking and sighing," said romantic Barbara.

"Ah! I'm afraid not, Babie, dear. No—no! I dare say she does not care—she doesn't care much, at least. Do you really think she does?" sighed Roger, and pressed her hand again.

And Babie patted the back of his sunburnt paw with tender compassion, and a great misgiving at her heart, which she dared not tell him. And Babie would have gone on romancing, and Roger listening to her delightful dreams, heaven knows for how long, had not the maid just at that moment popped in at the door, to tell them that dinner was ready; so, with another great sigh, and a grateful pressure of Babie's hand, Roger in haste took his place and followed in the wake of more important people, besides Charles Mordant, whom, as they went, he patted gently on the shoulder, saying—"Glad to see you again, old fellow!"

For all but my good friend Roger, that quiet evening glided very pleasantly into the past. There was talking—old recollections and new stories. There was the merry, and sometimes plaintive, jingle of the old piano. There were songs, and one duet, which Miss Barbara encored—remarking, in a pleased aside to Stour, how charmingly their voices went together; so Rachel and Mordant sang it over again, and were much applauded, even by Roger, who remembered Miss Marlyn's voice in that duet, beside the same piano, and who for her sake sighed also an encore.

"Poor Stour!" exclaimed Miss Barbara, next morning at breakfast. "Not content with his own work, which, I do assure you, is nearly killing him, he has promised Mr. Clarke, who is in such affliction, you know, to visit for him, two days in the week, at Applebury prison; and so he's gone off, with an early breakfast, and we sha'n't see him now, I suppose, till dinner-time, or perhaps later."

And so it was. Stour was by this time visiting the "spirits in prison," so few of whom care to be preached to—in a prison not of common locks and masonry only—spirits imprisoned in the iron cage of evil education and habits, and screwed down, as Andersen says, each "under the coffin-lid of his connections."

"The prisoner named Carmel Sherlock," said Stour to the prison officer, when he had made the round of the wards, "not a convict—only committed for trial—who, you tell me, has refused to see the chaplain, would, I think, see me. I've known him for a long time, and take a deep interest in the unhappy man; and I would be so glad to see him, if he would admit my visit. Will you ask him?"

The man returned—Sherlock would be glad to see him. So the vicar walked down the flagged corridor and entered the small square room, where the thin figure of Carmel Sherlock met him.

Sherlock looked thinner, and his black hair was longer, but his pale face showed no change in expression, and no altered lines of suffering.

"I am glad, Mr. Sherlock, you have admitted me; I could not leave this place without asking whether you would see me," said the vicar.

"Thanks, yes; and how are the family at Raby?" said Sherlock, fixing his earnest eyes on him.

"All quite well," answered the vicar.

"Mr. Shadwell?" the prisoner inquired.

"Yes."

"And Mrs. Shadwell?"

"Always an invalid, you know; but not worse than she has been for some time."

"And Miss Rachel?"

"Quite well."

"Quite well," he echoed, mournfully; "and happy—ay, happy?"

"I am here, you know," said the vicar, after a pause, "as a clergyman—doing duty for the chaplain."

"Ah! yes, as a clergyman—and no doubt making many people happier—but that is not for me. You see God in your printed Bible, Mr. Temple, and I, in the pictured pages of His Creation; and my ideas and yours are different."

"My dear Mr. Sherlock, all this trouble has not, I hope, befallen you in vain. Surely you reflect on your present situation."

"That, sir, is all fair—yes, sir: the bitter for the sweet; the darkness for the light; a balanced account, with small profit or loss to any, when it is closed. When you come into a family you must accept their rules; and being born in the world, you are the οἰκέτης of the great house, and taste of its good cheer and also of its *horrible flagellum*. So it is, sir, I am here. You think it just; and if killing be always murder, it is just. And there is the weakness of the Bible. It makes you, don't you see, the slave of a few generalities; but I discriminate. Which is more spiritual? You call all the immortal sights and voices that are about us, fancies proceeding from our own perishable brains; but I perceive, and consider them, as belonging to God's outer household of immortal spirits."

The vicar answered nothing. He was looking down, disappointed. He ought to have remembered, he thought, how mad this wretched man was. He was but throwing good seed into the deep and barren sea.

"Sir Roke Wycherly, what was he? Ay, he came at the behest of others. Why should that hoary old goat haunt the house when there was so short an exorcism? Your evangelists and apostles were wiser than you, Mr. Temple. They knew the unclean spirits by the sense that was given them. They believed in demons, because they knew the signs of their tenancy, and saw that they fought murderously against expulsion—yes—with some of them, anything for a body—the tenement of clay, the mechanism of sense. They did it with a spell: 'Thou unclean spirit, come out of him.' I was told to cast him out another way."

"Pray," said the vicar, peremptorily, "say nothing to me that may commit you upon the question of your innocence. I must not be made partaker in any secret which I ought not to keep."

Carmel Sherlock's dark eyes glared askance on him a look of suspicion, and then dropped to the floor. In silence he ruminated, and with a sigh, he looked up and said:

"To a man who has always liked solitude, this kind of thing," and he waved his fingers slightly toward the wall, "has nothing formidable; and to one who has lost all but life, death looks friendly. I miss the picture, now and then, once in an hour;

once in a day, once in a night. Sometimes I would look from my window—I miss Wynderfel—enchanted ground—and the black tarn, in Feltram Glen—Lake Avernus. The spirits! Haunted ground—friendly spirits. They came to know the solitary man who did not fear them—who trusted them; and they sometimes told him thoughts. A star like that the wise men saw, I followed; but mine went out. I miss the Stradivarius.

"It followed my memory in all its windings, with its own storm and lamentation. You have showed me kindness, now and always, sir, in the same way. Your religion is comfortable to you, and you have wished to make me a partaker in it. No small kindness; and, I never forget a kindness, so I have left you the Stradivarius. Mr. Shadwell will have all the rest—the books, the creese, and the other things. But to you, for you have music,"—he was looking dreamily at Stour Temple's head, as he might on a phrenologic cast—"that wonderful creation, the Stradivarius!"

The vicar, remembering the strange sounds emitted by this same violin, as he stood with Mark Shadwell on the steps at Raby one melancholy night, was very near smiling.

The impulse was but transitory, and with decent gravity he thanked Carmel Sherlock, and hoped that it would be very long before his bequest took effect.

"You are kind, sir, but I sha'n't leave this new home of mine—this home of stone and iron—alive. This lamp will not be broken—it will go out."

The vicar already regretted his visit. In Carmel Sherlock's enigmatical speeches were hinted revelations which he ought not hear without divulging.

"I don't quite see your meaning," said Stour Temple, and hesitated. He suspected a covert threat of suicide.

"No, sir," said Sherlock, reading his suspicion with a strange penetration. "I mean that I shall die—die, as you would say, a natural death."

"You are not ill, I hope?"

"Ill? Oh, no! There's no man in England better: an elastic life that adapts itself to all forms of pain, which will bear sudden transition from the hermitage to the camp, and from the camp to the prison, and never feel it. If a man could sell such things, sir, there are men who would give a sack of gold for it. But money has its hour like every other thing; and for me it would come too late. Life in one hand, gold in the other, I would drop both into the abyss for one moment's certainty of a thing which never was—never can be—sir; and might have been a curse if it came.

"Haven't you seen celestial faces that changed when you came near? Everyone knows what horror is—these transformations. Therefore, sir, it is better to wait for the spiritual world, when the essence of things will appear, and into that world I go smiling, bidding my eternal farewell to the illusions of mortality. I go, sir, as I say, serene; at peace, Mr. Temple, with all the world and with myself; reconciled to the wonderful conditions of life, and expecting confidently those which are sublime!"

The vicar listened to what in his ears sounded like audacious impieties, with eyes cast down and a look of pain; and, shaking his head, he replied:

"Ah! Mr. Sherlock, your faith must repose on something more solid than your own wild theories, and you must have some more satisfactory convictions than the dark retrospect of a life and mind so fancifully preoccupied can offer to justify the confidence on which you may reasonably rest."

"Confidence and—curiosity, sir," said Sherlock.

"Well, Mr. Sherlock, you have said things today which have made me very anxious. You will not, from curiosity, make a jump, like Empedocles, into the crater?" And the vicar looked on Sherlock as he spoke. Sherlock smiled, and repeated—

"*Relictâ non bene parmulâ*;

No, sir. If I know myself, I sha'n't do that."

"If I had found you in a mood, Mr. Sherlock, as you say, from curiosity, if from no other motive, to talk on the one subject which can never lose its interest—I mean the lamp of truth, which is the Bible, which alone can light us through the valley of the shadow of death, to safety—it would have been a great happiness to me."

He paused; but Carmel Sherlock, listening respectfully, with downcast eyes, said nothing. "You are very good, sir, you are wonderfully good, to care for such a man as I. I can't understand it; I can only thank you from my heart. I was on the point today of telling you some things which, as yet, no one knows but myself, and when you checked me, I resolved to postpone. I shall perhaps tell my benefactor, Mr. Shadwell, instead, when he comes. I'm sure he'll come to see me, sir! He'll surely come! and for the rest, sir,—time—time. I have got some old books; you would think them of no value, but they have many deep meanings hidden one under the other, like the wisdom of Brutus or of Hamlet under a mad exterior."

"Then another time, perhaps, you will talk with me more as I could wish?" said Temple.

"Not now—not today, sir; perhaps never. But I am very grateful; and, will you show me another great kindness—knowing not in what shape, nor how soon, death may arrive—for I hear his steps in the air— if it should be with short notice—will you come and see me? There is something which I want to tell Mr. Shadwell—*he* will be glad to hear it—about the death of Sir Roke Wycherly, and if I can't write, and that you hear I am dying, will you come?"

"Certainly; you may rely upon me," answered Temple.

"That is all, sir. I hear the man at the door," said Carmel Sherlock.

Not without extracting a promise, in return, that Sherlock would read a little book which he would send him, did the good vicar take his leave.

"Solitude!" said Sherlock, with a smile, when he found himself alone, casting his Latin folio on the table. "With living comrades like you, with memory, with dreams that come through the golden gate, listeners are never alone. It is your talkers who are lonely. This romance is ended—so let us go and begin another."

# CHAPTER 62
## ROGER TEMPLE LOOKS IN

While Miss Barbara, with Rachel and Charles Mordant, drove to visit the ruins of Elverston Castle, my forlorn friend, Roger Temple, sauntered towards Wynderfel. From the heights beyond the ruined hall, he gazed sadly at the woods and chimneys of Raby, till, unable to resist the yearnings of his love, he trudged slowly on towards the sombre scene of his own romance.

As he approached the house, he began to regret that he had not asked Barbara to give him a message to excuse his visit. He would not go in, however; he would merely inquire at the door, and try his chance. Barbara would, of course, wish to know how Mrs. Shadwell was; and so he would inquire in her name; ay, and if he encountered Mark, he would say that she sent him. Very slowly he walked by the windows of the house, but no sign of life met his eye. Round the corner, along the side of the mansion, he proceeded quite solitarily, and so to the front. The hall-door was half open. He hesitated. He heard the well-known sound of the piano accompanying a rich clear voice.

Honest Roger was on the point of walking into the school-room, whence the music proceeded, unannounced. He recollected himself, however, and rang the bell, while his heart throbbed faster than was comfortable.

The old butler arrived at his leisure, and Roger greeted him in a very friendly way, and told him he had come to give a very particular message for Mrs. Shadwell, which his sister had specially directed him to give to no one but Miss Marlyn.

Roger was now fibbing away quite unscrupulously, which shows how dangerous, even in intention, is the slightest departure from the narrow path of truth. "I think I hear Miss Marlyn at her music?" he said. "Will you try and let me know whether she can see me for a moment?"

"Yes, that she would," said the servant; and without asking Miss Marlyn's leave introduced Roger Temple, nothing loath, to her presence.

Miss Marlyn stood up from her music very much surprised, it

seemed. Five, minutes before, she had not been playing or singing. She was in one of her reveries, talking perhaps with her little
black cat, when she saw the top of honest Roger's wide-awake
glide by, and, peeping, saw the worthy fellow himself. Thus it
happened that the schoolroom door was opened a very little,
and thus it came that the ring of music escaped from the schoolroom, and was quite audible on the steps of the hall-door.

"My sister sent me—a little message—and I am so sorry to
have interrupted that really heavenly music—quite heavenly!"
(a pause and an expressive look occurred here), "and I am so
fortunate—so very fortunate. Miss Marlyn, in having found you
at home—so very happy."

"I think you said there was a message?" suggested Miss Marlyn, for another pause had occurred, and Roger seemed to have
forgotten everything but those happy sensations which he described.

"Oh! oh, yes—to ask you particularly how Mrs. Shadwell is
this morning?"

"Mrs. Shadwell is just as usual. Shall I run up to give her your
message?"

"Oh, dear, no! pray, don't think of it—pray, don't—merely
when you do see her, to be so good as to mention that I called. I
heard the delightful music from the steps; I knew very well who
the musician must be. No other music affects me. Miss Marlyn,
like yours—none, upon my honour!"

"It is very good of you to say so, Mr. Temple. You kind people
in this part of the world are all so very good to me. I don't know
how I shall bear to leave Raby."

"Oh, Miss Marlyn, you must not leave us."

"I think I shall leave Raby about this day week. I like Raby.
I had grown so fond of it. I think I was formed for a country
life," said Miss Marlyn, with a sad little smile that moved honest
Roger extremely.

"I am sure, Miss Marlyn, you have not an idea how some of
us will miss you—how awfully—how really awfully!"

Miss Marlyn laughed prettily.

"There's one, at least, Miss Marlyn—there's someone—one I could name; there is, indeed, and I don't know what he should do—what would become of him—"

Here there was a pause, and poor Roger looked unspeakable things. He ought to have considered that he was making a rather awkward silence for Miss Marlyn.

"You left Miss Temple quite well, I hope, and Rachel?" she said.

"Yes, quite, thanks—quite well. They went to see Elverston Castle; but I couldn't—I couldn't, indeed. I couldn't come anywhere but in this direction—I was so low—so very unhappy. It was such a disappointment your not coming yesterday,—and my sister admires and likes you so much—you have no idea— we all do, and—and—oh! I wish I could tell you half what I feel. I wish. Miss Marlyn, I dare. I—I think you so beautiful, and—and so glorious—an angel of beauty and of goodness!" he rhapsodized, quoting a phrase unconsciously from one of the old novels in Miss Barbara's bookcase. "I can't tell you half—only, I can think of no one else—of nothing else. I quite worship you. There's nothing on earth I would not give just to hear you say you could ever like me. I—I have talked it all over a hundred times with dear Babie, and— and she would be so delighted, and we could live with them so pleasantly. I have four hundred a year of my own; and—and—you like the country so; and oh, dear! how happy we should be, and—and—for God's sake, don't say, 'No!'"

Perhaps it struck Miss Marlyn at the moment, that, all things considered,, the thing was worth weighing. If for a clever, friendless, beautiful girl like her, there were some brilliant prizes, there were also dismal blanks. But she was ambitious and enterprising, and for such a spirit mere safety has no very distinct attractions.

While some vague calculations were rolling in her mind, my friend Roger. in his rapture of entreaty, had seized her hand in both his, and was pressing it, and pressed it, even, tremblingly, two or three times to his lips. I suppose there was some little decent show of withdrawal! Miss Marlyn was standing with her back toward the door, and toward it also and toward her, honest Roger's bald head was presented as he made his hurried adorations. It was a very marked change in the expression of his face as he raised it, that caused her to look round as she withdrew her hand quickly.

They both saw Mark Shadwell standing there. There was an awkward pause for a moment, during which Miss Marlyn glided from the room.

"I just came in," he said, "Miss Marlyn, to say that my wife, I think, wishes to say a word to you,—how do you do. Temple?—but I suppose there's no great hurry.—You've had a walk across by Wynderfel, I suppose, or did you ride?"

"Oh! I—I walked," said Roger, not quite clear for a moment how he had come there. "I—yes. I walked. It is so beautiful; so—so very pretty."

"Yes, very pretty," acquiesced Mark, with a slight sarcasm.

"It is, indeed—sometimes, I think, quite irresistible," floundered poor Roger.

Mark smiled cynically.

"All your people quite well at the Vicarage, I hope?" said Mark.

"Oh! perfectly; thanks—thanks."

"Won't you come to the drawing-room, you'll be more comfortable?"

"No—well, no—I believe not," said Roger.

There was a short silence and Mark inquired abruptly:—"Can I do anything for you?"

"Anything for me—anything? Oh. no! many thanks. There's nothing—only, merely—nothing, in fact, but my sister, who wished me to inquire how Mrs. Shadwell is today."

"Very kind of her. She's pretty much as usual," said Mark.

"Oh! yes, thanks—I've heard; and now they'll be looking for me back again. What splendid timber you have got here, to be sure! and the walk over Wynderfel—one's led on."

"Yes, one's led on," repeated Mark. One never perceives the distance," and Roger coughed a little. "I'm detaining you."

"Only too glad to see you ," said Mark, affecting his ordinary manner on a sudden, though he felt very odd and very sore. "Any news of that poor fellow, Sherlock?"

"No, nothing since, except that he is quite well," said Roger, trying to recover himself; "that little hurt was not of any consequence; and—and—that's all; and I think I must be off, they'll wonder what has become of me," and flushed and nervous, Roger took his leave on the doorsteps, and whistled for his dog, and remembered he had not brought him with him, and took leave again.

With a sour and rather malicious smile, Mark stood for a time on the steps, and turned briskly and walked into the house, whistling. He stopped in the hall—

"Where's Miss Marlyn?" he inquired, rather sharply of the old butler.

"Haven't seen her, sir."

"Well, have her made out, and tell her I'd thank her very much to bring me to the library Mr. Smithwick's letter which she said she would be so good as to copy the other day."

And Mark walked into his room, and shut the door with a sharp emphasis.

## CHAPTER 63
### MISS MARLYN EXPLAINS.

A tap came to that door speedily, and in obedience to his call, Miss Marlyn entered. She had some papers in her hand.

"Oh! thanks. This is the letter—Mr. Smithwick's—that you were so good as to say you'd copy?"

"Yes, sir."

"A thousand thanks!"

He took the papers to the window, pretending to read them. Miss Marlyn's glance read his countenance, and she was pleased.

"So very nicely copied, I ought to be very grateful, indeed," he said, laying the papers down. "By-the-bye, I ought to apologize, shouldn't I, for having disturbed you just now, at a very interesting moment?"

Miss Marlyn made no reply.

"My handsome friend, Roger Temple, has withdrawn. I almost pitied him, not for his agitation; but getting over that hill at Wynderfel will blow him so; poor fellow, he was so hot! and this is anything but a hot day. He ought to make his excursions in a palanquin—don't you think?"

"Is there anything more for me to copy?" asked Miss Marlyn.

"Oh! you are very good—too good—but is it quite fair to Temple, to ask you to take all this trouble for me? He may think it a great impertinence; and it is rather dangerous, doctors say, putting a fat fellow of a certain age in a passion."

Miss Marlyn here appeared a little offended.

"If there is anything more, Mr. Shadwell, perhaps you will send it to the schoolroom?"

"Oh! I'm not going to let you off so—don't go just for a moment; no, pray don't."

Miss Marlyn stopped.

"You know how I am placed here. I think I ought to know what passes," said Mark Shadwell, with a cold sort of decision, and at the same time, perhaps, a little embarrassed.

He closed the door, and then added:

"What was that fellow saying?"

Miss Marlyn looked down upon the ground in a beautiful confusion, embarrassed for words to begin. She seemed on the point of speaking, but failed.

"Does he want to marry you? there's nothing to hide. It may be ridiculous, but *you'll* not be laughed at," persisted Mark. "Come, you know I ought to hear. Did he ask you to marry him?"

"Yes," said Miss Marlyn, faintly, "he did."

There was a short silence. Mark Shadwell felt very oddly; but he did not show it in his looks.

"And, I suppose, he has had an answer?"

"No, sir."

"Indeed—I'm afraid I came in, as I said, at an unlucky moment; but there's pen and ink, and you may write your answer now, if you like," said Shadwell. "Don't you think it's a sort of question that requires an answer?" He paused with his open hand indicating the table on which lay paper, pens, and envelopes.

"Oh! Mr. Shadwell, what shall I say?"

"Really, Miss Marlyn, you are the best judge of that," said he, drily.

"I mean how shall I express it?"

"I don't think young ladies usually have much difficulty in finding words," he said, with a sour smile. "Of course you have made up your mind?"

"How?" said the young Miss, raising her deep dark eyes suddenly to his and dropping them again.

"How can I tell? I can't say the least. Only it's a case for 'yes' or 'no;' and, I suppose, you know which you mean to say."

"I shall never marry," she said, still looking down.

"Come, come, you don't mean that," said he.

"Yes, Mr. Shadwell, I shall never marry," she repeated, very low.

"Well," said he, oddly relieved, "I'm not surprised at your being a little *difficile*; if you were not, considering all you are, you would be the most foolish girl in the world."

"I shall never marry, sir. I've quite made up my mind."

"Made up your mind, have you? And for how long, you wise little woman, have you been of that way of thinking?"

"Sir, it is not worth talking about."

"Madam, it is very well worth talking about. Seriously, I take an interest in you—I should be a brute if I did not—a deep interest. I am too deeply obliged—too deeply grateful."

He paused suddenly; he had taken her hand in both his.

The histrionic element was strong in Miss Marlyn. When she played a part, she entered, as the phrase is, thoroughly into it. Miss Bateman grows pale in *Leah*; Miss O'Neil used to shed real tears in *Jane Shore*, It is not easy for a looker-on to define the point of insincerity, or to say exactly where mere imitation kindles into veritable emotion. This I know, that as Mark Shadwell gazed he saw the soft carmine mount to her cheeks; but she did not raise her eyes, and he saw only their long, soft, black lashes.

"Don't you intend consulting any one?" said Mark, hardly understanding why he said this.

"Oh, no, sir!"

"Well, I have no right to ask why, and, certainly, about Roger Temple, he *is* such a fool, and so ridiculous—such a figure."

"He's very good, and very kind, and I am very grateful," she began.

"I never heard that he was particularly good or kind, or anything but fat which is often taken, I remark, for those qualities; but if you think him all that, perhaps you will reconsider the question."

Mark Shadwell spoke a little bitterly, which pleased Agnes Marlyn, as she looked down with an unchanged blush on the carpet.

He had dropped her hand for a moment, but he took it again, and said in a lower tone:

"Do you mean to think over that question?"

"No," she said, very low again.

"And why, '*no*'?" he said.

"Because—because I shall never marry any one whom I cannot love; that is to say, I shall never marry."

"How can you tell," he said, after a pause, "that you might not come to like him very well?"

"I never could love him," she said, with kindling audacity, "you know, Mr. Shadwell, I never could. Nor should I ever marry any one to whom I dared not, and could not trust the dearest and most awful secret of my life, for whom I would not incur danger, disgrace, and death itself, and think it martyrdom and glory!"

He felt her hand tremble, and she drew it towards her; but he held it still between his own. She turned away. He thought she was weeping. Was he imposed upon by coarse theatricals, or had he just witnessed a genuine burst of those passions which stir most men so deeply. Was he the possible man, after all? Was all the wild worship of this adoring and terrible soul for him?

"*You* are capable of loving; you are a heroine, Agnes," he almost whispered.

"I have been talking wildly; do, pray, release my hand, Mr. Shadwell. It was your strange advice that made me say all that—do, pray, forget it."

"I'll *never* forget it!" he said, still holding her fast. "I now understand you! I have been conjecturing, and guessing, and mistaking for months, but one moment of excited feeling has revealed you—generous, impulsive, daring, true."

"Pray speak of me no more—think of me no more. I shall soon have gone, leaving behind me no trace, but carrying with me my ineffaceable recollections and my sorrow."

"If it had been my fate, Agnes, to meet with sympathies like yours, that fate would have been different, and *I* a better man."

"I think I have now told you all, Mr. Shadwell, that you said I was bound to tell," she said, a little proudly and coldly; "and although you have spoken so kindly, sir, I yet feel that I have said a great deal that was very foolish, and, from my heart, I wish it all unspoken!"

"Never wish it unsaid; you know—none so well—how miserable a man I have been; you would not deny me that one gleam of a better light? Fate has forced us into a mutual confidence; you have told me that which binds us together in a secrecy that keeps your image always present to my mind."

"Listen!" said she, withdrawing her hand decisively from his grasp, while her fine eyes were directed with an expression of alarm upon the door.

He heard a step approach, and a knock at his door. He waved his hand backward, in warning to the young lady, as he advanced to see who was there.

But she passed him quickly, saying aloud:

"As you are interrupted, sir, another time perhaps will answer. I may go now, I suppose?"

Mark Shadwell looked both agitated and annoyed, and he said, also aloud:

"Certainly, Miss Marlyn ;" and at the same time he opened the door wide and suddenly.

"Well?" said he, looking straight in old Wyndle's face, rather sternly, for it was she who had knocked. "What do you want of me?"

"Oh!" said old Wyndle, prolonging her note of wonder as Miss Marlyn passed slowly from the door.

Miss Marlyn and the housekeeper did not like one another.

The young lady, I think, was pleased, and from her fine eyes just glided across the old retainer's face a glance of hardly disguised disdain and triumph. Mrs. Wyndle drew back, a little pallid, with her nose turned up, and her mouth pursed, and a sharp frown.

What do you want, Wyndle? I'm not going to stand here all day," said Mark, sharply, cutting short this little bit of by-play.

"Only my mistress wanted to know if *she* could see you here, sir?" said the old servant, following, with a disdainful sweep of her little grey eyes, the leisurely retreat of Agnes Marlyn.

"Of course she can; what the devil's to prevent her? Everyone can see me here—provided I'm not busy; and I'm always glad to see her—as she knows. Such rot! Just tell her, I'll go to her room if she likes it, or she can come here, if she likes it better."

And, angrily, Mark shut the door in the face of this privileged domestic.

"What factionists they are, with their d——d jealousies and little rivalries, and spites!" he muttered. "There is that stupid old Wyndle—she'll be off with a story, I suppose, to Amy, and she'll be crying and grimacing, like a martyr, for a week. I sometimes wish this cursed old house would fall and bury us all under its rubbish; I'm tired to death of it, I know!"

Mark Shadwell hated a scene. He hated being talked over by his servants; his neighbours he did not care about, for he did not see them. He had never been a vulgar profligate. He thought that vice and all its ways should be kept dark; and Roke

Wycherly had thought him, even at his worst, a rather cold and straight-laced fellow. And now, too, being like many men a medley of inconsistencies, he had his ideas of morality—his philosophy and self-control—and at the bottom of his soul was a dastardly hope—which he would not avow even to himself. Amy Shadwell had been very ill; more than once, lately, the doctor had been called in, and had gone away. In the life of a confirmed invalid, people take little note of these occasional shocks, and things are assumed to return to their old channel. But Mark saw—with sometimes a compunction, sometimes a glow of resignation—that this sad incumbrance could not trouble him very much longer.

"Well, Wyndle ?" inquired Mrs. Shadwell, as she entered.

"*Well*, ma'am, yes, and might be better, may be. It's an ill world, ma'am, and the worse the folk the better they thrive. The impittence of that Frenchwoman!" said Mrs. Wyndle, grimly.

"Whom do you mean, Wyndle?"

"Agnes Marlyn, ma'am. She's always a peepin' and pokin'—I *will* say it—after the master."

"Oh, Wyndle, what do you mean?" said her mistress, haughtily.

"Just that, ma'am; and I'd pack her off, if I had my way, without no more delays, ma'am. What business had she shut up in the library wi' the master this minute, when I went down o' your message?"

"Of course, Wyndle, he had sent to give her a direction; you are not to talk so," said the lady, haughtily still, and also uneasily. "I suppose she was leaving the room as you came?"

"Not till after I knocked, ma'am. Then her and the master came to the door together, and out sails my lady, and gives me a look as if I wasn't fit to wipe the dust off her shoes," said the housekeeper.

"Well, you know, you need not quarrel, Wyndle, for she is going to leave us. She wishes to leave us, and she's going."

"And joy go wi' her," she continued, with her privilege. "We all thinks she was just getting her word in about everything, and tryin' to turn master round her little finger."

This little parenthetic talk left a pain at Amy Shadwell's heart.

Shadwell waited now in his room, but no message came.

"Cool—isn't it? keeping a fellow waiting here to know her pleasure! That old fool, "Wyndle, I suppose, has been telling her a story. What a mystery the love of mischief is! and my meek wife has found a temper at last. She had better not try it on me, though."

I can't say how far his conjecture was right. He took his hat and stick, however, and loitered into the orchard, and spoke to the men who were removing the great pyramids of apples piled upon the grass, and thus trying to cheat himself into the fancy that he was busy and useful, and so into the farmyard, and then away among his distant woodlands.

On the whole, it had been a day of strange triumphs. Could Agnes Marlyn's half-confessions bear any other meaning than that which his vanity read in them? Could he ever forget her deep eyes, her colour, and the sudden breaking out of her fiery spirit? Talk of Swift and Vanessa! Was ever romance more desperately genuine than this? Had he not terrible proof of her devotion? Was not this wild, gentle, fierce girl, the most beautiful he had ever seen? Could he escape from her spell? Was not that Hebe always standing by him, filling for him to the brim the cup of madness? But no, she should not wreck herself. Were not these relations of mystery, of subjugation, of half-divulged passion, the most luxurious imaginable? The more she trusted him, the more would he reverence her. A supernatural being, knit to him by mysterious ties. Her devotion should be honoured, her defencelessness sacred.

## CHAPTER 64
### NEWS OF CARMEL SHERLOCK

Unromantically in this walk was Mark Shadwell's path crossed by the village attorney, who, in local litigations, was wont to act for him. With a qualm of anticipated annoyance he saw him, for he was pursuing the footpath that leads towards the house; and, with the sure presage of a man in difficulties, Mark knew that a visit from a man of law meant trouble, perhaps danger.

"How d'ye do, Twinley?" said he, stopping short. "Looking for me? Anything unpleasant?"

"Hope I see you well, Mr. Shadwell. Well, I hope not, sir, only Mr. Mervyn is going to file a bill to compel execution of the leases for Headlam."

"He sha'n't get them? I'll—I'll see you tomorrow about it—today I can't—if you look in about twelve. We'll talk, if you please, tomorrow," he repeated, a little peremptorily, repressing the attorney's incipient discussion. "I suppose it will do tomorrow One must sometimes take a little exercise, you know; one can't be always over law and accounts—shall we say tomorrow?"

Mr. Shadwell spoke as tartly as if it was Twinley and not Mr. Mervyn, who wanted these renewals.

"Very good, sir. I'll look up at twelve o'clock, Mr. Shadwell, as you say, tomorrow. Nice day, sir."

"Charming," he assented; and so they took leave, and went their several ways.

Mark Shadwell, being a haughty man, did not open his wounds to everyone, and never cursed Mr. Mervyn to his attorney. He relieved his feelings now, however, and he talked in soliloquy, in a strain by no means charitable, of the long head and the long purse that had spoiled his morning's walk, and dashed the luxury of his indolent dream with bitterness.

This little reminder of his relations with Mr. Mervyn had its effect by-and-bye. On his return, he found that his daughter had just arrived. He had written in the morning, rather stiffly, to request that she should come home, charging that request upon her mother's state of health, and her very lonely condition in Rachel's absence.

He had not been ten minutes at home, when Rachel arrived. She came into the library to see him. She was looking more than usually pretty, he thought, with a particularly beautiful colour, and an indescribable depth and fullness in her eyes, and something of confusion that was new to him. Her good looks, however, did not interest him now. There was no great chance that her beauty, buried where it was, should ever contribute to extricate her family from the quag in which it was sinking. For one dreamy moment, as he gazed with a sort of speculative admiration upon her beauty, he thought, "Were I to make her heiress of Raby—a thousand a year, at least—might not something come of it?" But Mark had no notion of fettering himself or his miserable property, by adding to her dot of four thousand pounds charged by his settlement.

Was he to divest himself of power to raise a thousand pounds if he wanted it? or to marry hereafter, should he recover his melancholy liberty? a step by which, he chose to think, even his daughter might benefit.

Dryly enough, he said:

"You had better run up and see your mother; she has been very lonely."

"Miss Temple came with me, and I think she is still in the hall," hesitated Rachel.

"Oh, is she? Has anything been heard about Carmel Sherlock since?"

"I think not," began Rachel.

"Well, just ask; and, if there has, come back to me," said he.

He had not waited five minutes, when a visit from Charles Mordant, in his room, gave a new turn to his thoughts. The sight of old Mervyn's nephew was not pleasant, and his countenance and manner showed it. He received him coldly, and without a smile.

It was plainly no common visit, for he was pale and preoccupied and nervous. It was plain, too, that there was something on his mind which he must speak,—and speak it he did.

A proud and fiery man is a bad custodian of his own interests. Had Mark been in a reasonable mood, he would have thought twice before dismissing any chance of relieving himself of the care and embarrassment of his daughter's guardianship. But the immediate temptation to snub Mervyn's nephew was too much for him, especially as that nephew had nothing but his commission and three hundred a year to offer.

"You are a very young man, Mr. Mordant, or you could not suppose that I could seriously entertain such a thing; and I can hardly suppose that your uncle, Mr. Mervyn, who has seen fit to challenge me to a lawsuit only the other day, can possibly have advised your making me this proposal, and, in any case, I must say it is one which I can't think of; and, without meaning anything unkind, I do say that I beg there may be no more about it. Has not Miss Temple called? I must go and see her. Shall we come?"

And, with his unpleasant smile and a peremptoriness of tone not to be mistaken, he uttered this little sentence, and preceded poor Mordant, who was in a state of dreadful bewilderment, from the room.

I cannot say that, in point of prudence, there was much to recommend this marriage. Perhaps a wise and kind father would have given it as decided a negative as Mark Shadwell did. But wild lamentations, in which romantic old Barbara joined, and profound dejection followed. Mark, however, was clear and peremptory, and in a very short time an idea entered his mind, which quite sealed his determination upon this point.

Weeks passed, and Miss Marlyn still lingered on. It was not her doing, neither was it owing to any indecision on the part of Mrs. Shadwell. When the day appointed for Miss Marlyn's departure had nearly come, Mark told his wife that he had been disappointed in money, and that the simple, vulgar truth was that he could not pay Miss Marlyn, and she must wait a week or two longer. "You must tell her when she's to go. Amy," he said. But Amy entreated him to undertake that task himself; and as he secretly wished to take it out of his wife's hands, he did consent to do so.

Miss Agnes Marlyn consented to remain a little longer at Raby, to old Wyndle's loud discontent, and poor Mrs. Shadwell's secret anxiety.

In old Raby church, when Rachel and Miss Marlyn attended morning service there on the Sunday following, they saw a young gentleman in solitary occupation of the square pew next theirs. His get-up was unexceptionable, and he was undoubtedly good looking, with something of the interesting air and languor of an invalid.

Very soft, large eyes, a delicately-formed nose, rather high, pale, gentle, handsome face; rich, silken, wavy, brown hair, and a decidedly elegant exterior, could not fail to excite a gentle curiosity in young ladies so near,—even in church.

Rachel had rallied since the occurrence I have last described. The cheerful support of Miss Barbara, most generous of matchmakers, and the romantic sympathies of Mrs. Shadwell, were all in favour of Charles Mordant, and Rachel was persuaded by these ministering spirits that the opposition of her father was simply one of those jolts and hitches in the path of true love which uniformly turn up and uniformly disappear. She was by no means, therefore, in that state of interesting apathy, begotten of despair, which refuses to take note of the outer world. And she did speculate a little like Miss Marlyn, when she ought to have been better employed, about this stranger.

There is in Raby, as everybody knows who has ever dipped into a book on the mineral waters of England, a well, known as the Raby Spa, whose peculiar virtues attract generally some four or five visitors at a time, during the summer months, to the inn, or, as we now term it, the hotel, of that quiet and quaint little town. Whenever a stranger, above the level of a religious missionary or a prosperous farmer, appears in the church of Raby, he is assumed to be, and pretty uniformly rightly, a flying visitor to "the Spa."

The stranger stole a few of those very quiet and cautious glances, which a well-bred man, leaning over the side of a pew and at his devotions, will permit himself in such a case.

The young ladies were delayed some ten minutes at old Mrs. Ford's cottage, and, having visited the sick, they drove home.

As they drove up the avenue, whom should they pass but the

interesting stranger.

"There he is again, Rachel!" said Miss Marlyn. "I suppose he has got leave to walk over the place."

"Yes—I dare say," said Rachel, both young ladies seeing, without appearing to look at the object of their curiosity. This conjecture turned out, however, to be erroneous.

They had not been in the house many minutes, when the stranger walked boldly up the steps, knocked and rang, and asked for Mr. Shadwell, telling the servant to say Captain Clayton, of the —— (mentioning a distinguished cavalry regiment), and then, on second thoughts, he wrote on his card "On sick leave," and gave it to the servant.

Forth came Shadwell, and was rather pleased to see him. He made him come in and take a biscuit and a glass of sherry, and then brought him for a walk through his wild and beautiful park.

This gleam of hospitality was not a mere caprice. A dull docile man is sometimes better company than a brilliant one, with his eyes about him and a vein of satire.

Clayton looked about four-and-thirty, but was in reality a good deal more. Shadwell had known him, very intimately, some sixteen years ago, when they used to play a great deal of billiards together, at his club, and Mark always beat him, and he thought Mark a wit and a philosopher. There was not much in Clayton; but this kind of admiration was the most agreeable quality imaginable, and healed the wounded vanity of the recluse.

Clayton could narrate things accurately enough, and answer his questions about the Crimea, and could not help knowing a great deal that was interesting. But his chief excellence was that he admired easily, and was absolutely without the faculty of satirical observation.

Clayton had been sent to Raby by his doctor, merely to try the Spa for a week; and, if it promised to do him good, he was to return after his visit to Scotland, and complete his recovery.

He was just the man, also, to answer the style of Raby hospitalities. He affected simple fare, and was under rule not to exceed two glasses of sherry. Mark could, therefore, have no fears about having him to dine, and, next day, accordingly he came. It is inexpressible the relief which Mark found in this hum-drum companionship, which, nevertheless, in so many essential points, so exactly suited him. It was human society and associations recovered suddenly, in a solitude which had but one capricious charm, and, except when that intervened, had become almost insupportably horrible.

With this Captain Clayton, who could tell so much about those memorable battle-fields and incidents of siege-life which were then so fresh in people's minds, and a great deal of other gossip also, and who was so communicative, and so disposed to be pleased, something like the glow of social life and interest returned to those sombre rooms.

Every evening during his stay he passed at Raby, and now at last Mark Shadwell did observe unquestionable evidences of something more than a fancy—a very decided penchant—for his daughter in this very eligible person; and although a recent deception had made him wary, still there was a very marked difference between this dull and comparatively simple man, and the unscrupulous and active intriguer who had now done troubling, and tempting, and lay white and simpering, with his dark heart pierced through, under his triple coffin-lid.

"How you must all have suffered," said Captain Clayton, one day after dinner, as in his *tête-à-tête* with Mark he sipped his cup of coffee, "while that miserable business was going on here. I was at Malta when it happened. There's a fellow in prison for it, isn't there?"

"Yes."

"And do you think he'll be hanged?"

"I hope not, poor devil, for he's perfectly mad."

"Oh, really? The man at the hotel here says he was a wonderfully clever fellow."

"Yes, wonderfully clever, but very odd, and actually mad," said Mark Shadwell.

"Have you seen him in prison?"

"No. We shall hear all about it, however, early in spring, when the judges come down to Applebury."

And Mark grew suddenly silent, and his face looked old and sombre, and after two or three minutes lost in profound abstraction, he suddenly roused himself, saying: "As you won't take any wine, if you have finished your coffee, suppose we come into the drawing-room."

Clayton looked very well pleased at the proposal.

"I shall miss my pleasant quarters awfully when I leave," he said.

"But that is not for some time, and you mustn't talk of it," said Mark, with something of anxiety as well as of politeness, for Clayton was in a measure to him what the friendly watcher in the nursery is to the nervous child, and he dreaded the hour when his long solitary evenings were to return.

Was not his secretary an occasional resource? Yes; she interested him perhaps more than ever. But Mark felt that old Wyndle and the other servants—all intense partisans of his wife—watched him, and compared notes, hating Miss Marlyn. He had, he assured himself, nothing to conceal. He defied them. But this sort of prying not only exasperated, but embarrassed him, and sorely abridged his opportunities.

Besides, Clayton had certainly begun to like Rachel, and with this fancy, which seeing that she was an only child, did not appear by any means imprudent, had visited him visions of Arcadian life very like those which false Sir Roke had affected. To be half frozen, wounded, rendered incapable, by a shot in the ankle, of ever dancing again, to have passed three months in pain in an hospital, and more than a year in a very precarious invalided state, is not a bad sedative.

When they went to the drawing-room he saw Clayton as usual address himself to Rachel, and he was glad. Clayton, though not rich in the exalted sense, was yet very well. He had more than two thousand a-year, "and possibilities." And that night, in his farewell talk with Mark—for he was to start for Scotland next morning—he admitted his admiration a little, and then a little more, and so on, till he made a full confession of his liking. He had not spoken to Rachel. He had heard something about an engagement, in fact, though he did not mention her name, it was Miss Marlyn who had told him that Rachel liked Charles Mordant, and was to be married to him.

Mark made short work of this suspicion, and they parted with a kind of understanding that Clayton after his visit to Scotland, to which he was committed for at least seven months, was to return to Raby, and make him a less hurried visit.

Next day Clayton was gone, and Mark left alone with his cares.

In his sudden allusion, on the night before, to the death of Roke Wycherly and to his murderer, Clayton had unwittingly disturbed an anxious question in Mark Shadwell's mind. Should he go forthwith, and visit Carmel Sherlock in Applebury prison. There were *pros* and *cons*. His judgment told him very distinctly that he ought to go, and without anymore procrastination; but a reluctance he could not surmount, restrained him day after day and week after week. And as the interval grew, so did the care that loaded his heart. Clayton's unexpected question had startled him more than his own occasional thoughts.

On this morning Mark had been in his library among his books and papers, when this note reached him from the vicar.

My Dear Shadwell,

I have just returned, very late, from Applebury, where, I am sorry to say, poor Carmel Sherlock is extremely ill, and the doctor says, in imminent danger. His illness is gastric fever, which he must have had for a considerable time. For several days he had been eating absolutely nothing, but declined to report himself ill; and it was supposed to be one of those obstinate cases of temper which I am told sometimes occur in prison, and are always subdued in the natural course—by hunger.

But suddenly he began to sink, and is rapidly losing ground; and on a visit made yesterday by the doctor, is ascertained to be too probably dying. I saw him today. He is very weak, and seems to speak with difficulty, but expressed twice so *very* earnest a wish to see you—in fact, conjured me so to persuade you to see him—that I trouble you with this note, which has grown into a letter. I shall be at Applebury again tomorrow at ten, to see the poor man, and I shall tell him that I gave you his message.

Believe me,

My dear Shadwell,

Yours truly,

S. Temple.

P.S.—It is, I find, too late to send tonight.

"That man will die, something tells me; I don't mind doctors or clergymen—but he's going to die!" So spoke Mark Shadwell, flushing suddenly and fiercely. Mark stood up, and read the note again, and then looked at his watch. "I ought to have had that at seven this morning. "

He rang the bell furiously, and not waiting for an answer, he strode across the hall, and shouted down the passage to command someone to order the fellow in the stable to get his horse instantly. He got on his hat and coat in the hall, waited for a few minutes in a deep reverie at the door-steps, then walked round hurriedly to the stables, and in a few minutes more was riding at a rapid trot in the direction of Applebury.

## Chapter 65
### Sherlock's Story

Mark Shadwell dismounted at the inn-door, in the market-place of Applebury , and inquired whether the vicar had been there. He learned that he had been in the town before nine o'clock, having an appointment to keep with Thomas Foukes, of the Mills, and he had shortly afterwards visited the prison, and returned by ten o'clock.

"Is Mr. Temple still here?"

"No, sir, he went up the town a bit. He said he'd be leaving, maybe, in twenty minutes, and his horse is at his feed."

"Did he say anything of a prisoner who was ill?" asked Shadwell, anxious to lighten his suspense.

"No, sir."

Throwing the bridle to the man, he walked quickly towards the narrow street in which stands the jail of Applebury. At the comer he met Stour Temple returning.

"Oh!" said he, stopping. "Thanks for your note—I'm here in consequence. How is he?"

"He'll never speak more, the doctor says," answered Stour Temple, with a shake of his head; "he has sunk into a lethargy, and is dying."

Shadwell sighed like a man who puts a load off, and looked down on the pavement for a little.

"Have you seen him more than once?—I hope he did speak."

Shadwell looked pale and anxious as he raised his eyes to ask this question.

"Yes, he did; and I was anxious to see you," answered the vicar, in a low tone, "Shall we get into the room at the inn? There is no use in your going on to the prison. He can neither hear nor speak—poor, unhappy man!"

They turned and walked down the steep little street toward the market-place. Mark, in a very low tone, said:—

"I suppose he confessed everything?"

"He told me a very odd story," said the vicar; "you shall hear all when we get in—it's only a minute?"

"Certainly,—very true."

Mark felt very oddly; and in his suppressed agony of suspense, as they walked toward the inn, he looked with what carelessness he could assume up toward the sky, and across from one gable-point to another among the quaint houses, as if in a sudden anxiety to read the weather.

They had now reached the inn-door. There was no one in the small room with the bow-window looking across the une-qually-paved square.

"We can have this quietly—to ourselves?" asked the vicar. The waiter acquiesced; and Stour Temple, shutting the door, drew near the window, where they sat down.

"The wretched man was quite aware that he is dying—in fact, it was only because he thought death so near that he despaired of your coming in time, and told me the circumstances."

"He confessed the murder, did he?" asked Shadwell.

"No—that is, he did confess the moral guilt," began the vicar.

"I don't understand," said Shadwell, growing paler.

"Well, I'll explain; I'll tell from the beginning—you know it was not always easy to follow poor Sherlock's meaning."

"No—there I agree—one must be a cabalist, or a Rosicrucian, to guess at it—quite mad," acquiesced Mark Shadwell.

"Well, my translation of his meaning is just this: from the moment he heard of Sir Roke Wycherly's visit, he had a foreboding of evil he could not account for."

"Yes—I know—his dreams and demons," said Mark. "He told me—go on, pray."

"Well, I know it is your wish that I should be quite frank. Of course there were foolish, or, as you say, mad things mixed up in what he said; and you'll forgive me for telling you one of them, because it evidently accounts for part of what has happened."

"Pray, tell me everything. I know—better than ever lately—that he was quite out of his mind; I sha'n't be surprised at anything."

"Well, then, he did not say so distinctly, but there is no other way of accounting for his language; in fact, he conveyed the admission that he had cherished a secret and absurd, but most passionate, attachment to Miss Shadwell."

"Oh!—Indeed!—Very flattering."

"No one, of course, suspected anything so preposterous, for he described it as a secret, as well as I could make out, between him and his violin, or his demon, and kept it close within his own heart Then came a suspicion that Sir Roke Wycherly had come to Raby to pay his addresses to your daughter."

That is strange!" said Mark, quickly, for poor Roke had actually taken a violent fancy; and had, in fact, made up his mind to ask my daughter to marry him. I can't say, of course, that so young a girl, and one so entirely out of the reach of all merely worldly influences would have dreamed of it; but, I may tell you now, he talked to me in a way that could not admit of a doubt as to his intentions. All that was laid in the dust with poor Roke himself, and what you say throws quite a new light on the motive."

"Yes, there was jealousy; but he says that, quite apart from that, there was another influence prompting him to that crime."

"That's pretty plain," said Mark, with a grim shrug.

"He told me it was an impulse which he found it eventually impossible to resist. He was so persuaded that he was drifting towards that dreadful crime, that he told you and Mrs. Shadwell that he must leave Raby, but not until after he had actually attempted to enter Sir Roke's room at night, with the distinct purpose of taking away his life."

"Lamentable that he should not have told his reason for urging his departure. It was my detaining him, then, that caused this miserable affair—but who could have fancied anything so perverted and dreadful?" said Mark, who was looking more and more miserable as their conversation proceeded.

"On the night of the murder he had resolved to confine himself strictly to his room, until the early morning, when he meant to leave Raby. But his temptation assailed and overcame him. He stole through the passages, and came to Sir Roke's door, which he found open. He had in his hand that Malayan dagger which was found in Sir Roke's room. He entered noiselessly;—there was light. Sir Roke was not in his bed; he saw him, as he fancied, dozing in his chair. He said as he approached, the resolution to put him to death grew more inflexible. He described himself as all the time freezing with horror at his own meditated act. On reaching the chair he found that Sir Roke was already dead, and weltering in his blood, as we found him."

Shadwell, as this narration proceeded, had risen; and, standing with his shoulder to the window-frame, was staring down on Stour Temple almost as one might have fancied Carmel Sherlock looking down on the dead face of the baronet.

When Stour Temple looked up, he was shocked. Was it Mark Shadwell or a ghost? That old face—frowning, trying to smile, with the eyes of a detective. His doubtful glance awakened something in Temple's startled countenance that recalled Mark Shadwell, and he laughed suddenly.

"A cock-and-bull story, eh?—rather?" he said. "The fellow's madder than I had an idea, and, also, more cunning. You don't quite believe all that—do you?"

"I—I hardly know what to believe," said Temple; "I have not had time to think it over yet. I only know that odd as his language was, and odder still his mystic ramblings, the story itself was perfectly consistent. He said that he remembered dropping the knife from his hand, and concluded that he must have picked up the dagger, with which the murder had actually been committed, by mistake. He fancied it was his own, and thought he had effectually concealed it afterwards in the stable-yard."

"Yes, it's all a muddle; I wonder you had patience to listen to him. The man's dreaming; always mad, and now in a fever," said Mark.

"Very weak, it is true; but he appeared to me as collected as I remember him at any time."

"Not saying very much, though."

"This, however, is no matter of theory or imagination. There, I grant you, he was always wild enough; but one simply of recollection, as you shall hear. He said that as he approached the door, through the gallery, someone went hurriedly out. He saw the shadow on the wall, after the figure quickly turned the corner of the gallery. He fancied, I can't say why, that it might be Sir Roke himself, in his dressing-gown, and followed quickly; and he distinctly saw that it was Miss Marlyn. He knew that she was awake and up. She had been, he says, at his own door not very long before. He thinks she had some quarrel with Sir Roke Wycherly—"

"Why, she did not know Sir Roke," interrupted Mark.

"Oh! pardon me, I thought I had mentioned *that*. She did

know him—he admired her when she was at that school, in France. I thought, in fact, I had mentioned—but, on second thoughts, I believe I did not—the unpleasant rumours affecting him, which I did mention to Sir Roke himself."

Mark looked down; the contents of Miss Marlyn's desk had apprized him of this discreditable acquaintance—a scandal now condoned. He had not been aware, before, however, that it was known to Stour Temple, and this discovery was embarrassing.

"What can I know of Miss Marlyn's acquaintances before she came to Raby, except what you told me, of which you seemed not to be very certain yourself, and what the principal of the school herself disclosed? There was nothing about Roke Wycherly there. There was absolutely nothing but what might be said, by a spiteful old woman, of any good-looking girl who had the misfortune to reside under her authority. Nothing but malice could account for Sherlock's talking such stuff, if we did not both know that he is crazy."

"Well, I can't quite agree with you. An acquaintance there certainly was; and, it would seem, an understanding, at one time at least; and Carmel Sherlock is quite distinct upon one point, and that is that she was the person who, he believes, came out of Sir Roke's room. He has not the slightest doubt that she was the person whom he saw in the gallery. She was walking very quickly, and he could not hear her tread."

"All very fine if poor Sherlock had been in his senses," said Mark.

"I always thought Carmel Sherlock a man of very acute observation and accurate memory," said Stour.

"Yes, and one who saw visions, in a matter where his imagination was excited. I would not hang a dog on his evidence."

"I'm merely submitting what Sherlock very positively stated; I don't offer any remarks of my own; but he said, in distinct terms, that he had no doubt the murder was committed by that person—Miss Agnes Marlyn."

"Why, my good God, sir! you can't seriously mean anything so hideous and absurd?" said Mark Shadwell, with a pale sneer.

"The meaning is not mine. I simply repeat what the dying man told me," remarked the clergyman.

"Simply," sneered Mark again.

"And, you know, it would be quite out of the question my presuming to suppress it," said the vicar.

"True churchman Temple," muttered Shadwell, bitterly. "Your true Christian loves punishment—sacrifice, you know— and as one victim slips through our fingers, we try to lay hold on another. I don't think you ever liked that poor young woman much?"

Stour Temple looked with an unconscious sternness for a moment, and Mark lowered his eyes before his surprised and searching gaze.

"One would naturally feel an interest in her," began the vicar, who made it a rule never to be offended with Mark.

"Well, I think so: an orphan girl, cast on the world so very young, without kindred or friends, I do think it rather appeals to—I don't say our Christianity—though I have read something somewhere, like *thinketh no evil*—but to our manliness and de- cency. I say, I think it appals one, even whispering such a charge, upon the evidence of a lunatic, against a creature so defenceless and inexperienced."

White and angry looked Mark as he spoke, and as if he hated the vicar, who, in his cold way, simply added:

"You see, I tell you all this as a magistrate. It does appear quite incredible; but is there anything so mysterious and paradoxical as crime? What new and terrible ideas of human nature it gives us."

"Oh! yes—philosophy and psychology—all very fine; but you will not get twelve men, in a Christian country, to believe on the evidence of a mad assassin, that a poor, little good-natured governess overpowered and slew a baronet of six feet high, and without any assignable motive. Come, what do you seriously ad- vise me to do with this notable piece of evidence? Had I better ask you to swear an information, and invite the crown to take it up? Do you think the country would ever allow such a joke to die against you and me?"

"I care very little," said the vicar, "who laughs, provided I have acquitted myself of my duty. Different men will value that dying declaration differently, I have a full note of it with me, and am ready to make affidavit to its accuracy, whenever I may be called on.

"Yes—yes—of course; I am quite sure that Carmel Sherlock said every word you repeat; but surely you must see that to pretend we had a case for indicting Miss Marlyn—my good God I as much a lady, in all respects, as you and I are gentlemen—would be simply to utter a frantic libel. We don't believe it;—we can't believe it—you no more than I."

"What steps do you mean to take?" asked the vicar.

A silence followed.

"Well, it is not easy, at a moment," said Mark, with a change of manner, and he walked to the window and looked out over the red blinds into the drowsy old market-place, across the jolty pavement, and to the picturesque gables, the tinted fronts and latticed windows, that looked to him like an odd dream. And he added, returning, "You would not mind giving me that copy of Sherlock's story?"

"I'll make a fair copy, and you shall have it," said the vicar.

"Yes, that's what I mean—thanks. I'll—I'll take an opinion upon it—an able opinion—and we'll put our heads together. And, I suppose, we both consider it right to be perfectly silent on this subject until I shall have got professional advice to guide me?" said Mark, looking hard at him.

"*Certainly*," said the vicar, with a reassuring emphasis.

"I knew you'd agree with me," said Mark. There was a pause, and then he said: "I wonder how Sherlock is now? Let us go and see."

Sherlock was worse, and could not live through the night. He lay in an uneasy lethargy, moaning, mumbling half sentences, turning feverishly, and nowhere and nohow finding ease—like a man dying in the fever of over-fatigue,—too exhausted for sleep, too exhausted for consciousness.

The doctor had looked in for the last time, while Mark and the vicar were talking in the inn "parlour," and Carmel Sherlock, in a few hours more, was to die. In the night he would go—in the darkness which he had peopled with shapes and voices, and pass through the throes and shades of chaos into the wonderful life of spirits.

So, drowning now in Lethe, the struggle, growing faint and fainter, would end surely in a few hours more, and he have sunk.

Farewell the queer old room at Raby, the battered quartos, the desultory life, the enchanted Stradivarius, the moonlit vigils, and that wild despairing love, that mingled with its music like a distant song and cry—all is hopeless jumble now, colours mingling, sounds confused, floating, and moving away toward the final darkness and silence.

Mark loitered on, from hour to hour, in the little town of Applebury. I think so long as Carmel Sherlock lived, there was a feeling of suspense. It were something, if that were ended before he mounted his horse. A few hours saw the short day out. The vicar's business in the neighbourhood was ended. They mounted their horses at the little inn-door together.

A melancholy sunset, a wild red glare faded into darkness, and a frosty starlight followed. The vicar and Mark rode away, side by side, in silence. I don't think a word was exchanged until they reached that point where the road to Raby diverges; and there they bid one another good night, and pursued their solitary routes homeward.

It was growing cold. Mark buttoned his wrapper closely across. One look over his shoulder he took toward the distant town of Applebury, and with a heavy heart thought of the matchless fidelity of poor Carmel Sherlock dying there in prison. Then he spurred homeward; and as he looked before him into the darkness, trees and hedges dimly gliding by, a different feeling succeeded; for was there not a beautiful face at the end of this night-ride that interested him, and made the darkness romantic?

## CHAPTER 66

## A CRISIS

Next morning came news from Applebury. Carmel Sherlock was dead, and Mark Shadwell was both glad and sorry. The sense of relief was disturbed, however, by the consciousness that Stour Temple had heard Sherlock's confession, and was watching him.

It was some weeks before Shadwell saw the vicar again. He met him under the old trees, now stark and leafless in the clear wintry air, as they both rode into the little town of Raby. They had not yet reached the houses, and with one accord they both drew bridle, and came to a walk.

"I sent that case up to my attorney in town," said Shadwell, almost the first thing after their greeting, "and had it submitted to Skelton, the Queen's Counsel, for general advice, and he says that, taking into account the facts that are proved as to poor Sherlock's state of mind, and unsupported as his statement is by a single particle of circumstantial evidence—considering how long it was delayed, and that the attempt to criminate another came from a person about himself to stand his trial for the crime on strong and clear evidence, there was no excuse for moving in it; in fact, he scouts it. I did not, of course, name the person whom the miserable man indicated."

"Quite right," said Temple.

"I knew you would think so. The fact is, we all know now the state of the poor fellow's mind; and to act on his dreams as if they were facts, would be a most monstrous cruelty."

"Can the servants throw any light upon it?" asked the vicar.

"None in the world, except negatively," said Mark. "They saw or heard nothing, no commotion, not the slightest sound. There was only that fellow Clewson, you remember, who heard or saw anything. What do you think of him?"

"Well, I thought he gave his evidence in a very distinct, unembarrassed way. I don't think anyone suspected him," said the vicar, slowly, thinking as he spoke.

"Yes, I know, and *I* don't suspect him now, but that's because

I don't believe one word of poor Sherlock's story," said Mark. "I'm quite certain the whole thing was one of his visions; but if I fancied—which, mind you, I do not—that Sherlock's narrative was a reality, my first suspicion would lighten upon Clewson."

"Why on Clewson?" said Temple.

"Roke had a fancy for expensive seals and rings, and all that sort of jeweller's finery; he had banknotes, for he told me so— he hated letters of credit, and all that sort of thing that gave him the least trouble. I think somewhere about seventy pounds was all that came to light on the inquest; but Heaven only knows! what it might have been. Don't you see a possible motive? Remember, not a creature on earth knew, but he, what money or valuables Roke may have had with him, or what his trinkets were like; a lot of them he may never have worn in England, don't you see?"

"Yes, of course, to rob him; but I remember, it appeared in evidence that Roke used to secure the door between himself and his servant," began the vicar.

"Very true," interposed Mark; "but so he used the door opening on the gallery. Now, it is clear that on the fatal night he must have neglected one or the other; and why not that? If Clewson were the man, he would naturally, being no fool, I suppose, open the other door, and leave it so, to suggest the idea that the murderer had entered from the gallery."

"But how about the person whom he saw leave the door?" said the vicar.

"Assuming, for the sake of testing the hypothesis, that this was so, I fancy it easier to believe that a young, harmless person like that passing near, and hearing perhaps some strange ejaculations and sounds, on reaching the door and seeing it partly open, should have listened there a moment, and possibly, even peeped, and gone away quickly on hearing Sherlock's step approaching."

"There may be something in that about Clewson," pondered the vicar gravely. "Do you believe it?"

"Not a word of it; and so I should swear as a witness, because

Sherlock has told me—and, in fact, whenever his imagination was in the slightest degree moved, he never failed to tell me— of marvels he saw. He saw Roke Wycherly come in at his door in the shape of a cock fluttering his wings, with his comb bleeding. He has had conversations at the tarn at Feltram with the lady who threw herself out of the window at Wynderfel, four hundred years ago, and saw her walk over the water with the most perfect distinctness, and several hundred equally wonderful revelations. In fact, in such a situation, with nerves admittedly excited to the highest pitch, and believing himself at the moment in actual communication with demons, I could not place the smallest reliance upon any evidence of his, or the reality of anything he fancied he had seen or heard; no human being who knew anything whatever of him could."

Here ensued a considerable interval of silence.

"The next time you are passing our way, Temple, you must look in. I'll give you my case and Skelton's opinion to read, and you'll see it all in a moment'; and in the meantime, I need not say how imperatively every consideration of honour, pity, and decency imposes silence upon us respecting the poor girl whose name Sherlock has mingled in his tale."

"I quite agree with you," said the vicar.

"Yes," said Mark, "I knew you would."

"A tragedy—full of instruction," said the vicar, awaking, as it were, from a little reverie. "Had Sir Roke married early someone whom he loved and respected, how different his life, and his fate too, would have been!"

"You speak out of the fullness of your heart. Temple. You went right from your college to a curacy. If you had seen something of the world, or even married, yourself, you'd hardly have made so innocent a speech. Why, a vicious fellow becomes ten times more vicious if he marries; it's a snare simply, and an aggravation of our miserable, hampered, sickly existence."

The vicar sighed, and said: "We are not agreed upon many points, I'm afraid."

"Not upon that, certainly. It is part of priestcraft—I mean

superstition—making everything irrevocable and irremediable. Vows and dedications! What can be more ridiculous and damnable than joining an unsuitable man and woman together in that irrevocable association.

"And so our discussion leaves us, as usual, pretty much where it found us," said the vicar, with a faint smile and a shake of his head, and a short silence followed.

"Miss Marlyn is still at Raby?" said the vicar.

"Yes; it depends on my wife how soon she goes. I suppose she will take her leave whenever it is quite my wife's convenience. Commend me to women for taking good care of themselves."

So Miss Marlyn lingered on at Raby. I don't think, notwithstanding this satirical speech of Mark Shadwell's, that his wife had even a voice in the matter. He would have liked people to think that the poor little nonentity who pined out her remaining days, with some complainings and little usefulness, gently in her sick room at Raby bullied him in this, and thwarted him in other things, and had been, negatively at least, the fatal incompatibility to whom he owed his failure, and all the mortifications attendant on it.

"Mark, dear," she said to him hesitatingly one day, "has anything been settled about Miss Marlyn since?"

"*Un*settled, I suppose you mean," said Mark, sharply. "About sending her away, eh?" and he laughed a little angrily. "There's just this difficulty. When that miserable fellow Sherlock died, I locked up his room, and should have given myself simply up to ruin, if she had not been here to undertake—as she has done, very cheerfully—a portion of the drudgery which must be got through, day by day, to save my affairs from falling into inextricable confusion. I don't happen to know anyone else in this house who would take the trouble of copying papers and writing letters—sixteen letters only yesterday—do you?"

"I wish I could, but the doctor won't let me write; I'm such a wretched. creature, Mark —such a burden—so useless."

"I did not say you could help it; I only venture to think it's but reasonable I should have a little help provisionally wherever

I can find it."

"Of course, dear Mark; certainly."

"You can do just as you please, whenever I have found any one to take Sherlock's place—the sooner that is, of course, the better for me. In the meantime I sha'n't undertake impossibilities, nor kill myself in the attempt, nor let myself drift into utter insolvency, merely to get rid of Miss Marlyn."

And, muttering to himself, he left the room angrily and suddenly.

Careless and contemptuous Mark's treatment of his wife had long been. But of late there was something of impatience and acrimony, and a perpetual harping on the folly of unsuitable marriages, and the indolence or uselessness of wives. These allusions were general, but the insult was particular, and she writhed under these cold barbarities.

There was a terrible change here. Indifference was assuming the sneer of intolerance. "He hates me—oh! he hates me— he hates me!" she used to sob, in her solitary agonies. "I made an idol of him—I adored him—and now I'm punished. Oh, Mark—Mark, darling; how have I deserved it from *you*? I could not help change and sickness—a weary life—useless, as you say. I know how it must try your patience, with all your cares, my poor, harassed darling! You are not yourself—you are not yourself: your life is one long trouble, and I know it is my fault—so helpless and wretched"—and so on, neither very logically nor coherently, but in great bitterness of spirit.

Then Rachel would come in, and her mother would smile piteously from her tears, drying them hastily; for these griefs were not for her ear, nor for any other's.

There was also another change—a very decided one—in Miss Marlyn. Perfectly quiet, perfectly submissive, there was an irony in her docility and an exaggeration in her submissiveness that were intangibly insulting. Even had Amy Shadwell been shrewd, hard, and irascible, instead of the most timid and gentle of women, it would not have been easy for her to fasten upon a particular ground of quarrel. For this premeditated impertinence was always arranged with a view to evasion.

Sometimes the young lady, as her spirits varied, approached Mrs. Shadwell in a different vein. She would affect quite her old manner, and talk volubly, and as if in the consciousness that her conversation was exactly the thing which Mrs. Shadwell most enjoyed, though she must have seen that these interviews gave her more pain than others, and were met with very decided discouragement.

This was not wonderful, for in these communicative moods Miss Marlyn never failed, before her talk was ended, to suggest or insinuate something mysterious and untold to the prejudice of Mr. Shadwell. These vague and intangible hints, whose meaning, for one moment legible and terrific, seemed in the next to dissolve and disappear, affrighted Mrs. Shadwell, like the intrusions of a half-seen spectre.

Were these ambiguities accidental? Were they produced by chance looks and phrases? Did Miss Marlyn herself see their odd significance? They helped the effect of other changes in Miss Marlyn's conduct, and invested that beautiful lady in the eyes of the invalid lady, with an indefinable character that was formidable.

Mrs. Shadwell in her room was sitting by the fire, listening to a little narrative of Rachel's, when Miss Marlyn looked in, paused, and retreated.

I don't know whether Rachel was talking about Miss Marlyn at the moment, but that young lady, during her few moments' hesitation at the threshold, looked from one to the other with an amused smile—a scarcely perceptible sneer—which seemed to say: "I've surprised you in high chat upon me; shouldn't I be rather *de trop* here?"

She acted provokingly well. Her air was that of a person trying to seem unconscious of her discovery, and suppressing every evidence of her amusement.

"Call her back; tell her to come in," said Mrs. Shadwell. Rachel did so, and in came Miss Agnes Marlyn.

"Pray sit down; you had better sit near the fire, hadn't you?

It's so very cold—isn't it, Miss Marlyn?" said Mrs. Shadwell.

"Very cold," acquiesced Miss Marlyn, with a gentle emphasis which conveyed a covert meaning.

Miss Marlyn sat down timidly—ceremoniously a little—and remained silent, after the manner of one admitted into a superior presence.

"I hope you keep a good fire downstairs?" said Mrs. Shadwell.

"You take a great deal too much trouble about me," she answered, with a faint, unpleasant smile; "you do, indeed, Mrs. Shadwell."

"I should be very sorry, so long as you stay with us, that you were anything, by any accident, but perfectly comfortable. Miss Marlyn," answered Amy.

"I should be very happy to abridge that so kind anxiety," said Agnes Marlyn, sadly, "if I could."

Mrs. Shadwell was silent—perhaps a little embarrassed—for assuredly she also, perhaps with more sincerity, wished Agnes Marlyn's stay at Raby shortened; and yet she had no distinct ground of quarrel to allege.

Miss Marlyn, looking down, smiled again. Rachel leaned back in her chair, with nearly closed eyes, as if in a reverie; she, too, was embarrassed—that kind of feeling is so contagious.

Then followed a silence of some minutes, during which you might hear the hum of the little jet of flame that spurted from between the bars.

"Don't you think we are all going to sleep?" said Rachel, after some minutes had passed in this way, turning to Agnes.

"I am not sleepy; my thoughts always amuse me," said Agnes Marlyn, in her ambiguous way.

Rachel looked at her a little vexed.

"I suppose you were thinking of some of the amusing people you knew in France; at least, I hope you were not thinking of us; for it is not pleasant to be laughed at, or even smiled at, as you sometimes smile," she said.

Miss Marlyn did actually laugh very faintly here, turning

away her head.

"Rachel, dear!" said Mrs. Shad well, in a tone of gentle reproof.

"I've remarked lately that you laugh, Agnes, when I am serious, and are grave when I am merry. It is not pleasant," said Rachel.

"People such as I are not pleasant company. It is not my fault that I am here. You and your mamma, I hope, know how unwillingly I find myself detained; but as you are so frank, I will be candid also. Your papa is not able to pay me the small arrear of my salary. If I had other means I should go away today, and willingly forgive that little debt; but I have no money, and without money there is nothing to be done."

"Oh! Miss Marlyn! I had hoped you were not so anxious to leave us; and I assure you I would have spoken to Mr. Shadwell, had I known you were made uncomfortable by his delay."

Miss Marlyn, turning away slowly, smiled again, faintly and bitterly.

"Many thanks; but I should not hesitate to speak myself to Mr. Shadwell, if I thought that speaking on the subject could be of any use; as it is, he asks me to await his convenience, and I suppose I must, You can't be more anxious to dismiss me, than I am to resign; the difficulty is, perhaps, a little ridiculous, but we can't help it, can we?"

"You're extremely impertinent," said Rachel, with a fiery glance and a brilliant colour.

"Rachel, dear, you mustn't!" entreated her mother.

"She has my leave to call me impertinent as often as she pleases," said Miss Marlyn; "it only shows that I have reason in wishing to go, and when I please I can retaliate, for language is at everyone's service, ain't it? But I sha'n't, though I need only pick up two or three unpleasant adjectives—insolent, beggarly, and so forth—and throw them back to you, but your caprices and insults shall not tempt me into such a meanness," said Miss Marlyn, with the same bitter smile, and growing very pale, with an angry glare in her eyes.

"Caprices and insults. Miss Marlyn!" echoed Mrs. Shadwell, in amazement.

"Caprices and insults, *yes*. I did not want to be petted. I came here as a governess: to take me up without a cause was caprice, to drop me without a cause, is insult; therefore I say caprice and insult. It is caprice, for instance, inviting me in here, when I know you dislike me; and insult from your daughter, calling me impertinent—I, who have authority here to direct your hours and instruction while I stay—and you'll come down now, if you please, Miss Shadwell, and practise your duet."

Miss Marlyn spoke in a cold way, her beautiful face white with anger, and a steady fire gleaming from her eyes, as she rose from her seat, and with a slight motion, indicated the door to Rachel.

"Authority!" repeated Mrs. Shadwell. "You forget, Miss Marlyn, that my daughter is quite past that age, and that I have never given you any such right."

"Oh, dear! I did not mean you, madam. I received it, of course, from Mr. Shadwell," said Agnes, with the same insolent smile.

"Your authority, I think, can hardly overrule mine. Miss Marlyn I wish my daughter to remain here," said Mrs. Shadwell, gently, but with a slight flush in her cheek.

"I think, however, I am doing my duty, madam, in desiring Miss Shadwell to come to her music. It would, of course, be much pleasanter for me to sit idle, reading my book."

"Do, pray mamma, tell her to leave your room," said Rachel, in her own way nearly as angry as Miss Marlyn.

"I shall be too happy to leave this room," said Miss Marlyn.

"Anything so ridiculous!" exclaimed Rachel.

"But it shall be to ascertain on exactly what footing I really am placed while I remain here," continued Agnes Marlyn, and with a courtesy, she left the room.

"Did you ever hear anything so impertinent in your life?" exclaimed Rachel. "I could not believe my ears. I wonder, mamma, you did not order her out of the room."

"She was angry, darling, and very rude; but I'm sure she will regret it when she reflects a little," said Mrs. Shadwell.

"She's so ungrateful and odious! I could not have believed it of her. I suppose she's gone down straight to papa, to the library; he'll soon bring her to her senses—impudent creature!" said Rachel. "Is it true, I wonder, that papa has not got money to pay her.—I don't believe it, do you?"

"I don't know, darling, I can't say, I'm sure," said Mrs. Shadwell. "She is so angry just now, that she would say almost anything; but it's only too possible, there is nothing more miserable than worries about money, but I ought not to complain; they press so much more on your poor papa, they have quite worn out his spirits. It is so miserable, this fine place and house, and all the rents passing through his hands, merely to pay interest on mortgages and annuities to strangers, and so very little left to us to live upon."

"Agnes Marlyn, talking in the odd rude way she sometimes used—I don't mean, of course, as she did just now—said that papa did not know anything about his own affairs; that he thought he had only twelve hundred a-year clear, and that he might easily have sixteen or seventeen hundred more, and that there is nearly five hundred a-year coming whenever an old man—I forget his name—dies; so that we might hold up our heads again, if only we had sense to look after our own business."

"Did she, really?" said Mrs. Shadwell, and, for a moment, looking down in a pained meditation. She seemed to reflect on something different from an accession of wealth.

"Yes," said Rachel; "but it is not always easy to know when Agnes Marlyn is joking, and when in earnest."

Just as she reached this point the door opened, and Mr. Shadwell, followed closely by Miss Marlyn, entered the room.

## CHAPTER 67
### MISS MARLYN'S TRIUMPH

Miss Marlyn had been weeping, and her handkerchief just touched her eyes, and was removed as she entered. Mark Shadwell looked pale and sternly on his wife and daughter, and said sharply, but slowly,

"I've merely looked in to say, that Miss Marlyn, being here as your instructress, Rachel, is by you, while she remains, to be obeyed."

At the last emphatic word he paused.

"Do you mind? *Obeyed*," he repeated. "I have no notion of anything else, or of being plagued by your tempers and contradiction. I think. Miss Marlyn, you required her to go down to her music, didn't you?"

"I asked Miss Shadwell to come to her usual practice," said Agnes Marlyn, with a suffering air, in a very subdued tone. "I do not wish to have power, I hate it; I only wish to know what is required of me, if what I say is to be done, then I am accountable; but I should so much prefer to have none, to have no authority, no power, no right. You do not know, sir, how unhappy it makes me; I am so miserable, so hated, so helpless."

A few tears fell here on Miss Marlyn's soft cheek, and her little speech suddenly broke down.

"Pray, don't distress yourself. Miss Marlyn. I insist that you shall be treated with proper respect while you remain here. You'll remember, if you please—"he continued, addressing his daughter, "that you are to obey Miss Marlyn as your instructress, and to treat her as my guest, and in all respects as your own equal where she is not your superior—your equal in birth, your superior in attainments. Do you think it can be any pleasure to her listening to your discords and blunders at the piano, and performing the thankless task of teaching you? What do you mean? What are you dreaming of? Go down this moment; and while Miss Marlyn remains, you shall obey her implicitly."

"But mamma was here," said Rachel,. frightened, but also excited and angry; "and Miss Marlyn was extremely rude to her, and ordered me out of the room in the most insulting way, and wished to annoy mamma by doing so; and I always thought I should obey mamma, and not her, when mamma was by."

"Your mamma knows how to take care of herself, I hope—"began Mark Shadwell in a sterner tone.

"Oh, Mr. Shadwell, pray—pray do not consider me!" pleaded Miss Marlyn, pathetically. "I only wish to know what my duties are; it is so miserable any misunderstanding. I am always so unfortunate! Do, I implore, with me whatever Mrs. Shadwell likes best."

"You shall be respected here, Miss Marlyn," said Mark, in a high tone.

"And so, I'm sure you think should mamma," said Rachel. "And Miss Marlyn has been most impertinent to her, and overbearing to me."

"Oh! Rachel, darling! how can you say so?" exclaimed Miss Marlyn, with an appealing look.

But this little dialogue was peremptorily brought to a close by Mark Shadwell's commanding his daughter, with a stamp on the floor, to go instantly, as Miss Marlyn had already desired her, downstairs to her music.

As Miss Marlyn followed her pupil from the room, she stole a glance at Mrs. Shadwell strangely at variance with her recent tears—a look of lurking triumph and insult that stung her to the heart.

This sudden scene, more violent in action by force of its looks and tones than its mere dialogue thus set down would convey, was fruitful in feminine tears; not only were Agnes Marlyn's young cheeks wet, but Mrs. Shadwell wept and trembled.

She had been bullied, and mortified, and humbled before that insolent young lady, who had provoked that collision for the direct purpose of appealing to the partial judgement of her husband.

Oh! cruel, wicked girl, what had that poor sick lady done to provoke the torture of that triumph? Oh! Mark, Mark, she thought, how could you forsake the wife of your youth, and requite her unchanged adoration with that deep and ruthless perfidy?

"Oh, Mark!" she exclaimed; "Oh, Mark! you don't know how you have wounded me. If you knew all you would not have slighted me so before Rachel, and before that insulting, wicked girl."

And speaking this, for her, unparalleled invective, she threw her arms about her husband's neck, and wept passionately on that breast which her head had not lain upon for years. Mark was disconcerted for a moment, and placed his hand almost fondly on her head. But recollecting himself, he gently removed her, his hand still resting not unkindly on her shoulder. She was clinging to him, looking up with such an imploring agony, and her poor swollen eyelids and wet cheeks moved Mark for a moment with a feeling of compunction.

"Come, Amy!" he said, "don't let us have a scene all about nothing. You women are all made up of exaggerations; that *wick ed* girl, as you call her. Miss Marlyn"—Mark's face as he looked down upon his wife was ghastly pale—"has, I think, simply done her duty, and so will you when you reflect. I can't, of course, say what you were all talking about before I came in. It's merely, so far as I can see, making mountains of molehills; but I'm quite certain—whether you had a scene or not before I came—that you will see the absurdity of treating this wretched little squabble as if it were something of—of importance."

"Oh! Mark, it *is* of importance! it is—it is—it is—you *know* it is; yes, darling, very important. Oh! Mark, do send her away, I implore of you; you don't know how miserable I am."

Mark was again disconcerted, perhaps agitated; but he affected to laugh.

"Come, come. Amy! you mustn't be foolish; you're not a child!"

"Oh, Mark, darling! this isn't foolish. Oh, darling! do as I ask you, and you'll say it was wise."

"Well, of course, if you make it important, it is important," said Mark, with a sudden and odd change of manner. "There's a crisis in everything. I *will* do as you say;—she shall go. She leaves Raby tomorrow morning. Long threatening comes at last, as old Wyndle says. I am utterly sick of this state of things."

Don't blame me, Mark, dear!"

"I blame no one; no, I know too well things come about of

themselves, and—and I hate suspense. It was to be, I suppose, and it has come," said Mark.

"Thank you, Mark, dear! I'm so grateful." "Don't thank me; you needn't. You're not to suppose, because I don't talk about what's passing, that I don't see it. I have observed—I could not help it—how from having petted and caressed Miss Marlyn—making, perhaps, too much of her— you have come to hate her, and to show her that you hate her—caprice and insult"—(how had he come to find these words?) "Of course, it's another worry; but I have resolved to put an end to the whole thing."

"I'm sorry you think I'm to blame; but, indeed, I'm not. And, Mark, there are some little jewels—I never wear them—and would it not be well to send them up to town and sell them, and that would make paying Miss Marlyn quite easy."

"That's my affair; no, keep them. You need not speak to Miss Marlyn. I don't wish another scene. I'll tell her to be ready to go by the two o'clock train tomorrow. She must leave this at eleven."

And, so saying, Mark abruptly left the room. Amy Shadwell watched his departure with a strange alarm. There was more in the impression that remained upon her than the occasion seemed to warrant. What resolution had he taken? What was about to happen? A sinister presentiment terrified her.

The scene that had just agitated her, in her weak state, was followed by violent nervous palpitations, and intense hysterical excitement.

Very late that night Amy Shadwell, under the influence of a strong narcotic, lying in her husband's room, with only a faint night-light burning, and the uncertain flame of the fire, awakened she knew not how, saw her husband standing by her bed. Her face was turned from the light, which flickered dimly on his face, as he looked down closely into hers. His countenance was sorrow-stricken and sullen, she could see; and standing erect, his gaze unrewarded, for her features were quite in darkness, he sighed heavily, and remained looking down with the same dismal aspect, for a time; then once more he stooped his face, and whispered very low:

"Amy! Amy!"

In the action of the opiate she had taken there was something that resembled a luxurious catalepsy. With a sufficient effort of will, no doubt she could have roused herself to reply, but the languor and serenity of her state held her in a drowsy spell. There was a dim sense of pleasure in protracting the unwonted scene. There was something of grief and tenderness in Mark Shadwell's countenance that held her in a strange suspense, and she watched his movements, and heard his words, with the curiosity that accompanies an interesting dream.

"Have I done her justice—have I understood her quite? Too late now," he said, faintly.

And again he stooped down and gazed into her darkened face, and seemed to glisten for her breathing.

"She's asleep—so best. Her lot is happier than mine!"

So saying, he walked gently to the fireplace, and stood there, looking ruefully into the embers.

She watched him with increasing intensity—her heart beat fast in the suspense. She expected him to return to her bedside; she debated within her own mind whether she should speak to him, but a sort of spell restrained her. He looked on her again, long and steadily. And now she saw his shadow on the wall moving—was it towards her? No—the door opened, and he was gone.

## CHAPTER 68
### MARK SHADWELL LEAVES RABY

Mark Shadwell, when he closed the door of his wife's room, went direct to his own, where were candles burning. He opened his desk, and taking a letter from it, written by his own hand, and not yet folded, he read it through, and with the deep sigh and anxious look of a man still irresolute, he placed it in its envelope and sealed it.

The window of his room looked out upon the yard in which Clewson, from his own, had seen Carmel Sherlock, on the memorable night of the murder, make his preparations for departure. There Mark Shadwell now saw a man busily getting a horse between the shafts of his tax-cart, while a portmanteau and bag lay on the ground beside the wheel.

Now Mark looked at his watch. He put on a loose coat and his hat, as he saw the vehicle get into motion to leave the yard. He put out the candles, and, with more caution than before, walked lightly through the gallery.

At the head of the great staircase stood the slender figure of Miss Agnes Marlyn. The moonlight entering through the great window on the landing showed her pretty form distinctly. She dressed in her ordinary costume; there was no bonnet, no cloak, no sign of meditated flight. The lady in the grey, high-up dress, with the little bit of crimson ribbon showing like a wound at her breast, met his sudden and eager advance with a little sign of caution, her slender figure raised. He took the warning, and checked his hurried step, looking over his shoulder. She glided a little way towards him by the wall, against which leaning her shoulder lightly, and repeating her warning gesture, she awaited him.

The lowest and softest possible "hush!" she breathed rather than whispered. He would have taken her hand, but she withdrew it, with a gentle but decided gesture, and another "hush!" while the moonlight showed the faint knitting of her beautiful eyebrows, betokening caution.

"The letter?" she whispered, her fingers a little extended.

"Yes," said he, and placed in them the letter he had just taken from his desk.

She turned it towards the light of the moon—that emblem of purity—and read the address; it was:

"Mrs. Shadwell,

"Raby."

and in the left-hand corner the sternly marked initials "M. S."

"I'll put it in the Raby post-office as I go," said she, as she softly dropped it within the breast of her dress.

405

"Just so—yourself?" he answered.

"Myself?—yes," she repeated.

"Don't give it to any servant, mind—old Wyndle would get it, and know all about it; and just do as you said."

She nodded.

"And, so, goodbye," he whispered, hesitating. Had he ever seen that strange girl look so beautiful before?

She merely nodded again, raising her head a little, in the moonlight delicately beautiful—a tinted statue.

"Not a word—nothing?" he whispered, lingering still in that fascination.

He extended his hand gently towards hers. She withdrew it again, merely whispering—

"Go!"

But, changing her mind before he turned, she took his hand, and pressed it tremblingly—vehemently—whispering:

"Goodbye! God bless you!"

Yes, "God bless you!" A benediction, an appeal to God; what a chaos in that mind!

And she glided swiftly away into the dark.

With a strange pang of shame, rapture, agony, he gazed for a moment back through the familiar oak-carved arch into the darkness which shrouded from him a shattered home—an anarchy of past and future, and the shapes of a dream wild and wicked.

Drawing his coat about him now, he ran lightly down the stairs. The hall-door was open, and the tax-cart stood there, and lean, wiry old Jem Truelock, who had served the Squire's father before him, was standing by the horse's head, whip in hand.

"The things there?" said Mark, not thinking of his luggage, but reminded of it by seeing it there. "Shut the door—very gently."

"All right, sir."

"You see, Jem," said his master, as he took his seat and the reins beside him, "I'm forced to steal away for a bit. You are an old friend, so I don't mind telling you: I've got a hint—the beaks, you know. All settled in a week or a fortnight, though— running up to town to manage it. These d—d fellows will be down tomorrow, perhaps, and I shouldn't much mind if, among you, you managed to give them a devilish good licking. Get along!"

Jem smiled shrewdly, and nodded with a fierce wink, and a touch of his finger to his hat; and away they went. Was there any truth in this story? Not a word. Mark was angry at having to practise this meanness—a shabby deception—upon his own servant; angry and ashamed, and he felt that he was lying badly, and doubted whether the man believed him.

He lighted a cigar as they drove out of the dark avenue of Raby. He felt relieved as the gate closed behind him, and they emerged from the solemn groining of the huge old trees, upon the road and into the clear moonlight. He felt better, and his cheroot helped him to serenity.

He did not look back at Raby. He looked toward the sky, and the stars, and the distant hills, and warmed and soothed his thoughts with tobacco; every now and then applying a reflection he had taught himself: "No woman ever loved a man whom she could not understand, and she never understood me."

At Raby all was quiet until the grey of the late wintry dawn. It was to be a day of change. Miss Marlyn was to leave Raby at eleven o'clock; and perhaps the consciousness of this approaching relief made Amy Shadwell's waking happier that morning than it had been for many days before.

Rachel ran into her mamma's room:

"Papa had to go away all on a sudden last night to London," said she. "Jem Truelock drove him to the station—sudden business. Did he tell you?"

"No. I hope nothing bad—no." She answered, looking as if she was going to faint. But he was here last night, and I fancy intended to speak to me. But though I saw him, that laudanum made me drowsy—and I did not say a word—I'll get up. I must go into the next room, and see old Truelock. I'm certain he told him; he tells Truelock everything."

So Mrs. Shadwell got on her dressing-gown, and made a

hasty toilet, and in her morning-room she saw old Truelock, and cross-examined him, she and Rachel, and he gave them a clear opinion upon the cause of his absence, founded on Mark's brief talk as they started, and he reminded her of another expedition on a similar occasion to London twelve years ago, which turned out all right in the end.

"Oh! yes, poor fellow! that must be it; that is certainly the cause. Old Truelock is so shrewd, he could not be mistaken, and Mark would not deceive him, he tells him everything."

With these and similar reflections she chased away the vague alarms that still returned. Later in the morning in came old Wyndle.

"Well, ma'am, that Frenchwoman—Agnes Marlyn—has her things on ready to start, and glad and gay she seems, and I thought first 'twas no more than swagger; but it's more than that, I'm thinkin'; and I tell you what it is, ma'am, if I was you, I'd keep her a bit longer at Raby."

Old Wyndle nodded, and looked darkly wise.

"I don't know what you mean, Wyndle."

"Only just that, my lady," said Wyndle, grimly. "I'd keep her here, and let the master send her away himself."

"Really, Wyndle, I don't understand you," said the lady, looking very hard at her, and a little agitated.

"Whiew! ma'am, she's a feather-pated wench, a wild dare-devil lass wi' her brain half-turned wi' vanities; and she was so forward—always pokin' after the master here, wi' her secretary stuff and nonsense, as if that giddy lass had a head for business, like poor Mr. Sherlock—God forgive him—had, and figuring and the like—not she; and if she goes away now, mind—God knows where she'll be going to."

"What do you mean, Wyndle?" said Amy Shadwell, sitting up in her bed, with a bright hectic in her cheek, for after her little talk in the next room with old Jem Truelock, she had lain down again, being still very ill.

"I know what I mean," said blunt, old Wyndle, mysteriously. "I don't trust them furriners."

"Oh! Wyndle, it's very wrong to speak of Miss Marlyn as you are doing, and as for your master, he's the soul of honour."

"Oh, yes!—I'm only meanin' her, ma'am. To be sure, she may be all very good and nice, but I'm an old woman, ma'am, and has seen more in my time than you, and I tell you, she doesn't like a bone in your skin, nor none of us: she hates us all; me because I see through her, an' you because 'appen you're a bit in her way."

"Oh! Wyndle, I really think you are going mad!" said Mrs. Shadwell, affecting incredulity, but feeling as if she were going to faint.

"Well, ma'am, there it is. I may be wrong, and I may be right; but anyhow, if I was in your place, ma'am, I wouldn't let her budge till master was here to write her discharge and pay her wi' his own hand—not a foot," said old Wyndle, resolutely.

"But he has paid her; he paid Miss Marlyn yesterday: I have got her acknowledgment, and there is no such thing as a discharge needed—a governess does not require one. If she chooses to refer people to us, of course we'll say all we can for her, and I know nothing against her."

"Well, ma'am, if ye will ye will; an' what'll ye have for your dinner?" And so old Wyndle, with a disconcerting transition, passed abruptly to other matters, leaving her mistress frightened and agitated, quite in the dark.

She sickened as she doubted whether the spirit of prudence might not have spoken in the coarse but kindly counsel of the privileged old servant. But what would Mark say or think if, on his return, he were to find Miss Marlyn still at Raby, under a countermand from its capricious mistress. So, as usually happens with irresolute people in a perplexity, it ended by her doing nothing.

It was between nine and ten o'clock, when a gentle tap came to Mrs. Shadwell's door, and, in obedience to her call, Miss Agnes Marlyn came in.

"I should not have thought of coming to bid farewell, Mrs. Shadwell, until you had sent for me; but I saw Mr. Shadwell, for a few minutes before his departure, this morning very early." Miss Marlyn spoke very slowly. She liked, I believe, protracting this communication. "And he requested me particularly to place this note in your hand—and, accordingly—here it is."

So saying, she gave her Mark's letter—which she was to have dropped, by his direction, in the Baby post-office—with a dark steady look, all the time, turned on Mrs. Shadwell's countenance. I am pretty certain that Miss Marlyn knew the contents of that letter perfectly, and that she had a fancy to witness its effect upon Mrs. Shadwell. In this, however, she was disappointed. Mrs. Shadwell glanced at the address, and felt very oddly. She laid it on the coverlet beside her, however, unopened, and she said gently—

"I suppose I am to say goodbye, now, Miss Marlyn—"

"You are very good," she said; "but I should not care to go till eleven—if you don't mind; the waiting at the station would be so very long."

"Oh! dear—of course—I only meant to say goodbye now. I am very sorry that you've seemed to misunderstand me—of late—and—and—we were not so happy—but I trust you may be very soon happier than you could ever have been in this *triste* place—and I wish you every good—"

She fancied she saw the smile of a disdainful incredulity faintly playing at the comers of Agnes Marlyn's lips, and hardly perceptibly dimpling her soft chin and cheek.

"Yes, indeed, Agnes Marlyn, I do wish you all good and happiness; and although we have not been so happy for some time—I am sure it was neither my wish, nor my fault—I shall never forget your kindness and attention— until the unhappy change came—and if you think of any way in which I can be of use, you may rely upon me."

So saying, she extended her open hand on the coverlet to Miss Marlyn; but the young lady did not take it.

"I don't think it would be fair to think of giving you any trouble, Mrs. Shadwell. In fact I rather think and hope I sha'n't need any help. I don't, of course, count good wishes and prayers, for they really hardly involve any trouble; but you, I assure you, Mrs. Shadwell, on account of your health and everything, are one of the very last persons on whom I should venture to impose the slightest real trouble on my account. Oh! no—thank you all the same, Mrs. Shadwell, very much."

"Well, Agnes—Miss Marlyn—goodbye," said Mrs. Shadwell; and again she extended her hand to take that of the young lady.

"*Adieu, Madame*," said Miss Marlyn, in the sweetest, softest imaginable tone; and at the same time she made her the very prettiest, saddest little courtesy you could imagine; her beautiful eyes lowered to her tiny foot, not choosing, I think, to see Mrs. Shadwell's friendly gesture; and so she passed through the door that opened into Mrs. Shadwell's sitting-room, where she stopped— having closed the door—affecting to admire some early flowers, the bells of which she turned up caressingly with the tips of her fingers, while she was listening for what might be heard from the next room, expecting that Mrs. Shadwell would open her letter forthwith, and in this her anticipations were verified.

## CHAPTER 69
### BREAKING THE SEAL.

In some good-natures a farewell is a forgiveness; and Amy Shadwell had experienced this unrequited at the moment when she was to look her last on Miss Marlyn. The door, however, had hardly closed upon her, when she opened her husband's letter, and read as follows:

Amy,—I have long made up my mind to take a step which, however painful at the outset to you and to me, will ultimately, I am convinced, conduce to the happiness of both. We have been living together without sympathy and without confidence. This state of things was painful to me. I saw that it was painful to you. It was not in my power, nor in yours, to improve our unhappy relations. What imaginable good purpose, therefore, could have been consulted by continuing to practise what had ceased to be even an experiment, and had become a miserable hypocrisy? I am quite incapable of reproaching you with that for which you are in no way to blame.

The entire incompatibility, not of tempers, but of sympathies and of tendencies, which had long separated us, had been seconded for years by the aggravations of ill health, and of incessant and harassing cares. Living under the same roof, we have for years been as effectually separated as if we had resided in separate cities; nay, worse, our occasional miserable meetings aggravated for each that sense of loneliness which was the root of our misery. I have left Raby, therefore, with the fixed and unalterable resolution of seeing it no more until the separation, which I am satisfied is essential to the happiness of each of us, shall have been legally and finally accomplished.

Your own fortune shall return to you, together with such a portion of my wretched income as may be fairly awarded for your further support and that of Rachel. I have written on the subject to your former guardian and surviving trustee, General Hardwicke. You and Rachel must arrange to leave Baby. I should finally arrange to do so myself, but the state of the property compels my personal presence and care. Your arrangements shall be absolutely at your own disposal. I shall not of course, interfere. Hardwicke will no doubt advise with you on any subject connected with the measure I have adopted. The cavils of a censorious and pharisaical world I utterly despise. I have taken the course which is best for both, and no expostulation can alter me.

Mark Shadwell.

Holding the paper before her eyes with one hand, and with the other pressing her temple, with white lips she read the dreadful letter through. "My good God!" she exclaimed when she had read it through. And she attempted to begin it over again, but she was seized with such a trembling that she could not.

"Why—why—what does he mean? I can't make it out," she repeated, still pressing her hand to her temple, with that look of horrible incredulity which borders on idiocy, and saying, "Where, where, call him," she got partly out of bed. But uttering a long, wild scream, she fell back in a violent convulsive fit.

Miss Marlyn, in the next room, heard the unearthly scream, and for a moment was scared. She would have returned and given an alarm, but she heard the bedroom door, at the other end of Mrs. Shadwell's room, open, and old Wyndle's voice— and then another voice and hurried steps entering.

From the distant door in the sitting-room, therefore. Miss Marlyn glided out upon the gallery, and down by the back stairs, and then round by the great staircase, to her own room, without passing again Mrs. Shadwell's door. There, pale and agitated, she sat down upon the side of her bed, with a beating heart, and listened, but could hear nothing. Then she opened her door, and stood at it listening again; but it was too far; and so she stole, on and on, till she could hear old Wyndle's voice, and that of the maid; and so, by little and little, she drew near enough to the door to hear what was passing.

"She's getting out of it, God be praised!" said old Wyndle.

"Oh!—oh!—oh!" groaned Amy Shadwell's voice. "What is it—what is it? Something dreadful has happened."

"No, no, sweet-heart; nothin'—nothin'—all quite right again; there now—there now —don't mind disturbin' yourself; just lie quiet; don't let her get out o' bed at that side."

And then Mrs. Shadwell's voice said—

"Oh! this dreadful news! What is it? Poor Mark will be so shocked to hear it, when he comes in!"

"There—there now—there—my darling good lady!" said Wyndle's voice. "Don't let her sit up!" And so on, until, all on a sudden, the same appalling scream again thrilled Agnes Marlyn's ear, and she knew that the convulsions had returned.

She was frightened, and for a moment irresolute, but she turned to retrace her steps towards her bedroom, hearing, as she did so, the hurried talk of the frightened women, and the sounds of a terrible mute struggle.

Miss Marlyn sat down on the stairs very pale. She had not

413

been there long, when Rachel, who had heard nothing of the scene now going on in her mother's room, came up. Quite disregarding the terms on which they had been, Agnes Marlyn stood up, and taking her by the arm, said—

"Rachel, I'm afraid Mrs. Shadwell's very ill. She's in her own room—you must send to Raby for the doctor."

Rachel ran to her mother's bedside, having entreated Agnes to send.

When the doctor came, he found the poor lady hurried from one epileptic fit into another, and in about an hour after his arrival, sudden symptoms of a fatal kind appeared; a vessel in the brain had given way, and the case was hopeless!

Miss Marlyn went into the room. The hour of her intended departure had long passed. She put a few questions to the doctor. She looked for a moment at the dying and unconscious lady, and then she said to Rachel—

"We must telegraph for your papa."

"He's gone to London, but we don't know where," said Rachel.

"No; he's in Birmingham, at Wycombe's Hotel. He told me he was going to stay there for some days," said Agnes Marlyn, reciting this solitary confidence with an evil pride, resulting from a strange mixture of feelings.

Old Wyndle looked at her savagely, and muttered to herself. But Agnes Marlyn, with a calm, pale face and collected manner, went downstairs and wrote a message for the Telegraph Office to Mark Shadwell.

"Mrs. Shadwell is dying: return to Raby instantly."

She hesitated; she would not be herself the sender of this message; it would associate her in his mind with a shock with which she would not be connected. The drawing-room door was open, and as she stood musing, with the paper in her fingers, she saw the doctor, and went into the hall, as he was getting his hat and coat.

"Don't you think, sir, that Mr. Shadwell should be sent for?" she said.

"Certainly; telegraph," he said.

"From what I am told, sir, I am afraid this message says no more than truth?"

And Miss Marlyn placed what she had written in his hands.

"Too true; but he'll not be in time—Birmingham's a good way: he'll not find her living," said he, with a shake of his head.

"But he ought to be here," said Miss Marlyn, decisively; "will you sign this?—we'll find a messenger here."

So the doctor signed it, and filled in dates, and so forth.

"She'll be gone before an hour, poor little thing!—She was the nicest creature, I think, I ever met almost."

So the doctor went, and Miss Marlyn saw old Jem Truelock, and with the fresh horse that was to have brought her to the station, away he rode with his message.

Mark Shadwell's letter, which the maid had seen in Agnes Marlyn's hand as she entered Mrs. Shadwell's room, was found on the counterpane, and old Wyndle took it.

That night, the Rev. Stour Temple called. He had heard the sad news, and rode over, not knowing that Mark was away. Rachel had fallen into that deep sleep which succeeds grief and excitement, and is the closing compensation for that frightful suspense. Old Wyndle had her voluble and bitter story to tell.

"She was better this morning than I saw her for two years or more, when in came that Agnes Marlyn, wi' this letter in her fist—Jane Cherry saw her, before ten o'clock—and I picked up the letter off the quilt. It's from the master—God forgive him!—telling her he blames her for everything, as I think—he left last night—but the two that God joined together, should be sundered by such villainy! and that letter was the death o' her; and here it is—I can't make much o't myself—but you must read it, and see how it is wi' poor Miss Rachel."

After a few more questions, therefore, he did read that shocking letter, and after a long silence, he said that he would call again next day—having considered the matter carefully meanwhile—and see and talk with Rachel.

Late that night Mark returned. He knew by the face of the

servant who opened the door, that his wife was dead.

He heard the short tale in silence. There was a sense of re-covered liberty; there was something of remorse; also an angry shame, which tortured his pride, and made him uneasy in the presence of his own servants.

Sullen as a wounded beast, Mark Shadwell made his way to his bedroom, where, not in sleep nor in prayer, but in an agitated hurry of thought and emotion, he passed a long and troubled night.

When Stour Temple called next morning, and learned that Mark Shadwell had arrived, he contented himself with inquiries at the door, and did not ask to go in.

Wyndle in her own way had told him something of Miss Marlyn's movements. The more he heard of that young lady's doings, the less he liked or trusted her. It pained him that she should be at Raby. Still he hoped that it was the confusion of this sudden death that had postponed her departure. There were suspicions afloat in his mind which he would not have liked to tell to anybody.

Rachel was past the strange curiosity of childhood. She could not bring herself to look at her dead mother and companion. She lay sobbing on her bed, now and then reading more serenely in her Bible, and then, as the truth—incredible for a moment—returned, bursting into a wild convulsion of weeping again.

Old Wyndle often looked in, and stood or sat by her bed, talking in her own rough, quaint way. But now she had gone, and, with Jane Cherry, the housemaid, was busy in poor Mrs. Shadwell's room.

And now their sad office was ended, and she lay, cold and sad, in the white robes of her purity.

The blinds were lowered, the room darkened, and old Wyn-dle, having sent Jane Cherry away, remained for a few minutes, looking with rueful and bitter thoughts upon the young, forlorn face, with the light of a wonderful smile upon it.

There came a low tap at the door, and, expecting to see Jane Cherry come in, Wyndle walked a few cautious steps towards the door, and in a low tone, such as is heard in sick chambers, she bid the visitor come in.

It was not Jane Cherry who entered, but Agnes Marlyn. The old housekeeper, very erect, made one step backward, and a silence of some moments followed.

"And ye've actually come in!" exclaimed old Mrs. Wyndle, with a strange gasp, and her arms across, the fingers of one at the elbow of the other, and a gaze dark and stern, as if she had seen an evil spirit in the room.

"Mrs. Wyndle, you'll please not to speak to me," said the young lady, coldly. "Once for all, I come here at your master's desire, to lock these drawers, and wardrobes, and boxes," she said, with a stem deliberateness, "and to take charge of the keys for him. I shall do my duty, whatever other people may. Will you be good enough to move a little aside, and let me reach that wardrobe?"

"I don't believe the master ever sent ye in here, nor desired ye no such thing," said old Wyndle, pale and fierce.

"Come—come, Mrs. Wyndle; you must know it can't be pleasant to anyone coming in here."

And, turning suddenly on the old woman, with eyes that flashed, she added:

"What can you propose to yourself, woman, by trying to quarrel with me?"

"No, bad as he's bin, I can't believe that of him," said the old servant, sturdily.

"Bad as he has been!" repeated Miss Marlyn. "Why, you ungrateful old woman, of what use on earth are you? If he had not been a great deal too kind, you'd have been in the workhouse long ago. There—do, for goodness sake, just be decently quiet."

That brilliant, beautiful girl, with a strangely heightened colour and flashing eyes, pushed by her, locked the wardrobe, locked the drawers, gathered up some rings, chains, and trinkets that were on the dressing-table.

"Look here, please," she said, "I place them in this box."

Old Wyndle only lifted up her hands and eyes, and said:

"Oh! my mistress! my poor, little, good mistress! Did I live to see this day?"

Carrying her head high, and angrier than she cared to show. Miss Marlyn proceeded to lock up everything that seemed of any value.

Then said Miss Marlyn, coldly:

"He said particularly, there's the—a gold ring, and a diamond guard on her finger."

"Her weddin'-ring! Oh! master!—the ring you put on her finger!" She was speaking almost in a scream. "Oh! Mr. Shad well—oh, *man*! could ye let her fingers on it?"

"There's a guard-ring, too, a brilliant hoop, that he says I must take."

"Take them! Touch her? Touch her hand? My God! you would not dare to touch her!" shrieked old Wyndle.

"Take them off yourself—why, that's what I said," exclaimed Miss Agnes Marlyn, with a very wicked look at the old woman, though in a calm voice,

"Oh! my poor mistress! my darling! angel bright!" cried old Wyndle, standing at the foot of the bed, with her hands clasped, and tears trickling down her cheeks. "To think such things could be! No—no—I say! I'll take 'em off wi' my own old fingers, and I'll put them in the hand that gave them—the hand she loved—the hand that laid her there; but you sha'n't touch them or her. Yes, my darling!—ye'll give 'em up—gentle—gentle—like your beautiful self. Look at her! Ye've killed her. Look at her there—the poor little thing! Arn't ye afeard she'd stand up like an angel, and a strike ye wi' a look o' her white face? Look—look, woman—look! Lyin' there, wi' the light o' heaven on her face—murdered by ye! To think o't!

"Why does God *stan'* such things? She—the blessed creature, simple and lovin', that wouldn't hurt a fly, as meek as a little child—a little child! May God judge them that did it—gone—ye poor, little thing! and you that done it—there, to see! standin' on yer two feet, hale, and strong, and happy—my God! and full o' life. But she's the upper hand o' ye still: she's raised in power

418

—better off than the best o' you, with her crown incorruptible and robes of white, to tell her story before the throne. Oh! look at the poor, grieved, little face of her, you cruel, dreadful creature!"

"I never was anything in my life but kind to her, you stupid, wicked, old woman. Look at her! why shouldn't I? I've done my duty by her better than ever you did, who never did anything of any earthly use. Of course I'll look at her."

And with a quick step she came by the bedpost at the foot of the bed, and with a bright flush and a strange defiance, did look on that saddest and most angelic sight vouchsafed to mortals.

When Miss Marlyn left the room, old Wyndle grimly shut the door after her, and stood at the foot of the bed, thinking.

"I see how 'twill be—I a' seen it long enough. I can see a bit still, though my old head's little good now; but think I must—if I don't, who will?—about the poor lassie, Rachel. I'll set my wits to work on't, and 'appen counsel may come; and so it will, for God can't mean to leave his creature, without help or care, to them that'll grudge her her bit and sup, and the clothes on her back!"

## Chapter 70
### Mark Shadwell Takes a Decided Step

Good-natured as old Wyndle was, she had a proper regard for herself, and her thoughts naturally turned to her own future, a subject which the changes she saw at hand involved in utter uncertainty.

She was recalled, however, by fancying that she heard Agnes Marlyn's voice in the gallery. She looked on the face before her, and a gush of kindly recollections and bitter feelings found vent in a flood of tears.

Drying them hastily, and half-hoping to meet Miss Marlyn, she issued from the room, closing the door reverently. But she did not encounter that young lady on her way to Rachel's room, which, without ceremony, she entered.

Though not undressed, Rachel lay upon her bed with her

face to the pillow, you would have said in a deep sleep, had it not been for a convulsive sob every now and then.

"Get up, Miss," said old Wyndle, sternly, laying her hand on her shoulder; "this is no house for you."

The young lady sat up on the side of the bed, like a person called up from a swoon, and looked in old Wyndle's face, without speaking.

"Mind ye. Miss," said old Wyndle, inspired with sudden decision, "ye don't stay here; ye just come wi' me, and look your last on your poor mamma, and then go ye straight to Miss Barbara, down at the vicar's."

"Hold your tongue, Wyndle," said a stern voice, near the door. "Come, rouse yourself, Rachel, and listen to me."

Old Wyndle, with half a glance, saw Mark Shadwell standing within the shadow of the door.

"Ah!" groaned old Wyndle, bitterly, shaking her head slowly.

"Do you hear me, Rachel? Collect your thoughts," he repeated.

"Oh! yes—papa—papa!" And she caught him in a wild embrace, and lay close to his breast, sobbing, and straining him in her girlish arms.

He had not expected any such thing. This sudden burst of affection disconcerted and pained him.

"Go, Wyndle," said he, sternly. "Miss Rachel will ring for you when she wants you. Shut the door."

"Sit down, Rachel—do command your feelings—and attend to what I say, which sha'n't be much," he said, leading her to a chair.

"And first, you must not allow that ungrateful old woman, Wyndle, to talk to you about my plans, as they affect you or myself; and, also, I request that you'll not make a *confidante* of her. When you know as much of the world as I do, you'll learn that old persons in her rank are pushing and prying, conceited, and officious, and must be kept in their proper places. Wyndle is a prejudiced, impudent old woman, and I don't choose any confidences with such a person, d'ye mind. And, Rachel, and to

420

yourself—ourselves, I mean. I must run up to town forthwith, to consult about business; my stay and visits here, in fact, must be uncertain, and may be interrupted by very long intervals.

"Miss Marlyn and you don't get on pleasantly, and, even if she could remain in her late position, she is too young to take charge of you, and, the fact is, I must look about for another home for you—for the present, at least—for the idea of leaving you here at Raby, alone, is quite out of the question; and, at the same time, I wish, of course, to consult your feelings in making a choice. I am sure Miss Temple, so old a friend, would be glad to have you at the Vicarage, if you liked it, and I could arrange. And—think it over, and tell me tomorrow whether you would like it—or any other arrangement better; only, you see, staying here is not to be thought of, and whatever is to be done, must be arranged immediately."

He got up gloomily, and stooping over her, touched her forehead with a cold kiss, and then left the room.

In a few days this arrangement was actually made. I need hardly say that Mark Shadwell had first ascertained that Charles Mordant had rejoined his regiment—and Rachel Shadwell found herself, to the great delight of kind Miss Barbara, domesticated at the Vicarage.

Miss Marlyn at the same time left Raby, and honest Roger Temple, like the captain in the song, *lost his spirits daily*, and moped about, and sighed, and grew to be a silent man; and one day, walking with Doctor Stalton towards Wynderfel, less because he affected the doctor's company than because he loved a stroll in that particular direction, the doctor said:

"Miss Marlyn has left Raby some time—the same day that Miss Shadwell came to the Vicarage."

"Oh?" said Roger, interrogatively; for though he knew the fact only too well, he wished to hear more on that tender theme, and so tried to lead the physician on.

"Devilish pretty, whatever else she may be," continued the doctor, knowing nothing of poor Roger's little secret.

Roger sighed, and looked down, in soft and silent expectation, on the grass, as they walked along.

"Mark Shadwell is still at Raby," resumed the doctor; "but—between you and me—I'm afraid that d—d woman has got a fast hold of him."

"Oh?" said Roger Temple, quite quietly, but feeling all the time, as if he had got a hard box in the ear; he was stunned, tingling, but could not resent it. In secret he coined it over, and grew frightened and sadder.

Time, the healer, the destroyer, the constructor, had been working his potent changes.

The doctor's remark about Miss Agnes Marlyn and Mark Shadwell, expressed pretty distinctly the surmises of the little town of Raby and its neighbourhood. And soon the scandal darkened.

Mark had now been for many weeks absent from the country. No letter had reached Raby, or the vicar, or his attorney at the village, for all that time.

At length there arrived a letter from Mark Shadwell to the vicar, which surprised that rustic clergyman a good deal. It was a long letter, for a lazy man like Mark, and was written, it seemed, in dejection.

It began by assuming that Stour Temple would not be much surprised if he, Mark Shadwell, acted as most men do when, in middle life, placed in his sad and solitary circumstances. His ideas of right and wrong, and those of the vicar, though drawn from different sources, were very much alike, in fact, in most points identical; and the step he was going to take, after the most careful consideration of what was best and most proper, was one, he was confident, which the vicar would thoroughly approve. He was about, in fact, to marry. He was a man of few acquaintances, and he did not care to look up any of his old London friends.

A wife educated in that atmosphere would never do at Raby. What was needed there was a person who could content herself with plain clothes, plain fare, servants few and clumsy, and no society, and who, in addition to all this, could make herself positively useful to a man who had often more business to look after than two men could be reasonably expected to get through. Would the vicar mention all this to his sister, and consult with her as to how best to open it to Rachel. Girls are so odd, and in these circumstances so seldom see what is really so much for their own advantage. But where there was a temper—and Rachel had one of her own—they run away with things, and required to be reasoned with; and so he would kindly use his discretion in communicating this news to Rachel. He would, for his daughter's sake, advise her denying herself an indulgence in that anger and jealousy on this occasion, to which women are prone—which affect a higher inspiration, but are, in fact, so narrow, selfish, and vulgar.

Such was the tenor of the letter.

"Who can it be?" said Barbara, looking hard at the vicar, as they conferred, in his study, over the letter.

The vicar did not return her dark look of inquiry or conjecture, but looked on the letter which he held in his fingers.

"He does not say," said the vicar; "we shall know, time enough. I hope he has made a wise choice."

"Ah, poor Amy! Well—well, how such things can be, I don't understand!" murmured Miss Barbara Temple. "Such idolatry! So soon forgotten."

She did not know the story of the letter that was found upon poor Amy's bed, nor did Rachel. Old Wyndle had spelled through a part of it without comprehending its exact meaning. Rachel had looked at it—no more, for her mind was distracted with another panic at the time; and except that it was an unkind letter, she remembered nothing very distinctly of it. It lay in the vicar's desk—one of those secrets of other people which he always kept religiously.

"Ah! My poor Amy! Well—well, how such things can be, I don't understand!" murmured Barbara.

The news was told to Rachel very kindly and briefly by the vicar that evening, Miss Barbara being present, who hugged and kissed Rachel vehemently when the story was over, and spared no sympathy, indignation, or consolation.

I sometimes think that the more despotic and selfish parents are, the more they are revered and admired by their children. It is one of those strange perversities and injustices which appear in the laws of human nature. Rachel cherished for her father an awe and veneration which a better man might have failed to inspire. She wept over this intelligence in the despair and tribulation of youth, which, however, are transitory.

Then came conjectures as to whom he had selected for his wife. Miss Barbara listened reservedly to these speculations, for she had a pretty decided opinion upon the point, aided by that scandal, which of course had not reached Rachel's ear.

In a little while, however, it was established, and past the period of debate. The bride was Miss Agnes Marlyn, and she came down with her husband to Raby, and forthwith began with rapidity and decision to remodel the household. One by one the old servants were removed, and new ones came in their places. Mr. Twinley, the attorney, spoke of her reservedly as "a very clever woman," and "a lady who would, if anyone could, make the estate pay."

The new Mrs. Shadwell was looking more beautiful than ever, and appeared in the Squire's pew in Raby Church, dressed very richly, but in excellent taste. But rumours had preceded her, and a great scandal had traced a circle round her, and she was isolated.

She was not a person, however, to forego an object without an effort. As the wife of Shadwell of Raby, she was, in some respects, the first lady of her county. That she should be snubbed by such people was really too good!

But though she tried patiently and many ways, by taking a graceful interest in the charities of the neighbourhood, by visiting the girls' school, by looking in upon the sick room of old Martha Cripps, and by fifty other expedients, she failed to make any way with the ladies whom she was disposed to know. They were shy— they did not visit her.

She did not acquiesce in these relations. But she saw that she must wait and proceed circuitously. If only the clear income of

Raby could be got up to three thousand a year—and that, she thought, was quite on the cards before four years were over—with Mark Shadwell's connections he should have a seat in the House, and make a fresh start in the great world. Then these mean little people of Raby and the vicinity would have their eyes opened, and be made to see things as they were. This would be beginning at the right end, and Agnes would pay those small people off when the proper time came.

The vicar painfully reconsidered the whole case. The recent rumours to which I have referred were unpleasant; but he found no proof of them. The stories about the French school were better supported; but, after all, they proved no more than extreme giddiness, and were, in some measure, attributable to the mad spirits and inexperience of a schoolgirl; and must he not assume that Mr. Shadwell—a proud and fiery man— had satisfied himself upon these points? and had he any right, upon mere conjecture, to go behind his mature decision? And if his clerical position obliged him to special reserves, did it not also exact special charities?

The result was, that Miss Barbara paid a visit; but Rachel did not come. The vicar had reasoned with her to make the effort, but she could not, and his sympathies were with her.

Mark Shadwell saw Miss Barbara after she had paid her cold and embarrassed visit, as she crossed the hall. He talked to her there for a few minutes, and then asked sharply where Rachel was. So Barbara, with a feminine dexterity, pleaded for her young friend, hiding altogether the fiery element which had mingled in her refusal to come to Raby, and urging only the pain of reviving so recent a grief and other similar apologies, in which Mart, unsatisfied, darkly acquiesced.

So the good old lady took her leave of him at the steps, and drove away, with an unpleasant conviction that Mark understood only too well the spirit in which his daughter had stayed away, and resented it fiercely.

It was about this time that Captain Clayton returned from Scotland. He put up at the comfortable little inn at Raby, and passed his days at "the great house" as before. Agnes Shadwell took up the idea of his marrying Rachel with energy. Clayton opened his rental and his plans to Mark Shadwell, who, in consequence, walked over in the afternoon to the Vicarage, and paid his respects to Miss Barbara. Honest Roger had made an agitated exit by the back-door as Mark arrived at the steps, Mark Shadwell saw and spoke to Rachel, who trembled a great deal, and for a long time could hardly control the hysterical gush of tears which were every moment at the point of bursting forth.

It was a short but a tedious visit. He had something more to say, however, and on taking his leave he made Rachel accompany him as far as the little brook on the way to Wynderfel.

## Chapter 71
### Plain Language

Rachel was very much frightened as she walked beside her father, who maintained an unbroken and a stern silence till they reached the stile under the gentle hill of Wynderfel.

"I sha'n't trouble you to come further; just sit down there, or stand, if you like it better, and listen to what I have to say."

She did not sit on the broad plank of the stile, but stood looking at him with a face of awe and large and frightened eyes.

"As you don't like coming to Raby—your friends here at the Vicarage, I am sure, must admire your spirit vastly—I have asked you to accompany me here. Mind, I don't want you to come to Raby. I quite understand the petty malice which, under fine names, indulges itself in inflicting what it conceives to be mortifications; under such circumstances it is a great pleasure to women, and I hope it does them good. Not a word, please. I don't care a farthing, mind; it's nothing to me, absolutely, or to—to anyone else. You have got your four thousand pounds, and you are independent of me; you can do what you like, what your friends here advise you; but my consent, by the settlement, is necessary."

He paused. She was looking at him half bewildered. "I say, by the terms of the instrument, the deed, which gives you that provision, you forfeit it the moment you marry without my consent; do you quite understand?"

"Yes, sir; yes, papa," whispered Rachel, with a gasp, and looking as frightened as her worst enemy, if she had any, could wish her.

"You need not look so stupid, then. Should any of the wiseacres about the Vicarage, there—the people whom you choose to consult and trust—persuade you to marry that very impudent and foolish young man, Charles Mordant, you will do precisely the thing which I forbid, and one guinea you sha'n't get. You'll find that by that spirited act you will have disappointed the religious, primitive people up there— left yourself without a shilling—improved my estate to the extent of four thousand pounds, and let that charming young man, who knows, I presume, the value of money, in for a very romantic and disinterested adventure."

In spite of her alarm, a flush of crimson dyed Rachel's cheeks as her father spoke. She remained standing, and perfectly silent.

"Well, so much for romance, and—and contempt of my wishes; and I have left a note for Stour Temple, telling him shortly those facts. So that anyone who aids in accomplishing that folly will have done so, at all events, with their eyes open."

He paused, and there was a little silence, in which Rachel felt utterly confounded, and the croon and gurgling of the little brook close by filled her ears with a strange distinctness.

"And now, the other part. I don't mean to reason with you, observe. I'm simply putting facts before you; and if you decline to act according to common sense, it's all the better, in one sense, for me. Captain Clayton, whom you saw some time ago—every day for a month—likes you; he has returned to Raby for a time, and I see him, as before, every day. He has spoken to me, and satisfied me that there is nothing in point of prudence against it. Quite the reverse—very advantageous, indeed, and with extremely good prospects, that proposal is now before you; if you choose to accept it, you have my entire approval; but one word more, I won't talk about it at present.

"I won't take your answer now; you had better think it over, and all the consequences. He knows your friends, the Temples, and will very likely look in tomorrow afternoon, and speak to you himself—that is, if they choose to give him an opportunity, and that you like the idea; but I wished to tell you exactly all about it, and how I view the subject; not because I suppose my opinion of any weight—in fact I don't care a farthing whether it is or not—but because I wish you to understand the exact effect of acting under ill-advice in this matter, or indulging an idiotic and unworthy fancy, for which there is not even the miserable excuse that you see, or are ever likely to meet the object of it; for he is in India, and very well content to live there without troubling his head about you."

As soon as he had said that, Mark Shadwell went away. Whether her father kissed her at parting she could not remember, nor how he looked at her. For some time, with a dreadful sense of suffocation, she stood still, and at length her excitement and anguish found relief in a convulsive burst of tears.

An hour after she told, as well as she could, all that had passed to Barbara Temple. And they cried together in Rachel's room for more than an hour. Then Barbara, in the evening, communicated the matter to the vicar, who was pained and helpless. What could these good people do but speak, not even comfortably, but only kindly, to the poor girl.

The next morning a note was despatched by the vicar to Mark Shadwell, saying a great deal to the point, and with a very moderate expenditure of words. He knew that Mark Shadwell would excuse his writing, as Rachel was so distressed and agitated that she felt herself unequal to write as she would wish, and had begged of him to say that the proposal of Captain Clayton had come upon her by surprise—that she had never looked on him as a possible suitor, and could never consent to view him in that light, and a great deal more that was deprecatory and dutiful; but quite clear and decided on the point that she could not listen to Captain Clayton's suit.

Mark was intensely angry. Clayton was at the breakfast-table with him and his wife, exhibiting, his suspense considered, a wonderfully good appetite, when the vicar's note was handed to Mark, he took it to the window, exchanging a glance with his guest, and there read it.

Very angry under one of his bitter impulses, he said, with a kind of laugh:—

"I've had my answer, and there it is."

At the same time he presented the note open to Clayton, who said, as he took it, looking towards Agnes:—

"Am I to read this?"

"Certainly," said Mark. "They intend it, evidently."

Clayton did read it. He looked annoyed, but by no means so much moved as Mark.

His beautiful young wife was the only one of the party who talked much during the time they continued at the breakfast-table, and seemed quite as gay and happy as usual. About an hour later, however, alone with her husband, she said a little tartly:—

"What possessed you to show him that letter?"

"It won't make the least difference," said Mark. "Those Temple people have got fast hold of her; it's quite enough thinking I wish it."

"You give up things too easily. Clayton can be of immense use to us. You must be in parliament; you forget your own plans—everything—when you grow angry," his wife rejoined.

"My giving up or not has nothing to do with it; that rests with him, not me, and as to hiding it from him, that would be all very well if Stour Temple weren't sure to make him out before he goes, and tell him all about it," answered Mark Shadwell, moodily.

"Well, leave him to me; he must not be allowed to think her answer final; he must be kept on; he must come back to Raby. I dare say all will go right in a little while. I'll talk to him by-and-bye, and you need not say a word more about it."

Instead of his intended walk to the Vicarage, Clayton joined Mark Shadwell in a ramble to the woods, which was made short, however, by the early winter nightfall. In the drawing-room that evening, before he bid goodnight and went away to his inn in the village, Agnes had a long talk with him, Mark affecting to be busy in writing some letters. Next day, again, in the drawing-room, she had a very long farewell interview with Clayton.

The result of her persuasions was that he would return to Raby in the autumn. Mark was pleased. He knew that earlier he could not come. He had to join his sister, now at Naples, where she was to winter. Then northward for the summer, and to be joined by her mother in October, who was to relieve him, and having regained his liberty, to Raby he would return.

At Raby time moved slowly. Mark had his fits of gloom, more abrupt and more terrible perhaps than ever; but also more transient. His young wife watched him with an observant eye. She was always cheerful, and nearly always in an amiable temper. Her influence upon him was gradually developing itself. An artful, clever woman could have little difficulty in managing that vain, proud man.

"So you write to Clayton?" said he one day, as the autumn which was to bring him back again to Raby approached, tapping an envelope addressed in his hand-writing to her, which lay upon her desk.

"Write to Clayton? I should think I do; how else could we know whether he is coming?

Mark extended his fingers towards Clayton's envelope, but his wife, laughing, took it up, and popped it into her desk.

"Is he jealous? How delightful," said she, with a little laugh.

"Well, no! He's not quite such a fool," said Mark; "but what does Clayton say, for I really am curious?"

"He says he will certainly be at Raby in October," she answered.

"In two months," said Mark, ruminating. He was thinking whether it might not be well to prepare Rachel for his return. And something of this he hinted to Agnes.

She laughed.

"Don't be vexed; but I understand her better, I'm afraid, than you do. I don't think she really cares about Mordant, and I'm quite sure that if she did not think that you and I both wished her to marry Clayton, she would marry him; but she does think it, and the less time she has to think it over the better. She thinks of course that I'm at the bottom of it, and she hates me. I have never given her any cause, but one."

Suddenly her tone changed from one almost of gaiety to one of sadness, and her fine eyes filled with tears; "and that for all the world I would not undo."

As she said this, looking up fondly, she folded her hands about his arm, and he stooped and kissed her very tenderly.

"Never mind; I love you only the more, the more ungracious they all are. I know how dull this life is, but fortune will yet make us amends, and I shall see you where you ought to be;" and kissing her again, he walked down, in a sudden access of energy, to the little town of Raby, where he had an interview with his attorney, who pleaded in excuse for dilatoriness, that he had not got full instructions yet, and brought out a bundle of papers, and spread them before his client.

A few days afterward the attorney, happening to meet the vicar on the Applebury road, said, after some little talk:

"There was a matter I thought I might as well give you a hint of, but you must not let Mr. Shadwell know, I rely for that on your honour—you'll promise?"

The vicar assented.

"Well. He made no settlement," said the attorney, in an undertone, "on his recent marriage, but he's going to deal with his property now, and, you know, there's his daughter, poor Miss Shadwell, and she ought to be considered; he ought not to put everything out of his power for the advantage of the present Mrs. Shadwell, and he has powers which, under a well-considered settlement, he ought not to have had; and, as you take an interest in the poor young lady, I wished to give you a hint that you may put in a word for her, if you have an opportunity, naturally, you know, only you must not let him suspect that you got it from me."

Here was a new uneasiness, and what could the vicar do?

## CHAPTER 72

THE DAGGER HALF UNSHEATHED.

Mark Shadwell was still enamoured of his young wife. He had reason to admire her cleverness. For the first time a gleam of hope pierced the darkness that overhung him. Mr. Twinley, the Raby attorney, has often said that he never met a professed accountant who could match that girl in disentangling complications, and reducing confusion to order. But her genius for figures was but one of her curiously-admirable faculties for business. Than the management of that large portion of the Raby estate which was in Mark's hands, nothing could have been more slobbering and wasteful; all this underwent a keen and wise revision, and the result was an immediate saving of several hundreds a year.

The two mills of Drimsworth, that had been locked up for nearly three years and were falling to decay, within four months had tenants. All the leases were carefully overhauled. In several that had expired, and were held from year to year, it was found that the holdings were under-measured, and immediate accessions to the rental were the result. It would be tedious to enumerate the various operations of the new and active regime which began with the accession of the second Mrs. Shadwell.

Had no one at Raby eyes or brains till this young lady arrived among them? No doubt there was no lack of either. But the attorney only knew the state of things in glimpses and patches, as isolated cases came before him, and Carmel Sherlock, clever and rapid at accounts, had no turn for other business, and Mark Shadwell—though not deficient, perhaps, in talents of a different kind—was indolent and incapable in this.

The result was an immediate improvement in Mark Shadwell's income, and a prospect of a much larger one to be effected in the course of some half-dozen years. So Mark began to hold up his head, and it is not wonderful if he built castles in the air, or if his clever wife constructed several for his habitation. For she was resolved to get her husband on in the world, and was not a person to allow the grass to grow under her feet.

In his library, in the lower part of his *escritoire*, lay a square parcel of books, papered and corded, which Carmel Sherlock, a few days before his death, had himself made up and directed to him.

It was a heavy parcel, for some of Sherlock's few books were folios. Mark fancied that there were papers in it beside. He had often weighed it in his hand, and every time he opened the part of the *escritoire* where it lay, he read the address.

A faint curiosity each time prompted him to open it, and a reluctance, intuitive and superstitious, restrained him. Carmel Sherlock was such an odd fellow. There was probably one of his mystical letters there. They amused Mark, it is true, but in those follies there was a half-defined second meaning that teased and depressed him. In his fun was a *gout de revers*, and his laughter and derision sounded with an echo like the mirth in old Red Gauntlet's spectral hall, and scared him secretly. He had come to look on this parcel with a sort of helpless dislike and suspicion.

This day it caught his eye, as usual. He was tired of its silent upbraidings. So, yielding to the momentary temptation to know the worst, he pulled it out of its hiding-place and put it on the table. Carmel Sherlock was about to speak. Mark Shadwell cut the string.

Some rubbishy old folios, as he had expected, emerged. He opened and shook them with their backs upward, but no letter dropped out.

A few papers remained. One contained some valuable hints as to how to make use of two ledgers in his room, so as to facilitate the keeping of the Raby estate accounts.

A smaller one was folded in blank paper, and contained a large closed envelope addressed to "Miss Agnes Marlyn,—Private."

Mark did not hesitate to open this, and he found this note addressed, in Carmel Sherlock's hand, to the lady who was now his wife:

Miss Agnes Marlyn,—I return hereby the note you asked me to give to Sir Roke Wycherly on the night when he lost his life. That being impracticable, I now return it un-opened, as you gave it to me. Your messenger was faithful—but the other messenger, Death, outstripped

Yours,

Carmel Sherlock.

"The d—d fool!" said Mark, between his set-teeth, but whether he meant Carmel or his wife, I can't say.

Enclosed was a tiny note, sealed and addressed "Sir Roke Wycherly," but the writing was so disguised, that Mark could not recognise a resemblance to that of his wife. It was rather a dark day, and Mark drew toward the window, and carefully opened and read this little note.

It contained but three or four lines. Here was his wife's hand-writing without any disguise. It would not, probably, have done to leave Sir Roke at all in doubt as to its identity, and it had the initials "A. M." at its foot.

These lines were very significant. Mark looked pale with anger as he read them. He thrust the little note into his coat-pocket, sneering. The servant crossing the hall saw his pale face over the banister, as he came down, and knew that something had gone wrong.

"Your mistress in the drawing-room?" he asked.

"Yes, sir."

"Well, well, that will do," said Mark, as if he would have sent him anywhere else.

His beautiful young wife sat at her writing- table, deep in a letter, when Mark entered. In the isolation of that drawing-room, never now entered by a female visitor, she sat. She looked up at Mark with a rather bored expression, and turned her letter with its face downward.

"Oh, I've interrupted you!" he said, a little dryly.

"Not much—what is it?"

"It is only a letter like that, which was intended to turn its face downward when I came near," he answered.

"I don't care if you read it from beginning to end," said she, carelessly; "but what's the matter?"

"Oh, nothing;—you'll think it nothing, of course— women have their own code of honour, it is not ours, that's all," said

434

Mark.

Agnes made a hurried mental survey of liabilities and blots that might be hit, but felt pretty safe.

"I really don't know what you mean, Mark; I wish you would speak plainly."

He placed his hand on her shoulder, not caressingly, and looked down in her face.

"You remember that evening when you swore to me that my—my idea about that man—was false?"

"What man?—whom do you mean?"

"You know, very well."

"Roke Wycherly?" she said, and turned away a little contemptuously.

"Well, well, don't look away, look here—at *that!*" He laughed coldly, as he held the note before her eyes for a minute.

A brilliant scarlet coloured her cheeks as she said it, but she tossed her head a little, and said, looking askance on it.

"Well?"

"Upon my soul, that's cool!" he said, bitterly, and with a very savage eye.

"My foolish little note to Roke Wycherly?" she said. "I see it—well?"

"Well!" he echoed, growing paler; "reconcile that with your oath, if you can."

Agnes had recovered her nerve.

"Reconcile that! I'm not going, if you can't. No harm ever came of that note; don't be a great old fool, Mark Shadwell! I think it's agreed to let bygones be bygones. Let us understand one another. What have I gained by marrying you? Simply a share in the solitude and mortifications of an excluded man. I never see a creature here. It would be insulting, but that I know it was so before, and is meant not for me, but for you. As your wife, however, I am simply avoided, as you are, and here I sit under the insult of that neglect and avoidance, merely to be a drudge over your accounts and letters, which you can't understand or write yourself—to try to save you, and to retrieve your ruined prop-

435

erty. I don't care if that note were stuck up at Raby post-office, for every squire, and boor, and woman—you have no ladies—in the county to read. I'm sick of this place already, and tired of its secrets, and I should not mind bidding you goodbye any morning, my good sir. Your note indeed! What a discovery!"

She shut her desk with a clap, down upon the letter she had half written.

"I sha'n't show you my letters. I shan't tell you anything; we know quite enough of one another. If you want to see my letters, I suppose you can break my desk, as usual. I'm afraid of no discovery. I have no atrocious secrets."

And thus speaking, she walked out of the room with an air of defiance, and even menace, in which was no trace of vulgarity; it was perfectly graceful.

Mark Shadwell stared after her, his ears tingling as if he had received a blow; the tremor of fury was in his hand. Upon a vain man, proud, full of the egotism of solitude, an insult which tears alike his vanity and his dignity, tells with a power of which men in a less morbid state know nothing.

He hardly breathed; he did not even curse—that relief vouchsafed to squires. His lips were closed, and he sighed once or twice, and going to the table, he turned over the leaves of a book of prints slowly, seeing dark pictures of quite another kind all the time.

Then, perhaps for the first time, his heart was wrung with a sudden and great remorse. Poor Amy, that adored him, in spite of the cold decay of his love, through all his dark and unreasonable moods, with an unchanging worship: who had never given him one ungentle look or word. The remembrance came with a vivid pang. He was not a man to confess himself wrong. Even in the solitude of that room he would not have spoken all he felt; but he missed her.

Mark, in his slow and lonely walk, met the messenger returning from Raby with the letters. There was one for him from Captain Clayton. It was not very long. He was coming to Raby to see him. He had been ailing, and his physician hinted that he must winter at Naples.

Not a word about Rachel! Was all that cooling? Mark would soon see. There was no absolute need, however, that he should say anything upon that subject in his letter, coming as he intended so soon.

The autumnal sun had set, and the sky clouded with faded gold and crimson, piled and floating in seas of faintest yellow and pale green, rose sad and solemn before him, and toned the lightest minds to melancholy, and others, sad already—with a profounder gloom. Mark was leaning by the window, and looking over the dimly glowing undulations of sward and woodland toward haunted Wynderfel. Dreams of the dead and lost; of Carmel Sherlock and his crazy visions and inalienable fidelity; of the predestinated decay of his family, and the legend of the angry spirit—the lady of Feltram hollow—with the star of Bethlehem on her left hand,—when he felt the fingers of a little hand playfully pluck his ear, and a soft, sweet voice said:

"Come, Mark, we can't afford to quarrel; you remember the two companions in the Eddystone Lighthouse? don't let us imitate them. I dare say I was very cross, and I beg your pardon" (she made him a little comic, plaintive curtsey). "But wasn't it you who began?—Mark, you know it was—and now we'll make it up, and we understand one another ever so much better, and we'll never quarrel again."

He looked at her, with the odd lights of Wynderfel upon her strangely beautiful face. Her words and manner were playful, but her face was cold and even cruel.

"I don't know, Agnes," said he, surprised by the suddenness of her speech, "in what mood you are talking, but I accept it as in earnest, and I agree. It is too late for me to think of making new friends, Agnes; and if I lose you, I lose my last."

She smiled. The odd, wild lights reflected from the sky distorted that smile. It looked arch and sinister. Her right hand was round his neck, and still in gentle play plucked at his ear. Her left he had taken in both his, and fondled it caressingly; its palm was up, with the little star-like scar, five-rayed, in its centre. She kissed his cheek, and whispered something in his ear, and he smiled in his turn.

So the little quarrel was made up, but each remembered it. It had scarred a deep line in Mark's heart; it had opened in their nuptial chamber, for a moment, a closet where he saw a whip of scorpions hissing on the wall. It had swelled the soft, clear tones of Agnes to a piercing yell of thunder, at sound of which the sky blackened, and the earth trembled under his feet.

Was that proud man to live henceforward under a threat?

## CHAPTER 73
### MARK AT APPLEBURY

So the apple leaf grew yellow, and the hawthorn tree was brown, at Raby. October had arrived, and at no season of the year does that melancholy old place, with its fine forest *vistas*, and its vast stretch of wooded hill, look so grand.

In this becoming costume did Captain Clayton, on his arrival at his inn in the pretty little town, find the ancient seat of Raby; and if he had been blessed with a sense of the picturesque, one might have supposed that he had made his arrangements— and it would have been well worth his while—so as to make his visit at that sad and glorious crisis in the forest world, when decay and maturity—its death and glory—are blended with a funereal splendour.

Clayton went up at once, and paid his respects at the great house. When Mark returned from the Mills, he found him established in the drawing-room.

"You've promised to come to us, mind, just as you did last time—every day to luncheon, and to stay dinner," urged Mark, hospitably; and only too happy was Clayton to accept the frank invitation.

He had a good deal to tell about people whom, or, at all events, their fathers or mothers or uncles or aunts, Mark had known long ago; and though his manner of relating was not particularly brilliant, yet the stories were more or less amusing, and afforded him glimpses into a world that had been closed for him for ever so many years. But Rachel's name he never once mentioned!

When a silence came, as they sat together by the spluttering wood-fire, Mark sometimes stole a glance at his handsome apathetic face, as his large azure eyes gazed indolently on the burning logs, and the lingering smile left by his last story still showed the edges of his even teeth. But the long expected reintroduction of the subject on which he desired to hear him, came not.

"He seems to think all quite at an end, and I can't blame him," said Mark peevishly.

"I'm certain," answered his wife, cheerily, "that he does not think *we* think so."

"I don't see how that affects the case, except in making us appear excessively absurd."

"So it would, if Captain Clayton were a different sort of person. But he would not wish us to think he has behaved ill; and, you may depend upon it, he will speak to you."

"But I don't say that he's obliged to say any more about it. Why should he?"

"It was a great pity."

"What?" said he.

"Poor Rachel sacrificing herself to vex you," said Agnes, with a shrug. "You're going to Applebury today, ain't you?"

"Yes. I can't be here for luncheon; tell Clayton so, when he comes. Rachel's a fool—a greater fool than she thinks, as she will find, by-and-bye."

"I don't blame her for hating me," said Mrs. Shadwell, "although I have never been anything but kind to her, according to my poor opportunities. But she ought not to speak of you—her father—as she does."

"Oh! of course, she hates me! Every miss who fancies she is to rule her father's house and himself, by Jove! hates him, as a matter of course, if he marries," said Mark, affecting to think nothing of it.

"Yes, but I don't think the Temples should encourage that kind of thing. Even before servants, she and they talk us over—

you particularly."

"Well, I'm going to Applebury now, and I sha'n't be back till near dinner-time, and I don't care a farthing what they say."

And with this magnanimous speech, looking, nevertheless, very much annoyed, as she could see by every line of his face, he took his departure.

Applebury is a cheerful, quaint, little place, as I have said, with an antique cosiness and a wonderful variety of aspect within so small a compass. But of all places on earth, except one, Applebury was to Mark Shadwell the most repulsive. What was he to do, however, when people, whom he wanted to see, fixed that spot—the most convenient half-way trysting place—for a meeting?

I sha'n't trouble any one with the particulars of the business that brought Mark here. It was an anxious one. His attorney from Raby was here to aid him with advice and documents. Mark hated business as much as every rational man, who has nothing to gain by it, does. Besides, in his ease, it too generally meant danger. He had sat up late the night before, over it, and had been wakeful and feverish by reason of it, almost till day broke.

It was past six o'clock that evening, when Agnes received a note from him in these terms:

Applebury, 4 o'clock.
My own beautiful little Witch,—Pity your poor old fellow, shut up in this vile little town. A telegram says that the people from London won't be here till next train, six o'clock. I can't be home till eight or nine, at soonest; awkward, isn't it? Make my apologies to Clayton. I had no notion such an awkward delay could happen; but I shall break away from my tormentors as early as possible. Already my life darkens—my star of Bethlehem shines too far away. I did not know how much every hour of my life depended on my enchantress. For the world I would not have left you alone; but here I am on compulsion. Looking for light, I remain here; in exile, still the captive of my

440

beautiful witch.

P.S.—I fear I sha'n't be home till nine.

This was a sufficiently ardent love-letter from a fellow of Mark Shadwell's years; and what is more, in great measure genuine; which is more than can be said for all such performances. It might not have been quite so long, however, if Mark had not found his young wife a little exacting, as brides are, at least, while they continue to be in love with their husbands! and also there was this, that Agnes was a precisian in her ideas of what she owed to prudence. She worried him sometimes with scruples, and compelled him to go to places with her, where he thought she might perfectly well have gone alone. These little exactions vexed him sometimes; but, on the whole, it was a fault on the side of the virtues, and pleased him. So he wisely cultivated those nun-like ideas, and laid more stress on his regret for his absence from dinner than he thought the accident quite deserved.

Another disappointment awaited him. By the six o'clock train no one arrived for him; but, half an hour after, another telegram told of an unavoidable delay in London, and the postponement of the meeting until next day.

It was dark now. Across the market-square of Applebury you could not distinguish any longer, windows or doors, except where candle or firelight shone through them. You could only see the gables against the, as yet, moon- less sky, like the shoulders of gigantic sentries. The sounds of the little town had died out; Mark was peevish, hungry, and tired. His attorney had taken his leave, and ridden home to Raby half an hour ago. While the good people of the inn were getting ready a beef-steak for the exhausted Squire, he, with his feet on the fender, fell into a nap, troubled, after a while, by a confused and ugly dream.

He fancied himself in a strange room; how he came there he could not remember; and, with the anticipation of danger which sometimes overpowers one in a dream, he was listening to a heavy tread, approaching on the lobby, and under which the floor on which he stood trembled. While he listened in suspense, from the further side of the room, on a sudden, the voice of

441

Carmel Sherlock scared him, crying, "Beware, sir! it's the beak." At the same time the door seemed to open, and a huge gaunt figure, with a black crape over his face, and a parchment process in his hand, entered.

At his elbow was Sir Roke Wycherly, with a white malignant face, peering by his side, and with a long hand, the fingers of which were grimed with old blood-stains, extended towards Mark—he continued crying, "Tonight's your time! you have the warrant, there's your man." The big-boned figure, in the black mask, was close to him, and Mark, in his agony, seized a knife; it was the dagger of Roke Wycherly—an image always present to his eye—which seemed to lie on the table before him. The room and its belongings were growing like the fatal room at Raby. But it seemed to him that his endeavours to defend himself were frustrated by his young wife, who from behind clung wildly about his arms, screaming with a terrifying laugh in his ear, "The knife, Mark, defend yourself! the knife—or he'll have you!" At the same time a dreadful roar of waters was drowning all the voices, and the room seemed to topple and roll like a sinking ship. And with a struggle, like strangulation, he suddenly awoke with a cry of "God!" repeated fearfully.

For a while he did not know where he was; he had sprung to his feet. The roar and darkness of the sinking room were still in his ears and eyes, and he distinguished nothing.

Even after all this had vanished, the sense of danger remained, and he listened breathlessly, wondering whether those accursed London fellows could have sent down a bailiff after all.

Mark, like other avowed sceptics, had a strong vein of superstition. One way or another, the instinct of belief in the unseen will assert itself. Out to the inn-door walked Mark, to shake off the lingering images of his evil dream, and to allow its influence to exhale in the free night air.

An undercurrent of his thought had been busy for half the day with his own possible arrest, and he still held, crumpled between his finger and thumb, one of those reminders printed on a little square of paper, which good men drop about, on the chance that one seed in a thousand may strike root. He had picked it up on the chimney-piece of the inn room, and in the act of reading the words, so early heard and so accustomed, that their very meaning seems, like an aroma too long exposed to the air, to have quite exhaled, and spent itself; and we have but a residuum of sound.

*But know this, that if the good man of the house had known in what watch the thief would come, he would have watched, and would not have suffered his house to be broken up.*

So his dream was accounted for; and Mark, somewhat better, returned, at the summons of the waiter, to partake of his good cheer. But as he rode home this dream, in spite of his reason, depressed his spirits with an ever-recurring sense of having witnessed, in reality, something dreadful; and his mind, every now and then, was busy with the fanciful problem—which he affected to despise—did this dream reflect, as it were, some approaching disaster.

When he reached the gate of Raby, he was glad. The sombre outlines of the great house, and the towering trees which surrounded it, as a rule, gladdened few people, and him least of all. But he called up the image of the fireside and the lighted drawing-room, and his beautiful wife, no doubt uncomfortable by reason of his protracted stay. "Yes, the pretty little fool, she'll be glad to see me. She don't know what to think; and Clayton—will Clayton be still here?" He rather wished he might. He shouldn't mind a game of *écarté*, or even a homely rubber of backgammon.

And as these cheerful fancies crossed his mind, a thought struck him. Should he play them a little trick, and knock at the drawing-room window? So letting his sober horse find his way to the stables as best he might, he dismounted and walked round the side of the house, and on the grass under the windows, at the back, till he reached those of the drawing-room, through the blinds of which he could see the glow transmitted from the inner light.

# CHAPTER 74
## A STORM

This drawing-room had three windows; a larger and drearier room beyond it was disused. The window-blind did not quite cover the lower end of the glass, and Mark stood and peeped in. His mood was instantly and sternly changed.

Clayton and his wife were standing beside a cabinet, very near the window. He was talking, holding her hand in his, and she looking down, her cheeks dyed with a brilliant blush.

Could it be that they were talking of Rachel? No. It was the hope and agony of an instant. There is no mistaking the gaze of a lover who looks upon the object of his passion. With such eyes, Clayton, speaking low and earnestly, leaning over her, gazed; and, as if to preclude all doubt, stooping still nearer, he passionately kissed her unresisting lips.

If Mark's fury had been one degree under its acme, he would have dashed in the window, and, with his lacerated hands and ghastly face, have confronted his betrayers. He drew back, staring at the dull light of the blind that now interposed. But the picture was not in the room, but in his eyes. Backward he stepped and waited—and waited still—trying to understand and feel the whole of his appalling position. Freezing and stupefied, he saw the black image of the great old house stand up before and above him. All its hateful and dreadful associations were vaguely gathered in its shadow. He had dreamed of despair—talked of despair—fancied that he was intimate with despair for years. He had now, for the first time, met that tremendous stranger.

Someone approached the window; he saw the shadow on the blind and he glided away into the dark, like a ghost, and was hid. Clayton raised it and looked out for a few moments, dropped it, and returned.

For a long time Mark stood where he was; at last he was seized with a violent shivering. It was a crisis in his catalepsy. A dull dead light was breaking on his mind, and he began to walk swiftly away. It was a mild night, and yet he was pierced and shuddering with cold. Walking among the trees as fast as he could stride, he felt better, and the dreadful rigor subsided.

The one idea present to his mind was his revenge. Immense it must be, orderly and complete. His mind must clear. He must see, quite, how the land lay. He must do nothing hand-over-head. It must be a comprehensive and methodical revenge. But something he must be doing. To be quite inactive was to go mad.

He was now near the gate that opened on the silent highway, and the sight of the road to the little town of Raby suggested his first measure.

The distance was trifling. He was now in the street of the quiet little town he had so recently trotted briskly through. It was still early, not nine o'clock. Lights were shining from the drawing-room windows of his attorney, Mr. Twinley.

He knocked—sent up his message; and in a few moments more was seated in that gentleman's office. The attorney, as he set the candles on the table, eyed him with a shrewd and grim scrutiny. He suspected some disaster. He feared the bailiff in charge of his person might be, at that moment, keeping ward in the hall; for Mark's face looked as if he had stolen from his bed in the crisis of a fever.

"Nothing from London—since—sir?" hesitated the attorney, seeing that Mark did not accost him. He had left him only two hours ago at Applebury.

"No. You have that draft-deed, in favour of my wife, ready?"

"Yes, sir—and—"

"And engrossed?"

"Engrossed? Yes, sir, but—"

"Put it on the table, please," said Mark.

"Certainly, sir; but will you permit me only one word?"

"Do as I tell you, sir," said Mark, sternly; "we can talk afterwards."

"Certainly, sir," said the attorney, a little high and huffed; and, getting on a chair, he took down from shelves well stored with others like it, a mahogany-coloured tin-box, with "M. Shadwell, Esq., Raby," in large yellow letters on the front; and drawing forth the deed, placed it before Mark, who opened the milk-white parchment folds, and displayed that handsome piece of engrossing with its blue stamps and silver foil, ready at the touch of his pen to become fixed and inflexible as those chemical fluids which solidify at the turning of a stopper.

"You can get a couple of witnesses——"

"Well, I——" The attorney looked at his watch.

"Oh! yes," interrupted Mark, fiercely. "Of course you can—and—I'm not going to sign this thing;" and he pushed the deed with the back of his hand a little from him. "I've changed my mind, and I want you to draw the shortest will you can, leaving everything I possess, without exception, to my daughter. I've made up my mind tonight, and she shall have it rather than a—a stranger."

By this time, Mark's mind was clear, and his hand steady, and he wrote across the deed without a tremor these words to which the date was prefixed:

"Having changed my mind this evening, I do not intend to execute this deed, and have countermanded my instructions, with the intention of dealing differently with my property in my will. M. Shadwell."

Beneath them, at Shadwell's request, the wondering and curious attorney wrote: "Present while Mr. Shadwell wrote and signed the above memorandum;" and at foot of this, the attorney himself signed his name.

Mark Shadwell walked up and down the room, sometimes stopping to look out of the window with the same unchanged and stony face, while the attorney copied a short form of a will, which Shadwell read, and perfected then and there, and, taking it and the deed with him, departed, leaving the attorney at the doorsteps, with his candle blown out in his courteous hand, bursting with wonder and surmise as he watched Mark's tall, slight figure receding homeward.

But Mark did not go home. A fitful melancholy wind had got up, and the moon was just showing its edges above the distant mountains and lighting the filmy streak of cloud that lay over them, as he entered the gate of Raby, and passing the great dark house, which no longer showed a gleam, but seemed to have closed its eyes, thinking of its secrets, he took the path to Wynderfel.

A man who walks with one idea in his head, and in a high state of excitement, gets over the ground quickly. The moon was now up, and a mournful wind piped through the roofless gables and open windows of the old Manor House of Wynderfel, under whose walls he already was. From the lady's window an arm seemed wildly to wave him toward it. It was only that long ivy tendril, white in the moonlight, which had got a trick of beckoning when the wind was up.

He passed by these haunted walls, and down the lonely path to the Vicarage—a solitary figure—in that region deserted of life. Below him lay that happier land without the circle of Wynderfel, where were farmsteads and hedgerows, and the snug and kindly Vicarage, from which he could dimly see a lonely light.

The servant who opened the Vicarage door did not happen to know Mark Shadwell. So much the better for him. The cheery sounds of voices and laughter came through the little drawing-room door as the maid opened it to say that a gentleman, who would not give his name, was in the hall, and wanted to say a word to the vicar on particular business. The vicar's "Show him into the study" followed instantly, and the vicar himself, with the pleasant radiance of the beloved faces he had just left still on his own thin features, entered, and looked with an uncertain gaze upon the figure, buttoned up in a loose coat, and imperfectly lighted.

"It is I—*Shadwell*," said Mark, in a low tone, as the vicar shut the door. "Just a word or two."

"Oh!" exclaimed the vicar, "I'm so glad. Won't you come into the drawing-room? Do."

"Two documents that I want to leave with you," continued Mark, whose speech went right on, like the chimes of a clock, "an odd hour; but I happened to be near this. You'll take care of them—great care, I know; this is the deed I was thinking of executing; but that's past. You'll see what I have written across the face of it; and this is my will. You can read them—time enough when I've left you. You take an interest in Rachel. You'll be glad when you see what I have done; and—I thank you, Temple, for your kindness to her, and you'd have been a good friend to me if I had allowed you. I must go."

"But it's a very nasty night. Did you drive?"

"I walked. Goodbye."

"You must take my cob; it's no night for a walk over those uplands."

Mark had reached the hall-door, and without waiting opened it. The wind was not on the front of the house, but it had increased to something like the gusty beginnings of a gale. The vicar held the door open, and the glass bell in the hall, with its modest candle, swung in the unruly air that it admitted, and threw its flaring light on Mark's pale face as, with the strangest smile the vicar ever saw, he nodded his farewell over his shoulder, while his loose coat flapped about him, and waving back his hand as if to forbid ceremony, he strode away.

The vicar shut his door with some little exertion, and locked it and drew the bolts, and having indorsed in pencil the date at which Shadwell had placed the documents in his hands, he locked them up also, intending, by-and-bye, to read them as Mark seemed to wish. And he crossed the hall, anticipating the attack which the curious women were sure to make, and think how best to fence pleasantly with his intending examiners.

The wind gradually increased in violence. It became a storm. Even in the sheltered Vicarage its fury was heard, on high, loud and awful, and Miss Barbara was up twice in the night in her dressing-gown and slippers patrolling the lobbies, and with great disgust and terror wondering at the apathy of the other human occupants of the house.

At midnight Mark had not returned to Raby. Agnes did not know what to think. His horse, without a rider, had found his way to his stable door. In such sinister conjunctures of doubt and alarm, what a magic mirror does the imagination hold up!

Happy those who, in a spirit of prayer, can lift the veil and look in. She could not look with pure eyes, and in its depths saw only phantoms that appalled her.

At half-past twelve she sent down a frightened note to the attorney, who, she knew, had accompanied him to Applebury. Mr. Twinley scrawled a line in pencil from his bed to say he had seen him at nine o'clock, when he called, after his return from Apple bury, for a few minutes, and here the note stopped.

What had he called about? Whither had he gone? Had bad news come from London? Was he a prisoner? Was he forced to fly? Or—or—and she dropped the veil over the spectres that were astir upon the speculum.

Mr. Twinley had turned upon his other side, and was deep in the peaceful sleep of a robust attorney, when he was again awakened by an energetic note from the lady of Raby. It called on him to come up to Raby and see her, otherwise she would come down to his office and see him.

Mr. Twinley might admire the new Mrs. Shadwell, but he did not like her. If he had been sure that the Squire would stick to his resolution of the evening before, he would have taken this message very coolly. But human passion is transitory—*amantium iræ* proverbially so, and wills are revocable. The queen might enjoy her own again, and the Raby connection was worth preserving.

So, though rather peevishly, the attorney did get up, and dress in haste, and walked down to Raby, where the lady received him awfully pale, and thoughtful, and inquisitive. He wisely kept the subject of his conference with Mark that evening strictly to himself, and wondered intensely what the secret could be. It plainly was not a quarrel. Mark had spoken to him in the morning about the deed, and had not seen his wife since.

"He must have heard news, however," said the pale lady, with decision, "or he is consulting with Mr. Temple at the Vicarage, and they don't know how late it is. He'll turn up immediately, or they have made him stay there, it is such an awful night."

"Yes, indeed—a frightful night it is, ma'am," said the attorney, with feeling.

"Won't you take a glass of sherry, Mr. Twinley," said the lady, thoughtfully.

"No, thank you, ma'am."

"You think he'll be here soon?" urged the eager wife, holding the candle at the dining-room door, as the attorney entered the hall where the servant waited to let him out.

"Oh! yes, ma'am, I'm sure you're right about his waiting at the Vicarage. Slates were flying, I assure you, in the street of Raby as I came, and I should not be surprised if some of the trees here were blown down before morning."

And the attorney's countenance darkened as, with this idea in his mind, he thought of his walk under the huge trees that line the avenue.

## CHAPTER 75
### A KNOCKING AT THE DOOR

Not that night did Mark Shadwell return to Raby. Various were the moods that lightened or darkened the soul of Agnes Shadwell through these long hours as the flying scud above the wild and agitated landscape. Where was Mark? What had become of him? What was he meditating?

From the summit of the sylvan uplands that overlook Wynderfel there opens, gradually, descending toward that ruined mansion, a ravine which expands into a dark glen. This glen at one spot widens into an amphitheatre, walled darkly up at its southern side by a precipice, over whose stained front brambles hang and thick ivy grows; and over its upper edge the old trees stoop and gather, deepening the solemn shadow which makes the tarn that washes its base look black as ink. The tiny stream that feeds this sombre lake steals out from the rocks at its foot, and makes its way deviously through the glen, which narrows again at the other end of the tarn, leaving, however, a level carpet of grass.

Of all that lonely region this is the most entirely lonely spot. The overshadowed tarn looks smooth as ice, and black as ink, and there are fabulous stories of its depth at some points. On the green floor of soft sward that lies on the eastern side of the sheet of water stands the kyst-shaped black tomb of the suicide, Lady Mildred of Wynderfel. There is inscription neither of name nor of date. In rude bass-relief reposes a female figure, life-size, with the left hand raised above the shoulder, and in the centre of the palm a five-rayed star, such as heralds term a star of Bethlehem.

In this solitude of solitudes repose the outcast bones of the suicide. If she pined for quiet and oblivion, never did mortal drink deeper of both. From a silence like the grave, from an abyss into whose depths scarcely at highest summer noon does the sun ever peep, at night you may look up, through masses of wild trees and clambering underwood, to the glimmering face and moon-lighted peaks of the precipice, and see the narrow disk of dark-blue sky and stars that roof in this solemn hall of silence. Over it the scud was flying and the storm roaring, and now and then a huge gust broke in, whirling the withered leaves, and tossing the boughs frantically in the dark, and lashing the deep pool into sudden eddies.

Toward morning the gale subsided; a sullen calm succeeded, and the leaves that had danced in such mad circles, whirling up in columns nearly to the summit of the precipitous glen, now slept without a stir, on the soft grass by the tomb of lonely Mildred, and by the margin of the tarn that looked up to the cold morning sky with a surface as dead and black as if it had never been agitated. A broken bough, floating with its sear leaves upward, alone gave token of the recent fury of the storm. Over it broke the cold wild dawn; the pale sun glittered across the landscape as it might over a field of battle; many a tall tree lay low, and great drifts of yellow leaves were huddled together in clefts and hollows, to dance on forest boughs, in air and sun, no more.

No tidings meanwhile at Raby were heard of Mark Shad-well.

Again the attorney was called up to see the perplexed lady at Raby. This time she sent the tax-cart for him, and he came

451

in better temper. He had asked the servant, and already learnt that Mark had not been heard of. She had sent to inquire at the Vicarage. He had left that last night at about ten o'clock, as the vicar supposed at the time, intending to return direct to Raby. But he could not say what direction he took.

There was an agent at Chester, with whom Mark often had business. He must be telegraphed to. It would not do to publish far and wide, however, that Mr. Shadwell of Raby had absconded without apprising his wife of his intention. The message therefore said: "If Mr. Shadwell should call, telegraph instantly to me, as a message awaits him here."

In the same terms messages were sent to the hotel at which, in his unfrequent visits to London, he was accustomed to put up; and also to the office of his London attorney.

Two hours passed—three hours—four hours—and brought no answer. At about twelve o'clock Captain Clayton arrived, as usual, having heard nothing of the alarm and perplexity that prevailed at Raby. He came straight into the drawing-room, where Agnes was talking to the attorney, and was struck by a certain pallor in her face, and by the intense coldness of her smile, and her manner to him as she greeted him.

The attorney, as he entered, was taking his leave, and Mrs. Shadwell, who stood on no forms that day, accompanied him into the hall to say a last word.

"That is Mr. Clayton, you know" (she preferred saying Mr. to calling him Captain)—"my husband's particular friend—can we make any use of him. May I ask him to call on you just now? perhaps you can devise some employment for him: he would be horridly in the way here, you know."

And having seen him out of the house, she returned to the drawing-room, and, without waiting for question, she placed her hands on his shoulders, looking with her deep eyes into his handsome but apathetic face, at that moment full of stolid wonder, and said:

"Oh! Alfred!—he's gone. I have never seen Mark since: what can it be?"

And though she spoke interrogatively, her eyes suggested dreadful, positive suspicions.

"I—I assure you, I haven't heard from him; if you are apprehensive of anything of that kind. I haven't, darling, really—upon my honour!" he answered, in great bewilderment.

"You remember when I made you look out of the window last night, and you said you saw nothing?"

"Well—I swear there was nothing; I think so. In fact, I'm nearly certain," he hesitated.

"It must have been just about that time his horse came home. They found it in the yard, at the stable-door. I—I don't know what to think: he's probably with his London lawyers by this time. Alfred—Alfred! My God! Alfred, what has your madness involved me in!"

"No—now, my darling, you're talking the most arrant nonsense, I do assure you; now just you be quiet; you must not talk so, for fifty reasons. I'll just consider it a little: I'll think what's best to be done, and come back and talk it over with you. Isn't that the best way?"

And so he went; but he did not come back any more than Mark Shadwell. She drove down in her miniature brougham—an acquisition on which she had insisted some months before—to the attorney's office. Captain Clayton had been there. He had run up to London to make inquiries, and having scarcely time to catch the train, had requested the attorney to inform Mrs. Shadwell that he would exert himself to the uttermost to make the inquiry effectual, and let her know the result forthwith. Mrs. Shadwell concealed her anger.

Next evening's post, however, brought a letter from Clayton to the attorney, which said: "I was on the point of sending the enclosed note direct to Mrs. Shadwell, but reflected that if the uncertainty still continues, her agitation may have increased since yesterday, and knowing the very confidential position occupied by you in Mr. Shadwell's family, I thought I had better leave the note open, that you might use your discretion as to the best manner of apprising Mrs. Shadwell of its purport."

The open note enclosed in this, said:

My Dear Mrs. Shadwell,

I have ventured to make inquiry at all the places usually frequented by Mr. Shadwell in town, and have failed to learn anything. When his solicitors last heard from him, he had no intention of coming to town. Deeply regretting that I have not been fortunate enough to learn anything positive, I can only add, that anything that may strike you or Mr. Twinley as being in my power to aid further in this anxious affair, I shall be only too happy to undertake.

Believe me,

My Dear Mrs. Shadwell,

Yours very truly,       A. L. Clayton.

This cavalier treatment incensed Mrs. Shadwell, and one of her intense, sarcastic notes replied. But It did not reach him till next spring, for Captain Clayton had gone abroad; and it lay upon the hall-porter's table, with a row of similarly neglected letters, of all shapes and sizes, that awaited there the return of their careless owners.

Another idea now visited the anxious brain of Mrs. Shadwell. Could Mark have made away with himself? No; Mark was not mad. There was no aptitude for inflicting on himself any avoidable pain or privation. He was vindictive; he was violent; he was, from long isolation, careless what people might say or think. Heaven alone knew what he might be about.

She went down to Raby and saw Twinley, and cross-questioned him about the deed, and, on hearing that her husband had taken away the engrossed copy, as yet unexecuted—Twinley took care to tell no more about that than he was strictly obliged—she demanded the draft-deed, which, taking her receipt for it, he gave her.

Mrs. Shadwell was suffering. She did not know what to think. Ominous as everything looked, it was still possible that Mark was merely complying with a necessity, and concealing himself till some special danger—which he had no time to communicate to others—had blown over.

Miss Barbara came over to see her, and found her rather silent, fierce and odd: but looking miserably. She told her brother, Stour, that if he had seen her he could not help pitying her. To which he replied, that: "Suspense is torture, and of course she is suffering; but I confess I pity our poor Rachel a great deal more, because there can be no doubt that her misery is unselfish."

I don't know what was passing in honest Roger's mind during the period of Mark Shadwell's disappearance. He originated no conjectures, but listened earnestly to those of others. His spirits recovered, not their gaiety—that would not have been decent—but their energy, and his attention to his toilet mysteriously revived. He was sorry on Rachel's account. He was shocked even. Mark might be in France, or in the Fleet—who could tell where? But he might also have killed himself, or been killed; and, in that case, might it not be reserved for honest Roger to comfort his widow? He had heard of the course of true love, diverted similarly from its proper channel, and returning thus circuitously to reward patient fidelity, after an interval of despair. He knew, as many men do, cases precisely in point. The nature of his suspense, therefore, was somewhat affected by these secret considerations.

Four days had now passed, and brought no tidings of Mark Shadwell.

The night had closed: serene moonlight silvered the wooded landscape. The air was still and frosty. It was a night of utter silence, and now twelve o'clock. Agnes could not sleep: nervously listening, she lay, still with her dress on, awake upon her bed, the coverlet thrown over her. Her maid was sleeping in the same room: Agnes could not bear to be alone.

Leaning on her elbow, she had been for a minute listening, and fancying a distant sound. But she had listened in vain, and placed her sleepless head again upon the pillow, and fell into dismal speculations and reveries, that frightened her; and, in the midst of these silent communings, a loud and long double-knock suddenly thundered at the hall-door, and the bell rang shrilly.

"Dorothy!—Dorothy!" shrieked Agnes, starting upright in

the bed. "My God! It's your master's knock!"

# Chapter 76

## Conclusion

"Get your things on as fast as you can—any way, no matter—you can throw a cloak over you."

And as the half-awakened maid obeyed, Agnes hurried to the window; but she had forgotten that it did not command a view of the hall-door. Before the shutters were well opened, the knocking and ringing were repeated.

"Quick, Dorothy! I can't go without you—do, for Heaven's sake!"

Expecting to see Mark in a few moments—not knowing what story he might have to tell, or in what spirit or character he might appear—her heart, which all this while was beating as if it would choke her, suddenly, with a deadly faintness, felt as if it stopped still.

But Agnes was not a lady to swoon easily. There is some truth in the theory of effort. When she and her maid had reached the head of the great staircase, a servant had already opened the hall-door, and she heard a voice; it was not her husband's, talking in the hall with the old butler, who was still retained.

Agnes descended, stopping now and then, for a moment, to listen. When she came into the hall, the old servant, in slippers, and without a necktie, in *déshabille*, with a solitary candle on the table, was talking to a stranger who had not removed his hat. They were talking earnestly, it seemed, and in tones little above a whisper.

Disappointed, and also relieved, she came forward more boldly, and the men looked round. The stranger removed his hat, and advanced to meet her. He was the vicar. Strange was the countenance of Agnes—the light of her candle so close to her face, and that face so pale, and contracted with the peculiar frown of pain.

"Tell me quickly? you need not fear," she said, very low, in a voice thin and cold, that thrilled Stour Temple.

She read instantly the dark look in the vicar's earnest eyes—she knew there was news of Mark, bad news for her, at least, she saw it must be.

"Yes—I've learned something about Mr. Shadwell—there has been an accident— a very bad one—fatal—I'm grieved to say."

He was led on to say this by the gaze that was fixed on him. He felt that the least delay would not soften but protract her agony.

She made an attempt to speak, it was but a contortion, her voice did not come; but she was pulling at his hand quiveringly, and he knew she wanted to hear the whole story, be it what it might, and he told it.

I will not relate it in his words, but these were the facts.

Two cows of the vicar's were pastured in Wynderfel park. One of these that evening had strayed away, and a man was sent in quest of it, but in vain.

About eight o'clock, favoured by the moonlight, he resumed his search. Having failed in other quarters, he meant to try the woods near Hazelden, which are approached through a glen. He missed his way, however, and found himself, on a sudden, by the awful tarn of Feltram.

The moon being high, lighted the opposite side of the precipitous amphitheatre, and those peaked, grey rocks, projecting through the trees here and there, to which Doré, drawing such a scene, would have given the outlines of sheeted grotesques, with upraised arms, stooping from midair over the black oval of the pool.

The man looked round, and saw the black tomb of the unhappy Mildred—like a patch of shadow on the grass, and "winter's tales" which he had heard of the "gaze-lady" which, as I have said, local antiquaries tell us is truly "ghaist-ladye," came crowding horribly on his memory; and these scaring fancies were brought suddenly to their climax by his seeing, just emerging above the smooth surface of the tarn, a human figure, floating face upwards.

It was not till he looked hard at it for some seconds, that he became certain that the white object which he saw was a half-submerged human face, looking upwards against that streak of moonlight which, wavering and flickering in the shadow of nearly leafless branches, yet so sharply defined it, that there could remain no doubt in his mind—except that the appearance might be one of the delusions practised by the goblin of that haunted glen.

Forgetting the cow, and everything but the ghost of the Lady Mildred, the man got away as fast as he could, and by the time he got quite out of that haunted territory, he began to reflect that the figure he had seen floating in the tarn might have been not a ghost, but a corpse. He made haste to the Vicarage, and there saw Stour Temple, who, though it was by this time past ten, got men together, and with his brother Roger, and proper appliances for drawing the body, if such it should prove to be, from the water and carrying it away, set off for the Glen of Feltram.

The vicar was very silent during the march. He had a presentiment—so had others—which no one uttered. Through the narrow glen, bearing their ropes and poles for an extemporized bier, silent and awed, like men passing into a cathedral at a midnight Amend, they entered that dark hall where stands the solitary tomb, and the tarn reflects the stars.

Taking their stand upon that patch of sward on which fell a narrow strip of light from the moon, now high in the heavens, they got the rope in a long loop round the object which floated at the surface, and drew it slowly to the margin.

Slowly, with a sort of undulation, sometimes under, sometimes over the water, it glided to the bank. With hardly a word, spoken under breath, they drew it up, with a trail of water streaming after, and laid it, a few yards on, in the patch of moonshine. It was the tall, slender figure, and proud face of Mark Shadwell, on which the moonlight fell!

The vicar looked down upon the familiar features of the man with whom so much of the past of his secluded existence was associated, with a vague mingling of deep emotion and deep thought. Every face is sublime in death. The whole case is there; the weakness and the fate. It awes and it softens us. We see, for the first time, how much was excusable, how tremendous is the penalty. The tale is told, to which words can be added never more, and it lingers still in our ears. We remember things we might have said, but which can never now, be said. The writing is finished, and rolled up, and sealed, till the tremendous day breaks over all.

Having given his men orders to convey the body to Raby, and left that matter in charge of his brother, he himself walked on to Raby, whose inmates were startled, as I have said, by his late knocking.

"Very rash," thought the vicar, struggling to get rid of a conviction that haunted him, as he rapidly trod the Wynderfel path to Raby, "very mad of him to take that devious and dangerous way on such a night!"

The truth is, there was no way of accounting reasonably for Mark Shadwell's having taken the Feltram path, if his object was to reach Raby either safely, in such a storm, or expeditiously. Stour Temple was trying to exclude the hypothesis, at which other people arrived, unanimously—I mean, that the Squire's death was not accidental. Knowing all I do of the circumstances, and of that impulsive, violent, and hypochondriac man, as well as of the intense agitation in which he took his leave of the vicar that night, and of the legal measures he had taken to secure the disposition of his property, I have myself no doubt whatever, that Mark Shadwell made away with himself, in his despair, deliberately.

In the mind of every man who wilfully ends his life, there are, I have no doubt, fluctuations, waverings, horrible recoils, and then relapses into suicidal frenzy, before the irrevocable plunge, or pistol-shot, or razor-gash. Human nature takes fright, and cries, No! with all its might; and morality pleads, and the whole man shudders and protests; and he thinks, and thanks God—the danger is over; but the mysterious temptation recurs—importunes, bewitches, transforms him,—and he is gone!

The body lay that night at Raby. A coroner's jury pronounced his death accidental, following strictly such evidence as was before them, though every man of them had his misgivings, and afterwards his convictions.

Time has passed—with many disturbances and adjustments, demolishing and repairing, obliterating and creating, and carrying on the great story of human passion, vanity, and sorrow, since then.

The beautiful Agnes—like a spirit in possession—was not easily to be cast out. She was active, truculent, unscrupulous; and seemed resolved to contest the rights of the heiress of Raby to the last. But Rachel had no intention of turning one who had been her father's wife—undeserving as she was—adrift upon the world with absolutely no provision. She knew nothing of that paroxysm of jealousy, and its cause, which had produced the catastrophe.

Perhaps Mark Shadwell's construction of what he saw was too nearly absolute and extreme, considering how strangely perfidious that woman was, and how capable of deception within deception, and of merely beguiling Clayton and befooling him for a purpose.

Clayton, however, kept her at arm's length ever after, and she hated him with a mysterious and intense acrimony.

So soon as the fury of this beautiful young woman, holding Raby against the siege of London attorneys, engineered by counsel learned in the law, a little cooled, and her cold, shrewd common sense asserted itself, she was more disposed to listen to reason, and so a treaty was concluded. Rachel charged the estate with an annuity to her, and she covenanted to trouble her and the estate no more. So this evil angel, so beautiful and fatal, her mission ended, vanished, and ceased to be seen and heard at Raby.

I have heard of her at different places—at Paris, at Florence, at Spa, at Vienna, at St. Petersburg, where occurred that *fracas* which I dare say you remember.

This ambiguous beauty is clever and admired, and carries

with her a gentle gaiety, an angry heart, and many secrets. I am always expecting to hear more of her. Scarlet lip and pearly smile, and softest eddies of dimples; those brilliant blushes, and dark eyes, with liquid glances, shy and fiery, are still weaving spells, and turning heads, and setting new dramas in motion.

And so she is going up and down, and to and fro upon the earth. There are disappointments and revenges; deep works the "little billow" of that bosom. The fire is not quenched, and she is not happy.

Rachel is married, very happily, to Mr. Charles Mordant, of whom I know little, except that he is a very good fellow. Old Mervyn, his uncle, stopped the suit he had commenced, and the estate has benefited by that forbearance; but he paid off, besides, a smart mortgage. He has the young people to live with him at free quarters, and takes an interest in nursing the Raby estate, which is already emerging. Rachel will never live at Raby: it has too many melancholy and terrible associations.

One secret of that ill-omened house is, happily for her, hid alike from herself and the world. It concerns the murder of Sir Roke Wycherly, which happened thus.

Sir Roke, after a short nap in his chair, awoke. He got up and locked his door, which opened upon the lobby. The other room, which communicated with Clewson's room, being bolted, you would have said that the baronet was tolerably secure. There was a fatality here, however. Just as he had completed the mysterious ceremony of unwigging, described at the inquest by Mr. Clewson, and donned that quaint cap in which he was found next morning dead in his chair, he heard a step approaching from the end of the gallery. The baronet had been expecting a note from Miss Marlyn all the evening.

It was awkward, his nightcap being on his head instead of that extremely clever wig in which he usually met his friends. Still, he could not risk missing that note. It struck him, however, that the step might be that of Carmel Sherlock, whose crazy visit at his door he remembered uncomfortably; and rather to quiet a nervous feeling, than with the slightest idea that it might actually be employed, he took up the dagger which, in an evil hour for him, he saw shining upon the dressing-table, and then went quickly to his door and peeped out upon the gallery.

The step was not that of Carmel Sherlock, nor yet that which he half expected. It was the figure of Mark Shadwell, now very near his door, that appeared. He had intended passing on to his own room, but Roke Wycherly stopped him, and invited him in, with what to Mark seemed an irritating insincerity—satirical, inquisitive—which he felt like an insult.

In a spirit of latent defiance then, Mark did turn into the room. Those who mean to tease others, and amuse themselves with their irritations, should be very sure of their own tempers. Roke Wycherly being, in some respects, a man of the world, though naturally, as Mr. Clewson knew, a gentleman easily exasperated, could affect good humour where it suited him. But under the strain of circumstances, all affectations are liable to break down.

The cards were there, but Shadwell did not care to play, and the baronet talked a little in his usual ironical vein. There are rules to be observed, of course, in this kind of game, as in others, and I have no doubt that had Mark respected them. Sir Roke would have managed to keep his temper. But Mark Shadwell's natural violence and isolated habits, were against all such regulated hostilities. He became utterly unparliamentarily, and was quickly very much the more provoking of the two, and broke into insult so direct and galling, that the baronet, with a pallid smile, told him he lied, and at the same moment chucked the pen that lay on the table in his face.

The wizened malevolent smile, the retorted outrage, Mark's long pent hate and ungovernable pride and violence, transported him.

As a man starts from his bed in the crisis of a frightful dream, in a moment, Mark stood freezing before his victim. The convulsive smile continued, there was something like a sob, and another, and a gush of blood flowed from the simpering mouth. Mark's hands wildly pressed the wound, and the blood flowed warm and sluggishly through his fingers and over his wrists, and the changeless face of Roke Wycherly seemed to smile at efforts vain as the dream of rolling back time and undoing the past; and Mark felt, with a transport like madness, that the work of that blind moment was for him and for Roke to go on, and on, and on—through inexorable eternity.

It was the few furious words of the altercation and the crash of the decanter, overturned by Mark's arm, that had startled Mr. Clewson from his slumbers. Then followed the quiet, and those mutterings of Mark's solitary horror, which had deceived him.

As Mark left the room, pale as a spectre, with the dreadful evidences of bloodshed on his hands, he was observed by Agnes Marlyn, herself unseen. When he had gone, her curiosity drew her to Sir Roke's door. It lay partly open. She listened—she knocked, to ascertain whether any one was in the room, and, finally, she entered. She thought something bad must have happened, but had no idea how bad. Courage was the attribute, perhaps, most remarkably pronounced in the strange character of that young girl. But the horrible revelation nearly overcame her. Even in that sickening moment her habit of never acting except on second thoughts, prevailed. Rapidly recovering herself, she distinctly saw the whole truth, and comprehended the value of her secret, and stole silently, her brain teeming with horror, wonder, and castles in the air, to her room.

The confession of Carmel Sherlock explains the rest.

I linger over, these scenes. When business or pleasure calls me northward, I sometimes make a halt at the quaint little town of Raby, and saunter through the grand old park of the bygone Shadwells, admiring with a renewed interest its picturesque nooks and hollows, its magnificent timber, its sombre uplands, and broad westward slopes.

My latest visit was made toward the end of last October. I looked in upon my dear old friends at the Vicarage. They are all well, and by a happy chance I found the vicar himself at home.

One bit of news in that part of the world I learned. An heir has been born to the Mordants, and, I suppose, Rachel is now as happy as mortal well can be. I should have walked over to pay my respects to the young gentleman, had time sufficed. But, alas! the Railway, though an educator, is also a tyrant, and makes us count our minutes and keep tryst, under very disagreeable penalties. So, consulting my watch, I took my leave of those loved and simple friends.

The vicar accompanied me in my walk toward the town of Raby, where he had a call to make. We pursued the well-known path by Wynderfel. And when we reached the ruins, with mutual consent we paused before the silent doorway through which Carmel Sherlock had emerged on the day when he was captured.

"You have read the old Latin inscription cut in the stone of that doorway. It refers, evidently, to the gaze-lady," said the vicar. "The more I think of that legend, the more curious it appears. I have, in my few leisure hours, been collecting materials. I shall find out something of the history of the two ladies who were supposed to have represented, in other centuries, that fatal spirit. Certainly, according to the old prophecy, she was due, as we say of ships, just at the time when Miss Marlyn appeared at Raby, and then, you know, it was to be for the disastrous extinction of the old family name; and see what accompanied it—I may say, what was brought about by it—a great scandal—murder, suicide, and the predicted utter obliteration of the ancient name of Shadwell; and she had the mark of a star in her left hand, also—it tempts one to superstition."

The vicar smiled sadly. "And I hear, at intervals, of the wanderings of that mysterious young lady with a kind of interest—though I never liked her—and I should not wonder any day to learn that her clothes were found standing upright and empty, in her room, the form, that had filled them, vanished, like the lady in the German legend, you recollect, who had returned to her husband from the grave. But the sun is near the edge of the distant wood, and I've been delaying you, so let us be gone."

So we turned toward Raby, and for a time, in silence, pursued our way thinking, and then talked of the neighbours, and their haps and mishaps, and sayings and doings, till the moment came for a kind farewell.

Raby is untenanted. But its wild and noble scenery, the picturesque ruins of Wynderfel, and the awful glen of Feltram, draw many a tourist and wandering artist to visit its haunted grounds. These memorials of a once famous race remain, but Shadwell of Wynderfel, or of Raby, a title which we meet with often in old county chronicles, and which mingles historically with others in the lists of splendour and of war, will turn up no more. It is "A Lost Name."

# The Last Heir of Castle Connor

There is something in the decay of ancient grandeur to interest even the most unconcerned spectator—the evidences of
greatness, of power, and of pride that survive the wreck of time,
proving, in mournful contrast with present desolation and decay,
what WAS in other days, appeal, with a resistless power, to the
sympathies of our nature. And when, as we gaze on the scion of
some ruined family, the first impulse of nature that bids us regard
his fate with interest and respect is justified by the recollection
of great exertions and self-devotion and sacrifices in the cause of
a lost country and of a despised religion—sacrifices and efforts
made with all the motives of faithfulness and of honour, and
terminating in ruin—in such a case respect becomes veneration,
and the interest we feel amounts almost to a passion.

It is this feeling which has thrown the magic veil of romance
over every roofless castle and ruined turret throughout our
country; it is this feeling that, so long as a tower remains above
the level of the soil, so long as one scion of a prostrate and im-
poverished family survives, will never suffer Ireland to yield to
the stranger more than the 'mouth honour' which fear compels.[1] I who have conversed *viva voce et propria persona* with those
whose recollections could run back so far as the times previous
to the confiscations which followed the Revolution of 1688—

---

1. This passage serves (*mirabile dictu*) to corroborate a statement of Mr. O'Connell's,
which occurs in his evidence given before the House of Commons, wherein he af-
firms that the principles of the Irish priesthood 'ARE democratic, and were those of
Jacobinism.'—See digest of the evidence upon the state of Ireland, given before the
House of Commons.

whose memory could repeople halls long roofless and desolate, and point out the places where greatness once had been, may feel all this more strongly, and with a more vivid interest, than can those whose sympathies are awakened by the feebler influence of what may be called the PICTURESQUE effects of ruin and decay.

There do, indeed, still exist some fragments of the ancient Catholic families of Ireland; but, alas! what VERY fragments! They linger like the remnants of her aboriginal forests, reft indeed of their strength and greatness, but proud even in decay. Every winter thins their ranks, and strews the ground with the wreck of their loftiest branches; they are at best but tolerated in the land which gave them birth—objects of curiosity, perhaps of pity, to one class, but of veneration to another.

The O'Connors, of Castle Connor, were an ancient Irish family. The name recurs frequently in our history, and is generally to be found in a prominent place whenever periods of tumult or of peril called forth the courage and the enterprise of this country. After the accession of William III., the storm of confiscation which swept over the land made woeful havoc in their broad domains. Some fragments of property, however, did remain to them, and with it the building which had for ages formed the family residence.

About the year 17—, my uncle, a Catholic priest, became acquainted with the inmates of Castle Connor, and after a time introduced me, then a lad of about fifteen, full of spirits, and little dreaming that a profession so grave as his should ever become mine.

The family at that time consisted of but two members, a widow lady and her only son, a young man aged about eighteen. In our early days the progress from acquaintance to intimacy, and from intimacy to friendship is proverbially rapid; and young O'Connor and I became, in less than a month, close and confidential companions—an intercourse which ripened gradually into an attachment ardent, deep, and devoted—such as I believe young hearts only are capable of forming.

He had been left early fatherless, and the representative and heir of his family. His mother's affection for him was intense in proportion as there existed no other object to divide it—indeed—such love as that she bore him I have never seen elsewhere. Her love was better bestowed than that of mothers generally is, for young O'Connor, not without some of the faults, had certainly many of the most engaging qualities of youth. He had all the frankness and gaiety which attract, and the generosity of heart which confirms friendship; indeed, I never saw a person so universally popular; his very faults seemed to recommend him; he was wild, extravagant, thoughtless, and fearlessly adventurous—defects of character which, among the peasantry of Ireland, are honoured as virtues. The combination of these qualities, and the position which O'Connor occupied as representative of an ancient Irish Catholic family—a peculiarly interesting one to me, one of the old faith—endeared him to me so much that I have never felt the pangs of parting more keenly than when it became necessary, for the finishing of his education, that he should go abroad.

Three years had passed away before I saw him again. During the interval, however, I had frequently heard from him, so that absence had not abated the warmth of our attachment. Who could tell of the rejoicings that marked the evening of his return? The horses were removed from the chaise at the distance of a mile from the castle, while it and its contents were borne rapidly onward almost by the pressure of the multitude, like a log upon a torrent. Bonfires blared far and near—bagpipes roared and fiddles squeaked; and, amid the thundering shouts of thousands, the carriage drew up before the castle.

In an instant young O'Connor was upon the ground, crying, 'Thank you, boys—thank you, boys;' while a thousand hands were stretched out from all sides to grasp even a finger of his. Still, amid shouts of 'God bless your honour—long may you reign!' and 'Make room there, boys! clear the road for the masther!' he reached the threshold of the castle, where stood his mother weeping for joy.

Oh! who could describe that embrace, or the enthusiasm with which it was witnessed? 'God bless him to you, my lady— glory to ye both!' and 'Oh, but he is a fine young gentleman, God bless him!' resounded on all sides, while hats flew up in volleys that darkened the moon; and when at length, amid the broad delighted grins of the thronging domestics, whose sense of decorum precluded any more boisterous evidence of joy, they reached the parlour, then giving way to the fullness of her joy the widowed mother kissed and blessed him and wept in turn. Well might any parent be proud to claim as son the handsome stripling who now represented the Castle Connor family; but to her his beauty had a peculiar charm, for it bore a striking resemblance to that of her husband, the last O'Connor.

I know not whether partiality blinded me, or that I did no more than justice to my friend in believing that I had never seen so handsome a young man. I am inclined to think the latter. He was rather tall, very slightly and elegantly made; his face was oval, and his features decidedly Spanish in cast and complexion, but with far more vivacity of expression than generally belongs to the beauty of that nation. The extreme delicacy of his features and the varied animation of his countenance made him appear even younger than his years—an illusion which the total absence of everything studied in his manners seemed to confirm.

Time had wrought no small change in me, alike in mind and spirits; but in the case of O'Connor it seemed to have lost its power to alter. His gaiety was undamped, his generosity unchilled; and though the space which had intervened between our parting and reunion was but brief, yet at the period of life at which we were, even a shorter interval than that of three years has frequently served to form or DEform a character.

Weeks had passed away since the return of O'Connor, and scarce a day had elapsed without my seeing him, when the neighbourhood was thrown into an unusual state of excitement by the announcement of a race-ball to be celebrated at the assembly-room of the town of T——, distant scarcely two miles from Castle Connor.

Young O'Connor, as I had expected, determined at once to attend it; and having directed in vain all the powers of his rhetoric to persuade his mother to accompany him, he turned the whole battery of his logic upon me, who, at that time, felt a reluctance stronger than that of mere apathy to mixing in any of these scenes of noisy pleasure for which for many reasons I felt myself unfitted. He was so urgent and persevering, however, that I could not refuse; and I found myself reluctantly obliged to make up my mind to attend him upon the important night to the spacious but ill-finished building, which the fashion and beauty of the county were pleased to term an assembly-room.

When we entered the apartment, we found a select few, surrounded by a crowd of spectators, busily performing a minuet, with all the congees and flourishes which belonged to that courtly dance; and my companion, infected by the contagion of example, was soon, as I had anticipated, waving his *chapeau bras*, and gracefully bowing before one of the prettiest girls in the room. I had neither skill nor spirits to qualify me to follow his example; and as the fullness of the room rendered it easy to do so without its appearing singular, I determined to be merely a spectator of the scene which surrounded me, without taking an active part in its amusements.

The room was indeed very much crowded, so that its various groups, formed as design or accident had thrown the parties together, afforded no small fund of entertainment to the contemplative observer. There were the dancers, all gaiety and good-humour; a little further off were the tables at which sat the card-players, some plying their vocation with deep and silent anxiety—for in those days gaming often ran very high in such places—and others disputing with all the vociferous pertinacity of undisguised ill-temper. There, again, were the sallow, blue-nosed, grey-eyed dealers in whispered scandal; and, in short, there is scarcely a group or combination to be met with in the court of kings which might not have found a humble parallel in the assembly-room of T——.

I was allowed to indulge in undisturbed contemplation, for I suppose I was not known to more than five or six in the room. I thus had leisure not only to observe the different classes into which the company had divided itself, but to amuse myself by speculating as to the rank and character of many of the individual actors in the drama.

Among many who have long since passed from my memory, one person for some time engaged my attention, and that person, for many reasons, I shall not soon forget. He was a tall, square-shouldered man, who stood in a careless attitude, leaning with his back to the wall; he seemed to have secluded himself from the busy multitudes which moved noisily and gaily around him, and nobody seemed to observe or to converse with him. He was fashionably dressed, but perhaps rather extravagantly; his face was full and heavy, expressive of sullenness and stupidity, and marked with the lines of strong vulgarity; his age might be somewhere between forty and fifty. Such as I have endeavoured to describe him, he remained motionless, his arms doggedly folded across his broad chest, and turning his sullen eyes from corner to corner of the room, as if eager to detect some object on which to vent his ill-humour.

It is strange, and yet it is true, that one sometimes finds even in the most commonplace countenance an undefinable something, which fascinates the attention, and forces it to recur again and again, while it is impossible to tell whether the peculiarity which thus attracts us lies in feature or in expression or in both combined, and why it is that our observation should be engrossed by an object which, when analysed, seems to possess no claim to interest or even to notice. This unaccountable feeling I have often experienced, and I believe I am not singular. but never in so remarkable a degree as upon this occasion. My friend O'Connor, having disposed of his fair partner, was crossing the room for the purpose of joining me, in doing which I was surprised to see him exchange a familiar, almost a cordial, greeting with the object of my curiosity.

I say I was surprised, for independent of his very questionable appearance, it struck me as strange that though so constantly associated with O'Connor, and, as I thought, personally acquainted with all his intimates, I had never before even seen this individual. I did not fail immediately to ask him who this gentleman was. I thought he seemed slightly embarrassed, but after a moment's pause he laughingly said that his friend over the way was too mysterious a personage to have his name announced in so giddy a scene as the present; but that on the morrow he would furnish me with all the information which I could desire. There was, I thought, in his affected jocularity a real awkwardness which appeared to me unaccountable, and consequently increased my curiosity; its gratification, however, I was obliged to defer. At length, wearied with witnessing amusements in which I could not sympathise, I left the room, and did not see O'Connor until late in the next day.

I had ridden down towards the castle for the purpose of visiting the O'Connors, and had nearly reached the avenue leading to the mansion, when I met my friend. He was also mounted; and having answered my inquiries respecting his mother, he easily persuaded me to accompany him in his ramble. We had chatted as usual for some time, when, after a pause, O'Connor said:

'By the way, Purcell, you expressed some curiosity respecting the tall, handsome fellow to whom I spoke last night.'

'I certainly did question you about a TALL gentleman, but was not aware of his claims to beauty,' replied I.

'Well, that is as it may be,' said he; 'the ladies think him handsome, and their opinion upon that score is more valuable than yours or mine. Do you know,' he continued, 'I sometimes feel half sorry that I ever made the fellow's acquaintance: he is quite a marked man here, and they tell stories of him that are anything but reputable, though I am sure without foundation. I think I know enough about him to warrant me in saying so.'

'May I ask his name?' inquired I.

'Oh! did not I tell you his name?' rejoined he. 'You should have heard that first; he and his name are equally well known. You will recognise the individual at once when I tell you that his name is—Fitzgerald.'

'Fitzgerald!' I repeated. 'Fitzgerald!—can it be Fitzgerald the duellist?'

'Upon my word you have hit it,' replied he, laughing; 'but you have accompanied the discovery with a look of horror more tragic than appropriate. He is not the monster you take him for—he has a good deal of old Irish pride; his temper is hasty, and he has been unfortunately thrown in the way of men who have not made allowance for these things. I am convinced that in every case in which Fitzgerald has fought, if the truth could be discovered, he would be found to have acted throughout upon the defensive. No man is mad enough to risk his own life, except when the doing so is an alternative to submitting tamely to what he considers an insult. I am certain that no man ever engaged in a duel under the consciousness that he had acted an intentionally aggressive part.'

'When did you make his acquaintance?' said I.

'About two years ago,' he replied. 'I met him in France, and you know when one is abroad it is an ungracious task to reject the advances of one's countryman, otherwise I think I should have avoided his society—less upon my own account than because I am sure the acquaintance would be a source of continual though groundless uneasiness to my mother. I know, therefore, that you will not unnecessarily mention its existence to her.'

I gave him the desired assurance, and added:

'May I ask you. O'Connor, if, indeed, it be a fair question, whether this Fitzgerald at any time attempted to engage you in anything like gaming?'

This question was suggested by my having frequently heard Fitzgerald mentioned as a noted gambler, and sometimes even as a blackleg. O'Connor seemed, I thought, slightly embarrassed. He answered:

'No, no—I cannot say that he ever attempted anything of the kind. I certainly have played with him, but never lost to any serious amount; nor can I recollect that he ever solicited me—indeed he knows that I have a strong objection to deep play. YOU must be aware that my finances could not bear much pruning down. I never lost more to him at a sitting than about five pounds, which you know is nothing. No, you wrong him if you imagine that he attached himself to me merely for the sake of such contemptible winnings as those which a broken-down Irish gentleman could afford him. Come, Purcell, you are too hard upon him—you judge only by report; you must see him, and decide for yourself.—Suppose we call upon him now; he is at the inn, in the High Street, not a mile off.'

I declined the proposal drily.

'Your caution is too easily alarmed,' said he. 'I do not wish you to make this man your bosom friend: I merely desire that you should see and speak to him, and if you form any acquaintance with him, it must be of that slight nature which can be dropped or continued at pleasure.'

From the time that O'Connor had announced the fact that his friend was no other than the notorious Fitzgerald, a foreboding of something calamitous had come upon me, and it now occurred to me that if any unpleasantness were to be feared as likely to result to O'Connor from their connection, I might find my attempts to extricate him much facilitated by my being acquainted, however slightly, with Fitzgerald. I know not whether the idea was reasonable—it was certainly natural; and I told O'Connor that upon second thoughts I would ride down with him to the town, and wait upon Mr. Fitzgerald.

We found him at home; and chatted with him for a considerable time. To my surprise his manners were perfectly those of a gentleman, and his conversation, if not peculiarly engaging, was certainly amusing. The politeness of his demeanour, and the easy fluency with which he told his stories and his anecdotes, many of them curious, and all more or less entertaining, accounted to my mind at once for the facility with which he had improved his acquaintance with O'Connor; and when he pressed upon us an invitation to sup with him that night, I had almost joined O'Connor in accepting it. I determined, however, against doing so, for I had no wish to be on terms of familiarity with Mr. Fitzgerald; and I knew that one evening spent together as he proposed would go further towards establishing an intimacy between us than fifty morning visits could do.

When I arose to depart, it was with feelings almost favourable to Fitzgerald; indeed I was more than half ashamed to acknowledge to my companion how complete a revolution in my opinion respecting his friend half an hour's conversation with him had wrought. His appearance certainly WAS against him; but then, under the influence of his manner, one lost sight of much of its ungainliness, and of nearly all its vulgarity; and, on the whole, I felt convinced that report had done him grievous wrong, inasmuch as anybody, by an observance of the common courtesies of society, might easily avoid coming into personal collision with a gentleman so studiously polite as Fitzgerald.

At parting, O'Connor requested me to call upon him the next day, as he intended to make trial of the merits of a pair of greyhounds, which he had thoughts of purchasing; adding, that if he could escape in anything like tolerable time from Fitzgerald's supper-party, he would take the field soon after ten on the next morning. At the appointed hour, or perhaps a little later, I dismounted at Castle Connor; and, on entering the hall, I observed a gentleman issuing from O'Connor's private room. I recognised him, as he approached, as a Mr. M'Donough, and, being but slightly acquainted with him, was about to pass him with a bow, when he stopped me. There was something in his manner which struck me as odd; he seemed a good deal flurried if not agitated, and said, in a hurried tone:

'This is a very foolish business, Mr. Purcell. You have some influence with my friend O'Connor; I hope you can induce him to adopt some more moderate line of conduct than that he has decided upon. If you will allow me, I will return for a moment with you, and talk over the matter again with O'Connor.'

As M'Donough uttered these words, I felt that sudden sinking of the heart which accompanies the immediate anticipation of something dreaded and dreadful. I was instantly convinced that O'Connor had quarrelled with Fitzgerald, and I knew that if such were the case, nothing short of a miracle could extricate

475

him from the consequences. I signed to M'Donough to lead the way, and we entered the little study together. O'Connor was standing with his back to the fire; on the table lay the breakfast-things in the disorder in which a hurried meal had left them; and on another smaller table, placed near the hearth, lay pen, ink, and paper. As soon as O'Connor saw me, he came forward and shook me cordially by the hand.

'My dear Purcell,' said he, 'you are the very man I wanted. I have got into an ugly scrape, and I trust to my friends to get me out of it.'

'You have had no dispute with that man—that Fitzgerald, I hope,' said I, giving utterance to the conjecture whose truth I most dreaded.

'Faith, I cannot say exactly what passed between us,' said he, 'inasmuch as I was at the time nearly half seas over; but of this much I am certain, that we exchanged angry words last night. I lost my temper most confoundedly; but, as well as I can recollect, he appeared perfectly cool and collected. What he said was, therefore, deliberately said, and on that account must be resented.'

'My dear O'Connor, are you mad?' I exclaimed. 'Why will you seek to drive to a deadly issue a few hasty words, uttered under the influence of wine, and forgotten almost as soon as uttered? A quarrel with Fitzgerald it is twenty chances to one would terminate fatally to you.'

'It is exactly because Fitzgerald IS such an accomplished shot,' said he, 'that I become liable to the most injurious and intolerable suspicions if I submit to anything from him which could be construed into an affront; and for that reason Fitzgerald is the very last man to whom I would concede an inch in a case of honour.'

'I do not require you to make any, the slightest sacrifice of what you term your honour,' I replied; 'but if you have actually written a challenge to Fitzgerald, as I suspect you have done, I conjure you to reconsider the matter before you despatch it. From all that I have heard you say, Fitzgerald has more to complain of in the altercation which has taken place than you. You owe it to your only surviving parent not to thrust yourself thus wantonly upon—I will say it, the most appalling danger. Nobody, my dear O'Connor, can have a doubt of your courage; and if at any time, which God forbid, you shall be called upon thus to risk your life, you should have it in your power to enter the field under the consciousness that you have acted throughout temperately and like a man, and not, as I fear you now would do, having rashly and most causelessly endangered your own life and that of your friend.'

'I believe, Purcell, you are right,' said he. 'I believe I HAVE viewed the matter in too decided a light; my note, I think, scarcely allows him an honourable alternative, and that is certainly going a step too far—further than I intended. Mr. M'Donough, I'll thank you to hand me the note.'

He broke the seal, and, casting his eye hastily over it, he continued:

'It is, indeed, a monument of folly. I am very glad, Purcell, you happened to come in, otherwise it would have reached its destination by this time.'

He threw it into the fire; and, after a moment's pause, resumed:

'You must not mistake me, however. I am perfectly satisfied as to the propriety, nay, the necessity, of communicating with Fitzgerald. The difficulty is in what tone I should address him. I cannot say that the man directly affronted me—I cannot recollect any one expression which I could lay hold upon as offensive—but his language was ambiguous, and admitted frequently of the most insulting construction, and his manner throughout was insupportably domineering. I know it impressed me with the idea that he presumed upon his reputation as a DEAD SHOT, and that would be utterly unendurable'

'I would now recommend, as I have already done,' said M'Donough, 'that if you write to Fitzgerald, it should be in such a strain as to leave him at perfect liberty, without a compromise of honour, in a friendly way, to satisfy your doubts as to his conduct.'

I seconded the proposal warmly, and O'Connor, in a few minutes, finished a note, which he desired us to read. It was to this effect:

O'Connor, of Castle Connor, feeling that some expressions employed by Mr. Fitzgerald upon last night, admitted of a construction offensive to him, and injurious to his character, requests to know whether Mr. Fitzgerald intended to convey such a meaning.
Castle Connor, Thursday morning.

This note was consigned to the care of Mr. M'Donough, who forthwith departed to execute his mission. The sound of his horse's hoofs, as he rode rapidly away, struck heavily at my heart; but I found some satisfaction in the reflection that M'Donough appeared as averse from extreme measures as I was myself, for I well knew, with respect to the final result of the affair, that as much depended upon the tone adopted by the SECOND, as upon the nature of the written communication.

I have seldom passed a more anxious hour than that which intervened between the departure and the return of that gentleman. Every instant I imagined I heard the tramp of a horse approaching, and every time that a door opened I fancied it was to give entrance to the eagerly expected courier. At length I did hear the hollow and rapid tread of a horse's hoof upon the avenue. It approached—it stopped—a hurried step traversed the hall—the room door opened, and M'Donough entered.

'You have made great haste,' said O'Connor; 'did you find him at home?'

'I did,' replied M'Donough, 'and made the greater haste as Fitzgerald did not let me know the contents of his reply.'

At the same time he handed a note to O'Connor, who instantly broke the seal. The words were as follow:

Mr. Fitzgerald regrets that anything which has fallen from him should have appeared to Mr. O'Connor to be intended to convey a reflection upon his honour (none such having been meant), and begs leave to disavow any wish to quarrel unnecessarily with Mr. O'Connor.

T—— Inn, Thursday morning.

I cannot describe how much I felt relieved on reading the above communication. I took O'Connor's hand and pressed it warmly, but my emotions were deeper and stronger than I cared to show, for I was convinced that he had escaped a most imminent danger. Nobody whose notions upon the subject are derived from the duelling of modern times, in which matters are conducted without any very sanguinary determination upon either side, and with equal want of skill and coolness by both parties, can form a just estimate of the danger incurred by one who ventured to encounter a duellist of the old school.

Perfect coolness in the field, and a steadiness and accuracy (which to the unpractised appeared almost miraculous) in the use of the pistol, formed the characteristics of this class; and in addition to this there generally existed a kind of professional pride, which prompted the duellist, in default of any more malignant feeling, from motives of mere vanity, to seek the life of his antagonist. Fitzgerald's career had been a remarkably successful one, and I knew that out of thirteen duels which he had fought in Ireland, in nine cases he had KILLED his man. In those days one never heard of the parties leaving the field, as not unfrequently now occurs, without blood having been spilt; and the odds were, of course, in all cases tremendously against a young and unpractised man, when matched with an experienced antagonist. My impression respecting the magnitude of the danger which my friend had incurred was therefore by no means unwarranted.

I now questioned O'Connor more accurately respecting the circumstances of his quarrel with Fitzgerald. It arose from some dispute respecting the application of a rule of piquet, at which game they had been playing, each interpreting it favourably to himself, and O'Connor, having lost considerably, was in no mood to conduct an argument with temper—an altercation ensued, and that of rather a pungent nature, and the result was that he left Fitzgerald's room rather abruptly, determined to demand an explanation in the most peremptory tone. For this purpose he had sent for M'Donough, and had commissioned him to deliver the note, which my arrival had fortunately intercepted.

As it was now past noon, O'Connor made me promise to remain with him to dinner; and we sat down a party of three, all in high spirits at the termination of our anxieties. It is necessary to mention, for the purpose of accounting for what follows, that Mrs. O'Connor, or, as she was more euphoniously styled, the lady of Castle Connor, was precluded by ill-health from taking her place at the dinner-table, and, indeed, seldom left her room before four o'clock.[2] We were sitting after dinner sipping our claret, and talking, and laughing, and enjoying ourselves exceedingly, when a servant, stepping into the room, informed his master that a gentleman wanted to speak with him.

'Request him, with my compliments, to walk in,' said O'Connor; and in a few moments a gentleman entered the room.

His appearance was anything but prepossessing. He was a little above the middle size, spare, and raw-boned; his face very red, his features sharp and bluish, and his age might be about sixty. His attire savoured a good deal of the SHABBY-GENTEEL; his clothes, which had much of tarnished and faded pretension about them, did not fit him, and had not improbably fluttered in the stalls of Plunket Street. We had risen on his entrance, and O'Connor had twice requested of him to take a chair at the table, without his hearing, or at least noticing, the invitation; while with a slow pace, and with an air of mingled importance and effrontery, he advanced into the centre of the apartment, and regarding our small party with a supercilious air, he said:

'I take the liberty of introducing myself—I am Captain M'Creagh, formerly of the—infantry. My business here is with a Mr. O'Connor, and the sooner it is despatched the better.'

'I am the gentleman you name,' said O'Connor; 'and as you

<hr>

2. It is scarcely necessary to remind the reader, that at the period spoken of, the important hour of dinner occurred very nearly at noon.

appear impatient, we had better proceed to your commission without delay.'

'Then, Mr. O'Connor, you will please to read that note,' said the captain, placing a sealed paper in his hand.

O'Connor read it through, and then observed:

'This is very extraordinary indeed. This note appears to me perfectly unaccountable.'

'You are very young, Mr. O'Connor,' said the captain, with vulgar familiarity; 'but, without much experience in these matters, I think you might have anticipated something like this. You know the old saying, "Second thoughts are best;" and so they are like to prove, by G——!'

'You will have no objection, Captain M'Creagh, on the part of your friend, to my reading this note to these gentlemen; they are both confidential friends of mine, and one of them has already acted for me in this business.'

'I can have no objection,' replied the captain, 'to your doing what you please with your own. I have nothing more to do with that note once I put it safe into your hand; and when that is once done, it is all one to me, if you read it to half the world—that's YOUR concern, and no affair of mine.'

O'Connor then read the following:

Mr. Fitzgerald begs leave to state, that upon re-perusing Mr. O'Connor's communication of this morning carefully, with an experienced friend, he is forced to consider himself as challenged. His friend, Captain M'Creagh, has been empowered by him to make all the necessary arrangements.

T—— Inn, Thursday.

I can hardly describe the astonishment with which I heard this note. I turned to the captain, and said:

'Surely, sir, there is some mistake in all this?'

'Not the slightest, I'll assure you, sir.' said he, coolly; 'the case is a very clear one, and I think my friend has pretty well made up his mind upon it. May I request your answer?' he continued, turning to O'Connor; 'time is precious, you know.'

O'Connor expressed his willingness to comply with the suggestion, and in a few minutes had folded and directed the following rejoinder:

Mr. O'Connor having received a satisfactory explanation from Mr. Fitzgerald, of the language used by that gentleman, feels that there no longer exists any grounds for misunderstanding, and wishes further to state, that the note of which Mr. Fitzgerald speaks was not intended as a challenge.

With this note the captain departed; and as we did not doubt that the message which he had delivered had been suggested by some unintentional misconstruction of O'Connor's first *billet*, we felt assured that the conclusion of his last note would set the matter at rest. In this belief, however, we were mistaken; before we had left the table, and in an incredibly short time, the captain returned. He entered the room with a countenance evidently tasked to avoid expressing the satisfaction which a consciousness of the nature of his mission had conferred; but in spite of all his efforts to look gravely unconcerned, there was a twinkle in the small grey eye, and an almost imperceptible motion in the corner of the mouth, which sufficiently betrayed his internal glee, as he placed a note in the hand of O'Connor. As the young man cast his eye over it, he coloured deeply, and turning to M'Donough, he said:

'You will have the goodness to make all the necessary arrangements for a meeting. Something has occurred to render one between me and Mr. Fitzgerald inevitable. Understand me literally, when I say that it is now totally impossible that this affair should be amicably arranged. You will have the goodness, M'Donough, to let me know as soon as all the particulars are arranged. Purcell,' he continued, 'will you have the kindness to accompany me?' and having bowed to M'Creagh, we left the room.

As I closed the door after me, I heard the captain laugh,

and thought I could distinguish the words—'By —— I knew Fitzgerald would bring him to his way of thinking before he stopped.'

I followed O'Connor into his study, and on entering, the door being closed, he showed me the communication which had determined him upon hostilities. Its language was grossly impertinent, and it concluded by actually threatening to 'POST' him, in case he further attempted 'to be OFF.' I cannot describe the agony of indignation in which O'Connor writhed under this insult. He said repeatedly that 'he was a degraded and disho-houred man,' that 'he was dragged into the field,' that 'there was ignominy in the very thought that such a letter should have been directed to him.' It was in vain that I reasoned against this impression; the conviction that he had been disgraced had taken possession of his mind. He said again and again that nothing but his DEATH could remove the stain which his indecision had cast upon the name of his family. I hurried to the hall, on hear-ing M'Donough and the captain passing, and reached the door just in time to hear the latter say, as he mounted his horse:

'All the rest can be arranged on the spot; and so farewell, Mr. M'Donough—we'll meet at Philippi, you know;' and with this classical allusion, which was accompanied with a grin and a bow, and probably served many such occasions, the captain took his departure.

M'Donough briefly stated the few particulars which had been arranged. The parties were to meet at the stand-house, in the race-ground, which lay at about an equal distance between Castle Connor and the town of T——. The hour appointed was half-past five on the next morning, at which time the twilight would be sufficiently advanced to afford a distinct view; and the weapons to be employed were PISTOLS—M'Creagh hav-ing claimed, on the part of his friend, all the advantages of the CHALLENGED party, and having, consequently, insisted upon the choice of "TOOLS,' as he expressed himself; and it was fur-ther stipulated that the utmost secrecy should be observed, as Fitzgerald would incur great risk from the violence of the peasantry, in case the affair took wind.

These conditions were, of course, agreed upon by O'Connor, and M'Donough left the castle, having appointed four o'clock upon the next morning as the hour of his return, by which time it would be his business to provide everything necessary for the meeting. On his departure, O'Connor requested me to remain with him upon that evening, saying that 'he could not bear to be alone with his mother.' It was to me a most painful request, but at the same time one which I could not think of refusing. I felt, however, that the difficulty at least of the task which I had to perform would be in some measure mitigated by the arrival of two relations of O'Connor upon that evening.

'It is very fortunate,' said O'Connor, whose thoughts had been running upon the same subject, 'that the O'Gradys will be with us to-night; their gaiety and good-humour will relieve us from a heavy task. I trust that nothing may occur to prevent their coming.' Fervently concurring in the same wish, I accompanied O'Connor into the parlour, there to await the arrival of his mother.

God grant that I may never spend such another evening! The O'Gradys DID come, but their high and noisy spirits, so far from relieving me, did but give additional gloom to the despondency, I might say the despair, which filled my heart with misery— the terrible forebodings which I could not for an instant silence, turned their laughter into discord, and seemed to mock the smiles and jests of the unconscious party. When I turned my eyes upon the mother, I thought I never had seen her look so proudly and so lovingly upon her son before—it cut me to the heart—oh, how cruelly I was deceiving her! I was a hundred times on the very point of starting up, and, at all hazards, declaring to her how matters were; but other feelings subdued my better emotions.

Oh, what monsters are we made of by the fashions of the world! how are our kindlier and nobler feelings warped or destroyed by their baleful influences! I felt that it would not be HONOURABLE, that it would not be ETIQUETTE, to betray O'Connor's secret. I sacrificed a higher and a nobler duty than I have since been called upon to perform, to the dastardly fear of bearing the unmerited censure of a world from which I was about to retire. O Fashion! thou gaudy idol, whose feet are red with the blood of human sacrifice, would I had always felt towards thee as I now do!

O'Connor was not dejected; on the contrary, he joined with loud and lively alacrity in the hilarity of the little party; but I could see in the flush of his cheek, and in the unusual brightness of his eye, all the excitement of fever—he was making an effort almost beyond his strength, but he succeeded—and when his mother rose to leave the room, it was with the impression that her son was the gayest and most light-hearted of the company. Twice or thrice she had risen with the intention of retiring, but O'Connor, with an eagerness which I alone could understand, had persuaded her to remain until the usual hour of her departure had long passed; and when at length she arose, declaring that she could not possibly stay longer, I alone could comprehend the desolate change which passed over his manner; and when I saw them part, it was with the sickening conviction that those two beings, so dear to one another, so loved, so cherished, should meet no more.

O'Connor briefly informed his cousins of the position in which he was placed, requesting them at the same time to accompany him to the field, and this having been settled, we separated, each to his own apartment. I had wished to sit up with O'Connor, who had matters to arrange sufficient to employ him until the hour appointed for M'Donough's visit; but he would not hear of it, and I was forced, though sorely against my will, to leave him without a companion. I went to my room, and, in a state of excitement which I cannot describe, I paced for hours up and down its narrow precincts. I could not—who could?-analyse the strange, contradictory, torturing feelings which, while I recoiled in shrinking horror from the scene which the morning was to bring, yet forced me to wish the intervening time annihilated; each hour that the clock told seemed to vibrate and tinkle through every nerve; my agitation was dreadful; fancy conjured up the forms of those who filled my thoughts with more than the vividness of reality; things seemed to glide through the dusky shadows of the room.

I saw the dreaded form of Fitzgerald—I heard the hated laugh of the captain—and again the features of O'Connor would appear before me, with ghastly distinctness, pale and writhed in death, the gouts of gore clotted in the mouth, and the eye-balls glared and staring. Scared with the visions which seemed to throng with unceasing rapidity and vividness, I threw open the window and looked out upon the quiet scene around. I turned my eyes in the direction of the town; a heavy cloud was lowering darkly about it, and I, in impious frenzy, prayed to God that it might burst in avenging fires upon the murderous wretch who lay beneath. At length, sick and giddy with excess of excitement, I threw myself upon the bed without removing my clothes, and endeavoured to compose myself so far as to remain quiet until the hour for our assembling should arrive.

A few minutes before four o'clock I stole noiselessly downstairs, and made my way to the small study already mentioned. A candle was burning within; and, when I opened the door, O'Connor was reading a book, which, on seeing me, he hastily closed, colouring slightly as he did so. We exchanged a cordial but mournful greeting; and after a slight pause he said, laying his hand upon the volume which he had shut a moment before:

'Purcell, I feel perfectly calm, though I cannot say that I have much hope as to the issue of this morning's rencounter. I shall avoid half the danger. If I must fall, I am determined I shall not go down to the grave with his blood upon my hands. I have resolved not to fire at Fitzgerald—that is, to fire in such a direction as to assure myself against hitting him. Do not say a word of this to the O'Gradys. Your doing so would only produce fruitless altercation; they could not understand my motives. I feel convinced that I shall not leave the field alive. If I must die today, I shall avoid an awful aggravation of wretchedness. Purcell,' he continued, after a little space, 'I was so weak as to feel almost ashamed of the manner in which I was occupied as you entered the room. Yes, I—I who will be, before this evening, a cold and lifeless clod, was ashamed to have spent my last moment of reflection in prayer. God pardon me! God pardon me!' he repeated.

I took his hand and pressed it, but I could not speak. I sought for words of comfort, but they would not come. To have uttered one cheering sentence I must have contradicted every impression of my own mind. I felt too much awed to attempt it. Shortly afterwards, M'Donough arrived. No wretched patient ever underwent a more thrilling revulsion at the first sight of the case of surgical instruments under which he had to suffer, than did I upon beholding a certain oblong flat mahogany box, bound with brass, and of about two feet in length, laid upon the table in the hall. O'Connor, thanking him for his punctuality, requested him to come into his study for a moment, when, with a melancholy collectedness, he proceeded to make arrangements for our witnessing his will. The document was a brief one, and the whole matter was just arranged, when the two O'Gradys crept softly into the room.

'So! last will and testament,' said the elder. 'Why, you have a very BLUE notion of these matters. I tell you, you need not be uneasy. I remember very well, when young Ryan of Ballykealey met M'Neil the duellist, bets ran twenty to one against him. I stole away from school, and had a peep at the fun as well as the best of them. They fired together. Ryan received the ball through the collar of his coat, and M'Neil in the temple; he spun like a top: it was a most unexpected thing, and disappointed his friends damnably. It was admitted, however, to have been very pretty shooting upon both sides. To be sure,' he continued, pointing to the will, 'you are in the right to keep upon the safe side of fortune; but then, there is no occasion to be altogether so devilish down in the mouth as you appear to be.'

'You will allow,' said O'Connor, 'that the chances are heavily against me.'

'Why, let me see,' he replied, 'not so hollow a thin', either.

Let me see, we'll say about four to one against you; you may chance to throw doublets like him I told you of, and then what becomes of the odds I'd like to know? But let things go as they will, I'll give and take four to one, in pounds and tens of pounds. There, M'Donough, there's a GET for you; b——t me, if it is not. Poh! the fellow is stolen away,' he continued, observing that the object of his proposal had left the room; 'but d—— it, Purcell, you are fond of a SOFT THING, too, in a quiet way—I'm sure you are—so curse me if I do not make you the same offer-is it a go?'

I was too much disgusted to make any reply, but I believe my looks expressed my feelings sufficiently, for in a moment he said:

'Well, I see there is nothing to be done, so we may as well be stirring. M'Donough, myself, and my brother will saddle the horses in a jiffy, while you and Purcell settle anything which remains to be arranged.'

So saying, he left the room with as much alacrity as if it were to prepare for a fox-hunt. Selfish, heartless fool! I have often since heard him spoken of as A CURSED GOOD-NA-TURED DOG and a D—— GOOD FELLOW; but such eulogies as these are not calculated to mitigate the abhorrence with which his conduct upon that morning inspired me.

The chill mists of night were still hovering on the landscape as our party left the castle. It was a raw, comfortless morning —a kind of drizzling fog hung heavily over the scene, dimming the light of the sun, which had now risen, into a pale and even a grey glimmer. As the appointed hour was fast approaching, it was proposed that we should enter the race-ground at a point close to the stand-house—a measure which would save us a ride of nearly two miles, over a broken road; at which distance there was an open entrance into the race-ground.

Here, accordingly, we dismounted, and leaving our horses in the care of a country fellow who happened to be stirring at that early hour, we proceeded up a narrow lane, over a side wall of which we were to climb into the open ground where stood the now deserted building, under which the meeting was to take place. Our progress was intercepted by the unexpected appearance of an old woman, who, in the scarlet cloak which is the picturesque characteristic of the female peasantry of the south, was moving slowly down the avenue to meet us, uttering that peculiarly wild and piteous lamentation well known by the name of 'the Irish cry,' accompanied throughout by all the customary gesticulation of passionate grief.

This rencounter was more awkward than we had at first anticipated; for, upon a nearer approach, the person proved to be no other than an old attached dependent of the family, and who had herself nursed O'Connor. She quickened her pace as we advanced almost to a run; and, throwing her arms round O'Connor's neck, she poured forth such a torrent of lamentation, reproach, and endearment, as showed that she was aware of the nature of our purpose, whence and by what means I knew not. It was in vain that he sought to satisfy her by evasion, and gently to extricate himself from her embrace. She knelt upon the ground, and clasped her arms round his legs, uttering all the while such touching supplications, such cutting and passionate expressions of woe, as went to my very heart.

At length, with much difficulty, we passed this most painful interruption; and, crossing the boundary wall, were placed beyond her reach. The O'Gradys damned her for a troublesome hag, and passed on with O'Connor, but I remained behind for a moment. The poor woman looked hopelessly at the high wall which separated her from him she had loved from infancy, and to be with whom at that minute she would have given worlds, she took her seat upon a solitary stone under the opposite wall, and there, in a low, subdued key, she continued to utter her sorrow in words so desolate, yet expressing such a tenderness of devotion as wrung my heart.

'My poor woman,' I said, laying my hand gently upon her shoulder, 'you will make yourself ill; the morning is very cold, and your cloak is but a thin defence against the damp and chill. Pray return home and take this; it may be useful to you.'

489

So saying, I dropped a purse, with what money I had about me, into her lap, but it lay there unheeded; she did not hear me.

'Oh I my child, my child, my darlin',' she sobbed, 'are you gone from me? are you gone from me? Ah, mavourneen, mavourneen, you'll never come back alive to me again. The crathur that slept on my bosom—the lovin' crathur that I was so proud of—they'll kill him, they'll kill him. Oh, voh! voh!'

The affecting tone, the feeling, the abandonment with which all this was uttered, none can conceive who have not heard the lamentations of the Irish peasantry. It brought tears to my eyes. I saw that no consolation of mine could soothe her grief, so I turned and departed; but as I rapidly traversed the level sward which separated me from my companions, now considerably in advance, I could still hear the wailings of the solitary mourner.

As we approached the stand-house, it was evident that our antagonists had already arrived. Our path lay by the side of a high fence constructed of loose stones, and on turning a sharp angle at its extremity, we found ourselves close to the appointed spot, and within a few yards of a crowd of persons, some mounted and some on foot, evidently awaiting our arrival. The affair had unaccountably taken wind, as the number of the expectants clearly showed; but for this there was now no remedy.

As our little party advanced we were met and saluted by several acquaintances, whom curiosity, if no deeper feeling, had brought to the place. Fitzgerald and the Captain had arrived, and having dismounted, were standing upon the sod. The former, as we approached, bowed slightly and sullenly—while the latter, evidently in high good humour, made his most courteous obeisance. No time was to be lost; and the two seconds immediately withdrew to a slight distance, for the purpose of completing the last minute arrangements.

It was a brief but horrible interval—each returned to his principal to communicate the result, which was soon caught up and repeated from mouth to mouth throughout the crowd. I felt a strange and insurmountable reluctance to hear the sickening particulars detailed; and as I stood irresolute at some distance from the principal parties, a top-booted squireen, with a hunting whip in his hand, bustling up to a companion of his, exclaimed:

"Not fire together!—did you ever hear the like? If Fitzgerald gets the first shot all is over. M'Donough sold the pass, by ——, and that is the long and the short of it.'

The parties now moved down a little to a small level space, suited to the purpose; and the captain, addressing M'Donough, said:

'Mr. M'Donough, you'll now have the goodness to toss for choice of ground; as the light comes from the east the line must of course run north and south. Will you be so obliging as to toss up a crown-piece, while I call?'

A coin was instantly chucked into the air. The captain cried, 'Harp.' The HEAD was uppermost, and M'Donough immediately made choice of the southern point at which to place his friend—a position which it will be easily seen had the advantage of turning his back upon the light—no trifling superiority of location. The captain turned with a kind of laugh, and said:

'By ——, sir, you are as cunning as a dead pig; but you forgot one thing. My friend is a left-handed gunner, though never a bit the worse for that; so you see there is no odds as far as the choice of light goes.'

He then proceeded to measure nine paces in a direction running north and south, and the principals took their ground.

'I must be troublesome to you once again, Mr. M'Donough. One toss more, and everything is complete. We must settle who is to have the FIRST SLAP.'

A piece of money was again thrown into the air; again the captain lost the toss and M'Donough proceeded to load the pistols. I happened to stand near Fitzgerald, and I overheard the captain, with a chuckle, say something to him in which the word 'cravat' was repeated. It instantly occurred to me that the captain's attention was directed to a bright-coloured muffler which O'Connor wore round his neck, and which would afford his antagonist a distinct and favourable mark. I instantly urged him to remove it, and at length, with difficulty, succeeded. He seemed perfectly careless as to any precaution. Everything was now ready; the pistol was placed in O'Connor's hand, and he only awaited the word from the captain.

M'Creagh then said:

'Mr. M'Donough, is your principal ready?'

M'Donough replied in the affirmative; and, after a slight pause, the captain, as had been arranged, uttered the words:

'Ready—fire.'

O'Connor fired, but so wide of the mark that someone in the crowd exclaimed:

'Fired in the air.'

'Who says he fired in the air?' thundered Fitzgerald. 'By —— he lies, whoever he is.' There was a silence. 'But even if he was fool enough to fire in the air, it is not in HIS power to put an end to the quarrel by THAT. D—— my soul, if I am come here to be played with like a child, and by the Almighty —— you shall hear more of this, each and every one of you, before I'm satisfied.'

A kind of low murmur, or rather groan, was now raised, and a slight motion was observable in the crowd, as if to intercept Fitzgerald's passage to his horse. M'Creagh, drawing the horse close to the spot where Fitzgerald stood, threatened, with the most awful imprecations, 'to blow the brains out of the first man who should dare to press on them.'

O'Connor now interfered, requesting the crowd to forbear, and some degree of order was restored. He then said, 'that in firing as he did, he had no intention whatever of waiving his right of firing upon Fitzgerald, and of depriving that gentleman of his right of prosecuting the affair to the utmost—that if any person present imagined that he intended to fire in the air, he begged to set him right; since, so far from seeking to exhort an unwilling reconciliation, he was determined that no power on earth should induce him to concede one inch of ground to Mr. Fitzgerald.'

This announcement was received with a shout by the crowd, who now resumed their places at either side of the plot of ground which had been measured. The principals took their places once more, and M'Creagh proceeded, with the nicest and most anxious care, to load the pistols; and this task being accomplished, Fitzgerald whispered something in the Captain's ear, who instantly drew his friend's horse so as to place him within a step of his rider, and then tightened the girths. This accomplished, Fitzgerald proceeded deliberately to remove his coat, which he threw across his horse in front of the saddle; and then, with the assistance of M'Creagh, he rolled the shirt sleeve up to the shoulder, so as to leave the whole of his muscular arm perfectly naked. A cry of 'Coward, coward! butcher, butcher!' arose from the crowd. Fitzgerald paused.

'Do you object, Mr. M'Donough? and upon what grounds, if you please?' said he.

'Certainly he does not,' replied O'Connor; and, turning to M'Donough, he added, 'pray let there be no unnecessary delay.'

'There is no objection, then,' said Fitzgerald.

'*I* object,' said the younger of the O'Gradys, 'if nobody else will.'

' And who the devil are you, that DARES to object?' shouted Fitzgerald; 'and what d——d presumption prompts you to DARE to wag your tongue here?'

'I am Mr. O'Grady, of Castle Blake,' replied the young man, now much enraged; 'and by ——, you shall answer for your language to me.'

'Shall I, by ——? Shall I?' cried he, with a laugh of brutal scorn; 'the more the merrier, d—n the doubt of it—so now hold your tongue, for I promise you you shall have business enough of your own to think about, and that before long.'

There was an appalling ferocity in his tone and manner which no words could convey. He seemed transformed; he was actually like a man possessed. Was it possible, I thought, that I beheld the courteous gentleman, the gay, good-humoured retailer of amusing anecdote with whom, scarce two days ago, I had laughed and chatted, in the blasphemous and murderous ruffian who glared and stormed before me!

O'Connor interposed, and requested that time should not be unnecessarily lost.

'You have not got a second coat on?' inquired the Captain. 'I beg pardon, but my duty to my friend requires that I should ascertain the point.'

O'Connor replied in the negative. The Captain expressed himself as satisfied, adding, in what he meant to be a complimentary strain, 'that he knew Mr. O'Connor would scorn to employ padding or any unfair mode of protection.'

There was now a breathless silence. O'Connor stood perfectly motionless; and, excepting the death-like paleness of his features, he exhibited no sign of agitation. His eye was steady—his lip did not tremble—his attitude was calm. The Captain, having re-examined the priming of the pistols, placed one of them in the hand of Fitzgerald.—M'Donough inquired whether the parties were prepared, and having been answered in the affirmative, he proceeded to give the word, 'Ready.' Fitzgerald raised his hand, but almost instantly lowered it again. The crowd had pressed too much forward as it appeared, and his eye had been unsteadied by the flapping of the skirt of a frieze riding-coat worn by one of the spectators.

'In the name of my principal,' said the Captain, 'I must and do insist upon these gentlemen moving back a little. We ask but little; fair play, and no favour.'

The crowd moved as requested. M'Donough repeated his former question, and was answered as before. There was a breathless silence. Fitzgerald fixed his eye upon O'Connor. The appointed signal, 'Ready, fire!' was given. There was a pause while one might slowly reckon three—Fitzgerald fired—and O'Connor fell helplessly upon the ground.

'There is no time to be lost,' said M'Creagrh; 'for, by ——, you have done for him.'

So saying, he threw himself upon his horse, and was instantly followed at a hard gallop by Fitzgerald.

'Cold-blooded murder, if ever murder was committed,' said O'Grady. 'He shall hang for it; d—n me, but he shall.'

A hopeless attempt was made to overtake the fugitives; but they were better mounted than any of their pursuers, and escaped with ease. Curses and actual yells of execration followed their course; and as, in crossing the brow of a neighbouring hill, they turned round in the saddle to observe if they were pursued, every gesture which could express fury and defiance was exhausted by the enraged and defeated multitude.

'Clear the way, boys,' said young O'Grady, who with me was kneeling beside O'Connor, while we supported him in our arms; 'do not press so close, and be d——d; can't you let the fresh air to him; don't you see he's dying?'

On opening his waistcoat we easily detected the wound: it was a little below the chest—a small blue mark, from which oozed a single heavy drop of blood.

'He is bleeding but little—that is a comfort at all events,' said one of the gentlemen who surrounded the wounded man.

Another suggested the expediency of his being removed homeward with as little delay as possible, and recommended, for this purpose, that a door should be removed from its hinges, and the patient, laid upon this, should be conveyed from the field. Upon this rude bier my poor friend was carried from that fatal ground towards Castle Connor. I walked close by his side, and observed every motion of his. He seldom opened his eyes, and was perfectly still, excepting a nervous WORKING of the fingers, and a slight, almost imperceptible twitching of the features, which took place, however, only at intervals.

The first word he uttered was spoken as we approached the entrance of the castle itself, when he said; repeatedly, 'The back way, the back way.' He feared lest his mother should meet him abruptly and without preparation; but although this fear was groundless, since she never left her room until late in the day, yet it was thought advisable, and, indeed, necessary, to caution all the servants most strongly against breathing a hint to their mistress of the events which had befallen.

Two or three gentlemen had ridden from the field one after another, promising that they should overtake our party before it reached the castle, bringing with them medical aid from one quarter or another; and we determined that Mrs. O'Connor should not know anything of the occurrence until the opinion of some professional man should have determined the extent of the injury which her son had sustained—a course of conduct which would at least have the effect of relieving her from the horrors of suspense. When O'Connor found himself in his own room, and laid upon his own bed, he appeared much revived-so much so, that I could not help admitting a strong hope that all might yet be well.

'After all, Purcell,' said he, with a melancholy smile, and speaking with evident difficulty, 'I believe I have got off with a trifling wound. I am sure it cannot be fatal I feel so little pain-almost none.'

I cautioned him against fatiguing himself by endeavouring to speak; and he remained quiet for a little time. At length he said:

'Purcell, I trust this lesson shall not have been given in vain. God has been very merciful to me; I feel—I have an internal confidence that I am not wounded mortally. Had I been fatally wounded—had I been killed upon the spot, only think on it'—and he closed his eyes as if the very thought made him dizzy—'struck down into the grave, unprepared as I am, in the very blossom of my sins, without a moment of repentance or of reflection; I must have been lost—lost forever and ever.'

I prevailed upon him, with some difficulty, to abstain from such agitating reflections, and at length induced him to court such repose as his condition admitted of, by remaining perfectly silent, and as much as possible without motion.

O'Connor and I only were in the room; he had lain for some time in tolerable quiet, when I thought I distinguished the bustle attendant upon the arrival of someone at the castle, and went eagerly to the window, believing, or at least hoping, that the sounds might announce the approach of the medical man, whom we all longed most impatiently to see.

My conjecture was right; I had the satisfaction of seeing him dismount and prepare to enter the castle, when my observations were interrupted, and my attention was attracted by a smothered, gurgling sound proceeding from the bed in which lay the wounded man. I instantly turned round, and in doing so the spectacle which met my eyes was sufficiently shocking.

I had left O'Connor lying in the bed, supported by pillows, perfectly calm, and with his eyes closed: he was now lying nearly in the same position, his eyes open and almost starting from their sockets, with every feature pale and distorted as death, and vomiting blood in quantities that were frightful. I rushed to the door and called for assistance; the paroxysm, though violent, was brief, and O'Connor sank into a swoon so deep and death-like, that I feared he should waken no more.

The surgeon, a little, fussy man, but I believe with some skill to justify his pretensions, now entered the room, carrying his case of instruments, and followed by servants bearing basins and water and bandages of linen. He relieved our doubts by instantly assuring us that 'the patient' was still living; and at the same time professed his determination to take advantage of the muscular relaxation which the faint had induced to examine the wound-adding that a patient was more easily 'handled' when in a swoon than under other circumstances.

After examining the wound in front where the ball had entered, he passed his hand round beneath the shoulder, and after a little pause he shook his head, observing that he feared very much that one of the vertebrae was fatally injured, but that he could not say decidedly until his patient should revive a little. 'Though his language was very technical, and consequently to me nearly unintelligible, I could perceive plainly by his manner that he considered the case as almost hopeless.

O'Connor gradually gave some signs of returning animation, and at length was so far restored as to be enabled to speak. After some few general questions as to how he felt affected, etc., etc., the surgeon, placing his hand upon his leg and pressing it slightly, asked him if he felt any pressure upon the limb? O'Connor answered in the negative—he pressed harder, and repeated the question; still the answer was the same, till at length, by repeated experiments, he ascertained that all that part of the body which lay behind the wound was paralysed, proving that the spine must have received some fatal injury.

'Well, doctor,' said O'Connor, after the examination of the wound was over; 'well, I shall do, shan't I?'

The physician was silent for a moment, and then, as if with an effort, he replied:

'Indeed, my dear sir, it would not be honest to flatter you with much hope.'

'Eh?' said O'Connor with more alacrity than I had seen him exhibit since the morning; 'surely I did not hear you aright; I spoke of my recovery—surely there is no doubt; there can be none—speak frankly, doctor, for God's sake—am I dying?'

The surgeon was evidently no stoic, and his manner had extinguished in me every hope, even before he had uttered a word in reply.

'You are—you are indeed dying. There is no hope; I should but deceive you if I held out any.'

As the surgeon uttered these terrible words, the hands which O'Connor had stretched towards him while awaiting his reply fell powerless by his side; his head sank forward; it seemed as if horror and despair had unstrung every nerve and sinew; he appeared to collapse and shrink together as a plant might under the influence of a withering spell.

It has often been my fate, since then, to visit the chambers of death and of suffering; I have witnessed fearful agonies of body and of soul; the mysterious shudderings of the departing spirit, and the heart-rending desolation of the survivors; the severing of the tenderest ties, the piteous yearnings of unavailing love-of all these things the sad duties of my profession have made me a witness. But, generally speaking, I have observed in such scenes something to mitigate, if not the sorrows, at least the terrors, of death; the dying man seldom seems to feel the reality of his situation; a dull consciousness of approaching dissolution, a dim anticipation of unconsciousness and insensibility, are the feelings which most nearly border upon an appreciation of his state; the film of death seems to have overspread the mind's eye, objects lose their distinctness, and float cloudily before it, and the apathy and apparent indifference with which men recognise the sure advances of immediate death, rob that awful hour of much of its terrors, and the deathbed of its otherwise inevitable agonies.

This is a merciful dispensation; but the rule has its exceptions—its terrible exceptions. When a man is brought in an instant, by some sudden accident, to the very verge of the fathomless pit of death, with all his recollections awake, and his perceptions keenly and vividly alive, without previous illness to subdue the tone of the mind as to dull its apprehensions—then, and then only, the deathbed is truly terrible.

Oh, what a contrast did O'Connor afford as he lay in all the abject helplessness of undisguised terror upon his deathbed, to the proud composure with which he had taken the field that morning. I had always before thought of death as of a quiet sleep stealing gradually upon exhausted nature, made welcome by suffering, or, at least, softened by resignation; I had never before stood by the side of one upon whom the hand of death had been thus suddenly laid; I had never seen the tyrant arrayed in his terror till then.

Never before or since have I seen horror so intensely depicted. It seemed actually as if O'Connor's mind had been unsettled by the shock; the few words he uttered were marked with all the incoherence of distraction; but it was not words that marked his despair most strongly, the appalling and heart-sickening groans that came from the terror-stricken and dying man must haunt me while I live; the expression, too, of hopeless, imploring agony with which he turned his eyes from object to object, I can never forget. At length, appearing suddenly to recollect himself, he said, with startling alertness, but in a voice so altered that I scarce could recognise the tones:

'Purcell, Purcell, go and tell my poor mother; she must know all, and then, quick, quick, quick, call your uncle, bring him here; I must have a chance.' He made a violent but fruitless effort to rise, and after a slight pause continued, with deep and urgent solemnity:'Doctor, how long shall I live? Don't flatter me. Compliments at a deathbed are out of place; doctor, for God's sake, as you would not have my soul perish with my body, do not mock a dying man; have I an hour to live?'

'Certainly,' replied the surgeon; 'if you will but endeavour to keep yourself tranquil; otherwise I cannot answer for a moment.'

'Well, doctor,' said the patient, 'I will obey you; now, Purcell, my first and dearest friend, will you inform my poor mother of—of what you see, and return with your uncle; I know you will.'

I took the dear fellow's hand and kissed it, it was the only answer I could give, and left the room. I asked the first female servant I chanced to meet, if her mistress were yet up, and was answered in the affirmative. Without giving myself time to hesitate, I requested her to lead me to her lady's room, which she accordingly did; she entered first, I supposed to announce my name, and I followed closely; the poor mother said something, and held out her hands to welcome me; I strove for words; I could not speak, but nature found expression; I threw myself at her feet and covered her hands with kisses and tears. My manner was enough; with a quickness almost preternatural she understood it all; she simply said the words: 'O'Connor is killed;' she uttered no more.

How I left the room I know not; I rode madly to my uncle's residence, and brought him back with me—all the rest is a blank. I remember standing by O'Connor's bedside, and kissing the cold pallid forehead again and again; I remember the pale serenity of the beautiful features; I remember that I looked upon the dead face of my friend, and I remember no more.

For many months I lay writhing and raving in the frenzy of brain fever; a hundred times I stood tottering at the brink of death, and long after my restoration to bodily health was assured, it appeared doubtful whether I should ever be restored to reason. But God dealt very mercifully with me; His mighty hand rescued me from death and from madness when one or other appeared inevitable. As soon as I was permitted pen and ink, I wrote to the bereaved mother in a tone bordering upon frenzy. I accused myself of having made her childless; I called myself a murderer; I believed myself accursed; I could not find terms strong enough to express my abhorrence of my own conduct. But, oh! what an answer I received, so mild, so sweet, from the desolate, childless mother! its words spoke all that is beautiful in Christianity—it was forgiveness—it was resignation. I am convinced that to that letter, operating as it did upon a mind already predisposed, is owing my final determination to devote myself to that profession in which, for more than half a century, I have been a humble minister.

Years roll away, and we count them not as they pass, but their influence is not the less certain that it is silent; the deepest wounds are gradually healed, the keenest griefs are mitigated, and we, in character, feelings, tastes, and pursuits, become such altered beings, that but for some few indelible marks which past events must leave behind them, which time may soften, but can never efface; our very identity would be dubious. Who has not felt all this at one time or other? Who has not mournfully felt it? This trite, but natural train of reflection filled my mind as I approached the domain of Castle Connor some ten years after the occurrence of the events above narrated.

Everything looked the same as when I had left it; the old trees stood as graceful and as grand as ever; no plough had violated the soft green sward; no utilitarian hand had constrained the wanderings of the clear and sportive stream, or disturbed the lichen-covered rocks through which it gushed, or the wild coppice that over-shadowed its sequestered nooks—but the eye that looked upon these things was altered, and memory was busy with other days, shrouding in sadness every beauty that met my sight.

As I approached the castle my emotions became so acutely painful that I had almost returned the way I came, without accomplishing the purpose for which I had gone thus far; and nothing but the conviction that my having been in the neighbourhood of Castle Connor without visiting its desolate mistress would render me justly liable to the severest censure, could overcome my reluctance to encountering the heavy task which was before me. I recognised the old servant who opened the door, but he did not know me. I was completely changed; suffering of body and mind had altered me in feature and in bearing, as much as in character. I asked the man whether his mistress ever saw visitors. He answered:

'But seldom; perhaps, however, if she knew that an old friend wished to see her for a few minutes, she would gratify him so far.'

At the same time I placed my card in his hand, and requested him to deliver it to his mistress. He returned in a few moments, saying that his lady would be happy to see me in the parlour, and I accordingly followed him to the door, which he opened. I entered the room, and was in a moment at the side of my early friend and benefactress. I was too much agitated to speak; I could only hold the hands which she gave me, while, spite of every effort, the tears flowed fast and bitterly.

'It was kind, very, very kind of you to come to see me,' she said, with far more composure than I could have commanded; 'I see it is very painful to you.'

I endeavoured to compose myself, and for a little time we remained silent; she was the first to speak:

'You will be surprised, Mr. Purcell, when you observe the calmness with which I can speak of him who was dearest to me, who is gone; but my thoughts are always with him, and the recollections of his love'—her voice faltered a little—'and the hope of meeting him hereafter enables me to bear existence.'

I said I know not what; something about resignation, I believe.

'I hope I am resigned; God made me more: so,' she said. 'Oh, Mr. Purcell, I have often thought I loved my lost child TOO well. It was natural—he was my only child—he was——' She could not proceed for a few moments: 'It was very natural that I should love him as I did; but it may have been sinful; I have often thought so. I doated upon him—I idolised him—I thought too little of other holier affections; and God may have taken him from me, only to teach me, by this severe lesson, that I owed to heaven a larger share of my heart than to anything earthly. I cannot think of him now without more solemn feelings than if he were with me. There is something holy in our thoughts of the dead; I feel it so.'

After a pause, she continued—'Mr. Purcell, do you remember his features well? they were very beautiful.' I assured her that I did. 'Then you can tell me if you think this a faithful likeness.' She took from a drawer a case in which lay a miniature. I took it reverently from her hands; it was indeed very like—touchingly like. I told her so; and she seemed gratified.

As the evening was wearing fast, and I had far to go, I hastened to terminate my visit, as I had intended, by placing in her hand a letter from her son to me, written during his sojourn upon the Continent. I requested her to keep it; it was one in which he spoke much of her, and in terms of the tenderest affection. As she read its contents the heavy tears gathered in her eyes, and fell, one by one, upon the page; she wiped them away, but they still flowed fast and silently. It was in vain that she tried to read it; her eyes were filled with tears: so she folded the letter, and placed it in her bosom. I rose to depart, and she also rose.

'I will not ask you to delay your departure,' said she; 'your visit here must have been a painful one to you. I cannot find words to thank you for the letter as I would wish, or for all your kindness. It has given me a pleasure greater than I thought could have fallen to the lot of a creature so very desolate as I am; may God bless you for it!' And thus we parted; I never saw Castle Connor or its solitary inmate more.

# The Phantom Fourth

They were three.

It was in the cheap night-service train from Paris to Calais that I first met them.

Railways, as a rule, are among the many things which they do *not* order better in France, and the French Northern line is one of the worst managed in the world, barring none, not even the Italian *vie ferrate*. I make it a rule, therefore, to punish the directors of, and the shareholders in, that undertaking to the utmost within my limited ability, by spending as little money on their line as I can help.

It was, then, in a third-class compartment of the train that I met the three.

Three as hearty, jolly-looking Saxon faces, with stalwart frames to match, as one would be likely to meet in an hour's walk from the Regent's Park to the Mansion House.

One of the three was dark, the other two were fair. The dark one was the senior of the party. He wore an incipient full beard, evidently in process of training, with a considerable amount of grizzle in it.

The face of one of his companions was graced with a magnificent flowing beard. The third of the party, a fair-haired youth of some twenty-three or four summers, showed a scrupulously smooth-shaven face.

They looked all three much flushed and slightly excited, and, I must say, they turned out the most boisterous set of fellows I ever met.

They were clearly gentlemen, however, and men of education, with considerable linguistic acquirements; for they chatted and sang, and declaimed and "did orations" all the way from Paris to Calais, in a slightly bewildering variety of tongues.

Their jollity had, perhaps, just a little over-tinge of the slap-bang jolly-dog style in it; but there was so much heartiness and good-nature in all they said and in all they did, that it was quite impossible for any of the other occupants of the carriage to vote them a nuisance; and even the sourest of the officials, whom they chaffed most unmercifully and unremittingly at every station on the line, took their punishment with a shrug and a grin. The only person, indeed, who rose against them in indignant protestation was the head-waiter at the Calais station refreshment-room, to whom they would persist in propounding puzzling problems, such as, for instance, "If you charge two shillings for one-and-a-half-ounce slice of breast of veal, how many fools will it take to buy the joint off you?"—and what *he* got by the attempt to stop their chaff was a caution to any other sinner who might have felt similarly inclined.

As for me, I could only give half my sense of hearing to their utterings, the other half being put under strict sequester at the time by my friend O'Kweene, the great Irish philosopher, who was delivering to me, for my own special behoof and benefit, a brilliant, albeit somewhat abstruse, dissertation on the "visible and palpable outward manifestations of the inner consciousness of the soul in a trance;" which occupied all the time from Paris to Calais, full eight hours, and which, to judge from my feelings at the time, would certainly afford matter for three heavy volumes of reading in bed, in cases of inveterate sleeplessness—a hint to enterprising publishers.

My friend O'Kweene, who intended to stay a few days at Calais, took leave of me on the pier, and I went on board the steamer that was to carry us and the mail over to Dover.

Here I found our trio of the railway-car, snugly ensconced under an extemporized awning, artfully constructed with railway-rugs and greatcoats, supported partly against the luggage, and partly upon several oars, purloined from the boats, and turned into tent-poles for the nonce—which made the skipper swear woefully when he found it out sometime after.

The three were even more cheery and boisterous on board than they had been on shore. From what I could make out in the dark, they were discussing the contents of divers bottles of liquor; I counted four dead men dropped quietly overboard by them in the course of the hour and a half we had to wait for the arrival of the mail-train, which was late, as usual on this line.

At last we were off, about half-past two o'clock in the morning. It was a beautiful, clear, moonlit night, so clear, indeed, that we could see the Dover lights almost from Calais harbour. But we had considerably more than a capful of wind, and there was a turgent ground-swell on, which made our boat—double-engined, and as trim and tidy a craft as ever sped across the span from shore to shore—behave rather lively, with sportive indulgence in a brisk game of pitch-and-toss that proved anything but comfortable to most of the passengers.

When we were steaming out of Calais harbour, our three friends, emerging from beneath their tent, struck up in chorus Campbell's noble song, "Ye Mariners of England," finishing up with a stave from "Rule, Britannia!"

But, alas for them! however loudly their throats were shouting forth the sway proverbially held by Albion and her sons over the waves, on this occasion at least the said waves seemed determined upon ruling these particular three Britons with a rod of antimony; for barely a few seconds after the last vibrating echoes of the "Britons never, never, never shall be slaves!" had died away upon the wind, I beheld the three leaning lovingly together, in fast friendship linked, over the rail, conversing in deep ventriguttural accents with the denizens of Neptune's watery realm.

We had one of the quickest passages on record—ninety-three minutes' steaming carried us across from shore to shore. When we were just on the point of landing, I heard the dark senior of the party mutter to his companions, in a hollow whisper and mysterious manner, "He is gone again;" to which the others, the bearded and the smooth-shaven, responded in the same way, with deep sighs of evident relief, "Ay, marry! so he is at last."

This mysterious communication roused my curiosity. Who was the party that was said to be gone at last? Where had he come from? where had he been hiding, that *I* had not seen him? and where was he gone to now? I determined to know; if but the opportunity would offer, to screw, by cunning questioning, the secret out of either of the three.

Fate favoured my design.

For some inscrutable reason, known only to the company's officials, we cheap-trainers were not permitted to proceed on our journey to London along with the mail, but were left to kick our heels for some two hours at the Dover station.

I went into the refreshment-room to look for my party; I had a notion I should find them where the Briton's unswerving and unerring instinct would be most likely to lead them. It turned out that I was right in my conjecture. There they were, seated round a table with huge bowls of steaming tea and monster piles of buttered toast and muffins spread on the festive board before them. Ay, indeed, there they were; but *quantum mutati ab illis!* how strangely changed from the noisy, rollicking set I had known them in the railway-car and on board the steamer, ere yet the demon of sea-sickness had claimed them for his own! How ghastly sober they looked now, to be sure! And how sternly and silently bent upon devoting themselves to the swilling of the Chinese shrub infusion and to the gorging of indigestible muffins. It was quite clear to me that it would have been worse than folly to venture upon addressing them while thus absorbed in absorbing. So I resolved to await a more favourable opening, and went out meanwhile to walk on the platform.

A short time I was left in solitary possession of the promenade; then I became suddenly aware that another traveller was treading the same ground with me—it was the dark elderly leader of the three. I glanced at him as he passed me under one of the lamps. He looked pale and sad. The furrowed lines on his brow bespoke deliberation deep and pondering profound. All the infinite mirth of the preceding few hours had departed from him, leaving him but a wretched wreck of his former reckless self.

"A fine night, sir," I said to break the ice—"for the season of the year," I added by way of a saving clause, to tone down the absoluteness of the assertion.

He looked at me abstractedly, merely re-echoing my own words, "A fine night, sir, for the season of the year."

"Why look ye so sad now, who were erst so jolly?" I bluntly asked, determined to force him into conversation.

"Ay, indeed, why so sad now?" he replied, looking me full in the face; then, suddenly clasping my arm with a spasmodic grip, he continued hurriedly, "I think I had best confide our secret to you. You seem a man of thought. I witnessed and admired the patient attention with which you listened to your friend's abstruse talk in the railway-car. Maybe you can find the solution of a mystery which defies the ponderings of our poor brains- mine and my two friends."

Then he proceeded to pour into my attentive ear this grue- some tale of mystery:

"We three—that is, myself, yon tall bearded Briton," pointing to the glass door of the refreshment-room, "whose name is Jack Hobson, and young Emmanuel Topp, junior partner in a great beer firm, whom you may behold now at his fifth bowl of tea and his seventh muffin—are teetotallers———"

"Teetotallers!" I could not help exclaiming. "Lord bless me! that is certainly about the last thing I should have taken you for, either of you."

"Well," he replied with some slight confusion, "at least, we *were total* teetotallers, though I admit we can now only claim the character of partial abstainers. The fact is, when, about a fort- night ago, we were discussing the plan of our projected visit to the great Paris Exhibition, Topp suggested that while in France we should do as the French do, to which Jack Hobson assented, remarking that the French knew nothing about tea, and that a Frenchman's tea would be sure to prove an Englishman's poi- son. So we resolved to suspend the pledge during our visit to

France.

"It was on the second day after our arrival in Paris. We were dining in a private cabinet at Desire Beaurain's, one of the leading restaurants on the fashionable side of the Montmartre—Italiens Boulevard. Our dinner was what an Irishman might call a most 'illigant' affair. We had sipped several bottles of Sauterne, and tasted a few of Tavel, and we were just topping the entertainment with a solitary bottle of champagne, when I became suddenly aware of the presence of another party in the room—a *fourth man*—who sat him down at our table, and helped himself liberally to our liquor. From what I ascertained afterward from Jack Hobson and Emmanuel Topp, the intruder's presence became revealed to them also, either about the same time or a little later. What was he like? I cannot tell. His figure and face remained indistinct throughout—phantom-like. His features seemed endowed with a strong weird mobility that would defyingly elude the fixing grasp of our eager eyes.

"Now, and to my two companions, he would look marvellously like me; then, to me, he would stalk and rave about in the likeness of Jack Hobson; again, he would seem the counterfeit of Emmanuel Topp; then he would look like all the three of us put together; then like neither of us, nor like anybody else. Oh, sir, it was a woeful thing to be haunted by this phantom apparition. Yet the strangest part of the affair was that neither of us seemed to feel a whit surprised at the dread presence; that we quietly and uncomplainingly let him drink our wine, and actually give orders for more; that we never objected, in fact, to any of his sayings and doings. What seemed also strange was that the waiter, while yet receiving and executing his orders, was evidently pretending to ignore his presence. But then, as I dare say you know as well as I do, French waiters are *such* actors!

"Well, to resume, there he was, this fourth man, seated at our table and feasting at our expense. And the pranks that he would play us—they were truly stupendous. He began his little game by ordering in half-a-dozen of champagne. And when the waiter seemed slightly doubtful and hesitating about executing the order, Topp, forsooth, must put in his oar, and indorse the command, actually pretending that *I*, who am now speaking to you, and who am the very last man in the world likely to dream of such a preposterous thing, had given the order, and that I was a jolly old brick, and the best of boon companions. Surprise at this barefaced assertion kept me mute, and so, of course, the champagne was brought in, and I thought the best thing to do under the circumstances was to have my share of it at least; and so I had—my fair share; but, bless you, it was nothing to what that fourth man drank of it. In fact, the amount of liquor *he* would swill on this and on the many subsequent occasions he intruded his presence upon us, was a caution.

"We paid our little bill without grumbling, though the presence of the fourth man at our table had added rather heavily to the *addition*, as they call bills at French restaurants.

"We sallied forth into the street to get a whiff of fresh air. *He*, the demon, pertinaciously stuck to us; he familiarly linked his arm through mine, and, suggesting coffee as rather a good thing to take after dinner, took us over to the Cafe du Cardinal, where he, however, took none of the Arabian beverage himself (there being only three cups placed for us, as I distinctly saw), but drank an interminable succession of *chasse-cafe*, utterly regardless of the divisional lines of the cognac *carafon*.

"Part of these he would take neat, another portion he would burn over sugar, gloating glaringly over the bluish flame, while gleams of demoniac delight would flit across his ever-changing features. Jack Hobson and Topp, I am sorry to say, joined him with a will in this double-distilled debauch; and when I attempted to remonstrate with them, they brazenly asserted that *I*, who am now speaking to you, who have always, publicly and privately, declared brandy to be the worst of evil spirits, had taken more of it, to my own cheek, as they slangily expressed it, than the two of them together; and the waiter, who had evidently been bribed by them, boldly maintained that *le vieux monsieur*, as he had the impudence to call me, had swallowed *plus de trois carafons de fine*; whereupon the fourth man, stepping up to him, punched his head, which served him right.

"Now you will hardly believe me when I tell you that at that very instant Topp forced me back into my chair, while Jack Hobson pinioned my arms from behind, and the waiter had the unblushing effrontery to stamp and rave at me like a maniac, demanding satisfaction or compensation at my hands for the unprovoked assault committed upon him by *me, coram populo*!- by *me*, who, I beg to assure you, am the most peaceable man living, and am actually famed for the mildness of my disposition and the sweetness and suavity of my temper. And, would you believe it? everybody present, waiters and guests, and my own two bosom-friends, joined in the conspiracy against me, and I actually had to give the wretch of a waiter ten *francs* as a plaster for his broken pate, and a salve for his wounded honour! Where was the real culprit all this time, you ask me—the fourth man? Why, he quietly stood by grinning, and they all and every one of them pretended not to see him, though Topp and Jack Hobson next morning confessed to me that they certainly had an indistinct consciousness of the presence throughout of this miserable intruder.

"How we finished that night I remember not; nor could Jack Hobson or Emmanuel Topp. All we could conscientiously stand by, if we were questioned, is that we awoke next morning—the three of us—with some slight swimming in our heads, and a hazy recollection of a gorgeous dream of brilliant lights and sounds of music and revelry, and bright visions of groves and grottoes, and dancing *houris* (or hussies, as moral Jack Hobson calls the poor things), and a hot supper at a certain place in the Passage des Princes, of which I think the name is Peter's.

"I will not tire your courteous patience by a detailed narrative of our experiences day after day, during our fortnight's stay in Paris. Suffice it to tell you that from that time forward to yesterday, when we left, the *fourth man*, as we, by mutual consent, agreed to call the phantom apparition, came in regularly to our dinner; with the dessert or a little after; that he would constantly suggest a fresh supply of Cote St. Jacques, Moulin-a-Vent,

Beaune, Chambertin, Roederer Carte Blanche, and a variety of other, generally rather more than less expensive, wines—and that he somehow would manage to make us have them, too.

"Then he would sally forth with us to the cafe, where he would indulge in irritating chaff of the waiters, and in slighting comments upon the great French nation in general, and the Parisians in particular, and upon their institutions and manners and customs.

"He would insist upon singing the *Marseillaise*; he would speak disparagingly of the Emperor, whom he would irreverently call Lambert; he would pass cutting and unsavoury remarks upon the glorious system of the night-carts; he would call down the judgment of Heaven upon the devoted head of poor Mr. Haussmann; he would go up to some unhappy *sergent-de-ville*, who might, however unwittingly, excite his ire, and tell him a bit of his mind in English, with sarcastic allusions to his cocket-hat and his toasting-fork, and polite inquiries after the health of *ce cher* Monsieur Lambert, or the whereabouts of *cet excellent* Monsieur Godinot.

"The worst of the matter was that I suppose for the reason that man is an imitative animal, a sort of [Greek: *pithekos myoros*], or Monboddian monkey minus the tail—my two companions were, somehow, always sure to join the wretch in his evil behaviour, and to go on just as bad as he did. No wonder, then, that we got into no end of rows, and it is a marvel to me now, however we have managed to get off with a whole skin to our bodies.

"He would insist upon taking us to Mabille, the Closerie des Lilas, and the Chateaurouge, where he would indulge in the maddest pranks and antics, and somehow lead us to join in the wildest dances, and make us lift our legs as high as the highest lifter among the *habitues*, male or female.

"One night, at about half-past two in the morning (*Hibernice*), he had the cool assurance to drag us along with him to the then closed entrance to the Passage des Princes, where he frantically shook the gate, and insisted to the frightened concierge, who came running up in his night-shirt, that Peter's must and ought to be open still, as *we* had not had our supper yet; and Topp and Jack Hobson, forsooth, must join in the row. I have no distinct recollection of whether it was our phantom guest or either of my companions that madly strove to detain the hastily retreating form of the concierge by a desperate clutch at the tail of his shirt; I only remember that the garment gave way in the struggle, and that the unhappy functionary was reduced nearly altogether to the primitive buff costume of the father of man in Paradise ere he had put his teeth into that unlucky apple of which, the pips keep so inconveniently sticking in poor humanity's gizzard to the present day.

"And what I remember also to my cost is, that the *sergent-de-ville*, whom the bereaved man's shouts of distress brought to the scene, fastened upon *me*, the most inoffensive of mortals, for a compensation fine of twenty *francs*, as if *I* had been the culprit. And deuced glad we were, I assure you, to get off without more serious damage to our pocket and reputation than this, and a copious volley of *sacres ivrognes Anglais*, fired at us by the wretched concierge and his friend of the police, who, I am quite sure, went halves with him in the compensation. Ah! they are a lawless set, these French.

"On another occasion we three went to the Exhibition, where we visited one of our colonial departments, in company with several English friends, and some French gentlemen appointed on the wine jury. We went to taste a few samples of colonial wines. *He* was not with us *then*. Barely, however, had we uncorked a poor dozen bottles, which turned out rather good for colonial, though a little raw and slightly uneducated, when *who* should stalk in but our fourth man, as jaunty and unconcerned as ever. Well, *he* fell to tasting, and he soon grew eloquent in praise of the colonial juice, which he declared would, in another twenty years' time, be fit to compete successfully with the best French vintages.

"Of course, the French gentlemen with us could not stand *this*; they spoke slightingly of the British colonial, and one of them even went so far as to call it rotgut. I cannot say whether it was the spirit of the uncompromising opinion thus pronounced, or the coarsely indelicate way in which the judgment of our French friend was expressed, that riled our phantom guest—enough, it brought him down in full force upon the offender and his countrymen, with most fluent French vituperation and an unconscionable amount of bad jokes and worse puns, finishing up with a general address to them as members of the *disgusting* jury, instead of jury of *degustation*.

"Now, this I should not have minded so much; for, I must confess, I felt rather nettled at the national conceit and prejudice of these French. But the wretch, in the impetuous utterance of his invective, must somehow—though I was not aware of it at the time—have mimicked my gestures and imitated the very tones and accent of my voice so closely as to deceive even some of my English companions: or how else to account for the fact of their calling me a noisy brawler and a pestilent nuisance? *me*, the gentlest and mildest-spoken of mortals!

"Before our departure from London we had calculated our probable expenses on a most liberal scale, and we had made comfortable provision accordingly for a few weeks' stay in Paris. But with the additional heavy burden of the franking of so copious an imbiber as our fourth man thus unexpectedly thrown on our shoulders, it was no great wonder that we should find our resources go much faster than we had anticipated; so we had already been forcedly led to bethink ourselves of shortening our intended stay in the French capital when a fresh exploit of the phantom fourth, climaxing all his past misdeeds, brought matters to a crisis.

"It was the day before yesterday, the 4th of September. We had been dining at Marigny, and dancing at Mabille. Our eccentric guest had come in, as usual, with the champagne, and had of course, after dinner, taken us over to the enchanted gardens. We were all very jolly. *He* suggested supper at the Cascades, in the Bois de Boulogne. We chartered a *fiacre* to take us there and back. We supped rather copiously. *He* somehow made our coachman drunk, and took upon himself to drive us home.

Need I tell you that he upset us in the Avenue de l'Imperatrice, and that we had to walk it, and pretty fast too? It was a mercy there were no bones broken.

"Well, as we were walking along, just barely recovering from the shock of the accident, he suddenly took some new whim into his confounded noddle. Nothing would do for him but he must drag us along with him to the great entrance of the Elysee Napoleon (which erst was, and maybe is soon likely to be once more, the Elysee Bourbon), where he had the brazen impudence to claim admittance, as the Emperor, he pretended, had been graciously pleased to offer us the splendid hospitality of that renowned mansion. What further happened here, neither I nor either of my friends can tell.

"Our recollections from this period till next morning are doubtful and indistinct. All we can state for certain is, that yesterday morning we awoke, the three of us, in a most wretched state, in a strange, nasty place. We learn soon after from a gentleman in a cocked hat, who came to visit us on business, that the imperial hospitality which we had claimed last night had indeed been extended to us—only in the *violon*, instead of the Elysee. Our phantom guest was gone: he would always, somehow sneak away in the morning, when there was nothing left for him to drink—the guzzling villain!

"The gentleman in the cocked-hat pressingly invited us to pay a visit to the *Commissaire du Quartier*. That formidable functionary received us with the customary French-polished veneer of urbanity which, as a rule, constitutes the *suaviter in modo* of the higher class of Gallic officials. He read us a severe lecture, however, upon the alleged impropriety of our conduct; and when I ventured to protest that it was not to us the blame ought to be imputed, but to the *quatrieme*, he mistook my meaning, and, ere I could explain myself, he cut me short with a polite remark that the French used the cardinal instead of the ordinal numbers in stating the days of the month, with the exception of the first, and that he had had too much trouble with our countrymen (he took us for Yankees!) on the 4th of July, to be disposed to look with an over-lenient eye upon the vagaries we had chosen to commit on the 4th of September, which he supposed was another great national day with us.

"He would, however, let us off this time with a simple reprimand, upon payment of one hundred *francs*, compensation for damage done to the coach—drunken cabby having turned up, of course, to testify against us. Well, we paid the money, and handed the worthy magistrate twenty *francs* besides, for the benefit of the poor, by way of acknowledgment for the imperial hospitality we had enjoyed. We were then allowed to depart in peace.

"Now, you'll hardly believe it, I dare say, but it is the truth notwithstanding, that we three, who have been fast friends for years, actually began to quarrel among ourselves now, mutually imputing to one another the blame of all our misadventures and misfortunes since our arrival in Paris, while yet we clearly knew and felt, each and every of us, that it was all the doings of that phantom fourth.

"One thing, however, we all agreed to do—to leave Paris by the first train.

"To fortify ourselves for the coming journey, we went to indulge in the luxury of a farewell breakfast at Desire Beaurain's. Of course we emptied a few bottles to our reconciliation. I do not exactly remember how many, but this I *do* remember, that our irrepressible *incubus* walked in again, and took his place in the midst of us rather sooner even than he had been wont to do; and he never left us from that time to the moment of our landing at Dover harbour, when he took his, I hope and trust final, departure with a ghastly grin.

"I dare say you must have thought us a most noisy and obstreperous lot: well, with my hand on my heart, I can assure you, on my conscience, that a quieter and milder set of fellows than us three you are not likely to find on this or the other side the Channel. But for that mysterious phantom fourth——"

Here the whistle sounded, and the guard came up to us with a hurried, "Now then, gents, take your seats, please; train is off in half a minnit!"

"What can have become of Topp and Jack Hobson?" muttered my new friend, looking around him with eager scrutiny. "I should not wonder if they were still refreshing." And he started off in the direction of the refreshment-room.

I took my seat. Immediately after the train whirled off. I cannot say whether the three were left behind; all I know is that I did not see them get out at London Bridge.

Remembering, however, that the appalling secret of the supernatural visitation which had thus harassed my three fellow-travellers had been confided to me under the impression that I might be likely to find a solution of the mystery, I have ever since deeply pondered thereon.

Shallow thinkers, and sneerers uncharitably given, may, from a consideration of the times, places, and circumstances at and under which the abnormal phenomena here recited were stated to have been observed, be led to attribute them simply to the promptings and imaginings of brains overheated by excessive indulgence in spirituous liquors. But I, striving to be mindful always of the great scriptural injunction to judge not, lest we be judged, and opportunely remembering my friend O'Kweene's learned dissertation above alluded to, feel disposed to pronounce the apparition of the phantom of the fourth man, and all the sayings, doings, and demeanings of the same, to have been simply so many visible and palpable outward manifestations of the inner consciousness of the souls of the three, and more notably of that of the elderly senior of the party, in a succession of *vino*-alcoholic trances.

My friend O'Kweene is, of course, welcome to such credit as may attach to this attempted solution of mine.

# 'The Quare Gander'

As I rode at a slow walk, one soft autumn evening, from the once noted and noticeable town of Emly, now a squalid village, towards the no less remarkable town of Tipperary, I fell into a meditative mood.

My eye wandered over a glorious landscape; a broad sea of corn-fields, that might have gladdened even a golden age, was waving before me; groups of little cabins, with their poplars, osiers, and light mountain ashes, clustered shelteringly around them, were scattered over the plain; the thin blue smoke arose floating through their boughs in the still evening air. And far away with all their broad lights and shades, softened with the haze of approaching twilight, stood the bold wild Galties.

As I gazed on this scene, whose richness was deepened by the melancholy glow of the setting sun, the tears rose to my eyes, and I said:

'Alas, my country! what a mournful beauty is thine. Dressed in loveliness and laughter, there is mortal decay at thy heart: sorrow, sin, and shame have mingled thy cup of misery. Strange rulers have bruised thee, and laughed thee to scorn, and they have made all thy sweetness bitter. Thy shames and sins are the austere fruits of thy miseries, and thy miseries have been poured out upon thee by foreign hands. Alas, my stricken country! clothed with this most pity-moving smile, with this most unutterably mournful loveliness, thou sore-grieved, thou desperately-beloved! Is there for thee, my country, a resurrection?'

I know not how long I might have continued to rhapsodize

in this strain, had not my wandering thoughts been suddenly recalled to my own immediate neighbourhood by the monotonous clatter of a horse's hoofs upon the road, evidently moving, at that peculiar pace which is neither a walk nor a trot, and yet partakes of both, so much in vogue among the southern farmers.

In a moment my pursuer was up with me, and checking his steed into a walk he saluted me with much respect. The cavalier was a light-built fellow, with good-humoured sun-burnt features, a shrewd and lively black eye, and a head covered with a crop of close curly black hair, and surmounted with a turf-coloured *caubeen*, in the pack-thread band of which was stuck a short pipe, which had evidently seen much service.

My companion was a dealer in all kinds of local lore, and soon took occasion to let me see that he was so.

After two or three short stories, in which the scandalous and supernatural were happily blended, we happened to arrive at a narrow road or *bohreen* leading to a snug-looking farmhouse.

'That's a comfortable bit iv a farm,' observed my comrade, pointing towards the dwelling with his thumb; 'a shnug spot, and belongs to the Mooneys this long time. 'Tis a noted place for what happened wid the famous gandher there in former times.'

'And what was that?' inquired I.

'What was it happened wid the gandher!' ejaculated my companion in a tone of indignant surprise; 'the gandher iv Ballymacrucker, the gandher! Your raverance must be a stranger in these parts. Sure every fool knows all about the gandher, and Terence Mooney, that was, rest his sowl. Begorra, 'tis surprisin' to me how in the world you didn't hear iv the gandher; and maybe it's funnin me ye are, your raverance.'

I assured him to the contrary, and conjured him to narrate to me the facts, an unacquaintance with which was sufficient it appeared to stamp me as an ignoramus of the first magnitude.

It did not require much entreaty to induce my communicative friend to relate the circumstance, in nearly the following words:

'Terence Mooney was an honest boy and well to do; an' he rinted the biggest farm on this side iv the Galties; an' bein' mighty cute an' a sevare worker, it was small wonder he turned a good penny every harvest. But unluckily he was blessed with an ilegant large family iv daughters, an' iv coorse his heart was allamost bruck, striving to make up fortunes for the whole of them. An' there wasn't a conthrivance iv any soart or description for makin' money out iv the farm, but he was up to.

'Well, among the other ways he had iv gettin' up in the world, he always kep a power iv turkeys, and all soarts iv poultrey; an' he was out iv all rason partial to geese—an' small blame to him for that same—for twice't a year you can pluck them as bare as my hand—an' get a fine price for the feathers, an' plenty of rale sizable eggs—an' when they are too ould to lay any more, you can kill them, an' sell them to the gintlemen for goslings, d'ye see, let alone that a goose is the most manly bird that is out.

'Well, it happened in the coorse iv time that one ould gandher tuck a wondherful likin' to Terence, an' divil a place he could go serenadin' about the farm, or lookin' afther the men, but the gandher id be at his heels, an' rubbin' himself agin his legs, an' lookin' up in his face jist like any other Christian id do; an' begorra, the likes iv it was never seen—Terence Mooney an' the gandher wor so great.

'An' at last the bird was so engagin' that Terence would not allow it to be plucked any more, an' kep it from that time out for love an' affection—just all as one like one iv his childer.

'But happiness in perfection never lasts long, an' the neighbours begin'd to suspect the nathur an' intentions iv the gandher, an' some iv them said it was the divil, an' more iv them that it was a fairy.

'Well, Terence could not but hear something of what was sayin', an' you may be sure he was not altogether asy in his mind about it, an' from one day to another he was gettin' more ancomfortable in himself, until he determined to sind for Jer Garvan, the fairy docthor in Garryowen, an' it's he was the ilegant hand at the business, an' divil a sperit id say a crass word to

520

him, no more nor a priest. An' moreover he was very great wid ould Terence Mooney—this man's father that' was.

'So without more about it he was sint for, an' sure enough the divil a long he was about it, for he kem back that very evenin' along wid the boy that was sint for him, an' as soon as he was there, an' tuck his supper, an' was done talkin' for a while, he begined of coorse to look into the gandher.

'Well, he turned it this away an' that away, to the right an' to the left, an' straight-ways an' upside-down, an' when he was tired handlin' it, says he to Terence Mooney:

'"Terence," says he, "you must remove the bird into the next room," says he, "an' put a petticoat," says he, "or anny other con-vaynience round his head," says he.

'"An' why so?" says Terence.

'"Becase," says Jer, says he.

'"Becase what?" says Terence.

'"Becase," says Jer, "if it isn't done you'll never be asy again," says he, "or pusilanimous in your mind," says he; "so ax no more questions, but do my biddin'," says he.

'"Well," says Terence, "have your own way," says he.

'An' wid that he tuck the ould gandher, an' giv' it to one iv the gossoons.

'"An' take care," says he, "don't smother the crathur," says he.

'Well, as soon as the bird was gone, says Jer Garvan says he:

'"Do you know what that ould gandher IS, Terence Mooney?"

'"Divil a taste," says Terence.

'"Well then," says Jer, "the gandher is your own father," says he.

'"It's jokin' you are," says Terence, turnin' mighty pale; "how can an ould gandher be my father?" says he.

'"I'm not funnin' you at all," says Jer; "it's thrue what I tell you, it's your father's wandhrin' sowl," says he, "that's naturally tuck pissession iv the ould gandher's body," says he. "I know him many ways, and I wondher," says he, "you do not know the cock iv his eye yourself," says he.

"'Oh blur an' ages!" says Terence, "what the divil will I ever do at all at all," says he; "it's all over wid me, for I plucked him twelve times at the laste," says he.

"'That can't be helped now," says Jer; "it was a sevare act surely," says he, "but it's too late to lamint for it now," says he; "the only way to prevint what's past," says he, "is to put a stop to it before it happens," says he.

"'Thrue for you," says Terence, "but how the divil did you come to the knowledge iv my father's sowl," says he, "bein' in the owld gandher," says he.

"'If I tould you," says Jer, "you would not undherstand me," says he, "without book-larnin' an' gasthronomy," says he; "so ax me no questions," says he, "an' I'll tell you no lies. But blieve me in this much," says he, "it's your father that's in it," says he; "an' if I don't make him spake tomorrow mornin'," says he, "I'll give you lave to call me a fool," says he.

"'Say no more," says Terence, "that settles the business," says he; "an' oh! blur and ages is it not a quare thing," says he, "for a dacent respictable man," says he, "to be walkin' about the counthry in the shape iv an ould gandher," says he; "and oh, murdher, murdher! is not it often I plucked him," says he, "an' tundher and ouns might not I have ate him," says he; and wid that he fell into a could parspiration, savin' your prisince, an was on the pint iv faintin' wid the bare notions iv it.

'Well, whin he was come to himself agin, says Jerry to him quite an' asy:

"'Terence," says he, "don't be aggravatin' yourself," says he; "for I have a plan composed that 'ill make him spake out," says he, "an' tell what it is in the world he's wantin'," says he; "an' mind an' don't be comin' in wid your gosther, an' to say agin anything I tell you," says he, "but jist purtind, as soon as the bird is brought back," says he, "how that we're goin' to sind him to-morrow mornin' to market," says he. "An' if he don't spake to-night," says he, "or gother himself out iv the place," says he, "put him into the hamper airly, and sind him in the cart," says he, "straight to Tipperary, to be sould for ating," says he, "along wid the two gossoons," says he, "an' my name isn't Jer Garvan," says he, "if he doesn't spake out before he's half-way," says he. "An' mind," says he, "as soon as iver he says the first word," says he, "that very minute bring him aff to Father Crotty," says he; "an' if his raverince doesn't make him ratire," says he, "like the rest iv his parishioners, glory be to God," says he, "into the siclusion iv the flames iv purgathory," says he, "there's no vartue in my charums," says he.

'Well, wid that the ould gandher was let into the room agin, an' they all bigined to talk iv sindin' him the nixt mornin' to be sould for roastin' in Tipperary, jist as if it was a thing andoubtingly settled. But divil a notice the gandher tuck, no more nor if they wor spaking iv the Lord-Liftinant; an' Terence desired the boys to get ready the kish for the poulthry, an' to "settle it out wid hay soft an' shnug," says he, "for it's the last jauntin' the poor ould gandher 'ill get in this world," says he.

'Well, as the night was gettin' late, Terence was growin' mighty sorrowful an' down-hearted in himself entirely wid the notions iv what was goin' to happen. An' as soon as the wife an' the crathurs war fairly in bed, he brought out some illigint potteen, an' himself an' Jer Garvan sot down to it; an' begorra, the more anasy Terence got, the more he dhrank, and himself and Jer Garvan finished a quart betune them. It wasn't an imparial though, an' more's the pity, for them wasn't anvinted antil short since; but divil a much matther it signifies any longer if a pint could hould two quarts, let alone what it does, sinst Father Mathew—the Lord purloin his raverence—begin'd to give the pledge, an' wid the blessin' iv timperance to deginerate Ireland.

'An' begorra, I have the medle myself; an' it's proud I am iv that same, for abstamiousness is a fine thing, although it's mighty dhry.

'Well, whin Terence finished his pint, he thought he might as well stop; "for enough is as good as a faste," says he; "an' I pity the vagabond," says he, "that is not able to conthroul his licquor," says he, "an' to keep constantly inside iv a pint measure," said he; an' wid that he wished Jer Garvan a goodnight, an' walked out iv the room.

'But he wint out the wrong door, bein' a thrifle hearty in himself, an' not rightly knowin' whether he was standin' on his head or his heels, or both iv them at the same time, an' in place iv gettin' into bed, where did he thrun himself but into the poulthry hamper, that the boys had settled out ready for the gandher in the mornin'. An' sure enough he sunk down soft an' complate through the hay to the bottom; an' wid the turnin' and roulin' about in the night, the divil a bit iv him but was covered up as shnug as a lumper in a pittaty furrow before mornin'.

'So wid the first light, up gets the two boys, that war to take the sperit, as they consaved, to Tipperary; an' they cotched the ould gandher, an' put him in the hamper, and clapped a good wisp iv hay an' the top iv him, and tied it down sthrong wid a bit iv a coard, and med the sign iv the crass over him, in dhread iv any harum, an' put the hamper up an the car, wontherin' all the while what in the world was makin' the ould burd so surprisin' heavy.

'Well, they wint along quite anasy towards Tipperary, wishin' every minute that some iv the neighbours bound the same way id happen to fall in with them, for they didn't half like the notions iv havin' no company but the bewitched gandher, an' small blame to them for that same.

'But although they wor shaking in their skhins in dhread iv the ould bird beginnin' to convarse them every minute, they did not let an' to one another, bud kep singin' an' whistlin' like mad, to keep the dread out iv their hearts.

'Well, afther they war on the road betther nor half an hour, they kem to the bad bit close by Father Crotty's, an' there was one divil of a rut three feet deep at the laste; an' the car got sich a wondherful chuck goin' through it, that it wakened Terence widin in the basket.

'"Bad luck to ye," says he, "my bones is bruck wid yer thricks; what the divil are ye doin' wid me?"

'"Did ye hear anything quare, Thady?" says the boy that was next to the car, turnin' as white as the top iv a musharoon; "did ye hear anything quare soundin' out iv the hamper?" says he.

"'No, nor you,' says Thady, turnin' as pale as himself, "it's the ould gandher that's gruntin' wid the shakin' he's gettin'," says he.

"'Where the divil have ye put me into," says Terence inside, "bad luck to your sowls," says he, "let me out, or I'll be smothered this minute," says he.

"'There's no use in purtending," says the boy, "the gandher's spakin', glory be to God," says he.

"'Let me out, you murdherers," says Terence.

"'In the name iv the blessed Vargin," says Thady, "an' iv all the holy saints, hould yer tongue, you unnatheral gandher," says he.

"'Who's that, that dar to call me nicknames?" says Terence inside, roaring wid the fair passion, "let me out, you blasphamious infiddles," says he, "or by this crass I'll stretch ye," says he.

"'In the name iv all the blessed saints in heaven," says Thady, "who the divil are ye?"

"'Who the divil would I be, but Terence Mooney," says he. "It's myself that's in it, you unmerciful bliggards," says he, "let me out, or by the holy, I'll get out in spite iv yes," says he, "an' by jaburs, I'll wallop yes in arnest," says he.

"'It's ould Terence, sure enough," says Thady, "isn't it cute the fairy docthor found him out," says he.

"'I'm an the pint iv snuffication," says Terence, "let me out, I tell you, an' wait till I get at ye," says he, "for begorra, the divil a bone in your body but I'll powdher," says he.

'An' wid that, he biginned kickin' and flingin' inside in the hamper, and dhrivin his legs agin the sides iv it, that it was a wonder he did not knock it to pieces.

'Well, as soon as the boys seen that, they skelped the ould horse into a gallop as hard as he could peg towards the priest's house, through the ruts, an' over the stones; an' you'd see the hamper fairly flyin' three feet up in the air with the joultin'; glory be to God.

'So it was small wondher, by the time they got to his Raverince's door, the breath was fairly knocked out of poor Terence, so that he was lyin' speechless in the bottom iv the hamper.

'Well, whin his Raverince kem down, they up an' they tould him all that happened, an' how they put the gandher into the hamper, an' how he beginned to spake, an' how he confissed that he was ould Terence Mooney; an' they axed his honour to advise them how to get rid iv the spirit for good an' all.

'So says his Raverince, says he:

'"I'll take my booke," says he, "an' I'll read some rale sthrong holy bits out iv it," says he, "an' do you get a rope and put it round the hamper," says he, "an' let it swing over the runnin' wather at the bridge," says he, "an' it's no matther if I don't make the spirit come out iv it," says he.

'Well, wid that, the priest got his horse, and tuck his booke in undher his arum, an' the boys follied his Raverince, ladin' the horse down to the bridge, an' divil a word out iv Terence all the way, for he seen it was no use spakin', an' he was afeard if he med any noise they might thrait him to another gallop an finish him intirely.

'Well, as soon as they war all come to the bridge, the boys tuck the rope they had with them, an' med it fast to the top iv the hamper an' swung it fairly over the bridge, lettin' it hang in the air about twelve feet out iv the wather.

'An' his Raverince rode down to the bank of the river, close by, an' beginned to read mighty loud and bould intirely.

'An' when he was goin' on about five minutes, all at onst the bottom iv the hamper kem out, an' down wint Terence, falling splash dash into the water, an' the ould gandher a-top iv him. Down they both went to the bottom, wid a souse you'd hear half a mile off.

'An' before they had time to rise agin, his Raverince, wid the fair astonishment, giv his horse one dig iv the spurs, an' before he knew where he was, in he went, horse an' all, a-top iv them, an' down to the bottom.

'Up they all kem agin together, gaspin' and puffin', an' off down wid the current wid them, like shot in under the arch iv the bridge till they kem to the shallow wather.

'The ould gandher was the first out, and the priest and Terence kem next, pantin' an' blowin' an' more than half dhrounded, an' his Raverince was so freckened wid the droundin' he got, and wid the sight iv the sperit, as he consaved, that he wasn't the better of it for a month.

'An' as soon as Terence could spake, he swore he'd have the life of the two gossoons; but Father Crotty would not give him his will. An' as soon as he was got quiter, they all endivoured to explain it; but Terence consaved he went raly to bed the night before, and his wife said the same to shilter him from the suspicion for havin' th' dthrop taken. An' his Raverince said it was a mysthery, an' swore if he cotched anyone laughin' at the accident, he'd lay the horsewhip across their shouldhers.

'An' Terence grew fonder an' fonder iv the gandher every day, until at last he died in a wondherful old age, lavin' the gandher afther him an' a large family iv childher.

'An' to this day the farm is rinted by one iv Terence Mooney's lenial and legitimate postariors.'

# The Secret of the Two Plaster Casts

Years before the accession of her Majesty Queen Victoria, and yet at not so remote a date as to be utterly beyond the period to which the reminiscences of our middle-aged readers extend, it happened that two English gentlemen sat at table on a summer's evening, after dinner, quietly sipping their wine and engaged in desultory conversation. They were both men known to fame. One of them was a sculptor whose statues adorned the palaces of princes, and whose chiselled busts were the pride of half the nobility of his nation; the other was no less renowned as an anatomist and surgeon. The age of the anatomist might have been guessed at fifty, but the guess would have erred on the side of youth by at least ten years. That of the sculptor could scarcely be more than five-and-thirty.

A bust of the anatomist, so admirably executed as to present, although in stone, the perfect similitude of life and flesh, stood upon a pedestal opposite to the table at which sat the pair, and at once explained at least one connecting-link of companionship between them. The anatomist was exhibiting for the criticism of his friend a rare gem which he had just drawn from his cabinet: it was a crucifix magnificently carved in ivory, and incased in a setting of pure gold.

"The carving, my dear sir," observed Mr. Fiddyes, the sculptor, "is indeed, as you say, exquisite. The muscles are admirably made out, the flesh well modelled, wonderfully so for the size and material; and yet—by the bye, on this point you must know more than I—the more I think upon the matter, the more I re-

528

gard the artistic conception as utterly false and wrong."

"You speak in a riddle," replied Dr. Carnell; "but pray go on, and explain."

"It is a fancy I first had in my student-days," replied Fiddyes. "Conventionality, not to say a most proper and becoming reverence, prevents people by no means ignorant from considering the point. But once think upon it, and you at least, of all men, must at once perceive how utterly impossible it would be for a victim nailed upon a cross by hands and feet to preserve the position invariably displayed in figures of the Crucifixion. Those who so portray it fail in what should be their most awful and agonizing effect. Think for one moment, and imagine, if you can, what would be the attitude of a man, living or dead, under this frightful torture."

"You startle me," returned the great surgeon, "not only by the truth of your remarks, but by their obviousness. It is strange indeed that such a matter should have so long been overlooked. The more I think upon it the more the bare idea of actual crucifixion seems to horrify me, though heaven knows I am accustomed enough to scenes of suffering. How would you represent such a terrible agony?"

"Indeed I cannot tell," replied the sculptor; "to guess would be almost vain. The fearful strain upon the muscles, their utter helplessness and inactivity, the frightful swellings, the effect of weight upon the racked and tortured sinews, appal me too much even for speculation."

"But this," replied the surgeon, "one might think a matter of importance, not only to art, but, higher still, to religion itself."

"Maybe so," returned the sculptor. "But perhaps the appeal to the senses through a true representation might be too horrible for either the one or the other."

"Still," persisted the surgeon, "I should like—say for curiosity—though I am weak enough to believe even in my own motive as a higher one—to ascertain the effect from actual observation."

"So should I, could it be done, and of course without pain to the object, which, as a condition, seems to present at the outset an impossibility."

"Perhaps not," mused the anatomist; "I think I have a notion. Stay—we may contrive this matter. I will tell you my plan, and it will be strange indeed if we two cannot manage to carry it out."

The discourse here, owing to the rapt attention of both speakers, assumed a low and earnest tone, but had perhaps better be narrated by a relation of the events to which it gave rise. Suffice it to say that the Sovereign was more than once mentioned during its progress, and in a manner which plainly told that the two speakers each possessed sufficient influence to obtain the assistance of royalty, and that such assistance would be required in their scheme.

The shades of evening deepened while the two were still conversing. And leaving this scene, let us cast one hurried glimpse at another taking place contemporaneously.

Between Pimlico and Chelsea, and across a canal of which the bed has since been used for the railway terminating at Victoria Station, there was at the time of which we speak a rude timber footway, long since replaced by a more substantial and convenient erection, but then known as the Wooden Bridge. It was named shortly afterward Cutthroat Bridge, and for this reason.

While Mr. Fiddyes and Dr. Carnell were discoursing over their wine, as we have already seen, one Peter Starke, a drunken Chelsea pensioner, was murdering his wife upon the spot we have last indicated. The coincidence was curious.

★ ★ ★ ★ ★

In those days the punishment of criminals followed closely upon their conviction. The Chelsea pensioner whom we have mentioned was found guilty one Friday and sentenced to die on the following Monday. He was a sad scoundrel, impenitent to the last, glorying in the deeds of slaughter which he had witnessed and acted during the series of campaigns which had ended just previously at Waterloo. He was a tall, well-built fellow enough, of middle age, for his class was not then, as now, composed chiefly of veterans, but comprised many young men, just sufficiently disabled to be unfit for service. Peter Starke, although but slightly wounded, had nearly completed his term of service, and had obtained his pension and presentment to Chelsea Hospital. With his life we have but little to do, save as regards its close, which we shall shortly endeavour to describe far more veraciously, and at some greater length than set forth in the brief account which satisfied the public of his own day, and which, as embodied in the columns of the few journals then appearing, ran thus:

*On Monday last Peter Starke was executed at Newgate for the murder at the Wooden Bridge, Chelsea, with four others for various offences. After he had been hanging only for a few minutes a respite arrived, but although he was promptly cut down, life was pronounced to be extinct. His body was buried within the prison walls.*

Thus far history. But the conciseness of history far more frequently embodies falsehood than truth. Perhaps the following narration may approach more nearly to the facts.

A room within the prison had been, upon that special occasion and by high authority, allotted to the use of Dr. Carnell and Mr. Fiddyes, the famous sculptor, for the purpose of certain investigations connected with art and science. In that room Mr. Fiddyes, while wretched Peter Starke was yet swinging between heaven and earth, was busily engaged in arranging a variety of implements and materials, consisting of a large quantity of plaster-of-Paris, two large pails of water, some tubs, and other necessaries of the moulder's art. The room contained a large deal table, and a wooden cross, not neatly planed and squared at the angles, but of thick, narrow, rudely-sawn oaken plank, fixed by strong, heavy nails. And while Mr. Fiddyes was thus occupied, the executioner entered, bearing upon his shoulders the body of the wretched Peter, which he flung heavily upon the table.

"You are sure he is dead?" asked Mr. Fiddyes.

"Dead as a herring," replied the other. "And yet just as warm and limp as if he had only fainted."

"Then go to work at once," replied the sculptor, as turning his back upon the hangman, he resumed his occupation.

The "work" was soon done. Peter was stripped and nailed upon the timber, which was instantly propped against the wall.

"As fine a one as ever I see," exclaimed the executioner, as he regarded the defunct murderer with an expression of admiration, as if at his own handiwork, in having abruptly demolished such a magnificent animal. "Drops a good bit for'ard, though. Shall I tie him up round the waist, sir?"

"Certainly not," returned the sculptor. "Just rub him well over with this oil, especially his head, and then you can go. Dr. Carnell will settle with you."

"All right, sir."

The fellow did as ordered, and retired without another word; leaving this strange couple, the living and the dead, in that dismal chamber.

Mr. Fiddyes was a man of strong nerve in such matters. He had been too much accustomed to taking posthumous casts to trouble himself with any sentiment of repugnance at his approaching task of taking what is called a "piece-mould" from a body. He emptied a number of bags of the white powdery plaster-of-Paris into one of the larger vessels, poured into it a pail of water, and was carefully stirring up the mass, when a sound of dropping arrested his ear.

*Drip, drip.*

"There's something leaking," he muttered, as he took a second pail, and emptying it, again stirred the composition.

*Drip, drip, drip.*

"It's strange," he soliloquized, half aloud. "There is no more water, and yet——"

The sound was heard again.

He gazed at the ceiling; there was no sign of damp. He turned his eyes to the body, and something suddenly caused him a violent start. The murderer was bleeding.

The sculptor, spite of his command over himself, turned pale. At that moment the head of Starke moved—clearly moved. It raised itself convulsively for a single moment; its eyes rolled, and it gave vent to a subdued moan of intense agony. Mr. Fiddyes fell fainting on the floor as Dr. Carnell entered. It needed but a glance to tell the doctor what had happened, even had not Peter just then given vent to another low cry. The surgeon's measures were soon taken. Locking the door, he bore a chair to the wall which supported the body of the malefactor. He drew from his pocket a case of glittering instruments, and with one of these, so small and delicate that it scarcely seemed larger than a needle, he rapidly, but dexterously and firmly, touched Peter just at the back of the neck. There was no wound larger than the head of a small pin, and yet the head fell instantly as though the heart had been pierced. The doctor had divided the spinal cord, and Peter Starke was dead indeed.

A few minutes sufficed to recall the sculptor to his senses. He at first gazed wildly upon the still suspended body, so painfully recalled to life by the rough venesection of the hangman and the subsequent friction of anointing his body to prevent the adhesion of the plaster.

"You need not fear now," said Dr. Carnell; "I assure you he is dead."

"But he *was* alive, surely!"

"Only for a moment, and even that scarcely to be called life—mere muscular contraction, my dear sir, mere muscular contraction."

The sculptor resumed his labour. The body was girt at various circumferences with fine twine, to be afterward withdrawn through a thick coating of plaster, so as to separate the various pieces of the mould, which was at last completed; and after this Dr. Carnell skilfully flayed the body, to enable a second mould to be taken of the entire figure, showing every muscle of the outer layer.

The two moulds were thus taken. It is difficult to conceive more ghastly appearances than they presented. For sculptor's work they were utterly useless; for no artist except the most daring of realists would have ventured to indicate the horrors which they presented. Fiddyes refused to receive them. Dr. Carnell, hard and cruel as he was, for kindness' sake, in his profession, was a gentle, genial father of a family of daughters. He received the casts, and at once consigned them to a garret, to which he forbade access. His youngest daughter, one unfortunate day, during her father's absence, was impelled by feminine curiosity-perhaps a little increased by the prohibition—to enter the mysterious chamber.

Whether she imagined in the pallid figure upon the cross a celestial rebuke for her disobedience, or whether she was overcome by the mere mortal horror of one or both of those dreadful casts, can now never be known. But this is true: she became a maniac.

The writer of this has more than once seen (as, no doubt, have many others) the plaster effigies of Peter Starke, after their removal from Dr. Carnell's to a famous studio near the Regent's Park. It was there that he heard whispered the strange story of their origin. Sculptor and surgeon are now both long since dead, and it is no longer necessary to keep *the secret of the two plaster casts*.

# The Spirit's Whisper

Yes, I have been haunted!—haunted so fearfully that for some little time I thought myself insane. I was no raving maniac; I mixed in society as heretofore, although perhaps a trifle more grave and taciturn than usual; I pursued my daily avocations; I employed myself even on literary work. To all appearance I was one of the sanest of the sane; and yet all the while I considered myself the victim of such strange delusions that, in my own mind, I fancied my senses—and one sense in particular—so far erratic and beyond my own control that I was, in real truth, a madman. How far I was then insane it must be for others, who hear my story, to decide. My hallucinations have long since left me, and, at all events, I am now as sane as I suppose most men are.

My first attack came on one afternoon when, being in a listless and an idle mood, I had risen from my work and was amusing myself with speculating at my window on the different personages who were passing before me. At that time I occupied apartments in the Brompton Road. Perhaps, there is no thoroughfare in London where the ordinary passengers are of so varied a description or high life and low life mingle in so perpetual a medley. South-Kensington carriages there jostle costermongers' carts; the clerk in the public office, returning to his suburban dwelling, brushes the labourer coming from his work on the never-ending modern constructions in the new district; and the ladies of some of the surrounding squares flaunt the most gigantic of *chignons*, and the most exuberant of motley dresses, before the envying eyes of the ragged girls with their vegetable-baskets.

There was, as usual, plenty of material for observation and conjecture in the passengers, and their characters or destinations, from my window on that day. Yet I was not in the right cue for the thorough enjoyment of my favourite amusement. I was in a rather melancholy mood. Somehow or other, I don't know why, my memory had reverted to a pretty woman whom I had not seen for many years. She had been my first love, and I had loved her with a boyish passion as genuine as it was intense. I thought my heart would have broken, and I certainly talked seriously of dying, when she formed an attachment to an ill-conditioned, handsome young adventurer, and, on her family objecting to such an alliance, eloped with him.

I had never seen the fellow, against whom, however, I cherished a hatred almost as intense as my passion for the infatuated girl who had flown from her home for his sake. We had heard of her being on the Continent with her husband, and learned that the man's shifty life had eventually taken him to the East. For some years nothing more had been heard of the poor girl. It was a melancholy history, and its memory ill-disposed me for amusement.

A sigh was probably just escaping my lips with the half-articulated words, "Poor Julia!" when my eyes fell on a man passing before my window. There was nothing particularly striking about him. He was tall, with fine features, and a long, fair beard, contrasting somewhat with his bronzed complexion. I had seen many of our officers on their return from the Crimea look much the same. Still, the man's aspect gave me a shuddering feeling, I didn't know why. At the same moment, a whispering, low voice uttered aloud in my ear the words, "It is he!" I turned, startled; there was no one near me, no one in the room. There was no fancy in the sound; I had heard the words with painful distinctness. I ran to the door, opened it—not a sound on the staircase, not a sound in the whole house—nothing but the hum from the street. I came back and sat down.

It was no use reasoning with myself; I had the ineffaceable conviction that I had heard the voice. Then first the idea crossed my mind that I might be the victim of hallucinations. Yes, it must have been so, for now I recalled to mind that the voice had been that of my poor lost Julia; and at the moment I heard it I had been dreaming of her. I questioned my own state of health. I was well; at least I had been so, I felt fully assured, up to that moment. Now a feeling of chilliness and numbness and faintness had crept over me, a cold sweat was on my forehead. I tried to shake off this feeling by bringing back my thoughts to some other subject. But, involuntarily as it were, I again uttered the words, "Poor Julia!" aloud. At the same time a deep and heavy sigh, almost a groan, was distinctly audible close by me. I sprang up; I was alone—quite alone. It was, once more, an hallucination.

By degrees the first painful impression wore away. Some days had passed, and I had begun to forget my singular delusion. When my thoughts aid revert to it, the recollection was dismissed as that of a ridiculous fancy. One afternoon I was in the Strand, coming from Charing Cross, when I was once more overcome by that peculiar feeling of cold and numbness which I had before experienced. The day was warm and bright and genial, and yet I positively shivered. I had scarce time to interrogate my own strange sensations when a man went by me rapidly. How was it that I recognized him at once as the individual who had only passed my window so casually on that morning of the hallucination? I don't know, and yet I was aware that this man was the tall, fair passer-by of the Brompton Road.

At the same moment the voice I had previously heard whispered distinctly in my ear the words, "Follow him!" I stood stupefied. The usual throngs of indifferent persons were hurrying past me in that crowded thoroughfare, but I felt convinced that not one of these had spoken to me. I remained transfixed for a moment. I was bent on a matter of business in the contrary direction to the individual I had remarked, and so, although with unsteady step, I endeavoured to proceed on my way. Again that voice said, still more emphatically, in my ear, "Follow him!" I stopped involuntarily. And a third time, "Follow him!" I told myself that the sound was a delusion, a cheat of my senses, and yet I could not resist the spell. I turned to follow. Quickening my pace, I soon came up with the tall, fair man, and, unremarked by him, I followed him. Whither was this foolish pursuit to lead me? It was useless to ask myself the question—I was impelled to follow.

I was not destined to go very far, however. Before long the object of my absurd chase entered a well-known insurance-office. I stopped at the door of the establishment. I had no business within, why should I continue to follow? Had I not already been making a sad fool of myself by my ridiculous conduct? These were my thoughts as I stood heated by my quick walk. Yes, heated; and yet, once more, came the sudden chill. Once more that same low but now awful voice spoke in my ear: "Go in!" it said. I endeavoured to resist the spell, and yet I felt that resistance was in vain.

Fortunately, as it seemed to me, the thought crossed my mind that an old acquaintance was a clerk in that same insurance-office. I had not seen the fellow for a great length of time, and I never had been very intimate with him. But here was a pretext; and so I went in and inquired for Clement Stanley. My acquaintance came forward. He was very busy, he said. I invented, on the spur of the moment, some excuse of the most frivolous and absurd nature, as far as I can recollect, for my intrusion.

"By the way," I said, as I turned to take my leave, although my question was "by the way" of nothing at all, "who was that tall, fair man who just now entered the office?"

"Oh, that fellow?" was the indifferent reply; "a Captain Campbell, or Canton, or some such name; I forget what. He is gone in before the board—insured his wife's life—and she is dead; comes for a settlement, I suppose."

There was nothing more to be gained, and so I left the office. As soon as I came without into the scorching sunlight, again the same feeling of cold, again the same voice—"Wait!" Was I going mad? More and more the conviction forced itself upon me that I was decidedly a monomaniac already. I felt my pulse. It was agitated and yet not feverish. I was determined not to give way to this absurd hallucination; and yet, so far was I out of my senses, that my will was no longer my own. Resolved as I was to go, I listened to the dictates of that voice and waited. What was it to me that this Campbell or Canton had insured his wife's life, that she was dead, and that he wanted a settlement of his claim? Obviously nothing; and I yet waited.

So strong was the spell on me that I had no longer any count of time. I had no consciousness whether the period was long or short that I stood there near the door, heedless of all the throng that passed, gazing on vacancy. The fiercest of policemen might have told me to "move on," and I should not have stirred, spite of all the terrors of the "station." The individual came forth. He paid no heed to me. Why should he? What was I to him? This time I needed no warning voice to bid me follow. I was a mad-man, and I could not resist the impulses of my madness. It was thus, at least I reasoned with myself. I followed into Regent Street. The object of my insensate observation lingered, and looked around as if in expectation.

Presently a fine-looking woman, somewhat extravagantly dressed, and obviously not a lady, advanced toward him on the pavement. At the sight of her he quickened his step, and joined her rapidly. I shuddered again, but this time a sort of dread was mingled with that strange shivering. I knew what was coming, and it came. Again that voice in my ear. "Look and remember!" it said. I passed the man and woman as they stopped at their first meeting!

"Is all right, George?" said the female.

"All right, my girl," was the reply.

I looked. An evil smile, as if of wicked triumph, was on the man's face, I thought. And on the woman's? I looked at her, and I remembered. I could not be mistaken. Spite of her change in manner, dress, and appearance, it was Mary Simms. This woman some years before, when she was still very young, had been a sort of humble companion to my mother. A simple-minded, honest girl, we thought her. Sometimes I had fancied that she had paid me, in a sly way, a marked attention. I had been foolish enough to be flattered by her stealthy glances and her sighs. But I had treated these little demonstrations of partiality as due only to a silly girlish fancy. Mary Simms, however, had come to grief in our household. She had been detected in the abstraction of sundry jewels and petty ornaments.

The morning after discovery she had left the house, and we had heard of her no more. As these recollections passed rapidly through my mind I looked behind me. The couple had turned back. I turned to follow again; and spite of carriages and cabs, and shouts and oaths of drivers, I took the middle of the street in order to pass the man and woman at a little distance unobserved. No; I was not mistaken. The woman was Mary Simms, though without any trace of all her former simple-minded airs; Mary Simms, no longer in her humble attire, but flaunting in all the finery of overdone fashion. She wore an air of reckless joyousness in her face; and yet, spite of that, I pitied her. It was clear she had fallen on the evil ways of bettered fortune—bettered, alas! for the worse.

I had an excuse now, in my own mind, for my continued pursuit, without deeming myself an utter madman—the excuse of curiosity to know the destiny of one with whom I had been formerly familiar, and in whom I had taken an interest. Presently the game I was hunting down stopped at the door of the Grand Cafe. After a little discussion they entered. It was a public place of entertainment; there was no reason why I should not enter also. I found my way to the first floor. They were already seated at a table, Mary holding the *carte* in her hand. They were about to dine. Why should not I dine there too? There was but one little objection,—I had an engagement to dinner. But the strange impulse which overpowered me, and seemed leading me on step by step, spite of myself, quickly overruled all the dictates of propriety toward my intended hosts.

Could I not send a prettily devised apology? I glided past the couple, with my head averted, seeking a table, and I was unobserved by my old acquaintance. I was too agitated to eat, but I made a semblance, and little heeded the air of surprise and almost disgust on the bewildered face of the waiter as he bore away the barely touched dishes. I was in a very fever of impatience and doubt what next to do. They still sat on, in evident enjoyment of their meal and their constant draughts of sparkling wine. My impatience was becoming almost unbearable when the man at last rose. The woman seemed to have uttered some expostulation, for he turned at the door and said somewhat harshly aloud, "Nonsense; only one game and I shall be back. The waiter will give you a paper—a magazine—something to while away the time." And he left the room for the billiard-table, as I surmised.

Now was my opportunity. After a little hesitation, I rose, and planted myself abruptly on the vacant seat before the woman.

"Mary," I said.

She started, with a little exclamation of alarm, and dropped the paper she had held. She knew me at once.

"Master John!" she exclaimed, using the familiar term still given me when I was long past boyhood; and then, after a lengthened gaze, she turned away her head. I was embarrassed at first how to address her.

"Mary," I said at last, "I am grieved to see you thus."

"Why should you be grieved for me?" she retorted, looking at me sharply, and speaking in a tone of impatient anger. "I am happy as I am."

"I don't believe you," I replied.

She again turned away her head.

"Mary," I pursued, "can you doubt, that, spite of all, I have still a strong interest in the companion of my youth?"

She looked at me almost mournfully, but did not speak. At that moment I probably grew pale; for suddenly that chilly fit seized me again, and my forehead became clammy. That voice sounded again in my ear: "Speak of him!" were the words it uttered. Mary gazed on me with surprise, and yet I was assured that *she* had not heard that voice, so plain to me. She evidently

541

mistook the nature of my visible emotion.

"O Master John!" she stammered, with tears gathering in her eyes, reverting again to that name of bygone times, "if you had loved me then—if you had consoled my true affection with one word of hope, one look of loving-kindness—if you had not spurned and crushed me, I should not have been what I am now."

I was about to make some answer to this burst of unforgotten passion, when the voice came again: "Speak of him!"

"You have loved others since," I remarked, with a coldness which seemed cruel to myself. "You love *him* now." And I nodded my head toward the door by which the man had disappeared.

"Do I?" she said, with a bitter smile. "Perhaps; who knows?"

"And yet no good can come to you from a connection with that man," I pursued.

"Why not? He adores me, and he is free," was her answer, given with a little triumphant air.

"Yes," I said, "I know he is free: he has lately lost his wife. He has made good his claim to the sum for which he insured her life."

Mary grew deadly pale. "How did you learn this? what do you know of him?" she stammered.

I had no reply to give. She scanned my face anxiously for some time; then in a low voice she added, "What do you suspect?"

I was still silent, and only looked at her fixedly.

"You do not speak," she pursued nervously. "Why do you not speak? Ah, you know more than you would say! Master John, Master John, you might set my tortured mind at rest, and clear or confirm those doubts which *will* come into my poor head, spite of myself. Speak out—O, do speak out!"

"Not here; it is impossible," I replied, looking around. The room as the hour advanced, was becoming more thronged with guests, and the full tables gave a pretext for my reticence, when in truth I had nothing to say.

"Will you come and see me—will you?" she asked with earnest entreaty.

I nodded my head.

"Have you a pocketbook? I will write you my address; and you will come—yes, I am sure you will come!" she said in an agitated way.

I handed her my pocketbook and pencil; she wrote rapidly.

"Between the hours of three and five," she whispered, looking uneasily at the door; "*he* is sure not to be at home."

I rose; Mary held out her hand to me, then withdrew it hastily with an air of shame, and the tears sprang into her eyes again. I left the room hurriedly, and met her companion on the stairs.

That same evening, in the solitude of my own room, I pondered over the little event of the day. I had calmed down from my state of excitement. The living apparition of Mary Simms occupied my mind almost to the exclusion of the terrors of the ghostly voice which had haunted me, and my own fears of coming insanity. In truth, what was that man to me? Nothing. What did his doings matter to such a perfect stranger as myself? Nothing.

His connection with Mary Simms was our only link; and in what should that affect me? Nothing again. I debated with myself whether it were not foolish of me to comply with my youthful companion's request to visit her; whether it were not imprudent in me to take any further interest in the lost woman; whether there were not even danger in seeking to penetrate mysteries which were no concern of mine. The resolution to which I came pleased me, and I said aloud, "No, I will not go!"

At the same moment came again the voice like an awful echo to my words—"Go!" It came so suddenly and so imperatively, almost without any previous warning of the usual shudder, that the shock was more than I could bear. I believe I fainted; I know I found myself, when I came to consciousness, in my arm-chair, cold and numb, and my candles had almost burned down into their sockets.

The next morning I was really ill. A sort of low fever seemed to have prostrated me, and I would have willingly seized so valid a reason for disobeying, at least for that day—for some days, perhaps—the injunction of that ghostly voice. But all that morning it never left me. My fearful chilly fit was of constant recurrence, and the words "Go! go! go!" were murmured so perpetually in my ears—the sound was one of such urgent entreaty—that all force of will gave way completely. Had I remained in that lone room, I should have gone wholly mad. As yet, to my own feelings, I was but partially out of my senses.

I dressed hastily; and, I scarce know how—by no effort of my own will, it seemed to me—I was in the open air. The address of Mary Simms was in a street not far from my own suburb. Without any power of reasoning, I found myself before the door of the house. I knocked, and asked a slipshod girl who opened the door to me for "Miss Simms." She knew no such person, held a brief shrill colloquy with some female in the back-parlour, and, on coming back, was about to shut the door in my face, when a voice from above—the voice of her I sought—called down the stairs, "Let the gentleman come up!"

I was allowed to pass. In the front drawing-room I found Mary Simms.

"They do not know me under that name," she said with a mournful smile, and again extended, then withdrew, her hand.

"Sit down," she went on to say, after a nervous pause. "I am alone now; told I adjure you, if you have still one latent feeling of old kindness for me, explain your words of yesterday to me."

I muttered something to the effect that I had no explanation to give. No words could be truer; I had not the slightest conception what to say.

"Yes, I am sure you have; you must, you will," pursued Mary excitedly; "you have some knowledge of that matter."

"What matter?" I asked.

"Why, the insurance," she replied impatiently. "You know well what I mean. My mind has been distracted about it. Spite of myself, terrible suspicions have forced themselves on me. No; I don't mean that," she cried, suddenly checking herself and changing her tone; "don't heed what I said; it was madness in me to say what I did. But do, do, do tell me all you know."

The request was a difficult one to comply with, for I knew nothing. It is impossible to say what might have been the end of this strange interview, in which I began to feel myself an unwilling impostor; but suddenly Mary started.

"The noise of the latchkey in the lock!" she cried, alarmed; "He has returned; he must not see you; you must come another time. Here, here, be quick! I'll manage him."

And before I could utter another word she had pushed me into the back drawing-room and closed the door. A man's step on the stairs; then voices. The man was begging Mary to come out with him, as the day was so fine. She excused herself; he would hear no refusal. At last she appeared to consent, on condition that the man would assist at her toilet. There was a little laughter, almost hysterical on the part of Mary, whose voice evidently quivered with trepidation.

Presently both mounted the upper stairs. Then the thought stuck me that I had left my hat in the front room—a sufficient cause for the woman's alarm. I opened the door cautiously, seized my hat, and was about to steal down the stairs, when I was again spellbound by that numb cold.

"Stay!" said the voice. I staggered back to the other room with my hat, and closed the door.

Presently the couple came down. Mary was probably relieved by discovering that my hat was no longer there, and surmised that I had departed; for I heard her laughing as they went down the lower flight. Then I heard them leave the house.

I was alone in that back drawing-room. Why? what did I want there? I was soon to learn. I felt the chill invisible presence near me; and the voice said, "Search!"

The room belonged to the common representative class of back drawing-rooms in "apartments" of the better kind. The only one unfamiliar piece of furniture was an old Indian cabinet; and my eye naturally fell on that. As I stood and looked at it with a strange unaccountable feeling of fascination, again came the voice—"Search!"

I shuddered and obeyed. The cabinet was firmly locked; there was no power of opening it except by burglarious infraction; but still the voice said, "Search!"

A thought suddenly struck me, and I turned the cabinet from its position against the wall. Behind, the woodwork had rotted, and in many portions fallen away, so that the inner drawers were visible. What could my ghostly monitor mean—that I should open those drawers? I would not do such a deed of petty treachery. I turned defiantly, and addressing myself to the invisible as if it were a living creature by my side, I cried, "I must not, will not, do such an act of baseness."

The voice replied, "Search!"

I might have known that, in my state of what I deemed insanity, resistance was in vain. I grasped the most accessible drawer from behind, and pulled it toward me. Uppermost within it lay letters: they were addressed to "Captain Cameron,"—"Captain George Cameron." That name!—the name of Julia's husband, the man with whom she had eloped; for it was he who was the object of my pursuit.

My shuddering fit became so strong that I could scarce hold the papers; and "Search!" was repeated in my ear.

Below the letters lay a small book in a limp black cover. I opened this book with trembling hand; it was filled with manuscript—Julia's well-known handwriting.

"Read!" muttered the voice. I read. There were long entries by poor Julia of her daily life; complaints of her husband's unkindness, neglect, then cruelty. I turned to the last pages: her hand had grown very feeble now, and she was very ill. "George seems kinder now," she wrote; "he brings me all my medicines with his own hand." Later on: "I am dying; I know I am dying: he has poisoned me. I saw him last night through the curtains pour something in my cup; I saw it in his evil eye. I would not drink; I will drink no more; but I feel that I must die."

These were the last words. Below were written, in a man's bold hand, the words "Poor fool!"

This sudden revelation of poor Julia's death and dying thoughts unnerved me quite. I grew colder in my whole frame than ever.

"Take it!" said her voice. I took the book, pushed back the cabinet into its place against the wall, and, leaving that fearful room, stole down the stairs with trembling limbs, and left the house with all the feelings of a guilty thief.

For some days I perused my poor lost Julia's diary again and again. The whole revelation of her sad life and sudden death led but to one conclusion,—she had died of poison by the hands of her unworthy husband. He had insured her life, and then——

It seemed evident to me that Mary Simms had vaguely shared suspicions of the same foul deed. On my own mind came conviction. But what could I do next? how bring this evil man to justice? what proof would be deemed to exist in those writings? I was bewildered, weak, irresolute. Like Hamlet, I shrank back and temporized. But I was not feigning madness; my madness seemed but all too real for me. During all this period the wailing of that wretched voice in my ear was almost incessant. O, I must have been mad!

I wandered about restlessly, like the haunted thing I had become. One day I had come unconsciously and without purpose into Oxford Street. My troubled thoughts were suddenly broken in upon by the solicitations of a beggar. With a heart hardened against begging impostors, and under the influence of the shock rudely given to my absorbing dreams, I answered more hardly than was my wont. The man heaved a heavy sigh, and sobbed forth, "Then Heaven help me!" I caught sight of him before he turned away. He was a ghastly object, with fever in his hollow eyes and sunken cheeks, and fever on his dry, chapped lips. But I knew, or fancied I knew, the tricks of the trade, and I was obdurate.

Why, I asked myself, should the cold shudder come over me at such a moment? But it was so strong on me as to make me shake all over. It came—that maddening voice. "Succour!" it said now. I had become so accustomed already to address the ghostly voice that I cried aloud, "Why, Julia, why?" I saw people laughing in my face at this strange cry, and I turned in the direction in which the beggar had gone. I just caught sight of him as he was tottering down a street toward Soho. I determined to have pity for this once, and followed the poor man. He led me on through I know not what streets. His steps was hurried now. In one street I lost sight of him; but I felt convinced he must have turned into a dingy court.

I made inquiries, but for a time received only rude jeering answers from the rough men and women whom I questioned. At last a little girl informed me that I must mean the strange man who lodged in the garret of a house she pointed out to me. It was an old dilapidated building, and I had much repugnance on entering it. But again I was no master of my will. I mounted some creaking stairs to the top of the house, until I could go no further. A shattered door was open; I entered a wretched garret; the object of my search lay now on a bundle of rags on the bare floor. He opened his wild eyes as I approached.

"I have come to succour," I said, using unconsciously the word of the voice; "what ails you?"

"Ails me?" gasped the man; "hunger, starvation, fever."

I was horrified. Hurrying to the top of the stairs, I shouted till I had roused the attention of an old woman. I gave her money to bring me food and brandy, promising her a recompense for her trouble.

"Have you no friends?" I asked the wretched man as I returned.

"None," he said feebly. Then as the fever rose in his eyes and even flushed his pallid face, he said excitedly, "I had a master once—one I periled my soul for. He knows I am dying; but, spite of all my letters, he will not come. He wants me dead, he wants me dead—and his wish is coming to pass now."

"Cannot I find him—bring him here?" I asked.

The man stared at me, shook his head, and at last, as if collecting his faculties with much exertion, muttered, "Yes; it is a last hope; perhaps you may, and I can be revenged on him at least.

Yes revenged. I have threatened him already." And the fellow laughed a wild laugh.

"Control yourself," I urged, kneeling by his side; "give me his name—his address."

"Captain George Cameron," he gasped, and then fell back.

"Captain George Cameron!" I cried. "Speak! what of him?"

But the man's senses seemed gone; he only muttered incoherently. The old woman returned with the food and spirits. I had found one honest creature in that foul region. I gave her money—provide her more if she would bring a doctor. She departed on her new errand. I raised the man's head, moistened his lips with the brandy, and then poured some of the spirit down his throat. He gulped at it eagerly, and opened his eyes; but he still raved incoherently, "I did not do it, it was he. He made me buy the poison; he dared not risk the danger himself, the coward! I knew what he meant to do with it, and yet I did not speak; I was her murderer too. Poor Mrs. Cameron! poor Mrs. Cameron! do you forgive?—can you forgive?" And the man screamed aloud and stretched out his arms as if to fright away a phantom.

I had drunk in every word, and knew the meaning of those broken accents well. Could I have found at last the means of bringing justice on the murderer's head? But the man was raving in a delirium, and I was obliged to hold him with all my strength. A step on the stairs. Could it be the medical man I had sent for? That would be indeed a blessing. A man entered—it was Cameron!

He came in jauntily, with the words, "How now, Saunders, you rascal! What more do you want to get out of me?"

He started at the sight of a stranger.

I rose from my kneeling posture like an accusing spirit. I struggled for calm; but passion beyond my control mastered me, and was I not a madman? I seized him by the throat, with the words, "Murderer! poisoner! where is Julia?" He shook me off violently.

"And who the devil are you, sir?" he cried.

"That murdered woman's cousin!" I rushed at him again.

"Lying hound!" he shouted, and grappled me. His strength was far beyond mine. He had his hand on my throat; a crimson darkness was in my eyes; I could not see, I could not hear; there was a torrent of sound pouring in my ears. Suddenly his grasp relaxed. When I recovered my sight, I saw the murderer struggling with the fever-stricken man, who had risen from the floor, and seized him from behind. This unexpected diversion saved my life; but the ex-groom was soon thrown back on the ground.

"Captain George Cameron," I cried, "kill me, but you will only heap another murder on your head!"

He advanced on me with something glittering in his hand. Without a word he came and stabbed at me; but at the same moment I darted at him a heavy blow. What followed was too confused for clear remembrance. I saw—no, I will say I fancied that I saw—the dim form of Julia Staunton standing between me and her vile husband. Did he see the vision too? I cannot say. He reeled back, and fell heavily to the floor. Maybe it was only my blow that felled him. Then came confusion—a dream of a crowd of people—policemen—muttered accusations. I had fainted from the wound in my arm.

Captain George Cameron was arrested. Saunders recovered, and lived long enough to be the principal witness on his trial. The murderer was found guilty. Poor Julia's diary, too, which I had abstracted, told fearfully against him. But he contrived to escape the gallows; he had managed to conceal poison on his person, and he was found dead in his cell. Mary Simms I never saw again. I once received a little scrawl, "I am at peace now, Master John. God bless you!"

I have had no more hallucinations since that time; the voice has never come again. I found out poor Julia's grave, and, as I stood and wept by its side, the cold shudder came over me for the last time. Who shall tell me whether I was once really mad, or whether I was not?

# The Vision of Tom Chuff

At the edge of melancholy Catstean Moor, in the north of England, with half-a-dozen ancient poplar-trees with rugged and hoary stems around, one smashed across the middle by a flash of lightning thirty summers before, and all by their great height dwarfing the abode near which they stand, there squats a rude stone house, with a thick chimney, a kitchen and bedroom on the ground-floor, and a loft, accessible by a ladder, under the shingle roof, divided into two rooms.

Its owner was a man of ill repute. Tom Chuff was his name. A shock-headed, broad-shouldered, powerful man, though somewhat short, with lowering brows and a sullen eye. He was a poacher, and hardly made an ostensible pretence of earning his bread by any honest industry. He was a drunkard. He beat his wife, and led his children a life of terror and lamentation, when he was at home. It was a blessing to his frightened little family when he absented himself, as he sometimes did, for a week or more together.

On the night I speak of he knocked at the door with his cudgel at about eight o'clock. It was winter, and the night was very dark. Had the summons been that of a bogie from the moor, the inmates of this small house could hardly have heard it with greater terror.

His wife unbarred the door in fear and haste. Her hunch-backed sister stood by the hearth, staring toward the threshold. The children cowered behind.

Tom Chuff entered with his cudgel in his hand, without

speaking, and threw himself into a chair opposite the fire. He had been away two or three days. He looked haggard, and his eyes were bloodshot. They knew he had been drinking.

Tom raked and knocked the peat fire with his stick, and thrust his feet close to it. He signed towards the little dresser, and nodded to his wife, and she knew he wanted a cup, which in silence she gave him. He pulled a bottle of gin from his coat-pocket, and nearly filling the teacup, drank off the dram at a few gulps.

He usually refreshed himself with two or three drams of this kind before beating the inmates of his house. His three little children, cowering in a corner, eyed him from under a table, as Jack did the ogre in the nursery tale. His wife, Nell, standing behind a chair, which she was ready to snatch up to meet the blow of the cudgel, which might be levelled at her at any moment, never took her eyes off him; and hunchbacked Mary showed the whites of a large pair of eyes, similarly employed, as she stood against the oaken press, her dark face hardly distinguishable in the distance from the brown panel behind it.

Tom Chuff was at his third dram, and had not yet spoken a word since his entrance, and the suspense was growing dreadful, when, on a sudden, he leaned back in his rude seat, the cudgel slipped from his hand, a change and a death-like pallor came over his face.

For a while they all stared on; such was their fear of him, they dared not speak or move, lest it should prove to have been but a doze, and Tom should wake up and proceed forthwith to gratify his temper and exercise his cudgel.

In a very little time, however, things began to look so odd, that they ventured, his wife and Mary, to exchange glances full of doubt and wonder. He hung so much over the side of the chair, that if it had not been one of cyclopean clumsiness and weight, he would have borne it to the floor. A leaden tint was darkening the pallor of his face. They were becoming alarmed, and finally braving everything his wife timidly said, "Tom!" and then more sharply repeated it, and finally cried the appellative loudly, and again and again, with the terrified accompaniment,

"He's dying—he's dying!" her voice rising to a scream, as she found that neither it nor her plucks and shakings of him by the shoulder had the slightest effect in recalling him from his torpor.

And now from sheer terror of a new kind the children added their shrilly piping to the talk and cries of their seniors; and if anything could have called Tom up from his lethargy, it might have been the piercing chorus that made the rude chamber of the poacher's habitation ring again. But Tom continued unmoved, deaf, and stirless.

His wife sent Mary down to the village, hardly a quarter of a mile away, to implore of the doctor, for whose family she did duty as laundress, to come down and look at her husband, who seemed to be dying.

The doctor, who was a good-natured fellow, arrived. With his hat still on, he looked at Tom, examined him, and when he found that the emetic he had brought with him, on conjecture from Mary's description, did not act, and that his lancet brought no blood, and that he felt a pulseless wrist, he shook his head, and inwardly thought:

"What the plague is the woman crying for? Could she have desired a greater blessing for her children and herself than the very thing that has happened?"

Tom, in fact, seemed quite gone. At his lips no breath was perceptible. The doctor could discover no pulse. His hands and feet were cold, and the chill was stealing up into his body.

The doctor, after a stay of twenty minutes, had buttoned up his great-coat again and pulled down his hat, and told Mrs. Chuff that there was no use in his remaining any longer, when, all of a sudden, a little rill of blood began to trickle from the lancet-cut in Tom Chuff's temple.

"That's very odd," said the doctor. "Let us wait a little."

I must describe now the sensations which Tom Chuff had experienced.

With his elbows on his knees, and his chin upon his hands, he was staring into the embers, with his gin beside him, when suddenly a swimming came in his head, he lost sight of the fire, and a sound like one stroke of a loud church bell smote his brain.

Then he heard a confused humming, and the leaden weight of his head held him backward as he sank in his chair, and consciousness quite forsook him.

When he came to himself he felt chilled, and was leaning against a huge leafless tree. The night was moonless, and when he looked up he thought he had never seen stars so large and bright, or sky so black. The stars, too, seemed to blink down with longer intervals of darkness, and fiercer and more dazzling emergence, and something, he vaguely thought, of the character of silent menace and fury.

He had a confused recollection of having come there, or rather of having been carried along, as if on men's shoulders, with a sort of rushing motion. But it was utterly indistinct; the imperfect recollection simply of a sensation. He had seen or heard nothing on his way.

He looked round. There was not a sign of a living creature near. And he began with a sense of awe to recognise the place.

The tree against which he had been leaning was one of the noble old beeches that surround at irregular intervals the churchyard of Shackleton, which spreads its green and wavy lap on the edge of the Moor of Catstean, at the opposite side of which stands the rude cottage in which he had just lost consciousness. It was six miles or more across the moor to his habitation, and the black expanse lay before him, disappearing dismally in the darkness. So that, looking straight before him, sky and land blended together in an undistinguishable and awful blank.

There was a silence quite unnatural over the place. The distant murmur of the brook, which he knew so well, was dead; not a whisper in the leaves about him; the air, earth, everything about and above was indescribably still; and he experienced that quaking of the heart that seems to portend the approach of something awful. He would have set out upon his return across the moor, had he not an undefined presentiment that he was waylaid by something he dared not pass.

The old grey church and tower of Shackleton stood like a shadow in the rear. His eye had grown accustomed to the obscurity, and he could just trace its outline. There were no comforting associations in his mind connected with it; nothing but menace and misgiving. His early training in his lawless calling was connected with this very spot. Here his father used to meet two other poachers, and bring his son, then but a boy, with him.

Under the church porch, towards morning, they used to divide the game they had taken, and take account of the sales they had made on the previous day, and make partition of the money, and drink their gin. It was here he had taken his early lessons in drinking, cursing, and lawlessness. His father's grave was hardly eight steps from the spot where he stood. In his present state of awful dejection, no scene on earth could have so helped to heighten his fear.

There was one object close by which added to his gloom. About a yard away, in rear of the tree, behind himself, and extending to his left, was an open grave, the mould and rubbish piled on the other side. At the head of this grave stood the beech-tree; its columnar stem rose like a huge monumental pillar. He knew every line and crease on its smooth surface. The initial letters of his own name, cut in its bark long ago, had spread out and wrinkled like the grotesque capitals of a fanciful engraver, and now with a sinister significance overlooked the open grave, as if answering his mental question, "Who for is t' grave cut?"

He felt still a little stunned, and there was a faint tremor in his joints that disinclined him to exert himself; and, further, he had a vague apprehension that take what direction he might, there was danger around him worse than that of staying where he was.

On a sudden the stars began to blink more fiercely, a faint wild light overspread for a minute the bleak landscape, and he saw approaching from the moor a figure at a kind of swinging trot, with now and then a zigzag hop or two, such as men accustomed to cross such places make, to avoid the patches of slob or quag that meet them here and there. This figure resembled his father's, and like him, whistled through his finger by way of signal as he approached; but the whistle sounded not now shrilly and sharp, as in old times, but immensely far away, and seemed to sing strangely through Tom's head. From habit or from fear, in answer to the signal, Tom whistled as he used to do five-and-twenty years ago and more, although he was already chilled with an unearthly fear.

Like his father, too, the figure held up the bag that was in his left hand as he drew near, when it was his custom to call out to him what was in it. It did not reassure the watcher, you may be certain, when a shout unnaturally faint reached him, as the phantom dangled the bag in the air, and he heard with a faint distinctness the words, "Tom Chuff's soul!"

Scarcely fifty yards away from the low churchyard fence at which Tom was standing, there was a wider chasm in the peat, which there threw up a growth of reeds and bulrushes, among which, as the old poacher used to do on a sudden alarm, the approaching figure suddenly cast itself down.

From the same patch of tall reeds and rushes emerged instantaneously what he at first mistook for the same figure creeping on all-fours, but what he soon perceived to be an enormous black dog with a rough coat like a bear's, which at first sniffed about, and then started towards him in what seemed to be a sportive amble, bouncing this way and that, but as it drew near it displayed a pair of fearful eyes that glowed like live coals, and emitted from the monstrous expanse of its jaws a terrifying growl.

This beast seemed on the point of seizing him, and Tom recoiled in panic and fell into the open grave behind him. The edge which he caught as he tumbled gave way, and down he went, expecting almost at the same instant to reach the bottom. But never was such a fall! Bottomless seemed the abyss! Down, down, down, with immeasurable and still increasing speed, through utter darkness, with hair streaming straight upward, breathless, he shot with a rush of air against him, the force of which whirled up his very arms, second after second, minute after minute, through the chasm downward he flew, the icy perspiration of horror covering his body, and suddenly, as he expected to be dashed into annihilation, his descent was in an instant arrested with a tremendous shock, which, however, did not deprive him of consciousness even for a moment.

He looked about him. The place resembled a smoke-stained cavern or catacomb, the roof of which, except for a ribbed arch here and there faintly visible, was lost in darkness. From several rude passages, like the galleries of a gigantic mine, which opened from this centre chamber, was very dimly emitted a dull glow as of charcoal, which was the only light by which he could imperfectly discern the objects immediately about him.

What seemed like a projecting piece of the rock, at the corner of one of these murky entrances, moved on a sudden, and proved to be a human figure, that beckoned to him. He approached, and saw his father. He could barely recognise him, he was so monstrously altered.

"I've been looking for you, Tom. Welcome home, lad; come along to your place."

Tom's heart sank as he heard these words, which were spoken in a hollow and, he thought, derisive voice that made him tremble. But he could not help accompanying the wicked spirit, who led him into a place, in passing which he heard, as it were from within the rock, dreadful cries and appeals for mercy.

"What is this?" said he.

"Never mind."

"Who are they?"

"Newcomers, like yourself, lad," answered his father apathetically. "They give over that work in time, finding it is no use."

"What shall I do?" said Tom, in an agony.

"It's all one."

"But what shall I do?" reiterated Tom, quivering in every joint and nerve.

"Grin and bear it, I suppose."

"For God's sake, if ever you cared for me, as I am your own child, let me out of this!"

"There's no way out."

"If there's a way in there's a way out, and for Heaven's sake let me out of this."

But the dreadful figure made no further answer, and glided backwards by his shoulder to the rear; and others appeared in view, each with a faint red halo round it, staring on him with frightful eyes, images, all in hideous variety, of eternal fury or derision. He was growing mad, it seemed, under the stare of so many eyes, increasing in number and drawing closer every moment, and at the same time myriads and myriads of voices were calling him by his name, some far away, some near, some from one point, some from another, some from behind, close to his ears. These cries were increased in rapidity and multitude, and mingled with laughter, with flitting blasphemies, with broken insults and mockeries, succeeded and obliterated by others, before he could half catch their meaning.

All this time, in proportion to the rapidity and urgency of these dreadful sights and sounds, the epilepsy of terror was creeping up to his brain, and with a long and dreadful scream he lost consciousness.

When he recovered his senses, he found himself in a small stone chamber, vaulted above, and with a ponderous door. A single point of light in the wall, with a strange brilliancy illuminated this cell.

Seated opposite to him was a venerable man with a snowy beard of immense length; an image of awful purity and severity. He was dressed in a coarse robe, with three large keys suspensed from his girdle. He might have filled one's idea of an ancient porter of a city gate; such spiritual cities, I should say, as John Bunyan loved to describe.

This old man's eyes were brilliant and awful, and fixed on him as they were, Tom Chuff felt himself helplessly in his power. At length he spoke:

"The command is given to let you forth for one trial more. But if you are found again drinking with the drunken, and beating your fellow-servants, you shall return through the door by which you came, and go out no more."

With these words the old man took him by the wrist and led him through the first door, and then unlocking one that stood in the cavern outside, he struck Tom Chuff sharply on the shoulder, and the door shut behind him with a sound that boomed peal after peal of thunder near and far away, and all round and above, till it rolled off gradually into silence. It was totally dark, but there was a fanning of fresh cool air that overpowered him. He felt that he was in the upper world again.

In a few minutes he began to hear voices which he knew, and first a faint point of light appeared before his eyes, and gradually he saw the flame of the candle, and, after that, the familiar faces of his wife and children, and he heard them faintly when they spoke to him, although he was as yet unable to answer.

He also saw the doctor, like an isolated figure in the dark, and heard him say:

"There, now, you have him back. He'll do, I think."

His first words, when he could speak and saw clearly all about him, and felt the blood on his neck and shirt, were:

"Wife, forgie me. I'm a changed man. Send for't sir."

Which last phrase means, "Send for the clergyman."

When the vicar came and entered the little bedroom where the scared poacher, whose soul had died within him, was lying, still sick and weak, in his bed, and with a spirit that was prostrate with terror, Tom Chuff feebly beckoned the rest from the room, and, the door being closed, the good parson heard the strange confession, and with equal amazement the man's earnest and agitated vows of amendment, and his helpless appeals to him for support and counsel.

These, of course, were kindly met; and the visits of the rector, for some time, were frequent.

One day, when he took Tom Chuff's hand on bidding him good-bye, the sick man held it still, and said:

"Ye'r vicar o' Shackleton, sir, and if I sud dee, ye'll promise me a'e thing, as I a promised ye a many. I a said I'll never gie wife, nor barn, nor folk o' no sort, skelp nor sizzup more, and ye'll know o' me no more among the sipers. Nor never will Tom draw trigger, nor set a snare again, but in an honest way, and after that ye'll no make it a bootless bene for me, but bein', as I say, vicar o' Shackleton, and able to do as ye list, ye'll no let them bury me within twenty good yerd-wands measure o' the a'd beech trees that's round the churchyard of Shackleton."

"I see; you would have your grave, when your time really comes, a good way from the place where lay the grave you dreamed of."

"That's jest it. I'd lie at the bottom o' a marl-pit liefer! And I'd be laid in anither churchyard just to be shut o' my fear o' that, but that a' my kinsfolk is buried beyond in Shackleton, and ye'll gie me yer promise, and no break yer word."

"I do promise, certainly. I'm not likely to outlive you; but, if I should, and still be vicar of Shackleton, you shall be buried somewhere as near the middle of the churchyard as we can find space."

"That'll do."

And so content they parted.

The effect of the vision upon Tom Chuff was powerful, and promised to be lasting. With a sore effort he exchanged his life of desultory adventure and comparative idleness for one of regular industry. He gave up drinking; he was as kind as an originally surly nature would allow to his wife and family; he went to church; in fine weather they crossed the moor to Shackleton Church; the vicar said he came there to look at the scenery of his vision, and to fortify his good resolutions by the reminder.

Impressions upon the imagination, however, are but transitory, and a bad man acting under fear is not a free agent; his real character does not appear. But as the images of the imagination fade, and the action of fear abates, the essential qualities of the man reassert themselves.

So, after a time, Tom Chuff began to grow weary of his new life; he grew lazy, and people began to say that he was catching hares, and pursuing his old contraband way of life, under the rose.

He came home one hard night, with signs of the bottle in his thick speech and violent temper. Next day he was sorry, or frightened, at all events repentant, and for a week or more something of the old horror returned, and he was once more on his good behaviour. But in a little time came a relapse, and another repentance, and then a relapse again, and gradually the return of old habits and the flooding in of all his old way of life, with more violence and gloom, in proportion as the man was alarmed and exasperated by the remembrance of his despised, but terrible, warning.

With the old life returned the misery of the cottage. The smiles, which had begun to appear with the unwonted sunshine, were seen no more. Instead, returned to his poor wife's face the old pale and heartbroken look. The cottage lost its neat and cheerful air, and the melancholy of neglect was visible. Sometimes at night were overheard, by a chance passer-by, cries and sobs from that ill-omened dwelling. Tom Chuff was now often drunk, and not very often at home, except when he came in to sweep away his poor wife's earnings.

Tom had long lost sight of the honest old parson. There was shame mixed with his degradation. He had grace enough left when he saw the thin figure of "t' sir" walking along the road to turn out of his way and avoid meeting him. The clergyman shook his head, and sometimes groaned, when his name was mentioned. His horror and regret were more for the poor wife than for the relapsed sinner, for her case was pitiable indeed.

Her brother, Jack Everton, coming over from Hexley, having heard stories of all this, determined to beat Tom, for his ill-treatment of his sister, within an inch of his life. Luckily, perhaps, for all concerned, Tom happened to be away upon one of his long excursions, and poor Nell besought her brother, in extremity of terror, not to interpose between them. So he took his leave and went home muttering and sulky.

Now it happened a few months later that Nelly Chuff fell sick. She had been ailing, as heartbroken people do, for a good while. But now the end had come.

There was a coroner's inquest when she died, for the doctor had doubts as to whether a blow had not, at least, hastened her death. Nothing certain, however, came of the inquiry. Tom Chuff had left his home more than two days before his wife's death. He was absent upon his lawless business still when the coroner had held his quest.

Jack Everton came over from Hexley to attend the dismal obsequies of his sister. He was more incensed than ever with the wicked husband, who, one way or other, had hastened Nelly's death. The inquest had closed early in the day. The husband had not appeared.

An occasional companion—perhaps I ought to say accomplice—of Chuff's happened to turn up. He had left him on the borders of Westmoreland, and said he would probably be home next day. But Everton affected not to believe it. Perhaps it was to Tom Chuff, he suggested, a secret satisfaction to crown the history of his bad married life with the scandal of his absence from the funeral of his neglected and abused wife.

Everton had taken on himself the direction of the melancholy preparations. He had ordered a grave to be opened for his sister beside her mother's, in Shackleton churchyard, at the other side of the moor. For the purpose, as I have said, of marking the callous neglect of her husband, he determined that the funeral should take place that night. His brother Dick had accompanied him, and they and his sister, with Mary and the children, and a couple of the neighbours, formed the humble cortege.

Jack Everton said he would wait behind, on the chance of Tom Chuff coming in time, that he might tell him what had happened, and make him cross the moor with him to meet the funeral. His real object, I think, was to inflict upon the villain the drubbing he had so long wished to give him. Anyhow, he was resolved, by crossing the moor, to reach the churchyard in time to anticipate the arrival of the funeral, and to have a few words with the vicar, clerk, and sexton, all old friends of his, for the parish of Shackleton was the place of his birth and early recollections.

But Tom Chuff did not appear at his house that night. In surly mood, and without a shilling in his pocket, he was making his way homeward. His bottle of gin, his last investment, half emptied, with its neck protruding, as usual on such returns, was in his coat-pocket.

His way home lay across the moor of Catstean, and the point at which he best knew the passage was from the churchyard of Shackleton. He vaulted the low wall that forms its boundary, and strode across the graves, and over many a flat, half-buried tombstone, toward the side of the churchyard next Catstean Moor.

The old church of Shackleton and its tower rose, close at his right, like a black shadow against the sky. It was a moonless night, but clear. By this time he had reached the low boundary wall, at the other side, that overlooks the wide expanse of Catstean Moor. He stood by one of the huge old beech-trees, and leaned his back to its smooth trunk. Had he ever seen the sky look so black, and the stars shine out and blink so vividly? There was a deathlike silence over the scene, like the hush that precedes thunder in sultry weather. The expanse before him was lost in utter blackness.

A strange quaking unnerved his heart. It was the sky and scenery of his vision! The same horror and misgiving. The same invincible fear of venturing from the spot where he stood. He would have prayed if he dared. His sinking heart demanded a restorative of some sort, and he grasped the bottle in his coat-pocket. Turning to his left, as he did so, he saw the piled-up mould of an open grave that gaped with its head close to the base of the great tree against which he was leaning.

He stood aghast. His dream was returning and slowly enveloping him. Everything he saw was weaving itself into the texture of his vision. The chill of horror stole over him.

A faint whistle came shrill and clear over the moor, and he saw a figure approaching at a swinging trot, with a zigzag course, hopping now here and now there, as men do over a surface where one has need to choose their steps. Through the jungle of reeds and bulrushes in the foreground this figure advanced; and with the same unaccountable impulse that had coerced him in his dream, he answered the whistle of the advancing figure.

On that signal it directed its course straight toward him. It mounted the low wall, and, standing there, looked into the graveyard.

"Who med answer?" challenged the newcomer from his post of observation.

"Me," answered Tom.

"Who are you?" repeated the man upon the wall.

"Tom Chuff; and who's this grave cut for?" He answered in a savage tone, to cover the secret shudder of his panic.

"I'll tell you that, ye villain!" answered the stranger, descending from the wall, "I a' looked for you far and near, and waited long, and now you're found at last."

Not knowing what to make of the figure that advanced upon him, Tom Chuff recoiled, stumbled, and fell backward into the open grave. He caught at the sides as he fell, but without retarding his fall.

An hour later, when lights came with the coffin, the corpse of Tom Chuff was found at the bottom of the grave. He had fallen direct upon his head, and his neck was broken. His death must have been simultaneous with his fall. Thus far his dream was accomplished.

It was his brother-in-law who had crossed the moor and approached the churchyard of Shackleton, exactly in the line which the image of his father had seemed to take in his strange vision. Fortunately for Jack Everton, the sexton and clerk of Shackleton church were, unseen by him, crossing the churchyard toward the grave of Nelly Chuff, just as Tom the poacher stumbled and fell. Suspicion of direct violence would otherwise have inevitably attached to the exasperated brother. As it was, the catastrophe was followed by no legal consequences.

The good vicar kept his word, and the grave of Tom Chuff is still pointed out by the old inhabitants of Shackleton pretty nearly in the centre of the churchyard. This conscientious compliance with the entreaty of the panic-stricken man as to the place of his sepulture gave a horrible and mocking emphasis to the strange combination by which fate had defeated his precaution, and fixed the place of his death.

The story was for many a year, and we believe still is, told round many a cottage hearth, and though it appeals to what many would term superstition, it yet sounded, in the ears of a rude and simple audience, a thrilling, and let us hope, not altogether fruitless homily.

# Some Gossip About Chapelizod

Ghosts in Chapelizod, my good sir! "Why who knows not so?" A place that is itself a shadow of things past, the living spectre of old times. Chapelizod is all a ghost. If anyone desires to see a suburban village of the once proud city of Dublin reduced to a marrowless skeleton, without a single speculation in its eye by which it can ever hope to rise again, let him go to Chapelizod. Dead walls; dead trees overhanging them; dead lights instead of windows in the houses; the men grave, the women lifeless, the little spirits squeaking and gibbering in the muddy streets! A veritable *caput mortuum* is Chapelizod. No wonder that Bob Martin should fancy he saw ghost, for he was always looking at one.

It is just fifty years since Chapelizod was marked for the silent tomb, and condemned to perish by a lingering death. The cold hand of Centralisation, long before the insatiable monster was known by that name, clutched its first victim in Chapelizod. I barely remember the event. A heavy storm came down from the west; great rains had previously descended, and the angry spirit of the river screeched. I heard it myself running under the skew arch of the old bridge. There was lightning in the sky, and the clouds flew across the face of the moon like mad things. As yet the air was calm on the surface of the earth, but towards midnight the gale arose and tore up a number of trees in the Park. Before twenty-four hours we all perceived how easy it would have been to foresee what was coming, for in the course of the forenoon the order arrived for disbanding the *Royal Irish Artil-*

*lery*. It was now no longer a mystery why it had *blown great guns* all the night.

That was the first special act of centralisation—always excepting the fatal centripetal movement from the house in College-green—which was perpetrated against Ireland. The glory of our national service was then extinguished, and Woolwich was made the arsenal sole of the United Kingdom. The royal regiment was broken up, its guns transferred to *Sarah Bridge,* its veterans drafted—as many of them as thought proper to merge their name in an undistinguished throng—into the general service, and not a few who had grown old in the troop found an asylum in the Royal Hospital at Kilmainham.

The transition of an old soldier from Chapelizod to Kilmainham was easy, the principal change consisting in putting off a blue coat to put on a red. They were not required to seek unaccustomed seats, or new associations among strangers, in whom the very accents of their tongue would awaken a prejudice against them, and make them objects of vulgar derision; but they dropped gently down the vale of years, amongst their unit countrymen, near scenes hallowed, to memory, still looking upon those hills which had exhilarated their hearts in the pride and prime of life, and inhaling breezes, wafted down the stream, which had braced and invigorated their lusty sinews, when they were "strong swimmers."

They had friends and kindred at the old quarter, whom they continued to visit on festive occasions, "at the season of the year;" and it was pleasant to see the hearty old fellows, in their now "coats of scarlet," on the king's birthday or a Whitsun-Monday, mixing with the crowd of villagers; one leading a little grandson by the hand, another engaged in cheering converse with a married daughter, or linked with some civil *remanet* of the bygone century, with whom, peradventure, he had quaffed many a social cup of ale; and all climbing the green slope that overhangs the Liffey, on their way to the grand review.

By degrees, as years rolled on, the bright red spots in that moving picture died out; but it was a consoling reflection to those who turned their thoughts to the evidence thus afforded of the sure and silent work of death, that the ties of life had not been abruptly or prematurely torn asunder by the cold hands of centralizing economy. They who had served their country faithfully and loyally in their youth, were suffered to live out their full time, solaced by those attentions and sympathies, dearer far than the charity of dry *rations,* which public gratitude, aiding and giving effect to royal bounty, ungrudgingly secured for them.

But our new generation is wiser than to care for the feelings of men. The *heart* of this United Kingdom beats only and exclusively in the centre of its body; and thither all the life-blood of the land must flow. It may one day be found out, when pulsation refuses to answer at the extremities, that it is possible to overgorge the ventricles of that huge organ. At present, however, it is resolved to "take in all," regardless alike of charters, of rights, of common sense, and of common humanity. The Royal Hospital at Kilmainham is doomed to extinction.

It seems nothing that it was founded by royal charter, and by a rate levied upon the pay of soldiers serving in the army of Ireland, "to the end that such of the said army as have faithfully served their sovereign in the strength and vigour of their youth may, in the weakness and disaster that their old age, wounds, or other misfortunes may bring them into, find a comfortable retreat and a competent maintenance therein." It was endowed with lands, by an instrument which provides that "within the precincts of those lands shall be from henceforth, and shall *forever* hereafter continue and be an hospital, in deed and name, for the receipt, abiding, and dwelling of such a number of poor, aged, maimed, and infirm soldiers, to be lodged, harboured, abide, and be relieved therein."

The charter by which Trinity College holds its estates is not more sacred, nor the perpetual uses to which they must be applied more distinctly defined. Yet the Queen's government, upon its own mere motion and authority, has taken upon itself to root out this time-honoured foundation. The maimed and aged Irish soldier must henceforth find a "comfortable retreat" in Chelsea, where the voice of kinsman or friend will greet him no more. The sights and sounds, which bring back the days of youth with such a homefelt and soothing power to the memory of the aged, will be excluded from his eyes and ears, and he will die in cheerless exile, an unhappy and unthankful recipient of imperial alms.

It was well for the survivors of our National Artillery, that the faith of royal charters, and the kindly feelings of human nature were respected in their days. They had the satisfaction to feel, to their latest moment, that they possessed a country, and that their country had no disposition to disown them; so their end was peace.

Beside those who took service in the British army, or who retired for the remainder of their lives into the shelter provided for them in "the Hospital of King Charles the Second," there were many who, laying aside the military character, merged in the general body of society, and occupied themselves variously in civil employments, according to their natural leanings or abilities. Some few, who had adorned the old brigade in its palmy estate, disdained to quit the scene of its renown, but lingered about the ancient haunts till, one by one, they dropped into the grave.

There was General Bettesworth, and his orderly man John Norton. The general inhabited a pretty place, now sadly dismantled, by the river side, and John was his gate-keeper. It was a sight to see them both stepping out for the parish church at Christmas, and the other high festivals, in the full uniform of their respective ranks, powdered, pomatum'd. and bequeued, as if they were sallying forth to be reviewed by Frederick William of Prussia. If Corporal Trim left a representative after him, it was John Norton: stiff in opinion, erect in stature, simple and honest as a child, pious as a parson. His master had all the gentle parts of human nature blended with the same high courage which distinguished my Uncle Toby.

Is it not strange how many people claim relation to "Uncle Tobry?" Nobody thinks of calling him Tristram Shandy's uncle. He is "my uncle", your uncle, everybody's uncle. Sterne has managed to infuse that sweet touch into his nature, which makes the whole world kin to him, and proud to acknowledge it. But this by the bye.

An anecdote may here be related which illustrates the character of those primitive soldiers, and of the discipline of the service at the close of the eighteenth century. It happened one morning that John Norton was late at parade, and, as men sometime do when they are hurried, he made a mistake in his equipments having put on his cross-belts wrong.

"Why, John Norton," said the general, "how is this? you have put on your belts the wrong way."

The men began to laugh, and John's ire was kindled; but he was too proud to look at his right hand or his left, to examine into the truth of the case.

"No, general," said he, "I have not."

"Oh but, indeed, John, you have."

"By all that's bad, general," said John, who had a trick of interlarding his discourse with this extraordinary invocation, "I have not."

"Well, then," said the patient commander, "we'll try. Fall in, John Norton. Attention! Carry arms! Prime and load."

All these manoeuvres did John go through, like an automaton, until the last, when, laying his hand upon a bayonet where his cartouch-box ought to be, he exclaimed—

"By all that's bad, general, you're right."

According to the present strict rules of discipline in the British army a file of men would have been ordered to march so refractory a subject off to the guard-house; and if he were not tried by a regimental court-martial for insubordination, he might deem himself a fortunate individual. At all events, "good conduct" would never afterwards, should he continue in the service to the age of the Duke of Wellington, emblazon his discharge. But John Norton walked home beside the general's horse listening, with a meek and subdued spirit, to a friendly lecture upon the wisdom of sometimes supposing that others may be in the right as well as one's self.

At the other side of the river, nearly opposite to General Bettesworth's, but close to the village, are two adjoining brick houses, somewhat removed from the road. In one of these lived and died General Stratton. The other was occupied by Major Legge. The general was a venerable Ligonier-like man, and his wife a stately matron of the olden time, whom I seem to see this moment, with her stomacher and brocaded dress, and a long narrow scarf trimmed with the richest lace; her grey locks turned up, like flax round a distaff, over her forehead, and a towering bonnet of black silk over all. She was deemed a proud woman, but very good to the poor. As to her pride, I have heard no proof of it, except that she kept the village gossips at bay; but the reputation of her goodness is incontestable.

An *Emeritus* of a lower grade, but more formidable than the whole *Etat Major* to the juvenile imagination, was William Oulton Prosser, who from the post of a bombardier had retired to Ballyfermot Castle, where he opened an "academy" of liberal instruction. I still quail to remember him. It was only the other day that his name, written in round-hand across the title-page of a "Trusler's Chronology," purchased at Sharpe's auction-room, sent a thrill through me, as if it had been the wind of a round shot. He was a tall, stern-looking pedagogue, who never came down from his bedroom before eleven o'clock in the forenoon; and then he despatched a dirty servant-boy into the school-room, which was detached from the castle, to summon the boys on the black list to come in and be whipped. That operation he performed as if he had served in no other rank than that of a drummer all the days of his "sogering" upon earth; and it was administered in the breakfast parlour amid the *debris* of the repast (bread and butter and egg-shells), which the giant had just demolished to give him strength for the task.

It had been his wont to inflict condign discipline in the midst of the school; but it happened on a day, that a boy, whose name was included in the usher's report, lay in ambush behind a heap of coats, in the porch; and as the ogre passed through, flourishing the formidable taws, and "chewing vengeance all the way," the poor wretch, in a frenzy of terror and despair, flew upon him, as a cat driven wild by persecution, and bit a large piece out of the calf of his leg. The big tyrant limped away into his den, and swore upon the family Bible that he would never again set foot in the said schoolroom, and that he would whip the said boy. He kept both the oaths, "in a sort of way," being obliged to compromise the matter with the delinquent, who agreed to save his Christian master's conscience, only on condition that the word of promise should be broken to the hope. A shadowy castigation, therefore (the ghost of a whipping), was submitted to; but from that hour the main business of the academy was carried on by deputies, remote from the eye of the master. He still continued, however, to perform the part of an high justiciary, and to take cognizance of copy-books and arithmetical exercises, which the boys were required to exhibit to him in procession.

The remainder of his day was occupied principally in attending to the refrigerating process of some gallon of boiled water, in a huge white jug, which he filled every morning at the breakfast-table, and set upon the stone outside the window to cool. After dinner, this supply was placed on the table by his right hand, and corrected, *pro re natâ*, with whiskey, until, tumbler after tumbler, the whole of its contents disappeared. That was his stint; he never exceeded it; but as soon as it was finished, which was rarely before two or three o'clock next morning, he went to bed; and it depended on the quality of the spirit thus imbibed (the quantity being uniformly the same) in what degree of ill-humour he should apply himself to his professional duties of the following noon.

Such was the schoolmaster of one of the fashionable boarding-schools in the immediate vicinity of our capital some fifty years since. It was my fortune to be removed from under his *ferula* to that of another who had been an operative tailor—not an Alton Locke, though—and whose ignorance of everything but handwriting and Gough's Arithmetic, was far more astounding than that of the bombardier. He made up, however, in morality, for his shortcomings in erudition; and as they both kept tolerably competent ushers, and had an understanding of mutual profit with the bookseller, care was taken that their pupils should be supplied with a competent stock of tools for learning at all events; so we hobbled through the Latin and Greek course, *utcunque,* and Trinity College made the most of us afterwards.

If ever your ghost-seer extends his nocturnal saunterings towards Ballyfermot, about "the wee sma' hours ayont the twal," let him have an eye out for a large white jug with a red nightcap and a pair of green goggles; for as surely as drunken spirits are permitted to revisit the glimpses of the moon, in that place and at such an hour will the schoolmaster be abroad.

Upon the dispersion of our own royal regiment, the Macleod Fencibles took up their quarters in the barrack, which thereupon stank horribly of cockaleekie every morning. A raw, wild, breekless tribe they were, fresh caught from the Highlands, at a period when the Trossachs were as inaccessible to the foot of civilised man as the KyberPass. The chief of the clan had collected and regimented them, selecting his own officers from the sons of his tacksmen and reivers, and few members of the mess could speak a dozen consecutive words of good English. The colonel, a fiery old Gael, and "vengeance proud," did his best to *lick* them into form, using his knuckles occasionally, it was said, for that purpose; and, indeed, a vigorous discipline was needful.

They wrangled at dinner for the choice morsels of the various joints, three or four knives and forks being sometimes plunged at the same moment into one leg of mutton; and upon a certain occasion, when a large turbot was served, those who sate near the would-be carver saved him the trouble of apportioning it, by forking it away upon their own plates with their long bony fingers. This vexed the colonel exceedingly; for there were strangers at the table who had never dined at a Fencible mess before. For a whole week, therefore, he condemned them to leek-porridge, which was *eaten* with a spoon, while all the regimental pipers, seated (*more Scotico*) at the end of the apartment, blew "*Could Kail,*" and other appetizing *refreins,* to bring them to an improving sense of the privations they were enduring.

Many of those caterans were afterwards drafted into the general service, and attained the highest honours awarded to good soldiership. These, indeed, came to them by nature; but the acquisition of the manners of gentlemen was not so easy; yet more than one of the individuals, who scrambled on that memorable occasion for the turbot, have been deemed worthy to sit down at royal banquets, and were justly classed amongst the flower of North British chivalry.

The Carlow militia came next, a polite corps, but numbering some strange twists among its subalterns. The adjutant, one Clifford, had been raised from the ranks by the favour and discernment of Colonel Latouche. He was a humorous fellow, of a manly, independent mind, and scorned to hang his head at the remembrance of his origin. The General of Division, dining at the mess on the occasion of a quarterly inspection, complimented Clifford upon the excellent state of drill in which he found the regiment, and, alluding to his name, asked "if he had any relations on the staff?"

"No, General," he replied, "but I have a great number on the spade."

It happened, on some occasion, that he displeased his colonel, who, in a hasty moment, declared his regret at having raised him from the state in which he had found him.

"Then, Colonel Latouche," said Clifford, "you are the first of your name that ever was sorry for doing a good action."

It is scarcely necessary to say that so adroit and just a compliment replaced him at once in his good patron's favour.

The pride of the old barrack was sorely tried afterwards, by various incursions of feather-beds which came in successively with the Wicklow, South Mayo, North Downshire, and Limerick regiments. Your shell-jacket dandies of this day would stare at the half-moon-shaped cocked hats, black leggings with innumerable small buttons, and draggle-tailed coats of their predecessors. But the hair-powder was worse than all. Can I ever forget Bob Gloster, of the *Garryowens*, on his return from the grand review one broiling *Fourth of June*, wiping away, with the sleeve of his new scarlet uniform, the streams of liquefied flour that meandered down his cheeks, and bewailing the day that he had "ever left the sweet *English Town*,[1] where he might have been reared up to an imminent marchant, to be melted out of creation like an althar-candle."

Bob volunteered, shortly afterwards, into *the Line*, and became well used to the "melting mood" in Spain, where he soon earned for himself a pair of spurs; and when he came home, after the peace of Paris, Major Gloster, quite a polished cavalier, with a fine military accent, I should have liked to see the man who would remind him of his early chances of *imminence* in the mercantile line. It was of such materials that heroes were manufactured; and I could enumerate at least a dozen "ragged colte" who left that old barrack, in the midst of scenes of riot and drunkenness incidental to the volunteering system, and turned out "bra'chargers" at Vittoria, or on the plain of Waterloo.

But Chapelizod was not always a mere depot of Fencibles and militia. It was for a good while the headquarters of the 92nd, or *Gordon Highlanders*, so truly described in Captain Grant's charming romance. They marched in, all brown and shrivelled by the sands of Egypt, though some years had passed since they had been there. A grave, orderly, religious body of men they were, who seemed always conscious that they were only here for a breathing time, and could not long he spared from the field of death. Their leader was Major Cameron, *the Fassifern*, who ended his career of glory at Waterloo. Authors who write "stories founded on facts" take a license to embellish their materials, and to exaggerate the moral as well as the physical attributes of the persons whom they introduce, according to the exigencies of the fable.

But there is no exaggeration in Captain Grant's portrait of Cameron. It is a true representation of the man. His outward semblance and his frank and generous spirit, his nobility of mind

---

1. "The English Town" is a part of the ancient city of Limerick, which, so far as cleanliness it concerned, is justly considered "*Hiberniâ ipsâ Hibernior.*"

and person, are painted with equal fidelity. To see that man in front of his regiment was a sight worthy of the olden time. John Kemble did not impart a more exalted notion of the figure of *Caius Marcius* as he rallied the Roman legions before *Corioli*, than Cameron's robust but stately form, the dignity of which was in no degree impaired by a slight and scarcely perceptible halt, the effect of a musket-shot in the knee which he had received in Egypt, gave the spectators of the men who had scattered England's chivalry at Bannockborn. If Walter Scott knew him, his picture of Fergus Mac Ivor, all perfect as it is, can scarcely claim the merit of originality.

No regimental biographer has attempted a history of *The Army of Reserve*. It is a theme worthy of the pen of *Lorrequer* (now that poor Maxwell is gone, there is none other capable of doing it justice), and the materials for constructing it are fading rapidly out of the memory of mankind; yet Chapelizod still remembers "*the Blackbelts.*" Who that ever saw can forget them? It is scarcely worth being sixty, indeed, or thereabouts, to have seen them; but since that would be in any case, it is a pride and a joy to have enjoyed the vision; for

*Eye ne'er shall look upon their like again.*

The *Blackbelts,* so called because those decorations of military equipment in which the song exults as

*Your belts of white leather,*

were polished off as glossy as the raven's down across the shoulders and breasts of this distinguished corps, were known at the Horse Guards as the Second Garrison Battalion. They were physically, as the Sixtieth Regiment in those days was in a moral sense, the sweepings of the service. Every soldier who was blind of an eye, lame of a leg, maimed in an arm, crooked in form, or diminutive in size, and yet considered able to carry arms in the service of his sovereign, was drafted into the "*Blackbelts,*" and the officers were pretty nearly of a piece with the men. They reminded me of the little hairy men who came in swarms on board Sinbad's vessel and devoured everything, carnal and vegetable, they could stick their claws into. But they were a well-disciplined battalion, and efficient enough for the sort of duty they had to perform.

Excellent shots too they were, every man of them. No rifle corps in any service could have surpassed them with the brown Bess; a target was knocked to splinters by them in half-an-hour. They were specially employed, on this account, to escort deserters; for escape was not an uncommon thing while the corporal's guard were engaged in social chat along a dusty road. The prisoner would slip his wrist through the handcuff, bolt up a lane, and dodge his pursuers from hedge to hedge till he got clear off. But let a *Blackbelt* catch but a glimpse of his person emerging from a thicket or doubling round a corner, and he had him down as unerringly as O'Gorman Mahon would bag a woodcock.

Two or three incidents of this kind occurred during the stay of the battalion in Chapelizod. One of the occasions was very remarkable. A deserter broke loose in a crowded street and fled amongst men and women, who threw themselves purposely in the way, in order to facilitate his escape. But this manoeuvre did not save him. The corporal levelled his musket, waited coolly till the wretch glanced for a moment into a vacant space, and then shot him dead. The fame of the *Blackbelts*, as sharp-shooters, and the unrelenting sternness with which they acted on such occasions, soon made them the terror of the service, and their prisoners ceased to hope for safety in sudden flight.

Before taking leave of the military reminiscences of Chapelizod, let me throw a Parthian glance upon the yeomanry corps commanded by Captain Wilcocks (the late Sir Richard), whose handsome and portly figure I still seem to behold, like a Colossus looking down upon the evolutions of his men. The vicar of the parish, a loyal man, who took a lively interest in the military education of those heroes, offered a gold medal to be shot for, at a distance of a hundred yards, upon the Palmerston fair-green. It was a great occasion, and all the beauty and fashion of three villages adorned it with their presence. There stood the captain to see fair play and encourage the nervous, while his permanent sergeant, Ned Bullard, was ready with a jeer and a joke at the service of every one that shot wide of the mark. The zealous parson, adumbrated by a *shovel* of such dimensions as we see not in these days of skimping economy, rode up and down the line exhorting the brave to fear nothing, but, remembering that the eyes of their country were upon them, to acquit them like men.

Point blank was the practice on that memorable day. Had the target been a thing of life, it would have required to be of the feline species to have survived; for I have no doubt that at least nine out of the hundred bullets struck some part of its circumference. The victor was one Pierce Butler, a round, fat, oily son of Crispin, who had never discharged a bit of lead from a musket barrel before, and who approached his task as we may suppose King Agag to have approached the Prophet Samuel. With averted eye he raised the gun to his shoulder, pulled the trigger, in an agony of desperation, and falling back by the force of the rebound amongst his sympathizing fellow-soldiers, exclaimed, "Hould me up!"

It was some time before he could collect his scattered senses sufficiently to comprehend the cheers which announced that he had pierced *the bull's eye*. But when the great fact was made perfectly plain to his understanding, it was wonderful how promptly his spirit rose with his fortune, and with what a fiercely modest alacrity he strutted forward to the place where the vicar's niece, a charming young lady of eighteen, stood ready to invest him with the trophy. And now let me tell you that the only ghost of that corps that walks this firm set earth is the individual Bob Martin, whom your ghost-seer has so prematurely sent to his account. Bob is still as much as ever he was, which is not saying a great deal for him, extant amongst "articulate men," and, according to his own somewhat indignant account, has "as little call to sperrits, maybe, as gentlemen that takes greater liberties wid them."

But there was a Bob Martin once; the old Bob of all, who served the office of sexton when the population of Ireland scarcely amounted to three millions of interrable bodies. That man could have enwrinkled you all over with grave statistics. It was he that buried Luttrell, and saw the blue light flickering out of the coffin, when the first shovelful of black earth was cast upon it; and formidable were the stories which he related of the same Luttrell. Bob was for a long while "the oldest inhabitant," but, unlike that personage in general, he could remember many things; and he would tell them with a gusto, when engaged knee-deep, or deeper still, in his professional avocation. To him is the world indebted for a few fragments of *Satanic History*, collected from the transactions of "The Hellfire Club," every tittle of which he was prepared to verify before any tribunal.

The building of "*The Devil's Mills*," on the Lower Road to Lucan, was one of those incontestable facts. They were built in one night, at the requisition of the redoubtable Luttrell, who being hard pressed to devise a task beyond the ability of the architect to perform (otherwise he could not get rid of his society, which began to be rather *ennuyant*), he commanded the mill to be erected. But that was no trouble. He looked out of the window, and saw it done.

"Throw a weir and dam across the river." *Presto*, there it was!

"Make me a rope of sand."

"Ah, there you have me," said the old gentleman, "for the devil himself cannot do that;" and so he was quit for that time. The ruined mill at Woodlands, on the Liffey bank, still attests the reality of this wonder.

Again, at an annual meeting of the club, at which whoever happened to be last in a certain saltatory movement of the whole assembly, became the lawful prey of the *grand master*, it was Luttrell's luck to be left behind. But his good genius did not forsake him.

"What are your eyes for?" he cried, nothing daunted. "Take the fellow that is coming after me."

The devil let go his prey and seized—*a shadow*; whence the

remarkable fact, that, to the hour of his death, Luttrell never had a shadow. Bob Martin had seen him a dozen times, without a shadow. He could not swear, indeed, that the sun shone on such occasions; but of the material fact, that Luttrell belonged to the *ascii* of the earth, there could not be a possible doubt.

On a third occasion, when immersed in study—it would be curious to know the name of the volume—the old one peeping over his shoulder, gave him a familiar tap, and said:—

"Come down, and finish it at my fireside."

"Stay," said Luttrell, whose ready wit was never at a "*nonplush*," I have a codicil to add to my will. Give me a delay till this inch of candle is burned out."

The request seemed so moderate, that it was granted without hesitation.

"Upon your honour?"

"As I'm a gentleman."

"Then, perhaps, you'll have no objection to sit a short time in the dark?"

So said, so done. He blew out the candle, locked it up in his desk, marked the sign of the cross over the keyhole, and requested his friend to ring the bell for fresh lights.

Now, though Bob was a staunch Protestant, and held mutterings in as much contempt as Lord John Russell, he believed most firmly that nothing could have hindered the old gentleman from following that inch of candle into the desk, and annihilating it with one puff of his breath, if the sign of the cross had not been so timely interposed to bar him out.

But Bob's conversation was rich in remembrances of better men. His father had been married by "the Dane," whereby he meant Dean Swift, and a considerable proportion of his store of traditionary anecdote was connected, more or less, with that great name; nor was he singular in that. All the old men of his time preserved a lively sense of the wit and patriotism of the eccentric Drapier. They could tell all that is written, and a great deal that is not written, illustrative of his peculiar humour. As for Bob, he was able to point out the particular spot on the

Castleknock road, where he stopped his horse to bargain with a cowboy for a secret whereby he was enabled to prognosticate the weather. The dean had passed by, lightly clad, in full confidence that the weather would continue fair.

"Go back for your cloak, sir," said the urchin; " it will rain."

Without heeding the warning, he passed on; and in an hour's time was wet to the skin. He returned to the spot, and demanded how the boy could foresee the shower? The youngster required half-a-crown for the information, which having obtained after some chaffering, he said:—

"You see that big stone, your reverence, in the middle of the field. Well, whenever you want to know if it is going to rain, come to that place, and if you find the bull scratching himself against that big stone, you may be sure of it."

To that big stone many a chuckling sexagenarian could point, as a memento of "the Dane," whose memory the whole community loved and revered, having been outwitted for once by a poor country boy. It may stand there yet, for aught I can tell.

It was surely something, when the peasantry of a whole district were accustomed to amuse one another with the sayings and doings of the greatest of the wits of Queen Anne. The schoolmaster may have done much for the world in the last half-century, but he certainly has not raised the minds or improved the taste of that class. There are very few Bob Martins, in whose mouths the names of Swift, and Sheridan, and Delany, and Archbishop Boulter are now as "familiar as household words."

LEONAUR

# ALSO FROM LEONAUR
## AVAILABLE IN SOFTCOVER OR HARDCOVER WITH DUST JACKET

**THE COMPLETE FOUR JUST MEN: VOLUME 2** *by Edgar Wallace*—*The Law of the Four Just Men* & *The Three Just Men*—disillusioned with a world where the wicked and the abusers of power perpetually go unpunished, the Just Men set about to rectify matters according to their own standards, and retribution is dispensed on swift and deadly wings.

**THE COMPLETE RAFFLES: 1** *by E. W. Hornung*—*The Amateur Cracksman* & *The Black Mask*—By turns urbane gentleman about town and accomplished cricketer, life is just too ordinary for Raffles and that sets him on a series of adventures that have long been treasured as a real antidote to the 'white knights' who are the usual heroes of the crime fiction of this period.

**THE COMPLETE RAFFLES: 2** *by E. W. Hornung*—*A Thief in the Night* & *Mr Justice Raffles*—By turns urbane gentleman about town and accomplished cricketer, life is just too ordinary for Raffles and that sets him on a series of adventures that have long been treasured as a real antidote to the 'white knights' who are the usual heroes of the crime fiction of this period.

**THE COLLECTED SUPERNATURAL AND WEIRD FICTION OF WILKIE COLLINS: VOLUME 1** *by Wilkie Collins*—Contains one novel 'The Haunted Hotel', one novella 'Mad Monkton', three novelettes 'Mr Percy and the Prophet', 'The Biter Bit' and 'The Dead Alive' and eight short stories to chill the blood.

**THE COLLECTED SUPERNATURAL AND WEIRD FICTION OF WILKIE COLLINS: VOLUME 2** *by Wilkie Collins*—Contains one novel 'The Two Destinies', three novellas 'The Frozen deep', 'Sister Rose' and 'The Yellow Mask' and two short stories to chill the blood.

**THE COLLECTED SUPERNATURAL AND WEIRD FICTION OF WILKIE COLLINS: VOLUME 3** *by Wilkie Collins*—Contains one novel 'Dead Secret,' two novelettes 'Mrs Zant and the Ghost' and 'The Nun's Story of Gabriel's Marriage' and five short stories to chill the blood.

**FUNNY BONES** *selected by Dorothy Scarborough*—An Anthology of Humorous Ghost Stories.

**MONTEZUMA'S CASTLE AND OTHER WEIRD TALES** *by Charles B. Cory*—Cory has written a superb collection of eighteen ghostly and weird stories to chill and thrill the avid enthusiast of supernatural fiction.

**SUPERNATURAL BUCHAN** *by John Buchan*—Stories of Ancient Spirits, Uncanny Places & Strange Creatures.